PRAISE FOR
CHARLOTTE BINGHAM

To Hear A Nightingale

'A delightful novel . . . pulsating with vitality and deeply felt emotions. I found myself with tears in my eyes on one page and laughing out loud on another.'
Sunday Express

'A lovely sprawling saga with a heroine you can't fail to love.'
Prima

The Business

'Probably more sun-tan lotion will be spilled on the pages of Charlotte Bingham's *The Business* than any other book this summer . . . the ideal beach read.'
Homes and Gardens

'A compulsive, intriguing and perceptive read.'
Sunday Express

In Sunshine Or In Shadow

'Superbly written . . . a romantic novel that is romantic in the true sense of the word.'
Daily Mail

'Marvellous . . . a very accomplished novel.'
Jilly Cooper

Stardust

CHARLOTTE BINGHAM

Doubleday

LONDON · NEW YORK · TORONTO · SYDNEY · AUCKLAND

TRANSWORLD PUBLISHERS LTD
61–63 Uxbridge Road, London W5 5SA

TRANSWORLD PUBLISHERS (AUSTRALIA) PTY LTD
15–23 Helles Avenue, Moorebank, NSW 2170

TRANSWORLD PUBLISHERS (NZ) LTD
3 William Pickering Drive,
Albany, Auckland

DOUBLEDAY CANADA LTD
105 Bond Street, Toronto, Ontario, M5B 1YE

This edition published 1992
Hardcover edition published 1992 by Doubleday
a division of Transworld Publishers Ltd
Copyright © 1992 Charlotte Bingham

A catalogue record for this book is available from the British Library

ISBN 0385 40395X

Typeset in Joanna by
Chippendale Type, Otley, West Yorkshire.

Printed in Great Britain by
Mackays of Chatham, Plc, Chatham, Kent

For the Duke who loves the stars

When he shall die,
Take him and cut him out in little stars,
And he will make the face of heaven so fine
That all the world will be in love with night,
And pay no worship to the garish sun.

Romeo and Juliet, Act III Sc II

OVERTURE

It seems she was always beautiful. There are photographs to prove it, photographs that were taken at the time. Even at three months old, when other babies are rarely even pretty, she was beautiful. And already the camera was in love with her.

They say that beautiful babies don't grow into beautiful children. But at three her looks were so arresting, she won first prize in a national competition.

No doubt you saw her picture then. Everyone did. Whichever magazine you picked up, or whatever hoarding you glanced at, there was that perfect little heart-shaped face, staring out at you, or down at you, with big serious dark-lashed eyes, eyes which already fascinated, eyes like a baby tigress. And no doubt you were captivated even then, everyone was, particularly by those eyes, those strangely vulnerable eyes, with their odd little flecks and strange markings.

Naturally flawless, her skin unnaturally stayed that way. She took great care to make sure that it did, she took care to preserve its almost translucent whiteness, never allowing it to get fashionably tanned, knowing that the real drama of her looks depended on that pearl white skin being shown off against her thick and lustrous dark hair.

Early studio photographs reveal that without doubt her hair was one of her greatest assets, that and the incredible delicacy of her features. Even more unusually, she had identical profiles, making her every director's and cameraman's dream. Because in the theatre wherever the audience sat, or on screen from whichever angle the camera photographed her, her beauty was indefectible. Even her voice, so often the thief of beauty, was light and full of charm.

9

So imagine then, if you can, someone so beautiful that in all her life as she grew up into womanhood, she never had a plain day. Not, that is, until she finally won him from her. And it was from that moment, from the moment that she finally won him for herself, that her lustrous beauty began quite inexorably to fade.

ACT ONE

England
Some time in the Fifties

ONE

All she did was walk across the room. As the other woman entered, she simply got up from her desk, smoothed down her dress, smiled at the other woman, walked her across the office and let her through another door, which she held open with one hand and a smile that lit up the sky. That was all she did. And she only did it once.

There were no other takes. It had been the end of the day's shoot, it was routine, so the director had shot and printed just the one take. But the image was the stuff of dreams. Even though the print had been hastily processed, and was silent, as was the way with the rushes, the tall, dark-haired man standing by the door of the viewing theatre had seen enough. The way the girl looked, the way she moved, the way her eyes found the lens, and once they did, the way she smiled at you right through the camera, that was all he needed to see, to know that this girl was something quite exceptional.

'Lights!' he shouted, and at once there were lights.

Charles Keyes, the film's director, shot bolt upright in his seat in the second row. He hadn't even realized Boska was in the room.

'I want to see that last scene again,' Boska said. 'So Mike? Wind back if you will, please?'

'Something wrong, Boz?' Keyes asked as casually as he could. 'I didn't spot anything.'

'Obviously not, Charles,' Boska said. 'Luckily I did.'

'What was it?'

'Who was it?' Boska corrected him, taking a fresh packet of Passing Cloud from his suit pocket and carefully removing an oval cigarette which he tapped at both ends on one manicured thumb-nail. 'Who was the girl?'

Keyes stalled. He hadn't been paying full attention since, to his mind, the scene was of absolutely no importance.

'You obviously don't mean our Sylvia, Boz,' Keyes replied, referring to his leading lady. 'I was watching her, naturally.'

'You were half asleep, Charles,' Boska replied. 'I was watching you as well. Mike?' Boska opened the door through to the projection room. 'Roll it if you're ready, please.'

'Yes sir!' came the reply. 'Yes, Mr Boska sir!'

This time everyone in the viewing theatre watched, because as they all knew from experience, when Dmitri Boska said there was something to see, there was something to see. And now that they watched, they saw a dark-haired, slender, angelic-looking girl who moved as if she was dancing, and who smiled as if the sun had come out for the first time after weeks of nothing but rain. The reason they hadn't seen her before was because they were looking for technical faults or blemishes, noting detail for continuity, or checking that all was right with Sylvia Dean, the leading lady. No-one had paid the secretary any attention because the girl was a walk-on and this was her only scene. Yet now their attention had been drawn to her, everyone in the viewing theatre wondered how they could possibly have missed her.

'Well?' Boska asked as the lights came on again, momentarily dazzling the assembled company. 'I hate to think what would have happened if I hadn't paid you a visit this morning. Because if I hadn't, I swear the world would have been a poorer place.'

'She's certainly pretty, Boz,' Keyes said, stretching his long legs out in front of him. 'In fact I'd go as far as to say she is very pretty.'

'Don't be a fool, Charles,' Boska sighed. 'That girl is not *pretty*, or even *very pretty*. That girl is beautiful. That girl is one of the most beautiful girls I have ever seen, anywhere. Her eyes, for instance. You saw how the camera captured their look? The camera loves her, and if the camera loves her, we love her. What you have just seen, what we all have just seen, we have seen a star being born, that's what. In just that one little scene. OK. So now what you do, Charles, is you build up her part in this film. You give her something to do, because I'm not wrong, believe me. You put her in two or three scenes, with dialogue. I don't care if it means getting another girl for the secretary, a reshoot, and casting this girl as something else. I don't mind what it takes. All I want is this girl back here, and under contract. So get moving.'

Boska dropped his half-smoked cigarette into the fire bucket, looked round the assembled company to make sure he had made his point, and then turned and swept out of the viewing room. When he had gone, Charles Keyes took a small pair of scissors from his top pocket and slowly began to trim his immaculate finger-nails.

'Imagine that,' he said finally and to no-one in particular. 'A star. And there was I going to cut that whole silly sequence.'

While the studio was doing their best to track her down, Elizabeth Laurence was out shopping with Lalla Henderson, her best friend from her drama school days. They window shopped in Bond Street, and Knightsbridge, but they bought nothing, because neither of them could really afford to do so, Lalla because she was a struggling actress, and Elizabeth because she was newly married and dependent on her husband for her clothes allowance.

'You'd look sensational in those,' Lalla stopped to point at a pair of yellow velvet trousers with a high waist and tapered, zippered ankles. 'With your figure they're just made for you.'

'I can't,' Elizabeth said. 'I absolutely promised Sebastian.'

'What about the money you earned from your day on the film?' Lalla said. 'Surely that's yours to do what you like with?'

Elizabeth sighed and gazed longingly at the velvet trousers in the shop window.

'I suppose there wouldn't be any harm in trying them on,' she said.

Unfortunately Lalla was right, and Elizabeth, with her twenty-inch waist, slender hips and perfectly proportioned legs looked wonderful in the dull yellow trousers, particularly when the shop assistant suggested teaming them up with a close-fitting black jersey blouse.

'It's no good,' Elizabeth sighed as she turned and looked at herself from all angles in the mirror. 'I simply can't afford them.'

'If you did some more filming you could.'

Elizabeth looked up at Lalla and smiled radiantly.

'Get behind me, Satan,' she said.

They left the shop empty handed and caught a bus in Oxford Street to take them to Kensington where they planned to have lunch on the roof garden of Derry and Toms.

'When I get my big break,' Lalla said, after they had settled in the empty front seat on the top deck, the first thing I shall do is go to Bond Street and buy a dress by Balenciaga. And another by Givenchy. And another by Dior.'

'Perhaps this will be your big break,' Elizabeth said, holding on to the rail in front of them as the bus swung into Park Lane. 'Perhaps someone will see you in it, and put you under contract. Isn't that what happens?'

'That's what's meant to happen,' Lalla laughed, 'in fairy stories. No, I don't think *Made In Heaven* is going to turn yours truly into a star. I think it's going to take more than one scene and my one line – "Dr Hargreaves will see you now, madam." Still, it was fun, wasn't it?'

Elizabeth agreed. It had been fun. Loath though she was to admit it, she regretted having had to give up acting once she had got formally engaged. Even though she hadn't really taken drama school that seriously, and had been much more interested in making a good marriage, she had secretly enjoyed performing, and although her young husband, Sebastian Ferrers, was extremely handsome, comfortably off and deemed the catch of the season, the newly married Mrs Ferrers adjudged her life dull, especially when compared to the life her friend Lalla was leading.

That was why she had allowed Lalla to persuade her to attend a casting session for the comedy being shot at Richmond Studios, a film in which Lalla had what she described as a cough-and-a-spit as a doctor's receptionist. Sebastian was away on business, and Elizabeth was even more bored than usual, so there really seemed to be no good reason to say no.

The casting director obviously felt the same about Elizabeth as soon as he saw her, hiring her at once, although her appearance among a crowd of extras somewhat disconcerted him.

'But you're a trained actress,' he said. 'Weren't you at RADA with Lalla Henderson?'

'Yes I was, why?'

'It just seems odd, if I may say so,' the casting director said, 'for a girl with your rather exceptional looks— '

'I'm – married,' Elizabeth interrupted with a sweet smile. 'I was married within months of leaving drama school.'

'Ah,' the director said. 'I see.'

'This is just for pin money,' Elizabeth explained. 'Nothing more.'

Which is probably how it would have remained, had Elizabeth not given in to temptation and decided to upstage the leading lady, a habit she had fallen into at drama school whenever she considered she hadn't been given a part worthy of her talents. It didn't take much effort, at least not when the upstager was as strikingly beautiful as Elizabeth was. All it required was a sudden smile in an unexpected place, a slight widening of the eyes, a small but eye-catching gesture (in this case, a simple straightening of her dress), or just a special way of walking. Elizabeth had a special way of walking. Elizabeth walked as if on air. And, of course, she had learned how to look into the camera when she was a baby, with the consequence that whatever trick she might employ, Elizabeth discovered very quickly that there was no difficulty whatsoever in making audiences believe that it was she not the principal player at whom they should all be looking. As for Sylvia Dean, the leading lady, she never stood a chance from the moment Elizabeth came into shot.

'You could perfectly easily get some more work on the film,' Lalla persisted over lunch in the gardens high on the roof of Kensington's most fashionable department store. 'They're shooting the big party scene next week, and all of us cough-and-spitters are doubling up for the crowd. I know that Gerry, the casting director you saw, remember? Gerry'd have you back like a shot.'

'I'd love to,' Elizabeth admitted. 'But Sebastian will be back by then.'

'You sound as if you're dreading it,' Lalla said with a frown.

'Do I?' Elizabeth said, without showing how pleased she was Lalla had picked up the nuance.

'Well, yes,' Lalla replied. 'You do as a matter of fact. Is everything all right?'

Elizabeth sighed, pushed her half-eaten salad to one side and lit a Balkan Sobranie, the only cigarette she would smoke.

'Do you promise you won't say anything, darling?' she asked, after exhaling a long plume of smoke.

'There's nothing to promise, I don't believe there can be anything wrong between you and Sebastian.'

'It isn't Sebastian,' Elizabeth replied. 'There's absolutely nothing wrong with poor Sebastian. No-one could be sweeter. And kinder. Or more thoughtful.'

'So what is it then, Liz?'

'It's me, darling. And it's really rather awful, so you're not to say *one word* to anyone. Promise?'

'I promise,' Lalla agreed, and she rummaged in her handbag for her own cigarettes while never taking her eyes off Elizabeth. 'Well?'

'The trouble is, darling, whatever, and whenever, and however, the problem is I've discovered I don't like – I don't like *it*.'

'Oh *God*,' Lalla said. 'You can't be serious?'

'I'm very serious, darling, I assure you,' Elizabeth sighed. 'It's not Sebastian. Because as I said, Sebastian is kind, and gentle, and very considerate. It's me. I simply can't stand doing it.'

17

'Not at all?' Lalla frowned. 'Not ever?'

'No. To be perfectly honest, I find it incredibly boring. It just does nothing for me. Nothing – nothing happens. I just lie there, getting more and more bored. And rather revolted finally.'

Elizabeth looked up at Lalla, wide-eyed over her cigarette, challenging her to say something, but all Lalla could do was frown and shake her sleek blond head.

'You obviously don't find it boring,' Elizabeth continued. 'Or repellent, you lucky thing.'

'I'm not married.'

'That's not the point, darling,' Elizabeth put in quickly. 'You've had lovers.'

'Only one really, I only really slept with David.'

'But you enjoyed it. You told me.'

'I certainly didn't find it boring, or – or—'

'Or revolting,' Elizabeth sighed again and raised her eyebrows, as if in wonder at herself. 'I don't think anyone else does, darling. That's what worries me. I think I must be some sort of freak.'

'Have you talked to Sebastian about it?'

Elizabeth stared at Lalla as if she were mad, and then burst into a peal of laughter.

'Can you *imagine*?' she asked. '*Sebastian, darling, I want to talk to you. I simply have to, because I'm so bored by you in bed!*'

'What I meant was,' Lalla said, immediately defensive, 'what I meant was, don't you ever talk about – you know – *it*?'

'Of course not.' Elizabeth crushed her cigarette out while tossing back her dark hair. 'It's not something one talks about is it? It's just something you do. We do.'

'But what about Sebastian?' Lalla asked after a short silence. 'I mean surely if you're that bored—'

'Sebastian doesn't suspect a thing,' Elizabeth answered pre-guessing her friend's thoughts. 'I make quite sure of that. One good thing as far as I'm concerned about having gone to drama school, darling, is that it did teach us just a little about play-acting.'

'Play-acting?'

'Lalla darling, you don't think I'm going to just lie there yawning and looking at my watch, do you? Poor Sebastian. The last thing in the world I would do would be to hurt poor darling Sebastian.'

They fell to silence while a waitress served them coffee. Elizabeth lit another cigarette and stared at some of the other women lunching in the roof gardens.

'I wonder how many of them were virgins when they got married?' she finally wondered.

18

'You think that's what your problem is?'

Elizabeth nodded.

'Of course.'

'I don't,' Lalla replied. 'I think your problem is you have nothing to do. With Sebastian away so much, now they've made him a junior partner, you have nothing to do with yourself all day, and so you're bored. And because you're bored at home, by yourself—'

'That doesn't make sense, Lalla. If that was the case I'd be delighted when Sebastian made love to me, and broke the dreadful monotony of my day to day existence.'

'All right. But you admit to being bored.'

'Of course I'm bored, darling. I'm bored totally rigid. So what do you suggest I do? Join the Women's Institute?'

'No, I think you should start acting. Seriously.'

'Sebastian wouldn't hear of it.'

'Sebastian would understand perfectly.'

'I promise you he wouldn't.'

'In that case, the only other thing I can suggest is that you should get pregnant.'

It was this last remark that did it. The last thing Elizabeth wanted in the world was to have children. The very thought of something else growing inside her body and making her gradually, uncontrollably fatter and fatter filled her with horror.

'If I had known, if I had only known,' was what she dimly remembered her mother murmuring, and then sighing and saying, always the same words, 'your birth was the most degrading, the most disgusting, the most horrifying moment of my life. I had rather someone shot me than that they put me through such torture ever again.'

Her foster mother took up the theme. Birth, pregnancy, babies, they were a terrifying ordeal. God didn't love women which was why when He came down to earth He made sure He came down as a man, because He couldn't have stood being a woman. Unfortunately she ignored her own terrible warnings. At a late age, in her middle years, she conceived for the first time and died in childbirth.

Little wonder then that when Sebastian touched, lightly but firmly, on the subject of their projected family Elizabeth found herself having to employ her play-acting skills. Naturally she found herself quite able to discuss the matter with all the necessary enthusiasm, while always managing to find a reason as to why she had not been able to make them both even more ecstatic with a

Happy Event. For better or worse a confirmed fear of childbirth was not the only legacy Elizabeth's late, great foster mother had left her with, she had also taught her how to make it impossible to conceive.

'All right. I'll ask Sebastian when he returns,' Elizabeth agreed in the taxi on the way back to her house in Chelsea. 'I'll whisper it in his ear, after I've whispered all the sweet nothings.' She stared out of the taxi window. 'About how strong he is. And how clever.' Then she turned back and stared at Lalla. 'I'll say it's just a bit of fun. He won't mind if he thinks I'm doing it just for fun.'

As the taxi pulled up outside the pretty, white-painted house in Chelsea, Elizabeth invited Lalla to come in for tea so that they could go on talking. She hated being alone, and now she was married, she hated it more than ever.

'What are you doing for the rest of the day?' Elizabeth asked Lalla as her maid opened the door. 'If you're not doing anything, why don't we go to the cinema after tea? *The African Queen* is on at the Odeon.'

'I think Maggie wants to say something,' Lalla replied, having noticed Elizabeth's maid trying to attract her mistress's attention.

'Thank you, Miss Henderson,' the girl said gratefully. 'It's the telephone, madam. It's been ringing all day. Someone called Mr Keyes at Richmond Studios is very anxious to speak to you. I wrote it all down by the telephone.'

Elizabeth watched the sweat forming on Sebastian's brow and wondered if it was going to fall on her. Sometimes, occasionally, a bead would roll slowly down his nose and drop on her face and she hated that when it happened, although when she was particularly bored she would have a bet with herself as to whether or not she could move and avoid it without Sebastian knowing. This time, however, such was her husband's ardour, having been absent from her for well over a week, the sweat began to run off him freely, and Elizabeth, closing her eyes as tightly as she could, resigned herself to the awful feeling of being dripped over.

'Darling,' he was whispering. 'Darling.'

'Oh yes, darling,' she whispered back, 'oh yes, oh yes, oh yes.'

The only good thing, Elizabeth thought, as Sebastian suddenly collapsed with a gasp on to the pillows was that they were in his bed and not hers. Because she wasn't expecting him back until the weekend, only that morning she had ordered Maggie to make up her bed in her best and favourite hand-embroidered Italian cotton sheets. Luckily she had left Sebastian's bed as it was.

'Oh my God, darling,' Sebastian sighed. 'I can't tell you how much I've missed you.'

'I've missed you too, darling,' Elizabeth replied. 'But what a lovely surprise. You coming home three days early.'

'I have to go away again next week, I'm afraid,' Sebastian said, wiping his cheek and his forehead with the back of one hand. 'We've got this new commission. A private house in North Oxford, and we've got a site meeting over two days.'

'But how *exciting*,' Elizabeth whispered, looking up from where she lay on her husband's chest to put one finger under her chin, just like she had spent hours practising in front of the mirror when she was bored at school. 'Didn't you tell me the house in Oxford was one of your designs?'

'Well, it's – it's not entirely all my own work,' Sebastian replied with his usual modesty. 'James did help considerably.'

'I shall miss you,' Elizabeth murmured.

'I shall miss you too,' Sebastian whispered back.

Elizabeth deemed it only diplomatic to allow Sebastian to make love to her again that night before she broached the subject.

'Darling,' she said. 'I have a confession. I'm afraid I've been rather naughty.'

'Nonsense, darling,' Sebastian replied. 'Angels just can't be naughty.'

'This one can, I'm afraid.' She put her face closer to him on the pillow so that their noses touched. 'I'm in a film.'

'A film? What film?' Sebastian propped himself up on one elbow and looked down at his young wife.

'Oh, it's nothing. It's an awfully silly film. And it was only for a bit of fun. But Lalla was working on it, and she thought it might be a hoot if she got me a tiny part. Which she did. That's all.' She leaned up and kissed him on the cheek. 'It really was only for a bit of fun.'

Sebastian smiled, put his arm round her, and lay back beside her in the bed so that her head lay on his shoulder.

'I don't see that there is any great harm in that, angel,' he said. 'Just so long as it doesn't become a habit.'

'I don't think that there's much chance in that, darling,' Elizabeth giggled. 'It's all a bit different from drama school.'

'I'll bet. No, I don't see any great harm in that, angel. Not if it's just a bit of fun.'

Elizabeth closed her eyes, took a deep breath, and kissed her husband on his bare chest. In return he kissed the top of her head, and then put his other arm around her, and held her fast. She sighed contentedly, and Sebastian sighed contentedly back, stroking her hair with a hand which he then let fall lightly on to one of her breasts. Elizabeth bit her lip and stared out into the darkness, and waited, and waited. But thankfully there was no further movement. Even so she waited for a good half an hour, until she was quite sure her husband was sound asleep, before she eased herself from his arms and back into her own bed, where she sighed once again with the sheer pleasure of being back in her own crisp, cool, pristine sheets, by herself.

As she spread her wonderful hair out behind her on her pillow, she thought all in all it, or rather *it*, was only a small price to pay for freedom.

At the eleventh hour, Cecil Manners, Lalla's agent and recommended choice of representation for Elizabeth, found he was after all unable to see them.

'I told you this might happen, Miss Henderson,' his secretary explained. She was a thin, plain girl in a home-made dress of an open lacey design, which was probably why she was suffering from a heavy cold. 'I said he was busy all morning. I told you you'd be taking a chance,' she sniffed.

'That's perfectly all right,' Elizabeth said sweetly, sitting down and indicating to Lalla that she should do the same. 'We're not in any hurry.'

'I don't think you understand, Miss,' the girl continued.

'Miss Laurence,' Elizabeth said helpfully. 'Miss Laurence.'

'You don't understand, Miss Laurence, but Mr Manners has got someone with him, and then he's got to go out to lunch.'

'Then we'll wait until he comes back from lunch,' Elizabeth replied, again with a smile. 'As I said, we're really not in a hurry.'

The secretary glared at them both, and then suddenly sneezed.

'Bless you,' Elizabeth said. '*What* a horrid cold.'

Meanwhile inside the elegant main office, Cecil Manners, whom most people would take to be forty-something, but in fact was only rising thirty, was doing his best to get rid of one Oscar Greene, playwright and budding genius in his own eyes, if not yet in Cecil's. Cecil represented Oscar, but that didn't mean he could allow Oscar to make him late for his luncheon appointment.

But Oscar was not a man to be hurried. He was a big man, more like a boxer than a writer, an Anglo-American with a mat of thick, dark, curly hair and a friendly, lightly jowled face. Oscar considered himself ugly, which in a way he was, until like most men of character he started to talk, when he became, as most of the women

22

of his acquaintance would vouchsafe, almost irresistibly attractive.

Not that it particularly worried Oscar how he looked. He had long ago concluded that he was ugly, and therefore not very attractive to women. And because of this modest self-assessment, and perhaps because he wore spectacles, and certainly because, despite the excellent cut of his clothes, he still managed to look like an unmade bed, women loved him.

He was opinionated, of course, as befitted a playwright not yet out of his twenties and with only one qualified success behind him – a romantic comedy which had filled on tour, but failed to make the West End. Success was just around the corner, and he knew it. It was just a question of which corner.

At this moment in time he was not in a mood to let Cecil go until Cecil was quite sure of Oscar's opinion of Jimmy Locke, the management who had been in charge of his oh-so-nearly-a-hit.

'Your lunch is going to have to wait, Cecil,' Oscar said, tapping out the last Lucky Strike from a crumpled pack. 'I'm blocking this door until you agree at the very least that I must have some say in the casting. Let's just call it consultation. I'm not going to stand by and see that silly ass Jimmy Locke putting yet another of his untalented boyfriends in any play of mine.'

'When you have your first West End hit, Oscar—' Cecil began, giving his watch another anxious glance.

'But don't you see? I'm not going to have any goddam West End hit, Cecil, you chump,' Oscar interrupted, 'not while Jimmy Locke puts his current favourites in my leading roles, OK?'

Oscar eyed him over the cigarette which he was finding impossible to light since it was as crumpled as the packet from which he'd taken it.

'Clive Willett—' Cecil said.

'Clive Willett,' Oscar groaned, breaking the Lucky Strike in half and trying again. 'Clive *Willett*.' The memory was too much for Oscar, who sank on his haunches before the office door.

'Clive is very popular in the provinces,' Cecil insisted, wondering how he was going to get past the hundred-and-forty odd pounds blocking his exit.

'Not in any of the provinces we play, Cecil,' Oscar replied, tilting his face sideways to avoid the flame of his Zippo lighter. 'They laughed at him – not with him, at him – from Sheffield to Brighton. Clive Willett would be overcast in the back row of the chorus. Well?' He looked up at his agent. 'I'm not moving, Cecil, not until you promise at least to *try*.'

The telephone rang on Cecil's desk.

'I told you I can't possibly see anyone now,' Cecil informed his secretary after a moment. 'And not after lunch either. Tell them to try ringing tomorrow, or the next day.'

Dropping the large white telephone back on to its cradle, Cecil pulled on a pair of expensive leather gloves.

'My car's here,' he told Oscar. 'And I will suggest it to Jimmy. I promise.'

'OK,' Oscar said with a sigh, pulling himself to his feet.

'But I can't promise more than that,' he added quickly.

'You never do, Cecil, *old boy* ,' Oscar grinned. 'And you never have.'

He opened the door behind him without turning, so that Cecil could leave, which Cecil started to do, until he saw what was waiting for him in the outer office.

'Hey,' Oscar frowned. 'You look as though you've seen a spook.' Then he turned as well, following Cecil's gaze, and saw what Cecil had seen.

'No,' Oscar said, nodding slowly. 'That is not a spook. That is something that just fell out of the sky.'

'You must be Mr Manners,' Elizabeth said, rising and coming forward. 'I'm Elizabeth Laurence. A friend of Lalla's.'

'How do you do?' Cecil asked, taking Elizabeth's gloved hand in his, and feeling suddenly gauche and clumsy as his six foot frame towered over the diminutive figure before him. 'Haven't we met before?'

'I don't think so,' Elizabeth smiled up at him, her chin tilted upwards, her green eyes meeting his from under the brim of her pretty blue hat. 'If we'd met, I'm quite sure I wouldn't have forgotten.'

She said it without being in the least flirtatious, which excited Cecil, causing him to hold her slender hand in his much longer than necessary, and never even giving Lalla a glance.

'I believe you're just off to lunch,' Elizabeth continued. 'So we mustn't detain you. It's just—'

Then she stopped, and smiled, as if she thought better of it than to continue.

'Please,' Cecil said, finally remembering to relinquish her hand. 'I'm in no great hurry. Come in.'

He stood aside and ushered both the girls into his office. Oscar backed off and stood in the corner by the hatstand, preferring to observe rather than be seen.

'This is terribly sweet of you,' Elizabeth said, sitting in the prof-fered chair, and as she did, Oscar suddenly realized who it was he was staring at with such intensity. He was staring at the heroine of his yet unwritten new play.

'I know you're frightfully busy. Lalla told me you're always frightfully busy. So this is really very sweet of you,' his heroine was saying.

Cecil went back and sat behind his desk again. As he did so Lalla drew up another chair, and sat unprompted beside Elizabeth. So far she hadn't said a word, nor had a single word been addressed to her. But Lalla didn't mind one bit, because like the two men in the room, Lalla knew she was riding the wake of a star.

'It's just that I need an agent,' Elizabeth sighed, deciding it was time to remove her little hat and allow Cecil full sight of her shiny dark hair. 'Dmitri, Dmitri . . .' She petered out and looked helplessly at Lalla.

'Boska,' Lalla prompted with a smile. 'Dmitri Boska.'

'Thank you, Lalla darling,' Elizabeth said, before returning to look Cecil right in the eyes.

'Dmitri Boska wants to put me under contract,' she continued. 'Apparently he saw this scene I did—'

'Elizabeth has a small part in this film,' Lalla interrupted helpfully, 'and Boska saw the rushes. And, well, you know Boska.'

'What I don't know is what all the fuss is about.' Elizabeth sighed.

'May I ask what the film is?' Cecil enquired, unable to take his eyes off Elizabeth.

'*Made In Heaven,*' Lalla told him. 'Known on the floor as *Made In A Hurry* – of course.'

'Lalla's right,' Elizabeth smiled. 'Even from the little I know, it's obviously really not very good. So I honestly don't know – well, why all the fuss.'

'Dmitri Boska only calls the fire brigade once he's quite certain there's a fire,' Cecil said, leaning across the desk and offering Elizabeth a cigarette from a modern engraved silver box.

'Do you mind if I smoke my own?' Elizabeth asked. 'Anything else makes me cough.'

While Cecil rose with alacrity to cross in front of his desk and light Elizabeth's cigarette for her, Lalla continued the story.

'We were at RADA together, Cecil,' she told him. 'And everyone thought Elizabeth was brilliant. But then she got engaged in her last term, and married shortly after we left.'

'You're married?' Cecil asked, his face falling slightly, but he carefully replaced his Ronson desk lighter in the exact position which it had just occupied.

'Shhh!' Elizabeth laughed, 'you're not meant to know.'

'I thought if Boska was going to put her under contract—' Lalla continued, before Elizabeth interrupted her.

'I haven't agreed about the contract, Lalla,' she said. 'You know that.'

'Even so, Cecil,' Lalla said. 'I told her she'd need an agent. And that you were the best in town.'

Cecil smiled, but still didn't bother to look at Lalla. And still Lalla didn't mind. The more Cecil looked at Elizabeth, the better it would be for her, while half hidden behind a wall of coats and hats, Oscar Greene wished that they would all get the hell out so that he could start writing his play.

'I should be delighted to represent you, Miss Laurence,' Cecil said. 'As from today, you shall be under my exclusive management.'

'Thank you, Mr Manners,' Elizabeth replied, with a sudden smile which literally took Cecil's breath away. 'I know I shall be in good hands. Lalla has spoken so highly of you.'

She held his eyes with hers, while expertly rebuttoning one tiny pearly button on her glove, pulling the suede even tighter round her slender wrists, and smoothing the material up her forearms.

'How about some lunch?' Cecil asked, having refound his voice. 'I'm meeting Jimmy Locke at the Ivy. He's a very important management. And I know he would be delighted if you joined us.'

'How terribly sweet of you,' Elizabeth replied. 'I can't imagine anything nicer, can you, Lalla darling?'

She turned to look at Lalla who smiled back broadly.

'No, I don't think I can,' said Lalla.

'Excellent,' Cecil replied, trying his best to sound pleased at Lalla Henderson's inclusion, which had not been intended, since he had all but forgotten she was even present.

Cecil had also forgotten all about Oscar, who was still in place behind the hatstand.

'I hope I'm not included,' Oscar said, from behind one of Cecil's overcoats. 'I have work to do.'

Elizabeth wheeled round in surprise in time to see the dishevelled playwright emerge from his hiding place.

'Hi,' he said to her. 'I'm Oscar Greene. Otherwise known as Cecil's Shame.'

'Forgive me, Miss Laurence,' Cecil said hastily as he came across to glare at Oscar. 'I'm sorry, I should have introduced you.'

'You never introduce me to pretty girls, Cecil,' Oscar complained, not taking his eyes off Elizabeth. 'He doesn't introduce me to pretty girls, because I'm a playwright. And Cecil is one of these fellows who think that playwrights should be heard and not seen.'

'How do you do?' Elizabeth asked, holding out her hand. 'I'm Elizabeth Laurence.'

'No, you're not Miss Laurence,' Oscar told her, taking her gloved hand and holding it. 'You – are our Emerald Glynn.'

Oscar had been carrying the idea for the play around in his head for some time now, but he had constantly put off writing it, because nowhere could he find an actress even remotely suitable for his needs.

Until today. Now that he had met Miss Elizabeth Laurence, he knew he could begin. Doing his best to contain his excitement he carefully typed the title page, and then printed: 'Act One, scene one. The deck of a transatlantic liner', before picking up the telephone to speak to the ever miserable cold-ridden Miss Jeans.

'Miss Jeans,' said Oscar. 'I shall be working here in Mr Manners' side office, and I'm not to be disturbed, OK? Not for anything, got me? I'm going to sleep on the couch in here, and so I'll need a blanket, a toothbrush and some paste, and four packets of cigarettes. And an endless supply of that stuff you dare to call coffee.'

'Is there some reason you can't fetch these things yourself?' Miss Jeans sniffed wearily in his ear.

'There most certainly is, Miss Jeans,' Oscar replied with certainty. 'I'm going to be far too busy writing a smash hit.'

By the time Cecil Manners had returned from lunch, Oscar was well into the first scene of the play.

'Well?' Cecil asked. 'And what do you think about our Miss Laurence?'

'Just shut the door, will you?' Oscar growled staring myopically at what he had just typed. 'And preferably with you on the other side of it.'

'I have to say,' Cecil continued blithely, carefully hanging his overcoat up, 'that without a doubt she is the loveliest girl I have ever seen.'

'The loveliest girl,' Oscar muttered, exxing over a typo with a resounding and monotonous clatter. 'I thought she was more like a whole new light up in the goddam sky. Now if you don't mind Cecil, *old boy—*'

'Well, yes, I do mind, as a matter of fact, dear boy,' Cecil said, peering over his shoulder. 'What exactly do you think you're doing, hammering away in here?'

'I thought you'd learned to recognize this activity by now,' Oscar told him. 'It's called Creative Writing. And this particular bit of Creative Writing is especially for Miss Laurence. And in it, she is going to be not just beautiful, but witty, and intelligent. She is going to say astonishing and memorable things, things which will imprint themselves on her audience's minds even more than Gladys Arden's ridiculously expensive costumes.'

'Should I book Gladys Arden?' Cecil asked ingenuously.

'Why not?' Oscar replied. 'You invariably do. Now come on, Cecil. Run along and leave a genius in peace.'

Oscar drew on his cigarette and wound a fresh sheet of paper into the Remington, as Cecil made as if to pick up the pages Oscar had already written. But Oscar beat him to it, slapping a hand down smartly on the small pile of paper.

'Uh huh,' he said warningly. 'I'll call you when it's finished.'

'Very good,' Cecil said. 'Well, if you want anything—'

'I won't,' Oscar interrupted. 'I have everything I want. I have Miss Elizabeth Laurence.'

That was at a quarter to three on Wednesday afternoon. By nine o'clock the following Sunday evening the play was finished.

T W O

Once again they watched what she did, but this time they needed no prompting. In fact, for the first view of the rough cut, there wasn't an empty seat in the viewing theatre. Word was already out.

Word had got out during the first day of the re-shoot, when those who had been on Soundstage 2 had witnessed Elizabeth Laurence's first dialogue scene on camera. No-one doubted she was beautiful when they saw her that day in her navy blue dress with a white fichu collar which showed off to perfection her dramatic colouring and her exquisite figure. But everyone who had seen it all before refused to pass final judgement until they had heard Boska's latest discovery speak, knowing as they did how certain mouths once they opened could cruelly distort what had only one happy silent moment ago been a lovely face.

Now there was an almost audible sigh of relief, because when Elizabeth spoke it was in a voice of infinite charm. And she spoke with her eyes too, eyes that reflected not only what she was saying, but seemingly even what she was thinking. Even when she laughed she was without fault. Laughs can all too easily spoil good looks, by their sounds, or again by the way they can distort the face. Elizabeth Laurence's laugh was as perfect as the rest of her. It was music, it was light, a sound with a sublime cadence, and an infectious quality that made everyone want to laugh with her. She seemed therefore to be flawless. She had the looks of an angel, the grace of a dancer, and a voice to beguile the listener.

Even so, all this would have been meaningless had she been unable to act. Dancing angels who sound like musical instruments may be delightful, but they will not have the power to suspend the audience's disbelief if they cannot convincingly deceive their audience. Happily from the first moment she spoke she proved she had the power. Boska was right. Elizabeth Laurence was going to be a star.

The viewing over, the screen flickered to a bright white and then a barely visible blank as the projectionist shut off his machine. For once no-one called for the lights. Instead everyone sat in silence, waiting for Boska's pronouncement, watching the end of his Passing Cloud glow bright as he drew on it, and then dull as he exhaled. Finally the cigarette was extinguished and the verdict for which they had all been waiting was passed.

'So, OK,' Boska said. 'Now all our shooting star needs is a leading man.'

THREE

Dmitri Boska was only one of the many luminaries in the audience that had jam-packed the Marie Leborne theatre to see the final year's production of *Romeo and Juliet*. The graduating drama students' last and most major production was a fixture in the diaries of every important producer, director, casting agent, and personal representative in town, although more often than not it turned out to be something which they had to endure rather than enjoy. But this year it was different. This year there was a buzz going round before the curtain rose. This year the word was that there was a Discovery.

But as usual, Dmitri Boska had stolen a march on his rivals, his spies having informed him well in advance. Which was how the tall, elegant, exiled Pole came to be waiting in the wings for Romeo to come off-stage long before the actor had wished his Juliet that sleep should dwell upon her eyes, and peace in her breast. A few other impresarios had the same intention as the wily Boska, but being British they observed the proprieties and waited until the house lights came up for the interval, by which time Boska had beaten them all to it, having whisked the young actor off to lock him in his dressing room, where, by the time the call boy was calling Act Three beginners, Boska had Jerome Didier signed to a five-year exclusive contract.

'It's wonderful, yes?' he mused, as his chauffeur drove him and his young and beautiful fashion model companion on to dine at the Savoy, just as the Curtain was rising on Act Three. 'It's always the same, you know,' he continued, lighting a fresh cigar. 'Spotting talent is something even you could do, my dear. And will I tell you

31

why? Of course I will. Because talent stinks. And when you smell this, you sign it up.'

But that, for a while, was all Dmitri Boska was to do for Jerome Didier, just sign him up. Undoubtedly it was a stroke of incredible fortune for the young actor to be put under contract by the most powerful film impresario in the country before he had even finished his last performance at drama school, but after six months of solid unemployment, Jerome Didier was beginning to doubt the wisdom of the move.

Of course Boska paid him. He gave the young actor an allowance, just enough money to finance the purchase of a second-hand red MG sports car, some new clothes, including a much-needed dinner jacket, and to ensure that once or twice a week Jerome Didier could afford to be seen in the right kind of places with the right kind of people. Boska saw to the young actor's social arrangements personally, as well as his professional ones, which included an introduction to and inevitably a subsequent contract with the man most people considered the most up and coming young agent in town, Cecil Manners, whom Boska knew was honest enough to look after the best interests of the actor without jeopardizing Boska's own.

Jerome chafed at the restrictions his contract with Boska imposed, which was exactly what his new employer wanted. Once he had signed them up, Dmitri Boska liked to keep his actors waiting, believing that an appetite for success was born out of want. And Boska knew that what Jerome Didier wanted, like every other promising young actor Boska had signed before, was to get up there and act. And so he made absolutely sure that no offer was made until the young actor was on the verge of artistic starvation.

But Boska was acting from the best, not from the worst of motives. Although he loved to play the sadistic, heartless employer, he was really nothing of the kind, for he loved both his profession and the members of it, and when it came to producing good films on impossibly low budgets he was infinitely more skilled at doing so than his English rivals. Dmitri Boska loved film, and was determined to produce films which finally would be every bit as good as those produced transatlantic, believing that his adopted country had both the artistic and technical ability to match the Americans.

Which was one of the reasons he was so excited by Jerome Didier. He had put many young and promising players under contract over the years, but none of them had ever really fulfilled their promise. But Didier, he felt, was different. Jerome Didier would become a star, he just knew it. And not only that, Jerome Didier would become his first truly international star.

Cecil Manners thought so, too, but worried over Boska's tactics.

'Don't worry!' Boska laughed, pinching one of Cecil's rather pink cheeks. 'The waiting bit makes them humble!'

'I'm not so sure about Jerome,' Cecil replied. 'He's a little short on patience, and he indicated to me the other day that he's not sure he can stand being idle a moment longer.'

'Good!' Boska squeezed Cecil's other cheek, making it also burn red. 'For if he *is* a star – this is how we want him. Ready to burst, no? You know those stars up there? The ones above us?' Boska gestured in a wide circle above his head. 'So how are they made? I tell you. After *centuries* of silence. Light *years* of nothing doing. And then suddenly! All that energy! Whoooff! It explodes! And another bright and brand new star he is born!'

Of course Boska was right, and Cecil Manners knew it. Nobody, however brilliant they might be, or might be going to be, nobody ever shone bright in a bad film or play. So Boska was right to wait for the ideal conditions. Because when the moment came, which it surely would, all that pent-up frustration and unused energy would positively rocket Jerome Didier into orbit.

'And not only that,' Boska would invariably add as his final word, 'the waiting bit makes them humble!'

Jerome didn't know that he was meant to be learning humility. All Jerome knew was that he was suffering, and not just from frustration, he was also suffering from loneliness. Since leaving drama school he had lived in a rented, one-bedroomed flat in a converted Victorian house which smelt of stale cabbage and was situated down the wrong end of the Bayswater Road, and because by now most of the friends with whom he had graduated had started working, he felt worse and worse the longer he remained unemployed. He had even stopped going out, preferring to stay in and read, and save his unearned income just in case he was still unemployed by the time his contract with Boska came to an end.

Happily, Cecil Manners was more than just a good agent. Cecil Manners was also a compassionate human being, and he took pity on his latest client.

'You're looking pale, dear boy,' he said one day when he was lunching Jerome. 'Why not come down to Sussex for the weekend? Mother's having one of her house-parties. But we live on the edge of the Downs, so one can easily slip off for a good ramble. Get some colour into your cheeks.'

'That's very kind of you, Cecil,' Jerome replied. 'If I'm free, I'd enjoy that very much.'

Jerome was, of course, free, and from the moment he arrived at Mrs Ursula Manners' large Edwardian house in West Sussex, he enjoyed himself enormously. It was like stepping into the set of a West End play, pure theatre, Jerome decided, from the impeccably costumed maid and sonorously voiced manservant, to the game of croquet which he could spot being played on the manicured lawns outside.

The settings were perfect too, he observed, as he followed the butler through from a hall complete with family portraits and reproduction suit of armour and into a large eau-de-Nil drawing room furnished with chintz covered furniture and embellished with enormous Constance Spry flower arrangements. Even the gathered guests all looked perfectly costumed and cast.

They also all looked at him, particularly the women. They were all far too well bred, of course, actually to stop talking and stare open mouthed, but a definite hush settled on the company as Jerome made his entrance, pausing at the doorway to light a cigarette before glancing up at his fellow guests with an open but quizzical look, which brought a blush to the cheek of several of the women, all of whom were convinced the look was meant for them.

More looks followed him as he was led over to meet his hostess.

'Mrs Manners,' he said, half bowing over her proffered hand and deliberately kissing it, confident from what he had already seen of Cecil's mother, with her slightly oversized jewellery, the somewhat overbright colour of her dress, and her quite definitely over-made-up eyes, that she was exactly the type of woman who would enjoy rather than be taken aback by the gesture.

'Cecil has told me so *much* about you,' Ursula Manners murmured, and she finally and reluctantly withdrew her heavily ringed hand.

'There's really so very little to tell,' Jerome said with a smile, bending forward as if confiding a secret. 'Alas, I am still waiting in the wings.'

'But not for long,' his hostess countered. 'Cecil tells me it's only a matter of finding the right *vehicle*.'

Jerome smiled, but really the smile was for himself. Cecil's mother made it sound as though Jerome were in the motor trade.

'Oh, for a muse of fire, Mrs Manners!' Jerome dropped his voice, but the whisper carried, as it was trained to do. 'And then watch! I shall ascend the very brightest *heaven* of invention!'

At this moment, Cecil came into the room from the gardens, and looked around for Jerome. Jerome saw him, and noted that Cecil was wearing just the sort of casual and worn English clothes which in theatrical terms would be known as *distressed*, and which made the wearers all look as though they belonged to the same club. Seeing his agent so correctly attired, Jerome suffered a moment of sudden anxiety, for he knew his own clothes were wrong, not only because they were the wrong sort of clothes, but also because they were far too new.

His discomfort was somewhat mitigated, however, by Cecil's obvious embarrassment with his mother, who was by now positively gushing at Jerome. As soon as he could do so politely, he broke into their conversation, and with the excuse that he must introduce Jerome around, whisked him out of the drawing room and into the gardens.

'Dear boy,' Cecil said, leading Jerome down the stone steps. 'How very good to see you. You found your way all right? Now come along, there are lots of people I want you to meet.'

Jerome paused on the stairs, while his agent unwittingly wandered on ahead of him. This was something which Jerome was beginning to understand, the importance and style of one's first entrance. So he hung back deliberately, turning his best profile to the group waiting below while he lit a cigarette. Then leaning his head back slightly, he exhaled a long plume of smoke upwards into the sunlight and, having made quite sure he had everyone's attention, skipped lightly down the remaining steps to be introduced.

'Sarah Landen,' Cecil said. 'Jerome Didier.'

A long legged, slim and typically English blonde took Jerome's hand in hers and did her best to make as little as she could of Jerome's dark and stunning and very un-English looks. But once Jerome met her cool blue eyes with his own dark brown ones, she was totally, and to her companions' amusement, very visibly mesmerized.

'Marguerite Dundas – Jerome Didier,' Cecil continued, and Jerome, rather than letting go of the blonde's hand, allowed it seemingly to just slip from his grasp before turning to meet the rest of the group.

'Georgina Branscome – Jerome Didier. Toby Walters – Jerome Didier. Neil Cameron – Jerome Didier.'

And so the introductions were effected, as Jerome turned from one to another, greeting the men with the same kind of mysterious disdain he used on the girls. And such was the impression he made on them, none of them ever forgot him, and would forever boast of how they met Jerome Didier once at a house-party when he was just Jerome Didier, a totally unknown actor.

The men remembered equally as well as the women, although they would sometimes try and dismiss the recollection with the rider that Didier even then was very much *the actor chappie*. The girls never forgot him, and certainly never tried to make less of the impact Jerome had made, preferring rather to exaggerate, leading their audience to believe that Jerome had singled them out with one of his famous dark looks, or paid them that extra and secret bit of attention.

While on the other hand, Jerome forgot them all. Not in time, but from the moment he glanced over Cecil's shoulder and saw a slender girl with a mane of dark unruly hair that kept falling in her eyes, as she bent over her croquet mallet to line up her shots. She was completely absorbed in her game, paying the group by the steps not even the slightest attention, including Jerome.

Cecil noticed Jerome's sudden and prolonged stare, and called to the girl.

'Pippa? Come over here and meet Jerome!'

Even then, she didn't even look up. She just pushed the hair from her eyes and relined up her shot.

'I am trying to rescue you, Cecil!' she called back in a deliciously husky voice. 'You've got so far behind!'

'That is Pippa,' Cecil said finally, and just a little hopelessly. 'Pippa Nicholls.'

They waited while with one old gym shoed foot she rolled her red ball against the black before *roqueing* the black yards up field out of play into some bushes on the edge of the lawn.

'There!' the girl exclaimed, before running across to join them. 'That'll teach them to bash *us* into the bushes!'

'Pippa,' Cecil said patiently, as if addressing a restless child. 'This is a new client of mine, Jerome Didier. Jerome, this is a neighbour of mine, Pippa Nicholls.'

Jerome stared at her. She had grey eyes, a face full of tiny freckles, and in direct contrast to the rest of the guests, she was dressed most unconventionally, even for a weekend and casual house-party. Besides her faded gym shoes, she wore a pair of even more faded boys grey shorts, and an old white aertex shirt, which

Jerome could only assume to be an elder brother's cast-offs. But whoever's they were or had been, the faded grey shorts showed the girl's slim brown legs off to perfection.

'Be careful of Miss Nicholls,' Cecil said, half jokingly but also half seriously, having noted the look on Jerome's face. 'She is quite heartless. That is if she's not on your side.'

Pippa frowned and shook Jerome's hand briefly.

'Hello,' she said, as if he hardly existed, and then turned back to Cecil. 'Come on, Cecil,' she urged. 'It's still my go, and we can win now, thanks to my *roqueing* Charles. And if you'd only put your mind to it. Come on.'

Once the game re-started, Jerome sat on the stone wall along the lawn's edge, and made polite conversation with the other girls to whom he had been introduced, all of whom seemed most anxious to talk to him. Girls had always fallen for him. Ever since he was fifteen, the year after he had moved to Carriagetown with his mother, girls had been fascinated by him. He had noticed, of course, but he hadn't been in the least interested. All he still wanted to do was fish and swim. And while he liked girls well enough, and would go swimming with them, or play beach tennis when his friends weren't available, girls couldn't take the place of boys, friends like Charlie Willcox or Sam Hoskins. Girls didn't like fishing, and Jerome could outswim any girl by miles.

And then one day, not long after his seventeenth birthday, he went for a long swim with a girl who had just moved to Carriagetown. She was called Trix, she was pretty and blonde and athletic, she could swim almost as fast as Jerome, and sometimes even outrun him. After their swim, they lay in the hot sun-drenched sand dunes, and Trix kissed him, and with her kiss, and the other, longer kisses that followed, Jerome stopped being a boy and became a young man.

They spent the rest of the afternoon kissing, so that by the time Jerome got back for his tea in the converted railway carriage which overlooked the English Channel and was his home, his mouth was reddened and his neck covered in love bites, which Jerome did his best to hide under the buttoned-up collar of his shirt, while his mother sat in eloquent silence.

Six weeks later, in the same dunes where he had tasted his first kiss with Trix, he lost his virginity to her, although strangely the only image that remained of that particular afternoon was not the loss of his chastity, but rather his memory of the sight in the skies above him of a squadron of Spitfires flying full throttle to intercept the incoming German bombers.

'Oh – *fiddle*!'

A husky voice from below on the lawn focused Jerome's attention once more on the freckle-faced, tousle-haired girl below him on the lawns.

'What did I do wrong, Cecil?' she appealed to her partner. 'That's the easiest hoop of all!'

Jerome hopped down from the wall and wandered over the grass.

'You're not swinging the mallet back far enough,' he told her as he reached her side.

'Of course I am!' she retorted, without even looking up at him.

'No, really,' Jerome insisted. 'You need more backswing.'

But before he could show her what he meant, Pippa had played the shot and the ball curled towards the hoop and clean through it.

'See?' she asked gleefully, pushing back yet another long strand of curling hair from her eyes. 'You don't know this lawn. Too much backswing on this side, and it won't take the borrow.'

She walked on beyond the hoop to where her ball lay, and then surveyed the state of the game.

'Oh blast,' she sighed, hooking the errant strand back over one pretty little ear. 'I suppose I'd better go back for poor Cecil. Honestly, he's hopeless.'

Her partner's ball lay two hoops behind, and Jerome watched as Pippa lined the impossibly long shot up, and stared intensely from mallet to ball, and back again.

'You really will need a lot of backswing for this,' Jerome murmured, but Pippa just ignored his advice except for rewarding him with a brief glare, before striking the ball with a long sweet stroke, which carried it all the way back down the lawn to take another hidden borrow and kiss the yellow.

'Hurrah!' she cried, charging across the grass while Jerome watched, enthralled by a feeling he had often tried to act out in class but had never before felt. 'I'll put you through, Cecil!' she shouted to her partner. 'And then I'll come back for Sarah!'

Jerome sat down alone on the bottom of the flight of steps, as the object of his growing adoration cannoned her partner's ball through the hoop, and then came back to knock the blue ball right up to the other end of the lawn. Within minutes the game was concluded, victory going to the home team, due, Cecil had to admit, entirely to the skills of his long brown-legged and tousle-haired partner.

'Tea, Mr Didier!' a voice called from up above him, and Jerome turned to see Ursula Manners waving at him from the top of the steps. 'We're taking it up here on the terrace!'

Jerome stood up, brushing some moss from his trousers, and by the time he looked back up, the girl was gone. Or rather going, for he could still just see her, strolling off against the sun towards the copse at the end of the lawn. She had her hands deep in the pockets of her shorts, and a freshly picked long grass in her mouth. For a moment she stopped, combing her long mane of dark hair back with one slender brown hand, as she stared up into the trees at a bird calling above her, before disappearing through a wicket gate at the side of the woods.

'Et tu, Brute?' Cecil said, as he stood on the steps behind Jerome, following the young man's gaze. 'You shouldn't, you know, really. For your own sake, dear boy. Not at this point in your career.'

'I was just thinking what a perfect Juliet she'd make, as a matter of fact,' Jerome lied.

'No, no,' Cecil laughed. 'Not Pippa's style at all. The moment Romeo began all his nonsense from below Pippa's balcony, she'd send him on his way with just a look from those extraordinary eyes.'

Jerome looked round and seeing the expression on Cecil's face, half raised an eyebrow.

'I see,' he said.

'Yes.' Cecil sighed. 'I'm afraid I fell for her the first moment I saw her, winning the bending race on that mad pony of hers.'

'And how does she feel about you?' Jerome enquired, over-politely. 'Is your picture on her piano?'

'Don't be absurd, dear boy, she treats me like an uncle. Probably my thatch, or rather my lack of it. Heigh ho.'

Cecil ran his fingers through his prematurely thinning hair and sighed again.

'Is there anyone else's picture on her piano?' Jerome enquired.

'No-one,' Cecil replied. 'There is no-one else in Pippa Nicholls' life except her mother and her dog. And they're both murder to get past.'

'Good,' Jerome said, and then drew the back of an index finger across his mouth, a habit which was to become a trademark. 'Then all's fair.'

'What?' Cecil said. 'You said something.'

'I was talking to myself,' Jerome smiled. 'Shall we go and join your mother for tea?'

39

Later that evening, after a large, formal dinner party, the house party repaired *en masse* to a dance held in a large and rambling Tudor manor nearby. It was an elaborate affair, with flowers everywhere, silk-lined marquees on the lawn, two dance bands, and champagne at every turn. But to Jerome it might as well have been a hop in the local parish hall, until he saw Pippa.

She was standing talking to a very tall, upright young man at the entrance of one of the marquees, wearing a long muslin evening dress which to Jerome looked distinctly old-fashioned and almost certainly a hand-me-down. It did nothing for her slim figure, and worse, she had put her hair up, which Jerome at once decided didn't suit her. In a fit of pique and with quite unjustifiable possessiveness, he at once made his way to her side.

'Good evening,' he said, unable to stop the greeting from sounding like an insult.

Both Pippa and her escort turned to stare with surprise at the intruder.

'I'm sorry?' Pippa said after a moment. 'Should I know you?'

Jerome saw from the expression on her face she hadn't remembered him. He was so astounded further words failed him, and he felt a look of dismay which he couldn't control come over his face. She had forgotten him. They had met only a few hours ago, and yet she had palpably failed to remember him. Him. Jerome Didier. The handsome, the beautiful, the irresistible. She could barely have even noticed him. Either that, or the girl was a consummate actress.

He passed the back of one hand lightly along the top of his brow, against the edge of his dark hair, and smiled, his poise seemingly recovered.

'We met earlier this afternoon, Miss Nicholls,' he said. 'At Cecil Manners'. When you were playing croquet.'

He spoke slowly, dividing the speech into a series of prompts, hoping that all he would have to say was that they had met earlier. But she didn't pick up any of the prompts, and so Jerome realized he would have to carry on until the famous penny finally dropped.

'I told you you weren't taking enough backswing,' he said as sweetly as he could, while seething internally. 'But nonetheless you made the hoop. Along a right-handed borrow.'

'Of course!' she suddenly remembered, rewarding him with a deep frown rather than the smile for which he had hoped. 'You're that new client of Cecil's.'

Thankful that he had worked so hard on his breathing technique at drama school, for otherwise he would certainly have betrayed the depth of his rising panic, Jerome managed a smile, as if grateful simply that Pippa had managed at least to recall him.

'I'm terribly sorry,' she said after a moment. 'You know I really can't remember your name.'

'Jerome Didier, Miss Nicholls.'

'Yes, of course,' she replied, as if she had never heard it before. 'This is Captain Bodell. A great friend of my brother's. Rodney, this is Jeremy Didier.'

'Jerome, Miss Nicholls,' he corrected her, as he shook hands with the tall elegant guardsman. 'My name is Jerome.'

'As in *Three Men In A Boat*?' Pippa asked.

'Precisely,' Jerome replied, before turning back to the guardsman. 'I'm sorry,' he said. 'Did you say Bodell? Someone was looking for a Captain Bodell a minute ago. It appears you're wanted on the telephone.'

'Oh blast,' the soldier said. 'Really?'

'Absolutely,' Jerome assured him, and then having watched poker-faced as Bodell excused himself from their company he turned back and found Pippa watching him with an equally straight face.

'Did you learn that in a play?' she asked him.

'Most probably,' Jerome replied, half smiling.

'It can't have been a very good play.'

Before Jerome could reply, and indeed before he could even think up a reply, the band struck up a new tune, coming to his rescue.

He turned to the bandstand, and then back to Pippa.

'Would you like to dance?' he asked.

She looked at him a little dubiously.

'I'm not a very good dancer, actually,' she replied. 'I don't get much practice. My mother's widowed you see, and she can't afford to give me a proper sort of dance. And if you don't give a dance, well, you don't get asked to them much, I find.'

'No?' Jerome asked, slipping his right arm round her waist.

'You dance rather well.'

'Thank you.'

Jerome had taught himself to dance in Carriagetown, at parties inside the converted carriages, or outside on the beach, before honing his technique to near perfection at drama school.

'But then you would,' Pippa added after a moment's thought.

41

'Would what, Miss Nicholls?'

'Dance well, Mr Didier. People like you should dance well. Because you obviously get asked to lots of dances.'

'People like me?'

'Who go to lots of dances. Deb dances.'

'I'm an actor, Miss Nicholls,' Jerome sighed. 'Not a socialite. Actors rarely get asked to dances, at least not in *my* experience.'

Pippa smiled, and then frowned, as she began to concentrate on her dancing in the same way that she had concentrated on her croquet. Jerome found this oddly touching, as he found everything about the girl in his arms, from her hand-me-down clothes, and her great tousle of hair which appeared to have a life of its own, to the optimism which seemed to shine in her oddly coloured grey eyes, as if she expected life to be an eternally interesting challenge, one to be undertaken with the same determination she had shown on the croquet lawn, and was now showing again on the dance floor.

There was something else about her, which Jerome couldn't specify, which made him long to talk to her, to sit down somewhere quite alone, and tell her all about his family and his childhood, about Terence Vaughan, National Service in the RAF, why and how he went to drama school, and what had happened to him since. But the more he thought about talking to her, the more silent he became, and he found himself instead just looking into a face full of such sweetness, feeling just the very lightness of her young slim body in his arms, and through the fabric of her dress the warmth and firmness of her small round breasts.

'Thank you,' she said, and Jerome frowned. He hadn't even noticed the band had stopped playing. He hadn't even noticed what the band had been playing.

'That was lovely,' Pippa continued, retightening the sash around her waist in another effort to get her dress to hang properly. 'Now I'm sure you want to dance with somebody else. And I think perhaps I'd better as well.'

'Why?' Jerome asked.

'Because,' Pippa replied patiently, as if addressing a child, 'we have just danced three dances on the trot, that's why.'

'So why not four, may I ask?'

'Because it's bad manners.'

She looked up at him, smiling, and as she did, the smile vanished and was replaced by a sudden, puzzled look, a look which seemed to say that she didn't quite understand what was happening to her.

And then that look also vanished, and was replaced by the smile, although this time the smile was a little less certain.

The band began to play a waltz, and Pippa turned away to listen.

'We haven't danced a waltz,' Jerome said from behind her, leaning closer so that he could whisper it in her ear. 'Let's just dance this waltz, and then I'll hand you back to the heathens.'

Pippa turned back, about to dance with him, when the young guardsman returned and cut in.

'My dance I think,' he said, giving Jerome one brief but hard stare. 'Pippa?'

He gave her his arm and led her on to the floor, while Jerome stood watching helplessly, unable this time to think up some ready ruse. Instead he went and fetched himself a drink, and stood by the bar watching Pippa being danced by the tall, upright soldier. Finally he could take it not one moment longer, and having downed his champagne, he fought his way across the crowded dance floor until he was once more at Pippa's side.

'Excuse me,' he said, cutting in.

Bodell gave a glance to see who it was, and seeing it was Jerome, his face hardened.

'Look,' he said coldly. 'Sorry, but this is not an Excuse-me.'

'I never said it was,' Jerome replied equally coldly, taking the bewildered Pippa by the arm. 'I simply said excuse me.'

He marched Pippa off the dance floor holding her by the arm, as if she was a child who had just committed some social solecism. He marched her right through the crowd until they were out of the marquee and across the far side of the moonlit lawns, under the long shadows cast by a line of tall conifers.

'I don't think Rodney took that very well,' Pippa said, looking back to the tent.

Jerome groaned.

'Now what's the matter?'

'Dear lord – he would have to be called Rodney, wouldn't he?'

'What's wrong with Rodney?' Pippa asked, starting to pull some of the pins out of her hair, and putting them in her mouth. 'Someone has to be called Rodney.'

'What are you doing?'

'My hair,' Pippa replied. 'It doesn't seem to want to stay up.'

'I don't blame it,' Jerome said, putting his hand on her arm. 'Leave it down. It's so much prettier.'

'You don't like my hair up?'

43

'I like your hair up, but I like it even more – *down*.'

Pippa stopped rearranging her hair for a moment and looked at Jerome. Then she sighed.

'Yes, I know,' she said. 'I'm a bit of a mess.'

'Of course you aren't,' Jerome replied quickly, and valiantly.

'Of course I am,' Pippa insisted. 'I mean look at this dress.'

'It's a lovely dress. There's absolutely nothing wrong with the dress.'

'Liar.'

'You look lovely, I promise you. So how can there be anything wrong with the dress?'

'Don't you think it's a little – a little old?'

'That is probably—' Jerome smiled and paused, as he bent slightly towards her, 'half its – charm.'

Jerome was secretly pleased as he heard himself. He had, he realized suddenly, recaptured precisely the painfully sensitive and strangely intense character he had given Eugene Marchbanks so successfully in the drama school production of Shaw's *Candida*.

But Pippa seemed to be still too concerned with her appearance to notice, giving yet another sigh as she pulled the straps of her dress back up on to her shoulders.

'It's my grandmother's, if you really want to know,' she said. 'Which probably makes it pre-First World War.'

She looked at him, awaiting a response, but Jerome had fallen silent, choosing just to stare at her with a slight frown. While they stood there in silence, an owl called in the woods beyond them, while across the lawns came the distant sound of the band playing.

'Is something the matter?' Pippa asked finally.

'Oh yes I think so,' Jerome replied, dropping his voice dramatically. 'Yes I think there most definitely is.'

'What?'

'Don't you know?'

'No.'

'You must know,' Jerome insisted. 'I saw it on your face while we were dancing. I saw it on your face after we had danced. I saw it on your face a moment ago.'

Now it was Pippa's turn to frown.

'What did you see?'

'You know,' Jerome whispered.

'No I don't.' said Pippa, contradicting not only Jerome, but something inside herself, something in the way she was beginning to know she felt. 'Now if you'll excuse me, I really must get back.'

'Of course you mustn't,' Jerome replied dismissively. 'Sit here and talk.'

'We can talk back there.' Pippa indicated the house and marquees across the lawns. 'We can talk on the way back there.'

'Pippa.'

This time Jerome managed to make the whisper into a sound of anguish, as if the very act of saying her name caused him pain.

'You're very serious, aren't you?' she said curiously, turning back to face him.

'Am I?'

'Yes.' Pippa studied him for a moment, before continuing, finding herself momentarily startled by quite how good looking Jerome was. 'Are you going to be a very serious actor?' she asked.

Jerome laughed, showing a row of perfect and straight white teeth.

'I'm going to be a very famous one,' he replied.

He preferred it now that she was teasing him, because now that she was teasing him it meant she was at least taking notice. And teasing was a type of intimacy, a sort of foreplay almost, although from the look in Pippa's eyes Jerome sensed she was still trying to find the best way to approach him, which now made him suppose that the teasing might rather be a form of self-defence, to keep him at arm's length emotionally, because she was not yet ready for any wholesale emotional intrusion into her life, preferring to stay as she was, a single entity.

To test her, he reached out his hand and tried to take hers, but she withdrew, stepping back and away from him.

'No,' she said, although considerably less firmly, Jerome was happy to note. 'We really should get back.'

'Very well,' he replied, rolling the r around his mouth. 'If you must. But not I. I do not *wish* to go back.'

He wanted to surprise her, to wrongfoot her by his waywardness, but all he did was make her laugh.

'Now what's funny?' he demanded. 'What are you laughing at?'

'I'm sorry,' Pippa said. 'It was just—' She stopped, and did her best to look serious. 'I'm sorry but you did sound like something straight out of a play.'

She was smiling again, and because of it Jerome felt himself growing increasingly infuriated.

'Go on,' he ordered her. 'Go on – back to your dance. Go on.'

'What are you going to do?'

Her tone managed to infuriate Jerome even more, because she sounded not in the least bit concerned, but merely curious. So hoping to madden her in return, he just gave a shrug and turned to walk away into the moonlit woods beyond.

'Where are you going?' she called after him, still not sounding in the least bit anxious.

'Never mind me!' he called back over his shoulder. 'Please! Go back to your dance!'

His voice echoed rather thrillingly in the woods, Jerome thought as he walked away, tempting him to cry out once more. But he resisted the temptation, and waited instead for the summons he felt must surely come from Pippa for him not to be so foolish, and to return.

But nothing came. The only sound was that of twigs snapping beneath his feet as he headed ever deeper into the darkening woods.

Finally he could bear it no more, and turned back to see if she was at least still waiting for him. But when he got to the edge of the woods he saw the lawn where they had been standing was now deserted, and there was no sign of Pippa anywhere. She had let him go.

She had allowed him to go, deeper and deeper into the woods, further and further from her side, and had returned to the dance, and the party, and most probably that tall idiot of a guardsman – damn it! he thought. She must have gone at once! As soon, in fact, as he had turned and headed for the woods – because it was a long way back across the lawns, and if she had stood hesitating, waiting and wondering whether or not to go after him, she could not have made it back to the marquees. She would still be crossing the lawns, a slender figure in a strange old-fashioned dress.

Instead she had gone, vanished back into the party, not bothered by his refusal to return there with her, abandoning him, leaving him utterly alone under a bright full moon, heartsick and dismayed.

Jerome stood and lit a cigarette. He smoked half of it, practising precisely how to exhale with the maximum of effect, before growing bored. He was bored with feeling heartsick and dismayed, bored with being abandoned, bored even with his cigarette.

So he threw it away into a flowerbed, and straightening his bow-tie, turned and walked back to rejoin the party, no longer feeling bored, just merely slightly ridiculous.

He found her number easily enough the following morning, in Ursula Manners' telephone book on the hall table.

'Jerome Didier,' he said when he heard her voice on the other end of the telephone. 'And before you say anything, I'm sorry about last night.' Which he wasn't at all, in fact he felt that she should be sorry, particularly since when he had made the sacrifice and returned to the dance, he couldn't find her, and later discovered she had long since gone home.

'Sorry?' her husky voice said in his ear. 'Who is this?'

'Jerome,' he said, stifling an impatient sigh. 'Jerome Didier.'

'Oh.' There was a short pause, and then: 'Hello.'

'I was ringing to say sorry,' Jerome repeated.

'Why?' she asked him. 'What on earth for?'

Now Jerome really sighed, unable to help it. The sound of that lightly husky voice made him instantly go weak.

'Because,' he said slowly, while studying his reaction in the oval mirror above the hall table. 'I behaved appallingly. I really don't know what came over me.'

He left a little pause, knowing she wouldn't answer, hoping that she wouldn't. 'No, that's not true,' he continued, pleased with his reading of the scene so far. 'I know *perfectly* well what came over me. But that was still no excuse for my shockingly bad behaviour.'

'You really don't have to apologize for anything,' said the husky little voice. 'I don't see what there is to apologize for. Unless—'

'I shouldn't have walked off like that,' Jerome interrupted. 'And left you. That was very rude.'

'Not really,' she laughed. 'I mean not as rude as interrupting poor Rodney's dance.'

'That –' Jerome announced firmly, 'I am not sorry for.'

'You should be,' Pippa replied. 'I mean if you want to apologize for anything—'

'I don't want to apologize for that,' Jerome reiterated.

All right,' Pippa said and Jerome could almost hear her shrugging her shoulders. 'Well, if you don't want to apologize for that—'

'Look,' Jerome came in quickly, in case Pippa suddenly got it into her head to conclude the conversation. 'I have to see you again.'

'Have to?'

'I would *like* – to see you again.'

'Not want to?'

She was back to teasing, and Jerome smiled, tilting his head back slightly.

'Yes, yes,' he agreed quickly, on the breath. 'I *want* – to see you. All right? Will you come for a walk?'

'Very well,' she agreed, but only after a very long pause. 'After church,' she said, after what seemed like an enormous pause, a wait which made Jerome once more grow desperate. She seemed so poised, and so distant. Was this because this was the way she had decided to play it? Detached and disinterested? Or was it, he thought with a rising hope, perhaps because someone else was standing there listening to her conversation? Like her mother? Cecil had said he would have to get by her mother. So perhaps that was who was listening, and why Pippa couldn't betray any interest in his call.

Or was it perhaps because she simply wasn't interested in him? He would find all this out on the walk, he determined, once and for all.

'Where shall I meet you?'

'Oh, I don't know. By the wicket gate on the far side of Cecil's tennis court. At about quarter-past twelve.'

Jerome saw her first, because he had been waiting for her, half hidden away in the changing hut beside the tennis court. She arrived at the gate exactly on time, a dog lead hung around her neck, and her hair falling in a tumble down her back, but perhaps because it was Sunday, today there were no old faded grey shorts to show off the slim brown legs, just an old pale blue cotton dress and a pair of sandals.

Jerome stayed hidden for a moment, watching her, as she swung on the gate while her small black and white mongrel dashed in and out of the woods chasing what were either real or imaginary rabbits. He watched her with what he realized was a growing sense of dismay, for half of him had hoped that when he saw her again she would turn out to be nothing at all out of the ordinary, that on this the second day of their acquaintance she would prove to have been an emotional mirage, leaving him to wonder why and how he could have felt as impossibly heartsick as he had felt the day before, and as helpless as he had felt that very morning at just the thought of her. But as he looked at her, as he watched her, he knew that the half of him which had hoped her to be a will-o'-the-wisp was now doomed to disappointment. Looking at her he realized he felt even more heartsick and utterly helpless than ever.

Her face with its myriad of freckles, its inquisitive and mischievous grey-green eyes, and its pretty and perfectly proportioned mouth which turned up just very slightly at the corners, had haunted him all night, so much so that now he saw it again he wanted nothing more than to cup it in both his hands and kiss it to pieces.

'Hello!' he called as he appeared in front of her, having slipped quietly out of the hut and made his way unnoticed round the court. 'I hope you haven't been waiting! Blasted telephone!'

He caught hold of the gate Pippa was swinging on, and smiled at her, and his heart leapt when he saw her smile back. Then the little black and white mongrel dashed from out of the woods and hurled itself at Jerome, barking excitedly, while jumping up and down against his legs.

'How odd,' Pippa said with a frown. 'Bobby likes you.'

'That's odd?'

'He doesn't usually like boys.'

'How is he with men?'

Pippa brushed some hair out of her eyes and turned to look at Jerome rather thoroughly.

'Sorry,' she said after a moment. 'I meant men.'

'And I'm sorry about last night,' Jerome said, happily falling into step beside Pippa as she began to walk off ahead of him.

'That's all right,' Pippa said. 'Rodney's a bit of a drone, as a matter of fact.'

She smiled at him, and the warmth of her smile prevented Jerome from remonstrating any further about what he felt the need to apologize for and what he did not. Instead he bent down and finding a stick nearby, threw it for her dog.

'What a great dog,' he said, brushing some of the mud it had left on his immaculate trousers. 'Have you had him since a puppy?'

'He's my mother's dog really,' Pippa replied, only half answering the question. 'But because of her arthritis, she can't walk him. You know – and look after him really.'

'I'm sorry,' Jerome said, which made Pippa frown.

'You can't really be sorry about that,' she replied. 'It's hardly your fault.'

'I meant –' Jerome corrected her. 'I'm sorry *for* your mother.'

'Don't be,' Pippa said. 'She can't stand people feeling sorry for her.'

She stopped and looked round for her dog, who seemed to have disappeared. Then a moment later the air was rent by a piercing whistle which Pippa had concocted by sticking her first two fingers

49

in her mouth. Jerome roared with genuinely surprised laughter.

'Bravo!' he cried. 'Please – you have to teach me how to do that!'

For the next twenty or so minutes, as they strolled towards the Downs, Pippa tried to teach Jerome how to whistle in like fashion, but he was a hopeless pupil, and between fits of helpless laughter, all he could manage was a sound like a train letting off steam.

'I'll get this if it takes all day,' he swore, trying once again. 'I have to. I might need to do this one day in a film. And just think –' he tried once more, only to fail once more. 'Just think,' he continued. 'You might see the film, and you'd be able to say – to whoever you're with – I did that. I taught Jerome Didier to whistle.'

Pippa laughed, and threw the stick again for the dog.

'You're quite certain you're going to be famous, aren't you?' she asked.

'I wouldn't be doing it unless I was. I should imagine acting might be more than just a little silly if you weren't famous.'

'And when do you plan to start being famous?'

'Thursday,' Jerome grinned. 'Now that's enough about me. I want to hear *all* – about you.'

'What?' Pippa stared at Jerome as if he were demented. 'There's absolutely nothing to tell!' she exclaimed, and then started to laugh as if the idea of telling somebody about herself was the funniest notion in the world.

'Every town has a story,' Jerome intoned in his best radio voice. 'And why even this quiet-seeming little town of ours has plenty of strange tales to tell.'

'There's nothing strange about my tale, I'm afraid,' Pippa laughed. 'My life's been really rather ordinary actually. Apart from my father being killed in the war, but then there's nothing really out of the ordinary in that either, is there? When you think how many people were killed in the war.'

'Was he killed in action?'

'Yes. He was a fighter pilot. Well, a squadron leader actually. He was shot down over Germany. Which meant Mother brought us up, us being my brother and I. Which I don't suppose can have been easy for one minute, since there's never been much in the kitty. Of course, in one way it will be easier when she has me off her hands—'

'When you get married, you mean?'

'No.' Pippa rounded on him, and looked at him sharply. 'I meant when I start earning my living. I want to paint. Well I do paint, so it's not a question of wanting to, and what I'd really like to do is set design. My art teacher at school thought that's what I should do as well. And Cecil says he'll help me get started. Because he has all the right contacts.'

Pippa suddenly stopped talking and stared into the distance, except this time she wasn't looking for her dog.

'Penny for them,' Jerome prompted her, wondering whether Pippa had any feelings for Cecil which were at all like the ones Cecil so obviously had for her. 'Are you thinking about Cecil?'

'Cecil? No, I was thinking of something quite different, actually,' Pippa replied.

'What?'

Again she looked at him, surprised by the blunt enquiry.

'We're not going to get to know each other,' Jerome said, 'unless we tell each other everything about ourselves.'

'Who said anything about getting to know each other?'

'I did,' Jerome replied with a slow smile, 'just now. Didn't you hear? So what was the different thing you were thinking about?'

'Nothing.' Pippa walked on. 'It was something about my mother if you really want to know.'

'Of course,' Jerome agreed. 'You were wondering how – or indeed if, more like – if and how your mother could cope if you did ever leave home. Of course,' he continued, sensing that Pippa was about to interrupt him. 'Of course, you could paint – professionally – at home, and still look after her. But then a time might come when you might have to leave home for quite a different reason.'

'I suppose Cecil told you that my mother needs care.'

'No. You did.'

'I did? I don't remember saying any such thing.'

'You didn't. Not in so many words.' Jerome sunk his hands in his trouser pockets. 'It's what in rehearsal we call the subtext,' he added.

'What's that?'

'It's not so much what you say,' Jerome explained, 'but rather what you don't say.' He gestured one handed, as if producing something from his chest. 'What you feel.'

'Why don't you have another go at whistling?' she asked after a moment spent staring ahead. 'You never know, you might get it.'

As Jerome obliged, putting his fingers up to his mouth once more, Pippa stopped him, taking his hand and looking at his second finger.

'Did you break this? It's terribly crooked.'

51

'I broke it when I was in the RAF. Fooling around.'

'You were in the RAF?'

'Only for my National Service.'

'Did you learn to fly?'

'I wanted to be a full-time pilot.'

'So why didn't you?'

It was Jerome's turn to talk, and he talked easily because he found that to Pippa he could. He talked far more easily and more honestly than he had ever talked with anyone before, including all the girls with whom he'd had affairs at drama school, who had always wanted to know everything about him, and because they had been so insistent, he had found he could hardly even begin to talk to them.

But Pippa was different. She didn't pepper him with questions, or put an interpretation on things, she just listened, which as he had found out at drama school in class when another student listened to him, improved the level of his performance dramatically, which was precisely the effect Pippa was having on him. Jerome was telling her things about himself he had never told anyone before, he was even admitting things he had never even admitted to himself.

They must have walked miles that midday, high on the Downs where he learned Pippa walked or rode whenever she had the chance. With the breeze ruffling both their hair, he remembered out loud the ugly red brick house where he had been born, and where he had spent the first twelve years of his life. Situated in a Kentish village not five miles from RAF Hawkinge, it was hardly surprising his abiding passion as a boy had been for aeroplanes, and for as long as he could remember all he wanted to be was a fighter pilot.

'I watched the Battle of Britain daily,' he told her, 'in the skies above my head. I'd watch it from the top of my favourite tree, or sitting alone in the cornfields. I'd see Spitfires engaging the enemy fighters, and Hurricanes attacking their bombers. And I wished – oh, how I wished I'd been born those five years earlier, so I could be up there with them, fighting the Battle for Britain!'

'You'll be awfully good as Henry V,' Pippa said, in answer to the way Jerome had raised his voice in a fine crescendo.

Jerome laughed and took her arm, and then encouraged because she didn't remove it, continued up a gentle slope in the Downs.

'And then my life changed suddenly, totally,' he continued. 'One night, when I was fast asleep, my mother woke me, and told me not to say a word. She had packed our suitcases, and without telling me why, she took me and walked out of the house deep in the middle of one dark winter night.'

'Where did you go?' Pippa asked, as Jerome lapsed into silence, stopping on the side of the hill as he remembered the event of that night long ago. 'And why the middle of the night?'

'That I didn't find out until later,' Jerome replied. 'When it happened, I was much too muddled at first, then excited, and then bewildered to ask why. When you're that age—' He shrugged, and looked to Pippa for agreement. 'You know,' he continued. 'You might *want* to know things, but you don't always know how to ask them. Or even if you should. So for a long time I never actually knew what the cause of it all was, why my mother who was such a quiet and loving person, should suddenly and inexplicably leave my father. And my father was such a quiet, *ordinary* man. Or so it seemed. His life was like clockwork. In and out of the house the same time each day, out twice a week to his meetings, you literally could set your watch by him. He only suffered one setback apparently, which emerged to be the all important one, and that was failing his army medical for some trifling little infirmity. And he took it very badly. That I did realize at the time, because I remember walking with him the day after he had failed, along the foreland at Dover, and he fell behind when I was playing aeroplanes or some such nonsense. And when I ran back to him, he was crying. Real tears. Right down his face. It's oddly frightening, you know, for a boy. To see his father crying. I didn't ask why. I couldn't. I just took his hand – and we walked home in silence. My mother told me the reason later. About the medical.'

'And when did you find out why she left him? When did she tell you that?'

'Oh, a long time after. But it all stemmed from that day. The day he failed that wretched medical. Because it was from that moment he started to lead a double life. He was a bigamist, you see, my father. It was as if because the Army had turned him away, he had to prove himself twice the man he was. And so he found himself another wife.'

They had reached a turning point, a small wood at the top of the long hill they had climbed, and from which when they both turned round, catching the freshening breeze in their faces, they could see Cecil's home far below, and another house nestling in a fold of fields and woodland nearby, which Pippa pointed out as hers.

For a while they sat on the trunk of a fallen tree, Pippa making daisy chains, and Jerome smoking a cigarette.

'My god,' he breathed, 'England is such a beautiful country. *A fortress built by Nature for herself against infection, and the hand of war.*'

Pippa put the long chain of daisies round the neck of her little dog, who sat panting at her feet.

'Where did your mother take you?' she asked. 'Where on earth did you go that night?'

'We went to the most extraordinary place, a place I must take you one day,' Jerome said, getting up and stretching. 'It's a settlement of obsolete railway rolling stock, and it's called Carriagetown. Or rather that's what it was called by everyone who lived there. And it was the most *wonderful* place you can imagine. And for kids – well, it was paradise. No official school. Just the sea, and the beach, no conventions, and this collection of wonderful people! All runaways, vagrants like ourselves, mostly, I have to say, women who had run off from their drunken, or violent, or unfaithful husbands to live in this settlement of abandoned railway carriages right on Denge Beach.'

'Where?'

'Denge Beach. The end of the line near Lydd, where I suppose they used to just take the old rolling stock and dump it. They made the most marvellous homes once they were converted, much more solid and comfortable than caravans. We were known as the Railway Gypsies, we owned nothing, and we were owned by nothing. All we had were three sets of clothes, like the Chinese. One set on, one in the wash, and one set to spare. It was such a happy place. I think everyone was happy there, once they got there. We were, the kids I mean. Imagine, we had the sea, we fished, we swam, we played games on the beach, it was heaven.'

'You must have had some schooling,' Pippa wondered. 'You're hardly an illiterate.'

'As a matter of fact we had a very good schooling,' he explained. 'The women saw to that. There were some men there, not many, some who'd failed their army medicals, some who objected to the war and whom the authorities were content to let "disappear", and some older men who wished to live alone for private unspoken reasons. They taught us our three Rs. And some of the mothers did too. Between them all they managed to give us a very good education. I should imagine our teachers were the best you could find anywhere, because they all had souls, you see. Particularly Terence Vaughan.'

Jerome stopped talking, not for effect this time, but because the memory of Vaughan was suddenly too much for him. So he walked on ahead, and threw yet another stick for Pippa's little dog, who bounded after it across the springy old turf, barking for joy. Pippa hurried after them both, and catching up with Jerome, slipped her arm through his.

'I'm sorry,' Jerome said.

'What for now?'

'I've been banging on about myself, I'm terribly sorry.'

'Who was Terence Vaughan?'

'I really have talked far too much about myself,' Jerome sighed. 'Come on, let's hear a bit more about you.'

'Not until you've told me about Terence Vaughan,' Pippa replied. 'He must have been important, because your voice went all funny.'

'All right,' Jerome said, exhaling deeply. 'Terence Vaughan was perhaps the finest actor who never was.'

'You're certainly going to have to explain that conundrum,' Pippa said.

So Jerome did. He told her all about the man who was his mentor, how he had trained to be an actor, and how the First World War had put a stop to his ambitions when he stood on an enemy mine and lost both his legs. And how after he was invalided out of the Army he became an English teacher at a school in a town not far from Lydd, and how one day when he was visiting an old pupil who had just moved to Carriagetown, he met Jerome's mother, fell in love, threw over his job and moved into Carriagetown.

'For some reason,' Jerome said, 'I became his star pupil. But I have to say the admiration was mutual. I absolutely worshipped him. He was strict, but kind, firm, but understanding, and he had a simply marvellous sense of humour. He was a brilliant teacher. He taught me everything I know. He taught me voice, he taught me how to move, how to speak verse, blank verse, where to breathe and how, how to take the breath where no-one else would, which is the essence of it all, to take a breath and carry on the line through, *past* the full stop, and somewhere into the next sentence. Best of all, he taught me the secret of surprise, how to do something on stage *unpredictably*, which he swore was the key to great acting. Always to be *unpredictable*. I would say that goes for most things, wouldn't you, Pippa?'

'Yes, I think I would, Jerome,' Pippa agreed, letting go of his arm. 'I think I agree with that entirely.'

She walked alongside him for a while, detached from him, playing with her dog, and paying him no attention. Jerome glanced

55

at her, but she was still involved with the dog and their game. And then just when he thought he had lost her, he felt her slipping her hand in his, and turned to see her smiling at him.

'So when did you decide you were going to be an actor?' she asked. 'Rather than a fighter pilot?'

'I never really gave it a thought,' Jerome confessed. 'I thought it was *marvellous*, learning all that stuff, but it was just a sort of game to me, you see. And because I adored Terry, and because he loved my mother, I went along with it because it was such fun, and to please them both, I suppose. And I didn't take it very seriously, even though Terry was forever booming at me that I had the romantic power for Romeo, and the melancholy for Hamlet.'

'Until?'

'Until one day when we'd been out on a long fishing trip, and late in the day after we'd turned for home, I suddenly confided in Terry that what I really wanted to do more than anything else – still – was to be a fighter pilot. He nearly fell out of the boat.' Jerome assumed Terence Vaughan's voice, changing to a deep booming basso profundo. 'A fighter pilot? You cannot possibly be a *fighter pilot*, you ass! Those looks were not meant to be lost in some fire above the clouds! You were given looks like yours to make people gasp!'

Pippa laughed, but it was true, and it was the first time Jerome had been made aware of his looks. Until that moment he had just leaped straight from his bed and into his clothes to go fishing, or into his bathing trunks to go swimming before breakfast. He'd never had either the time or the inclination to stop and look at himself in a mirror. Like so many exceptionally handsome children, he had been careless of his greatest asset.

But that evening after supper, in the mirror of the old first-class carriage which was his bedroom, a yellowing glass which hung between advertisements for Players cigarettes and the Grand Hotel at Brighton, Jerome took a long good look at himself, and saw a dark-haired, dark-eyed, high-cheekboned face staring back at him, one with a hint of arrogance already around the mouth, and an air of brooding melancholy around the eyes. He looked at himself long and hard, and then asked himself the question.

'To be, or not to be?' he asked, before getting into bed and lying wonderingly in the dark.

'Was that when you decided?'

'I didn't *decide* then, Pippa,' Jerome told her. 'But I seriously considered it. Although during my National Service in the RAF

I went back to square one, forgot all about it, and seriously considered signing on for seven years. And I think I would have done, I know I would have done, if Terry hadn't drowned.'

'I don't understand. Because he drowned—'

'He drowned one day when I was home on leave,' Jerome continued. 'He'd been out fishing by himself, and his little white and blue dinghy came back empty. We were all sitting outside, having a picnic, and when we got to his boat, and pulled it in, it was empty. They found his body two days later.'

'But if he had come back,' Pippa wondered, 'you're saying you wouldn't have become an actor?'

'I think I became an actor for him', Jerome said with great simplicity. 'I think it's as simple as that.'

'No, I don't,' Pippa said, shaking her head and looking at him very seriously. 'I don't think you'd have signed up for the RAF. I think you were always going to be an actor, Jerome Didier. And if I think that, I think you must always have thought so, too.'

He watched her play croquet again, all afternoon. He would gladly have watched her all afternoon whatever she had been doing. He would have spent the entire afternoon watching her if she had just been sleeping, because the longer he watched her, the more certain he became that he loved her.

He loved her intensity. The way she played croquet, it was as if she was playing for her life. Her involvement was total. During the game she hardly looked to where Jerome sat, she simply watched what her opponents were doing and how the game was progressing. Until it was her turn, she would adopt the same pose, sitting on her upturned mallet with her sun-tanned arms folded across her breasts, with her pretty head tilted forward. And then when it was her turn, she would hurry into position, having already worked out her ploy, line up her shot, stick her tongue firmly in one cheek, turn her left toe in and strike.

Jerome was entranced, bewitched. Soon the summer afternoon began to fade slowly into evening, but still they played, and still he watched, and the longer he did so, the more he found to love about her. Besides her intensity, there was her air of innocence. She argued like a child guilelessly, wide-eyed, her face a study in bewilderment, as she wondered at the waywardness of some of Cecil's shots, before giving a deep sigh and playing them out of trouble, at which point she would then turn and grin cheekily at Cecil, which would at once allay Cecil's obvious and mounting anxiety. Poor Cecil, Jerome thought from the sidelines. He was so helpless and so utterly in Pippa's thrall.

She also had such a pretty laugh, Jerome noticed, an attribute lacking in so many of the girls he had taken out. It was a light laugh, infectious and full of merriment and good humour, and he loved that too, just as he loved the way she moved, with a natural athleticism and grace. From his position on the wall, Jerome decided *lithe* might be an appropriate description for her, as she prowled the croquet lawn, looking to see how best to make her shots, watching to see how the game developed.

But most of all he loved the sudden way she would look round at him where he sat perched up on the brick wall. As the evening drew on, she would look up more and more, from under her tumbling head of dark brown hair, and she would smile at him carefully, shyly, as if more and more pleased to see that he was still there.

'Come on,' he said, as her opponents finally conceded defeat. 'Let me walk you home.'

'You don't have to,' she said, but only out of politeness, not to deter him. 'It's only one field.'

'I don't care if it's only fifty yards,' Jerome said, taking her arm. 'I want to be with you until the moment I have to leave for London.'

It was deep dusk as they walked along the edge of the hayfield, hand in hand. The woods alongside the path were full of the even-song of birds, and the faint clatter of small animals hurrying about their business before night fell. In the darkening sky above, where already the evening star shone brightly, birds gathered suddenly from nowhere, and formed into huge, dark squadrons, before wheeling and turning for home. Bobby added to the action by put-ting up a few rabbits which fled bob-tailing before him, deep into the safety of the thickets, and thence underground, while the air was thickening with the smell of wild columbine, and dog roses.

'You're very quiet,' Pippa said after a long while.

'That is because for once,' Jerome replied, 'even I can think of nothing to say. Because for once, everything is quite perfect.'

Pippa's mother was in the drawing room, sitting by the open french windows with a book in her lap, when they appeared from the garden.

'This is Jerome Didier, Mother,' Pippa told her, having long ago freed her hand from Jerome's. 'A friend of mine.'

'Hello, Mrs Nicholls,' Jerome said, his hands clasped before him and he half bowed to her, having quickly noticed how badly

Pippa's mother's hands were affected by arthritis. 'I'm glad to meet you.'

'How do you do?' Mrs Nicholls looked over the top of her reading glasses at Jerome. 'You must be the actor.'

'An actor,' Jerome corrected her, tongue in cheek, pleased that Pippa had obviously spoken to her about him.

'Do you mind if I make Jerome some sandwiches, Mother?' Pippa asked. 'He's got to go back to London, and the croquet game went on rather long.'

'Hasn't Cecil's mother been feeding him?' her mother asked, returning to her book.

'Good heavens, yes!' Jerome laughed. 'I've done most terribly well!' He turned to Pippa his hands clasped behind his back, and now bent himself slightly towards her. 'I really am not at all hungry,' he told her in a stage whisper.

'You will be by the time you get back to London,' Pippa replied with complete certainty. 'Cecil's the most frightfully slow driver. It'll probably be breakfast time by the time you get back to London. Will cheese be all right?'

Jerome raised a hand in polite assent, and Pippa left quickly to make the sandwiches before, it seemed to Jerome, her mother could stop her. He then pulled a foot-stool up next to where Mrs Nicholls was sitting, and perched on it, having first removed the pile of old magazines from the top of it.

' "Now the hungry lion roars" ' he said. ' "And the wolf behowls the moon. Whilst the heavy ploughman snores, all with weary task fordone." '

Mrs Nicholls was forced to look up from her book.

'Tell me,' she said eventually, looking at him once again over the top of her spectacles. 'Aren't actors always away on tour?'

'Not always,' he replied, realizing at once what Mrs Nicholls was getting at, namely that because of the nature of their profession, actors were not the sort of people with whom mothers necessarily wished their daughters to consort.

Which when he had taken in the photograph on the nearby table of a handsome young man in Hussars' uniform whom he assumed to be Pippa's elder brother, Jerome considered to be ironic to say the least.

'We're not *always* on tour,' he smiled. 'Not like these poor chaps.' He held up the photograph. 'We're not like soldiers after all. They're forever off "on tour", aren't they?' he continued. 'And even worse, poor blighters' job is to fight wars. I mean we actors, we might often *die the death,* but we don't actually get killed.'

A fact, Jerome considered, carefully replacing the photograph, which really had to make anyone in the armed forces the most ineligible people of all.

'When may I see you again?'

He had been meaning to ask Pippa all the time they had sat in the kitchen eating their sandwiches, but he only dared ask now, as they stood by the gate at the bottom of her garden, which was now flooded by moonlight.

'I don't know,' Pippa replied quite truthfully. 'I'm really not sure.'

Jerome was tongue-tied. He had taken out so many girls, so many of them beautiful, really beautiful, he had made love to most of them, never having any trouble whatsoever talking them into his arms and then into his bed, and yet now here he was with a fresh, freckle-faced nineteen year old, who wore boys' shorts and aertex shirts, and smelt of sunshine and lavender soap, a girl who most probably had never been kissed, at least not properly, and he couldn't think of one word to say to her, nor the next move to make.

'You're going to be late,' Pippa warned him. 'If Cecil says he's leaving at ten, he doesn't mean five-past.'

'Can I ring you?'

'If you want to,' Pippa shook out her mane of hair and began to turn away.

'I don't know your number.'

'Of course you do, you chump. You rang me this morning.'

'Of course I did, but that's a hundred years ago.'

'Three two one,' Pippa reminded him. 'Midhurst three two one. It's terribly easy to remember. And if you do forget it—'

She turned back.

'I shan't forget it, Pippa. Don't worry.'

'You're going to miss your lift,' she warned him.

'I don't care.' Jerome opened the gate, and then turned back. 'Do you ever come up to London?' he asked. 'I mean would you come up to London?'

'I do occasionally,' Pippa admitted, 'but it's really not easy. It's a question of leaving my mother, you see. Her arthritis has just got worse and worse, ever since my father was killed really. It's as if her body is – oh, what's the word?' She paused, and looked up to the stars in the skies. 'Yes,' she remembered. 'It's as if her body is manifesting her feelings, at least that's what I think. That what she's feeling inside, it's showing outside. And she can't be cured. At least she can, but not until she's together again with my father.'

That was the moment Jerome knew that deep down in his heart he really loved this wonderful girl. She had such honesty and compassion, and a depth to her he had never found in anyone before, at least not in any girl. He also knew that he had to see her again soon, and that he simply couldn't go on living without seeing her.

'If you don't come up to London,' he said, 'then I shall simply have to keep coming back down here.'

Pippa smiled at him, as if she had no objections to the idea, and then carefully closed the gate.

'You really must go,' she said. 'It's practically ten o'clock.'

'I'll ring you,' he said, taking her hand in his. 'Tomorrow.'

'All right,' she agreed. 'Fine.'

Jerome kissed her hand, and then turned and ran, not looking back, not daring to because he knew that if he did, he would never leave her. So he just ran, and as he reached the edge of the woods, he raised one hand in farewell before disappearing into the darkness.

What Pippa did after he was gone, Jerome never knew. He never knew that as she watched him vanish into the night, she gave a sudden deep sigh, nor did he know that she stood at the little wicket gate for a full half an hour after he had vanished.

F O U R

Oscar's new play was in trouble. It had been in trouble from the word go, right from the initial read-through, but nobody would face up to it, except Oscar. Everyone else was going around with that dewy-eyed optimism so peculiar to the theatre, which makes playwrights despair, and long to throw themselves headlong into the nearest bar. Which is how Oscar felt at the end of each day as he sat in the rehearsal room, head in hands, longing for the director to send them home, so he could go and plunge into a Dry Martini.

He was not alone. Elizabeth Laurence knew the play was heading for the rocks, and while she played along in rehearsals with the corporate optimism, when they broke to go home, she would privately seek out Oscar, following him at first to the bar where he drank, and on in after him. Here they would meet every evening after everyone else had left, and talk over the impending tragedy. For that's how Elizabeth saw it, in tragic terms, because she genuinely loved Oscar Greene's play, not because he had written it specially for her, but because Elizabeth knew instinctively that it was a very special play.

'Who shall we blame today, darling?' Elizabeth asked him one night, as Oscar set up her orange juice and his Martini. 'Are you still determined to brutally murder my leading man?'

'No, no,' Oscar corrected her. 'Lewis Paine is not a leading man, Elizabeth. Lewis Paine is a *mis*leading man.'

Elizabeth laughed, and took a sip from her drink, as Oscar took a swig from his.

'No,' the writer continued, 'I've had it with Lewis Paine-in-the-ass. I've nothing left to say about him. I think it's time to savage that fool of a director. You heard the latest, I guess? He's now blaming the failure of Act Two, scene two on my insistence that it should be played against the rain? I mean would you believe that? He says it creates a feeling of misery. While I insist it creates a feeling of *sexy*.'

Elizabeth laughed again, this time at Oscar's deliberate misuse of words, then swizzling her drink with a cocktail stirrer gave a deep sigh.

'We all know what's *wrong*, Oscar darling,' she said, dropping her voice to a whisper. 'Come on.'

'I can't say anything, sweetheart,' Oscar said in his best Raymond Chandler voice. 'I'm-only-the-writer.'

'I could say something to Cecil, I suppose,' Elizabeth ventured, turning her green eyes on Oscar. 'I'll tell him they're murdering your play, and he won't stand for it. He loves the play as much as I do.'

'Uncle Cecil wouldn't know a good play if it ran for ten years,' Oscar sighed, and then proceeded to drop hot cigarette ash down the inside of his open necked shirt. He jumped to his feet and pulled the front of his shirt out of his trousers.

'Oh-my-God,' he intoned slowly. 'One day I'm going to set my chest on fire.'

'Oscar, darling,' Elizabeth insisted. 'I'm serious. Cecil won't have it. Cecil really cares.'

'My dear, beautiful Elizabeth,' Oscar replied, signalling to the barman for a refresher. 'The only thing Cecil cares about is how near to the kerb his chauffeur parks his goddam car. I mean you really have to worry about Cecil. Hell, the guy's not yet thirty, and he has a *car rug*. You know something else? He has tissue paper in the sleeves of his suits.'

'Well, if Cecil doesn't care, Oscar darling, I do,' Elizabeth said, putting an elegant hand on Oscar's. In fact Elizabeth cared greatly. Chances to play heroines like Oscar's Emerald Glynn came along once in a lifetime, if at all. So Elizabeth was utterly determined to get her way, and persuade the management to get rid of the conceited ass who was playing opposite her, by whatever means she had at her disposal.

'Don't worry, Oscar,' she reassured the writer, 'I shall rescue your precious play.'

'No,' Sebastian said, as firmly as he could.

'Darling,' Elizabeth pleaded, as she stepped out of her silk slip.

'I really can't, Elizabeth,' her husband insisted. 'It really is none of my business.'

'I'm none of your business?' Elizabeth opened her eyes as wide as they would go, stripping down finally to nothing except her silk stockings, and then dropping to lie down on her front on the quilted bed, with her chin supported by her two small clenched fists.

'I don't often ask you favours,' she whispered.

'This acting business—'

'I've told you, darling, it's just fun. *Please* don't let's go through all that again.'

'I'm sorry, but you gave me the impression—' Sebastian began, only to be interrupted once again.

'Darling,' Elizabeth said, but this time the endearment contained a note of warning. 'I didn't know it was going to be so much *fun*.'

This was the line she had adopted and pursued, and was holding to remorselessly, to pretend it was all a whim, that acting was just fun, a game from which she could extricate herself at any time she so desired. She looked up once more at her husband, and shook out her long black hair.

'Please?' she begged, deliberately childlike. 'Pretty please?'

'Oh, very well,' Sebastian relented, sitting on the bed and reaching for the telephone, knowing perfectly well he was the luckiest man alive, to be married to one of the most exquisite women ever born. 'What's the wretched chap's number?'

Cecil listened carefully to what Sebastian had to say, and then having replaced the receiver, picked it up again immediately and dialled Richard Derwent.

'Richard, dear boy,' he groaned. 'Trouble.'

They met for dinner at the Garrick Club.

'He wasn't my idea,' the director complained, 'just for the wretched record.'

'It doesn't matter,' Cecil replied. 'If something isn't done, Elizabeth Laurence will leave.'

'Locke's will sue. She does have a contract.'

'What's a contract? Nothing, dear boy, not when a play's in trouble. Elizabeth can get "pregnant", she can go down with suspected appendicitis, or she can simply get a fishbone stuck in her throat and lose her voice.'

Derwent glared at Cecil, but reluctantly had to agree. There were all sorts of well-known diplomatic excuses which an actor or an actress could employ in order to leave a cast when they were unhappy, usually the very same excuses managements gave when dispensing with the services of any actor or actress with whom they were unhappy.

'You don't want to lose Elizabeth,' Cecil continued, opening out his stiff linen table napkin. 'She's giving a wonderful performance. Despite – the lack of support.'

Cecil had heard this from everyone concerned. He also knew that she was arriving at her performance without any help from the director whatsoever.

'She needs a lot of direction,' Derwent said, as if reading Cecil's thought. 'It's not as if she's a natural. I can't *tell* you the work I'm putting in.'

'You don't have to, dear boy,' Cecil assured him. 'Elizabeth tells me everything.'

'Look,' Derwent said, dropping his voice so as not to be over-heard, 'I don't give a *toss* what you do about Lewis. Just so long as we have it on record that he was not *my idea*. He was Jimmy Locke's idea. I *never* liked him. He's tedious, a slow study, a moaner, and a typical bloody actor, he can't *wait* to blame the play.'

'I have a – very untypical bloody actor I would like you to see,' Cecil said importantly, pushing his soup bowl two inches from him with perfectly manicured hands. 'He's under contract, like Elizabeth, to Boska. You won't know him. But soon everyone will. He's called Jerome Didier.'

'Never heard of the guy,' Oscar said, staring at the photograph with which Cecil had presented him. 'But I sure like his looks. In fact I like his looks so much I'd like them for myself.'

'Be serious, Oscar,' Cecil said, glancing at his watch. 'Just for once.'

'I am being serious, Cecil!' Oscar protested. 'I'd give my goddam writing arm to look like this guy! If I looked like this guy, just think! I could wear my spectacles shaving! Maybe he doesn't look this good in the flesh.'

Oscar held the photograph away from him, as if unable to believe the actor's good looks.

'He looks even better than that, Oscar,' his agent assured him, holding his arms out straight in front of him, so that he could shoot his immaculate white cuffs. 'He is the very best looking young actor I have ever seen. And I'll be very surprised if you don't like him.'

'You mean I'll be very surprised if I don't like him.' Oscar grinned, and tossed the photograph down on Cecil's desk. 'If I don't like this guy, I'll be looking for a new agent.'

Cecil Manners rose, smoothing his double-breasted dark blue pinstriped suit, before crossing to look down at the scene in the street two floors below them.

'You have to like him, O.G.,' he said, placing his hands which were manicured daily on to the window sill. 'Even more so, since Derwent seems to have got to Elizabeth first.'

Oscar looked out of the window and saw Derwent paying off a taxi on the opposite side of the road, while Elizabeth stood gazing in a dress shop window.

'What else is there but to like him?' Oscar asked hopelessly. 'Come on, I only wrote the play. So what does it matter whether the guy is right or not? Just so long as I *like* him.'

'You can always have another of Jimmy Locke's protégés if you'd rather,' Cecil said, coming away from the window. 'You could have Clive Willett. And don't imagine we haven't been threatened with him, because we have.'

'I like Jerome Didier,' Oscar announced, holding up his hands in self defence. 'I love the guy. Don't even bother to introduce us.'

Elizabeth was first through the door. Dressed in a simple but expensive yellow silk coat and dress, she was the first day of spring. Cecil as always was rendered speechless, while Oscar looked at her, and then slowly mistimed lighting his cigarette, burning the end of his nose instead.

'So what will happen to poor Lewis?' Elizabeth asked, ingenuously, but almost before she was seated. 'The poor dear.'

Oscar shook his head and smiled privately at Elizabeth's consummate acting skill. She had managed to make her idle curiosity sound like very real concern.

'That's Locke's responsibility,' said Richard Derwent, who had just pulled up a chair by Cecil's desk. 'We leave all that to Jimmy.'

'But what will he say?' Elizabeth persisted. 'I mean to someone like Lewis. It's not as if he's exactly *unknown*.'

'Leave it to Jimmy,' Derwent repeated, helping himself to a cigarette from the silver box on the desk. 'It's really nothing for you to worry your pretty little head about.'

'Come on, you guys,' Oscar said, having finally managed to light his cigarette. 'Tell the little lady the truth. Forewarned is forearmed, right?'

'Oscar—' Cecil said warningly.

'They have this guy, Miss Laurence,' Oscar continued, deliberately formal. 'Locke's have a special guy to do their dirty work. It's done very well.' Elizabeth was looking round at him, enthralled. 'A man, very correctly dressed, in a black bowler hat, and a black coat and striped trousers comes round backstage to your dressing room. You'd never suspect a thing about him. He looks as though he's just come straight from work in the City. And after an exchange of pleasantries, he takes you out to dinner, somewhere good and expensive, and having filled you with the best food and wines, he explains that Locke's have made a dreadful, *terrible* mistake, and it's all their fault. You can't possibly come into town with this show. It would be the end of your career, they must find you something new, something better for you. At once. But whatever you do, you mustn't come in with this play. And you're happy. You agree. You don't even *know* you've been sacked. You feel you have *left* this disastrous play just in time, and you are *thrilled*. To pieces. You leave the show thinking what philanthropists these guys of Locke's are! I mean what Locke's care about is your career!'

'Oscar—' Cecil made one last half-hearted attempt to stop Oscar, but it was far too late. The beans had been spilt.

'Listen,' Oscar told him. 'This is good. This is all part of Miss Laurence's theatrical education. You see it's a great tactic, Miss Laurence. You leave the show, Locke's gets to re-cast—'

'And nobody's feelings get hurt,' Elizabeth put in.

'Right. And you never get to work for Locke's ever again.'

Oscar took his glasses off, and tugging part of his shirt free from his trousers, proceeded to wipe the lenses clean while Elizabeth stared at him wide-eyed.

'It isn't *true*!' she whispered.

To show her that it was, Oscar drew one arm of his spectacles across his throat like a razor, before tucking in his shirt.

Which was where the discussion ended as Miss Jeans appeared at the door with a hankie to her nose, to announce the arrival of Mr Jerome Didier.

It was love at first sight. The moment the dashing and handsome young man came into the room, Elizabeth lost her heart. As he took her hand in his, holding it all the while as he gazed into her eyes, Elizabeth felt as if she was looking at a twin soul. Her surroundings vanished, and with them all sound, leaving her with the momentous feeling she was about to fulfil her destiny. Jerome released her hand, but Elizabeth was still enthralled, even though the only words they had exchanged were those in greeting.

And yet they were already a couple.

Everyone noticed, and fell silent, finding difficulty in exchanging even the lightest theatrical banter. There was hardly any conversation at all, and what little there was, was strained as Cecil and Richard Derwent began to organize the reading of the play.

Finally they began to read, and when they did the atmosphere became recharged, but this time with electricity. Even Oscar, whose habit was normally to want to hide under his chair or in a closet whenever actors began to read his work out loud, sat wide-eyed and breathless, an unlit Lucky Strike in the corner of his mouth, as at last, at long, long last he heard his play coming properly to life. Jerome Didier was everything Cecil had promised. He was sensational. And even more so when matched against the sublime Elizabeth Laurence. Oscar sat back and beamed at the ceiling. The play couldn't now fail.

Everyone knew it. By the time Elizabeth and Jerome had finished reading even the first scene, the people in the room knew the play was a smash. And by the time the two actors closed their manuscripts shut and the reading was finished, in the joint imagination of everyone there the curtain was rising and falling, and rising and falling to the sound of continuous cheering.

This was why they had all gone into the theatre. This was the moment they had all dreamed about. This was the once in a lifetime moment, when you had a hit. And nothing could ever take the feeling away. Not all the failures in the world could ever snuff out the light of a palpable hit.

The silence in which they all now sat, unlike any other silence the writer, the director or the manager had ever previously known, was finally broken by Jerome.

'Ah,' he said with a sigh, having quickly consulted his watch, 'if that really is the time, I have to be going.'

He rose, smiling at them all, while he carefully rebuttoned his jacket.

'Thank you, thank you, thank you, Mr Greene,' he said. 'This is a wonderful play. Wonderful. And a privilege to have read it for you. And thank you, Miss Laurence. So nice to meet you.'

Elizabeth was silent, but Cecil wasn't. He was on his feet, hurrying round his desk.

'You can't go yet, dear boy!' he cried. 'We have so much to talk about!'

'I'm sure you would really rather talk about all you have to talk about, Cecil, amongst yourselves first,' Jerome replied, with the most courteous of smiles, first to his agent, and then to the others in the room. 'Telephone me when you're free, about that other thing, remember?'

Jerome was as cute as a barrel of monkeys, Cecil thought, as he watched him prepare to take his leave. There was no other 'thing', but the young actor was learning fast how to play the game.

Finally, at the door, he turned the magic of his smile on everyone, without favour to anyone in particular, and then he was gone. Everyone fell to talking all at once, everyone except Elizabeth, who first sat staring silently at the door, at the place where Jerome had been last, before rising and crossing to the window which overlooked the street below.

She saw him come out of the building and get into a little red sports car. Before he pressed the ignition, he turned the driver's mirror to himself to check his appearance, rifling his hair with his fingers, and then drove off, at high speed.

Elizabeth watched him all the time. And if any of the other three present had been paying her attention, instead of talking animatedly amongst themselves, they might have seen her bright green eyes glitter in the sun, and then narrow, the way cats' eyes do when they spy a bird which they intend to devour.

Jerome drove straight down to Sussex. He had thought of ringing Pippa first, but then it occurred to him that her mother might answer, and be unable to tell him, as mothers so often were, precisely where her daughter might be. He had seen the look in Mrs Nicholls' eyes when Pippa had introduced them. It was a look which as a young and good-looking actor, he had seen all too often on the faces of the mothers and fathers of girls who had taken him home, a mixture of fear and disdain, a look which up until now had always amused him.

But the look on Mrs Nicholls' face he knew he had to take seriously, because mixed with the usual fear and disdain, he could sense an implacable resistance. So he decided against ringing, and for arriving unannounced. And if he should find Pippa out when he arrived, then he would simply wait outside in his car until she returned. Whatever happened, he would not be deterred, simply because he could go no longer without seeing her. It had surprised him quite how much he had missed her, even though he had mentally prepared himself for their separation. But he had actually been astounded by how he finally felt when he got back to London and found she was no longer within reach. He had felt quite simply wretched, and with the exception of reading against Elizabeth Laurence that day, everything that had happened to him between leaving Pippa and the chance of seeing her again had been without any importance.

He also wanted Pippa to be the first person in the world to know that he had landed a plum part. No-one had, of course, told him officially, and he knew it would still be some time yet before they finally decided to do so, but he had known the moment he had begun reading the play with Elizabeth Laurence that not only was he right for the part, but that he was right for Elizabeth and she for him.

He arrived at Bay Tree Cottage just in time to meet Pippa walking down to the gate on her way to the shops. She stopped stone dead when she saw him, and stared first with amazement and then with delight.

'Jerome!' she called, and then hurried to the gate.

'Splendid,' Jerome said, hopping out of his car to hold open the gate. 'At least you remembered my name.'

She ignored the jibe, and continued to stare at him, as if he wasn't altogether real.

'Why didn't you ring?' she asked.

'Don't you remember what I told you about Terry Vaughan?' he said. 'Always surprise your audience.'

'Is that what I am?' Pippa enquired, coming through the open gate. 'Part of your audience?'

'No,' Jerome said, taking one of her slim brown hands. 'That's the very last thing you are, Pippa Nicholls.'

'You look different,' she ventured. 'As if something has happened.'

'It has!' Jerome cried. 'And you're brilliant!' He took her other hand, and dropped his voice back to its normal pitch. 'I am about to be offered the part of a lifetime – and I wanted you to be the first to know.'

'I'm sorry,' Pippa said with a frown, 'but I don't understand. How do you know you're "about" to be offered the part? I don't know how these things work. Does that mean that you know, but it isn't official, or something?'

'It means I know,' Jerome replied, a little too sharply, piqued by Pippa pulling his surprise to pieces.

'I'm sorry,' she said again, 'but as I said, I don't know how these things work.'

'Let me put it this way,' Jerome said expansively. 'If I *don't* get this part, I will buy you anything you want. I'll buy you a fur coat.'

'I don't really want a fur coat.'

'Then I'll buy your mother one.'

'She wouldn't want one either.'

Jerome leaned back against the car and regarded her. 'You don't appear terrifically pleased to see me,' he said.

'It's not that,' Pippa said, with an anxious and tell-tale glance back at the house. 'You really should have telephoned.'

'Oh, I think you know, we both know,' Jerome replied, 'why I didn't. Now come and have some tea.'

Again Pippa hesitated, and then whistling for her little dog, put him on his lead and got into the car.

'It will be all right,' Jerome reassured her, as he got in the driver's seat. 'I take it from the basket on your arm you're meant to be going shopping?' Pippa nodded. 'Well,' Jerome continued, starting the car. 'Having tea with me, by car, is hardly going to take you any longer, is it?'

He looked at her, overdoing his conspiratorial frown in the hope of making her smile, but Pippa just frowned, and settled down deep into her seat, as if afraid of being seen.

They drove into Midhurst and had tea at a café called somewhat inappropriately for West Sussex The Mandarin. And Pippa refused to settle, spending the first quarter of an hour checking her watch every five minutes, and seeming not to pay full attention to what Jerome was trying to tell her. And when she wasn't checking the time, she was popping outside to the car to make sure her dog was all right and hadn't escaped through the somewhat flimsy roof. Finally Jerome lost patience, since this was not at all how he had imagined their first reunion was going to be.

'For God's sake, Pippa,' he snapped suddenly. 'Will you for pity's sake just sit down and relax?'

Pippa looked up at him, and her face softened.

'I don't blame you getting cross,' she told him with what he now understood to be her usual candour. 'It's leaving my mother. She hasn't been at all well today.'

Jerome leaned back and then slowly forward, putting his face close to Pippa's.

'Then why on earth – didn't you *say*?'

'Because I wanted to see you,' Pippa replied. 'I couldn't ask you in to tea, because of my mother. I mean how she is, I mean. But I wanted to see you.'

'I'm sorry,' he whispered. 'I *should* have rung.' He bit his lip. 'You must think me very heartless.'

'Don't be silly. I'm sure that's the last thing you are.'

'Would you rather go home?' he asked. 'If you're worried.'

'No,' she said. 'I'd rather be with you.'

After that, Pippa relaxed, and Jerome relaxed, and they ordered some more tea and some fresh hot toast, and Jerome told Pippa all about the play and the reading.

'I can't wait to see it,' Pippa said, when she had listened enthralled and in silence to the whole story. 'It sounds wonderful. And I'm sure you'll be wonderful in it.'

71

'What makes you so sure, Miss Nicholls?' Jerome asked with a smile.

'Just from what you said,' Pippa replied simply. 'From what you told me, and the way you told me. I just think you will.'

'I will be,' Jerome assured her. 'Now I have your belief.'

He smiled at her, as their eyes met, and he rested both his square tipped fingers on the round oak table. Pippa refused to drop her eyes, and stared back at him levelly, over the top of her willow patterned tea cup.

'Good,' Jerome said. 'Now when are you coming up to London?'

'If my mother improves,' Pippa replied, 'actually I might be coming up next week. To do some shopping.'

'But what time will you have to get back? Because I shall be rehearsing—'

'You're sure?' Pippa teased.

'Certain,' Jerome replied, raising his eyebrows. 'So if I'm rehearsing all day—'

'When I come up to London, or go anywhere for that matter,' Pippa said, 'there's always someone with my mother. Like my aunt, or someone from the village. So as long as I'm not back *too* late—'

She left the sentence unfinished, and put down her empty tea cup.

'We could have dinner,' Jerome suggested. 'I should imagine we won't rehearse later than six.'

Pippa shook her head wonderingly.

'You're really certain you've got this part, aren't you?'

'Of course.' Jerome looked back at her as directly as she was now looking at him. 'I'm as certain of it as I am of the fact that you and I are going to be married.'

She didn't look down, or away, but continued to look straight at him, although now she was no longer smiling. But neither was Jerome. Pippa thought he must have been joking, but now she saw that he was looking at her very seriously, without the suggestion of a tease in his dark brown eyes, resting his perfectly sculpted chin on the thumb and index finger of one hand.

And for his part, although he didn't show it, Jerome was delighted to see the look of blank astonishment which now clouded the pretty freckled face of the girl sitting opposite him, this extraordinary girl who had inspired in him such an extraordinary passion.

At long last late that same evening Cecil finally got Jerome on the telephone.

'Where have you been, dear boy?' he asked, although he had his suspicions, thoughts he would rather not face. 'I've been trying to raise you since tea-time. Didn't your landlady pass on my messages?'

'I've only just got back, Cecil,' Jerome replied. 'This minute. What is it? You sound frightfully – *tense*.'

Cecil missed the tease. He was still trying to dismiss from his mind the thought of where he knew Jerome must have been.

'Look, it's wonderful news, dear boy,' he told him, after taking a long, deep breath. 'Derwent definitely wants you.'

'Good,' Jerome replied, sounding to Cecil for all the world like someone who has just been told their car was ready for collection from the garage.

'Good?' Cecil repeated, unable to keep the astonishment from his voice. 'Do you realize what this means, Jerome? This play is going to be a very big hit.'

'No please, Cecil,' Jerome replied. 'Don't misunderstand me. I'm delighted they want me. Really.'

And so he should be, Cecil thought at his end of the line. Straight out of drama school without a credit to his name, and here he was being offered the lead in a brand new play opposite the most exciting and beautiful young actress in London, and all he could say was *good*. Cecil sighed, and rued the fact that he had been born a gentile. Jews made so much better agents. At times like this Jewish agents told their whippersnapper young clients exactly how they should be, while all Cecil could do was to express his pleasure that Jerome was at least delighted.

'I just don't think we should get carried away,' Jerome continued. 'We have to consider this play in exactly the same way we shall have to consider every play that I'm offered. Is it right for me?'

'You said so yourself!' Cecil protested. 'You said so to Oscar Greene! You said—'

'I only read two scenes, Cecil,' Jerome interrupted. 'I haven't read the whole play. And there's something else. What do you know about this girl?'

'This girl?' Cecil stuttered, reaching across the desk for his Mappin & Webb cigarette box. 'This girl?'

'Yes,' Jerome replied, over-investing the word with far too much patience. 'This *girl*.'

Cecil told him what he knew about the girl everyone was speaking of as the most exciting discovery in London. He told him exactly what he knew, and this time he made less effort to keep the exasperation out of his voice. But by the time he had finished

73

telling Jerome all about Elizabeth Laurence, instead of being suitably chastened, the young actor simply laughed.

'Cecil, my dear,' he sighed when he no longer found the subject of further amusement, 'that is not what I *meant*. It is *I* who they want for this play. *I* shall be the person up there on-stage every night, doing my best to make sense of what is written. Not anyone else, least of all anyone in management or representation, or whatever. So what I want to know, dear boy, is not what you all think of this girl, or who you all think she may be, the next Sarah Bernhardt, or Mrs Pat, or whoever. What I want to know is, is she – *difficult?*'

Once again, Jerome let drop one of his telling pauses, which gave the chosen word a particularly distinctive emphasis.

'I am assured,' Cecil replied, 'that Miss Laurence, besides being undoubtedly the most talented young actress to be discovered in a decade, is in every way a perfect lady.'

'Yes?'

'Yes. And not only that, but she was extremely impressed with you.'

'I have to say that she read well,' Jerome agreed.

'You should also know that she too is under contract to Dmitri Boska,' Cecil added, as his *coup de grâce.*

'Meaning?'

'Meaning that unless we are all crazy, those of us who were privileged to hear you both read this morning, to see you both as a couple—' Cecil paused.

'I'm waiting,' Jerome finally prompted.

'Unless we are all completely without judgement, dear boy,' Cecil concluded, 'after this play the next step will undoubtedly be straight into films.'

This time it was the actor's turn to pause, which he did to good effect, so much so that Cecil momentarily thought he had over-baited his hook.

'Very well,' Jerome said finally, when he thought Cecil had sweated long enough. 'Have them send me round the play tomorrow morning.'

'Good,' Cecil replied, not knowing whether to admire or despair at the young man's self-assurance. 'I'll see to it first thing.'

Cecil put down the telephone and considered the conversation he had just had. Jerome had been in high spirits, before he had received the good news, and as Cecil had suspected all day, there can have been only one reason for those high spirits. Jerome had just come back from Pippa.

Rising with a sigh from behind his desk, he went and poured himself a whisky, and then went and sat back down to review the prospect which now lay ahead. Elizabeth Laurence was quite utterly stunning, of that there was no doubt in Cecil's mind, let alone the mind of anyone who had come into professional contact with her. Even Jerome Didier had not been immune, Cecil decided as he sipped his drink. Jerome may have tried to underplay the impact of their meeting, but Cecil could swear he had seen the young actor taking several long, sideways glances at Elizabeth, long before they started reading the play, as if he couldn't quite believe his own eyes, while for her part Cecil had observed that Elizabeth Laurence couldn't take her eyes off Jerome.

As a pair, if not actually made in heaven, they were definitely heaven sent, Cecil decided. But they were definitely a pair, quite definitely. They fitted each other sublimely, and enhanced each other's talent incredibly. Everyone present had seen and felt their immediate rapport, and were all holding their corporate breath to see what the divine Miss Laurence and the stunningly handsome Jerome Didier would make of Oscar's play, a play, Cecil noted with quiet satisfaction, which was a love story, a love story which contained several passionate love scenes, and involved Elizabeth Laurence and Jerome Didier hardly ever being on-stage without each other. Cecil leaned back in his chair and permitted himself a smile. He knew what that meant. Everyone in the theatre knew what that meant. Everyone in the theatre knew what ultimately happened when plays like this went into rehearsal, and subsequently when then they went out on tour. Because of a fear of the unknown, the cast were thrown together in an enforced intimacy, particularly the leading players, and most particularly the leading players in a romantic drama who, as was so often the case that some people believed it to be an inevitability, entered into an affair, simply because they were no longer able to differentiate between what was fact and what was fiction.

So the odds were heavily in favour that long before the play reached London, Elizabeth and Jerome would have been unable to stay out of each other's beds.

On the strength of his conclusions, Cecil fetched himself a second whisky, which was most unlike him. But he felt he had earned it this evening, particularly in the light of his final conclusion, which was that all the time Jerome and Elizabeth were being forcibly closeted together by the needs of the production they were part of, Pippa would be safe, safe and free from Jerome. Pippa would be at home, looking after her mother at Bay Tree

Cottage, walking her little dog, doing the shopping and running the household like she normally always did.

And as the play moved out on to the road, to play dates more and more distant from Sussex, Cecil would drive home for the weekends, just like he always did, and he would keep asking Pippa over for lunch and the inevitable croquet match, while Jerome would be up in the north of the country somewhere, caught in the throes of the inevitable extra Sunday rehearsals which the casts of new plays being tried out away from London invariably had to endure.

Cecil would make it his personal business to see that Pippa was weaned off Jerome, not because he thought that by doing so he would strengthen his own chances with her, but for altruistic reasons, because Cecil knew that someone like Jerome was neither good nor right for someone like Pippa. Cecil didn't even mind if later Pippa turned on him, and blamed him for interfering, because it would have been worth it. Cecil would have rescued her from a liaison which by rights could only be a catastrophe.

Cecil finished his drink and set the empty glass back on the tray which his secretary set out religiously each midday and late afternoon, before turning off the lights and leaving his office feeling considerably less disturbed than he had been feeling half an hour earlier.

As things turned out, he would have been better locking himself in his office and getting blind and hopelessly drunk.

On the day before he began rehearsals, Jerome telephoned Pippa early in the afternoon, a time he knew it was safe to call her, since Pippa had told him that her mother rested every day between two and four o'clock. The first and only thing he wanted to know was when he might see her again.

There was a short silence before Pippa replied, and when she did, Jerome noted that she sounded almost surprised with herself.

'As a matter of fact,' she said, 'I'm coming up to London tomorrow.'

'Tomorrow!' Jerome could barely keep the unalloyed joy out of his voice.

'I told you, if you remember,' Pippa continued, very levelly. 'I had to come up some time for some shopping. There are some things I have to get my mother.'

'But what time do you have to get back?' Jerome asked. 'You know I'm rehearsing all day.'

'Well no, I didn't.' Pippa confessed. 'I didn't know when you

76

started. Or what the hours were, or are, rather. I could meet you when you finish though. Because I can always catch the later train.'

'How much later is the later train?'

'I could catch the half-past nine. I mean my mother's not going to be alone. There'll be one of our neighbours here. As usual.'

'Good,' Jerome said, hardly able to believe how overjoyed he felt.

'That is,' Pippa added hesitantly, 'I mean that is if you still want to see me.'

'I cannot *think*, Pippa Nicholls, at this moment in time,' Jerome replied, closing his eyes slowly and dreamily, 'of anything I want more.'

Then having instructed her when and where to meet him, Jerome went off to rehearsals as if it was the first day of spring where, with the first real show of his prodigious talent, he proceeded utterly to confound and astonish the assembled company, but most particularly Miss Elizabeth Laurence.

He astonished her even before rehearsals began. On his way there, Jerome had stopped at a small but expensive florists and bought a dozen of the best red roses, which upon his arrival he presented to his leading lady. Elizabeth was privately annoyed at how unprepared she was for the gesture, since the night before she had resolved that she would not let Jerome Didier past her guard twice. Yet here she was again, speechless, and with the breath catching in her throat, as Jerome presented the roses to her mock-gallant, bowing formally to her, while allowing himself a small, and quizzical smile. For her part Elizabeth went through the motions she had so carefully practised, laughing at his tongue-in-cheek dalliance, and allowing herself to be captivated by his easy charm, while hoping against hope to herself that she was skilled enough to carry off the deception. She hoped dearly that she was, because everyone was watching her, and she prayed her face was not betraying any sign of the utter helplessness she felt.

'Oh dear,' Oscar sighed to Cecil, as they wandered over to pour themselves a coffee from the urn, 'and her a married lady.'

'Oh nonsense,' Cecil laughed, 'they're actors! This is just part of their ritual.'

'Sure,' Oscar said, filling a cup with coffee. 'Let's just hope they both remember that out in the sticks. Or we have had it.'

'You'd rather they didn't get on?'

'I'd rather they just stayed actors,' Oscar sighed, over-filling his cup disastrously so that he flooded the saucer. 'Goddamit,' he continued, shaking some hot coffee off his hand. 'Didn't you see her face when he came into the room? Long before he even gave her the flowers? Oh boy, actors. All they want is to be loved. Why can't they just settle for the affection of the audience. But they can't. They never can. And believe me, Cecil, if and when Juliet loves Romeo for *real*, it's a five alarm fire, I'm telling you.'

'I'm sorry,' Cecil rejoined feebly. 'But I'd rather the cast all got on any day.'

He was rewarded with one of Oscar's most withering looks, but happily the playwright's worries proved to be short-lived, because as the day's rehearsal grew longer, it became abundantly clear that off the set Jerome was profoundly disinterested in Elizabeth as a woman. What Jerome was interested in, like almost any other leading actor, regardless of his talent, was not in seducing his leading lady but simply outshining her.

In rehearsal proper, it was a quite different story. From the moment they started the usually mundane task of just blocking their scenes, there was a chemistry between them, but by the time they began to act in earnest that had given way to a palpable electricity. The atmosphere in the rehearsal room fairly crackled, and everyone watching knew they were seeing something very much out of the ordinary. The two young actors were immediately empathetic, giving to and taking from each other as if they had been doing it all their professional lives. Quite obviously they were unique, and so much so that time and time again Oscar noticed that their fellow actors, when they were not required, instead of wandering off to do the crossword puzzle, or have an idle gossip outside in the corridor, remained instead on the sidelines, watching Elizabeth and Jerome in an almost reverential silence. Because they knew they were watching a sort of theatrical history, a moment of fusion, the moment when an exceptional partnership is born.

But as soon as they stopped rehearsing, the moment they returned to the real world, there was a powercut, and as far as Jerome was concerned, the lights went out. Jerome simply walked off to study his text, and never gave Elizabeth a second glance until their next call.

Then just before they broke for the day, they rehearsed their first kiss, and when they did everything fell apart.

'I'll never forget it,' Oscar said to Cecil later, as they sat recovering over their drinks. 'I will never forget that look on Elizabeth's beautiful face. I mean one moment she's taking a glance at her script, right there in her hand, and then – wham. Next moment, she's picking herself off the *wall*.'

78

In the stage instructions, Oscar had simply written *they kiss*. He had envisaged it as a tentative kiss, a moment of speculation on behalf of the characters he had created. He had thought of it as a moment of tenderness, calm before the emotional storm which lay ahead. But Jerome had other ideas.

'I tell you, I've never seen a moment like it,' Oscar recalled in the bar afterwards. 'First of all, it's early days. Like the first day of his involvement. I was expecting something a little more hesitant, a touch more diffident. But oh, no. No, this was war. You saw for yourself, Cecil, Jerome didn't merely try and kiss her. Jerome hit her, he hit Miss Laurence amidships. And boy – she was calling for the life-rafts.'

Elizabeth Laurence's distress, however, was short-lived. When she realized this was the way Jerome intended to play their first embrace, she gave every bit as good as she got. She kissed him back. Jerome had released her, and was about to pick his script back up off the table, when Elizabeth dropped hers, and throwing both her arms around Jerome's neck, kissed him back, long and hard. And when she did, everyone stopped whatever they thought they were doing, and stood and stared, as if it was the very end of time.

Suddenly the silence was broken by Richard Derwent springing to his feet, and clapping his hands together sharply. His eyes were practically standing out of his head.

'Would one of you please kindly tell what the *hell* is going on?' he asked with heavy sarcasm, as the actors parted. 'That is, if it's not an inconvenience. *If* – you can spare the time.'

Elizabeth went to speak, but Jerome signalled her to be silent, then turned to stare at the director, his hand protectively resting on one of Elizabeth's forearms.

'I am kissing Miss Laurence, Richard,' Jerome said, looking both puzzled and innocent. 'Why?'

'And that is what you call kissing, dear heart, is it?'

Derwent advanced on Jerome, finally standing almost on the actor's toes as he stared maniacally up at him.

'Forgive me if I'm wrong here, Richard—' Jerome glanced down at the script in his hand. 'But it does say, "Paul looks at Emerald for a long, difficult moment. And then unable to resist her any longer—"'

'"They kiss,"' Elizabeth quietly volunteered.

'Children—' Derwent hissed at them both, 'they may kiss, but *not* – like that! That is not how we kiss on-*stage*, duckies!'

'If I may say so, Richard—' Jerome began, only to be immediately interrupted.

'No, you may *not* say so, ducky!' Derwent shouted. 'You are still wet behind your pretty little ears, heart! So you will keep quiet – and *I* will do the talking! And what I have to say to you is this! On-stage, when we kiss, we give what is called a *stage* kiss, ducky! You kiss the little lady with your top lip on her bottom lip! Or even – with your top lip *below* her bottom lip, *savez*! What you just did looks perfectly *disgusting*! We do not want the dear old dears passing out in the stalls now, do we?'

Jerome continued to stare at the director for a moment as if he was not quite sure of Derwent's sanity, before turning to his co-star.

'I'm sorry, Elizabeth,' he said. 'We should, of course, have discussed this between us. I do hope I didn't embarrass you – but I'm afraid – I'm afraid I was completely caught up.'

Jerome stopped and sighed, brushing his mouth thoughtfully with the side of an index finger, as if recalling the moment and the very texture of the kiss.

'The strange thing is,' he went on, 'it *felt* right.'

On the last word of the sentence, on the word *right*, he turned slowly back and fixed their director with a cold and piercing look.

'It didn't *look* right,' Derwent muttered, after a short but significant silence.

'Why don't we ask the writer?' Elizabeth suddenly asked brightly. 'Oscar?' she called in her pretty, light voice.

'Oscar is not directing this play,' Derwent hissed. 'I happen to be the director.'

'Of course you do, Richard,' Elizabeth purred. 'And Oscar happens to be the writer. Oscar dear, did you see how we kissed?'

'Both acts, Elizabeth,' Oscar replied, wiping the lenses of his glasses with his fingers. 'I thought it was great.'

'Ah!' Elizabeth sighed, putting her hands together under her pretty chin.

'It looked like a kiss should look, Elizabeth,' Oscar continued, 'it looked very real. And very sexy.'

'Yes. But even so—'

Jerome raised his voice in interruption, before Derwent had time to collect his thoughts, and turned once again to Elizabeth, bending slightly forward and clasping his hands behind his back.

'The point is—' he said with great concern, 'did Elizabeth mind me kissing her like that?'

'Of course not,' Elizabeth replied, factually, and professionally, but with just the merest hint of shyness.

'That was another thing,' Oscar recalled to Cecil over their second drink. 'He took it right away from having anything to do with stagecraft, and made it a matter of *chivalry*, goddamit! The guy is not only a magic actor, Cecil. When he's not working, the guy should be running the UN! You remember the smile he got in reward?'

Elizabeth had smiled at Jerome, she had given him her best smile, her most intimate smile, the smile she had rehearsed from early puberty in front of the mirror, the smile reserved for special occasions. But Jerome did not return her smile. He just nodded at her the once, before turning back to the now out-gunned director.

'The consensus of opinion, Richard,' he said pleasantly, 'would appear to be that we got the kiss right.'

'Dear heart—' Derwent began, only to be once again interrupted by Jerome, but this time on a change of tack.

'Even so, Richard,' Jerome continued, 'we will also do it your way, the way you advise, because then we may compare the two approaches. Just in case – you know.' Jerome paused, to smile ingenuously. 'Just in case, Richard,' he concluded, 'our – *inexperience* is showing.'

Before Derwent could voice an objection, Jerome took Elizabeth by the hand and began to play the scene. By the time they had finished kissing as *directed*, the cast and the bystanders, with the exception of the director, were helpless with laughter.

'You are wrong!' he shouted. 'And quite, quite mad! Bringing sex – so brazenly into a play like this! At this point!'

'But surely?' Jerome wondered politely, 'isn't that what this play is about, Richard? This play is not a drawing-room comedy. This is not a french windows, anyone for tennis and cucumber sandwiches play. This play is about love, and passion. Correct me if I'm wrong, but it's about two people's passion for each other. And how it *consumes* them. I don't see how we can *depict* passion, Richard, in all honesty, by kissing each other on the chin.'

Oscar started the round of applause, but he had barely clapped more than twice before the rest of the cast joined in enthusiastically. Jerome nodded to them all, with a grateful and graceful smile, and then the whole body of the assembled company turned to look at the director, awaiting his final judgement.

'I think you're quite mad,' he said, but the day was won. And well won, because one of the reasons for the phenomenal success Oscar's play was to enjoy was the passion with which Elizabeth Laurence and Jerome Didier played their love scenes.

'Thank you,' Jerome said to Elizabeth as they prepared to leave rehearsals.

'You're thanking me?' Elizabeth laughed. 'I'm afraid I played very little part in the triumph. The day very much belongs to you.'

'Nonsense,' Jerome replied, hurriedly pulling on his coat and glancing again at his watch. 'We both fight for the same cause. Truth. Now if you'll excuse me – I shall see you tomorrow.'

He hurried from the rehearsal room, in the way a person does when they are late for the person they have to meet. Elizabeth hurried to the window in case whoever it happened to be was waiting, and sure enough, sitting in the window of the café opposite, sat the figure of a girl, who got up hurriedly and left as soon as she in turn saw Jerome coming out of the building.

She was a slim girl, with long brown hair, about the same height as Jerome who, with his mackintosh slung over his shoulders, was hurrying across the road to greet her. The girl was wearing a dark blue waterproof which was undone, revealing below it a matching dark blue cotton dress with small white polka dots. It was hard for Elizabeth to see from that distance how pretty the girl was, although as she hurried along the pavement to meet Jerome where he was crossing, Elizabeth saw she had exceptionally good legs, and moved with a natural athleticism.

For a moment she assumed, or perhaps more accurately hoped that the girl was a relation of Jerome's, maybe his sister, or a cousin. She did after all, Elizabeth decided, look a little too unsophisticated to be anything more to someone as dashing and talented as her new leading man.

The moment Jerome arrived at the girl's side, Elizabeth knew she was wrong. She could tell immediately from the way Jerome kissed the top of her tousled hair, and the way he put his arm through hers and, even from her vantage point two floors above the street, from the way he smiled at her. They were not relatives, nor even just friends. They were lovers, or lovers-in-waiting.

After a moment, Elizabeth collected her things together and turned to see who was left in the rehearsal room. In the far corner she saw the person she wanted, Oscar, who was busy packing his script into a blizzard of loose papers already stuffed inside his battered old briefcase. Elizabeth smiled to herself and then walked over to him.

'Oscar dear,' she said, 'are you dashing off, too? Or do you have time for a coffee?'

'A coffee? At this hour?' Oscar peered at Elizabeth through finger-printed eyeglasses. 'You have to be kidding. Anyway, much as I'd love to take you for a drink, I'm already spoken for.'

'You go on ahead with Elizabeth,' Cecil said, overhearing. 'I still have one or two things to do here.'

'OK,' Oscar smiled to Elizabeth. 'Let's go and get out of our wet things and into a Dry Martini.'

The actress waited until they were in the bar and seated with their drinks in front of them before setting about her self-appointed task. But first she smiled at him, her best kitten's smile.

'Oscar?' she said. 'Do you mind if I ask you something?'

'Anything,' Oscar replied, searching his pockets hopelessly for his cigarettes, which he had already placed most carefully on the table in front of them. 'You may ask me anything, just so long as it doesn't involve a rewrite.'

'You know I love your play,' Elizabeth replied, with just the right amount of hurt in her voice. 'I wouldn't have you change a word of it. Your play's wonderful.'

'It might be now,' Oscar agreed, accepting one of his own cigarettes from the packet Elizabeth was holding beneath his nose. 'It has a chance of being something now you and Jerome Didier are doing it.'

'It would be a wonderful play with *anybody* doing it, Oscar,' Elizabeth assured him. 'Jerome and I are very lucky people.'

'Oh shucks,' Oscar said, 'as they say in all the best comic strips.'

Elizabeth smiled, and then picking up Oscar's battered old Zippo lighter, lit both their cigarettes, before flipping the lighter back shut.

'I *love* American things,' she said. 'Animate and inanimate.'

'And so what can this rather inanimate American do for you?' Oscar enquired.

'I don't remember saying I wanted you to do anything for me, Oscar.'

She gave him another kittenish smile, but this one said you-clever-old-thing.

'Sure,' Oscar nodded, swizzling the olive in his drink a little too vigorously so that he nearly spilt the entire cocktail. 'I'm a writer, as you probably recall. So I get to work out plots in advance.'

'And so what's this plot, Mr Writer?'

'You tell me, ma'am. If it's good and I use it, I might even cut you in.'

'It isn't a plot,' Elizabeth whispered, 'I just want some advice. Not just for my own good, but because I think it will help make your play even *more* wonderful.'

'How can I resist?'

Oscar couldn't, he knew that. This was a girl for whom he would walk on red-hot coals, fly to the moon and go to the end of the earth all rolled into one. Not that he was in love with Elizabeth as a person, because he wasn't. But as an actress, as an instrument for his work, he gave thanks every minute of his waking life for the day she was born.

'Come on,' he said, lighting his cigarette again even though it was still alight. 'Try me. Let Auntie hear your agony.'

'It's Jerome,' Elizabeth confessed. 'I think he's wonderful, and I think we're going to be good together.'

'Good?' Oscar frowned deeply, as if she was mad. '*Good*? They haven't a word to say what you two are going to be.'

'I hope you're right, Oscar.' Elizabeth grew very serious, and then fell silent for a moment. 'I don't know how to put this.'

'I'm no good at writing dialogue,' Oscar said, 'unless I have the motivation.'

'I want us to be *so* good, Oscar. I can't tell you how much I want it. And I know we can! It's just – it's just.' She stopped and looked at him across the table, then put her hand on his. 'I don't know whether Jerome will let me get close enough.'

Oscar nodded, as he saw the picture, and he knew that if ever there was a time to keep his mouth shut, this was it. But she had her hand on his, and she was looking with those strange hypnotic bright green eyes into his, and she was so goddam beautiful he really did want to help her, even though he knew it was going to cost him dear.

So much against his better judgement he told her exactly what she wanted to hear, and he knew even as he was doing it that he was busy making himself into his own executioner.

Meantime Jerome was falling ever more deeply in love with Pippa as they dined over bacon, egg and french fries in a Lyon's Corner House.

'I wish I had the money to buy a Rolls-Royce,' he sighed, putting down his knife and fork.

'Is that your ambition?' Pippa asked. 'To own a Rolls-Royce?'

Jerome shook his head as he wiped his mouth on his table napkin, but Pippa could see that he was smiling, because it was in his eyes.

'I don't want a Rolls-Royce, Pippa Nicholls,' he replied, still from behind his napkin, while arching both his eyebrows. 'I just wish I had the money.' He leaned forward and put a finger to her lips as Pippa laughed. 'No,' he warned her. 'Don't laugh. If I had the money, then I could take you somewhere. Somewhere more – *glamorous*.'

'I'm happy here,' Pippa said. 'I like Lyon's Corner Houses.'

'You'll like the Ritz even better,' Jerome informed her. 'When the play has opened, to ecstatic notices, on the second night I shall take you to dine at the Ritz.'

'Supposing it opens to terrible notices?' Pippa asked.

'If it does, I shall kill myself.'

'Of course you won't.'

'I most certainly shall, Pippa Nicholls. I promise you. And the reason why I can promise you that, is because the notices will be ecstatic.'

'You're very confident, aren't you?' she asked him. 'It doesn't occur to you that it might fail.'

Pippa looked across at him, with a deep frown. In return, Jerome pursed his lips, and tapped them with the end of one finger. Then he shook his head.

'You would need to have been there today, Pippa,' he said. 'You see, I am good. It's not a conceit, it's a fact. I have a talent, a God-given talent, like Elizabeth Laurence, who is also very good. Very, *very* good. Individually, we are both very, very good. But together, together we are going to be – *sensational*.'

'You know this after just one day's rehearsal?'

'As I said, you'd need to have been there, Pippa. It was extra-ordinary. It was like being in the middle of an electric storm. You could have lit the Albert Hall from the amount of electricity that was generated. The light – and it *was* a light – it actually shone in everyone's eyes. And on everyone's faces.'

'I can't imagine it,' Pippa said with a frown, carefully putting down and together her own knife and fork before looking back up at him. 'Was it awfully exciting?'

'No,' Jerome said, *sotto voce*. 'Compared to being with you, it was nothing.'

Halfway through the second week of rehearsals Elizabeth suddenly and totally lost her performance. For a day or so nothing was said, and everyone carried on as if nothing had happened.

'This sort of thing happens all the time,' Richard Derwent sighed to Cecil. 'All the time. Probably better if you hadn't come in today, really. This sort of thing happens all the time.'

'She asked me to come in, dear boy, crying on the telephone at two in the morning. Even her husband was worried.'

By Friday her director was too. Not only had Elizabeth lost her performance, by the end of the week, for some extraordinary reason she seemed to have lost her memory too, and was back rehearsing play script in hand.

'Heart?' the benighted director kept reminding her. 'We open in Oxford in a week. Remember? One week, heart of oak. But we can't the way you're going, unless we get Oscar to rewrite this whole play as a frigging pantomime!'

Elizabeth's eyes welled full with tears. Richard Derwent turned away from the now all too familiar sight.

'Oh God,' he muttered hopelessly. 'God preserve us from all female actresses.'

Of course, had Oscar Greene been there to ask, the playwright would have been able to explain exactly what was going on, but because of the way Derwent worked, Oscar had been asked to stay away until Derwent considered the play was ready for him to see. Which, of course, Elizabeth knew, and which, of course, explained her perfect timing.

Not unnaturally, Jerome had become extremely worried by his co-star's apparent disintegration, but had been advised by his director not to bring attention to it lest his concern precipitated an even more catastrophic decline. But finally, at the end of this particular day's rehearsals, which ended as all recent ones had done with Elizabeth in a welter of tears and semi-hysterics, Jerome could bear it no more, and caught up with Elizabeth in the street as she searched in full flight for a taxi.

'Come and have a drink,' he said, catching her arm.

'Why?' Elizabeth asked, biting her lip until it started to turn scarlet. 'What's the point?'

'Taxi.'

Jerome caught the first passing cab and swung open the back door.

'Please,' he said to Elizabeth. 'We should have done this ages ago. I don't know what I can have been thinking.'

He took her to the Ritz, although he had so little money he had to turn away and count it before they went through the doors. He sat her in the corner of the bar, and persuaded her very much against her wishes to order a brandy, which she didn't drink.

'I'm sorry,' she whispered, searching her handbag for a handkerchief. 'I don't know what's happening to me.'

Neither did Jerome. But he thought he did.

'You're afraid,' he said, very gently.

'Yes,' Elizabeth agreed, equally *sotto*. 'But I'm afraid that's all too obvious, wouldn't you say? I seem completely to have lost my nerve.'

She smiled at him, bravely, over the top of her immaculately laundered hankie.

'You haven't lost your nerve,' Jerome frowned, leaning towards her. 'You have lost your performance – temporarily, for one reason, and for one reason alone. You got there too *early*. And that is what frightened you.'

'I – I don't understand,' Elizabeth lied. 'Please explain.'

'There was nowhere left for you to go, darling, it happens all the time,' Jerome told her, sitting further forward in his chair and putting both his hands on the edge of the table. 'Nowhere. At least not when I joined the cast. Perhaps with Lewis – perhaps you'd found it all a mite too easy? And you had got your performance—' Jerome snapped his finger and thumb to illustrate his point. 'Like that. And so then – where was there to go?'

'I don't know,' Elizabeth demurred. 'I don't think it's just that.' Elizabeth fell to silence.

'Yes?' Jerome prompted, almost below his breath. 'So what then? What do you think it is?'

Elizabeth looked down at the handkerchief clasped between her hands.

'If only I could believe it was as easy as that,' she murmured.

'It is!'

'If you were me – perhaps. If this was you, if this had happened to you—' She shook her head sadly, and looked down. 'I'm afraid it goes deeper than that.'

'Elizabeth,' Jerome commanded, and Elizabeth looked back up at him, showing surprise at the authority in his voice. 'You know about holding back. Surely you were told, were you not, never to give it all too early? You have to hold back so that you may *build*, just like a painter builds a picture, from sketches, and outlines – long before he paints it. And even then, then he still leaves room for *repainting*. Which is what you must do. You must make the canvas blank again, and start again from *scratch*. Until you arrive *organically* – at your performance.'

Word for word Jerome was parroting Terence Vaughan, advice he had always followed at drama school, where he had found it never to be lacking. Others loved to rush headlong into their performances, showing everybody every trick they had all at once. But Jerome had learned how to surprise them. He would show brilliance at the read through, even early on in rehearsals, so they might catch a glimpse of his armoury. Then he would shut the door and go back to scratch, slowly and seemingly painstakingly crafting his performance, while all the time knowing if the truth be told and he was called on suddenly to produce the finished goods, they were there ready and waiting, where they had been since he had first read the part.

To Elizabeth, however, there was no scent of trickery about Jerome's advice, at least so it seemed from the way she had decided to react, which was to show nothing but trust on her beautiful but still melancholy countenance, while letting her eyes travel slowly like a camera over Jerome's. Then she sighed and she frowned, once more.

'It's really so odd, don't you think?' she asked. 'What's happened, I mean. Oscar wrote his play, or rather this part especially for me, so it's really so peculiar that all of a sudden it should start slipping away from me.' She bit her lip, while still looking directly into Jerome's eyes. 'And the point is, you see I still *did* have something in reserve. That's what's so odd. Actually until I lost it, I was holding back really rather a lot.'

A sudden darkness clouded Jerome's eyes, and Elizabeth was delighted to see it. She had allowed him to think he had diagnosed her perfectly, but now she was about to prove him wrong.

'You see, what I think has happened is that you have thrown me,' Elizabeth said, placing her cool hand on Jerome's. 'I think when you joined the cast – you threw me.'

'Me?' Jerome gasped. '*Me*? But whatever could *I* have done? You're not saying – surely you don't mean – no, no, no! You can't mean that I am responsible for you losing your performance?'

'Not in the way you mean, Jerome,' she replied. 'You haven't thrown me by doing something wrong, or by bringing something unsuitable to the play.' She looked down at their lightly touching hands, and then once more up into his dark and bewildered eyes, fixing them with hers, before dropping her voice to a whisper, which was almost a purr.

'I have lost my performance,' she told him, 'because of your *brilliance*.'

She felt his hand tense under hers, and saw his eyelids drop slightly, half hooding his deep, dark eyes. But the eyes never left hers, and although he moved his hand it was only to turn it upwards in order to hold her own, which he did, slipping his long fingers through her pale and slender ones.

'No,' he said in a low voice, 'what nonsense.'

'I promise you. I just feel I can't live up to you,' she replied. 'I feel as if I have been run down. I'm like the moon in an eclipse. When the sun passes between it and the earth.'

'This is nonsense,' Jerome protested, but the tightening of the grip on her hands, the light of excitement in his eyes betrayed him. 'In fact,' he continued, now holding her one hand in the two of his, 'if you must know, Miss Laurence, the boot – is entirely on the other foot. When we read in Cecil's office – yes?'

'You don't imagine I can have forgotten that?'

'When I heard you read,' Jerome went on, silencing her by tightening the hold on her hand even more, 'I thought, no. No, I can never *possibly* live with this. Not possibly.'

'I'm afraid you're just being kind,' Elizabeth replied, apparently giving the possibility no credence. 'And it's very sweet of you. To try and give me back my confidence by saying such sweet things. But it's not as easy as that. Because I now know my limitations. Because you've made me aware of them.'

Jerome let go of Elizabeth's hands and leaned back in his chair, staring for a moment at the ceiling.

'I don't think it's me,' he announced finally. 'In fact I don't think it has anything to do with *me* – whatsoever.'

For a moment Elizabeth caught her breath, afraid that her best laid plan was about to go awry, but said nothing, and did nothing, except widen her luminous eyes slightly in feigned disbelief at Jerome.

'No, no! It's true!' he laughed, catching the nuance, and then leaning forward once again. 'It has nothing to do with me – nor you, Elizabeth darling! You are *brilliant*. It isn't me that's throwing you.' He dropped his voice conspiratorially. 'It's *Richard*,' he whispered.

'Do you think so?' Elizabeth asked, furrowing her brow deeply. 'Do you really honestly think so, because if you're right – oh! Oh, if only you are *right*!'

'Of course I'm right,' Jerome replied, almost testily. 'Richard Derwent is an oaf. It's him who's inhibiting you. If you think about it, what's he said to you since you began to lose confidence? Not a word, not a single piece of direction. And why? Why do you think this is?'

'Why? Jerome? Why?'

'Because he doesn't *like* women. And because he does not – *like* – women, he has just let you—' Jerome made a rather round sort of gesture with his right hand as he searched for the suitable words. 'He has just let you – quite literally – fall to *pieces*.'

He bared his teeth into a miniature snarl, hissing the word 'pieces', giving it just enough of the right inflexion to make the state of going to pieces sound like the onset of a fatal disease. Elizabeth shuddered privately and pleasurably, finding she was even more thrilled by Jerome in private than she was in rehearsal.

'So what do you suggest?' she wondered softly. 'What should we do? I mean – he is the director.'

Jerome leaned his head back and smiled at the ceiling, because he had already decided what course of action they should take. To his way of thinking there was only one course of action open to them.

'What are you doing now?' he asked suddenly. 'This evening?'

'Why – nothing.' Elizabeth looked puzzled, as if she didn't have any idea at all of what Jerome was about to suggest. 'I was going home to study.'

'Then you must take me with you. The only way back, my darling, is for you and I to work on the play, and our performances, *both* our performances – together.'

Elizabeth stood up, and smiled to herself as she thought of how completely right dear Oscar had been. He had told her that the best possible way to get someone in your debt was not as you would suppose, to help them, but on the contrary to allow them to help you.

'That way,' he had concluded, 'they will feel obligated to you. And it'll be quite a considerable sense of obligation. Because it'll be based on the very real fear that in advising you they may well have given you the wrong advice – and in doing so, messed up the rest of your life!'

Jerome had never given the off-stage life of Elizabeth Laurence a second thought. There had been no reason to do so. Elizabeth and he were simply members of a cast doing a play, and when work was done they went their separate ways. Besides, his head was always too full of Pippa. Until the moment Elizabeth invited him to her home, therefore, he hadn't thought of her as having an existence outside the rehearsal room.

He hadn't even been curious as to how she lived, or where she lived, or with whom, and although at some point he had been told that she was married, he had long since forgotten the fact. To Jerome, Elizabeth Laurence was an actress, a leading lady of the play in which he had been somewhat precipitously cast. She was very beautiful, and she was gifted, but it was this that concerned Jerome the most. For while there were plenty of pretty actresses, and while there was a handful of beautiful ones, there were few who were also genuinely gifted, and almost none who combined both beauty and exceptional talent. This was what had prompted Jerome to take her under his wing. He was on her side, he wanted her good, she had to be good to make the play work, although he

90

must be careful that she wasn't altogether *too* good.

He was so busy thinking about this that it wasn't until after he had paid the taxi off and Elizabeth was actually knocking at the door of a pretty little white painted Regency villa that Jerome took stock of his surroundings. He immediately assumed this had to be her parents' house, for certainly no relatively untried or unknown actress of Jerome's somewhat limited acquaintance lived in anything but lodgings, or at the very most, a garret in someone else's house. And this was such a perfect little house, with its black-glossed, brass-knobbed front door, and window boxes teeming with lobelia and bright red geraniums. It was in fact precisely the sort of house about which Jerome dreamed.

Elizabeth rapped on the door once more with the brass knocker, and then turned to Jerome with an apologetic smile.

'I've only forgotten my key again,' she said. 'I suppose one day I'll remember it.'

The door was answered by a smartly uniformed housemaid, which only went even further to confirm Jerome's original suspicion that the house was not Elizabeth's own.

'Good evening, Mrs Ferrers,' the maid said, standing aside. 'I'm afraid you've just missed Mr Ferrers, ma'am.'

Elizabeth handed the maid her coat and gloves, while Jerome half closed his eyes, and rocked slightly back on his heels, just as he had seen Daniel Morrow do as Hamlet when he learns of Ophelia's death. Of course! She was married – of course! How could he have forgotten? Most probably, Jerome thought as he crossed the threshold of her house, because she never once had mentioned her husband.

'Poor Mr Ferrers,' Jerome heard Elizabeth sigh to her maid. 'I'd quite forgotten he was dining with his old regiment tonight. Did he say what time he would be back, Maggie?'

'Late ma'am,' the maid replied, now taking Jerome's coat. 'He has to take his father home, so he said as not to wait up.'

'This is Mr Didier, Maggie,' Elizabeth said, adding in explanation that he was the star of the play she was rehearsing. Jerome practised his best matinée idol smile on the apple-cheeked girl, and at once brought even more colour to her face.

'Mr Didier and I are going to rehearse our parts in the drawing room, Maggie, so would you mind bringing us up some sandwiches? And a jug of very strong coffee, please?'

'Is this all right?' Jerome asked, as Elizabeth led him into the drawing room. 'I mean you are sure your husband won't mind my being here?'

'It's not really any of his business, wouldn't you say?' Elizabeth asked, taking the sting from the question by gilding it with a naughty-kitten smile.

'But of course, you will tell him?' Jerome said.

'Do you think I should?' Elizabeth enquired, still being a kitten.

'Of course you must!' Jerome laughed. 'If you don't tell him, your maid most certainly will!'

Elizabeth laughed, all the time watching Jerome in the antique looking-glass while tidying her perfectly tidy lustrous dark hair. Once she had finished, she flopped down into a large chintz covered armchair, and closing her eyes, stretched her arms out wide so that the fabric of her thin blouse tightened over the shape of her firm young breasts.

'Heavens,' she sighed, stifling a small yawn, 'isn't acting absolutely exhausting?'

'If you're that tired—'

Jerome picked up his script which he had placed on the table beside him, and tapped it against his hand.

'Oh no!' Elizabeth opened her eyes and looked up at him, happy to see he was still looking at her. 'I didn't mean I was tired, Jerome. I just meant that *acting* – is *exhausting*! Heavens – I intend to work until I *drop*.'

She smoothed out her skirt, and picked up her play script.

'Where do you think we should start?' she asked.

'I think we should take the King's advice,' Jerome replied gravely. 'And begin at the beginning, and go on until we come to the end. And then we should stop.'

'Excellent!' Elizabeth clapped her hands with delight. 'Even if it takes all night.'

It took a lot less time than that for Elizabeth to recover her lost performance. Long before Maggie appeared with the welcome tray of sandwiches and coffee, Elizabeth was back on song, so much so that she and Jerome forgot all about eating until they had worked right the way through to the end of Act One.

'You did that without a note, hardly a note,' Jerome told her, helping himself from the tray. 'I didn't have to tell you one thing.'

Elizabeth took a sandwich from the plate, eating just the chicken and leaving the bread.

'I think,' she said, after a moment, having digested the sliver of chicken breast. 'I think it's because of the way you're playing it. I think that's what it is.'

'I'm not doing anything different,' Jerome countered.

'Yes, you are.' Elizabeth shook her head, and carefully pulled another sandwich apart. 'You are doing something different, darling. You're listening. And I'm listening to you. We didn't listen to each other before.'

'Yes?'

'Yes.'

Jerome looked back at her and saw an added sparkle in her eyes. He could sense her excitement, and he was sympathetic to it, because he too felt the excitement.

'I'm probably playing it less—' he searched for the words, one hand once more describing a circle. 'I'm playing it less forcefully, perhaps.'

'Yes,' Elizabeth agreed. 'Much less.'

'Less bombastic?' Jerome enquired.

'Less bombastic, yes,' Elizabeth frowned up at him, 'and *much* less forcefully.'

Jerome frowned back at her.

'It's probably because I'm here, that we're doing it here,' he said. 'In your house. On your home ground.' Elizabeth turned away and taking the coffee she had just poured herself, went and sat on the floor in front of the fire.

'I don't think so, darling,' she said thoughtfully. 'I really don't think we were listening to each other before. I think it's as simple as that.'

Jerome brought his coffee over and came and sat down on the rug beside her.

'Well, well,' he sighed. 'I thought it was going to be me helping you.'

'You have,' Elizabeth assured him, quietly, putting a hesitant hand up to his cheek and touching it. 'You've got us both to *listen*.'

By the time Jerome left just before midnight, they had worked right through to the end of the play. And when they reached the end, they had stopped and sat in silence, staring into the dying embers of the fire before Jerome had finally got to his feet.

'It's late,' he said. 'I have to go home.'

When she had seen him out, Elizabeth went upstairs to her bedroom, undressed at once and slipped straight into her single bed, putting out her light immediately, in case Sebastian returned while she was still awake. Elizabeth didn't want to talk to her husband, not now, because there was no way she could explain what she felt, no way she could describe her state of intense excitement, or what had caused it. For Elizabeth believed in truth she had won Jerome.

She lay there in the dark remembering. She remembered the looks he had given her, and the way he had given those looks. She remembered the touch of his hand as he had held hers, and the softness of his cheek when she had put her hand to it. But most of all she remembered the feeling of power, the power she felt she now had over Jerome. All Elizabeth felt she had to do was choose the moment for him to fall, and when she did, he would.

She was certain of it. She was so certain, she was so overjoyed. She felt like laughing out loud in the dark as she lay there in her bed, her brilliant black hair spilt in thick strands on the hand embroidered Italian pillowcase, her slender hands lying flat, palms down on the silk counterpane, floating blissfully in the dark. Jerome Didier was hers, to do with as she liked, as she had done that very evening, for from the word go he had done exactly what she wanted him to do, and she had got him to do that by pretending that she would do exactly what he said. It was as simple as that.

Elizabeth smiled, because she believed she had achieved both her objectives, namely to enslave Jerome publicly as well as privately, to make him hers on-stage as well as off. She was certain she had been doubly successful, because in the end, by pretending she was going to do exactly what he advised, she had instead turned the tables on him, and got him to do exactly what she wanted, which was to stop overplaying, to stop being selfish, and to start listening, all of which things he had begun to do, and as a result there was once again room for her.

So now, she thought as she lay watching the lights of passing cars playing on her ceiling, perhaps people would start watching her again, and she could go back to doing in the play what she had been doing before she had been – as she liked to think of it – *run over*. After all, it was her for whom Oscar Greene had written the play, her, Elizabeth Laurence, not Jerome Didier. And it was her that people would be queuing up to see, not Jerome Didier. Elizabeth would make sure of that, however much and madly she loved her leading man.

FIVE

When the telephone finally rang for her, Pippa was in bed reading. It wasn't late, but she had preferred to go to bed and read *Anna Karenina* than to stay up on her own by the dying fire. Her mother had for once gone out for dinner, to a small party at The Vicarage, to which fortunately for once Pippa had not been invited. She had driven her mother over, but had been excused fetching her home by the offer of a lift from one of their neighbours.

When the telephone finally rang, at first Pippa hardly noticed it. She was so deeply involved in her book she never heard it ringing, until it stopped. Then she suddenly looked up from her reading, aware there was a silence where a moment ago there had been ringing, and in that moment she knew it was Jerome.

By now she was half out of bed, long legs dangling over the edge, her feet trying to find her slippers, pulling her old, warm dressing gown on around her shoulders, as if there was still a point in getting up. And then when she came back to her senses, and realized the phone had long since stopped ringing, she suddenly sat very still and stared at the floor.

'Blast,' she said. 'Hell.'

Bobby, who was sleeping on the end of her bed, had woken up in the sudden flurry of activity, and lain with his head half cocked, watching for developments. When he realized Pippa was not going to go anywhere, he yawned very wide, and then rolled over on to his back, sticking four short legs into the air. Pippa rubbed his little, fat tummy affectionately, and with a sigh kicked her slippers back off again.

Which was when the telephone rang again. This time Pippa was taking no chances, rushing barefooted straight down the stairs to the hall. Bobby followed at once, barking joyously at the thought of an unscheduled walk or game, reaching the telephone table well before his mistress, and jumping up and down against her bare legs as she reached to pick up the receiver.

'Ow!' she exclaimed, pushing the dog down. 'Knock it off, Bobby.'

'Hello?' said a voice before Pippa could ask who it was. 'Is that you? I thought I must have dialled the wrong number.'

'Hello.'

It had been Jerome, she knew it had. Pippa just wished she didn't feel quite so giddy whenever she heard his voice.

'Look,' the beautiful voice said. 'I hope you weren't asleep – except it's much too early for sleep. It's just that I couldn't get to a phone before.'

'Before when?' Pippa asked, managing to get the lightness back into her voice. 'Before this evening? Or before this week?'

'I know, I'm sorry. *Mea culpa*,' he groaned. 'But please try and understand. If I haven't rung you, it's not because I haven't thought of you every moment of the day, because I have. I couldn't ring you before because we had a *dis-as-ter*.'

'What sort of disaster?'

'Ohhhh . . .' a long, deep moan came back down the line. 'Elizabeth *lost* it. But *completely*.'

'You're talking in code,' Pippa said. 'Translate.'

'She lost her performance,' Jerome explained. 'It was as if suddenly she had forgotten how to act. It was a disaster! I had nothing to play against, nothing! So I started to overact to compensate. It's been misery.'

'Poor you,' Pippa laughed. 'How rotten.'

'I'd have cut my throat,' Jerome said darkly, 'if I hadn't had the thought of you.'

'I'm sure that's not true,' she said.

'It's all *too* true,' he replied. 'It was only the thought of you, and of seeing you again, believe me – that carried me through.'

'You make it sound like war,' Pippa chided.

'Oh, the theatre's a lot worse than war, Pippa Nicholls,' Jerome laughed. 'In war at least you know who's on your side.'

Pippa fell silent. She was sitting on the woodblock floor now, with Bobby beside her. She got hold of one of his silky ears and twisted it gently in her hand.

'So when am I going to see you again?' Jerome demanded, breaking the silence.

'I don't know,' Pippa told him, in all honesty. 'Aren't you going off on tour next week?'

'Yes, absolutely. Oxford first stop. Pippa—' Jerome paused, and then continued quickly. 'Why don't you come up? Come up to Oxford and see the play.'

'How can I?' she asked. 'You know I can't.'

'You must. You have to. I have to see you. I have to tell you how I feel.'

Lights from a car pulling into the drive alerted Pippa and she quickly got to her feet.

'I have to go,' she said. 'Sorry.'

'You must come up to Oxford, Pippa,' Jerome urged. 'Please. I must see you.'

Pippa looked round behind her as she saw the lights of the car sweep round outside the front door.

'Why?' she asked. 'Can't it wait till you're back in London?'

'No, it cannot wait!'

Jerome sounded almost peremptory.

'Why not?' Pippa asked, as Bobby began to bark.

'Because I love you.'

'I really do have to go, Jerome,' Pippa told him, without having time to tell him why. 'Goodbye.'

Just in time, Pippa banged the telephone down and ran back upstairs, leaving Bobby downstairs to bark even more excitedly as Mrs Nicholls opened the front door of her house.

Once in bed, Pippa put her light out, and lay in the darkness with her heart pounding in her chest. She would love to go to Oxford and see Jerome open in the play, but she knew it was out of the question, because her mother quite simply would never allow it, not even if she arranged for someone to look after her. She disapproved most strongly of Jerome, and told Pippa daily that she wanted her to have nothing to do with him.

'There is only one thing actors ever take seriously,' she had told Pippa several times over, 'and that is themselves.'

'Your mother tells me you're walking out with an actor,' Pippa's Aunt Bea said as they walked out on the Downs. 'Impossibly good-looking, I'll bet.'

Her aunt had arrived from London that Friday afternoon, unexpected and unannounced but as welcome as always. Everyone who knew her loved her, Aunt Bea was very dear, and always had been. Pippa was always particularly pleased to see her, because as her late father's sister, she could more or less always be relied on to be in Pippa's corner, even down to providing the necessary so that Pippa could keep her beloved Welsh cob, Bumble, in livery just down the road. Although a very pretty blonde, Bea had never married, because as she said she had never wanted to do so, agreeing with the dictum which asserted that marriage was not a word but a sentence.

'I'm not a crank,' she would explain when pressed. 'I'm just too afraid of loneliness to get married!'

At which *bon mot* she would laugh deliciously and infectiously, before proceeding to draft one of her notorious *fun plans*, as she always referred to her schemes. Aunt Bea dearly loved a scheme, and schemed constantly.

Her latest scheme was centred around how to fix up Pippa's trip to Oxford.

'I don't see why you shouldn't go,' she said to Pippa as they walked. 'You're a big girl now, and you've never been a silly one. As long as you remember the sort of people actors are. And don't go getting yourself over-involved.'

'Oh, don't you start, Bea!' Pippa laughed. 'I have it all day from my mother!'

'That's one thing your mother's right about,' her aunt replied. 'You want to watch actors. They're inclined to take the wrong things seriously, and they're forever away on tour.'

'I just think perhaps actors have a totally different defence mechanism,' Pippa said, quite surprising her aunt. 'I think that's why so many people don't really understand them.'

'I see,' Aunt Bea nodded and smiled. 'They are inclined though, are they not, to use their emotions up on stage, leaving little for afters?'

'I'll tell you what, Bea,' Pippa replied, with a smile. 'I'll let you know when I get to know Jerome better.'

'Jerome?'

'Jerome Didier.'

Her aunt nodded.

'I have always believed in names, you know, Pip,' she said. 'You can't be a great actor if you've got a name like Dobbs. Or Ruggins, or whatever. And I must say, Jerome Didier does have a ring about it.'

'He says he's going to be a star,' Pippa said. 'I'm dying for you to meet him.'

'So am I!' her aunt laughed. 'But first we must concentrate on getting *you* to meet *him*.'

The plan as devised was for Aunt Bea to stay a few days in Sussex, which every so often she did whenever she felt the need to escape London, and while in residence, Pippa could auspiciously go to London to see the new Christopher Fry play, for which Aunt Bea had been given some complimentary tickets.

'Which will provide us with the perfect alibi,' she said. 'I saw it on the first night, you see, so I can tell you *all* about it, without you having to go and see it at all. Because what you will be doing, sweetheart, is popping up to Oxford to see your jolly actor.'

'I'll never do it,' Pippa said when they were roughing out an itinerary. 'I'll never make it across from Paddington. I'll never make the last train.'

'Of course you won't, you chump,' Aunt Bea laughed. 'You're going to have to "miss" your last train, and stay overnight in my flat, aren't you?'

'Am I?' the bewildered Pippa asked her.

'Yes,' her aunt replied. 'Provided Scouts' Honour you come back from Oxford *ay-lone*, and you stay in the flat – *ay-lone*. Not that I really need to make that a condition,' she added, when she saw how quickly and brightly her niece's face was colouring.

'No,' Pippa said. 'You don't, Bea. Even so—'

Pippa broke off, to wonder on the feasibility of their plan.

'Are you sure it will work?'

'Darling. I shall tell you the whole play from boring beginning to boring end, just in case your mother quizzes you about it, which she won't, because theatre bores her *rigid*. She's really only interested in what's going on in the parish, and what that ghastly vicar has to say.'

Not for a moment did Pippa believe her mother would approve the proposed trip, but even so she learned a potted version of Christopher Fry's *A Sleep of Prisoners* just in case, and ironed her best summer dress the next afternoon when her mother was resting.

But as it happened, and to Pippa's well-concealed delight, her mother agreed. Naturally she had initially voiced doubts, but since Bea had come to stay and would be there to help her, she could voice no sustainable objection to the proposed trip, particularly after her sister made a great display of lending Pippa the key to her flat as a safety precaution, just in case Pippa missed her last train. This buried the last of any doubts Pippa's mother might still have been nursing, and she finally gave her consent, which was how Pippa found herself on Wednesday afternoon of the following week, making her way from the railway station across Oxford to catch the matinée of *All That Glitters* at the New Theatre, having rung and left a message at the stage door for Jerome to that effect.

The theatre was about two-thirds full for the afternoon show, but to judge from the excitement generated by the play and even more so by the unknown leading players, it could as easily have been an opening night in the West End of London. Not that Pippa had ever been to a first night, but she had often attended matinées in the company of her Aunt Bea on her occasional visits to London, and the matinées she had frequented had borne no resemblance to the performance she witnessed that afternoon in Oxford. For once the ladies in the audience were held spellbound, and nothing distracted them as they watched the play unfold. They even hurried through their interval tea, anxious to finish everything that was on their trays so that the clatter of cup and saucer would not distract either the performers or their audience. And when the final curtain fell, the predominantly female audience refused to release the cast until they had taken six curtain calls, even cheering and calling *bravo!* when Jerome and Elizabeth stepped forward to take their joint calls.

From her seat in the fifth row of the stalls, Pippa clapped and cheered with the rest of the delighted audience, many of whom Pippa noticed were in tears. The woman next door to Pippa was still crying openly, as indeed she had been since halfway through the final and very moving scene. Pippa smiled shyly at her, as she prepared to make her way from the auditorium.

'Do you know something, my dear?' she asked, dabbing at her eyes with a small lace handkerchief. 'That's the most beautiful play I have ever seen.'

'It was wonderful,' Pippa agreed. 'It was funny, and yet so touching.'

'Yes it was,' the woman agreed, 'and I shall never forget it. Not for as long as I live. And most of all, I shall never, ever forget that beautiful young man.'

Pippa was almost shocked by how she felt as she found herself saying his name.

'Jerome Didier, you mean?' Pippa asked, finding herself suddenly disorientated by the surge of emotion she felt just saying Jerome's name.

'Jerome Didier,' the woman replied, now consulting her programme, and opening it at Jerome's photograph, which made him look almost impossibly handsome. Pippa stared at it as well, becoming increasingly bewildered by how she was feeling, a mixture, she discovered, of fierce possessiveness and helpless adoration. The power of these unexpected emotions surprised and frightened her, and suddenly all Pippa wanted was to escape, to get out of the theatre and to run away as far as possible.

She picked up her handbag which she had almost forgotten and made to leave.

'Excuse me,' she said to her neighbour, but the woman wasn't quite ready yet to allow her to leave.

'You know something, my dear?' she asked, tapping Jerome's photograph with a sigh. 'They'd better all look to their laurels, you know. All of them. Because what we've seen here this afternoon, we haven't seen a star being born, my dear. What we've seen is something which is going to light up our heavens. What we've seen is the launch of a meteor.'

Staring down at the photograph of Jerome's beautiful face, Pippa still wanted to run, but where she wanted to run was not away any more, but straight round backstage to Jerome.

'We could have taken at *least* another two calls, darling,' Elizabeth teased as she and Jerome climbed the stairs to their dressing rooms. 'If you hadn't been in such a perfectly *beastly* hurry.'

'You can take as many as you like tonight, my darling,' Jerome smiled back, squeezing his co-star's hand, 'but this afternoon I have a visitor.'

Elizabeth stopped as they reached the stage door-keeper's booth and looked Jerome in the eye.

'Business?' she asked. 'Or pleasure?'

'Cecil B. de Mille,' Jerome replied, before leaning into the booth to see if he had either any mail or messages. There was nothing for him, but there was a note for Elizabeth which he handed her.

She took it, barely even glancing to see whom it was from, before looking back at Jerome, inclining her head to one side.

'By the way,' she said. 'You were even more brilliant than usual this afternoon.'

'We both were,' Jerome assured her. 'Your timing in the last scene—' He put his index finger to his thumb and closed his eyes. '*Mmmmm!*'

'You were far too good for a matinée,' Elizabeth smiled. 'In fact, I'd say you were inspired.'

'I was simply doing my best, my darling,' he whispered, leaning over to kiss her lightly on one cheek, 'to keep somewhere *near* up with you.'

Elizabeth paused for a moment, tempted to wait and see who

101

was coming round to see Jerome, but at that moment the telephone rang.

'It's for you, Miss L,' the old door-keeper said. 'Shall I put it through to your dressing room?'

'Please, Albert,' Elizabeth replied, before squeezing Jerome's hand in farewell. 'I'll see you later, my darling,' she said.

Jerome wandered out into the alleyway as Elizabeth disappeared up to her dressing room, and lit a cigarette while he waited for Pippa. As had been the case since the day after the play had opened in Oxford, there was already a crowd waiting for autographs, and Jerome charmingly and dutifully obliged, while all the time keeping an eye on the end of the alley for the arrival of his visitor.

When Pippa finally appeared, looking slightly bewildered and just a little bit lost, Jerome detached himself from his group of admirers, and went to collect her.

'Pippa Nicholls,' he said, stopping in front of her, and folding his hands behind his back. 'I was beginning to give you up for lost.'

'I'm terribly sorry,' Pippa said with as much assurance as she could manage. 'I only went round the wrong side of the theatre.'

'You look – wonderful,' Jerome said, now taking her arm and leading her back to the theatre. 'You have brought the sunshine from the South Downs with you.'

He stood aside by the stage door and Pippa walked in past him, looking inquisitively at her surroundings.

'I've never been backstage before,' she said. 'It's really quite bleak, isn't it?'

'Bleak?' Jerome laughed as he followed her up the stone stairs. 'Backstage at any theatre – it's like an institution!'

Reaching the first landing, Jerome steered Pippa along the corridor which contained the first set of dressing rooms.

'Number One,' he said, as they passed the first door. 'That's Miss Laurence's—'

Pippa held back for a moment to look at the greasepainted star on the dressing-room door, and the message in the middle.

'Told you!' it read. 'Love, love, love – J.'

'What did you tell her?' Pippa enquired. 'If you don't mind me asking.'

'I told her,' Jerome said, steering Pippa away from the door, 'that she was going to be a star, which she is. And this—' he added, throwing open the very next door, 'is *Chez Moi.*'

There was a similar star drawn on Jerome's door, in a different colour, in what looked like lipstick. And the hand-drawn star also contained a message.

'Same to you, my love,' the inscription read. 'With things on it.'

Underneath the star was a string of red x kisses. Jerome sighed as he saw Pippa staring at them, and took her by the hand to tug her into the room.

'Actors,' he sighed. 'We're just like children.'

'You're right though,' Pippa said as Jerome closed the door. 'She is going to be a star – Elizabeth Laurence. I don't think I've ever seen such a beautiful girl.'

'She is beautiful,' Jerome agreed. 'She is certainly the most beautiful actress that *I* have ever seen.'

'Yes,' Pippa said, looking at the poster for the play which Jerome had pinned on his wall. 'She's completely stunning. And she can act. At least, I mean, I think she can.'

'She can,' Jerome agreed once more, nodding seriously. 'She is the most beautiful and talented young actress I have ever seen. But she is nothing beside you.'

'I'm not an actress,' Pippa said, being deliberately obtuse.

'Thank God,' Jerome breathed, now standing behind Pippa as she stared at the poster on which she was now unable to focus. 'Elizabeth is a beautiful actress, Pippa. But you are just quite simply beautiful.' He turned her round slowly to him, holding her by the shoulders. 'You, Pippa – are the most beautiful *girl* – I have ever seen.'

'Don't be silly,' Pippa replied, but her answer sounded faint, and weak, and much less categorical than she had intended, because Pippa found she could now hardly breathe, let alone speak. It wasn't because of what Jerome had just said, or the way he had just said it, and it wasn't because of the way he was now looking at her or the way he had looked at her when he met her in the alleyway, or because he was holding her by her shoulders and standing so very, very close to her, it was none of these things. It was simply because he was Jerome, and no-one else. Because no-one else except this person, this someone called Jerome Didier, no-one else had ever made Pippa feel quite as overpoweringly helpless as he was making her feel right now.

'Do you mind if I sit down?' she suddenly asked. 'It was really quite hot in the theatre.'

'Of course,' Jerome said, very seriously, as he cleared a place on the old *chaise-longue*. 'It is an exceptionally warm day. We noticed it on-stage. There.'

He sat Pippa in the space among his belongings and then stood back. He thought he was doing well so far. He hadn't fluffed or bungled his lines, he had been dispassionate yet fond and polite, and he had not as yet rushed in where the angels fear to tread. Even though from the very moment she had rounded the corner and come back into his life, Jerome had wanted nothing more than to take her in his arms and kiss the breath out of her.

'Tea?' he said, walking over to where his dresser had laid the tea tray, which was set for two. 'I can even offer you some Fuller's cake. And some *chocolate* – biscuits.'

He flourished the plate of confections in front of Pippa, as if he were a butler or a waiter, and Pippa smiled, hoping the colour which she knew had vanished from her cheeks, was beginning to return. Jerome saw that it was, and wanted to touch the lightly reddening skin with his hand, to brush his fingers – or even better – his lips against her soft, smooth skin. She looked even sweeter and more innocent than before. In fact, he assured himself, he had forgotten how pure she was, how much without guile. She was the personification of kindness, of sweetness, of true simplicity, of all innocence, and he loved her so much he wanted to throw back his head and cry out and tell her now what he felt.

Instead, he asked her what she felt. But not about him, what she felt about the play.

'Well?' he said, pouring the tea. 'You must tell me. *Did* you like it?'

'Yes,' Pippa answered.

'Well?'

'It's very difficult to describe precisely what you feel about something. Particularly straight after.'

Pippa took the proffered tea cup, placing it beside her.

'But you "liked" it?' Jerome persisted.

'Very much. It must be very difficult to write a play like that. And to perform it. It's such a fine balance. Such a fine line between sentimentality and real feeling. But it comes off. Terribly well. All I can say is that I laughed, and I cried. We all did. The handkerchieves were out all round me at the end.'

'Good.'

Jerome took a sip from his own tea, and then put the cup down on his dressing table, before turning and leaning nearer the mirror in order to check his make-up.

'It is a very difficult piece to play,' he said, removing the mascara from under his eyes. 'You're right. It requires a rather light touch.'

He glanced at her in the mirror, wondering if that would be sufficient enough cue for her to change the subject to the matter of his performance.

'I should imagine it will do awfully well in London,' she said instead. 'I should think it will run for ages.'

Jerome said nothing more. He just continued to take off his make-up, plunging three fingers of one hand into a large tub of vanishing cream and then rubbing it into both hands, finally working it into and all over his face. Pippa watched with fascination.

'Hand me that towel, Pippa Nicholls,' Jerome requested from behind his mask of remover. 'From beside you somewhere on the sofa.'

The towel was actually hanging on the wicker chair, wedged behind Jerome's back. Pippa tugged it free and put it in his outstretched hand.

'It's such a wonderful smell, theatrical make-up,' she said, picking up a stick of Leichner Number 5. 'It's so atmospheric.'

'All part of the red and the gold thing,' Jerome replied. 'All part of what Cocteau called the Red and the Gold thing. What attracts you to the theatre – is either the *Red* – or the *Gold*. The smell of make-up's a part of that.'

'Is it red or gold though?' Pippa wondered. 'I think it's probably gold, don't you?'

'Yes,' Jerome nodded. 'Definitely.'

Pippa held the stick closer to her face, to smell it better.

'It takes me back to school,' she said, inhaling the pungent aroma. 'To when we did our toe-curling productions of Shakespeare. Mmmmm.' She took another smell, closing her eyes. 'Oh and it reminds me too, of Christmas. Of Cecil's amazing pantomimes.'

'Cecil puts on pantomimes?' Jerome laughed, widening his eyes at Pippa above the edge of his make-up towel. 'Don't tell me – I'll bet he plays the dame.'

'It was one of the ugly sisters last year,' Pippa replied, rifling through the rest of the sticks of Leichner. 'What a wonderful red!' she exclaimed, picking one out, and then another. 'But when on earth would you use *this*? And what for? What would you use green for?'

'For jealousy,' Jerome told her, poker-faced. 'In case you thought Elizabeth Laurence was better than I was.'

'You were both awfully good,' Pippa replied, trying some of the green on her eyelids. 'You don't need me to tell you that.'

'Of course I do!' Jerome laughed once more, giving his face a final rub with a clean, dry towel. 'I don't know what you thought of me!'

'Would it matter?' Pippa half closed her eyes to try and see the effect of the green make-up. 'You know you're good. You told me so. You told me what a good actor you are. Anyway, you heard that applause. You heard how good everyone thought you were.'

Pippa sat down on the rickety chair next to Jerome and began carefully to apply the carmine to her unmade-up lips. While she did, Jerome went and washed his face in a small sink in the corner. Behind him, Pippa suddenly began to laugh infectiously.

'Look,' she said. 'What would you think if I looked like this?'

Jerome bent down so that he could see Pippa fully in the mirror. She had given herself bright green eyelids and a large carmine-red butterfly mouth.

'I wouldn't think anything different,' Jerome whispered in her ear, 'to what I already think.'

'I'll bet you would,' Pippa replied, smiling broadly at him now so that he could see she had also blacked out one of her front teeth.

'I wouldn't care,' Jerome said, managing to keep his face straight, 'if you had no teeth whatsoever – and every one of those wonderful freckles of yours was bright purple.'

'Why wouldn't you care?' Pippa asked, before she could stop herself, before she saw the trap.

'Because,' Jerome said simply, 'I would still love you, Pippa Nicholls, that's why.'

Pippa fell silent and looked down, away from Jerome's steady gaze. She reached for some tissues and wiped the black from her teeth, but before she could remove the rest of her make-up, Jerome took her hand and turned her to him, lifting her to her feet.

'I meant what I said on the telephone,' he told her, taking her other hand.

'What?' Pippa asked, as defiantly as she could. 'When you said what on the telephone?'

'You know what I said on the telephone, Pippa Nicholls,' Jerome replied, putting an arm round her waist. 'And when. And you know that I meant it. Otherwise you wouldn't be here.'

He had both his arms round her waist now, and was holding her close to him. Pippa tilted her head back, trying to stop the unstoppable.

'You mean—' she began. 'Just because I came to see you in your play—'

'Precisely,' he interrupted her, and then kissed her.

His arms were both still round her waist, but he was only holding her lightly. Pippa could easily have broken free had she wanted to do so, but she didn't. From the moment she felt his mouth on hers, she knew that was the place she wanted to be, in his arms, being kissed by him like he was kissing her, gently, softly, and again now, with a little more passion so that she no longer knew quite where or quite what she was. She could hear his breath, and feel it, warm now on her neck, and on her cheek, and then once more within her, as he kissed her again and then again.

'Oh dear,' said a voice behind her. 'Sorry – I should have knocked.'

'Yes,' Jerome agreed, looking round at Elizabeth, but not letting go of Pippa. 'You should have done really, darling.'

Elizabeth held his look, and then despite biting her lip, began to laugh.

'What have you two been doing?' she asked. 'It looks as though someone's punched you both in the mouth.'

Jerome bent down to look at himself in the mirror, while Pippa put a hand to her lips, remembering the carmine make-up.

'By the way Elizabeth,' Jerome said, still bent over in front of the mirror. 'This is Pippa Nicholls, a friend of mine.'

'Hello, Pippa Nicholls,' Elizabeth said, gaily, extending a hand to be shaken. 'How do?'

'Hello,' Pippa replied, shaking hands, and then reaching for a tissue to wipe her mouth.

'We've been doing some *Ay-matuer Dramaticals*,' Jerome said, over his shoulder.

'So I see,' Elizabeth replied, directing one of her sweetest smiles at Pippa. 'Were you in this afternoon?'

'I'm sorry?' a still disconcerted Pippa asked. 'What did you say?'

'I asked if you were in this afternoon,' Elizabeth repeated. 'If you were out front.'

'Was I in the audience,' Pippa translated thoughtfully. 'Yes. Yes I was. In. Out front.'

'I'm so glad,' Elizabeth said, graciously. 'You were a *wonderful* house. Jerome—' Elizabeth caught Jerome's eyes in the mirror, ignoring the markedly dangerous gleam. 'Are you coming out to eat, my darling?' she asked. 'Or – or what?'

'No, I'm not coming out to eat, my darling,' Jerome answered in measured tones, having also by now removed all traces of the carmine from his mouth. 'I am going out to eat. With Miss Nicholls.'

'Oh,' Elizabeth said, with an inflexion of only slight surprise. 'Righto.'

She didn't give Pippa another look until she stopped in the open doorway to turn back as if she had forgotten something.

'Tell me,' she said, 'I should have asked, but I forgot. Did you enjoy our little play?'

'I'm sorry?' Pippa ventured, oblivious of the question, stunned into silence as she realized that contrary to the law which governed all things fair, Elizabeth Laurence was even more stunningly beautiful off-stage than she was on. Pippa had never seen eyes so bright, nor a skin so perfect.

'I asked you,' the actress was repeating, 'whether or not you enjoyed our little play.'

'Yes,' Pippa half stammered in reply. 'Yes I did. Very much. I thought it was wonderful.'

'Good,' Elizabeth purred. 'Goodee.'

One more smile, and one more look, and she was gone. The smile had been to cover the look, which had, Elizabeth hoped as she shut the dressing–room door behind her, been just long enough for the odd, freckled-faced girl with the unkempt hair and the unmade-up face to feel she was being inspected, and for her to feel that Elizabeth had noticed the small darn on the ankle of one of her stockings, the odd button on her cotton dress, and her cheap little piece of costume jewellery. *What*, Elizabeth wondered as she swept off to meet the rest of the cast across the road in the café, could someone as beautiful and as talented as Jerome possibly see in such an absurd little *mouse*?

Instead of eating, which neither of them wanted to do, Jerome and Pippa walked round Oxford. Pippa had never visited the city before, and was enchanted by it.

' "Noon of my dreams, O noon!" ' Jerome quoted, taking Pippa by the other hand now, and leading her around New College Square.

' "Proud and godly kings had built her, long ago,
With her towers and tombs and statues all arow,
With her fair and floral air and the love that lingers there,
And the streets where great men go." '

'Who was that?' Pippa asked. 'You seem to know every bit of verse ever written.'

'That was somebody or other,' Jerome replied, looking up at the stone buildings surrounding them. 'Don't ask me who. Except for Shakespeare, everything I know is Terry Vaughan. He was forever spouting verse, and getting me to do the same. But it's rather good though, isn't it? Whoever's it is. "With her fair and floral air and the love that lingers there." And I love you, Pippa Nicholls.'

'I wish you wouldn't say that.'

Pippa withdrew her hand and walked away towards the main gate.

'Why not?' Jerome called, enjoying the echo his voice made in the square as he hurried after her.

'Why not?' he whispered to her, once he had caught her up.

She told him as they sat on the banks of the Isis.

'I don't want you to fall in love with me,' she said.

'Too late, Miss Nicholls,' Jerome sighed, turning to lie on one side, propped up by an elbow to stare at her. 'It's a little too late for that.'

'All right,' Pippa argued, tossing a stone into the river. 'Let's put it this way. I didn't want you to fall in love with me. And I didn't want to fall in love with you.'

'Have you?'

'I've all my life ahead of me. I hadn't even thought about being in love. Don't you understand?'

'You haven't answered my question, Pippa Nicholls. *Have* you fallen in love with me?'

'Why do you all speak with such deliberate emphases?' Pippa asked, getting up and walking away from Jerome, who at once got up and followed her. 'Everything is always so *frightfully emphatic*. As if you lived all your lives in quote marks. Or italics.'

'*All* of us?' Jerome laughed.

'There you go again!' Pippa retorted.

'How many actors have you known? You asked why do we *all* speak with such deliberate emphases!' Jerome danced round in front of her, and held up his hands, like a traffic policeman. 'Stop!' he commanded. '*I demand you tell me how many actors you have known!*'

'It really is frightfully tiring,' Pippa muttered, sinking once more to the grass. 'It's like being in a play all the time.'

Jerome now knelt in front of her, and took both her hands in his.

'Please answer my question,' he begged, with puzzled eyes and a very deep frown. 'Please, Pippa Nicholls. Please say that you love me.'

'Until that day at Cecil's,' Pippa said after watching a young man about Jerome's age row a girl about her age slowly past them, 'I hadn't even thought about being in love. At least I had, but I'd dismissed it from my mind, as being a state I didn't want to be in. Not yet, anyway. Not until I'd found out what I wanted to do. I didn't want to be distracted, not by anything, least of all by being in love.'

'You can do the two things at once, you know, Pippa Nicholls,' Jerome replied. 'You can rub your tummy *and* pat the top of your head at the same time.'

'I can't,' Pippa said, with a glum little smile. 'I've never been able to do that sort of thing. I can only concentrate on one thing at a time. And I wanted to concentrate on my art, my sculpture that is, once I found that was what I wanted to do.'

'I have my art, I have my acting,' Jerome argued. 'Yet I can still love you.'

'Can you?' Pippa asked, with an intensity that made Jerome look up at her, sharply. 'Can you?' she asked him again, and then once more got up to walk away further down the riverbank. Jerome watched her for a while before he got up, and when he did, this time he didn't hurry after her, but allowed her to walk ahead of him, while he kept a good twenty or so yards behind her.

Finally she stopped, and stood right by the water's edge. Jerome walked up to her, and put his arms round her, from behind.

'I don't think you understand,' she said.

'That used to drive Terry Vaughan mad,' Jerome said. 'He used to tell me every time he had a set-to with my mother, and she would go into one of her silences, and he would ask her what was wrong – she would tell him there was no point in explaining because he wouldn't understand. It used to infuriate him so much he swore that if he'd had two good legs instead of two tin ones, he'd have taken her out, every time that she did it, and thrown her in the sea.'

'Will you throw me in the river?' Pippa asked, 'because I told you.'

'Probably, Miss Nicholls,' Jerome replied. 'There is certainly a very good chance.'

Pippa did her best to explain as they turned and walked back, what her reasons were, but Jerome would accept none of them, telling her each day had to be dealt with as it dawned, and insisting she tell him what her true feelings were. His persistence bothered Pippa, because it bewildered her. She had never had anyone pay serious court to her before. There had been boys, local boys, who had come shyly to the house and asked her mother if they could take Pippa to the cinema, and occasionally she was allowed to go as long as she went in a party, and then as she matured, there had been young men, and plenty of them too, some like the boys before them local young men, and others from farther afield, young men who were staying down with their friends for a dance or a party, or just for the weekend. They too would come to call and seek permission to take Pippa out, and once again permission was granted provided there were others present. But no-one was allowed to call often enough lest they grew too serious.

'You're seeing too much of that young man,' her mother would say. 'And no good will come of it. You'll end up rushing into some totally unsuitable marriage, and regretting it for the rest of your days. There are other things for girls, intelligent girls like you, you know, Pippa, besides marriage.'

With which Pippa would argue with no little passion that the very last thing she wanted to do was get married. She wanted to do something with her life, rather than let somebody else do something with it. Her mother would agree, wholeheartedly, often delightedly, before informing her daughter in which case there was no point in going on seeing whichever particular young man it was who was then taking her out, lest they got too serious over each other.

'Yes, but even so,' Pippa would wonder over dinner in the kitchen, 'it's not just that, is it? Don't take this wrong, because it's not a grumble. But you know I won't leave you.'

'Can't, you mean,' her mother would correct her.

'Won't,' Pippa insisted. 'I don't want to leave you. I wouldn't. Not with no-one to look after you.'

'But you would if there was someone to look after me,' her mother would reply. 'You'd be off like a shot.'

It was an impossible conversation to continue, not only because it was too painful a subject, but because they both knew that a time would come when Pippa would be forced into making a decision, when circumstances would dictate that she must choose between her own young life and what was left of her mother's. But not just yet, Pippa used to say when her mother was determined to prolong the debate.

'We don't have to discuss this now, Mother,' she would say. 'This is something we'll deal with if and if ever it arises.'

But not just yet.

'Please God I'll die soon,' her mother would say as her final words whenever they spent the evening debating their futures. 'I only hope to God I die soon, so that you can have a life of your own.'

And often, particularly recently, and most particularly since she had met Jerome, Pippa would lie awake in the dark of her bedroom and wonder whether in fact that would not be the most acceptable solution. She knew her mother didn't want to go on living. She knew all her mother wanted to do was to die so that she could be, as she hoped, with her late husband. Even if she had been fit and strong, Pippa knew that would still have been what her mother wanted, because her mother had regularly said so. And if her mother was dead, and if there was a heaven, then her mother would be happy, and even though she would mourn for her mother, finally Pippa could also be happy, possibly, although she hardly dared think about it, possibly with Jerome Didier.

But not just yet.

'You're staying for the evening performance?' Jerome asked, more as a matter of course than for information. 'We can dine afterwards rather splendidly. At The Mitre.'

'I can't, Jerome,' Pippa replied. 'I have to get back.'

'You said you weren't going back to Sussex tonight?'

Jerome put his make-up down and looked at Pippa in the mirror. She was once again sitting on the sofa in his dressing room, but this time she was much more relaxed, he noted, settled into one corner with her long elegant legs tucked up underneath her.

'I know I said I wasn't going back to Sussex,' Pippa replied. 'But you didn't let me finish telling you. I have to get back to London. I'm staying at – I'm staying with my aunt,' she corrected herself. 'At her flat.'

'Fine,' Jerome said, returning to the process of making-up. 'I'll drive you back down to London, after we've had dinner.'

'No,' Pippa said quickly, trying to kill the idea at birth, instinctively sensing danger. It had been difficult enough to control her emotions after seeing Jerome on-stage that afternoon, and she knew that after an evening performance to a house already sold out by the time they had returned to the theatre, and a dinner à *deux*, there was every chance that the little resolution she had left would dissolve completely, and she would stay the night in Oxford, with Jerome, and that they would go to bed together.

'No, I really can't, Jerome,' she repeated. 'I wouldn't get back until far too late. And my aunt would be furious.'

'We'll see,' Jerome said, this time without even bothering to look at her. 'You might feel quite different after the show.'

But it wasn't Pippa who felt different after the show, it was Jerome. Elizabeth had been a disaster, either practically inaudible, or else playing everything right over the top, as if she was hysterical. On top of all that she either walked through all her laughs, or killed every one of Jerome's stone dead, by coming in before the audience had barely drawn breath.

'Every line,' Jerome seethed in the interval to the actor who was playing Jerome's rival. 'Every laugh and every damn line she's in like a Sherman tank! We lost them in the first scene, and we haven't got them back since! I'm going to have a word with madam, and see what she's playing at.'

'Sorry, Mr Didier,' Elizabeth's dresser, Muzz, said, politely barring Jerome from coming into his co-star's dressing room. 'Miss Laurence is very upset and she doesn't want to see anyone.'

Jerome sighed and leaned his forehead on the doorframe.

'What, Muzz,' he sighed, 'has got into her? *You* tell me. Is she sick or something?'

'She's not sick, Mr Didier,' Muzz replied. 'She's just rather upset.'

'Have *I* upset her, Muzz?' Jerome asked, managing to ease the door open a fraction more, allowing himself sight of Elizabeth curled up in a silk gown on the couch with her back to them. 'Because if I'm the cause of the upset—'

'She's best left alone at such times, Mr Didier,' Muzz reminded Jerome, taking control of the door once more. 'You know that.'

'Dear God,' Jerome muttered, as the door was shut against him. 'Actresses.'

As Jerome was heading back for his dressing room, racking his brain for the best plan of action, Elizabeth turned her face from the back of the couch where she lay to smile sweetly at her dresser.

'Thank you, Muzz dear,' she murmured. 'What *would* I do without you?'

Or rather more to the point, she thought as she sat up to allow her dresser to plump up the silk-covered, monogrammed cushions behind her on the couch, what would Muzz do without her? Elizabeth considered it had been one of her rather more inspired notions, instructing Cecil to ensure she was allowed to choose her own dresser. Lalla had pointed out to her the importance of such a move, telling Elizabeth that at all costs and at all times it was vital to have someone backstage in whom she could confide, someone whose loyalty would never be questioned. So who better than old Muzz? After all, it had been Muzz who had rung Elizabeth first to sound out (albeit indirectly) whether or not there was anything in Elizabeth's new found career for her, so what could possibly be better than the job of her dresser? Elizabeth knew she could confide in Muzz, she knew she could trust her and count on her total loyalty, because she knew Muzz needed the job as much as Elizabeth needed her to do it. And so far, Elizabeth thought as her dresser draped a pretty lace shawl around her shoulders, so far and like most things at present in Elizabeth's life, it was working out absolutely perfectly.

'I don't actually think it's right, making you go on at these times,'

Muzz said, opening a jar of aspirins which were on Elizabeth's dressing table. 'I'm quite sure men wouldn't if men had it. But then I'm afraid that's typical men.'

'Yes, I'm afraid it is, Muzz,' Elizabeth agreed, pulling the shawl around her shoulders. 'But you know the saying, darling, the show *must* go on.'

Elizabeth gave a sad little yawn and smiled bravely. She had deliberately allowed her dresser to believe that the reason for her loss of control in Act One was a feminine one, which indeed it was, but not the one her dresser believed it to be. The reason Elizabeth had decided apparently to lose control on-stage and disconcert Jerome had to do not with Elizabeth's womb, but her heart.

She lay back on her mountain of feather-filled cushions and sighed with the pain of it all, a sigh which earned another look of the deepest sympathy from her dresser, who hurried over to her with two aspirins and a glass of water. Elizabeth pretended to take them, while in fact hiding them, one in either cheek, until Muzz had turned away and Elizabeth had a chance to get rid of them.

'Five minutes please, Miss Laurence!' the boy called with a knock on her dressing-room door. 'Act Two beginners five minutes please!'

Elizabeth held a lace hankie to her mouth, as if feeling nauseated, but in reality to conceal the fact she had pouched the aspirins.

'They'll have to hold the curtain, Muzz darling,' Elizabeth stage-whispered to her dresser, one hand to her mouth and the other pressing the newly refilled hot water bottle to her stomach. 'Just for a few minutes. Just until the aspirin begin to work.'

The tablets were starting to melt in her mouth and the taste was disgusting, but then, Elizabeth decided, when you were acting, obviously you had to put up with all sorts of horrid things.

Act One had left Pippa totally confused, as it had indeed left most of the audience. At least the play still made sense, she thought as she sat and slowly ate an ice cream from a tub, but no sense could be made of Elizabeth Laurence's performance. If Pippa hadn't seen the matinée, she would have had to conclude that Elizabeth Laurence, despite the rave notices quoted on the billboards outside the theatre, was one of the worst young actresses she had ever seen.

Fortunately this conclusion could only really be reached by those who had seen how brilliant she normally was, for they had a yardstick. Others who had not witnessed Elizabeth's true talent, in other words every other member of that night's audience, could only speculate, and wonder whether or not such an eccentric performance wasn't in fact part of the character the beautiful young actress was playing, so that when the curtain rose on Act Two, instead of there being a feeling of utter disbelief, which was what Pippa was experiencing, there was instead an atmosphere both hushed and expectant.

Neither Elizabeth nor Jerome appeared in the first part of the Act Two, scene one, which was devoted to a sub-plot concerning the supporting characters. It was a very funny scene, and the audience, reassured by the lightness of the comedy and the adroitness of the players, relaxed and prepared once again to enjoy themselves.

They were not disappointed.

Elizabeth Laurence was utterly brilliant. From her very first entrance in the second act she took the play by the throat and never once let go, exciting, amusing, bewitching, enthralling and finally breaking the hearts of her audience. And it was her audience, totally hers, because in her wake Jerome Didier all but disappeared from view.

It was obvious to Pippa what was happening, but not to that evening's audience, who simply more or less forgot all about him. They weren't to know that from his reappearance all Jerome was concerned about was holding the play together, and trying to control someone who in the first act had been totally aberrant. Neither were they to know that the look of utter astonishment on his face as he saw Elizabeth leaving him for dead wasn't part of the character he was playing, nor was the half-stutter he began to develop, and the sense of complete bewilderment he began to display. The audience understood this part of the play, that this was the effect that this wonderful, beautiful and divine creation called Emerald Glynn had on her lover, that she reduced him to shreds, that she turned him from a proud, self-confident, assured Adonis into a stammering, mumbling, uncertain shadow of a man, wrecked by the love of a woman who finally left him in order to save him.

The cheers were all for Elizabeth as she stepped forward, ushered from the line of actors by Jerome who even though he walked forward with her, found himself standing one step behind. Several, many and finally most of the audience got to their feet to call their *bravos!*, and as Elizabeth smiled her sweetest smile, many of the men unplucked their buttonholed flowers and threw them on-stage. Elizabeth smiled again and bent to pick up one of the many red roses. As she did so, she caught the eyes of Pippa who was seated in the middle of the front row, and just for a moment the smile became fixed, and her green eyes glinted like uncut emeralds.

Then she stood, and tossing her dark hair back, held the red rose against her pale white face and blew the audience a kiss they could all share, as the final curtain fell.

'What *happened* to you, darling?' Elizabeth said immediately to Jerome, barely before he had drawn breath. 'Where *were* you?'

She had him by the hand and was drawing him aside from the rest of the cast, who were trying not to be caught watching, but were nonetheless all watching.

'Where was *I*!' Jerome hissed in amazement. 'Where were *you* in the first blasted act!'

'I was waiting for you, my darling,' Elizabeth whispered as she led him off-stage. 'You seemed so oddly distracted tonight. As if your mind was elsewhere.'

Jerome stopped and stared at her, as if she were mad.

'I have never played the first act better,' he said, breathing in deeply and fixing her eyes with his. 'You were the one who seemed – distracted. As if your mind – was elsewhere.'

Elizabeth smiled, kissed him on the cheek, brushed his cheek with the back of one slender hand, and then squeezed one of Jerome's hands.

'It doesn't matter, my darling,' she said, turning him towards the stairs. 'We all have the odd off night.'

By now, as they started to climb the stone stairs, they were surrounded back and front by other members of the cast, seemingly chatting, but more obviously keeping one ear cocked on the conversation of the stars. Aware of this Jerome politely but firmly removed his hand from Elizabeth's and suggested that they should have a talk.

Elizabeth had an even better idea.

'I think we should have dinner,' she said.

By the time Pippa had fought her way backstage through the crowd and up to Jerome's dressing room, Jerome was stripped to the waist and washing himself briskly in the small sink in the corner. He paid no attention at all to his state of undress, but grabbed Pippa by both hands as soon as she appeared at the door, closing it behind her.

'You saw what happened,' he said, letting go of her hands to finish towelling himself dry. 'You did see what happened?'

'I saw what was going on,' Pippa said, 'but I couldn't say what was happening.'

'Trouble,' Jerome said grimly, taking a clean shirt from his dresser, a short, sharp-faced man in a sandy wig. 'She must have done it deliberately.'

'That's us girls for you, Mr Didier,' his dresser sighed. 'We're much more deadly than you boys.'

Unsure of what to do while Jerome finished dressing, and unsure of what they were going to do when he had, Pippa turned her back on him and was staring once again up at the play poster on the wall when a voice behind her asked when her last train was. Just in time, she stopped herself from asking why, and instead looked carefully at her watch.

'Twenty minutes,' she told him. 'I'd better go.'

'Sandy will get you a taxi,' Jerome said, knotting his tie quickly and efficiently. 'You'll do it with time to spare – if Sandy gets a move on.'

'Goin', massah,' Sandy replied, pouting his lips and shuffling to the door. 'I's a goin' now, boss.'

Jerome brushed his hair, and then ran his fingers through it, checking how he looked in the mirror once more.

'Look,' he said, loosening the knot on his tie just a fraction, 'I'm dreadfully sorry about dinner—'

'It's perfectly all right,' Pippa interrupted. 'It's much better this way.'

'You do understand, don't you?'

He straightened up from looking at himself in the mirror and now looked at her.

'We do have rather a crisis.'

'Of course,' Pippa replied. 'I quite understand.'

'I'll ring you tomorrow afternoon,' Jerome told her, opening the door. 'And I'll make it up to you when we get to London. I really am most *dread*fully sorry.'

'Don't be,' Pippa said, allowing him to kiss her but only on the cheek. 'It's much better this way.'

She was gone before Jerome could ask her why that was so, why and how possibly it could be better that they didn't dine together, that they didn't spend the rest of the evening together, and perhaps even the night, gone with her heels clattering down the stone steps, gone past Sandy in the alleyway as he returned from reserving her a cab in the rank, gone to the main line station and the last train back to London.

He was about to go straight into Elizabeth's dressing room, and then thinking better of it, shut his door and poured himself a stiff Scotch from the bottle Sandy had told him to keep for important visitors. Then he sat down once again in front of his mirror to stare at his image, rubbing one index finger along the line of his lips while he did so, while he thought about the best way of

117

discovering what precisely Miss Elizabeth Laurence was playing at, and what Pippa Nicholls had meant precisely by what she said.

Finally, deciding it was time, he went to collect Elizabeth to take her on to the dinner he should have been having with Pippa, but which he knew he would have to side-step halfway through Act Two when his world seemed to be collapsing around him.

Muzz answered his knock, and when he went into the Number One dressing room there was no-one else there besides her.

'Where's Miss Laurence, Muzz?' he asked, thinking perhaps she might still be changing behind her ornamental screen.

'I'm afraid she's gone home, Mr Didier,' Muzz replied, carefully folding up some of her charge's handmade lingerie. 'She went back to the hotel without even removing her make-up.'

'Back to the hotel for dinner, you mean?' Jerome asked. 'I take it you mean she's gone on ahead of me?'

'I don't think so, Mr Didier,' the dresser replied, 'I think she went straight back to bed. She's rather indisposed, I'm afraid, poor girl.'

All the way back to London, Oscar Greene tried not to keep staring at one of the most beguiling faces he had ever seen. But it was such a nice face, so unspoilt, so fresh, and so innocent that his eyes kept being drawn back to it, over the top of the manuscript he was trying to correct, to steal another secret look at the girl with the light grey eyes and the tousled brown hair, and all those tiny freckles.

Oscar loved freckles. Back home in Connecticut, one of his very first serious girlfriends had a face like this girl, different eyes, admittedly, Joni's eyes had been blue, but Joni'd had a face with more than a dusting of freckles, tiny tawn specks that ran in a ribbon across her snub nose, and on to her bright cheeks, just like this grey-eyed girl's did. Except this girl's nose wasn't snub. This brown-haired, sweet-faced girl's nose was totally perfect, small and only slightly tip-tilted, with the sort of perfect and pretty little nostrils Oscar imagined you would find on a fledgling angel.

He didn't dare talk to her. For all his official world-weary cynicism, for all his drollery, for all his so-called hard-nosed opinions, outside the world of the theatre, away from the playground, Oscar was a shy and diffident man, the very last sort of man to open a conversation with a complete stranger, particularly a tousle-headed, grey-eyed, speckled-face, long-legged creature who really was most probably, Oscar decided, like a manifestation in a Frank Capra movie, something heaven-sent to this earth in order to test his morality.

Besides, she was all wrapped up in herself, Oscar decided, judging by the way she was sitting half curled up in the window seat, pretending to watch the night-time go by when he could plainly see from the reflection of those wonderful eyes in the window glass that her look was turned inwards, that she was thinking of something which had just happened, rather than of something which might be going to happen. Once or twice when she shifted position, or made a desultory attempt to read the book on her lap, the girl glanced at Oscar, but whenever she did Oscar made sure he was back, busy scribbling away on his manuscript.

But he never once could put her out of his mind. Oscar was too much of a writer to allow such a beguiling creature to sit opposite him all the way back to London without inventing a whole history for her, and by the time the train was approaching Paddington, he had written her entire story, of the lonely childhood in India, her cruel stepmother who had stolen the love of her weak father, of her ambition to be a ballerina until those wonderfully shaped legs grew too long, and now of this fearfully unhappy love affair in which she was in the throes, with a man obviously older than she, perhaps even a man who was married, a shocking fact the grey-eyed neophyte angel only discovered after she had become involved with the son of a bitch. As she put her book away in the pocket of her coat, and retied her head scarf when the train began to pull into the terminus, Oscar had even identified her lover. He was an Oxford don, a surrogate father figure, whom the girl had just visited in order to try and say goodbye for ever, which explained her sad countenance, the wistful look in her extraordinary eyes, her entire aura.

Once the train had stopped, Oscar opened the carriage door for her and stood aside, his one moment of near contact throughout the length of the journey. The grey-eyed girl smiled shyly at him in thanks but said nothing. She just alighted from the train and disappeared into the crowd and the dark of the night.

Oscar stood and watched her go. He died to follow her, to overcome his shyness and introduce himself, and take her somewhere for a late night coffee, somewhere warm and comforting where he could sit and listen to her while she spoke of her unhappiness. But he didn't. He could have started a conversation on the train with her, as the people in his plays often did, but he hadn't. He could have offered to share a cab with her, just like other characters in his plays often did, but he didn't. He could run after her now, and explain his reticence, introduce himself to her and tell her the sort of things his make-believe people sometimes told each other, that of all the people in the whole wide world, they surely were meant for each other, that he couldn't let her go without talking to her, without telling her she was the most beguiling creature he had ever seen, but he couldn't. Instead he watched her go, and let her go, and then wandered off to find a cab himself once the crowd had swallowed her up, unmindful of the fact that into that warm summer night had disappeared the girl who was later to become his greatest and best loved heroine, the girl upon whom he was to base his world famous creation, *Tatty Gray*.

S I X

It was the sight of his wife in another man's arms which brought the reality home to Sebastian. There she was, there they both were, larger than life and for all the world to see. And all the world was seeing. Sebastian was not alone as he stood looking at Elizabeth kissing her lover, indeed a small crowd had gathered round to stare along with him at the picture of this beautiful couple embracing. But it was Sebastian who was staring the hardest.

He hadn't been allowed to see the play on tour. Elizabeth had forbidden him to visit, her reason being that she wanted the play and her performance to be at their best by the time he sat among the audience, and Sebastian had concurred. In fact he had been so busy with his work, a timetable which included two short trips to France, that he had more or less put the play out of his mind, attributing no more importance to it than Elizabeth's previous foray into the world of drama, what she described as her little 'cameo' in *Made In Heaven*.

He gave it no more importance, that is, until he saw the photographs, and once he did, once he set eyes on the array of pictures of his beautiful and beloved wife in various intimate poses with someone who was undoubtedly one of the best looking young men he had ever seen, Sebastian revised his opinion with regard to what precisely his wife was doing.

Fun was how she had described it, he remembered, still unable to tear himself away from the photographs, it was just going to be fun. But fun for whom? Elizabeth certainly looked as if she was enjoying herself, but Sebastian was not at all sure as to how he himself felt. He felt a fool, that at least he knew, in fact he had never felt quite so foolish as he did this moment, standing

121

among a crowd of men who were strangers to him, and yet who were all ogling his wife, some of them daring even to make personal remarks.

'She's got a fair old body,' said a slack-jawed young man who was standing close to a single photograph of Elizabeth. 'I wouldn't kick 'er out of bed.'

'Yeah?' his mate scoffed. 'A lardy tart like that? You'd be lucky if she let you bring the bleedin' coal in.'

They laughed and wandered off, leaving Sebastian clutching the handle of his umbrella as tightly as he could, lest he let fly with both fists at the impertinent youths. But then a voice inside him reminded him that if he was going to continue to allow Elizabeth her *fun*, then this was the sort of experience he would have to learn how to endure. It was the sort of experience he would have to learn to expect not just from the rank and file of strangers, but from friends and intimates, who having seen Elizabeth in her latest bit of *fun*, would feel bound to discuss her amongst themselves or worse, even with Sebastian, as if she were a commodity, a person in the public domain.

I saw Lizzie in Something or Other, he could imagine them saying. *And I must say, old man, I didn't half fancy her!*

Appalled with the notion, and deciding that this latest adventure of Elizabeth's was to be her very last, Sebastian turned away from the publicity display outside the theatre where *All That Glitters* was due to open that evening, and looked for a taxi. As he did so, a couple in their late middle age came out of the theatre, and paused where Sebastian had just been standing, in front of the photographs of Elizabeth and Jerome.

'I am so looking forward to this,' the woman told the man. 'I simply cannot tell you, James. Prue saw it in Brighton and she said it is quite, quite enchanting.'

'I must say,' her husband replied, leaning forwards the better to see the single portrait of Elizabeth. 'This gel is dashed pretty.'

'She's beautiful, James,' the woman sighed. 'Prue says she is the *most* beautiful gel she has ever seen.'

'Indeed?' Her husband took a closer look at the subject of their conversation, and then slipped his arm through his wife's. 'Tell you what,' he said, 'she reminds me of you.'

'Oh, what nonsense!' his wife laughed as they began to walk away, but Sebastian saw the look on her face, and saw how charmed and flattered she had been.

In answer to his raised arm, a cab pulled up at the kerb. But just before he climbed into it, Sebastian turned and took one last look at the array of publicity photographs, before reading the names in lights as yet unlit in the sign above the theatre entrance:

ELIZABETH LAURENCE and JEROME DIDIER

IN

ALL THAT GLITTERS

BY

OSCAR GREENE

Then he got into the taxi and ordered the driver to take him to Bond Street.

'Anywhere in particular, guv?' the cabbie enquired.

'Yes,' Sebastian replied. 'Asprey's.'

He had intended to go straight to his club for lunch once he had picked up his ticket for the first night, particularly after he had seen the photographs on display for all to see outside the theatre. The effect on him of seeing Elizabeth like that had been devastating, and he had been so taken by surprise at first he hurried away from the theatre without even calling at the box office.

But then a compulsive curiosity had drawn him back, and he had stood as described and stared at the blown-up portraits of his wife, in the company of passers-by, trying to come to terms with the effect such an exposure was having on him. As he sat back in the cab and remembered, he blamed himself, because he had never given the matter sufficient consideration, he had never thought the matter through. Elizabeth's *fun* had seemed to be just that, and as long as she had been happy having her fun, then Sebastian had been happy. What he had not realized, was that while Elizabeth was having her fun, she would belong to other people, people who didn't know her, but who felt they knew her, well enough to decide whether or not they would like to make love to her.

Elizabeth *Laurence*, the name on the unlit marquee had said. She wasn't even his anymore, at least not in public. She was unmarried, a single woman, a woman to be scrutinized, lusted after, remarked at, quantified and qualified. After tonight, she would no longer be his, his private property, his angel to be worshipped and carefully, most carefully seduced, his love and nobody else's. After tonight, if the play was a West End hit, which Cecil Manners had assured him it was going to be, then Elizabeth would be public property,

123

a property so public that people would wonder what she wore in bed and what she ate for breakfast.

And yet.

Yet Sebastian realized he was no longer horrified by the reality of the situation, appalled by the sudden and unexpected publicity, but in fact that he rather revelled in it. Even more than that, he felt proud.

It wasn't just the pleasure the middle-aged woman had received being favourably compared by her husband to the young and semi-divine Elizabeth which had changed Sebastian's thinking on the matter, although that had both touched and charmed him, it was the realization that although others, masses of others, thousands, maybe even hundreds of thousands of other men might want his wife, might lust after her, might harbour dark and passionate thoughts about her, none of them, not one of them would possess her. Because Elizabeth Laurence, the divine, ethereal, and exquisite Miss Laurence belonged only to him, because the divine, ethereal and exquisite Miss Laurence loved only him.

She told him so each day and every night they were together. She would whisper to him how much she loved him, how kind and understanding he was, how sweet and gentle, and how she would always and forever love him, and if she ever stopped loving him, even for a moment, he must take a dagger and plunge it through her unfaithful heart. She told him how faint she felt with love for him, how helpless she felt away from him, how warm and wonderfully secure she felt when she was once again with him.

' "Age cannot wither you," ' she would breathe softly in his ear, ' "nor custom stale your infinite variety." '

The fact that they made love only infrequently didn't worry Sebastian, firstly because he was uncertain of quite how frequently other young couples made love, since it was a subject which was never discussed, and secondly, aware of what Elizabeth referred to as her rather delicate nature, he was deliberately undemanding as far as his rights were concerned, happy enough just to be with his beloved wife, content just to have her with him, and to be able to talk to her and to admire her perfect beauty.

So although he had felt pangs of the very worst sort of jealousy and outrage when he saw Elizabeth so prominently displayed outside the Globe Theatre, he had now recovered himself entirely, due solely to the knowledge that Elizabeth was his and his alone. Everyone else might admire her, some might even love her, but he was the one she loved, and she was the one who was loved by him. Which was why instead of going straight to his club for a stiff gin and lunch with one of the other junior partners in the firm, he was going to Asprey's, to buy Elizabeth a first night present which she would treasure for the rest of her life.

'It has to be gold,' he told the assistant, but without explaining why. 'And I think a brooch, possibly. Oh yes – and if possible . . . I wonder – do you have a cat? A little gold cat would be absolutely the thing.'

Asprey's had the very thing, a small gold cat on a clasp, a cat couchant, a cat with ruby red eyes, a most exquisite artifice which Sebastian could ill afford, but which he was utterly determined to buy. It sat in his pocket all through lunch, gift-wrapped in a dark blue box, and it sat on his chest of drawers early that evening as he changed into his dinner jacket, and it sat in his inside pocket as he journeyed from Chelsea to Shaftesbury Avenue.

He had left plenty of time, as he wanted to see Elizabeth before curtain up. Naturally she had left the house well ahead of him, in fact according to their maid Maggie she had gone to the theatre just after lunch, so that she would have sufficient time to prepare herself. Elizabeth hated to be hurried, and she hated people hurrying her or hurrying around her, particularly when she was nervous.

Therefore Sebastian was more than a little concerned when he arrived backstage to find near chaos reigning. Curtain up was less than forty-five minutes away, and yet no-one seemed to know what they were doing or where they were headed. Delivery boys were rushing in off the street, with arms full of flowers, chocolates, or boxed bottles of wine, messenger boys and telegram boys were arriving one after the other, with greetings and good luck messages which they handed in sheafs to the stage door-keeper over the top of his half-door, actors, half dressed and half made-up jostled past each other on the stone stairways, calling for wardrobe, stage management, the director, their dresser, each other, or just vaguely and helplessly for someone, anyone to do something – anything – before it was too late.

Sebastian was carried along in the tide of bodies, and trapped against a wall at the end of the ground-floor corridor while a party of stage hands heaved an enormous hamper past him and on down a flight of stairs that was signposted private and to the stage only. There were a few other civilians (as Elizabeth had learned to call non-members of the theatrical fraternity), in evening dress like Sebastian, but they were there, so it seemed to Sebastian, with a purpose, since every so often some would grab and greet actors *en passant*, while others would shout purposeful orders to members of an army which was constantly on the move up and down the flights of stairs. The ones who were not giving orders, but who were familiar with each other Sebastian assumed to be agents, as they kept kissing actresses and shouting endearments (it was far too noisy for any intimate conversation) or embracing actors while being careful not to get make-up on their dinner jackets. An exhausted looking man in a half-buttoned and tie-less evening shirt kept appearing from and disappearing into various dressing rooms, with a sheaf of pencilled notes in his hand, while down the stone stairs from rooms high above clattered more of the militia, carrying carefully ironed articles of clothing, men's suits or women's dresses which they delivered to hands outstretched from half-open dressing-room doors.

'Half an hour please!' a boy began to call from somewhere downstairs, far below Sebastian. 'Act One beginners half an hour, please!'

This warning brought another sudden flurry of activity and hysteria, flattening Sebastian once again against the wall as he tried to fight his way back to the stage door-keeper's booth, only to discover upon finally reaching it that it was deserted. Looking around he saw a pretty girl in an oriental dressing gown taking a telephone call in a booth nearby, and excusing himself for interrupting her, asked where he might find Elizabeth Laurence. The girl indicated one flight up without breaking off her own rather fraught conversation, leaving Sebastian to fight his way up the indicated flight of stairs and along the dark, shiny-green painted corridor. As he looked for the right room, from another door along a man in only his trousers and singlet appeared, unmade-up and with soaking wet hair. Yet even in that state he was astonishingly handsome, and immediately recognizable as Jerome Didier, and also, amidst all the panic and confusion, able immediately to command attention, by the sheer force of his personality.

'Can somebody please tell me?' the actor demanded, hands on hip, calling those around him to his immediate attention. 'Where on God's earth our blasted director has got to now?'

A girl in a long shapeless cardigan, and holding a handkerchief to her nose, was trying to wriggle her way past Jerome, but he caught her by the arm and dragged her back to him, half playfully, half deadly earnest.

'Kathy *dear*,' he said. Where – is R-R-R-R-Richard?'

The girl muttered something back at Jerome, pointing to her watch and struggling to get free, while Sebastian watched transfixed, mesmerized by the almost palpable force of the young actor's presence.

'Well if *you* – don't know where he is, Kathy!' Jerome cried, his voice echoing off the stone walls, 'then find me somebody who *does*!'

And with that he released the girl and swept back into his dressing room, slamming shut the door. Sebastian, deeply impressed by the moment which, he thought, could have come straight from some classical tragedy, was about to ask the baggy cardigan girl who was trying to squeeze her way past him which was his wife's dressing room, when he saw her name in a card holder, under a big red star, under the number One. *Miss Elizabeth Laurence.*

A small, pretty, middle-aged woman with oddly piercing blue eyes came to the door in answer to his knock. She had a safety pin in her mouth, and a pair of stockings draped over one arm.

'Yes?' she said, without opening the door more than a foot.

'Mr Ferrers,' Sebastian said. 'Miss Laurence's husband.'

Even with the door only that far open Sebastian could see Elizabeth, or rather more correctly he could see her reflection. As soon as she heard his voice, she looked up, and he could see her eyes clearly in the glass, only they didn't look delighted, or even remotely pleased. They looked in a flash full of angry surprise.

The small woman took the safety pin out of her mouth, asked Sebastian to wait, and then closed the door. Sebastian waited, feeling most uncomfortable and ridiculous having to do so, since he could think of no good reason why a husband should be kept out of his wife's dressing room by a total stranger.

After a minute or so, the door was reopened and Sebastian was admitted. Elizabeth, who Sebastian now noted was wearing a long, pale-pink silk dressing gown which he couldn't remember seeing before, turned to him and smiled, before floating across to him, with both slender arms outstretched.

'Darling one,' she said, taking his hands, before moving her head quickly away. 'No!' she said. 'No kisses, darling one. I'm made-up.'

Sebastian felt himself colour, embarrassed by his gaffe, and by the presence of what seemed to be Elizabeth's personal theatrical maid, who was now sitting on the sofa sewing, paying him no attention whatsoever.

'Dearest,' Sebastian began, and then to make his point, inclined his head with a frown in the small woman's direction.

'Oh, don't worry about *Muzz*!' Elizabeth laughed, for some reason finding his concern amusing. 'The dear thing's seen and heard just about everything, haven't you, darling?'

'In one way or the other, yes, I suppose I have, dear,' her dresser replied, biting the thread with which she was sewing in half. 'In one way or another.'

Elizabeth smiled again at Sebastian, and then returned to her dressing table where she began the final stage of her preparation.

'Darling one,' she said, via the mirror, 'I don't want to be horrid, but they have called the Half.'

'I won't keep you, dearest,' Sebastian said, searching his pocket for the small gift-wrapped box. 'I just wanted to give you this.'

He handed the box to her, which Elizabeth took over one shoulder.

'A present! Oh, darling one!' she exclaimed. 'How – *sweet*!'

'How will you know?' Sebastian smiled at her reflection, 'until you open it? Whether it's – well, something you like, or don't – as the case may be.'

He was dying for her to open it, but instead Elizabeth put the package down beside her on the dressing table, and patted it once with one hand.

'I shall leave it there,' she said. 'Until after. I couldn't bear to open it now, my darling. In case it's something beautiful, and I might cry.'

'Which would never do, Miss Laurence,' Muzz said, through a new mouthful of pins, and giving Sebastian a look. 'Not when you've just made-up. Not just before you go on.'

For some reason Sebastian felt that he had committed another frightful gaffe which in actual fact unwittingly he had, one of which he was totally ignorant, one which Elizabeth put him right about as she rose and eased him gently towards the door.

'Sweetheart,' she said as she half closed the door behind her. 'It was *dear* of you to come round, really. And to bring a present. But you obviously didn't know. How could you? It's *frightfully* bad form. To come round before curtain up.'

She mouthed a kiss at him, pursing her lipsticked mouth, crinkled her eyes a little at him, but not too much in case it spoilt her make-up, and then blew a farewell kiss at him, making sure her hand didn't quite touch her lips.

'I love you,' she whispered.

'And I love you,' he said. 'Good luck.'

'No!' she almost screamed in return, startling Sebastian so much that he whipped back round in case something dreadful had happened.

'What is it?' Sebastian asked, seeing that he had upset her just when nothing should upset her. 'What is it, dearest? Now what have I done?'

128

'Darling one,' she said, recovering her poise. 'You don't come round before the show, darling, but that's as maybe. But what you never, *ever* do is wish an actor good luck.'

She smiled at him, briefly, for a moment, but there was none of the usual warmth in her smile, Sebastian noted, it was just a token smile, one to placate him before she disappeared back into her dressing room, leaving Sebastian no alternative but to make his way round to the front of the theatre to join the other civilians. And as he did so, even before he had reached and taken his seat in the auditorium to watch the curtain rise on what was to prove to be an unforgettable night in the history of the theatre, he knew that she had gone. Sebastian Ferrers knew that he had lost his Elizabeth for good.

What made it even more unbearable for Sebastian was that once the curtain had finally fallen to tumultuous cheering, to an acclaim which established beyond all reasonable doubt that Elizabeth Laurence had been launched into stardom, and that once all the nervous tension from which Sebastian concluded she had so obviously been suffering before she went on-stage had gone, Elizabeth was her old adoring and adorable self. Not once did she leave Sebastian's side at dinner afterwards, nor during the first heady couple of hours at the party Jimmy Locke threw for the company at his vast apartment overlooking Grosvenor Square. Elizabeth stayed by her husband, despite the fact that the rich, the powerful and the famous were all busy lobbying both Jimmy Locke and Cecil Manners to bring her over and introduce her to them at once, if not sooner. Instead Elizabeth insisted, politely but firmly, that whoever wished to meet her must meet her husband too, and at their table, so that Sebastian was never left stranded in the company of people who either didn't know who he was, or if they did, most certainly didn't care, nor was he made to follow Elizabeth everywhere like some embarrassing appendage. At dinner at Le Caprice, she sat with one leg secretly entwined around one of Sebastian's under cover of the tablecloth, or with her hand carefully out of sight on his knee, while at the party she made sure they were always either hand in hand or arm in arm.

And yet Sebastian knew he had lost her.

Whatever she did, whatever she said, she no longer belonged to him. She had ceased being his from the moment she had walked on-stage, and the audience had collectively claimed her. And although Sebastian had tried to anticipate this moment, knowing that when everyone saw his beautiful wife in the flesh they could not help but be captivated, nothing he could have mentally rehearsed could have prepared him for the reality of the actual moment the door opened and the bare footed Elizabeth, dressed in a simple, white, summer dress, and with her dark hair loose, stepped on-stage and the audience audibly gasped. The shock of the moment made Sebastian's head spin. It made his senses reel, and he never recovered them for the duration of the play, which he watched semi-dazed, half-conscious, as if, as he was later to recall, he had just been in the boxing ring with Rocky Marciano, rather than sitting in the stalls of a West End theatre.

He could make no sense of anything he saw for the next two and a half hours. He tried to forget that Elizabeth was his wife and did his best to see her as everyone else was seeing her, as someone called Emerald Glynn, but he couldn't. All he could see was Elizabeth, his Elizabeth, at home in Chelsea, sitting in front of the fire with her feet tucked up under her and Medusa on her lap, or in their bedroom, wrapped up in her thick, white bath robe with a towel round her freshly washed hair as she stood sorting out a dress to wear for their dinner à *deux*, or with him in the spring sunshine, picking bunches of daffodils from their country garden, walking back with armfuls of the bright yellow and white flowers which she loved to arrange in every room of the cottage, and then lying in silence in the evening, on the old sofa in front of the fire, with her black hair fallen across her beautiful pale-skinned face.

However hard he tried, he just couldn't see her as everyone else was now seeing her, as this other person, laughing and flirting with this other man, allowing this other man to embrace her, to put his arms round her, and stroke her hair and kiss her, exactly the way she might allow Sebastian to hold her and to kiss her, and stroke her dark shiny hair, while all the time being watched by hundreds of pairs of eyes, the eyes of other people who, as they watched their new heroine, became seemingly one person, someone who was falling head over heels and hopelessly in love with this ravishing, raven-haired, green-eyed girl who was his, who was Sebastian's, who was his wife. Sebastian could hardly bear it. As he felt the audience taking Elizabeth to its corporate heart, it was all he could do not to get to his feet and claim her publicly as his and his alone.

Being a gentleman, Sebastian naturally let none of this show in the aftermath of that famous first night. In fact he vowed never to make any mention of it, or ever refer to how he had felt as he watched her début. Instead he blamed himself entirely for his misfortune. He had been too lackadaisical altogether about the business of Elizabeth acting. He had no doubt that she had been talked into it, by being made to look upon it as only a 'bit of fun', because that would have been typical of Elizabeth. She was so lighthearted and blithe. It would never have occurred to her that her *fun* could turn into something quite the opposite, something so serious that it could, if not monitored, threaten the very stability of their marriage, which was why Sebastian truly believed he only had himself to blame. He should have adopted an altogether more responsible and mature attitude at the very beginning, he should have had more foresight, he should have used his imagination. He should have discredited the idea when it was initiated, and forbidden his beautiful and adored wife from having anything to do with the notorious and shallow world of the theatre.

'I know what you're thinking, dear boy,' Cecil Manners said, coming to sit beside him on the one occasion Sebastian found himself briefly detached from Elizabeth at Jimmy Locke's party. 'You're wondering what the devil you can have been thinking allowing such a wonderful creature as your beautiful wife to get mixed up in this caper.'

Cecil gestured with his cigarette holder at the crowd in the smoke filled room before them.

'You're thinking you must have been mad,' he went on. 'You think your wife belongs at home, that she should be at home having babies and being a wife, and that now, now life won't ever be the same. Well, I'm sorry to tell you, dear boy, first that I'm a bit drunk, and I'm sorry. But then how many times, if indeed ever, do you have a first night like this? Do you see acting like that. Like we have both, like we have *all* just seen?'

Sebastian shook his head and said that he didn't know, that he had no idea. But what he really hadn't had an idea about was exactly how good an actress Elizabeth was. That was something else to which he had never properly addressed himself. He had simply assumed she had a fancy to give acting a 'go', and that she would either be terrible, or at the most – passable. It had never for one moment occurred to him that she might have even a modicum of talent.

'I should imagine you never imagined,' Cecil continued, having poured them both some more champagne, and now reading his thoughts, 'not in your wildest imaginings could you have done, could you have imagined for *one moment*, how incredibly gifted Elizabeth was. Did you? You couldn't possibly, dear boy. And who could blame you? Apparently all you ever saw her do, all she ever did in fact, in the way of acting, was playing charades at Christmas! And now – now . . . '

Cecil broke off and shook his head in wonder.

'Yes?' Sebastian asked him. 'Now what? Please tell me, because believe me, I'm most interested.'

'I was going to tell you something else,' Cecil said, reordering his thoughts. 'First I must tell you what it was I was going to tell you, and then I'll answer your other question. What the devil was it I was going to tell you?'

'You were talking about life,' Sebastian reminded him. 'You were saying one's life might never be the same again.'

'Precisely,' Cecil nodded. 'Because that's what – and I could see it all over your face, dear boy. Because that's what you've been *thinking*. Ever since the entire audience got to its feet and cheered, and cheered, and cheered – you've been having very serious second thoughts, and wondering whether or not this was the best move. And whether or not your life is ever going to be what it was. Well, let me tell you, dear boy, it's not. And that's that. It is never going to be the same again, dear boy, because your wonderful wife – your beautiful, talented, brilliant wife – is going to be one of the biggest stars this country has ever seen. And your life – both your lives – your lives will never, ever be the same, boring, mundane old lives they were before! Because Elizabeth is going to be world famous, and you are going to be rich. Richer than you ever dreamed you could be.'

'Cecil!'

Cecil looked up, smiling, and when he saw who it was his smile grew ever more beatific.

'Elizabeth,' he sighed, taking both her hands and kissing them. 'My darling.'

'Cecil.' This time it was a reprimand, not a tease. 'Cecil,' Elizabeth said, withdrawing her hands, 'I do believe you are tipsy.'

'Yes, darling Elizabeth,' Cecil admitted, leaning back on the sofa, 'I am extremely tipsy. And you – are a star.'

Elizabeth eyed her agent, who now showed signs of falling asleep.

'Come along,' she whispered to Sebastian, bending down and kissing his cheek. 'Time for us to go home.'

'I thought you wanted to wait for the newspapers?' Sebastian said as he took her proffered hand.

'Fiddle the newspapers,' Elizabeth laughed. 'You have to work in the morning.'

It took the best part of half an hour for Elizabeth to make her exit, a delay which Sebastian took with his usual good humour and grace, standing aside while the final accolades were heaped upon his wife, and practically everyone in the room kissed her and hugged her. And then just as a maid had presented them both with their coats and they were finally about to leave, Elizabeth was spirited away from him by his host Jimmy Locke and the tall, mesmeric Polish exile to whom Sebastian had been introduced some time earlier, to a small room where they remained closeted for five or so minutes.

'I'm so sorry, my darling,' Elizabeth said to him as the lift dropped them to the ground floor. 'Jimmy and Dmitri just wanted one last, quick word.'

She slipped an arm through his as they crossed the marble-floored hall, and out into the night, her other arm holding the top of her fur coat closed, as if she felt a sudden chill. But Sebastian had already seen what she was trying to hide. He had seen her reflection in the hall mirror as he waited for her, as she re-emerged from the ante-room with their host and the tall Polish emigré. He had seen the necklace before Elizabeth had pulled her coat tightly together, and come back to his side so that they may take their leave.

'Forgive me, won't you, darling?' she pleaded as they waited for a taxi. 'Please.'

'There's nothing to forgive you for,' Sebastian said, telling her the first lie he had ever told her. 'Nothing at all.'

'Of course there is,' Elizabeth sighed, tightening her hold on his arm, 'I've kept you impossibly late, and you have to go to work in a few hours, you poor dear.'

'So I do,' Sebastian smiled, glancing at his watch. 'Back to Civvy Street.'

He let Elizabeth do all the talking on the way home in the taxi. She sat close to him, nestled up to him, one arm still though his, the other hand at the throat of her coat, as she recalled all the excitement of the evening, while Sebastian stared out of the side window and into the eyes of the night.

She was in the house and halfway up the stairs before he had got the key out of the front door. As he went to hang up his coat, she called down from the landing and asked him to bring her up a glass of warm milk and honey, and then disappeared into their bedroom. Sebastian went into the kitchen and did as he was asked, knowing exactly why he had been asked. He waited for the milk to boil, with Medusa wrapping herself happily round and round his legs, while he fingered the small gift-wrapped box which was in his jacket pocket, the box he had noticed lying still unopened on Elizabeth's dressing table as everyone prepared to leave for the celebratory dinner.

Elizabeth was already on her way, standing outside in the corridor talking and laughing with the rest of the excited cast, so Sebastian had been able to retrieve the box unnoticed. And now he waited as he heard Elizabeth run her bath, and for the bathroom door to be closed, before he slipped silently upstairs and into their bedroom, where first he placed the milk and honey on Elizabeth's bedside table and then put the gift-wrapped box where she couldn't help but find it, on her dressing table in her evening bag which lay open by her silver-backed hair-brushes. He knew she could not help but see it, because the last thing that Elizabeth did every night without fail was sit and brush out her wonderful hair.

'I put a saucer over your drink,' he said as she emerged from the bathroom. 'In case it got too cold.'

'You are an angel,' Elizabeth said with a smile, which didn't altogether hide the look on her face which suggested she had completely forgotten her request. 'I really don't deserve you.'

'On the contrary, dearest,' Sebastian said, turning a page in his book. 'It's I who don't deserve you.'

For a moment as she stood there by the end of his bed, Sebastian thought for the first time in their married life Elizabeth was going to get into bed without brushing her hair. And while he pondered that, he also wondered why she had chosen to wear the necklace when it had been given to her, and not just expressed her wonder and gratitude at such a gift before returning it to the case in which it was undoubtedly presented to her. Perhaps it was her vanity, he thought. Any beautiful woman would have wanted to see what such a piece of jewellery would look like round her neck, and against her skin, particularly against skin as fair as Elizabeth's, or perhaps it was merely her good manners. Perhaps the donors had urged her to wear their token, and rather than upset them, she had obliged, meaning to take it off the moment she could do so decently, and without causing anyone, himself included, offence. That was the most likely option, Sebastian thought as he closed his book over his bookmark. Elizabeth was the last person in the world who would upset anyone deliberately.

And yet she had forgotten his gift, his unopened present of the little gold cat. She had not only forgotten it, but she hadn't even remembered to bring it with her from the theatre, so that she might open it later. She must have forgotten it in the heat of the moment, Sebastian decided looking up at her, and seeing once again the face of an angel. How could he, an ordinary man, a *civilian* indeed, how could he even begin to imagine what a night as she had just experienced could possibly mean? Under the circumstances he had just witnessed, anyone could be forgiven for behaving irrationally, or abnormally, let alone forgetfully.

Which was why he had allowed her an escape route, because knowing his beloved Elizabeth the way he did, he knew there had to be a reason for her distraction. Knowing Elizabeth she would have been keeping his present until last perhaps, or until she was free to open it with him. And then in all that frenzy of excitement which followed the apparent triumph of the play, it had quite simply slipped her mind. Which is why he had placed it where he had, in her half-open little silver evening bag, along with her cosmetics and good luck charms, as if she herself had packed it away in order especially to open it in private with Sebastian.

If Elizabeth was astonished to see it in her bag, she showed no signs of such an emotion at all. She simply put down her hair brushes and looked for a long time at Sebastian in her dressing mirror.

'It's true,' she said finally, in a whisper, 'I really don't deserve you, you know.'

'Why?'

Sebastian laughed, doing his best to sound and look innocent, and failing miserably, because he had no talent for deception of any kind.

Elizabeth did.

'You thought I'd forgotten it, darling one,' she said, still looking at him in her mirror. 'You thought I'd left it behind, didn't you?'

'Of course I didn't!' Sebastian protested. 'It's just—'

Elizabeth put a finger to her lips to hush him, before coming to sit on the side of his bed.

'I had forgotten it,' she said, 'but only temporarily. In all the excitement, with everyone coming and going. And then when I realized, just as we were finally leaving, I sent Muzz back for it, and it was *gone*! Can you *imagine*? Poor Muzz. She turned the place upside down, and was in such terrible tears when she rang me at The Caprice. We all thought it had been stolen. And all because I was saving it. Because I wanted to open whatever it is, I wanted to open it with you, my darling one.'

She leaned over and kissed him, softly and sweetly on the lips. Sebastian suddenly felt dreadful, as he realized what he'd done, and even worse, why he had done it. He had jumped to a conclusion. He had assumed Elizabeth had forgotten all about his gift, and because of his now obviously quite unwarranted presumption, even though he had later given Elizabeth the benefit of the doubt, he had caused two innocent people untold and perfectly unnecessary misery. He could well have even taken the edge of Elizabeth's triumph.

'Oh!' she exclaimed. 'Oh, Sebastian darling – it is *beautiful*! *So* beautiful! Oh, my darling – how can I thank you!'

She thanked him by getting into his bed and by lying in his arms, holding in one small and slender hand the little gold cat with the emerald eyes, while lying across his chest, moving every now and then to kiss him again with her thanks, softly and sweetly on his mouth and his cheeks, but most usually on his cheeks.

He once made a move in response, just an arm round her waist, and a kiss to return one of hers. But her response was just a regretful sigh, and putting her free hand to his cheek whispered to him to wait until morning, because she was so completely and utterly exhausted. Sebastian understood and apologized for being so insensitive, to which she told him there was absolutely no need for any apologies, kissing him once more and then slipping back to her own bed, where before she fell asleep she reminded herself not to forget to tell Muzz exactly what had happened so that she would back up her story.

Jerome by now was very drunk, and sitting on the floor in a corner of Jimmy Locke's apartment, which was where Cecil, who was beginning to sober up, found him.

'Dear boy,' he said, 'I think you ought to go home.'

'Home, *dear boy*,' Jerome said, fixing him with a malevolent stare, 'is where the heart is. And I can't very well go there now, can I?'

Cecil put out a hand to help Jerome to his feet, but Jerome pushed it rudely aside.

'Can I?' he repeated, staring at Cecil even harder. 'I can't very well go there, can I?'

Cecil was about to make one last effort to get his client up and out of the party which was finally dying in the first light of dawn, when Jimmy Locke, still as immaculate as he had been when he welcomed his first guest, brought over yet another early edition.

'Another rave,' he said to Cecil, handing him the folded-open newspaper. '"The Best Romantic Comedy Locke's have given the West End since *Spring In The Park*." And wait till you hear what he calls Elizabeth.'

As Locke searched for the relevant quote, Cecil tried to steer him away from the corner where Jerome lay slouched, but to no avail. Jerome had heard every word and was slowly pulling himself to his feet with the help of the back of a sofa.

'And what now, Jimmy?' he asked. 'And what precisely is Miss Laurence to be called now that the last half dozen or so hacks have not called her? Yes?'

If Jimmy Locke was surprised by Jerome's appearance from behind the furniture, he certainly didn't show it. Instead he tapped the paragraph for which he had been searching and then handed it to Cecil.

'They're very nice about you too, old love,' he said, smiling at Jerome, while privately hoping the young actor was not just about to throw up all over his newly upholstered chesterfield. ' "Wonderful good looks" – isn't that what it says, Cecil?' he looked over Cecil's shoulder. ' "Wonderful good looks" . . . I was right, yes, and there you are – "whose wonderful good looks complemented a thoroughly well-rounded performance." '

Jerome's eyes, which only a moment ago had been dim and unfocused, suddenly became concentrated and glittered dangerously. Snatching the paper from his agent, he spread it along the back of the sofa and studied the latest notice.

' "A divine beauty," ' he read, ' "and a talent to match. I cannot recall seeing such a breathtaking and sublime début on the West End stage in all my many years as this paper's dramatic critic. And I prophesy that Miss Elizabeth Laurence will be no passing fancy but a true celestial being. She is no meteor, no shooting star, no sudden flash of brilliance in our theatrical skies, a light to take our eyes and distract us briefly before disappearing for ever into the void. No, the exquisite Miss Laurence is a fixed mark, that looks on tempests and is never shaken. Miss Laurence is a star." '

Jerome looked up, about to say something, about to pronounce on the inequality of all life, but when he did the faces in front of him swam, the room swam, the floor beneath his feet suddenly sloped sharply downhill, and he only just made it to the bathroom before being sick.

A long time afterwards, when everyone had stopped knocking on the door to ask if he was all right, as he sat on a chair with a soaking wet towel to his face, Jerome once again saw the empty seat. He knew he should have known better than to look, but since the seat in question was in the middle of the front row, it was practically impossible not to notice it at some point. Unfortunately, Jerome had noticed it at once.

The moment he walked on-stage he saw it. He couldn't fail to see it, it was as obvious as a missing front tooth. At first he thought it was Cecil who was missing, but no, he saw at a second, swiftly taken glance that Cecil was safely in place, and that so was everyone else in row A. There was just this one empty seat, right next to Cecil.

His next thought was that she was late. She had a long journey, trains were trains, and she could easily have got held up. There was no other explanation possible, because if anything else had prevented her from getting to his first night, Pippa would have rung and told him. Or even if she hadn't been able to reach him personally, she would have left a message for him. So that was it, Pippa was late.

It took him no more than a second to work this out once he had walked out on-stage and seen the empty seat in the stalls, and there was no risk in either the taking of his sideways glance, or the reaching of his conclusions. He had time to spare before his first line, since the action of the play demanded that he wait, somewhat impatiently, to be introduced to the other occupants of the drawing room. So because he was meant to be playing impatient, it was perfectly in character for him to glance at his surroundings, which in this instance he allowed to include the first row of the stalls, and which that night was his undoing.

For by doing so, and remarking on what he saw, Jerome allowed reality to intrude, and to enter his subconscious, so much so that although he felt completely at ease with his performance, and believed he was playing with his usual confidence and assurance, in fact he was not. He thought he was running on all six beautifully balanced cylinders, when at best he was only firing on five, because all the time at the back of his mind he was thinking about Pippa and where she was, rather than concentrating totally on being the character he was meant to be being. Jerome Didier had come on-stage with him, when there should have only been the fictional Charles Danby.

Jerome held the cold and soaking towel tighter against his face, allowing the water to drip from it down his neck and inside his evening shirt. Someone knocked once more on the bathroom door to ask after him, and from within the wet towel he called for them to go away, and continued to do so, long after whoever it was had gone. Then he turned his slowly clearing mind once more to the events of the evening, and tried to recall when precisely he knew he had gone.

His laughs were all in place, he remembered getting his laughs, particularly in the second scene, although they weren't as strong as he had expected. But then he had been warned, both Cecil and

Richard Derwent had warned him not to expect the best from a first night audience in the West End. It was not at all like opening a good date out on tour, where people were disposed to liking you. This was the amphitheatre, and they were the Christians being thrown to the lions. They had to fight to win their survival. It was far from being a cakewalk.

But the audience had been on their side almost immediately. He remembered that distinctly. He remembered Elizabeth coming off after the first scene and squeezing his hand in the wings.

'We've got them!' she whispered. 'We've *got* them, darling!'

And they had. They had got them. Derwent had also tipped him the wink as they hurried off to make their change. He had grabbed Jerome's arm as he made for the quick-change room, and whispered how marvellous he was being. So where had he gone wrong?

He had believed them, that's where he had gone wrong. In the solitude of Jimmy Lock's marble bathroom in Grosvenor Square, as a damp dawn broke over London, Jerome began to come to terms with the size of his folly. He had believed what they were saying, that he was carrying all before him, when in fact if he had listened to the voice inside his own head, he would have realized he was behind, he was lagging behind, and even worse – he wasn't carrying all before him, he was being *carried*.

He was being carried by the strength of the play, and more than anything by the sheer brilliance of Elizabeth. Elizabeth Laurence had found the big wave, and when she first appeared, she was already on the crest of it. For an absurd moment, when she materialized in the doorway, barefooted and in her simple white dress, Jerome had thought she was going to get a round. Even though to this audience she was totally unknown and untried, the impact of her entrance and her first appearance was such that Jerome could sense that the audience wanted to applaud her, before she had spoken even one word to them.

Elizabeth sensed it as well. Jerome saw it, he saw the sudden light that came into her eyes, and he heard it in the half-stifled gasp she gave as she spoke her first line, a line she took just that little bit earlier than she normally took it, as if modestly to stifle any feeling there might still be to applaud her mere appearance. At this moment, Jerome remembered suddenly, and vividly, at this moment he picked up, got his balance, and they were a team, he and Elizabeth, they were equals.

Dammit! he could still feel the sensation! He could still feel that thrust! That surge of previously untapped power! He threw the

139

soaking towel down into the basin and let himself out of the bathroom. There was no-one around, everyone seemed to have gone home. The drawing room was empty when he made his way back in there, so he walked straight to the french windows and out on to the wrought-iron balcony.

He retraced his thoughts. They were three-quarters of the way through the first scene, and it was a duet. They were in perfect harmony, and neither of them was getting away or ahead from the other one. You could sense the feeling of excitement in the auditorium. It was like a glow, an inaudible buzz. Jerome had never felt anything like it before. This was the *real thing*. This was the transport of joy. This was incomparable.

He would have been all right, he knew it now. He would have made it without ever slackening his grip, he would have made it and Elizabeth and he would have come home in a blanket finish. He was fine, he was flying, he was there on top of it, right up until the moment Cecil shifted his coat, and Jerome caught sight of him doing it. If he hadn't done that, who knows? Jerome wondered, as he stared down at the square below the balcony where he now stood, at the beginning of yet another London day. Anything might have happened if Cecil wasn't such an old woman, and hadn't wanted somewhere safe and clean to place his precious topcoat. Something could have happened later and thrown Elizabeth. Elizabeth was easily thrown, Jerome knew that. She had lost it before, badly, so badly she'd had to come to Jerome for help. So just suppose. Just suppose Cecil hadn't moved his topcoat. Just suppose.

But he had. The act was passed and over, it had been done. Cecil had moved his topcoat from his knee and placed it on the still unoccupied seat beside him, and Jerome had seen him do it out of the corner of his eye. And as he saw him do it, that was the moment Jerome knew Pippa would not be there, that Pippa wasn't coming to his first night, and that by the act of placing his coat on the empty seat, Cecil showed that he knew it, too.

That was the moment he let go of the rockface, just for a moment, just for a split second, but it was quite long enough. By the time he had regained his grip, Elizabeth was gone, higher and higher above him on the mountain, soon to be lost in the clouds shrouding the dizzy heights. Standing on the balcony in Grosvenor Square, eight hours or more after the event, Jerome could still recall it utterly, and as he did, as the feeling of complete helplessness overcame him, so once more his head began to swim and his senses reel.

140

From that moment, the moment he knew Pippa was not going to be there to see him, Jerome lost it, he lost both his conviction and his timing, and with it the full description of his performance, depriving himself finally of at least a fair share in the triumph of the evening.

'I trust you're not contemplating anything permanent, dear boy,' a tired voice said behind him. 'By and large your notices were really most encouraging.'

It was Cecil, red-eyed and exhausted, and for Cecil – very dishevelled.

'I fell asleep,' he said defensively, in response to Jerome's hard stare. 'Waiting for you.'

The two men faced each other on the balcony in silence, until Cecil, with a long uncontainable yawn, made as if to turn and go back inside, which was when Jerome pounced, grabbing him by the lapels of his dinner jacket.

'Why?' he demanded, 'why in hell didn't you *say*?'

'Look – we've been through all this, dear boy,' Cecil replied, trying not to look as taken aback as he felt by Jerome's sudden ferocity. 'I told you over dinner, remember?'

'Why didn't you tell me *before*, Cecil?' Jerome moaned, rocking slightly on his heels. 'Before I went on. I could have coped! It wouldn't have mattered!'

'Believe me, dear boy,' Cecil insisted, 'it was for the very best reasons. And it wasn't just me, you know. It was Pippa, too. When she found she couldn't get through to you on the stage-door phone, she rang me because that way she was certain you'd get the message. And when I suggested it might be better to tell you afterwards, particularly *vis-à-vis* her mother's accident, she thought it was better, too. She thought rather than you knowing *before* – I mean the last thing anyone wanted to do was throw you, dear boy.'

'Well it did, *dear boy*!' Jerome replied, suddenly full voice. 'It did, and God damn it, look at the *results*!'

He let Cecil go, pushing him back against the open windows, while he himself turned round once again to contemplate events in the square below.

Cecil took a cigarette from his wafer-thin case, tapped it against a thumb nail, and then lit it with his pocket Dunhill.

'Of course in retrospect,' he admitted, exhaling a plume of smoke, 'I should have realized. I should have remembered our seats were in the very front row. But in the heat of the moment . . . It really was with the very best intentions.'

141

'The road to hell, Cecil,' Jerome replied, swinging his dinner jacket over one shoulder, 'is *paved* with the damned things.'

'I'm sorry, Jerome,' Cecil said, 'if you think I acted foolishly. But I really did mean it for the best. I thought you would get upset if you knew in advance that Pippa wasn't going to be there. Which really is why I didn't tell you. Knowing that is exactly how you feel about Pippa.'

Jerome eyed Cecil, darkly, without any forgiving warmth, then pushed his way past him into the drawing room, leaving Cecil to smoke the rest of his cigarette on the balcony and wish that he had been telling Jerome the exact truth.

For while it was true to say that the reason Cecil hadn't told Jerome in advance of Pippa's enforced absence was indeed because he knew exactly how Jerome felt about Pippa, it wasn't true in the way that Jerome would think it to be so. Cecil hadn't told Jerome he knew *precisely* how Jerome felt about Pippa. Cecil hadn't told Jerome about Pippa out of spite.

The damage wasn't as bad as he had anticipated, and as they rode up on the Downs, Jerome told Pippa that, not with relief but with a feeling of aggravation, to which Pippa replied that not everything was always either black or white, but that there were in fact many shades of grey.

'I don't like grey,' he told her. 'Not at all. I only like things which are positive. Such as the fact that I love you, and you love me.'

'I don't remember saying I loved you,' she said, shortening the rein on her horse.

'I don't remember being *born*!' he exclaimed. 'But look at me – here I am!'

She laughed, and squeezed her horse into a trot. He followed suit and rode up alongside her.

'You're such an actor!' she called.

'And you're beautiful! Race you to the top of the hill!'

Pippa won easily, pulling up a good ten lengths ahead of Jerome.

'My God—' he panted as he reined his horse to a halt. 'Is there any sport at which you don't excel?'

'I know, it's awful, isn't it?' she agreed, tossing back her mane of hair. 'I suppose really I should have been born a boy.'

'I don't agree at all,' Jerome replied over-seriously. 'I think that is one of the very worst ideas I've ever heard.'

He leaned across and tried to kiss her, but both their horses fidgeted suddenly, and moved apart. Pippa laughed in delight.

'Well done, Drummer!' she said, leaning forward to pull one of the horse's ears. 'You really know how to look after me.'

Jerome ignored the tease, and swung his horse back round alongside Pippa's, so that they could stand together and overlook the wonderful sweep of the sunlit Downland all around them.

'Tell me about your mother's accident again,' he said, after a long silence. 'She fell over in the kitchen.'

'She fell over in the kitchen,' Pippa repeated, twisting some of the horse's mane around her fingers.

'About an hour before you were about to leave for London.'

'You know. I told you. We've been through all this.'

'What I don't understand is the fact that Mrs Whatshername?'

'Mrs Huxley.'

'Your neighbour, Mrs Huxley, was there, and was going to stay with her, and that once the doctor had been—'

'Jerome.'

Pippa looked round at him, and for the first time Jerome saw a warning light in her eyes.

'Sorree,' he said, putting on a rustic voice. 'I were only arskin'.'

'It wasn't as if I hadn't seen your play, Jerome,' Pippa continued. 'It wasn't as if I hadn't seen it in Oxford.'

'Oxford's Oxford, Pippa Nicholls!' Jerome cried. 'This was the West End! A West End first night! My first night! My first West End first night! And I wanted you there! And because you weren't there—'

'Oh fiddle!' Pippa interrupted. 'That's got absolutely nothing to do with it! My being there, or not being there!'

'It has everything to do with it, Pippa Nicholls!'

'No it doesn't, Jerome, and you know it! You're just making it the reason!'

'Making it the reason? What reason? Making what the reason, Pippa Nicholls?'

'You know perfectly well, Jerome Didier. This is getting boring, so I don't know about you, but I'm going to go and jump some logs.'

She cantered off along the ridge to a small copse a hundred or so yards distant. Jerome's horse wanted to follow, but Jerome didn't, so he reined him back and turned him round in order to settle him, and then once he was settled, Jerome relaxed his hold and sat back to think.

He knew what Pippa meant, and he was afraid she was right, which only made him love her the more. Of course, he had been heart-broken that she hadn't been able to make it, and for all that week he had convinced himself that was the reason why Elizabeth had walked off with the play, and why he had failed to fulfil his promise. But all the time, growing at the back of his mind, was a doubt, a doubt which grew larger and larger every time he stepped on-stage to perform Oscar Greene's hit play, a doubt which became certain knowledge by the time he was driving down to Sussex to see Pippa the following Sunday morning. When it came to the crunch, Elizabeth Laurence had triumphed not by default, but because Elizabeth Laurence was even more brilliant than he was.

At least in this play she was.

Which, Jerome reasoned as he had driven down from London, was not altogether surprising, because after all the play had been handwritten for her talent, not for his. The day would come perhaps, and perhaps soon, when someone would write a vehicle for him, and then he would triumph in his own right, but until then he would only be able to come to terms with himself by telling himself the truth. In this particular play, Miss Elizabeth Laurence was knocking Mr Jerome Didier into a cocked hat.

At first with Pippa he had gone back to his old ways, and tried to play it for her sympathy, trying to make her believe that it was her enforced absence which had so disconcerted him. But he saw from the outset she didn't believe him, and once he realized she didn't believe him, he himself could no longer believe in the pretence well enough to go on pretending. So now as she rode off with a final reminder for him to face the truth, Jerome left the disappointment of the play behind and turned to an even more pressing matter, namely how to marry Pippa. Because marry her was what he undoubtedly intended to do, despite the objections of her mother. In fact, he thought as he kicked his horse on to a canter, he would marry Pippa *because* of her mother's objections, and by doing so, he would show her and the world on what uncertain ground such ridiculous prejudices were based.

As he cantered faster and faster along the ridge to find Pippa, he laughed out loud, as he saw himself, lance in hand on a strong white charger, off to do battle, to joust for his lady's hand.

'Cry God for Harry!' he suddenly shouted, 'England! And Saint George!'

He found himself alone with her finally after tea, when Pippa had disappeared to wash up, alone but not quite face to face, because Mrs Nicholls continued to read, head bent over her book, as

144

if Jerome wasn't there. Even when he spoke, she didn't look up.

'Mrs Nicholls,' he began. 'I want to talk to you about Pippa and I.'

'Very well,' Mrs Nicholls replied, turning a page slowly.

'I think you know what I'm going to say,' Jerome said, and gave a smile, hoping to lighten the atmosphere.

'I have absolutely no idea at all what you're going to say, young man,' she corrected him, at last looking up and staring at him lengthily over her half moon spectacles. 'Why on earth should I?'

Jerome drew two deep and well concealed breaths, in and out through his nose, barely moving his diaphragm, just as he had been taught, and then put one hand into a trouser pocket and rested the other on the back of a small buttoned armchair.

'Mrs Nicholls,' he said, evenly and calmly, his nerves well in check thanks to his deep breathing. 'Mrs Nicholls, I would like to marry your daughter.'

There was a long silence, during which his adversary tilted her head even lower, the better to stare at him over her spectacles. Finally she raised her eyebrows briefly, sighed and returned to her reading.

'Mrs Nicholls—' Jerome began again.

'I heard what you said, young man,' Mrs Nicholls replied. 'Thank you.'

'Have you nothing to say on the matter?'

'If you must know, I have plenty to say on the matter.'

'So?'

'Very well.'

Pippa's mother closed her book and placed it carefully on the table beside her, next to the photograph of Pippa's brother, the position of which she adjusted fractionally before returning her gaze to Jerome.

'You say you would like to marry my daughter,' she reminded herself.

'Yes,' Jerome replied. 'That is exactly so.'

'Then what *I* would like to know, young man,' Mrs Nicholls asked, 'is why?'

'*Why*?' Jerome frowned deeply, and then leaned forward slightly, placing both of his hands now on the back of the chair. 'Why – for the very reasons most people wish to get married, Mrs Nicholls! Because I love her! Because I wish to spend the rest of my *life* with her! Because I want to have children with her!'

Mrs Nicholls shook her head.

'No, please,' she said. 'There's no need to shout. You're not on-stage now.'

As if in recognition of the reprimand but in fact to hide his look of fury, Jerome bowed his head for a moment, still holding the back of the chair, before straightening up once more and putting both his hands behind his back.

'Mrs Nicholls,' he said. 'I want to marry Pippa – because I love her.'

'Yes, I'm sure you do,' Mrs Nicholls replied, but now with a smile, which made Jerome feel he had said something odd or foolish, which was precisely her intention. 'But you see, people like you,' she continued, 'you shouldn't get married. People like you, actors, you're always away, or on tour, you're not really what I would call homebirds. You shouldn't really marry and have children. It really isn't fair. At least it isn't fair if you don't marry into your own world. People outside your world, they don't really understand. They know nothing of how people like you live, what you want, and why you want it. It really is much more sensible for people like you to stick to your own sort.'

'Like tinkers, you mean?' Jerome asked, over-lightly. 'Like the people of the road.'

'Young man,' Mrs Nicholls said, the smile gone from her face and a quite different look came into her eyes. 'There are hundreds of pretty girls in your profession. Beautiful girls, actresses, dancers, singers, what have you, girls who have the same kind of life as you, who understand the same things. Girls who would give their eye teeth to be married to a handsome young man like you. Girls who would be much more *suitable*. It really wouldn't work out with Pippa. She's very different to you. She was brought up in an entirely different manner. And I'm very much afraid that if you married Pippa, she would only end up being very unhappy.'

'I see,' Jerome said, floundering momentarily, *bouleversed* by the display of Mrs Nicholls' will and of her resolve. 'And is that all?'

'No,' Mrs Nicholls replied. 'Not quite. There is one other thing, something which I simply don't understand. And that is what a young man like you, surrounded as you are by beautiful girls, such as, I believe, this girl you're acting with at the moment, I just don't understand – I mean ... why Pippa?'

Jerome saw his exit, and was not going to forgo the opportunity.

'My dear Mrs Nicholls,' he said, turning a photograph of his beloved Pippa to face him, 'if you have to ask that, then you do not deserve to have such a daughter.'

Then with a final look at Pippa's image, he replaced the photograph and went out into the garden.

Pippa found him right down at the end of their gardens, sitting on an old swing which hung from a branch of a vast oak.

'I gather you two had words,' she said.

Jerome was pushing himself slowly backwards and forwards on the swing, staring all the time at the ground.

'All I told her,' he said, 'was that I wanted to marry you.'

'Move up,' Pippa ordered him, and then squeezed herself in beside him on the broad seat of the swing.

'Oh Pippa!' Jerome suddenly exclaimed, looking upwards into the bright blue sky. 'Why is love so *blasted* difficult?'

'If it wasn't,' Pippa replied, beginning to push with her feet, 'it would simply be just another form of friendship.'

She pushed against the ground harder, and the swing began to rise higher. Jerome joined in, pushing his feet against the ground in unison with hers. They crossed their hands and arms, each holding on to the chains either side, and as they did, Jerome looked at Pippa, and leaning towards her, buried his face in her hair.

'Do you know love?' he asked.

'It's a deceiver, isn't it?' she wondered.

'It?' Jerome pushed even harder against the ground. 'Love's a he or a she, surely? Not an "it". He's Eros, or she's Aphrodite, Cupid or the Sovereign Queen of Secrets. She who can *induce stale gravity to daunce.*'

'Push harder,' Pippa urged. 'I want to see if we can get as high as my brother and I used to get.'

'And how high was that, Pippa Nicholls?'

'So high that the chains used to buckle!'

Jerome and she pushed the ground some more.

'You want to be careful of swings!' Jerome laughed. 'They can induce some quite unexpected effects!'

Pippa turned and frowned at him as they flew ever higher.

'Really?' she asked. 'Come on – you're not pushing!'

They now swung in silence, until they were swinging so high and so fast they could barely get any more impulsion. So together they used their weight, shifting it at the prime moment, urging the swing even higher, until at the height of their arc they were all but parallel to the ground.

'Enough!' Jerome cried. 'I concede!'

'Don't be wet!' Pippa retorted. 'The chains are still straight!'

So on they flew, flying through the air face down and up again backwards until for one heartstopping moment the chains lost their tension and it seemed to Jerome there was nothing left holding them up.

Pippa gave a great cry of joy.

'Yes!' she shouted. 'We're there! We've done it!'

Slowly then they came back to earth, the momentum gone, the pendulum swinging easier and easier, silent again with nothing but the sound of the wind in their ears. Neither of them put a foot to the ground to break their progress. They just sat quite still, one arm around the other's waist, until at last the swing came to a rest, turning slowly left and right on its creaking chains before finally settling.

Jerome exhaled quietly, and pushed his hair back out of his eyes, while Pippa laughed and untucked her skirt from between her knees.

'Remarkable,' Jerome concluded. 'Remind me to do that when we're married.'

Pippa looked at him, very seriously, and then kissed him gently on the lips.

'I can't marry you, Jerome,' she said. 'Not yet.'

'When?' he asked impatiently, tightening his arm around her waist. 'I don't think I can wait until you're twenty-one.'

'No, don't,' Pippa said, looking suddenly puzzled. 'Please, Jerome.'

But it was too late, far too late, for by now Jerome was kissing her, while lifting her with the arm which was around her waist off the swing so they were standing and kissing, with their bodies pressed against each other.

'No,' she kept saying between his kisses, as he ran his hands first through her hair, and then along and around the shape of her body. 'No, Jerome, no please.'

'What do you mean by no?' he whispered. 'Do you mean no you want me to stop?'

'No,' Pippa whispered back. 'I just mean no I don't want you to go on.'

'Any further, you mean.'

'Yes. Yes.'

By now Jerome had undone the buttons down the front of Pippa's red and white cotton dress, carefully and slowly lest he frighten her, and then carefully and slowly he put one hand inside her dress and on to the soft, smooth, firm skin of her young body, surprised as always at exactly how exciting he found such a simple act. He caught his breath as his hand slipped around Pippa's waist

148

and he felt her catch her breath, too. He moved his hand round further, drawing her to him, and she leaned back her head, letting her waves of dark hair hang straight down in a tousled cascade, while she slowly closed her grey-green eyes, but only half closed her pretty pink mouth.

'Yes?' Jerome whispered, as he moved his hand down her back again, easing his little finger inside a line of softly covered elastic, feeling with the tip of his finger the top of a curve of warm, firm flesh.

'Yes what?' she sighed, letting her head now fall on to his shoulder as the top of one of his fingers became the whole of his hand, which he then moved slowly down to caress the whole of that warm curve of flesh.

'Yes will you marry me, Pippa Nicholls?' he murmured, letting his hand drop to the top of a thigh which he then drew slowly towards him. His other hand was on her shoulder, outside her dress, and with it he tilted her chin up so that her eyes met his. 'Yes will you marry me? I asked,' he said.

'Why do we have to get married, Jerome?' Pippa sighed. But that was all she was allowed to ask at that moment, since Jerome silenced her with another kiss, a long, lingering kiss which explored the dark red warmth of her mouth. 'We don't have to get married, Jerome,' she finally gasped as he finally stopped kissing her. 'We really don't.'

'Yes, we do have to get married, Pippa Nicholls,' Jerome countered. 'We have to get married because I love you, because I love you more than I thought it was possible to love anybody, because you love me, because you love me more than you thought it was possible to love anybody, and we have to get married so that I may take all your clothes off, and take you to bed, and get at this delicious, this *wonderful* body of yours, and make love to you endlessly, make love to you continually, infinitely, perpetually and eternally. That is why we *must* – get married.'

He kissed her again, now drawing his hand up and along her warm body, up round the front of her waist, up higher, up to the satin which cupped her warm breast, his thumb on the edge of another curve of her flesh, a softer curve, which moved with his touch.

'We don't have to get married, Jerome,' she breathed, putting her hand to his face, then round to the back of his neck. 'We could be lovers instead. I could come to London and see you. Visit you in your flat. We could have an affair. I don't mind, do you see? Because I want you, Jerome, as much as – as much as you want me. I want you to make love to me. Because I love you, Jerome, and I want you so very much. So you see you don't have to marry me. We don't have to get married just to make love.'

Jerome stepped back, and looked at her, taking his hands from her, staring at her quizzically.

'We don't?' he said.

'No,' she replied. 'You can make love to me whenever you want. You can make love to me now. Here.'

'I can?'

'Yes, Jerome. Yes. I promise you, we can make love without us getting married. You can make love to me here and now if you want to.'

He continued to stare at her without saying anything, and without expression. Then he suddenly leaned forward and put his hands to her waist.

'What are you doing, Jerome?' she asked.

'I am doing the buttons up, Pippa Nicholls,' he replied in a tone people usually reserved for slow children, 'on your dress.'

'But why?' she wanted to know. 'I don't understand you.'

'I am doing the buttons up on your *dress*, Pippa Nicholls,' Jerome sighed again, 'because I am not going to make love to you. And the reason I am not going to make love to you is because you will not agree to marry me. And because you will not agree to marry me, Pippa Nicholls, I shall not agree to make love to you until you do agree. And even then I shall not make love to you – until the night of the day – we are finally *married*.'

Having done up the last of her buttons, he smiled at her, kissed her briefly on the lips, and then walked away through the shrubbery, whistling 'Hello Young Lovers'.

After a moment Pippa ran after Jerome, determined to punch and pummel him with her tightly clenched fist, only to find that once she caught up with him, she was once more caught up in his arms.

Pippa's mother was not the only person who was deeply concerned about her daughter's involvement with Jerome Didier. There were others, the most prominent of them being Elizabeth Laurence. Try as she may, she simply could not understand quite what attraction the country bumpkin – as Elizabeth had dubbed her – had for Jerome. Besides the fact that Elizabeth considered her to be quite unexceptional looking, with her unkempt head of hair, her absurdly freckled face, her boyish manner and her hand-me-down clothes, the wretched creature wasn't even one of them. The

150

mouse wasn't just a bumpkin mouse, as she complained nightly to Muzz, worse – she was a civilian mouse.

'Poor Jerome,' she would sigh as she made herself up, 'he simply doesn't know what he'd be taking on, Muzz darling. Ask anybody. People like us – it's quite, quite hopeless marrying out of the business.'

If the irregularity of her own marital status ever occurred to Elizabeth, she never referred to it, nor did Muzz. As far as Elizabeth went, when she left her home in Chelsea each day to journey to the theatre, she ceased to be married, and by the time she had shut herself in her dressing room, Sebastian had ceased to exist. His name was never once mentioned, and after his disastrous appearance on the first night, he was never seen backstage again. He was never even seen in the vicinity of the theatre.

Elizabeth had managed to arrange this with her usual expert diplomacy. Firstly, as far as the mention of his name went, she let it be known via Muzz that because of the nature of the part she was playing, and the intensity of the relationship she had nightly to recreate on-stage with Jerome, she found the process of getting into her character in the hour before curtain up un-usually difficult, a process which she confessed to find well nigh impossible if her preparations were interrupted, particularly by the intrusion of any reality. Such as any mention of a husband, or a marriage.

'I cannot see or think of my darling Sebastian, I must only see Jerome,' she explained to Muzz, knowing that it would be around the entire company by the first interval. 'Or more correctly *Charles*, the character Jerome is playing. If for a moment I remember my darling Sebastian, then I stall, like a car running out of petrol. I become – oh, what is the word? *Inhibited* – yes! I find I cannot any longer be *Emerald Glynn*, giving herself to *Charles Danby*, but instead I become me, myself again, *playing* the part, not *being* it. So for the purposes of this wonderful play, I have to be just Elizabeth Laurence. *Un*-married.'

She used the same reasoning on her husband, the only difference being in the shading. She told him she had to appear to detach herself from him for the play to succeed, not for herself, but for Jerome.

'For me, darling one,' she told him, 'it is nothing but the *greatest* help having you there, either physically, or in my mind's eye. How else could I play those love scenes, do you think? If I didn't have you to think of? Every time I have to tell Jerome – or *Charles*, should I say – that I love him, I simply think he is you. As indeed

151

when I have to kiss him, or hold him, I just think of kissing and holding you, dearest one. But, of course, for poor Jerome it's just impossible. He is such a very sweet boy that if *he* thinks of you, he becomes most dreadfully inhibited! Can you imagine, my darling! But it's true. The poor boy goes to pieces! He said to me one night, *very* early in the run, in the first week I think it was, he said he thought he had seen you in the stalls, and he simply *froze*! I think it's a little jejeune actually, between you and me, my darling, just a *little* unprofessional, but then this is the poor lamb's very first part, and I suppose we must make allowances.'

And so Sebastian, being the kind and understanding person that he was, made the stipulated allowances, and promised he would never come to the play or visit the theatre again. When he was to meet Elizabeth afterwards, for dinner, or to go on to a party, he promised he would wait for her either at the restaurant or at his club from where she could collect him, the only other stipulation being that any parties which they attended together must be purely civilian ones.

'I hate to see you ignored,' Elizabeth told him. 'I cannot stand it, and I will not have it. So for your sake, we will not go to any of those silly sort of parties at all.'

Naturally Sebastian dismissed such a notion, on the understanding that it was important for Elizabeth to attend such events, since she was now so obviously determined to pursue a theatrical career, so rather than once again act as some sort of inhibitor, and aware of the sudden fame which had been thrust upon her, Sebastian very kindly stayed out of the limelight, and allowed Elizabeth to attend the necessary parties where she might be seen in company with Jerome, but only for the good of the play.

However, it was not all such plain sailing for the beautiful young woman who had become the toast of the town. Her adoring husband might understand the singularity of her needs, her fast growing army of admirers might worship at the shrine of her beauty, but the one person who really mattered to her, the object of all her desire, seemed impervious to her allure. Jerome Didier treated her as a friend, or even worse, like a sister.

Night after night he would sit in her dressing room in the interval, talking endlessly about Pippa, and seeking Elizabeth's advice as to what exactly he should do. For her part, Elizabeth would smile sympathetically, take his hands in hers, pretend to counsel him, sigh at his predicament, and promise to think of a solution, while all the time inwardly burning with a jealous rage. Then after Jerome had gone to prepare for the second act, Elizabeth would let her emotions go, and beg and beseech Muzz to try and explain to her what possible attraction someone such as this lanky, unkempt girl could have for someone as debonair and handsome as Jerome?

In reply, Muzz would just shake her head and come up with some bromide as there being no accounting for taste, while carefully folding away tiny perfectly ironed bundles of Elizabeth's handmade crêpe silk underwear into a special monogrammed satin case, initialled E.L.

'I could scream sometimes, Muzz dear, do you know that?' Elizabeth would tell her dresser nightly, sometimes twice nightly, sometimes even more on matinée days, as she sat staring at the only person who understood her, namely herself.

'I don't see why,' Muzz would reply, with little variation. 'We're sold out until Christmas.'

'Of course you know why, darling,' Elizabeth would sigh, leaning closer to her reflected image so that she could stare deeply into her eyes and into herself. 'And it has nothing to do with the bookings.'

Then there would be a knock on the door and the call boy's call.

'Five minutes, please, Miss Laurence! Five minutes please!'

Five minutes. And then just another ten before she would be back in Jerome's arms, which was all Elizabeth really cared about now, even though it was only make-believe. Nothing else mattered. All the adulation, the crowds at the stage door, the autographs, the photographs, the interviews, the fan mail, the flowers, the attention, the applause and the echoing cheers, none of it mattered as much as what was going to happen in the next two hours. Elizabeth was going to have Jerome all to herself, and they were going to be lovers. He was going to tell her he loved her, he was going to hold her, and kiss her, and vow to be hers for ever, which was only right and proper, because if any two people were made for each other, they were. They were each a half of the same seed, and Elizabeth knew Jerome wasn't just acting, because when he kissed her and then let her go, there was always that look in his eyes, that look a man cannot fake, the look Sebastian had whenever she allowed him to kiss her, the look everyone had ever had who had kissed her, or who had perhaps even just *thought* about kissing her, the look of astonishment which seems always to accompany true love.

Elizabeth saw it nightly in Jerome's eyes, and twice on Wednesdays and Saturdays. It didn't matter to her that the look vanished the moment the scene was over, or when the act was over, or when

153

the final curtain fell. Jerome might think he had been play-acting, but Elizabeth knew otherwise. Neither did it matter who he was going to meet after the show, or where he went at the weekends. Elizabeth had seen the look, and she knew, she just *knew* that by all rights Jerome Didier was hers.

All that needed to be done, therefore, was to think of some way to get that wretched country bumpkin out of his luscious hair.

Cecil Manners also strongly opposed the notion of Jerome marrying Pippa, his resistance being based on the fact that he wanted Pippa for himself. The notion had always been there, ever since the day of the famous gymkhana, but until Jerome had appeared on the scene, it had been a comfortably vague notion, a Romance rather than a romance. Cecil had been in love with the idea of Pippa, and with the idea of being in love with Pippa, rather than seriously in love with Pippa as a person. Cecil had been too busy furthering his career to give Pippa any really serious thought, but once he learned from her mother how serious Jerome's intentions were, Cecil thought it high time to reconsider the position. To Cecil's way of thinking Jerome marrying Pippa would constitute a disaster.

He found Dmitri Boska of the same complexion when they lunched together, although for quite different motives.

'We don't want him married to some hick,' Boska announced. 'A peasant with straws in her hair! This is not the image we want for this boy!'

Cecil stifled his own feelings, and said nothing to correct Boska about how wrongly he was representing his beloved Pippa, as he knew it would not be good business. Besides, Boska was so powerful that if he had decided he didn't want Jerome to marry Pippa, it was eminently possible that Boska could arrange that he didn't.

'Jerome Didier is style,' Boska continued, 'Jerome Didier is class. Jerome Didier everyone wants to screw. So my feelings, Cecil? If Jerome Didier wants to get his leg over something, then she too has to be style, she has to be class. She too has to be someone everyone want to screw. Yes? You see my thinking?'

Indeed Cecil did, he thought, as he adjusted the knot in his Garrick Club tie. He got Boska's drift all right. Everyone always did, Boska made sure of that. It was just he sometimes wished as he was wishing now in the subdued hush of The Mirabelle that Boska was not quite so professionally foreign. And that he wouldn't mispronounce his name as *Sissel*.

'OK, Cecil,' Boska said, tapping the table with one finger. 'So you tell me what I was thinking.'

'What you're saying, dear boy,' Cecil replied, brushing some invisible crumbs off the crisp linen table cloth, 'is that if Joan Public can't get into bed with Jerome Didier, then she wants whoever it is in his bed to be particularly glamorous.'

'Good,' Boska laughed. 'And why is this so? Because then she can *fantasize*! Yes? She can think in her head when she is imagining such things, that she is that beautiful woman. A beautiful woman. Not a hick. *A beautiful woman.* Such as Elizabeth Laurence.'

Now Cecil really was genuinely surprised, and the expression on his face as he looked up quickly must have said so, since Boska clapped his hands in delight.

'You got it!' he cried. 'This is who Jerome Didier should be screwing! He should be getting his legs around little Miss Laurence!'

'Ssshhh,' Cecil frowned warningly, looking over his shoulder to see who else had taken note of Boska's public pronouncement. 'Keep the old voice down, dear boy.'

'Nuts,' Boska scoffed, signalling the waiter for more cognac. 'We get Didier bunking Eliza Dolittle, and everyone's life gets easier. Not only easier, better! Richer! Think of the story! The public will lap it up! Two beautiful young people such as them? Devouring each other off-screen as well as on? You listen, Cecil, we could retire early tomorrow. Two stars like them bunking? You can't get it bigger.'

'I take your point,' Cecil replied, carefully and keeping his voice down. 'But aren't you forgetting something? Such as Elizabeth Laurence's husband?'

'You never hear of divorces?'

'I've heard of divorces, dear boy, but have you never heard of the scandal they create?'

Boska looked at him bug-eyed as the waiter carefully placed before them two large cognacs, and then he suddenly roared with laughter. Cecil felt most offended.

'I'm quite serious, dear boy,' Cecil said, toying with his glass. 'If what you said earlier is true, and you really are considering building my two clients up into a starring partnership, if – and I doubt the 'if' very much – but even so *if* they did ever . . . well – have a liaison, if you will, the ensuing scandal could be ruinous. Particularly internationally.'

Boska looked bewildered, laughed some more, and then slapped the table with both his hands. Cecil only just caught his glass in time.

'No, this I cannot take seriously, Cecil!' Boska announced. 'These people, your clients, my dear Cecil they are actors! Not nuns!'

'Of course they're not nuns, or monks, or whatever the case may be, dear boy,' Cecil replied, 'but you cannot forget the women's lobby. It's still very strong, you know. Most of all, in the States.'

'Oh nuts, Cecil! Such nuts!' Boska grinned. 'Plain women – they always forgive the beautiful ones. Everybody, they worship beauty. This is why they go to the movies – where else do they see such beauty? Yes? Movie stars? They are the modern saints, Cecil. They are sanctified. My mother – she would pray before a picture of Blessed Elizabeth of Gizycko. My daughter? She worship Yvonne de Carlo. We put Elizabeth to Jerome Didier, they'll be lighting candles to them everywhere.'

Cecil extinguished his cigarette and nodded slowly. He didn't necessarily agree with Boska's prognosis, but he couldn't help feeling that Jerome was far better suited to Elizabeth Laurence than he was to his beloved next door neighbour. And even leaving his own feelings aside for a moment, if Jerome went ahead and did manage to marry Pippa, it could well be disastrous in another way, for there really was no saying exactly how badly Elizabeth would take it, which would indeed bode ill for them all. At this very moment, Elizabeth was the hottest young property in the business, but she was still so young, and seemingly insecure, and as a result so easily upset, that a disappointment such as this might even lead her to abandon her career.

'Hell hasn't such a fury, Cecil,' Boska said, almost reading his mind.

'I know, dear boy,' Cecil replied. 'I'm just considering every eventuality.'

'Good,' Boska said, draining his cognac, 'we don't want our divine Miss Laurence getting herself to a nunnery, yes?'

'No,' said Cecil, 'most certainly not. But an idea's one thing, dear boy. An idea is all very well. *But.*'

'Which is why I suggest you take another of your clients out to lunch, Cecil,' Boska advised, looking round for the head waiter. 'That pretty blonde. That friend of Elizabeth's. The one she insisted to being also in the play.'

'Lalla Henderson?'

'Lalla Henderson. She's quite a lady.'

Boska had summoned the waiter over and ordered him to bring the bill.

'Yes, Cecil,' he said, reaching inside his jacket for his wallet. 'You take Miss Henderson out to lunch. She's a lady with quite a lot of surprises in her store.'

*

156

Cecil took Lalla to the Trocadero, which he thought a more suitable venue for their luncheon rather than any of his regular and more conventional restaurants. As she walked in on Cecil's arm, Lalla turned quite a few heads, a tall, leggy and well-proportioned blonde dressed up to the minute in a new suit by John Cavanagh.

'It's called, would you believe?' Lalla said as a waiter sat her at their table. 'It's called a *Claridge's* suit, isn't that fun? Apparently the designer intended this should only be worn when lunching at Claridge's.'

'You should have told me, Lalla dear,' Cecil said, offering her a cigarette. 'I could just as easily have taken you there.'

'Oh, I don't think so. Cecil darling,' Lalla said, accepting a light and then looking round at the velvet and gold of the restaurant. 'This is much more us, don't you think?'

For most of the lunch they discussed the play, and gossiped about nothing of any great note, at least not according to Lalla's book. But Lalla had been long enough in the theatre to know that important agents do not take their less important clients out to lunch without a purpose, so she ate her food, drank her wine, told a few tales, laughed at Cecil's unfunny jokes, and waited for the point to be reached.

It arrived with the pudding.

'We're all of us,' Cecil said, 'all of us that is on *this* side of the footlights as it were, we're really most concerned about Jerome and Elizabeth, you know, Lalla.'

'But they're both being wonderful!' Lalla exclaimed, playing the *ingénue.* 'They get better with each performance!'

Cecil looked at her and smiled. She was a lovely girl, but a really terrible actress, both on-stage and off.

'Let me put it another way, dear,' he said. 'We're rather concerned about Elizabeth in regard to her *emotional* state.'

For a moment Lalla's eyes caught Cecil's over the top of her wine glass, and when they did Cecil felt suddenly desirous, which was a most unusual state for Cecil. Objects of Cecil's desire usually came in the shape of contracts, rarely in that of nubile young actresses. Cecil had long ago taken a private vow of chastity as far as nubile young actresses went, since an indulgence in that particular direction had ruined many a good theatrical agent, most notably the man he had first worked for, Edward Goodbody, a notorious Lothario who died under the most embarrassing circumstances. Just to remember the circumstances of his passing made Cecil blush.

It did, however, help him get his mind off Lalla Henderson and her luscious *décolletage* and back on to the matter in hand.

'Lalla, dear,' he said, 'you're Elizabeth's best friend. So you're probably in a better position than anybody to say what might happen if Jerome Didier were to go through with his intended marriage.'

Lalla smiled suddenly, and leaned right across the table so that her pretty little face was only inches from Cecil's, close enough for him to become momentarily intoxicated by her scent.

'You really want to know what I think?' she breathed, 'I think if Jerome married the country bumpkin, as Liz calls her, I think it would be the very best thing that could happen.'

Cecil, expecting it to be the very worst, was now dumbfounded as well as confounded.

'But I was led to believe Elizabeth was madly in love with Jerome,' he said.

Lalla laughed.

'So she is, Cecil darling! She would *kill* to get him!'

'So? How could Jerome marrying—' he nearly said Pippa's name, but just stopped himself, lest the way that he said it and the look on his face as he said it might reveal what he felt. 'How could Jerome marrying this girl—' he corrected himself, 'I don't see how it could be the *best* thing that could happen.'

'Jerome marries Pippa,' Lalla sighed, spooning another fresh strawberry carefully into her mouth. 'Her mother is heart-broken, but not for long. Mothers by and large are pretty tough old things, don't you agree, Cecil darling? So Mrs Country Bumpkin gets over it, Jerome's happy because he's finally got the Bumpkin between the sheets, he's got someone to cook and bottle wash and mend his socks for him, and at night, before he goes back to his little love nest, he's got Elizabeth as well, hasn't he? With none of the imperfections of a wife and all the whatever the silly old opposite of imperfections is of a beautiful actress. And as a result, he'll start seeing Elizabeth in a different light, won't he, sweetie?'

'Will he?' Cecil asked, too fascinated even to light the cigarette he had taken from his case.

'Cecil darling,' Lalla drawled, 'Jerome won't be going around playing the unrequited lover any more, will he? And Jerome does love so to play the part, doesn't he? No, darling, all that will be left for dashing and handsome Jerome to play will be Good Old Hubbie, which is *not*, I imagine, a role to which he's most eminently suited, would you?'

Finally managing to light his cigarette, Cecil noticed with no little

158

curiosity, that his ever-steady hand was shaking in the excitement of the moment.

'Go on,' he said, 'I think I see what you're driving at.'

'Do you?' Lalla lit her own cigarette, and elegantly exhaled a thin thread of smoke. 'Well, just in case you don't, darling, I'll spell it out for you. We have Jerome playing Happy Hubbie. *Not* good casting. We have Bumpkin playing Mrs Newlywed – *very* happy casting. And we have Elizabeth, described as the best actress of her generation, playing what? Playing Milady-in-Waiting. And believe me, Cecil darling, she won't have to wait very long.'

'One thing everybody seems to forget,' Cecil said, frowning deeply, 'is that Elizabeth is actually married.'

Lalla just stared at him as if he was barking mad, and then suddenly laughed.

'Oh, Cecil!' she cried. 'You're so *wonderfully* old-fashioned! When Jerome gets bored with playing Lovely Happy Hubbie, what's the next role he'll have his eyes on? The Lover. And what do Lovers have to have? Mistresses. And who ever said Mistresses can't be married? After all, I always heard it was the married girls who were the best bet. Because they won't be nagging Loverboy to marry them all the time.'

Cecil pushed his cigarette out in the ashtray, ashamed of his part in what was turning into a conspiracy, and ashamed of himself for being unable – or worse unwilling – to withdraw from it.

'I can't imagine it, Lalla dear,' he said finally. 'Jerome is totally mad about – about this girl.'

'Yes. Until she becomes just the wife, Cecil, and is no longer the Great Unattainable. Until she's always at home, cooking. And one night when he comes home, he notices her hair smells of onions—'

'Oh no,' Cecil said, far too hastily. 'No, I don't think Pip – I don't think this girl's hair would ever smell of onions.'

This earned him a long and curious stare from Lalla, which Cecil pretended not to notice, instead taking a long drink from his glass of iced water.

'Do you play bridge, Cecil?' Lalla asked, and then continued without waiting for his reply. 'Well, of course you do. What a silly question. So let's put it in bridge terms. Mrs Bumpkin, once wed, is *vulnerable*. Because as Mrs Wife, she has it all to lose. The potential mistress doesn't. Give me the secondary role any day. Men are much less likely to cheat on their mistresses than their wives. Don't you think, Cecil darling?'

Cecil smiled, but only grimly, as he tried to recapitulate on the theory so far. If Lalla was right, and Jerome married Pippa, then everything would be all right because everything would go all wrong. That's really what she was saying, he decided. Jerome wouldn't be able to stay married, or at least stay faithful, Elizabeth would see to that, and then Pippa, being Pippa, would have to divorce him which, although a shocking thought, and not a path Cecil would willingly wish her to take, would finally leave Pippa free to marry him, which Cecil knew was the only way he could get her to be his wife, on the rebound.

'What about Jerome and Elizabeth?' he asked, as if from now on, having got the cast, it was simply a matter of rehearsing until they'd got it right.

'Darling,' Lalla said, as if he was missing the point. 'Jerome and Elizabeth are *made* for each other. They are *fated*, darling. Nothing, and no-one can stand in their way. It's there, in the stars. That's where their names are written. Everyone knows it, everyone who sees them act. And the papers are full of them. People can't *read* enough about them.'

'True,' Cecil nodded. 'And Dmitri Boska is already lining up their first film together. They certainly are news.'

'Darling,' Lalla sighed, 'they are unstoppable. Because they are that unique thing, darling. They are a *partnership*. And like all great theatrical partnerships they will fill everywhere. That – is a cast-iron certainty.'

Cecil was impressed, Cecil was convinced. It all seemed to make perfect sense. The fact that Elizabeth's husband hadn't even rated a specific mention seemed immaterial, because Lalla's argument was absolutely watertight. Everyone who had seen the two of them agreed. Didier and Laurence were a marriage.

'Good,' Cecil said, as if finishing the negotiations on a deal. 'So we all know where we stand.'

'Yes, poppet,' Lalla smiled, and put her hand on his. And once again, Cecil felt the stirrings of desire. 'And what would help simply enormously would be for someone in the know to go and talk to the Bumpkin's mother, don't you think? And if you don't mind me saying, soonest done, yes?'

Cecil put his hand on top of Lalla's and held it. To his de-light, which he did his best not to show, Lalla ran her thumb up and down the side of his index finger and looked him straight in the eyes.

'You're a very bright young lady, Lalla,' he said. 'If there's any-thing I can do in return.'

160

'Yes, darling,' Lalla returned promptly. 'Since you ask, I want another ten pounds a week, because what I'm on's a rotten wage, and I want you to guarantee me a part in Liz's next play. Or picture.'

Cecil nodded, unable to speak as Lalla started to run the tips of her fingers across the palm of his hand. But he knew there would be no difficulty on that score. If he could help manipulate events the way they all wanted, and keep Jerome and Elizabeth intact as a partnership, both Boska and Locke would be only too willing to find the necessary small part for Miss Lalla Henderson.

'Now I must dash, sweetie,' Lalla said, rising and leaning over to kiss Cecil on his forehead. 'Don't think me rude, but I have an appointment.'

Just before she left, Lalla put her arms on Cecil's shoulders from behind and kissed him once more on the top of his head. It amused her no end to see a bright red lipstick mark in the middle of Cecil's little bald patch.

It amused her no end as well as she sat in the taxi on her way to meet Elizabeth at how easy it had been to steer Cecil round to Elizabeth's way of thinking. He had been the proverbial putty in her hand, the silly old softy.

Then she sat back and thought also about how positively brilliant Elizabeth was. Only Elizabeth could have worked out that her best chance of getting Jerome would be to see him safely and finally boringly married to the Bumpkin. Only Elizabeth could have seen that as long as the Bumpkin remained unmarried, Jerome would be in her thrall.

'Once in bed, dead,' she had repeated often enough to Lalla, sometimes accompanied by a wicked laugh, sometimes by just a dangerous glint in those bright green eyes.

'Once in bed, dead.'

Poor Bumpkin, Lalla thought as the taxi turned down Piccadilly, poor funny old Bumpkin. With the cards Elizabeth held against her, she didn't stand a chance. For a moment, Lalla felt sorry for her. But it was only for a moment.

SEVEN

On the return drive to London, Cecil gave himself an excellent notice for the performance he had just given. It had not been the best of circumstances, a tea-time matinée with a hostile audience, but he had worked hard and well, and by the end he had won his audience over completely to his side. Admittedly he had been at a slight advantage, because his audience was not antagonistic to him personally, but rather to what he had to voice. In fact, had he just been allowed to be himself, he would have found himself warmly received from the moment he first appeared in the drawing room, because Mrs Nicholls had always liked Cecil and had regularly and openly made it quite plain that she would welcome him as a son-in-law. In fact when he first telephoned to ask if he might visit, saying that he wished to talk to her about Pippa, Mrs Nicholls had responded most affectionately and invited him down immediately. But unfortunately the moment Cecil ceased small-talking and began to perform what he had so carefully rehearsed, he lost his audience's sympathy.

Mrs Nicholls waited until Cecil had finished before she spoke, although such was her astonishment, she had tried to interrupt him and call him back to his senses on several occasions. But Cecil was in full cry, and like all amateur actors so totally enthralled by his own performance, that he was unstoppable. So Mrs Nicholls saved her breath until he had finished presenting his preposterous argument.

Then, after Cecil had poured them both a sherry, Mrs Nicholls told him what she thought. She said she found his reasoning difficult to accept, since she had always been under the impression that Cecil was keen on her daughter himself, and yet here he was making out an impassioned case as to why she should be allowed to marry someone else, and not only that but an *actor* of all people, a member of a profession for which Cecil avowedly had very little time, even though he earned his living from them. So often, she reminded him, she had sat in this very room and heard Cecil belittling actors, declaring himself to have no time for their introspection and self-indulgence. So why was this young man any different? Why should the lowly born Jerome Didier, who came from a broken home and had spent his formative years living in a disused railway carriage, brought up by a crowd of social misfits, why should he deserve such serious consideration as a possible husband for someone such as Pippa?

This was where Cecil had been most proud of himself, he reflected as he headed through Haselmere. For if there had been a moment where he might have weakened and revealed the truth of his feelings, this had been it. But he had triumphed. He had stayed, as it was known in the profession, *in character,* and argued most convincingly with Pippa's mother as to the worth of someone he privately considered worthless. Jerome Didier was an exception, he had assured her, not only as a talent, but as a human being. He was honest, dedicated to his craft, diligent, and possessed an integrity Cecil had never previously encountered before in an actor. But most importantly, he promised her, Jerome Didier loved Pippa with a passion and a truth which was far and away out of the ordinary.

Mrs Nicholls had fallen silent here, Cecil remembered, as he drove on for Guildford, because, and this hurt Cecil even to think of it, she knew it to be true. She would have seen it for herself, every time Jerome visited Bay Tree Cottage, she would have seen it in those dark expressive eyes of his, and heard it in that mellifluous voice. She knew both Jerome and Jerome's passion were distinctive and dangerously so. Cecil knew that from the tenor of her next question, which she had already answered in her mind before she even asked it, before she carefully enquired of him what would happen to Pippa and Jerome if she went on forbidding their union.

Two things, Cecil had answered, gravely and only after apparently careful consideration. Jerome would take Pippa to live with him in London, and marry her when she was twenty-one, or they would elope now, as Jerome had once suggested to Cecil that he might, and marry in Scotland. Those were the two eventualities. The one thing that was a certainty was that Jerome would never let her daughter go.

They drank a second sherry, mostly in silence, while Mrs Nicholls sat looking out into her beautiful garden and at the view of the Downs beyond, deliberating the situation. Cecil said no more, being careful not to try and prompt a response, lest he overplay his hand. He had said all he had rehearsed himself to say, and said it convincingly. That was perfectly apparent from the time Mrs Nicholls was giving to her considerations. Had he been less than convincing, she would have summarily dismissed his arguments out of hand.

'I know this is not for you to say, Cecil,' she had said finally, 'but I need to say it to somebody besides Pippa. Because – well, I do have to consider my own situation, and not just hers. I do have to think about what will happen when Pippa does finally leave here, however and with whoever. I have to consider carefully and properly and quite precisely what will happen to me.'

Happily Cecil had included this problem in his scenario, because his own mother was constantly reminding him of Mrs Nicholls' concern, although usually adding the rider that in her opinion her neighbour used her affliction quite cynically as a way of keeping her daughter at home as an unpaid servant. So having been well prepared for it, he had a ready answer, which was that since Mrs Nicholls would have to face this eventuality sooner or later, it might be more salutary to face it now, so that a decision could be made, as the law would have it, *without prejudice*. A companion was really all that was needed since Mrs Nicholls was under the constant supervision of the local doctor, and provided she had some basic help was still well able to cope with her daily routine, Cecil had gathered from his mother, so a companion was what he suggested. Since Mrs Nicholls was so fond of her daughter, Cecil argued, the least she could do was to allow her the full freedom of choice. If she wished to marry Jerome, she would do so anyway. That was the nature of Pippa and that was the nature of her relationship with Jerome. However, on the other hand, if she wished to stay at home and look after her mother more, then she would be able to make that choice unencumbered by feelings of guilt, if Mrs Nicholls found and employed a companion for herself.

There was no further argument. Cecil had won the day. Mrs Nicholls even offered him her forehead to kiss before he left, and thanked him most sincerely for the help and the guidance he had given her at this difficult time. Cecil rejoiced. For now if everything else fell into place, as he felt sure that it would, one day, and it didn't matter when, but one day, some day, Pippa Nicholls would most definitely be his.

To celebrate the fact, as he left Guildford behind him, Cecil sounded the horn on his Bentley dah-di-di-dah-dah, dah-dah, and doffed his hat at the driver of the solitary Riley passing by the other way. He had made the sacrifice, and he knew it would pay off. For – as someone had once written so sagely in his childhood autograph book – nothing real was ever gained without a sacrifice of some kind.

As soon as Pippa returned on her bike from the shops, her mother called her into the drawing room.

'Cecil Manners was just here,' she said. 'For tea.'

'In the middle of the week?' Pippa asked. 'Any particular reason?'

'He wanted to discuss you,' her mother replied.

Pippa laughed, as she poured herself some orange squash.

'Oh lord,' she said, 'don't tell me he's got *serious*.'

'Don't talk in that way,' her mother sighed. 'You're beginning to sound like your actor.'

'Well has he?' Pippa continued, ignoring the jibe. 'Has poor old Cecil got "serious"?'

'No,' her mother replied sharply. 'On the contrary, he was here to discuss you and that young man.'

Pippa looked round at her mother, and then came over to sit in the armchair opposite her. She took a sip of her drink and then looked up.

'I really don't see what business it is of Cecil's,' she said. 'I thought people's managers only managed their business affairs.'

'I don't think that's very funny, Pippa,' her mother ruled.

'Neither do I,' Pippa agreed. 'It wasn't meant to be.'

'This actor—'

'Jerome. You know his name, Mother, so you might as well use it.'

'I want to know how you feel about him.'

'So that you can send me up to my room without any supper?' Pippa wondered, half-teasingly.

'I want to know how you feel about him,' her mother insisted.

'Very well,' Pippa replied, looking her mother straight in the eye. 'The way I feel about him is that I love him, and I want to marry him.'

'That's rather what I thought,' her mother said, pulling her cardigan round her shoulders. 'And if that's the case, I think you should wait. I think you should wait for at least a year.'

'Why?' Pippa frowned. 'I don't see what difference it will make.'

'It could make all the difference.'

'It won't. All that will happen will be that we'll have lost a year. And I think that's unreasonable. I've never understood long engagements. You either want to get married, or you don't.'

'I never said anything about getting engaged.'

'You said we should wait a year.'

'I didn't say anything about getting *engaged*.'

'I see.' Pippa raised her eyebrows and shrugged. 'Well. Being engaged's only a formality. The point is, the real point, is how people feel about each other.'

'Pippa,' her mother warned. 'Remember you are not yet twenty.'

'I shall be twenty next week. You were only eighteen when you were married.'

'That was different.'

'Yes, it was,' Pippa agreed. 'You were nearly two years younger.'

'Your father came from a proper background. A military background. This young man is an actor.'

'You make him sound like some sort of pariah.'

'Well?'

Her mother stared at her challengingly.

'You think actors are pariahs?' Pippa asked.

'I do not think an actor would make the ideal match,' her mother replied.

'It's perfectly all right to put on a uniform and go round killing people, of course,' Pippa said, looking at the photographs of her father and brother.

In return her mother sighed in deep irritation.

'You're not only beginning to sound like your actor,' she said, 'you're also beginning to parrot him.'

'I'm sorry, but Jerome does have a point, mother,' Pippa replied. 'After all, the very worst an actor can do is bore you.'

'Or leave you,' her mother retorted.

'I don't think desertion's confined to the acting profession, do you?' Pippa wondered.

'Be serious, Pippa.'

'I am being serious.'

'No, you're not. Just consider what could happen. Suppose you did marry this boy, and just suppose he did leave you. Where would you be then?'

'Alone,' Pippa replied. 'Again.'

'You're not alone now, Pippa. Don't be absurd.'

'No, I'm not,' Pippa agreed. 'Because I have Jerome.'

Her mother looked at her once more, then having pulled her cardigan even more tightly round her shoulders, held up her empty glass and asked Pippa to pour her another sherry.

'I had no idea you were this serious,' she said, as she took the replenished glass, breaking the silence.

'Neither had I,' Pippa replied, going to stand by the french windows.

'No idea at all.'

Her mother sipped her sherry, while Pippa stared out into the gardens, wondering what or who really lay behind Cecil's call, and then wondering it out loud.

'You still haven't really said what Cecil wanted,' she said.

'It's not really any of your business, Pippa,' her mother replied. 'He came to see me.'

Pippa laughed, not derisively, but out of genuine amusement.

'Of course it's to do with me!' she returned. 'You said he came to discuss Jerome and me. I don't see who else's business it can be.'

'Very well,' her mother said, after sitting with her eyes closed for a minute. 'If you really must know, he's worried about your young man. About his future. He's not at all sure that getting married would be the very best thing for – for his client at this particular moment.'

'No, mother,' Pippa shook her head, and leaned her back against the doorway, still looking down the gardens. 'I don't really believe that, I'm afraid. If that was so, that would be between him and Jerome. He wouldn't have trekked all the way down here in the middle of the week to tell you about his professional worries.'

She turned her head back to see her mother's response, but apparently there was none. Her mother was just sitting in her chair, looking at Pippa stonefaced, while she sipped her sherry, holding the glass with both hands. It wasn't until Pippa had looked away out into the garden again that Mrs Nicholls responded, holding her half-full sherry glass over the hearth, and then deliberately dropping it.

'Damn,' she said as Pippa whipped round in surprise. 'I'm sorry for swearing, but I'm getting so clumsy.'

'I'm getting clumsy, Pippa,' her mother insisted. 'It has to be faced.'

They were now having dinner together in the kitchen, a fish pie Pippa had cooked and which her mother was apparently having some difficulty in managing. The subject of Pippa and Jerome had not been re-aired since the accident with the sherry glass.

'You're not getting clumsy, Mother,' Pippa reassured her. 'You were knitting this afternoon when I went out. And you managed your lamb cutlets at lunch all right.'

167

'Managed, yes,' her mother sighed. 'That's what it boils down to really, when all is said and done. Whether or not I *manage*. Whether or not I *can* manage.'

'I think you can manage,' Pippa said quietly, watching without being seen as her mother made another half-hearted attempt to spoon up some pie.

'It's easy for you to say, Pippa,' her mother replied, dropping her spoon and fork as if defeated. 'But I'm not sure I could manage without you.'

'You could get somebody,' Pippa said.

'That's exactly what Cecil said.'

Pippa now caught her mother's eye, deliberately, and reached across the table, putting one of her hands on one of her mother's.

'If Cecil had come here to say how much he didn't want Jerome and I to get married, Mother,' she said, 'then what was he doing recommending that you get someone in to help you?'

Now her mother really did abandon her dinner, pushing her plate to one side as she balefully regarded her youngest child.

'And what – pray – would exactly happen if you *don't* marry this boy?'

'Jerome.'

'Whatever his name is.'

'Jerome.'

'What will happen if you don't marry him?'

'Nothing will happen, Mother,' Pippa replied, shaking her head. 'If I don't marry him now, if you say I can't, the world won't catch on fire or anything. All that will happen is I shall simply wait until I can marry him.'

'I see.' Mrs Nicholls stared past her daughter for a moment, and then clasped her hands together in front of her on the table, looking down at them. 'Which means I suppose you'd go on living here.'

'No. It means I'd go and live with Jerome in London.'

'If you did that, Pippa, I'd make you a ward of court.'

'That would be very sad, Mother. But I don't think you would. Because we don't have that kind of a relationship. Do you want some apple pie?'

Her mother sat in silence once again while Pippa cleared up around her, finally serving her with apple pie which she had already cut into small pieces before sitting back down at the table.

'You're quite determined, are you, Pippa?' her mother asked, ignoring her pudding. 'You've set your heart on this young man.'

Pippa thought carefully before she replied, and then nodded.

'My heart is set,' she replied. 'Yes.'

'I see,' her mother said, and then pushed her pudding to one side.

The following weekend Doris Huxley moved out of her rented accommodation in the village and into Bay Tree Cottage.

'Mrs Huxley is your number one choice, is she?' Pippa asked her mother, when she discovered what was happening.

'Don't you like Doris Huxley?' her mother asked her back. 'She's got no-one either, you know. Not since she lost her husband last year.'

Ignoring the nuance, Pippa simply aired her concern that her mother's chosen companion might not prove the absolutely best choice for the job. She had heard rumours about Mrs Huxley ever since she was a small girl, although they were never very precise, since children's gossip is inclined to be rather unspecific, relying more on wild generalizations. One thing which Pippa had heard supposed since she had matured, however, was that Mrs Huxley drank.

She mentioned this to her mother.

'Nonsense,' her mother declared. 'Doris likes a drink when we're playing cards, that's all. She'd hardly be treasurer of the Parish Council if she was an inebriate, now would she?'

'Someone who drinks wouldn't be the ideal person, that's all I was thinking,' Pippa replied. 'You know, in case of an emergency or something.'

'It's simply because she's a woman,' Pippa's mother continued in defence of her chosen companion. 'If a woman is seen to take a drink, she's a drunk. If a man has a drink, he's a jolly good fellow.'

Pippa laughed in agreement, and put the doubts out of her mind. After all, the two women had known each other for years, ever since Pippa's mother had moved into Bay Tree Cottage, and in the last ten years had become close friends through their mutual love of bridge. The fact that Pippa didn't particularly like Doris Huxley was immaterial, since her mother did, and it was her mother she was going to be paid to look after.

More importantly, much more importantly, the appointment of her mother's bridge partner as her help and companion meant that her mother had consented to Pippa marrying Jerome. It was never said in so many words, but Pippa took Mrs Huxley's engagement to mean that the necessary consent was no longer to be withheld, and holding her breath, started privately and then publicly to make the necessary arrangements for her and Jerome to be married. To her infinite relief, her mother raised no further objections.

*

They had planned to go to Florence for their honeymoon. They had even bought a book about the city, by Guglielmo Amerighi, a beautiful volume wrapped in a paper cover of faint gold, which Pippa read avidly from cover to cover, not once but several times, with the result that she fell wildly in love with the city long before setting eyes on it.

'In that case, we won't go,' Jerome announced one Sunday on their walk.

'Jerome—' Pippa began.

'No listen, my darling,' Jerome interrupted. 'I'm perfectly serious. If the city means that much to you, and as you say if there are so many beautiful things to see, then it's not the place to go on honeymoon.'

Pippa was about to protest further when she saw the sense in what Jerome was saying, so instead of arguing she hugged his arm even more tightly with hers, and laughed with delight.

'I'd feel simply dreadful,' Jerome sighed. 'Lying in bed all morning, making love to you – going back to bed after lunch to make more love to you, and then lying there in bed, too exhausted to go anywhere. I couldn't bear the guilt! With that wonderful city out there! And all its wonderful treasures! *Unseen*! No, we can't go to Florence until we can bear being out of bed for at least four hours at a stretch. We shall go to Brighton instead.'

Pippa was hugely amused by Jerome's outrageousness, as well as secretly thrilled, because she herself could think of little else than lying in a bed somewhere and sometime soon in Jerome's loving arms. She also knew he was right about not going somewhere quite as wonderful as Florence for their honeymoon, because by the time they got there, they would have eyes not for the paintings of Fra Angelico, the carvings of Donatello, the frescoes of Masaccio, or the architecture of Brunelleschi, but only for each other. Florence would have to wait a little longer, until Jerome and she were grown accustomed.

They were married in Pippa's Parish Church, at the end of the first week in February. It was a small ceremony, attended by just family and close friends, which on Pippa's side included her mother, her Aunt Bea, and her brother, James, home on special leave from his regiment in Germany, who gave her away, and on Jerome's side his mother, his closest friends from Carriagetown and drama school, Cecil Manners who acted as his best man, and Elizabeth.

Elizabeth behaved impeccably throughout, the only tears she shed being recognizably theatrical ones when the couple took their vows. She made no attempt to upstage the bride, and impressed everyone present with the modesty of her behaviour and of her appearance, although of course everyone noted and privately commented on her astonishing beauty.

'She's the most beautiful young woman I have ever seen,' Pippa's mother confessed, as she helped her daughter get dressed to go away. 'I've never seen a complexion like it. And those *eyes*.'

'I couldn't agree more,' Pippa said happily, as she buttoned up her new, bright yellow wool coat. 'She's actually very nice as well. As a person.'

'She's very nice,' her mother agreed. 'She's not a bit like an actress. Now let me look at you.'

Her mother turned her daughter to her, then she looked at her, searchingly, her eyes roaming over Pippa's face, as if she was seeing her for the very first time.

'I just hope this young man deserves you, Pippa,' she said, brushing her daughter's wayward hair from her eyes.

'Jerome,' Pippa groaned. 'Just for once call him by his name. After all, he is your son-in-law now.'

'He looked very handsome in his morning dress,' her mother commented. 'Quite the part. And you looked lovely, too. It's just a pity your father isn't alive.'

'Yes,' Pippa agreed, pausing in her preparation. 'I know. But I felt him watching.'

'I wonder what he thought,' her mother mused, adjusting the angle of Pippa's hat. 'I just wonder.'

'Thought about what exactly, Mother?'

'You know. You being married. You being married so young. You're still so young.'

There was a knock on the door, precluding any more of this particular conversation.

'Everyone's waiting, Pip,' her brother said, putting his head round the door. 'Or are you going to be even later than usual?'

James grinned at his sister, and then came in to give her one last kiss and hug before she left home.

'Mind her hair, James,' Mrs Nicholls said. 'And her hat. For goodness sake.'

'I'm so glad you could make it, James,' Pippa whispered. 'And so is Jerome.'

'I only hope I marry someone as beautiful as he is handsome,' James replied. 'You just keep your eye on him.'

'No point in him keeping his eye on me I suppose?' Pippa asked, tongue in cheek.

171

'An ugly old frump like you?' James laughed. 'Heavens, no!'

Brother and sister kissed each other once more, and then James was gone, hurrying away to make sure all the tin cans were still in place underneath Jerome's sports car.

'Well,' her mother said, taking one of Pippa's hands. 'Well, there you are. You've got what you want, Pippa. Now all we must hope is you want what you get.'

'That's a happy little parting thought, Mother,' Pippa laughed. 'Where did you read that? In some Russian Christmas cracker or something?'

'We all make our own beds you know, Pippa.'

'I know, Mother.' Pippa picked up her new navy blue leather gloves and began to put them on. 'I know,' she agreed. 'And this is mine, and I'm more than happy to lie in it.'

'Good,' her mother replied. 'And just remember one more thing. Despair doesn't have to be tolerated, you know. There's no rule that says that it does. If, and I'm only saying if, if any situation becomes intolerable, there is no shame whatsoever in walking away from it. Just remember that. The way out can just as easily be the way in, sometimes.'

Pippa paused before picking up her handbag, and looked back at her mother, who was standing looking back at her. Then she put her arms around her gently and carefully, and held her in her arms.

'Goodbye, Mother,' she said softly, almost in a whisper. 'Take care of yourself.'

'Goodbye,' her mother wished her, reaching up to kiss her daughter on one cheek. 'Goodbye, darling Pippa.'

'Why do you think we love each other?' Pippa asked Jerome, as they walked the windswept seafront at Brighton with their arms wound tightly around each other. 'I wonder why it is.'

'It's because we're completely different,' Jerome announced later, as Pippa and he lay in each other's arms in the bed of the bridal suite in the Grand Hotel, safe from the storm that was raging outside. 'That's why we love each other, because we're so completely unalike. And that's why we'll endure. Because for any marriage or partnership to succeed, that's what it has to be. What we are. The union of opposites.'

'Do you think that's really what we are?' Pippa asked, suddenly afraid that she might be altogether too different from Jerome for her ever to understand him.

'We couldn't be *more* different, my love,' Jerome whispered, running his fingers through her hair as she laid her head on his chest. 'Which is the very reason I shall always be so utterly intrigued by you. I shall never get to the bottom of you, never. Nor you of me. Until our dying days, we shall never, *ever* fully understand each other.'

He kissed her luxuriant head of hair, and held her to him even more tightly.

'What about you and Elizabeth?' Pippa asked, turning her large grey eyes up at him.

'What about me and Elizabeth?' Jerome retorted, with a scold in his voice. 'Who's talking about me and Elizabeth?'

'Are you both very different?'

'What have Elizabeth and I got to do with it?'

Pippa frowned, as if Jerome was missing the obvious point.

'You're a partnership, aren't you?'

'No!' Jerome replied, raising his voice dramatically. 'No we are *not* a partnership, Pippa Nicholls—'

'Didier.'

'We are *not* – a partnership, Mrs Didier! And you are *never* – to refer to us, or even to think of us as such!' Jerome replied, turning Pippa on her back and pinning her by her arms down to the bed.

'Try and stop me.'

'I mean it, freckles,' Jerome warned. 'I am seriously – serious.'

'So am I,' Pippa replied, before biting him on the arm, and as Jerome let go, rolling away from under him.

'You savage!' he yelled delightedly. 'You are now going to pay for that!'

'Oh, I do hope so,' Pippa laughed, swiping him round the head with a feather pillow as he advanced on her. 'I really do hope so!'

Later, when Pippa stirred from the depths of her love-sleep, she found Jerome standing at the darkened windows in his dressing gown, staring at the invisible sea.

'Are you all right?' she asked a little anxiously, sensing a change of mood.

'Of course, Mrs Didier,' Jerome replied without turning. 'I am absolutely A.1.'

He took a battered packet of Senior Service from his dressing-gown pocket, and ferreted out a cigarette.

'It's just that – well,' he paused to light his cigarette. 'It's just that ever since we've come out of the play, all the talk's been of what we're going to do next. What *we're* going to do, Pippa. Not what Elizabeth's going to do, and what I'm going to do – separately. No. What *we're* going to do.'

'You've been offered that play. Just you, that is.'

173

'Yes. But in this case, my love, the play is not the thing. In this case the film's the thing. And the film – is for Didier and Laurence, as Boska is already billing us.'

'Can you afford not to do it?' Pippa asked, meaning exactly what she said.

'No, Mrs Didier,' Jerome sighed from the window. 'I can neither afford not to do it, nor can I not afford to do it, if you take my meaning. Anyway, I'm contracted! And who am I? Who am I to defy the mighty Dmitri Boska?'

Pippa sat up, pulled her robe on and around her, and then got up to go to Jerome.

'Jerome,' she said, putting her arms round him from behind. 'Tell me what you're afraid of. I'm not sure I understand.'

'I'm afraid of being half of something, Pippa,' he told her. 'I'm afraid of being a twin talent. I'm afraid of being *Them. Oh I saw Them in* Antony and Cleopatra. *Did you? No I saw Them in* Under The Bridges. *I'm dying to see Them in their new film. You mean you haven't seen Them in their new film? Oh, well* She *is Just Wonderful. Just Wonderful.'*

'And what's he like?' Pippa asked gently, resting her face against Jerome's back.

'*He's all right*,' Jerome replied, still in his *vox pop*. '*He's very good. But it's her I've always liked. I think she's* wonderful.'

'I think he's wonderful,' Pippa said, hugging him to her.

Jerome fell silent, smoking his cigarette, and gazing out at the darkness.

'Elizabeth walked away with the notices for the play, Pippa,' he said at last. 'She cleaned me. It was Laurence first, Didier nowhere.'

'That simply isn't true,' Pippa argued, turning her husband round to her. 'The critics praised you unanimously.'

'Second to eulogizing over Elizabeth,' Jerome replied.

'Nonsense, Jerome,' Pippa retorted. 'Sometimes you're really very childish. The critics were bound to go for Elizabeth over you. The people who wrote about you were all men – and Elizabeth is an exceptionally beautiful girl. Do use your head.'

Jerome looked at Pippa, and carefully brushed a braid of hair away from her face, before leaning over and kissing her softly.

'You're biased,' he said. 'You don't count.'

'You're cuckoo,' she replied. 'You don't think.'

She kissed him this time, without holding on to him, without touching any part of him with herself except her mouth on his. But with her kiss she still drew him towards her, daring this time to explore the dark of his mouth with the tip of her tongue, feeling the warm softness of the inside of his cheeks and sensing the curling reply his own tongue made, and the gentle bite of his teeth on her bottom lip. He put his hands on her waist as they kissed again, but she eased them away so that there was still no other contact but their kiss.

She loosed the sash on his dressing gown so that it fell open on his naked body underneath, and traced the contours of it lightly with her fingernails, down his back and up, down his small firm buttocks and around and up the inside of his thighs, up along the line between the top of his thighs and his pelvis, deliberately just missing his sex which she could feel hardening against her, drawing her nails carefully round it and up slowly on to his stomach, a teasing process which excited Jerome so much he gasped, throwing his head back from her and trying once more to take her in his arms. But again Pippa wouldn't allow this, whispering to him that he mustn't, that he must just stand there and do nothing, while she slipped the silky gown down from his shoulders and off his body so that he stood fully naked before her.

And when he did, she stood back, away from him, not far, just a foot or so, just enough distance for her to see him, to let her look at him up and down and then into his eyes, as they both just stood there, quite, quite still, Jerome naked and ready, opposite Pippa in her white *broderie anglaise* robe, looking at each other, standing, watching, waiting on the edge. Jerome raised his eyebrows at her unmoving look, feigning his best mock surprise, as if to say *imagine-that*, while widening his dark eyes at her and trying to force her to smile. But Pippa just stared back at him and stared him out, so that in another attempt to coax a smile from her, Jerome crossed his arms over his naked chest and then his legs as well.

Pippa refused to be amused by this either, showing her displeasure by suddenly pinching Jerome on his upper arm. Jerome was genuinely surprised by this reprimand, and put his other hand up to rub where he had been hit. But Pippa stopped him from doing that as well, taking his hand and putting it back down by his side, where she also made him put his other hand. Jerome widened his eyes further, turning the look into a mock glare, as if to frighten her, to intimidate her, to reassert his supremacy. But Pippa wasn't to be deterred by that either. Instead she took him by the hand and led him over to the vast walk-in wardrobe, where taking him utterly by surprise she shut him in.

175

'Pippa?' he called from within. 'Pippa?'

'Sorry!' Pippa called back. 'Not at home!'

'Pippa?' He rattled the heavy doors, but Pippa had them locked. 'What are you *doing*?'

Pippa refused to answer, getting into bed instead, and pinching herself hard under the sheets to stop herself from laughing.

'Pippaaaaa!' Jerome howled from inside the cupboards, with mock-tragic anguish. 'Why are you doing this to me? What have I *done*?'

'You've been a complete clot,' Pippa replied, still pinching herself to keep her voice straight, even though by now there were tears of laughter coursing down her cheeks. 'And you're not going to be allowed out and into bed until you apologize.'

'But what have I been a *clot* – about, Mrs Didier?' Jerome howled, making himself sound very childish and sad. 'I cannot begin to reason!'

Pippa sighed, play-acting every bit as well as Jerome. Then she sighed again, clicked her tongue and examined the state of her fingernails.

'What you've been a clot about is yourself,' she called back at last. 'And until you realize quite how wonderful you are, you are not allowed back into bed.'

'I realize it!' Jerome whooped from the cupboards. 'I realize it! I realize! And I'm sorry! I realize just how wonderful I am – and so now will you let me out of here?'

Pippa did, hopping out of bed quickly and unlocking the doors and then back in double quick time with Jerome in hot pursuit.

He caught her, just as she threw herself on to the bed, in a despairing last ditch effort to stay out of his reach.

'Right,' he said. 'You've asked for it.'

'Oh good,' sighed Pippa.

Jerome brought the subject up again over dinner, and for doing so he was rewarded with the gift of a brussel sprout in his wine glass.

'Mrs Didier,' Jerome began, grinning helplessly at the floating cabbage-bud.

'You can't say you haven't been warned,' Pippa interrupted. 'You can just thank your lucky stars we're not upstairs.'

'I simply wanted to say one thing,' Jerome assured her, after a waiter had tactfully replaced his desecrated glass with a clean one. 'I simply wanted to explain how I felt about this wretched partnership thing. In case at some point you mistook my motives.'

'What motives?'

'This is my last word on the matter, Mrs D. You see, the powers that be, Boska, Locke's, even Cecil, they really are lining us up to be the next or the new whatever.'

'Laurel and Hardy, you mean?' Pippa asked, carefully dissecting her sole. 'Her Laurel, you Hardy?'

'I think they're thinking more Tom and Jerry,' Jerome replied. 'Me Tom, her Jerry.'

'You have thirty seconds,' Pippa said eyeing him over a lightly laden fork. 'Starting now.'

Jerome took a deep breath and began.

'As I told you,' he said, running all his words together, 'I didn't become an actor to be part of some double act a double act that as sure as eggs will turn one of us into a stooge and even if it doesn't it won't allow either of us a full and separate identity we'll always be whisky and soda curds and whey salt and pepper vulgar and flash you name it we'll be it and *that's not what I want* I want to be me Jerome Didier and I want to do the work I want to do without having to be shoe-horned into an unending series of two handers because that's what it'll be Mrs Didier mark my words if I weakened and allowed them their wicked way I would spend the best part and by that I mean the worst part of my professional career as one half of a double bill and I don't want that and I won't do it so after this film *this one film* which I can't get out of and that's that after this one wretched film with Elizabeth *that is it* after that I do what I want to do and only what I want to do and if possible only when I want to do it and there's an end to it.'

'Bravo,' Pippa put down her knife and fork to clap her hands. 'It's your life, Jerome, so you must do exactly what you want with it.'

'Do you really mean that?'

'Of course I really mean it.'

'But do you really know what it means? If I turn my back on this particular devil?'

'It means you get to do what you want,' Pippa said. 'Everyone has the right to say no.'

'But their way,' Jerome warned her. 'You must remember that their way, Mrs Didier, we could get rich.'

'Socks,' said Pippa.

'*Socks?*' Jerome queried disbelievingly.

'Yes socks,' Pippa repeated, smiling at him suddenly. 'What do you mean – we could get rich? We're rich already.'

They spent the second week of an increasingly blissful fortnight in Devon, in the back bedroom of an old smugglers' inn, which nestled in the heart of a sleepy village not a quarter of a mile from the sea. There was no-one else staying, so they had the sole attention of the owners, a retired army major and his wife who spoiled them entirely. After a long breakfast in bed, brought to them by a permanently blushing maid called Brenda, they would go off for the day, to walk the pebble beaches and climb the long steep paths up to the top of the windswept cliffs. On these outings, Jerome would take photographs of Pippa when she wasn't ready, and Pippa would sketch Jerome when he wasn't looking. They would take bags of stale bread supplied by the major and his wife to feed the swooping, cawing army of gulls and gannets, along with their own packed lunches of slices of homemade pie, squashy ham or chicken sandwiches, bars of dark chocolate and baby bottles of Green Shield Worthington, to which Pippa took such a liking the bevy became known as Pip's Tip.

On their return in the late afternoon, they would tiptoe back to bed, where they would stay until just before dinner, for which they solemnly dressed up, even though they were the only people staying. Dinner was always delicious, and whatever they wanted, which in Pippa's case was invariably two puddings, and then afterwards they would play darts and shove ha'penny with the locals until they *corpsed rotten*, which as Jerome taught Pippa was the theatrical vernacular for suffering from a terminal fit of the giggles. Pippa had never even imagined that such a happiness could exist, and neither had Jerome. And there was no need to refer to their mutual state because it was perfectly self-apparent.

Instead they spent their time teasing each other, and playing games, Jerome discovering to his delight, although not to his surprise, that Pippa was not only well up to him, but in many cases way in advance of him when it came to what they christened *juss-kiddin'*. She once managed to *juss-kid* Jerome for a whole day, much to his astonishment when he found out the truth at bedtime.

'You amaze me, Mrs D,' he said, as they got into bed. 'You're quite an actress.'

'No I'm not,' Pippa replied. 'You're just a sucker.'

'Be that as it may,' Jerome told her, removing from her the nightdress she had only just put on. 'Maybe this new-found talent is too good to waste.'

'Oh, I don't think so,' Pippa disagreed, idly counting the hairs on Jerome's naked chest. 'I don't really have the need to act.'

'You mean I do?'

'Yes,' Pippa replied. 'Of course you do.'

*

In this way, as in every way, Pippa was good for Jerome. Having never been let off a hook in her life, even by herself, she expected the same from everyone else. She expected people to face up to whatever home-truths they needed to be told, since she believed this was the only way to discover who you really were.

'It's true, you know, Jerome,' she said one midday, as they sat in the shelter of an enormous rock having their picnic. 'The proper study of mankind is man.'

'I disagree,' Jerome replied. 'I think the proper study of mankind is women.'

'Really?' Pippa said, throwing a crust to the gulls. 'Do you regret getting married then?'

'Why should I regret getting married, Pippa Didier?'

'If you like studying women that much.'

Pippa shook her hair out, and turned to look at him.

'I'm sure I shall regret many things in my life, Pippa,' Jerome replied. 'But the one thing I shall never regret is having met and married you.'

Their return to London was not a bit like going back to school, which during dinner on their last night Pippa had said she very much feared that it might be. Jerome at once cheered her out of any impending depression by reminding her they had a brand new home awaiting them, a pretty little unfurnished mews house Jerome had rented for them, immediately off Kensington High Street. They were doubly lucky in that Jerome was also in work, with filming on Dmitri Boska's production of *The Eve of Night* due to start the following week. Not only that, as soon as they were unpacked and settled in the intention was to drive straight down to Sussex to have lunch with Pippa's mother and to collect Bobby, who much to Pippa's delight was to come and live with them in London.

'So there you are, Mrs Didier,' Jerome had said, raising his wine glass. 'It won't be even remotely like returning to school, or *Real Life* as you so gloomily predict. It will be the start of a whole new adventure.'

They had stayed up so late unpacking and sorting everything out on their return that they slept through the alarm the next morning. In fact, when Pippa heard the ringing, she reached out sleepily to turn off the clock only to find the bell had long ago sounded. A moment later she realized it was the telephone, and so she nudged Jerome awake to tell him.

'Why don't you answer it?' he mumbled from beneath the bedding. 'You live here too, remember?'

'It's bound to be for you,' Pippa replied, putting the pillow over her head. 'Like last night. Yet another change of call.'

Jerome groaned, rolled out of bed and staggered off to answer the phone. While he was gone, Pippa turned over to settle herself even more deeply under the thick warm blankets and found herself staring at Fred Bear, Jerome's one-armed and almost bald Teddy, which travelled with him everywhere.

'Good morning, Fred,' Pippa smiled and yawned. 'Welcome to Heaven.'

By the time Jerome returned, Pippa had fallen back into a gentle drowse, with Jerome's childhood toy held in the hand of an arm outstretched across his pillow. For a long time he just stood looking down on the girl he loved already so deeply, before taking a slow deep breath and sitting down on her side of the bed.

'Who was it?' she murmured, turning and putting her arms around his waist, still clutching the toy. 'Don't they know it's Sunday?'

'It was for you, my darling,' Jerome answered, staring at the white painted wall, wondering how to tell her.

'Was?' Pippa yawned, now resting her head against his back. 'If it's a "was" call and they didn't want to speak to me, it can't have been important. So come back to bed.'

But Jerome stayed where he was.

'It was important, Pip,' he said quietly. 'Something purely dreadful has happened.'

'What?' Pippa sat up at once, grabbing Jerome by the shoulders. 'What has happened?'

'Something quite, quite dreadful,' was all Jerome could find to say as he stared into eyes which were already wide with fright.

'It's Bobby, isn't it?' she said. 'Isn't it, Jerome? It's Bobby. He's been run over.'

She looked so bewildered, so puzzled and fearful, Jerome just wanted to take her in his arms and rock her, hold her to him, hold her and rock her and tell her that everything was going to be all right. But he couldn't. Not until he had broken the news. Not until he had told her what he had just been told. Until then, and even more importantly, afterwards, he must be strong. He must remain strong, and he must tell her as calmly as he could about the terrible thing which had just happened.

'Darling Pip,' he said, barely able to look at that precious face and those gentle grey eyes so full of love. 'My darling girl, Pippa

180

darling, it's your mother, Pip. Darling Pippa your mother's *dead*.'

It was unacceptable. To Pippa, like most people who face moments such as these, the fact of her mother's sudden death was unacceptable. As she kept saying to Jerome, over and over again, one moment her mother was there, in their lives, in life itself, and the next she was gone. She was gone totally, gone from her bedroom, her house, her village, gone from the very air she had breathed only a moment ago.

Not only was it unacceptable because it was so totally unexpected, it was inadmissible because of the mystery surrounding its circumstances. There was no suicide note, nor it seemed had there been any indication that anything might have been amiss, at least certainly not according to Mrs Doris Huxley. On the Saturday morning the two women had gone for a long drive in Mrs Huxley's old Morris round the lanes that run along the foot of the Downs, and had lunch in a pub at East Dean. On their return to Bay Tree Cottage they found the postman had called in their absence, and that the mail included yet another postcard from Pippa, the third one she had sent all told, sending her mother both their love and confirming that they would be back in London on Saturday night and down to Sussex the following day for lunch.

In the evening they had played bridge, as they did every Saturday evening, with Dr Weaver and his wife Nora. Dr Weaver, besides being Mrs Nicholls' GP, was also a close family friend of long standing. It had been a very relaxed and good humoured evening, according to Mrs Huxley, with the home side thrashing the visitors at the card table, and everyone enjoying the contest. So much so that Dr Weaver was moved to take Doris Huxley aside just before he left in order to tell her how impressed he was with his patient's wellbeing, and to opine that the new arrangement was obviously proving a great success.

Mrs Huxley related that Pippa's mother and she had sat up for a while longer talking over the events of the evening and having a general 'chinwag', as she deemed it, before retiring for the night. Doris Huxley looked in on her charge on her way back from the bathroom to make sure all was well, and found her sitting up in bed reading. Mrs Huxley had asked if Pippa's mother needed anything, and on receiving a negative answer, they had wished each other good night, and Mrs Huxley had then proceeded to bed.

This was all repeated at the inquest, which Jerome attended with Pippa's brother, James, home from Germany on compassionate leave, but without Pippa, it having been decided that since she

181

would not be called to give evidence, her attendance could cause her nothing but further grief.

'And that was all?' the coroner asked, when Doris Huxley had finished. 'There were absolutely no signs of anything untoward whatsoever?'

'Nothing at all,' Mrs Huxley assured him. 'I'm not the best of sleepers myself, anything wakes me. But I heard nothing at all that night.'

'I gather the deceased was in the habit of taking sleeping pills,' the coroner asked when Dr Weaver gave his testimony. 'Barbiturates.'

'Mrs Nicholls suffered from severe intractable insomnia,' Dr Weaver replied. 'She had done so for years, a condition which was instanced by the loss of her husband, and exacerbated by her later condition.'

'Arthritis, I believe.'

'Rheumatoid arthritis, more correctly. For her insomnia I had prescribed *amylobarbitone sodium,* otherwise know as *sodium amytal,* 120 milligrams thirty minutes before retiring, or when the pain was increasingly severe, and the insomnia totally intractable – 200 milligrams. The pills were bottled and labelled separately as 60 milligrams and 200 milligrams. As for her arthritis, I had been treating her with gold, and more latterly *penicillamine*, which is safe medication in that it causes no interactions between the two drugs.'

'What was the estimated dosage of barbiturates in the contents of the deceased's stomach, Dr Weaver?'

'The estimated dosage at time of death was 2000 milligrams of *sodium amytal.*'

'Which I understand is classed as a lethal dose, Doctor, particularly when taken with alcohol, as in this instance.'

'Indeed,' Dr Weaver agreed. 'But if I may, I would like to detail this case in the hope of clarifying the late Mrs Nicholls' situation. She had been playing cards that evening with myself and my wife, and her companion, Mrs Huxley. Mrs Nicholls had served us with whisky, which was her usual habit, but what was unusual was that she herself drank whisky that night. Normally she might have one, perhaps two, sherries before dinner, then nothing afterwards. But this evening she drank in company with the rest of us, taking I believe it was two whiskies all told during the course of the game. I mentioned this to her privately, remarking that this was not her normal habit, and reminding her of the dangers of mixing alcohol and barbiturates, recommending that she left her sleeping pills locked up when she retired, and relied upon the whisky to put her to sleep, which I assured her it most certainly would.'

'And yet,' the coroner wondered, 'the deceased ignored your advice, and went ahead and took the barbiturates. A dose which quite clearly caused her death. Can you offer us any explanation, Doctor? For this most uncharacteristic behaviour? And its subsequent, and tragic, aftermath? Unless this was, of course, the deceased's intention.'

'I doubt that very much,' Dr Weaver replied. 'Mrs Nicholls was a practising Christian, and would have been only too well aware what such an act would mean in the eyes of God. I can, however, hazard a guess, a guess based on my previous medical experiences, and that is the deceased became confused, firstly as a result of drinking whisky, which as far as I know was something the deceased was not in the habit of doing, not regularly anyway.'

'Are you saying the deceased was intoxicated, Doctor?'

'Mildly, yes, perhaps she was. She had taken a quota of sherry before dinner, a glass or so of wine over it, and a couple of whiskies afterwards, so yes, she could have been intoxicated enough later to forget my advice, and if this was so, she would perhaps have considered it safe enough to take her normal dose of sleeping pills.'

'But her normal dose would surely not have proved fatal, Doctor?' the coroner enquired. 'Even on top of alcohol.'

'Indeed not,' Dr Weaver replied. 'But this leads me to my second conclusion, namely that the deceased was doubly confused. You see, one of the contradictory side-effects of barbiturates is often the onset of a somewhat bewildering state prior to sleep itself, namely one of excitement, and extreme *disorientation*. The state of disorientation is the salient point here, for what often occurs is that the patient, particularly if having consumed alcohol earlier that evening, cannot recall whether or not he or she has taken the prescribed dose of sleeping pills. Consequently, they inadvertently overdose, normally with the complete absence of any ulterior motive.'

'Is it possible to overdose up to a level such as found in the deceased?'

'If the resultant confusion is severe enough, I would say yes, most certainly. The pills would not be taken all at once, but over a short span of time, perhaps half an hour or so.'

'And this on occasion has been your experience, Dr Weaver?'

'On several occasions. This is why I only prescribe barbiturates once the patient has fully understood the nature of the drug. But I have to admit that I was not unduly worried in this instance, because I knew the deceased to be a highly responsible person, and assumed once she had been reminded of the dangers of mixing her medication with alcohol, she would act on these advices. I can only assume in this instance I was wrong.'

The coroner thanked Dr Weaver for his testimony and recalled Doris Huxley.

'Would you be so kind as to tell this court, Mrs Huxley,' the coroner asked her, 'whether or not to the best of your knowledge the deceased partook of any more alcohol that evening?'

Like all hardened drinkers, Mrs Huxley thought she knew her own capacity, and that of everyone else. Like all hardened drinkers, she also forgot at the end of each session precisely how much she had drunk, knocking at least two if not three drinks off the grand total.

Most importantly, as far as that particular night had gone, Doris Huxley couldn't even remember going to bed, let alone what she had done or said in the hour or so previous to retiring.

So she answered in the way that all hardened drinkers answer when they are not quite sure. She lied with conviction.

'We had nothing more to drink that night, sir,' she told the coroner. 'Except for a cup of Ovaltine each as we sat talking by the fire.'

'Thank you, Mrs Huxley,' the coroner said.

On the strength of Dr Weaver's evidence, and in the absence of any note or notice of intention, the coroner instructed that a verdict of death through misadventure be returned.

'Yes,' Pippa said to Jerome as they walked in the garden on Jerome's return from Midhurst. 'Yes, well he would do, wouldn't he? This is a very small community, and Colonel Rogerson served under my father in the war. He was bound to err on the side of mercy.'

'I don't understand,' Jerome replied. 'If there was any doubt, wouldn't you rather he returned an open verdict?'

'There isn't any doubt, Jerome,' Pippa said, stopping by the gate which led on to the fields beyond. 'You know as well as I do. As well as everyone does. My mother killed herself.'

'There was no *note*, Pippa!'

'Why should there have to be a note. Jerome?'

'People always leave notes, Pippa my darling. Always.'

'In plays perhaps,' Pippa replied. 'Or in films, and books. But suppose she just decided it, there and then, as she lay there in bed? If that was the case, she wouldn't get out of bed and start writing notes. She'd just – she'd just – just do it.'

'But why, Pippa?' Jerome pleaded. 'Why? You still haven't been able to think of one good reason why.'

Pippa opened the gate and then turned back to face Jerome.

'Because of me, Jerome, that's why,' she said, and then walked away from him, out across the heavily frosted fields.

ACT TWO

EIGHT

Had Elizabeth wished someone to design such a turn of events, no-one, she thought, but no-one, not even dear, sweet Oscar Greene could have matched the masterstroke which fate had provided. No playwright on earth would have dared play such a trump card so early in the drama. Imagine, Elizabeth would think to herself as she lay happily soaking in her bath at night, or as she dozed on in her bed after Sebastian had left for work, the young lovers marry and go off on their honeymoon, and then – on the very eve of the lovers' first visit back home as husband and wife, the bride's mother inexplicably *kills herself.* Not even Ibsen would have dared, Elizabeth laughed, not even Shakespeare. (Well, perhaps Shakespeare.)

Neither was there any doubt in Elizabeth's mind that the Bumpkin's mother had committed suicide. There was no other explanation, at least that was Elizabeth's conclusion after Jerome had recounted the story to her in full detail, including a complete and wonderfully histrionic reconstruction of the inquest.

'It was utterly fascinating, Bethy,' he had recalled in her dressing room, during a break on the first day of filming *The Eve of Night.* 'And extraordinary to be there as an *actor*, of course! Because as you can imagine, there was so much *material*! So much to use at a later date! Amazing, don't you think? What a natural amphitheatre life is?'

But Jerome had been at his very best not in his physical recollections of the coroner, and the local doctor, Elizabeth considered, but in his wicked re-creation of the obviously quite beastly housekeeper, or companion, or whatever the wretched woman was. Mrs Huxtable, was it? Elizabeth tried to remember as she plumped up her feather-filled pillows, and resettled herself in her bed. No, she remembered, it was the same name as that famous writer – Huxley. Mrs *Huxley*. Elizabeth shuddered at just the thought of such a creature, pulling her bedclothes tightly round her as she recalled the portrait as described by Jerome in her mind's eye of a small-boned woman grown gross through drink, with rolls of fat on her neck, shifty little currant bun eyes sunk deep in fattened cheeks, and podgy hands clasped tightly on the handle of her cheap handbag.

'Of course, I knew she was lying, Bethy,' Jerome had announced, 'the moment she was called. Do you know how I knew? Because of what I'd been taught by Terry Vaughan. You remember what they taught you about lying, Bethy.'

'Of course,' Elizabeth had lied, having never needed to have been taught one thing about acting by anyone, while privately thrilling as always to the use of the nickname Jerome had bestowed on her.

'The feet,' Jerome had continued, 'you show you're lying through your *feet*. The feet have it, Bethy! Not the eyes! Not the eyes! Mrs Huxley couldn't keep her fat feet still for a minute! Her eyes – yes. She looked the coroner straight in the eyes, the picture of a good and honest woman. But her *feet*. When she was sitting down either one of her feet was forever jiggling, or waggling, or twisting, and when she stood up – look! They were like this!'

Every time she remembered Jerome's impersonation, Elizabeth laughed, as she did this morning as she lay in her bed, putting one slender hand up to her mouth to silence herself as she recalled the picture of Jerome in her dressing room, standing so still and so primly, holding an imaginary handbag just below an imaginary vast bosom, a figure of rural reliability except for his feet, which fidgeted and twisted in his shoes, like rabbits trying to escape from a sack.

'*Oh no, sir*,' Jerome had said in what Elizabeth knew had to be the most perfect imitation of the wretched woman, '*we had nothing more to drink that night, except, I seem to remember, a cup of Ovaltine while we sat by the fire. A cup of Ovaltine, Bethy? I'll bet you anything you like Mrs Huxley was completely and quite utterly *rats*! I'll bet you she'd been drinking all evening, and the next morning she hadn't the faintest idea of what had happened the night before! Or what sort of state poor Pippa's mother had been in!'

'Oh your poor wife,' Elizabeth had sighed, knowing she was judging her performance just right, conveying an exemplary blend of muted sympathy and strange bewilderment. 'Your poor wife. Your poor, sweet little wife.'

'I don't think she'll ever get over it, Bethy,' Jerome had announced, striding up and down the dressing room. He was in his costume for the film, that of an officer in the Duke of Wellington's army, and it did wonders for his figure, Elizabeth remembered with a happy sigh, particularly the breeches, which showed off his long, elegant legs to perfection, so much so that Elizabeth found it all but impossible to keep her hands off him.

'She blames herself, Bethy,' a puzzled Jerome had continued. 'I don't know why, but she's determined the whole thing should be her fault. Does that make any sense to you?'

He had then come and sat on the arm of her chair, one arm propping himself up on the back of it, and crossing his long white-breechered legs. Elizabeth had needed to clasp her hands together very tightly to prevent them from straying, and close her eyes to stop herself staring where a lady should not.

But she had used the closing of her eyes to good effect, to impart a sense of deep concern.

'Tell me, Jerome,' she had asked. 'If your poor wife's mother, if poor Mrs – Mrs . . .'

'Nicholls, Bethy. Mrs Nicholls.'

'If poor Mrs *Nicholls*, yes, if poor Mrs Nicholls really did kill herself, has anyone any idea *why*?'

'Not any hard and fast ideas, Bethy, no. Notions, yes. But no *real* idea, not one you can make stick.'

'A suicide must be terrible to come to terms with, don't you think?'

'If it was suicide, Bethy.'

'Your poor little wife.'

'There is nothing to say it definitely was suicide, darling.'

Jerome had sounded distinctly irritated at that moment, so Elizabeth had taken a risk, justifying her move as one intended to bring succour, and had briefly and very lightly laid one hand on his knee.

'Sweetheart,' she had stage whispered. 'No-one takes *that* amount of pills, not barbiturates certainly not – who doesn't intend something very serious *indeed*.'

'That wasn't the opinion of the coroner, Bethy.'

'Yes, but in your opinion, darling, the coroner was a cloth-head. You said so yourself. And quite right, too. If it was that obvious that beastly woman was lying.'

What had happened between them next was something Elizabeth kept locked in her mind. It was a fixed mark, which whenever she felt doubt or fear about the future she would look upon, to restore her belief.

Jerome had turned to her and taken her hand, the hand which she still had lightly resting on his knee. He had taken her hand, not to remove it, or press it gratefully before returning it to its rightful place, but he had held it, and looked at it as he held it, before looking up at Elizabeth and into her eyes, as still he held it.

'Bethy,' he had said. 'I need your help. As a woman you can help me. I'm frightened for Pippa, you see. I don't think something like this – how can she get over something like this?'

And still he had her hand in his.

'Jerome darling,' she had replied. 'I *wish* – oh, how I wish I *knew*. How I wish I could help you.'

'It's this business of girls with their mothers, you see. It's something I don't understand.'

'And something I'm afraid I can't really help you with.'

Elizabeth had smiled her helpless smile, as Jerome had looked deep into her eyes.

'Tell me about you and your mother,' he'd suggested. 'What sort of relationship do you have with your mother?'

'Jerome darling,' Elizabeth had sighed, 'I don't. My mother left me, us rather. She abandoned my brother and I when we were quite tiny. She upped and left us with a kind of aunt, you know. And she and Father just swanned back to their tea plantation in Ceylon, and never gave us another thought.'

'What? She left you both *behind*? She never sent for you? She must have come and seen you, they must have come back to see you some time, surely?'

Elizabeth had laughed, lightly, mockingly, a laugh she made a note she must learn to reproduce again. It was that good.

'Never once, Jerome darling. I have never seen either her or my father again.'

'So what about now? I mean how do you feel about them, particularly your mother, how do you feel about your mother now?'

'Jerome, my sweet, I don't. She might as well never have had me. So, don't ask me, please. Particularly not what I feel about my mother, darling. *Because I have no feelings.*'

'What about your father?'

'If you don't mind, darling, I'd rather not talk about it any more. My parents, as far as I'm concerned have never existed.'

Jerome had frowned here, still looking into her eyes, holding her gaze with his deep brown eyes that were so full of hurt.

'Of course,' he had agreed. 'It's just that with Pippa—'

'I know, my sweet,' Elizabeth had murmured, squeezing his

hand, but only lightly, as lightly as she had laughed. 'Heaven only knows how your poor little wife must feel.'

'Sometimes, Bethy,' Jerome had replied gravely, 'and I know it's all very recent and fresh in her mind, but sometimes, Bethy, when I look into her eyes, when I hear her tears at night, when I think of what it all implied, sometimes I imagine she will never get over it.'

'No,' Elizabeth had softly agreed, slipping her hand from his, taking the initiative from him, 'no, my darling, I don't suppose you do.'

And neither did Elizabeth, although sometimes, usually late in the night, when she was lying in the dark, thinking and plotting how the future must be made to go, she would suddenly curl up with fear at the thought that her adversary might be made of sterner stuff than she had so readily supposed. But not this particular March morning, as she turned on her side to ring the bell for the maid to bring her up some coffee and the *Daily Express*. This particular morning having slept well and apparently dreamlessly, Elizabeth felt utterly confident that no-one, however resilient they may seem, no-one could get over such a hammer blow, particularly a young and innocent girl, barely twenty, and married for a mere fortnight. It just wasn't possible.

The young lovers marry and go off on their honeymoon, and then – then on the very eve of the lovers' first visit back home as husband and wife, the bride's mother inexplicably kills herself.

As she lay back on her pillows to await the arrival of her maid, Elizabeth sighed deeply from happiness, and rejoiced in the Bumpkin's plight, a plight from which Elizabeth hoped there would be no remission.

On that very day, and at that selfsame time, had she known what Elizabeth was thinking Pippa would undoubtedly have agreed with her, despite her courageous efforts to fly in the face of her adversity. Since her mother's death, all days were bad days, but this the first Wednesday in March was a particularly bad one, since Pippa was returning to her childhood home for the first time since the funeral.

She had come down to collect some necessary papers and documents and, now that Mrs Huxley had departed, to shut the house up until probate was declared and her brother and she had decided what to do with their joint bequest. She had been dreading the visit, secretly hoping that Jerome might be able to accompany her, but his shooting schedule on the film was relentless, and since the lawyers were insisting they must start getting her mother's affairs in some sort of order, Pippa had grasped the nettle and taken the train down to Midhurst by herself.

It was all still so terribly unreal, she thought once again as the taxi headed out from the town towards the village and Bay Tree Cottage. She felt as if she were moving through a dream, with everything, including reality, just out of reach. It was such a convincing sensation that Pippa felt she would not have been in the slightest surprised if when she finally got to her old home her mother had opened the door to her and life had suddenly but not unexpectedly returned to normal.

Because surely it must all have been a mistake, Pippa wondered yet again, as the taxi sped through a wet and wind-swept landscape. There was just no reason why her mother should have killed herself, not under the circumstances, not at that most particular moment in time. And so if it had been a mistake, perhaps like all mistakes it could be corrected. Or perhaps the whole thing was a dream. It felt so much like a dream, and the dreams that she had been having, where her mother was still alive, and doing normal things, such as coming into her bedroom at Bay Tree Cottage to say good night, and looking up from a chair by the drawing-room fire, a chair which only a few moments ago had been empty, and walking up the Downs with her and Bobby, without a stick, with hands not yet deformed by disease, with James and Pippa young again, running hand in hand ahead of their mother, perhaps those weren't dreams as she supposed but moments of reality, despite their apparent dislocation. And so who could tell? When she got to the cottage, and knocked on the door, perhaps all this that Pippa accepted as real would all be shown to have been false, part of a dream, a passage in what appeared to be some terrible and prolonged nightmare but which in fact was being imagined in the length of time it took her to awake, and when she did all those fragmentary glimpses of happiness and normality would fuse into a whole, and life would return to what it was, to what it had been only the day before.

So much did Pippa hope this that she waited until the taxi had gone before walking up to the front door. She hardly dared look at the windows, in case her mother wasn't there, in case Bobby, whom in her dream she had left in London, wasn't to be seen with his wet black nose pressed against the glass. There were no lights on, but then her mother never put a light on in the day, not even during days when the landscape all but disappeared in the dark of a sudden summer storm.

But there was no answer to her knock, no sound of Bobby barking, no shouted reprimands at the dog from her mother as she made her way to open the door, no latch lifted and no face peering round the white painted front door anxious to identify the visitor. The door remained unanswered, and the house remained silent. Life was not a dream, and her dreams were not reality. Her mother was dead, her mother was gone.

The house was filthy. There was a thick layer of dust on everything, the waste baskets were still full, and the grates unemptied. There were even unwashed dishes in the sink and a dirty milk saucepan on the stove. Mrs Huxley, who had left the day after the funeral, hadn't even bothered to clear up after her last meal.

Deciding that the clearing up of the house could be her last job, Pippa went back to the drawing room to search the desk for the stipulated documents. As she came into the room, the first thing that caught her eye were her postcards, stuck where her mother had always stuck any postcards, under the clips of the oval mirror above the fireplace. Except there were only two. The first two. One of the front at Brighton, and one of the beach at Sandyscombe. But they had sent three, or rather Pippa had, as postcards were already a running joke with Jerome, and he had refused to send anyone any.

The third one had been of the pub where they had stayed for the second week, The Smugglers' Arms, which Pippa had posted on the Thursday, to make sure her mother got it by the weekend. But although her mother had received it, as witnessed by Mrs Huxley, she hadn't stuck it up on the mirror along with the others, which was very much out of character.

Pippa knew it must be somewhere, because her mother never threw anything away, at least not anything personal and certainly not anything familial. She hoarded letters and postcards and even old birthday and Christmas cards, although Pippa doubted that she had ever once taken them out from the drawers or the boxes where they were kept in order to reread any of them. Perhaps she had just intended keeping them as some sort of record for succeeding generations.

She began by looking in her mother's old writing case, and then in the walnut bureau, her mother's usual storage places, but she could find no trace of the missing card anywhere amongst all the jumble of recently received correspondence. She did start finding the bottles, however, beginning with the bureau, and graduating to hidey-holes all over the cottage.

They were all gin bottles, of various shapes and sizes, full size, halves and even quarters, and the more Pippa looked the more she found hidden. At the beginning of her search they were easy to find, at the back of drawers, behind books which stuck absurdly out from their shelves, albeit high-up ones, on the top of cupboards, and even in the bottom of the two log-boxes, but by the end of what proved to be an exhaustive search Pippa was finding them in the most bizarre places, taped under pantry shelves, stuck in the webbing underneath chairs, under loose floorboards and even in the cisterns of the WCs. By and large they were empty, but certain of them, most particularly the ones best hidden, were sometimes still a quarter or even half full. Pippa collected them all, every one she could find, and lined them up along the kitchen dresser.

She then made herself a cup of black coffee, and sat down opposite the long row of empty bottles to count them. All told there were seven full bottles, twelve halves, and eighteen quarter bottles, making a total of seventeen and a half bottles of gin altogether.

'There were thirty-seven green bottles,' she said to herself, 'up against the wall.'

Then as she realized the level of her concern, she put her head slowly in her hands and stared down at the top of the kitchen table. These had to be Mrs Huxley's bottles since her mother only drank sherry and the very occasional whisky, and she had warned her mother that she had heard it rumoured that Mrs Huxley drank, yet she had let her mother laugh her out of it, and left it at that.

She likes a drink when she's playing cards, her mother had assured her. *Of course, because she's a woman who likes a drink, she's a drunk, while if she was a man, she'd be a jolly good chap.*

So that's how much Pippa cared. Instead of finding someone else to look after her mother, someone more responsible, it had been yet another example of what her mother always used to call her basic weakness.

'Heaven help us if you ever joined the police,' she used to say. 'It would simply be a matter of you arresting whoever was nearest.'

In fact all Pippa's faults according to her mother were tarred with this particular brush, a love of convenience. She was always, according to her mother, inclined to go on first impressions, rather than waiting and seeing. She would rush to judgement rather than evaluate the arguments, she was too eager to please, too easily pleased, and too accommodating. And now because of this, because of what her mother had dubbed her hopelessly quixotic nature, her mother was dead because Pippa had not exercised sufficient judgement in the choice of a companion. She had left her mother quite wilfully in the care of a woman who was a drunk, while she had rushed off in typical Pippa fashion – according to her mother – to marry someone she barely knew. Anything could have happened being left in the charge of such a person. Anything had happened. Now as a result, Pippa knew she would find it harder than ever to forgive herself.

Fetching the first old grocery box that came to hand in the pantry, Pippa put it on the table and prepared to load it with the empty bottles, which was when she saw it. If she had picked any of the other half a dozen or so cardboard boxes, she would never have known, but somehow fate had seen to it that she chose this particular one and not any of the others. Even so, it was remarkable that Pippa spotted it, one small fragment amongst so much waste paper, one torn up shred.

But it was unmistakeable, unmistakeably her handwriting, and the word she had written was equally unmistakeable – *Jerome*.

Carefully she tipped the box up and sorted through all the old rubbish, the yellowing local newspaper, empty envelopes stained with discarded tea leaves, lipsticked stubs of Mrs Huxley's Craven As, potato peelings, and all sorts of other household detritus, until she thought she must have found every missing piece. Then having fetched some adhesive tape from the desk, she carefully stuck it all together, applying the tape to the side with the black and white photograph, until she had reassembled the last and until then the missing postcard.

Turning it over, she studied the back and thanks to her skilful reconstruction, found the message surprisingly legible. It read:

Weather still extraordinarily mild, and
Sandyscombe heaven, as is The Smugglers'
Arms – terrific board and lodging. We
shall be home Saturday, and with you
Sunday for lunch as arranged, but I'll
probably call you as soon as we're home.
Jerome sends his love, as do I. From us
both, The Didiers (!) xxxxxxxx

Pippa stared at the card until she couldn't focus any longer, wondering all the while how such an innocuous message could prompt such a savage reaction, because her mother must have been in a fury not only to have thrown away the card, but to have torn it into such small pieces before doing so. Yet it was so much out of character for her mother. If there had been anything on the card she hadn't liked, she'd have kept it to wave under Pippa's nose. Pippa knew her mother. She loved to take issue over something which might have inadvertently upset her, not maliciously, but gleefully. It was part of the family fabric.

But what could have upset her about this particular card and its simplistic message? Agreed, her mother might not have exactly warmed to Pippa signing it *The Didiers*, and knowing this, Pippa had deliberately included in brackets an exclamation mark, to remove the sting as it were. But there was no way, Pippa reasoned, that her signing who they properly and legally now were could throw her mother into such a rage that she would all but shred her card and throw it out with the tea leaves and the potato peelings.

Nor could the fact that Pippa had neglected to telephone her that Saturday evening have caused her to behave so illogically. Pippa knew her mother too well. Whenever she was away, which hadn't been that often in recent times, if she forgot to call when she had said she would, her mother would either ring her and berate her, or shake a finger under her nose when she returned home. But it was always soon forgotten. Underneath it all her mother understood perfectly well how easy it was to overlook things, which was why one of the family agreements had always been not to make anyone promise anything, because it was agreed that the best way to keep your word was not to give it. A missed telephone call would mean nothing, not in light of the fact that they were to be reunited the following day. This was just not typical of her mother. Pippa knew that, because Pippa knew her mother.

Except did she? Pippa suddenly thought, sitting and staring again at the message on the card. If she knew her mother like she thought she did, why was her mother lying inexplicably dead? If Pippa knew anything about her mother, she could at least begin to reason why this might be, but she could think of not one, *not one* possible explanation, or rather at least not one that she was willing to face.

For there was one, Pippa admitted to herself, and not for the first time. There was one explanation and if admitted it could be the only one, namely that her mother hated Jerome. Her mother hated Jerome and was passionately opposed to the marriage, as passionately as Pippa was determined to go through with it. But then why had she suddenly given in so completely? If she was so opposed to their union, the mother Pippa thought she knew would have fought on, she would have fought to the end rather than just surprisingly, and surprisingly tamely, conceding? So why? Why? Why? Why?

She began to clear up the house, starting right at the back, in the guest bedroom, and working her way down until she finished with the kitchen, in an attempt to purge her mind. But the longer and the harder she worked the more the questions came to her. Had her mother taken the decision to end her life before she and Jerome were married? Had her mother, a good Christian, really stood there in the house of God, watching her daughter getting married while contemplating her imminent suicide? What had she meant by what she had said to Pippa just before she left to go away – *you've got what you want, Pippa, now all we must hope is you want what you get*? Did she still think Jerome was a very different person to the one he really was? Or did she think that killing herself was her last refuge, the only way she was certain that she could blight their happiness? And if so, why? Her mother and she had always got along, they weren't inseparable by any means, and her mother never made a display of her affections, but even so – would she really take her own life just because she disapproved of Jerome? It simply didn't seem possible.

But then why had she given Pippa that strange, lingering look as she was about to leave on honeymoon, a look which Pippa had thought was as if she had never seen Pippa properly before, but which Pippa now realized was more the look someone might give you when they were looking at you for what they thought was the last time. All of which began to make sense, when Pippa recalled how her mother had wished her goodbye. How she had kissed her so tenderly and wished goodbye to her *darling Pippa*.

Normally, Pippa thought as she sat in the train heading back to London, such a goodbye could be ascribed to a moment of sheer sentimentality, to the sudden rush of affection a mother must feel when her daughter gets married, however unsentimental the mother in question might usually be, which was how Pippa had interpreted their embrace. But now, in light of what had happened since, that interpretation was no longer credible. With her mother now dead, Pippa knew that the look in her mother's eyes as she had reached up to kiss her goodbye, had the look of finality.

And yet, the wheels of the train rattled out rhythmically, *and yet and yet and yet and yet*. Yet all this was surmise, Pippa thought, as she stared out into the darkness, because she would never ever know the truth, because the only person who could tell her the truth was lying dead and buried.

She was in bed with all the lights out when Jerome finally got home from filming, in bed but still wide awake. So far she had done her best to minimize her grief, and to hide it from Jerome, because after all it was not his loss, and because after all he'd had to put up with a great deal of fairly implacable resistance early on from her mother. Not only that, but Pippa knew this was an important time in Jerome's life, whether he liked to admit it or not, the latter seeming to be the case. It was fairly obvious that the film he was making, *The Eve of Night*, or as Jerome had nicknamed it disparagingly, *The Crock of Shite*, dismissing it as nothing more than a schoolgirl's view of history, was going to do for him what Emerald Glynn had done for Elizabeth. It was going to make him into a star.

Cecil had told her. He had taken every opportunity to tell her, in the hope of helping to raise her spirits, and reported more or less daily to Pippa on the progress of the film so that she would have something else to think about other than her own remorse. Jerome was deeply grateful to his agent for his concern, as was Pippa, not for herself, but because it helped her see, even at a distance, how important this film could turn out to be.

Jerome, however, back in tandem with Elizabeth, was as doomy as ever about his prospects.

'You know what's going to happen, Pip, don't you?' he kept asking. '*The Crock* isn't going to be a crock after all. It's going to be the *most* enormous hit. It's bound to be, with its simplistic view of history, and its heart-on-the-sleeve patriotism.'

'And you in that wonderful costume,' Pippa used to tease.

'And Elizabeth looking even better than Garbo,' Jerome would correct her, and then sigh hopelessly, 'Yes – it's going to be *the* most tremendous smash hit and you know what that means, don't you? "They" – are going to do everything in their power to keep Elizabeth and I together, for the sake of their pig-skin wallets! And I for one – will not have it!'

Pippa would add nothing to this because she knew as an actor, Jerome was a cat. He walked alone, and liked to arrive at things by himself, and unsolicited advice ruffled his fur and put his back up. Instead she listened to his moans, and paid attention to his groans, and as far as his career went, only ever expressed an opinion once it was obvious Jerome had already made up his mind.

And so since the loss of her mother, she had tried to keep her grief as private as she could, in case Jerome should carry a part of her despair with him on to the studio floor. Even though they were now agreed that Pippa's absence on the first night of the play had not been the root cause of Jerome coming in second to Elizabeth, Pippa had recognized that such a thing could have been possible, and now that they were married and so deeply in love, she feared in case her misery might affect him.

But this night she had to talk, although Jerome still had to prompt her into it. And when finally she did, he sat the other end of the bed facing her, under the cover of the eiderdown, with a pillow at his back against the footrail, and Bobby lying on his back beside him. Pippa told him everything, from what she called her absurd fantasies in the taxi, to her deeply disturbing find among the debris in the old grocery box. Jerome listened intently, sipping his cocoa, and rubbing Bobby's upturned chest. He listened until Pippa had talked herself out, and fallen silent, staring down into her empty cocoa mug, and then taking the mug from her and putting it aside, he climbed into bed beside her.

'Well now, Mrs Didier,' he said, 'this won't do at all.'

'I know,' Pippa agreed. 'I'm sorry.'

'That's exactly what won't do, Mrs D,' Jerome chided. 'You being sorry. Not for yourself, because you never are. But sorry because in some way you think you're to blame. How long are you going to do this, Pip? No, that's a damn fool question, because you couldn't possibly answer that. Let me put it to you directly. You cannot go on for ever like this, you know. You cannot hold yourself responsible for your mother's death.'

'But why not, Jerome?' Pippa answered. 'I am. Who else is to blame?'

'You don't even know it was suicide, Pip.'

'I do. So do you. My mother was altogether too – too careful to have done something like that accidentally.'

'In your opinion.'

'In my opinion, yes.'

'Pippa, my darling,' Jerome said, taking her in his arms. 'What you're feeling, darling girl, is only *par for the course*.'

'Does that make any difference, Jerome?' she asked, looking up at him. 'If people always feel like this at times like this, it doesn't make it any easier.'

'I know,' Jerome said, holder her closer, 'I know, I know.'

'Jerome,' she began again, after a long silence. 'Jerome, do you think people ever recover from things like this?'

'I don't know, Pip,' Jerome said truthfully. 'I really don't know.'

'What happens if I don't, Jerome?' Pippa whispered. 'What happens then?'

He said nothing, because he didn't know what more there was to say. Instead he just held her, as tight as he dared, tighter than he'd ever held her before, as a sudden sob shook the whole of her body. He closed his arms around her, trying to stifle the grief in her, trying to kill the hurt, but despite the strength of his embrace, there was nothing he could do to stop her terrible sobs.

Finally she stopped crying, but didn't move from him, remaining with her head against his chest, both of them soaked with her tears.

'Perhaps the Ancients were right,' he said, slowly and rhythmically stroking her hair. 'Terry thought they were. Terry Vaughan. He thought the Greeks and the Romans were much more sensible about suicide, the Greeks arguing that to save a man against his will was as good as murdering him, and the Romans maintaining that amidst the suffering that is life, suicide was the gods' best gift to man. So just suppose, for whatever reason, suppose your mother *had* decided to end her life, perhaps it was a wise decision bravely made.'

Pippa lay in silence, and thought for a long time before she replied, and when she did, she did so without moving her head. She just curled one arm around Jerome and hugged herself to him.

'But why did she tear up our postcard, Jerome?' she asked, face turned sideways on his chest. 'If she was doing something wise and brave, why did she tear up and throw away my card?'

'I don't know, Pip,' Jerome answered slowly. 'I can't answer that.'

'No, Jerome,' Pippa replied. 'That's the trouble, you see. Who can?'

The person who could, the person who was in fact going to answer that very question, arrived in England six months later quite by chance on the same plane that brought Oscar Greene back from America, where he had gone as soon as his play had opened in triumph in the West End. The moment all the notices were out, he had taken Cecil Manners' advice and the first plane to New York, where within three months of his arrival and much to his delight and astonishment, he had another overnight success.

This person who was to change the course of Pippa's life was unknown to Oscar, and would always remain so, yet all the way across the Atlantic they sat no more than four feet from each other. Oscar, however, never very sociable at the best of times, was even more unsociable when flying, which for Oscar was the very worst of times. He either read or slept for the entire journey, and the few words he addressed *en transit* were reserved for the airline staff.

Consequently, when the plane landed and the passengers had cleared customs and immigration, the two people who were to play such vital roles in Pippa Didier's life soon went their separate ways, even though they walked almost alongside each other to the cab rank where each took a cab which in turn took each of them on towards their separate, although curiously interconnected destinies.

'Will Success Spoil Oscar Greene?' Cecil wondered aloud over lunch at the Connaught.

'I'm very Chinese about success, Cecil,' Oscar replied. 'You know what they say. The laundry only takes your custom as long as you've got the shirts to send them.'

'Even so,' Cecil told him, 'you have had, and in a very short space of time, a quite remarkable spate of success.'

'Sure,' Oscar said, munching his freshly baked roll, 'but the way I look at life, it's like a boxing ring. When you're the champ, everyone wants to see you knocked down. And then when you're knocked down, the ring's suddenly full of people wanting to help you up.'

Cecil smiled. He was delighted to see Oscar again, and delighted to see that despite having had a hit on Broadway as well as Shaftesbury Avenue, Oscar hadn't changed a bit. In fact, looking at Oscar's crumpled jacket, shirt and trousers, it didn't look as if Oscar had changed in any way.

'So what gives here, Cecil?' Oscar wondered, wiping a little of the soup he had spilled from his chin with one finger. 'How is the eternally gorgeous Elizabeth? And the super-lustrous Mr Didier?'

Over the rest of lunch, Cecil brought him up to date with the latest show business gossip and developments.

'Jerome *married*?' Oscar marvelled in point blank amazement through a mouthful of pastry. 'How can you marry yourself?'

'Come now,' Cecil chided him, although secretly delighted with Oscar's outrageous remark. 'Jerome isn't that much of a Narcissus.'

'Cecil, *old fruit*,' Oscar sighed. 'Show me an actor who isn't, and I'll give all my royalties to that famous dogs' home of yours. Don't misunderstand me. I like Jerome. Jerome Didier is fun. He's great company. He's a truly *wonderful* actor. I love the guy. But he's an actor. And not only that, Cecil, he's a star actor. Oh Jesus – heaven help the poor kid who married him. Unless, of course, she's an actress.'

Oscar looked up at Cecil, faintly hopeful that Jerome's chosen partner would at least be out of the same stable as her husband, but Cecil, who was doing his very best not to show Oscar just what music to his ears the words he had just spoken were, shook his head seriously in rebuttal.

'She's a very nice girl, O.G.,' he replied. 'A very nice girl indeed. She has nothing to do with the business. She's a simple country girl, who loves her animals, and painting, and the outdoor life. You couldn't meet a sweeter, nicer natured girl anywhere.'

'Oh Jesus,' Oscar groaned again, 'Jesus, Cecil, she is *cooked*.'

'Oh dear,' Cecil said, managing somehow to stop himself smiling from ear to ear, 'dear me, I do hope not. She's *such* a sweet girl.'

'Do you know something?' Oscar asked, draining the last of his Vosne-Romanée, 'I love actors, but they do have their limits. They're great to drink with, or to party with, but they shouldn't be allowed near your plays, or your women.'

'Talking of which, O.G.,' Cecil said, selecting some cheese, 'are we about to hear the pitter-patter of tiny keys again soon?'

'I don't think so,' Oscar said, dropping the handle of his cheese knife in the butter. 'Ever since they told me I could write, I don't seem to be able to any more.'

'There must be something you want to write about,' Cecil sighed, barely able to conceal the exasperation he felt whenever writers tried to make out that writing was difficult. 'Good Heavens, with everything that's going on in the world at the moment—'

'Listen, Cecil, *old fruit*,' Oscar interrupted, having cleaned off the handle on his knife, 'you may or you may not have noticed the sort of plays I write, and they aren't precisely what you would describe as topical. Right? I like to write about people, and women in particular. And at the moment, I'm right out of women.'

'Then we must find you some at once,' Cecil beamed, happy to find such an easy solution. 'That's no problem.'

'Sure,' Oscar agreed, eating some Stilton with his fingers. 'Have Harrods send me a selection on appro.'

Cecil did what he considered the next best thing, and that was to take Oscar that night to see the Command Performance of the film which had been nominated as that year's offering, *The Eve of Night*. Even Oscar was impressed, as he mingled in the foyer watching the stars arrive.

'This is big potatoes, Cecil,' he said, blinking as the flash bulbs popped at the arrival of the latest *glitterati*. 'Maybe now you'll be able to put some heating in that office of yours.'

Besides the royal party, the people the crowd were really waiting to see were the young couple who, according to the popular press, had captured the imagination and hearts of the nation, Elizabeth Laurence and Jerome Didier. The film had already opened to ecstatic notices, copies of which were reproduced all around the foyer, and which Oscar passed the time reading.

Without a doubt, the most distinguished British picture for a decade.

A beautiful picture, passionate and patriotic. The sort of film that makes you proud to be British, and proud of our British actors, particularly two who unquestionably must be the discoveries of the generation, Jerome Didier and Elizabeth Laurence.

A team made in heaven, if ever there was one. Two stars from the firmament come to earth to light up our lives. The memory of these two young people's tragic love story on the eve of one of this nation's greatest battles, Waterloo, will haunt you for evermore.

A superlative effort, deserving to rank among the British cinema's finest achievements. Miss Laurence lights up the screen.

Not for a long time have I seen a film so satisfying, so memorable, or so poignant. And in Jerome Didier we have not just a new star, but a star to shine with the best.

A star studded cast, and brightest of all, shine two brand new stars, Didier and Laurence – names which must become soon as familiar to us all as Huntley and Palmer, Crosse and Blackwell, Peak and Frean – names in other words destined to become household names.

'I give in,' Oscar said, staring myopically at the last enlarged press quote. 'Huntley and Palmer? Crosse and Blackwell? I never caught one of their movies.'

'You wouldn't, dear boy,' Cecil said, taking him to watch the arrival of the stars. 'They make food.'

'Even so, Cecil, old fruit,' Oscar sighed, 'next trip, I'm expecting radiators.'

They stood on the top of the first row of steps inside the cinema foyer, a good position from where to watch the arrivals. Within minutes of them taking their place, a black Daimler limousine drew up, off whose highly polished paintwork, within seconds, bounced the brilliantly flickering blinks of a hundred and one flash bulbs. The crowd pressed forward as one, a sudden heaving sea of humanity, all anxious to catch just a glimpse of the stars, who had arrived together and were now stepping out of the luxuriously appointed car, and on to the red carpet which had been laid to stretch from gutter to foyer. A uniformed usher stepped forward with military precision to hold open the car door for Elizabeth, and as she stepped out wearing what the fashion writers later reported as *a white mousseline-de-soie sheath bordered with mink*, first the crowd gasped, and then cheered, cheers which rang all the way round Leicester Square and its environs, cheers which grew even more in volume as after a very slight pause, Jerome then stepped out of the limousine after his co-star, turning as he did so like a ballet dancer turns, pivoting gracefully round to wave and blow one kiss at the crowd in one seamless movement. Then with one last wave from them both, he and Elizabeth disappeared inside to another battery of flashbulbs and the whirl of the world's newsreel cameras.

'Oh boy,' Oscar said thoughtfully after he had witnessed the arrival. 'You mean the Queen and her Duke have to follow that?'

The Command Performance was a triumph, and at the lavish party Boska threw afterwards, the toast was Didier and Laurence, who were radiant with excitement and rarely out of each other's company for even a moment.

'Design or intent?' Oscar asked Cecil as they mingled in the stars' court. 'Is Jerome's wife here for instance? Or at times like this do we have to stay at home?'

'Not at all, dear boy,' Cecil assured him, while trying to catch Jerome's eye. 'I doubt very much if she felt like coming, Jerome's wife that is. You see, something rather awful happened just after they'd got married. Her mother killed herself.'

'Oh, my God,' Oscar said, looking over at Jerome, who was laughing gaily with Elizabeth. 'Just how long after?'

'The day they got back from their honeymoon,' Cecil said.

About an hour later, Oscar was finally granted an audience.

'I guess it would have been easier to get to talk with your lovely young Queen!' Oscar shouted behind Jerome's back over the increasing din of the party. 'Or have you given up on writers now you've licked Napoleon?'

Jerome was already laughing joyously as he turned to embrace Oscar.

'Bethy!' he called at the same time. 'For God's sake will you look who it is?'

The three of them were reunited deliriously, at least that was the mood of Elizabeth and Jerome, because when it came to fond embraces, Oscar once more got overcome with his usual diffidence. Elizabeth immediately wanted to know what Oscar was writing at the moment, to which Oscar replied mostly cheques, while Jerome's questions were centred around what Oscar thought of the film.

'Or rather movie, as you Yanks will have it!' he shouted, giving his best Douglas Fairbanks grin.

Unfortunately for his friends, besides suffering from acute diffidence, and antisociability, Oscar was also a terminal claustrophobic, and as the size of the crowd began to grow out of all proportions, he began to suffer the usual symptoms, which he described as needing to get the hell out.

'Listen!' he yelled at Jerome, 'if such a thing is possible in here! I really have to go before I liquefy! Let's have lunch, OK!'

'Agreed!' Jerome shouted back. 'At once! Tomorrow in fact! And even better, Oz! Come and have lunch at home! I want you to meet my wonderful wife!'

Oscar agreed, saying how delighted he would be, wished them both *adieu*, and turned to go, having noted with interest the strange, cold gleam that had come into Elizabeth's now famous green eyes.

In fact lunch was cancelled, or rather postponed, Jerome calling the next morning to explain apologetically that he had completely forgotten he had to lunch with Roderick Mann who was proposing to do an interview with him for the *Sunday Express*, and to enquire if the day after tomorrow would be an acceptable alternative. Oscar assured him it would be perfectly fine, only too happy in fact to recurl up in his comfortable hotel bed and go back to sleeping off the excesses of the previous night.

The day after tomorrow was cancelled as well, and the day after that, all because of Jerome's meteoric rise to stardom. Suddenly it seemed he was wanted everywhere, and all at the same time. Oscar kept insisting if that was the problem why not just meet for a drink? A drink would do just fine, but no, Jerome was adamant they must lunch because they had so much to talk about. If Jerome had only known what was going to come out of that fateful lunch, and out of all the talk, he would have kept on cancelling indefinitely.

Of course Oscar knew who she was the moment she opened the door, and his first reaction, which with hindsight he was later to consider would have been the correct one, was to leave, to pretend he had called to the wrong house, mumble an apology and go. After all, she didn't know who he was because she didn't know what Oscar Greene looked like, and there was no sign of Jerome who could positively I.D. him, so Oscar could be just anybody.

In fact and in all fairness, he tried it, he tried to bolt. He made a vague and non-descript gesture in the air, muttered something incomprehensible about British house numbers, and turned to go, knocking over the empty milk bottles outside the door as he did, and sending them in a rolling and clattering cascade across the cobblestones.

'Oh heck,' he said, 'look, I'm sorry.'

'It's all right,' Pippa said, retrieving the rolling bottles, 'I'm always doing it. And you must be Oscar.'

Oscar knew he had gone bright red, just as he knew there was nothing he could do about it.

'Sure,' he replied. 'I guess I must be, mustn't I? This kind of thing is my visiting card.'

He took the bottles from her and carefully replaced them by the door, in the hope that if he took enough time his blush would fade. It didn't.

'Please come in,' Pippa said, pushing the front door open again. 'I'm afraid Jerome's not back yet.'

Still Oscar hesitated, knowing that once he entered the house there would be no going back. Once he crossed the threshold of this pretty little doll's house whatever happened and however it happened, Oscar knew their two lives would somehow become inextricably interwoven.

She was asking him something, but he didn't catch it, not first time round. He got it on the repeat.

'I said is something the matter?'

Oscar knew he was staring, but he couldn't help it, because he couldn't get over the hand fate had dealt him, that Jerome's wife should be the girl on the train. Except when he considered it further, he wondered why in actuality he should find it so extraordinary, because when she had sat opposite him on the train back from Oxford, she had obviously been to Oxford to see Jerome in the play. She was Jerome's girl, she'd been to see Jerome act, caught the train back to London, and had sat opposite Oscar. So where was the big deal in that? Furthermore, Oscar reasoned, if she was Jerome's girl and Jerome had got married, it was only logical for him to marry his girl. And if only God would help him find his tongue.

'I'm out of cigarettes,' he said, patting his pockets. 'I'd better go buy some.'

'Jerome has masses. You really needn't bother.'

'Sure. But I only use Luckies.'

'I know. Jerome told me. I went out and bought some this morning. And I made meat loaf for lunch.'

'You made meat loaf?'

'We have meat loaf and chilled beer.' Pippa smiled as she told him. 'The beer's English I'm afraid, but at least it's chilled.'

Oscar frowned, tongue tied once again.

'That's what matters, I gather,' she added, sensing his discomfort. 'Not the nationality, just that it has to be chilled. Do come in.'

Knowing this was it, Oscar did, and she followed, shutting the door behind him. He was glad of the dog, whom he had only very vaguely noticed barking, but who was now jumping with joy up and down against Oscar's legs, as if he, Oscar, were an old friend.

'I hope you don't mind dogs,' Pippa said, directing him through into a large, white-painted sitting room.

'I love dogs, it's just fine,' Oscar replied, still keeping all his attention on the dog while he tried to make just the slightest sense of his thoughts.

'He certainly likes you, which makes life a bit easier. Sometimes he can be awfully silly with strangers. He sits under the table and tries to stare them out.'

Oscar straightened up and felt brave enough now to take in his surroundings.

'This is a great room. Sort of like a ground-floor garret.'

'It is a bit,' Pippa agreed. 'Most of the houses in the mews still have their garages here. Or rather what used to be coachhouses, or stables. On the ground floor I mean. And you live above them. But one or two have been converted, like this, and we got one, luckily.'

'I love it,' Oscar nodded. 'If you were a painter, you could starve to death here in real comfort.'

They chatted some more, or rather Pippa chattered on some more while she fetched them both a beer, then offering Oscar the sofa, she sat down opposite him, curling both her long legs up under her.

'Jerome won't be long,' she assured him. 'He just had to go and see someone at rather short notice.'

As it happened, at that moment Oscar didn't care if he never saw Jerome Didier again as long as he lived, provided he could spend the rest of his own life in the company of this wonderful girl, now he had found her again. He had only seen her that once on the train, but even so he had never once forgotten her. He had thought about her constantly, picturing her in his mind's eye, so much so that he could remember her as if that train journey had taken place only the night before, he remembered everything about her, her beautiful grey eyes, her swash of freckles, her umber cataract of hair, and more than anything, what he always saw when he turned in his dreams, her fabulous face.

The telephone rang, startling Oscar and making him spill his beer down his tie. She frowned in sympathy, offering to sponge it for him, as she reached for the telephone. Oscar loosened his tie while she took the call, half turned from him, profiled against the September sun, while her dog took the opportunity of carefully washing one of the feet which she had slipped out of one shoe. Oscar watched her stroke the dog's head while she listened to the caller, fondle his ears, and tickle his chin, while in turn the dog now turned his attention from his mistress's foot to take one of her hands in his mouth, as gently as a gun dog does when retrieving a bird, pretending to chew it while rolling his tongue around the soft palm of her hand.

'That was Jerome,' she said with a frown, as she replaced the telephone and turned back to him. 'Look, he's terribly sorry but he's been held up with this producer, he has no idea how long he'll be, and says that we're to start without him.'

Oscar's heart leaped and his head began to swim, at one and the same time, so to steady himself, he grabbed both arms of his chair and sat as still as he could.

'Are you all right?' he heard her ask. 'You've gone a bit white.'

'It's nothing. Maybe a bit of asthma.'

'Can I get you anything?'

'Nothing, really. Perhaps if I could have a cigarette.'

He fumbled in his pockets before remembering that he was out.

'Should you smoke?' she asked. 'If you have asthma?'

'It's not really asthma. Not as such. At least not the sort of smoking that's affected by asthma. The sort of asthma that's affected by smoking.' He saw a pack of Lucky Strikes lying on the desk and reached for them. 'May I?' he asked.

'Of course. They were bought for you.'

She brought him a box of matches, and lit his cigarette for him, the way his kid sister used to light their father's, very carefully and earnestly, watching while she did it, before shaking not blowing the flame out.

'It's more of an allergic type of asthma,' Oscar continued with his lame explanation. 'Like – you know – brought on by ah – by blossom.'

'Really?' She frowned at him, uncertainly. 'But surely not this time of year? Not in September?'

'No,' Oscar shook his head. 'No, what I meant was it's particularly bad at the time of year *when* there's blossom.'

Privately he wanted to disappear through a hole in the floor. No doubt next he'd be hearing music.

'Ow,' he said instead.

'What's the matter? What have you done?'

'That damn fool thing with my cigarette. I'm forever doing it. You know—' Oscar rubbed the inside of his index and second finger with his thumb. 'When the goddam thing sticks to your lips and your fingers slip to the end. Ouch.'

'I don't smoke,' she replied. 'So I don't know. But I imagine it must be jolly painful.'

'It is,' Oscar agreed, blowing on the burn. 'Listen – tell you what. How about if I went out and came in all over again?'

They laughed most of the way through lunch, or rather Pippa did, since Oscar did most of the talking, keeping his hostess regaled with a constant stream of anecdotes, and every time she laughed the beat of Oscar's heart accelerated. He loved everything about this girl, from the way she looked to the way she listened, to the way she laughed, so infectiously, the way a child does when it senses the absurd. But, of course, he said nothing to her that could remotely reveal his feelings. He never would, he would make sure of it. The girl with the large grey eyes and the delighted laugh of a child belonged to someone else.

In fact the thought of someone like him trying to steal a girl like her from a man like Jerome made Oscar smile, while he sat waiting for the coffee Pippa had gone to make in the kitchen. And then it made Oscar sigh, and wonder why it was he always had to fall in love with the unobtainable. Maybe because it's easier, he thought, because that way you don't run any real risk of being hurt, but whatever, that's how it had always been. From the hatcheck girl at the plush restaurant where his father used to take him to lunch once he had entered his teenage, to Rita Hayworth, for whom he carried a torch right until this present day, a torch which had been lit the moment she appeared on screen in *Only Angels Have Wings*, and who had danced into his heart in *You'll Never Get Rich*.

And now there was this girl, someone else's wife, a girl with a wonderful mane of hair, such a slender but shapely frame, and large don't-hurt-me eyes, and who was as unobtainable as the girl who had checked his father's hat, and the girl whose feet never touched the floor when she danced.

'A penny for them,' Pippa said, putting a cup of coffee in front of him.

'For my thoughts, you mean?' Oscar asked, to his intense irritation feeling the blood rise once more to colour his cheeks. 'Listen, I'd be robbing you.'

'You were miles away,' Pippa informed him, sitting down opposite him once again. 'You were also humming something.'

Oscar was horrified. He'd probably been humming 'Since I Kissed My Baby Goodbye'.

'What was I humming?'

Pippa laughed. 'Don't ask me,' she said. 'I have the greatest difficulty recognizing the National Anthem. Under all this hair are a pair of totally tin ears. I'm only allowed to sing if Jerome's out, and not just out of the house, out of town.'

'Do you have any Irish blood?' Oscar asked, taking a spoon of sugar and stirring it into his coffee before taking another and turning the sugar brown. 'Heck, now look what I've done.'

'It doesn't matter,' Pippa told him, spooning out the damp patch of sugar with her dry spoon, and then feeding it to her dog from the palm of her hand. 'And no, I don't *think* I have any Irish blood.'

'Maybe some Latin?'

'Amo, amas, amat,' Pippa grinned mischievously. 'That's all the Latin I have.'

'And I don't speak it. What does it mean?'

'Amo, amas, amat?' Pippa enquired. 'It means I love, you love, he loves.'

Oscar regretted the question at once, and to cover his further confusion, started to drink his coffee while it was still far too hot.

Pippa took her cup and then sat back happily, for the first time in months feeling completely at her ease. Oscar was just the company Pippa saw she needed at this moment in her life. With the obvious exception of Jerome, since her mother's death there was no-one with whom Pippa could relax and behave naturally. All their friends and acquaintances treated her with almost excessive respect, due, Pippa suspected, to the embarrassment they felt over the circumstances of her mother's death, but now with Oscar, someone who less than two hours earlier had been a stranger except by reputation, Pippa found she could once again be herself, that she could laugh, and talk, and make light of things once more.

Not that she was blaming their friends. Pippa knew that the reason she had not been able publicly or even sometimes privately to be herself without feeling wretched and guilty as a consequence, was because of her inescapable sense of guilt. She still found it hard to laugh, even after six months, as if by laughing she would trivialize what had occurred. Even when they were alone, just she and Jerome, if they did find something to laugh at, their laughter seemed obscene, an act of betrayal. She knew Jerome found it hard as well, not because he mourned her mother's passing, but he knew that through Pippa losing her mother, he might be losing Pippa, at least the Pippa he had met and with whom he had fallen so passionately in love.

There had been nothing Pippa could do about it. She knew she was in danger of losing Jerome, she knew it every minute of the day, and of the night when she dreamed about it. She dreamed they would be walking along a path, a path which was always like one they had climbed on honeymoon, without ever being the same. They would both be walking at the same speed. That was something Pippa knew, that she was matching Jerome stride for stride. Yet he still forged ahead of her, relentlessly, while looking back every now and then, and calling for her to hurry, *hurry*. Pippa tried, but she couldn't, she couldn't get her legs which all at once felt heavy and weary, she couldn't get them to move any faster, because all the strength had gone from them, leaving her trailing far behind, and out of breath, until the next time she looked Jerome had gone. The path was deserted and Pippa was alone on the top of the cliff, with just a sea breaking silently far, far below.

They had stopped making love as well. Nothing was said, it was a tacit agreement, but for the first three months after her mother died, the most they ever did was lie in each other's arms. Jerome had been a model of patience and understanding, as time progressed never once bringing the subject up, nor ever trying to turn their nocturnal embraces into something more passionate. Pippa knew how impatient he must have felt, particularly after the discovery on honeymoon about exactly how congruous they were, but as she kept trying to explain voluntarily to Jerome, she simply wasn't ready yet in her mind.

'Darling girl,' he had said to her whenever she had tried to explain, 'darling girl, we have the whole of the rest of our *lives. Don't* – worry!'

But, of course, she had worried. Pippa loved making love with Jerome, and she could hardly bear not to do so, but the shadow hung everywhere, on every wall of the house, but most of all in the bedroom.

Yet now, this day, having had lunch and talked and laughed with Jerome's friend Oscar, Pippa at last felt the beginnings of a sense of liberation, as if a corner of the veil was finally lifting.

213

There had to be a turning point somewhere along the line, and as she watched Oscar fumble for another cigarette and fail to light it on the first half a dozen attempts, Pippa decided that Oscar was it. She whistled to him, chucking him a box of matches, and did her best not to laugh as somehow Oscar managed to break a handful of them before finally lighting up, at one point even contriving to send the lit head of a match spinning in the direction of Bobby who with a yelp promptly took off and hid under the table.

'You can see why I'd never have made it as an actor,' Oscar had commented. 'If I'd been required to smoke on-stage, I'd have burned the goddam theatre down.'

Oscar was just what the doctor ordered, Pippa thought, as she pulled her legs up under herself once more in the chair, or rather Oscar was just what the doctor should have ordered, instead of bottles of pills and bromides about time being the great healer. What everyone who was in shock needed was another shock, Pippa concluded, the shock of someone quite new and quite different.

So when Oscar turned the conversation round to her, Pippa found it as easy to talk to him as she had done, to laugh with him, telling him everything he wanted to know. Not that Oscar pried, or was indiscreet. On the contrary he was the epitome of discretion, particularly when it came to the inevitable subject of her mother. He listened to Pippa in thoughtful silence, never prompting her, and never commenting. Because he was a writer, he was a good listener, although Oscar kidded himself that the actual reverse was true. But whichever the case, what mattered was that Oscar listened, and consequently Pippa talked, so much so that by the time she had finished talking Oscar probably knew more about Pippa than anyone else, with the obvious exception of Jerome.

'I guess you'd like me to say something here,' Oscar offered as they fell to silence. 'I mean if I was writing this, I'd have me the visitor say something really illuminating and constructive, for which the heroine would be eternally grateful and the audience utterly stunned with my brilliance. But like all writers, when I need the words, they don't come. What I don't think you want me to say, is gee-how-sorry-I-am, because I don't think sympathy's your thing. Even though sure – I really do feel sorry for you, because what you're going through, and what you've been through, it must truly be just terrible.'

'I simply feel as if I'm in a maze,' Pippa frowned. 'I keep going round and round and ending up in the same place. I really wish there was something positive I could do. Instead of just staring into myself.'

'My Italian blood tells me to be careful here,' Oscar replied. 'You know what the Italians say? About helping people? They say *teeth-a placed befora-the-tongue give-a the best avvice*. But since you're wondering rather than asking, I'd have to suggest that maybe there is something you can do. You could give yourself a break, stop being so damn hard on yourself, and go out. Get out of here and do something. Anything. Just as long as you get out of here and do it.'

'I haven't felt like it,' Pippa said. 'I'm not sure I can. At least – not yet.'

'Sure you can. Go to the movies. There's nothing *wrong* in going to the movies. Or an art gallery. Or a concert. Even the theatre. Go see a play! Just check out of here. You know, don't you? That if you hide your sorrows away, they never get cured.'

'I'd go to the theatre,' Pippa smiled, 'if you had something on.'

'You saw my last play?' Oscar asked, all innocence.

Pippa stared back at him, suddenly putting a hand to her mouth.

'I haven't mentioned it, have I?' she asked in quiet horror. 'God, you must think I'm dreadful. I saw your play in Oxford. I thought it was simply wonderful.'

'It was better in London,' Oscar replied. 'But don't worry. I'm glad you saw it in Oxford.'

Jerome finally returned at tea-time, full of apologies for his unexpectedly long absence, but with a look of quiet triumph in his eyes. If Oscar hadn't known actors better, he might have mistakenly thought Jerome had been on the nest, such was the gleam in his eye. But Oscar knew that gleam, he knew it was the actor's gleam, a tell-tale sign of something quite different to a casual sexual liaison. The writer knew from the look in his eyes that the actor had been offered a part.

However, Oscar wasn't to be let in on the secret, since Jerome obviously wanted the revelation to be given in camera. He heard Jerome whisper to his wife as he kissed her so fondly that he had *some wonderful news*, before turning his attention back to Oscar, whereupon Oscar, sensing the moment had come for his departure, looked at his watch mock-aghast and asked for it to be confirmed that that really was the time.

'You don't have to go, Oz,' Jerome said. 'There's absolutely no hurry.'

Oscar regretfully assured him there was, that he had to rush off and meet someone, and started to collect his things together.

Jerome sighed in well-feigned disappointment and promised to fix another lunch date as soon as possible, which Oscar agreed would be good, not daring to take another look at Pippa in case something showed, and Jerome guessed how desperately Oscar had fallen in love with his wife.

'Are you writing anything, Oz?' Jerome asked him by the door, as he helped Oscar struggle into his coat.

'I wasn't,' Oscar replied. 'But now I'm all systems go.'

'Ah,' Jerome concluded, with a deliberately mock-serious look, the sort of look Oscar knew actors reserved for writers, the sort of look indulgent parents reserved for children. 'It came to you over lunch, did it?'

Oscar considered the question as he redid up the buttons he'd just done up all wrong on his raincoat.

'No,' he said, looking back at Jerome. 'The genesis of the idea I got on a train.'

Then he smiled, said goodbye to his muse, and took his leave.

Jerome was far too pumped up to notice that Oscar also had a look in his eyes, and even if he had, he would undoubtedly have ascribed the looks to a literary rather than a spiritual inspiration. So he shut the door, and Oscar out of his mind, and embracing his beloved Pippa once again, asked her to guess what.

Pippa couldn't, at least she pretended she couldn't, because even though she didn't yet have Oscar's experience with actors, she knew enough to know the only thing this look could mean. But Pippa was also a woman, and she knew instinctively that when someone asks you to guess something, the very last thing they want is for you to guess that something correctly.

'I give up,' she said. 'You tell me.'

Jerome smiled at her, let go her hands, and went and flopped down on the sofa, stretching his arms out either side of him, along the back.

'They want me to do *The Master of Kintyre*,' he announced.

'I thought *they* wanted you to do this other film. With Elizabeth.'

'Ah ha! They *did*. That is why I have been so *long*! That is why I have been out for most of the *day*, my darling girl! I fought them! I refused – flatly! No more, I said! I am *not* – the other side of a coin! We are not some – some double headed Hydra!'

'And you won?'

'Won? I *triumphed*, darling girl! Why else do you think they have offered me *The Master of Kintyre* unencumbered? With no strings attached! With no Elizabeth Laurence!'

Jerome, laughing with delight, tapped the seat beside him on the sofa for Pippa to come and sit down, which she did, first smiling at him, and then resting her head on his shoulder, in the crook of one arm.

'Are you pleased, my darling girl?' he asked.

'If you're pleased, Jerome, I'm delighted,' she replied. 'Is there a tour?'

'Very brief. Oxford again, Brighton, Richmond and then straight in. You'll come to Brighton, of course.'

'Of course.'

As she spoke, Pippa turned to face her husband, and as she did, he leaned across and kissed her, and kissed her a second time, before taking her upstairs to bed where at last, and to the great and joyous relief of them both, they once again made love.

'It was the only way, Boss,' Cecil said. 'I assure you.'

'Ha. Nuts,' Boska replied.

'You don't know him, dear chap. Not like I know him.'

'I don't want to know him. As like you know him. What I want, *all* I want is him to work.'

'If that is all you want, please – you really must rest assured. This is the only way you will get him.'

'Might we suppose Jimmy don't keep his word, huh? After all, might we suppose Jimmy has an interest in this Highland poop.'

'There is always that risk, I grant you. But I think you have somewhat minimized it by also letting Jimmy have an interest in *Lady Anne*.'

'We shall wait,' Boska sighed. 'And we shall see.'

'I've already seen, my dear fellow,' Cecil said. 'And I could hardly contain my mirth.'

Cecil Manners was not the only one who found *The Master of Kintyre* impossible to take seriously. The word on it was out before it even opened in Oxford, so that by the time it reached Brighton the profession and its acolytes were flocking down to the south coast town to witness what was rumoured to be by far and away the most hilarious tragedy staged in living memory. The critic for the *Brighton Echo* filed the following notice:

> I need hardly bother you with the preposterous plot, except to say it has something to do with a Scottish nobleman who is prepared to sacrifice himself, and does so, rather than have his beloved Highland estate plundered for oil. What should

concern us, however, is that the leading role is played by one of our most promising young actors in years, Jerome Didier, who besides being about a generation too young for a part requiring both depth and maturity, in his panicstruck performance has decided bombast equals passion, with the result that we the audience, instead of feeling any sympathy for the wretched Master of Kintyre, wish only that he would return to the drill square where he so obviously belongs. The sole redeeming feature of the appallingly miscast Mr Didier's performance is that in a kilt, which he perforce has to wear throughout the action, happily he is seen to have extremely good legs.

Pippa was allowed nowhere near the play, not even now it was in Brighton. After the Saturday performance, perhaps the most disastrous of the week, Jerome returned home to London and took to his bed where he stayed all day Sunday and late into Monday morning until in answer to his persistent telephone calls Cecil finally arrived round at the house at midday.

'Why don't you take Bobby to the park?' Jerome called back down to Pippa after she had yelled up to him to hurry and get dressed when she caught sight of Cecil's car pulling into the mews. 'I might have to lose my temper! And if I do – I'd rather do it in private!'

Pippa let Cecil in, excusing Jerome's absence by saying he was on the telephone, while she picked up her coat and Bobby's lead from the chair where she had dropped them when she had returned from her walk only ten minutes earlier.

'How are you, Pip?' Cecil asked, carefully taking off his dove grey gloves and avoiding her gaze. Ever since her mother had died, he had found it quite impossible to look Pippa in the eyes, however hard he tried. 'You're looking very well,' he said, taking off his expensive wool coat and handing it to her.

'I'm fine, Cecil, thank you,' Pippa replied. 'Can I get you anything? A beer? A glass of sherry?'

She had just poured Cecil his glass of sherry when the unshaven Jerome appeared, sliding an arm into the black polo neck sweater he had already pulled over his head.

'Cecil, *dear boy*,' he said in greeting. 'I do hope you've put in your *teeth*.'

'What are you talking about, my dear chap? You know perfectly well all my teeth are my own.'

'It was a *metaphor*, Cecil, *old boy*! Meaning you are going to have to bark for a change! Yes? Instead of just fawn!'

218

They were still arguing when Pippa and Bobby got back from the park, or rather Jerome was. Pippa could hear his voice as she walked towards the door. She hesitated before she put her key in the lock, waiting to see how far the argument had progressed, whether Jerome was winning or losing.

'I am not going into *tow-ern* – in this, Cecil!' Jerome howled, giving two full syllables to the place he wasn't going. 'There has to be *some* way out!'

Pippa couldn't hear Cecil's reply, but it was obviously not to Jerome's liking because the air was again rent with one of his wolverine wails of anguish.

'No, Cecil!' he cried. 'No, you got me into this, now you get me out!'

From where she stood by the front door, Pippa could see her husband in their sitting room. She watched him as he howled, and then as he stood with his back to the window, listening to what Cecil had to say. Cecil looked completely unflapped by Jerome's excess of emotion. He was seated in the library chair, smoking his cigarette as always through a holder, while he obviously told Jerome once again why there was no getting out of the play, at least, Pippa guessed, not under the terms Jerome wanted. She knew it would come to this. Even though she was not at all conversant with the way the theatre worked, from the moment the script of *The Master of Kintyre* had dropped through their letter box, Pippa had at once and for no known reason, been extremely uneasy.

Everything about the project seemed wrong. For a start, although she had no experience of reading playscripts, even Pippa could see that Jerome was not only far too young for the leading part, but that he was the wrong physical type. The play apparently required someone who commanded attention by his sheer presence, and while Jerome was undoubtedly magnetic on-stage, his appeal was diametrically opposite to that of the Laird of Kintyre. Jerome was broody, introspective and mercurial, while the Laird was meant to be a big red-haired Highlander, someone who could haul up the drawbridge on his castle singlehanded, not someone who would look better suited to sitting by a lonely lake writing sonnets.

'So what do you think?' Jerome had asked impatiently, having given Pippa the script to read. 'Don't you think it's simply *marvellous*? I shall play it in a wig, of course. And most probably a beard. And I shall have to go to the gym and put a bit of weight on. But don't you think it's *marvellous*! He's so strong. And contained. And – and all that *power*! He needs to be very quiet, when he isn't speaking. Very still. The silence of real authority. But when he speaks – he has this inner force. This – this *strength*.'

'Can you do a Scottish accent?' Pippa had asked, and Jerome had fallen across her in the bed, laughing and lying over her knees.

'What's a Scottish accent, Mrs Didier? What *sort* of Scottish accent? What's an English accent? There are hundreds of *English* accents! From Land's End up to the Borders! I shan't do a *Scottish* accent. I shall find where this man comes from, where *exactly* in Scotland, and I will do – *his* accent.'

'It seems such a strange part to offer you. It just doesn't seem to be your sort of part at all.'

'There is such a thing, Pip, as casting *against* type. And when it works, it's the most exciting sort of casting that there is.'

There was no point in any further discussion, because as Pippa well knew Jerome had made up his mind to do the part the moment it had been offered to him, not because the part was right for him, but because there was no part for Elizabeth Laurence. But if that was all there had been to it, Pippa would not have worried. Jerome was young enough to make a fool of himself once or twice without it damaging him permanently, Pippa had learned that from listening to what was said. One piece of miscasting was certainly not going to bury a talent as prodigious as Jerome's. Nonetheless, Pippa's suspicions had been raised, and they wouldn't lie down. She would have loved to have known, for example, precisely why all the people with whom Jerome was so closely involved, Cecil Manners, Jimmy Locke and the all-powerful Dmitri Boska, who normally went to great lengths to monitor Jerome's career, why they should all suddenly have decided that the very best thing for their most up-and-coming talent to do at such an important point in his career was be seen in the West End in such a ludicrous play. It just didn't make sense. Nothing about it made sense.

Except to Jerome. To Jerome it made perfect sense because it was going to prove two things, his versatility, and more importantly, his solo worth.

'It's a wonderful play,' he had announced time and time again to the increasingly doubtful Pippa. 'It's a marvellous, original allegory, and we shall fill everywhere!'

When Oscar had looked in one Sunday for drinks with some of Jerome's other friends, Pippa had asked him privately for his opinion.

'I haven't read the work in question, Pippa,' he had told her, 'but I'd be worried by that word *allegory*. George Kaufman, one of my heroes, one of our great comic playwrights, George says that Satire closes Saturday. And I have a very distinct feeling if you asked him about Allegory, he wouldn't even give it that long. He'd give it till Thursday at best.'

And now Jerome was trying to get out, and do it before Thursday. But he wasn't getting anywhere with Cecil. Pippa could see that from the way Cecil was smiling continuously, without really smiling at all, smoking his cigarette with distinct relish, while in front of him Jerome was visibly shrinking, until he finally flopped over the back of the sofa which was in front of him, and lay there, like a rag doll. Pippa watched them both through the window, unseen but all seeing, and as Jerome lay collapsed face downwards over the back of the sofa, she saw the smile disappear on Cecil's face, to be replaced by a cold look of seeming disinterest.

'Hello, Cecil,' Pippa said, as she shut the door behind her, having decided Jerome needed rescuing. 'You still here?'

The smile returned at once to Cecil's face as he got to his feet.

'We're almost finished, Pip,' he said. 'I won't keep him much longer.'

'I shall get a wishbone stuck in my throat, Cecil,' Jerome growled a warning from the sofa, 'I shall have a breakdown! I may even get pregnant!'

Cecil laughed easily, his old light-hearted self again, and leaned across to tap Jerome on the back.

'There is a way out, Jerome, you know that,' he said.

'No,' said Jerome, burying his face in a cushion. 'I would rather stay on the bridge while we sink with all hands.'

'Dear boy,' Cecil sighed and sat back down, while Pippa let Bobby off the lead and hung up her coat. 'You might have been able to put up with it in Oxford. You might just be able to endure it in Brighton, and shrug it off in Richmond. But you will not recover from a flop of this dimension in the West End. They will simply flay you alive. And from past clients' experiences, it is *not* the very best of things for the old confidence. Particularly in the young.'

'No, Cecil.'

'Think, dear boy. Think of afters. You may not get another offer for who knows? Six months? A year? Yes, of course you *will* get another offer. Someone as good as you is bound to get another offer, but of what? I mean you do not have a lot under the belt, do you? One play, one film.'

'Both hits.'

'A hit play, especially for Elizabeth, and a successful film.'

'A successful film – for *me*.'

221

'But what next, dear boy? You won't want second billing, but then after *The Master*, are they going to offer you top? Are they going to offer you anything? This business, believe me, this business is all start and stop and start again, if you're not very, *very* careful.'

'What's the alternative, Cecil?' Pippa asked in the ensuing silence. 'Because there obviously is one.'

'Pippaaaa—'

Jerome raised his head from his prone position for the first time for a long time.

'This is nothing to do with you, my darling girl.'

'I only wanted to know the one way out, Jerome. I don't think you should be unhappy in anything. Not at this stage.'

Jerome stood up and took a deep breath, closing his eyes.

'Does it ever occur to any of you?' he asked, and very loudly. 'That all is not lost? That the blasted out of town critics might just be *wrrrrrong*? That this is typical of tours – and that with a little extra rehearsal, and some judicious rewriting, not to say *recasting*, and one more date to play it all in before London, that might be all that is needed? Instead of hitting the panic button? Look at *The Parade Gone By*! Disaster! Everywhere it played – *disaster*! And what did they do? They replaced the juvenile lead, they wrote a new last act, they built a new set, they changed the first act and put in Alistair Stuart! And it ran for *two years*!'

'Thank God that was *all* they had to do,' Cecil sighed. 'Imagine if the play had really been in trouble.'

That was it, that was the blow in the solar plexus, the one to knock all the wind out of Jerome. Realizing suddenly the absurdity of the situation, he slowly collapsed backwards on to the sofa, both hands covering his face.

'This is the beginning of the end, Cecil, you know that, don't you?' he whispered from behind his hands.

'What is?' Pippa asked. 'Please, one of you tell me, what is going on? Why can't Jerome get out of this ridiculous play?'

'Who says it's ridiculous!' Jerome shouted at her, hands still to his face. 'How do you know what sort of play it is, darling girl!'

'Because if it was any good you'd have let me see it,' Pippa retorted. 'So come on, Cecil. Come clean. Why can't you get Jerome out of it?'

'I can get out of it, Pip,' Jerome stage whispered, 'if I agree to make *Lady Anne*.'

'With Elizabeth Laurence.'

'With – Elizabeth Laurence.'

'So which is the lesser of the two evils?'

'Elizabeth Laurence,' Cecil said.

'Go to hell!' Jerome roared, before dashing back upstairs to shut himself in the bedroom.

Cecil sighed, a long, exhausted sigh as he crushed his cigarette to death in an ashtray. Then he looked up at Pippa.

'What can I say?' he asked. 'I did my best, Pip. I tried to talk him out of this play. But he wouldn't listen. And you know Jerome.'

Pippa thought that she did, but now she realized that she didn't. She knew a bit of Jerome, the bit that showed just above the water.

Oscar, however, was not in the slightest bit interested in Jerome, nor his career problems. Oscar was only interested in Jerome's wife. He saw her every minute of his working day, and when his day was done he took her to bed with him, where she stayed locked away in his subconscious until it was time to let her free once more in the morning. Oscar literally lived and breathed Pippa. She was with him all of the time, wherever he went.

Occasionally he actually saw her, like the Sunday he was invited to drinks, and one blank day when he went walking in Hyde Park quite deliberately at the same time as she did. He knew her habits well, but this was the only time he abused the knowledge and accidentally on purpose bumped into her on her walk. She was pleased to see him, and although Oscar was pleased she was pleased, he didn't let it count for anything. He just fell into step alongside her and exchanged small talk. He told her nothing of what he was doing, except that he was writing again, and that it was going well, that is it had been going well until that morning, when he had come to a full stop, but that now he had taken a walk, he was sure that his inspiration would return. Oscar had every right to be sure, because his inspiration was at that moment walking alongside him.

She said he must come round to lunch again, as soon as Jerome had solved his differences over the play, and Oscar agreed that it would be fun to do so, before wishing her and Bobby goodbye. On the pretext of doing up his shoelace, he watched her walk away, and then sat on a park bench until she had disappeared entirely from his sight, before hurrying back to his recently rented apartment to take off his coat, roll up his sleeves, break open a fresh pack of Luckies and continue their love affair.

Except in Oscar's version he wasn't a writer, he was an unhappily married Oxford don, and Pippa wasn't Pippa. She was a student of Philosophy, she was the girl that night on the train, and she was called Tatty Gray.

NINE

Contrary to expectations, not all but most, *The Master of Kintyre* was a runaway hit. Jerome had been absolutely right. All the play needed was a new girl juvenile, a new last act, a different set, and just like *The Parade Gone By*, a different leading actor. Before the play reached Richmond, Locke's replaced Jerome with the increasingly popular Scottish actor Robert Maxwell-Law, who took the play by the scruff of the neck and turned it into an outrageous *tour de force*, to the delight of the West End audiences.

At first, even though he had wanted out, Jerome sulked, attributing the success of the play not to Maxwell-Law but to the things he had advocated, namely the rewriting and the recasting of the girl. Pippa paid the daily tirades little heed, as she knew that once Jerome was working again, albeit back in harness with Elizabeth Laurence, he would forget all about *The Master of Kintyre* and concentrate on the matters in hand. For the moment, however, he could not leave it alone, until Pippa, in an effort to kill or cure, dragged him along to see it.

'Absurd,' was Jerome's first reaction. 'Way over the top. I mean what is the superlative for Larger Than Life? The whole thing was surreal! It bears no resemblance to the way I saw it!'

'You could never have played that part, Jerome,' Pippa had told him, taking his arm as they walked back along Piccadilly. 'And you know it.'

'Nonsense!' he had retorted, before repeating the assertion but with considerably less conviction. 'Nonsense.'

'What made you think that you could?'

It had all come out as they walked all the way home, from Shaftesbury Avenue back to Kensington. Jerome had tried to refuse point blank to do *Lady Anne* with Elizabeth, but there was no way he could because of the terms of his contract with Boska. Boska had argued as always that the more films Jerome made with Elizabeth, the greater would be the stardom he achieved, and as a consequence, the better would be his position when it came to negotiating solo work. Finally Jerome had been forced to listen, even though he went down still arguing the toss.

'I wouldn't mind if they were films like *The Country Girl, On The Waterfront* or *Member of the Wedding*,' he said. 'But they're not. They're insipid melodramas, like *Time Will Tell, The Long Farewell, Above Us The Stars*, or historical garbage like *Lady Anne*.'

'It still doesn't explain how you got offered, and how you came to accept *The Master of Kintyre*,' Pippa persisted, as they walked round Hyde Park Corner.

It had been a bolt out of the blue. One day Cecil had called him and said that all concerned had come to respect his point of view, and that Locke's had just been sent a play for which they thought Jerome would be perfect. Actually, Jerome confessed to Pippa, his very own first impression of the piece was that he was entirely wrong, and that Maxwell-Law was the only actor who could possibly play the part. So how had he been persuaded? Very easily. Maxwell-Law was the *obvious* casting, they had told him, and as a consequence the play would suffer. It would be turned into yet another Maxwell-Law *tour de force*, which while undoubtedly entertaining, would certainly ruin the play as written. Much more interesting, surely, to cast *against* type, not to go for the cliché, but for the unexpected. Whoever would have thought that Marlon Brando could play Mark Antony? But it had been proved he could, hadn't it? So why not cast Jerome Didier against type? After all, surely not *every* Scottish Laird had to look like Robert Maxwell-Law?

'I see,' Pippa said. 'Well, of course. With that sort of argument, anyone could be persuaded. Particularly by Cecil.'

'Any *actor* can be persuaded.'

Jerome took Pippa's hand to lead her across the road and on up Knightsbridge towards the Albert Hall. It had taken Pippa to draw his attention to the salient point, as usual. It was Cecil who had persuaded him, and he was curious to know why. But that could wait, because the nightmare was behind him now.

'So what do you really feel now?' she asked. 'Now you've seen the play?'

Jerome smiled at her and put his arm round her slender waist now they were safely back on the pavement.

'I'm very glad you didn't see me in it,' he replied. 'You'd have left me.'

Pippa did see him in *Lady Anne*. It seemed most of England did. Wherever they went now, Jerome was recognized, and hunted for his autograph. They even found out where he lived, and soon there were small groups of fans gathered daily outside the mews house, waiting for a glimpse of their new idol.

They moved, of course, although neither wanted to do so. The mews was their first home, and they both loved it dearly. They called it The Snowflake, since because it was all painted white inside, and furnished with white rugs and carpets, bedspreads and sofas, Pippa said it was like living inside a snowfall, except that it was so snug and so warm. Their new home was very different, a large and very glamorous apartment on the first and second floors of a Regency house in Park Lane. It had wrought-iron balconies outside the windows which overlooked the park, a white marbled bathroom, and a dining room hung with a huge crystal chandelier.

'I'm not sure I can live here,' Pippa said, when they first saw it. 'It's like a stage set.'

'All the world is a stage, remember, Pip,' Jerome said, throwing open the drawing-room windows and stepping out on to the balcony.

'It just doesn't seem to be us, Jerome.'

'You don't *like* it?'

Jerome was amazed, and did his very best to look it.

'You don't like this place, Mrs Didier?'

'I love it, Jerome!' Pippa laughed. 'It's just – what's the word? It's just such a leap!'

It was a leap, and at first far too big a one for Pippa. Jerome made the transition easily, and took to their new life style as if he had been waiting for it, as if he had been expecting it to happen any moment, but Pippa missed their little snow house, she missed its warmth, its intimacy and its simplicity. Now and very suddenly there was champagne in the refrigerator, there was a uniformed housemaid, there was a secretary, a new car, paintings on the walls, expensive furniture, new clothes, white telephones, and within weeks nothing left from the snow house whatsoever, not even their marriage bed.

'You're worried we can't afford all this,' Jerome said to Pippa as men from Harrods positioned yet more reproduction antique furniture around the drawing room. 'Well don't.' He kissed Pippa, burying his face in the back of her hair as he stood behind her. 'Don't worry about anything, Pip,' he whispered. 'Because we can afford this six times over.'

But it wasn't the expense that worried Pippa. It was the swiftness of the transformation. One minute there had been the three of them, Jerome, Bobby and her, living modestly, peacefully and privately in the mews. Now there were seemingly thirty-three of them, living sumptuously, noisily and publicly in a luxury Park Lane apartment, a place where it seemed the telephone never stopped ringing, and the front door was forever open.

Everyone wanted to see Jerome and Jerome was happy to see everyone at home. Each and every day of the week, Sundays included, more and more and yet more strangers passed through the apartment, their numbers increasing by the week, passing Pippa by on their way to and from seeing Jerome, passing her by with scarcely a second glance, photographers, reporters, columnists, producers, directors, screenwriters, tailors, hairdressers, studio executives, publicists, manicurists, stockbrokers, insurance salesmen, doctors, throat specialists, masseurs and therapists of every size and description. All came and went, drilled into order by Miss Toothe, Jerome's awesomely efficient secretary, who made sure that none of the appointed, unless granted a special dispensation, stayed a minute longer than their appointments allowed.

'I can't believe this is happening,' Pippa said, as she saw each day turning into the day before.

'Neither can I,' Jerome agreed, as his tailor fitted him for his newest suit. 'It's like a play within a play.'

'Or like a fairy story,' Pippa offered, collecting her coat and Bobby's lead.

'Or like a fairy story,' Jerome smiled, raising an arm for the tailor.

'By Grimm,' Pippa concluded, leaving for her walk.

Nowadays she did her best to leave for hers and Bobby's walk before given her orders to do so by Miss Toothe. Bobby had become a nuisance, at least a nuisance according to Miss Toothe, barking at every new visitor, jumping up on everyone's legs, attacking trouser turn-ups, and laddering pair after pair of nylon stockings. At first as a precaution he was locked away in the kitchen with the maid, but all he did in there was howl or try and tear down the door at the sound of anyone's voice, so if Pippa didn't get him out of the apartment before the daily invasion began, Miss Toothe would despatch him by taxi in the charge of the maid to be locked away in Harrods' kennels until close of play.

227

It was Oscar who came to the rescue.

'It's no problem,' he said to her one day when they bumped into each other again in the park, and Pippa had explained Bobby's predicament. 'My own apartment's only a couple of blocks away, over there in Cumberland Place. So when you have one of those helluva-days on, drop the little fellow off with me.'

Since the very next day looked like being one of Oscar's *helluva-days*, Pippa took him at his word, and dropped Bobby round with him first thing in the morning. Oscar was at his desk when she called, so Pippa made her excuses and left, without accepting Oscar's offer of coffee.

'He's had a good walk!' she called back up the stairs as she hurried downwards. 'He'll probably sleep until I collect him!'

'Any idea when?' Oscar called back. 'Not that it matters!'

'Four o'clock all right?'

'Four o'clock is just fine.'

After she was gone, even though she hadn't stayed more than a minute, two at the most, Oscar lost his thread, and could only sit and stare at one blank sheet of paper after another.

'Goddamit, Robert,' he said to the dog who was busy trying to pull the valance of the sofa. 'Your mistress is meant to inspire me, not dumbfound me.'

Unable to settle back to work, Oscar taught Bobby how to play Crumples. This entailed teaching the dog to try and intercept a sheet of screwed up typing paper before it landed where Oscar was aiming it, namely in the waste basket at the far end of the room. But Bobby was not only a born retriever, he was a quick study, and it was a no-contest. Oscar couldn't get a crumple past him whatever tactic he adopted. By half-past eleven, Oscar called time and logged up the final tally on his blackboard.

'Robert thirty-one,' he wrote. 'O. Greene nil.'

'I don't understand why you're not happy,' Jerome said, as they dressed for dinner one evening.

'I am happy,' Pippa replied. 'That's not the point.'

'It's not going to go on like this, Pip, I promise.' He glanced at her in the mirror as he finished perfecting the bow in his tie. 'This will all die down. This is just in the wake of *Lady Anne*.'

'No, it isn't, Jerome,' Pippa said, stepping into her red velvet dress.

'You're not wearing that again, are you?'

'It won't die down, because you have to realize that whether you like it or not, and, of course, you like it, because that's why you're an actor.' Pippa turned her back round to him to be zipped up. 'You're a star, Jerome. In a way, this is just a foretaste.'

'Fiddlesticks!' Jerome laughed. 'I'm just the flavour of the month! Next month it will be somebody else! Somebody new! They're soon going to bore of me, don't you worry, darling girl! And haven't you *really* got anything else to wear?'

'What's wrong with this dress? You like this dress. At least you said you did.'

'I *love* that dress, Pip. I *adore* it! But you wear it all the time!'

'No I don't. I only wear it in the evening. And then only when we're going out.'

'You know perfectly well what I mean, smarty-pants.' Jerome grabbed Pippa as she turned to walk past him. He put his arms round her and looked into her eyes from very near.

'I want you to have everything you want, Pip, everything you need.'

'I have everything I want, Jerome. At the moment that is. And I have more than my needs.' She kissed him, and then brushed the light lipstick mark away with the tip of one finger. 'What I think you mean is you want me to have more clothes, which isn't something *I* want. It's something *you* want.'

'No, Pip, that just isn't so,' Jerome replied, knowing that it was. 'It's just typical of you. You're just simply not in the least acquisitive. Yes. Yes I want you to have more clothes, wonderful clothes, gorgeous clothes. But I want them for you. Because I want *you* – to have them.'

Jerome gave her *carte blanche* to choose what she liked, within a very generous budget. She was instructed to buy outfits for the day as well as the evening, hats, shoes and even lingerie.

'We can't have any more of this Orphan Annie look,' he confided. 'So for God's sake go out and buy clothes that *look the part*. That will look the part at all these premières that are coming up, and these receptions, let alone all these dinners!' Jerome threw his engagement diary back on the desk and walked to one of the windows overlooking the park, hands sunk deep in his tailor-made slacks. 'It's very sweet, but we can't have any more of this Little Orphan Annie nonsense.'

At that moment the drawing-room door opened and Bobby bounded in, followed by his mistress.

'Ah, there you are, darling girl,' Jerome said on the turn, picking up Bobby as he did so. 'Elizabeth's been waiting for you.'

*

229

Elizabeth wanted to take Pippa shopping to all the salons where Elizabeth did her own shopping, but Pippa refused. So Elizabeth reclosed the door of the taxi which had transported them to the environs of Bond Street and ordering the driver to wait, shut the intercommunicating window and turned to her companion.

'Pippa darling,' she sighed, 'I think it's time you learned the facts of life. As you know, your husband is now *nationally* famous, and fast on his way to being *internationally* famous. Now you may like this, darling, or you may not, whichever the case may be. For reasons best known to yourself you might want to keep out of the limelight and play little Miss Mousey. Well that would be fine, darling, if that was all right by Jerome, but you see it *isn't*.' Elizabeth smiled and put a hand on one of Pippa's. 'It isn't, darling, because Jerome loves you, darling,' she continued, 'and he wants to share all these wonderful things which are happening to him with you. But he can't do that, you see? Can he? If you're going to be Little Miss Stay-At-Home, or if when you do choose to go out every now and then you're always seen in the same dreary old thing. It doesn't *look good*, sweetheart, it looks a little funny. Do you see?' Elizabeth smiled her sweetest smile and squeezed Pippa's hand before continuing. 'Everyone looks at the woman, to see how well the man's doing. And if you're wearing last *century's* boring old velvet dress, they're all going to think what is this? This wonderful, handsome, dashing star that we all love – this is the best he can do? Allow his wife out in the same old frock, darling? They'll begin to suspect him of hiring his dinner jacket! It's all to do with what these clever old publicity people call *image*, so they tell me. And like it or lump it, one's better half is exactly that. Part of one's *image*. You're a pretty girl, darling.' Elizabeth sat back to take a better look at Pippa, who was still sitting stone-faced beside her. 'No, you are,' she said, as if she might almost have been wrong first time. Then she leaned over to Pippa and brushed her fringe of hair aside from her eyes. 'You have lovely eyes, a good figure, but we'll have to do something with this wonderful mop of hair, won't we! Gerard will know exactly what to do, don't worry. In fact I think that's where we'll go first.'

Elizabeth opened the window behind the driver once more and gave him their new destination.

'Elizabeth,' Pippa began.

'Ssshhh,' Elizabeth stopped her. 'You can thank me when we're finished, when you see how wonderful I'm going to make you look.'

'I'm really perfectly happy with the way I am, Elizabeth,' Pippa insisted.

'Yes, darling, I'm sure,' Elizabeth replied. 'But Jerome isn't. And Jerome does love you, you know. He wants you by his side all the time. Everywhere he goes. But I'm afraid – and I tell you this as a friend, darling. Believe me. I'm afraid if you won't go along with Jerome, and he is *so* proud of you. If he doesn't have you right there by his side – well. Darling. There are an *awful lot of people* who would be only too delighted to come forward and take your place.'

'You mean surely,' Pippa frowned, 'to *try* and come forward and take my place?'

'No, darling,' Elizabeth sighed, slipping her arm through Pippa's, 'I mean *will*. In this wretched business we're in, absence most definitely does *not* make the heart grow fonder.'

The following night, Jerome and Pippa attended the première of *The Greatest Gift* at the Odeon, Leicester Square. Pippa's hair had been beautifully cut and remodelled, swept above her ears and pulled round the back of her head into a small low-slung bun worn in the nape of her neck. Besides the jewellery Jerome had bought her, inch-and-a-half long pendant earrings and three gold bangles of different shapes and sizes worn on one wrist, everything else on her was either silk or satin, silk stockings and underwear, satin shoes and an exquisite suit of simple white satin made by Chanel.

After they had arrived, to the usual frenzied adulation from the huge crowd, as they mingled with the other stars and guests, someone tapped Pippa on the shoulder.

'Darling!' said an unknown voice.

Pippa turned round to see who it might be, and found herself staring at a totally strange young man.

'My mistake,' he said. 'I'm so sorry. I thought you were Elizabeth Laurence.'

T E N

In the spring of the following year, Pippa asked for a place of her own. Jerome was taken aback, worse – he was affronted by such a suggestion, completely misunderstanding Pippa's meaning. She laughed when she saw how slighted he was, and explained that all she wanted was a room of her own, somewhere she could have to herself, somewhere to go rather than having to hide in the kitchen or the bedroom when Jerome was being interviewed or photographed.

'You don't have to *hide*!' Jerome said, frowning his most perplexed frown. 'What *are* you talking about, darling girl? People want to take your photograph as well. Particularly now—'

'Yes?'

'Pippaaaa—'

'Particularly now that I'm presentable.'

'You've always been *presentable*, Pip! What nonsense you're talking today! It's just now that you look even *more* astounding than ever, and when people see how marvellous you can look—'

'Thanks.'

'I meant it as a compliment, Pip! You're the talk of the town! No-one can get over how beautiful you are! When people ask to photograph me, they *insist* – they make it a *condition* – that you are included!'

Pippa sighed and smiled, and came and sat down beside Jerome on the button back leather chesterfield. She took one of his hands, and turned it palm down on one of hers, so that she could look at and stroke his long, square-nailed fingers, while she explained what she meant. At first Jerome tried to interrupt her constantly, but Pippa wouldn't let him. She asked him to hear her out in silence, otherwise he would only once again misunderstand her. She explained that she had no life of her own. By that she didn't mean that she wanted a career, or that she was envious in any way of Jerome's astounding success. She wasn't. On the contrary she was inordinately proud of Jerome, and only wanted him to go from strength to strength.

'I shall,' he said, 'as long as I have you.'

'Ssshhh,' she replied. 'No interruptions.'

Pippa's problem was that she had always been active, even if her activities had been confined to riding or walking, playing tennis or simply just gardening at home. She had never been able to sit still and watch others do it, and now she was restless. Not bored, simply restless. She could tolerate the frills and the fripperies of being a rising star's wife, she didn't really mind having to go out dressed up like a fashion dummy, just as long as there was somewhere she could go of her own, somewhere private where she could let her newly fashioned hair back down, put on her old clothes, be herself and paint.

'Paint?'

'Paint.'

'Is that all you want?' Jerome laughed. 'You just want somewhere you can *paint*?'

'What's so funny?' Pippa asked, pinching Jerome on the leg at the same time. 'What's so hilarious about that?'

Jerome took hold of her upper arms and pinned her back in the corner of the sofa.

'I thought you wanted a place of your own for a quite different reason,' he whispered. 'I thought you wanted a place where you could take your lover.'

'I have a place where I can take my lover, you fool,' Pippa replied, struggling to get free. 'It's called our bedroom.'

'Then take me there now.'

Jerome had her hard held, despite Pippa's energetic struggle to be free.

'Only if you let me have somewhere I can paint,' she said.

'I shall let you have somewhere you can paint, only if it doesn't have a bed in it.'

'You don't trust me?'

'I don't trust other men.'

'If I'm not allowed a bed, and I allow you in, where are we going to make love?'

'Hmmm,' Jerome wondered. 'I hadn't thought of that. All right, Mrs Didier, you can have a bed. But it will have to be a *lockable* bed, to which I shall have the only key.'

233

Pippa smiled and stopped struggling. Jerome smiled and loosened his grip. He brushed one of her cheeks with the back of his hand, then he ran a finger over her lips. Pippa caught the finger in her teeth and held it, increasing the pressure gradually.

'Ow,' Jerome moaned softly. 'Ooh-ouch.'

He ran his free hand over the outline of one of her breasts, until he had caught her nipple between his first and second finger.

'Ow,' Pippa whispered. 'Ooh-ouch.'

'Your move,' Jerome said.

She moved, very quickly, not even running her hand up his thigh, just dropping it straight down to hold him, which she did, hard.

'Ah,' Jerome said thoughtfully. 'Playing dirty, are we? I see.'

Pippa closed her legs, pressing her knees together as hard as she could, while still keeping hold of Jerome. But Jerome was in no hurry. He just let things rest for a moment, while his eyes met hers, smiling slowly. But when he moved, he moved fast, letting go of her nipple and grabbing her doublehanded by the waist, hitting the spot at once.

'No!' Pippa screamed with laughter as he began tickling her. 'No! No – please don't!'

Unable hardly to breathe let alone keep her legs together, Pippa fell backwards, trying to escape from Jerome but too weakened by laughter to do so. He at once took advantage, moving one hand from her waist at the most opportune moment and sliding it between her stockinged knees. He was halfway up her silk lined skirt and she was begging for mercy and promising to do anything when the knock came on the door.

'Oh, I don't *believe* it!' Jerome whispered through his laughter. 'Who the hell—?'

'Mr Didier?' came Miss Toothe's measured tones. 'It is a five to three – and the gentlemen from *Life* are here!'

'Fuck,' said Jerome, which only reduced Pippa to an even greater state of helpless laughter as she struggled to make herself respectable. '*There is always a forgotten thing! And love is not secure!*'

'It will be,' Pippa whispered with a kiss as she took her leave. 'When I have a place of my own.'

Jerome wasn't the only visitor to Pippa's studio once she was settled in to the large purpose built room in Sydney Mews. Her other regular caller was Elizabeth Laurence.

Ever since their shopping expedition Elizabeth seemed to have taken a proprietary interest in Pippa, and now that Pippa had a quiet place of her own to which she could escape from the daily

234

bustle of Park Lane, Elizabeth, who, of course, lived nearby, began to drop in first once or twice a week, and then almost daily. At first she never stayed longer than it took to drink a cup of Pippa's freshly ground Blue Mountain coffee, to which Pippa was addicted, or she would stop by just before lunch to see if she could persuade her new friend to come and eat with her, and then perhaps do a little shopping, for herself, Elizabeth insisted, not for Pippa. Soon they were friends, good enough friends, Elizabeth considered, for her to extend the length of her visits, until they would cover either most of a morning or an afternoon.

'If I'm the slightest bit of a nuisance, or a distraction,' she had insisted, 'you must kick me out, expel me, lock me out. It simply will not do to have me putting you off.'

'Off what?' Pippa had asked. 'This is only really a sort of voyage of discovery. To see if I really can paint.'

'May I see?'

'If you want to.'

Elizabeth had looked at the painting in progress, an impression of the South Downs, drawn from memory only, without any artificial aids.

'You can paint,' she had said.

'Not yet,' Pippa had disagreed. 'But I think I might be able to. Constable always said you have to serve a long apprenticeship, to be a painter. Because painting is mechanical as well as intellectual. Which is why there are no and never have been any real child artists.'

'*Fascinating*,' Elizabeth had replied, not really giving it a second thought as she was far too busy studying Pippa studying the painting. 'Absolutely fascinating.'

Pippa had allowed Elizabeth to prolong her visits because Elizabeth turned out to be the perfect visitor. She seemed to know instinctively when to talk and when to be quiet, and when she talked, she was wonderful company. It was so good for her to have a friend outside the theatre, Elizabeth insisted, so they never talked about Jerome's and her business, but rather about every other sort of thing, the sort of things girls discuss best between themselves, without having to pay undue heed to a male point of view, which Pippa found most refreshing, because besides Jerome, and Oscar, of course, she had no other friends at all, particularly no girl friends.

What surprised Pippa more than anything, however, was that Elizabeth was immense fun. She delighted in finding things which amused Pippa and things which amused them both. They began to lunch regularly twice a week at the small French restaurant at the entrance to the mews, where over only the lightest of meals, since Elizabeth was on a permanent diet, Elizabeth would describe in the minutest detail her last purely social engagement, embellishing her accounts with wicked impersonations of her hosts and the other guests, until her mimickry and tart observations had Pippa all but crying with laughter. Alternatively, if it was a wet afternoon and Pippa had finished a painting but saw no point in going home because Jerome was rehearsing, Elizabeth, heavily disguised in vast dark glasses and swathed in at least two if not three head-scarves for fear of being recognized, would take Pippa to see the very worst double feature they could find that was showing, where Pippa would sit with a hankie stuffed in her mouth while Elizabeth *sotto voce* either barracked the films or supplied the actors with alternative lines of usually fairly *risqué* dialogue.

Worst of all were her practical jokes, which Elizabeth much preferred to call her *larks*. These were born either out of *ennui*, or simply from what Elizabeth called a passing attack of bad behaviour. Pippa was always shocked by Elizabeth's *larks*, even after weeks of either enduring or witnessing them, because she worried lest the victims might suffer as a result of the perpetrated pranks, even though Elizabeth constantly reassured her that this couldn't possibly be the case, since all her chosen quarry were fair game, a number which included the pompous, the greedy and the vain. It also included anyone unfortunate enough to ring Pippa's number in mistake for another's.

'You can't punish people for misdialling,' Pippa would protest. 'Everyone makes that sort of mistake!'

'Not in my book they don't,' Elizabeth would answer, her green eyes narrowing. 'Anyone who dials a wrong number does it because they've remembered the number *wrong*, or they've looked it up *wrong*, or they've simply dialled it *wrong*. And for that they must be punished.'

She was utterly unscrupulous in her dealings with misdiallers, her tactics being not to scold them, but to wrong foot them or even encourage them in their folly. If someone called up to speak to someone called Lorraine, Elizabeth would very sweetly inform them that Lorraine was upstairs in her room with another customer and ask them to call back in an hour. Alternatively she would tell the caller if it was a man that whoever he was (wrongly) calling never wanted to see him again because of his disgusting habits, that she had moved in with whoever he was (wrongly) calling and they didn't want him ringing any more, while her *pièce de résistance*, usually reserved for those who persistently got the number wrong, was to tell them at her most dramatic that the person he was (wrongly) calling had fallen downstairs and broken her leg and plead for them to bring a doctor over straightaway.

Pippa threatened to have the telephone removed from her studio if Elizabeth didn't stop, but Elizabeth dismissed this as nonsense, because while she knew she was shocking Pippa, she also saw how her telephone *larks* invariably reduced Pippa finally to a state of helpless laughter.

'They don't do any harm at all, Pippa,' she would say. 'In fact they probably do a little bit of good, brightening up otherwise *excruciatingly* dull little lives. I mean can you imagine what it's *like*? Being a *civilian*? And it's no good starting to look pettish – because we've long ago established you're *not* a civilian, darling, because you married into the ranks. Besides, darling, you paint.'

On days when Elizabeth was suffering from one of her more serious attacks of bad behaviour, the whole world became her playground. Unfortunately there was no way of Pippa recognizing the symptoms in advance because there were none. Elizabeth would behave perfectly normally and sweetly throughout an entire shopping trip until, if she was in such a mood, she spotted a possible victim, invariably some pompous over-dressed matron. Her favourite ruse with these women was to mistake them for shop assistants and either ask them to show her some particular and usually quite personal goods, or in her most inspired moments, to try physically to buy something off them. On one memorable occasion in Harrods she spotted a simply appalling fur-wrapped brute of a woman bullying an obviously very nervous young sales-girl. The woman was carrying a highly coiffured miniature poodle and both represented a prime target.

'Your grace!' Elizabeth cried in an impeccable French accent, indicating to Pippa the woman and her dog. 'Look, look! But this is just what you *want*!'

Whereupon she hurried over to the woman and demanded to know at once the price of the *leetle dawg*. The woman looked astounded, and inflating herself to her fullest size, grandly informed Elizabeth that the dog was not for sale.

'Oh my apologies,' Elizabeth sighed, still in broken English. 'But I assume you are a salesgirl.'

Of course, there was a price to pay for such entertainment, as Pippa discovered early on, long before she realized the actual height of the cost. In the early days of their relationship Pippa found that when someone was as expert as Elizabeth was at tom-foolery, it was difficult to know when precisely to take them seriously, and when not to do so. Not that Elizabeth ever involved Pippa directly in one of her *larks*. Whenever it was a *lark* pure and simple, Pippa's role would be that of witness, whether suspecting or unsuspecting. For example, if Elizabeth chose to launch into one of her sudden fantastical confessions on the way up or down in some department store's lift, she used Pippa as her foil, not as her victim. But when they were alone in the studio, or lunching quietly somewhere, at certain moments Pippa would get the feeling she was the victim of a sly tease, and would challenge Elizabeth. Elizabeth would usually deny the charge vehemently, swearing that she never played her *larks* on her friends, but very occasionally, just every now and then and without ever admitting she had perpetrated a deliberate joke as such, Elizabeth would sigh, look contrite and apologize – as she put it – for going a little *too* far.

'Darling, I'm *terribly* sorry, but I just couldn't help it,' she would say, usually with a hand on one of Pippa's. 'It was your *face*. I just had to go on because I love that expression of yours. Of *bewildered innocence*. You have such an incredible honesty. It simply shines out of you, darling. And I *do* wish I had it! You must forgive me, it's the awful, dreadful actress in me, I daresay. Always studying. And sometimes I just can't help being the tiniest bit naughty with you, just to see that look.'

She would then laugh it off, and it would be forgotten. Elizabeth would ensure that it was forgotten by immediately getting an attack of B.B., as her mischief had been initialled, bewildering some poor unsuspecting soul who was dancing attendance on them at that moment with a stream of incomprehensible double talk.

'Forgive me,' she would say at speed, 'but is your lartage percental? Or does it inclase the usual surmentation? I'm afraid I'm absolurate hopelack when it comes to accruing paravids.'

Jerome was delighted with the newly found friendship. It was cheering Pippa up considerably, and Elizabeth's consistently outlandish behaviour seemed to be pushing the memory of Pippa's mother's death further and further into the back of Pippa's mind. In fact everything seemed to be slipping gradually back into place, as it all had been a short time ago, except in some ways, providing the healing process continued, everything promised to be even better. Jerome's career had taken off, he was earning a great deal of money, they had a wonderful new home in which Pippa now seemed to be as happy as Jerome, but best of all, as far as their relationship went, he and Pippa were back as they were on honeymoon.

But the person who was most delighted with the new found friendship was Elizabeth. She had been wondering many things about Pippa, but most predominantly how the two of them could become intimate. She knew the suggestion could never come from Jerome, just as she knew she could not start a relationship with Pippa by simply dropping in at Park Lane. The Park Lane apartment was Jerome's and Pippa's home, not a place to watch and learn, Elizabeth guessed, because it would not be a place where she would be constantly welcomed. Elizabeth had done her homework. She had learned from Jerome how much Pippa resented the now constant invasion of their privacy, and that one more regular caller was the very last thing the Bumpkin would want.

So how to get near to her? Because Elizabeth knew for the next and most telling part of her strategy to work, she had to get near to the Bumpkin, gain her confidence, and observe her at close quarters, observe her closely, that is, without the Bumpkin suspecting for one short moment that she was a subject under close investigation.

When the idea first came to her, Elizabeth had not foreseen this difficulty. Somehow she had imagined that what she knew of Jerome's wife might be sufficient, and that she wouldn't have to bother herself to detail the Bumpkin further. But then the more she considered the piece, the more she realized how little she really knew about her model, and in order to convince, she would therefore have to get in very much closer.

But the gods were still smiling on her, as they had done, Elizabeth remembered fondly, since the fateful day she had picked up that copy of *The Times*. They smiled on her then as now, at the moment she learned from Jerome on the telephone that he had rented a studio for the Bumpkin very near to where Elizabeth and Sebastian lived in Chelsea.

'How sweet, Jerome,' Elizabeth had murmured. 'You're so *thought*ful. I didn't know the – that Pippa painted.'

'I don't know that she does, Bethy,' Jerome had replied. 'I just know she needs *some*thing. On top of everything else, she hasn't taken to the move at all.'

The spoilt, selfish, little cow, Elizabeth thought, examining her half-naked body for any trace of fatty tissue.

'Poor darling,' she said out loud into the receiver. 'She's very lucky to have you.'

'On the contrary, Bethy,' Jerome had replied. 'I'm the one who's lucky.'

Elizabeth had stuck her tongue out at Jerome down the telephone, sickened by what she considered his smug reply, before blowing him a *kissy-kissy* and hanging up. And before realizing what a windfall had just dropped in her lap.

Pippa working all alone in a studio nearby? What could be more opportune? Elizabeth thought, as she slipped out of her pink silk knickers and bra and padded catlike into the bathroom. A captive audience, she thought, and there was nothing Elizabeth liked more than a captive audience. Particularly when the Bumpkin was the one who was going to be her captive.

In fact the studio was most conveniently placed, immediately south of Onslow Square, almost back to back with a house which for the past six months had been one of Elizabeth's regular port of calls. Diana Shaw had started her going there when Elizabeth was making *Lady Anne*. The actress had played Elizabeth's mother, and while they were filming the two women had become good friends. At one point Elizabeth had complimented the older actress on the trimness of her figure, to which Diana Shaw smiled secretively, and tapping her flat stomach had whispered Elizabeth a name, the name of a Miss Page who practised in Onslow Square, an absolute genius who looked after simply *everybody*.

'What?' Elizabeth had asked. 'You mean your diet?'

'No, darling,' Diana Shaw had replied gaily. 'I mean the inner you. Your curly-whirlies. Your *bools*.'

At first the thought of going to such a person to be *cleansed*, as Diana Shaw put it, appalled someone as fastidious as Elizabeth, and she put it out of her mind, preferring rather to watch her weight by careful dieting and the drinking of plenty of fresh water. But then in private she later brought the subject up with her friend Lalla who was, of course, also working on the film, expecting Lalla to be as shocked as she had been. Instead Lalla had just laughed in her usual breezy manner and told Elizabeth that Diana Shaw was absolutely right, and that *everyone* went to Miss Page, or at least to someone exactly like her.

'It makes sense, Lizzie darling,' she had said. 'After all when you think about it, we give everything else a jolly good old wash, don't we? So why not our insides. I go twice a week, and you know me. I eat like a horse!'

The more Elizabeth thought about it and talked about it the more convinced she became that it could in fact only be to her good, so she too joined the ever-growing list of Miss Page's clientele, and just as forecast, Elizabeth found that anybody who was anybody did indeed go there. Whenever she visited someone famous had always either preceded her, or was the next in-waiting.

And it was terribly convenient to the studio, to the Bumpkin's bolt-hole, which meant that Elizabeth, once she had gained her entrée there, could happily while away any time she had deliberately set aside in the studio studying before going on to Miss Page's. There was no question of it being the other way round, of course, because after her treatment, like all of Miss Page's other patients, all Elizabeth wanted to do was go home immediately and rest until her strength returned. Besides, Elizabeth thought with no little satisfaction, even if she had felt strong enough to pay her visit after her treatment, this reverse order would have been far less satisfactory. Much better the way it was – visit the Bumpkin first and do with her what she must, and then visit Miss Page and be purged.

It had all worked out so neatly, it had dovetailed so perfectly that Elizabeth could hardly believe her luck. But surely the greatest inspiration had been hers, the revelation that had come to her after only her first few and fleeting visits to the studio.

'Darling,' she whispered down the telephone, as if by keeping her voice down she would disturb him less. 'I know how you *hate* being rung at this hour,but I have just had this *in*credible thought. This has nothing to do with my feelings about the work, because you know I love it to death. But how about and *please* at least consider it, just suppose, my darling, that you made this divine creation of yours whom I love as if *I* was giving birth to her, just suppose you made him a painter, and *her* – what if you made her an *art* student?'

Oscar kicked it around. In fact he kicked it around as hard as he could, trying to kick the life out of it, because he hated other people superimposing their ideas on his ideas, and most particularly he hated anyone, particularly an actress, imposing her ideas on this particular idea. In his head Tatty Gray had always been a university student, the reason being because that is how he first saw her, and the reason being not a good enough reason he now realized, the more he kicked Elizabeth's idea backwards and forwards and up and down. Everything about the play was right, and everything about what happened to the characters was right, and yet he knew it, he knew it at the back of his mind and he wouldn't face up to it, he knew that everything about the play was wrong, as was everything about the characters.

They simply didn't work, and neither did the play.

And until Elizabeth's telephone call, Oscar had just been papering over the cracks. He knew the atmosphere of the Oxford college was too rarefied, and that so were the two leading characters. They weren't enough feet-on-the-ground, as Oscar liked to think of it. In other words they weren't sufficiently rooted in reality for anyone to identify with them. Sure, painting still wasn't exactly like selling insurance, but at least by removing them from the groves of Academe, his characters could talk recognizable stuff, they could be more in touch with reality, which was vital to the success of the play, as Oscar knew. He knew it, but he hadn't been able to focus on it, because he had trapped himself inside his own original conception because he had fallen in love with it because he had fallen in love with his inspiration.

So why not an art student? It made much more sense. It was more real, it was sexier, it was more accessible. It made sense of the play, particularly of the reveal, when it slowly becomes apparent that Tatty Gray exists not in reality but only in the man's mind, that she is only a fabrication of his dream.

Oscar rang Elizabeth a week later.

'I shouldn't be telling you this, Lizzie,' he said, doing his best to growl. 'Because you'll only want a joint credit, or at the very least a percentage.'

'Which would be the least painful option, O.G.?' Elizabeth asked.

'A percentage,' Oscar replied, with feeling. 'But to hell, I'm going to tell you, because although to you mummers the only good writer's a dead writer, this writer is going to be very good to you mummers from now on, and to you in particular because not only are you beautiful, Mrs Ferrers, you also have beautiful thoughts. Your idea was wonderful. And I now have a play for you, which thanks to you, is the best play I have ever written.'

'Oscar darling,' Elizabeth sighed. 'I am *so* – excited.'

'So am I, sweetheart,' Oscar said, 'and I'll tell you for why. Not only is Tatty real now, she *really* exists, believe me, and, of course, you will breathe even more life into her, I know that. But because the man – because Sam isn't a don anymore, or a professor, or whatever – because he is this painter – Sam can be any age. For Chrissake Sam can be Jerome!'

'Of course!' Elizabeth exclaimed. 'Why of *course*.'

Even though she had never doubted that Jerome would not be Sam, not for one moment. Nonetheless, there was laughter still in heaven, and Elizabeth could now return to her studies with a greatly renewed sense of purpose.

Jerome was as excited as Elizabeth, if not more so. But not about Oscar's play. Jerome knew nothing about Oscar's new play, and even if he had, he wouldn't be interested, because Jerome had just heard from Cecil that Sir Fiacre O'Neill wanted him for his opening production of the new season at The Old Vic.

'It's *Romeo and Juliet*, isn't it?' he announced to Cecil before he had even taken his seat in Cecil's office. 'Well?'

'Absolutely right, dear boy,' Cecil agreed. 'It's *Romeo and Juliet*, not *Ant and Cleo* as first rumoured. And they want you for Mercutio.'

Jerome was staggered, just as Cecil had privately predicted he would be. But if he thought that was bad news, Cecil wondered, what was he going to say when he heard who was playing Romeo?

'Tony Hart!' Jerome was out of his chair, leaning halfway across Cecil's desk. '*Tony Hart*! He's old enough to be Romeo's blasted father, Cecil!'

'Don't shout at me, dear boy. I didn't cast it. The mighty Sir Fiacre did.'

'I don't care if God almighty did, Cecil! Tony *Hart*? Jesus Christ, Cecil, you know perfectly well who should be playing Romeo! Didn't the silly old windbag see *Lady Anne*! Didn't he see *The Eve of Night*! Hasn't he seen *any* of my work, Cecil?'

'There's not all that much to see, dear boy.'

'Because I have been careful, Cecil! Because I have been choosy! And not let you steamroll me into every damn thing that lands on your desk marked, 'Wanted! Tall, dark and handsome!' I can't play Mercutio to Tony Hart's Romeo, Cecil! Be sensible! Come on! How's he going to play it? With a walking stick?'

Cecil watched as Jerome paced his office, up and down, up and down, drawing deeply on his cigarette which he held in one hand, while he ran the fingers of his other hand back through his hair, over and over again.

'No,' he said. 'No, no, no.'

'Oh, I think so, dear boy,' Cecil corrected him. 'If it was anybody else directing, I could see your point. But the mighty Sir Fiacre . . .' Cecil paused to light himself a cigarette while he let the implication sink in. 'If he takes a shine, you know, you can more or less name your part.'

'You cannot play Mercutio against a senescent Romeo, Cecil! This fashion for older actors playing young parts is ridiculous. Romeo is a boy! *I'm* almost too old now – but at least I *look* boyish. Tony Hart looks as if he should be drawing his pension!'

'Anthony is only thirty-two, Jerome.'

Jerome laughed in scorn, and continued to pace the office.

'In Shakespeare's day, Cecil, people *died* at thirty-two! From old age! Romeo and Juliet are kids! So is Mercutio!'

'Alas this is not Shakespeare's day, dear boy, Sir Fiacre wants Anthony Hart for his Romeo, you for his Mercutio, Sally Stanway for his Juliet—'

Jerome came to a sudden halt in front of Cecil's desk, which he grabbed with two white-knuckled hands.

'Sally – Stanway?' he asked very quietly. 'Did you *see* – her Ophelia?'

'Of course,' Cecil replied. 'It was very moving.'

'Moving?' Jerome echoed. '*Moving*? I'll say it was moving! The whole stage shook every time she came on! Next thing you'll be telling me is that they want – oh, what was that frightful woman who's just done that terrible farce called? You know, *Ship Ahoy*! Hilda Hill! The next thing you'll be telling me is they want Hilda Hill for the Nurse!'

'They do.'

Jerome looked across the desk at Cecil, with his best suddenly-very-tired look, and then laughing at the absurdity of it all, he sat down in the chair opposite his agent.

'Very well,' he said. 'Tell me what else is on offer.'

'Not a great deal, dear boy,' Cecil told him, consulting some papers before him on his desk. 'Freddy Eynsford Hill in *Pygmalion*, a number one tour—'

'Dreadful part,' Jerome interrupted. 'Requires absolutely no playing whatsoever.'

'The lead in a new thriller by Paul Jeremy, *The Shaughnessy Bequest*.'

'Have you read it? I thought it was a comedy.'

'Or there's a film,' Cecil tossed him a red-bound script. '*Flight From Fate*. It's the lead.'

'What is he?' Jerome asked as he started to leaf through the pages.

'It seems he's a doctor, dear boy. With some rather curious habits.'

'No doctors,' Jerome slapped the script shut and chucked it back on the desk. 'You can only play doctors two ways. As monuments of patience and understanding, or with a mad gleam in their eyes. Is that all?'

'Mercutio is the best bet, dear boy. Trust me.'

'Romeo is the best bet, *dear boy*. Trust me.'

Pippa was alone in the house when the telephone rang. Jerome was still not back from his meeting with Cecil, and Miss Toothe was off sick with the flu, so Pippa and Bobby had the place to themselves. In view of this unusual event, Pippa had decided not to go to her studio, but to wait in for Jerome so that they could enjoy some time in the apartment alone for once.

It was after midday when it rang, and when Pippa answered it, she fully expected it to be Jerome to say he'd been delayed and that he was on his way home now.

Instead a strange voice spoke in her ear, a country woman's voice.

'Mrs Didier?'

The woman gave Pippa's married name the English pronunciation, not the French, like so many of the people who lived round Midhurst.

'Who is this?' Pippa asked.

'You don't know me,' the voice replied. 'You don't need to neither. But I knows you. And I knows who killed mother.'

Pippa sat forward on the sofa, pulling Bobby who was sitting at her side even closer to her.

'Who is this?' she asked again, eventually.

'I told you. You don't need to know that. What matters is I knows who killed your mother.'

'Very well,' Pippa said. 'Who did?'

'You,' the voice replied, then the line went dead.

She was still sitting tucked up in the corner of the sofa when Jerome returned an hour later, still in a barely controlled fury.

'Jerome?' she called as Bobby barked. 'Is that you?'

'Don't speak to me,' he said, coming into the drawing room still in his overcoat. 'Particularly about that idiot Cecil.'

He walked over to the large mahogany wardrobe they had converted into a drinks cupboard and poured himself a gin and tonic.

'You can pour me one, too,' Pippa said, resetting Bobby in beside her. 'A sherry.'

'Why?' Jerome was curious as to why Pippa wanted a drink, since she never drank anything in the middle of the day. 'Are you all right?'

'Not really,' she said. 'Are you?'

'Don't even speak about it. Do you know who their Romeo is going to be? No – not me, darling girl. No, Tony Hart.'

He went through his whole day in painstaking detail, telling her not only about his meeting with Cecil, but about the obnoxious taxi driver who took him into Mayfair, the rude woman in front of him in Fox's, where Jerome now bought his own brand of monogrammed cigarettes, the fool of an assistant in Hatchards where he had gone to try and buy a copy of Wilson Knight's essays on Shakespeare, and some half-drunk fan who recognized him as he was flagging down a taxi to take him home. Everyone was characterized and reproduced with Jerome's usual meticulous attention to detail, and embellished with just enough exaggeration that the monologue was totally compulsive, so much so that by the time he had finished recounting it, Pippa had all but forgotten her distress.

Jerome then flopped on the sofa next to her and scratched the back of Bobby's head. Pippa pulled her knees further up under her chin and frowned.

'I had a funny phone call,' she said. 'Someone rang, but wouldn't say who it was. She sounded like someone from home. You know – from the village. She said I – that I was responsible for my mother's death.'

She looked at Jerome from out under a fringe of hair which had half fallen across her eyes, not seeking an explanation but rather to watch his reaction. He looked back at her steadily, and thoughtfully, before clapping his hands together once and rising from the sofa.

'Balls,' he said. 'Let us have one of your delicious baguettes stuffed with this cheese I have brought home, and then out to the movies. I shall take you to see – *A Star is Born*.'

'Is that all you have to say, Jerome?' Pippa asked, as he pulled her up to her feet. 'Someone rings and says I'm the one who killed my mother, and all you can think of is—'

'Pippa. My sweet, darling child. It was some *crank*! That village of yours is full of Boeotians! It was obviously some daft old crone who has nothing better to do than cause trouble! She'll have seen our pictures everywhere, in the newspapers, the magazines – people are very funny about success, you know. Now do come along.'

Pippa did. She did precisely what she was told and went into the kitchen to make some lunch, while Jerome, having seen into Pippa's eyes, having seen that odd, flat, half-dead look staring once again back out at him, hoped to God that he was right and that the call was a one-off, the work as he had supposed of a crank.

*

It wasn't a one-off. The woman rang again. And again. Not at once, she delayed her second call until Jerome had begun rehearsals for *Romeo and Juliet* which he had agreed to do only if he could understudy Romeo as well. Cecil had thought the condition totally impractical, but Jerome had argued his case well, contending that if Tony Hart ever had to be off sick, far better for him to be covered by someone qualified to step into his shoes than a mere understudy. Let the understudy cover Mercutio, he reasoned, and Mercutio cover Romeo. Sir Fiacre O'Neill, far from being outraged, thought the idea a splendid one, and indeed after watching Jerome stand in one morning when Tony Hart was temporarily indisposed with laryngitis, was so impressed he let it be known, and not altogether privately, that he was contemplating the idea of the two actors alternating in the role.

That evening Jerome and Pippa celebrated the possibility by dining out at The Caprice. Towards the end of the meal, they were joined for coffee and a liqueur by Elizabeth, who had been dining in a large party hosted by Dmitri Boska. Boska grabbed Jerome by the hand as they were leaving to wish him luck in the play, and the moment, captured by an attentive photographer, appeared the next morning in the *Daily Express*.

Pippa was about to leave for her studio when the phone rang. Having all but forgotten the anonymous call, Pippa picked up the telephone in the hall before Miss Toothe could pick up her extension.

'Nice picture in the paper today, my dear,' said the soft voice. 'Lucky mother's not alive to see it.'

'Who is this?' Pippa asked, letting go of Bobby who was excitedly pulling at his lead. 'Who are you?'

'She didn't like your actor, you know. Not one bit. Said you'd never be able to trust him.'

'I don't understand why you're doing this. Why *are* you doing this?'

'She couldn't bear you marrying him. That's why she did away with herself.'

The phone burred dead in Pippa's ear as the caller disconnected. Pippa stared at the hateful instrument for a moment, then banged it down, picked up her dog's lead, and dashed out of the door.

'This is simply terrible,' Elizabeth said when Pippa told her at lunch. 'You poor, poor darling. What a simply *terrible* business. Of course, you must tell the police – and you must change your number. You simply cannot have this sort of thing happening to you. No-one can. It's like *Gaslight*, darling. You'll go *mad*. What a terrible business. Who do you think it is?'

Pippa had a thought who it was. She thought it was Mrs Huxley, her mother's friend and companion. She was certain it was her, because Mrs Huxley and Pippa had never really liked each other, because Mrs Huxley had only been left small items of sentimental value and no money in her late friend's will, and because Pippa couldn't imagine anyone else she knew in the village who would do such a mean and spiteful thing. She was positive it had to be Mrs Huxley, but there was no way she could prove it, so she said nothing to Elizabeth of her suspicions.

'The voice,' Elizabeth wondered. 'Do you recognize the voice?'

Oddly enough, Pippa didn't, but then it sounded as if the caller was making sure that her voice wasn't to be identified, since it sounded as if she were speaking from behind a hand, or perhaps a handkerchief. Both the calls had been oddly muffled, almost indistinct. In fact the more Pippa thought about the calls, the more she wondered at them. There was something unreal about them, something detached. Of course, Pippa was no expert on this sort of behaviour. She had no previous experience of anonymous telephone calls whatsoever, so she was in no position to give an opinion as to whether or not this was a normal hate call, that this was the way people always spoke when they rang up to frighten or to threaten you, flatly, unemotionally, distantly, carefully, as if they were repeating something over and over again, something which they had already prepared.

'One thing that does bother me,' Pippa admitted to Elizabeth, 'something that keeps bothering me. And that's how did the caller, whoever she is, and since we're ex-directory, how did she get our number?'

Elizabeth put down her lightly laden fork, and looked across the lunch table at Pippa, her green eyes catching the sunlight reflected in her wine glass.

The question gave her a long pause for thought, a time she filled by carefully wiping the corners of her mouth with her table napkin and then by signalling the waiter to clear her unfinished food away.

'Darling,' she said finally, after a scrupulous examination of the varnish on her nails. 'It's a horrible thought, but one that just has to be faced. She must either know a member of your staff, or it must be someone who has actually come to your house.'

When Pippa asked him, Jerome considered the matter at once of changing their number, but because they were now very near to opening *Romeo and Juliet,* and since it had in fact been decided that Anthony Hart and he should indeed play the leading role alternately, his professional life was once again extremely hectic, so he asked Pippa if they could delay making the change until things had settled down again, since circulating a new telephone number at such a moment might well cause untold chaos. As a consolation he made Pippa promise not to answer the telephone at all during the day when Miss Toothe was on duty, and told all their friends and acquaintances if they rang at any other times to let the phone ring twice and then hang up, before calling back, so that if Pippa was alone she would know from the code it was a friendly call. To the relief of both of them, the system worked perfectly and there were no more anonymous calls.

Instead Pippa's persecutor turned to the post. Not at once, in fact she gave Pippa quite a generous amount of breathing space, enough to lull her into a false sense of security before she sent the first letter, which arrived on the morning of the very day that Jerome was to make his first appearance as Romeo.

The letter was in a small, plain white envelope, postmarked Haslemere, and addressed in childish block capitals, as was the contained note, written on an inferior light blue lined writing paper, and read:

THINK OF MOTHER. THINK OF HER, A GOOD CHRISTIAN, A GOD FEARING WOMAN, TAKING HER LIFE, NOT SEEING HER MAKER. THINK THEN OF HER SHAME.

Jerome was still asleep when the post arrived, having left strict orders for him not to be disturbed until late morning. So after Pippa had sat staring pointlessly at the terrible message, she locked it away in her old blue writing case and took Bobby out to the park.

It was a fine autumn morning, and the park was bathed in a warm but fading sunshine. Pippa and Bobby walked all the way round, from opposite the apartment, down to Hyde Park Corner where they met the Household Cavalry returning from exercise, along Rotten Row to the Albert Memorial, round the Serpentine, up to Marble Arch and Speaker's Corner and then back down to their starting point, from where they commenced to walk all the way round once again.

The tears Pippa shed on her walk were long since dry by the time she looked into the bedroom on her return. Jerome was still fast asleep, so Pippa sat herself down on the *chaise-longue* under the curtained window and thought some more while she watched

Jerome slumber. She knew she would say nothing of the letter, not now, not on the morning of such an important day in Jerome's life. She ached to tell him, to have him comfort her, to hear him laugh and dismiss it with some mild obscenity, consigning it to the action of someone sick, someone unhinged. She needed him to tell her that it had no relevance, and that it contained no truth, because she was wounded, deeply, and she needed him, she needed his love.

But on this day he needed all his strength, Pippa knew that. Jerome had warned her right from the beginning, from the moment they knew they would marry, that there would be times she would find impossible. Pippa had denied this, confident that she could learn to deal with all the idiosyncrasies of an actor's life, but Jerome had insisted this would not be the case. There would be times she would find it difficult to understand him, he had warned her. There would be times, if he was to succeed, and not just succeed but if he was to achieve greatness, when he would no longer be himself but just a shell, a receptacle empty and ready to be filled by another persona, a mythical persona, by someone who didn't exist. And at these times she mustn't look for normality, rationality, regularity. She must detach herself from him, as he would do from her, and although they would know each other, there would be no familiarity, no contact, no dialogue, not while the actor prepared.

At first, Pippa hadn't altogether believed him, thinking that perhaps it was all a rather charming but nonetheless over-dramatic prophesy. Then once they were married and she saw exactly how Jerome worked, she realized how precise his prognostication had been. The nearer he got to a performance the more remote he would become, sometimes blanking himself out so entirely that early on in their relationship it would seriously worry Pippa. The same went for the immediate aftermath of a performance, except in reverse. Pippa would hardly recognize the person who greeted his friends and admirers backstage, an equally empty vessel but this time one full of sound and sometimes fury. If the performance had been a success, his energy would be formidable, and he would rarely come back to earth until the small hours of the morning, by which time Pippa would have been long ago ready for sleep.

She had learned quickly, though, that if she wanted to see the Jerome she knew and loved, she would have to keep Jerome's hours, otherwise all she would see would be the empty vessel, the blanked out receiver, or the hyped up, larger than life victor, the David who had entered the ring yet again to meet his Goliath and who had yet again triumphed over the odds. So she changed her routine, sleeping when Jerome slept, through long afternoons when he was in the theatre, and for short nights when he was filming, rising with him at the dawn, and then back to bed for a two hour doze before it was time to get up once again and take Bobby out.

Sometimes, when she knew they were going on somewhere after the theatre, she would go to bed for a couple of hours in the evening while Jerome was on-stage, in order that she would be able to keep pace with him wherever they went afterwards, always making her needs secondary to his, doing her best to understand what he did, and learning all the time that when he acted he no longer belonged just to her, but to everyone who owned a part of him, to all the girls and women who had his picture on their walls, by their beds or even under their pillows. But the more she watched and marked, the more she saw that he was a sculptor working in snow, and that when the snow melted, which it had each night by the time they tumbled exhausted into bed, Jerome once again was hers, and hers alone.

Not this morning, however, not the morning during which he must sleep until he could sleep no more, when he would awaken and begin a ritual which would take him through the day and away from her, ever further away and on to the theatre and up on to the stage. This morning she would just wait for him to wake, not kiss him awake as she could on ordinary days, nestled into the warmth of his back, an arm round his waist, her lips against his bare shoulder or neck. Today she would wait, and when he woke she would say nothing of the letter. She would make sure he had everything he needed on days such as these, she would run his bath, make him a light breakfast, and keep out of his way, unless there was anything he specifically wanted, anything she might have overlooked.

In fact after the triumph of his Romeo, and during its immediate frantic aftermath, when once again their home was besieged by the third estate, Pippa decided to go it alone, and confront her suspected adversary, whom by now she was utterly convinced could only be Mrs Huxley.

She rang from her studio.

'Yes?' said a voice on the other end of the telephone, a male voice.

'I'm sorry,' Pippa said carefully. 'Is that Mrs Huxley's house?'

'It was,' the man replied, 'until I moved in.'

'And that was—?'

'Who is this, please?'

'My name is Mrs Didier. I know Mrs Huxley. She was a friend of my mother's.'

'Oh yes,' the man said, after a short silence. 'I know. Well. I'm sorry I can't be of any help, but—'

Afraid he was about to hang up on her, Pippa cut in hastily. 'I'm sure you can. I mean, have you just moved in? I do need to know. It is rather important.'

The man laughed, without humour. 'No, no young lady. I moved in over a year ago. And I can't tell you the whereabouts of Mrs Huxley neither. Beyond the fact that she's living in Australia.'

The second letter arrived exactly one week later. It was identical to the first, all except for the message. This one read:

YOUR MOTHER DIED OF SHAME.

'Your mother died of shame.'

'Yes.'

'That's all it said?'

'Yes. It's enough, don't you think?'

'And the other one, the first one?'

Pippa could remember the exact wording without difficulty. It was etched in her mind. She told him. ' "Think of mother," ' she said. ' "Think of her, a good Christian, a God fearing woman, taking her life, not seeing her Maker. Think then of her shame".'

'Yes. That's why I don't think she killed herself.'

'The author of these letters does. Sorry, no – she thinks *I* killed her.'

'We're all in some way responsible for the fate of others.'

'I just don't see how I can be held responsible for my mother's death.'

'You can't. Unless you feel yourself that you are responsible. Do you?'

'I'm being made to feel that I do.'

'But do you?'

'I really can't say. Not with any honesty. I can't say because I don't know how my mother felt. I know she disapproved of me marrying—'

'She disapproved not of you marrying. She disapproved of *who* you married.'

'Did she *really*? Do you *really* think she did?'

'Pippa. I *know* that she did. She told me.'

Pippa rose from her chair and went to a window where she looked out unseeing, at a meaningless landscape. The man behind her offered her some more tea, which she declined, then she heard him sigh quietly as he poured himself a second cup.

'I was wondering when you'd come and see me.'

'You don't mean if?'

'No, no. No, I meant when. I knew you'd come. Heavens above, child, I've known you all your life. I helped bring you into this world. I'm not just the family doctor, you know. I'm a family friend.'

Pippa came and sat back down opposite Dr Weaver. She smiled at him as she crossed her long legs and folded her hands together over her knee.

'I know what you are,' she said. 'And I wish I'd come and talked to you sooner.'

'Why should you?' Weaver replied. 'You have a perfectly good husband. And a perfectly intelligent one. And a perfectly *nice* one. Look Pippa, I don't think for one moment your mother would have approved of whoever you had married. Because knowing you like I do, I don't think you'd have ever been the remotest bit interested in the sort of young men of whom your mother *did* approve.'

They both smiled then, knowing it to be true, knowing that Pippa's mother had only really ever approved of soldiers or clerics, and the memory of that knowledge gave Pippa hope.

'So what you're saying, Dr Weaver, is that even if my mother didn't approve of Jerome—'

'No *if*, Pippa. She didn't.'

'Yes, all right. So even though she disapproved of Jerome, you don't think that's a sufficient motive—' Pippa paused, not quite sure how to phrase exactly what she wanted to say. 'You don't think that would have been sufficient motive for what happened.'

It was a statement, not a question, because Pippa was at last beginning to feel surer of her facts.

'Like you, Pippa, I can only guess,' Dr Weaver replied.

'But at the inquest!' Pippa broke in, 'I'm sorry, but you said you were quite sure—'

Weaver held up a closed hand, with just the index finger pointing upwards.

'Your mother was a Christian, Pippa. I'm a Christian. So are you. And you know how the church stands on suicide. I didn't feel there was sufficient evidence for the coroner to return a verdict of suicide. I still don't. *But I don't know.* Like you, I cannot piece it together and make sense of it. You loved your mother and you can't bear to think she might have ended her own life, particularly

253

for reasons which might be to do with you.' Weaver paused, and took his old briar pipe from a side pocket, which he filled from a bowl of tobacco on the table beside him, carefully pushing the dark brown strands down with the end of one thumb before he continued, which he did after he had looked at Pippa long and hard from under a pair of greying bushy eyebrows. 'You know about your mother and I, do you?' he asked. 'Did you know we nearly married?'

Pippa's eyes opened wide, and then even wider as she frowned and shook her head. 'No. No I knew no such thing.'

Weaver smiled as he put the unlit pipe in his mouth.

'Her father talked her out of it. I was still a medical student. He said I was a bad risk.'

The irony wasn't lost on Pippa who returned his smile politely, but remained silent, waiting to hear what else Dr Weaver had to say.

'The point is, Pippa, since it couldn't be proved beyond reasonable doubt that your mother took her own life, then because of – because it couldn't be *proved*, I couldn't have her buried as a suicide. God is our judge, not a coroner's court, not the Palace of Westminster. And whatever happened that night, and for whatever reason, it will all have been explained by now. God is merciful, and your mother will be at peace.'

'But I'm not.' Pippa was suddenly terribly angry, furious with Dr Weaver's piety and the convenience of his rationalization. 'I think she did kill herself. I think she did it from—' She took a deep breath to control herself, a trick she had learned from Jerome. 'I think she did it for a purpose.'

'To get back at you?' It was Weaver's turn to look astonished. 'No, Pippa. No I really don't think so.'

'What about the postcard? No-one can explain the postcard! The only explanation can be that once she realized we really *were* married, and that we were coming down to see her, as husband and wife! Once that truth really dawned—'

It was Dr Weaver's turn to interrupt, which he did with a rueful smile. 'You mean because you signed the card in your married name? No, no. Believe me.' He lit his pipe, as if the act would underwrite his certainty.

'How can you be sure?' Pippa was on her feet. 'You didn't know my mother! No – no, you knew my mother, but not in the way I did! As her daughter! When she took against something, she took against it. And I think somehow that postcard for some unknown reason – I think it infuriated her! And she lost her reason! Why else

254

would she destroy it like that? Tear it up into tiny little pieces and throw it away?'

Dr Weaver took his pipe out of his mouth and studied the thin plume of blue smoke that was curling up nicely now from the bowl.

'Hmmm,' he said as he considered the contents of Pippa's outburst. 'I don't think so. Because you see, if she was that angry with you, then why did she keep your other two cards? Why didn't she throw them all away?'

This was something Pippa had never once considered, and to which she had no answer. Dr Weaver did, however, at least he had a piece of vital evidence which until now he had deliberately withheld.

'Sit down, Pippa,' he said, 'because I think there's something important you ought to know.'

Pippa sat down, and waited, while Weaver drew deeply on his pipe to make sure it was still well alight. Then he sat back in his chair, took a brief look at the ceiling, and then a much longer look at Pippa.

'You won't have known this,' he said. 'But your mother was an alcoholic.'

The bottles she had found around the house, Pippa explained to Elizabeth the next day when she visited Pippa's studio, were mostly her mother's, not Mrs Huxley's as she had first supposed. Mrs Huxley was a drinker, certainly, which was obviously why her mother had chosen her as a companion, although it appeared from what Pippa had learned that her mother had not been constantly alcoholic, but had managed long periods of abstinence, particularly in recent years, and particularly since Pippa had left school, which would explain why the growing Pippa never noticed either any untoward behavioural signs, or ever smelt drink regularly on her mother's breath. In fact according to Dr Weaver, her mother had started drinking heavily when she had lost Pippa's father, but for the past five or six years with Dr Weaver's help she had got it under control, until, it seemed, the fateful night of the bridge party, the eve of Pippa's and Jerome's return, when Dr Weaver had noticed with dismay that his friend and patient was back drinking spirits.

'She was perfectly all right, it seems,' Pippa explained, 'if she just had the occasional sherry, or even wine. But she couldn't touch spirits. If she had just one small glass of whisky or gin it would start her off again on another bout.'

'Which was obviously what happened that night,' Elizabeth said. 'She drank far too much, she probably went on drinking with Mrs Whatever long after everyone else had gone, and then forgot whether or not she'd taken any sleeping pills. So there you are, darling. There you have your explanation.'

'Not really,' Pippa replied. 'You see firstly, why did she *start* drinking again? If she'd been off it for so long? There would have to be something which would cause her to start up again. And then, of course, it still doesn't explain the postcard.'

'Ah yes,' Elizabeth pondered, her heart no longer sinking. 'You attach a great deal of importance to that postcard, darling, don't you?'

'Yes,' Pippa replied. 'It was the last thing my mother ever saw of me. And she tore it up. She tore it to pieces.'

Elizabeth put a hand to her mouth as if to stifle a small gasp, and then she reached across to Pippa and took both her hands. Nothing on her face betrayed her innermost thoughts, she knew that. She was far too consummate an actress. Nobody would ever have known that what Elizabeth was really thinking was that if this sort of thing went on, then it was going to take no time at all for the Bumpkin to become quite, quite demented.

After much heart searching, Pippa decided not to tell Jerome about the latest development. At first she had been convinced she should, since as she explained to Elizabeth they had no secrets from each other, but Elizabeth had persuaded her otherwise. She was afraid for Pippa, it seemed, in case Jerome, wrapped up as he was in the intricacies of his role as Romeo, might not give her news the attention it merited.

'Trust me,' Elizabeth had counselled her. 'He's an actor, and so am I, darling. And when you're deeply involved in a major role, the outside world seems a very distant place.'

On the strength of advice seemingly borne from experience, Pippa had decided at least to wait and see before involving Jerome any more in her personal anxieties, and the decision seemed to be the right one when Pippa saw both how totally immersed Jerome was in the part and how much playing it exhausted him. She also knew, the more time she spent by herself, either painting in her studio or walking Bobby in the park, that the problem of her mother was something which only Pippa could solve. Talking to Jerome was a great help, discussing her anxiety with him was immensely therapeutic, listening to what he had to say was enormously beneficial, but she knew even so he could never solve the problem for her, and that finally he would bore of it, and perhaps even of Pippa, at least he would bore of Pippa talking about it, which would mean that a part of him would be bored with a part of her, which was the very last thing Pippa wanted. She loved Jerome with all her heart, and she was sure he loved her with all of his, but she knew that to keep him, she must never lose his interest, not for a moment, because while a moment of boredom after passion is often tolerable, the reverse is never true.

Another undisputed fact was the success of Jerome as Romeo, or more properly, as *The Times* labelled it, his *unqualified triumph* in the part. Everyone who saw his performance agreed. He was simply brilliant, the best Romeo, some said, in living memory. He was also a superb Mercutio, as indeed was his rival Anthony Hart, but whereas Jerome scored maximum points in both roles, Hart was a total flop as Romeo. Nonetheless the whole run sold out, because the audiences were happy to see Jerome Didier in either role, although those fortunate enough to catch his Romeo remembered it for the rest of their lives.

Pippa knew she would never forget it. In all her life she had never seen or heard anything so beautiful, and she knew that if she lived to be a thousand she would never see anything as beautiful ever again.

She saw his every performance, and long before the end of the run she knew the play by heart.

'*Give me my Romeo,*' she would sometimes whisper to him as they were about to make love, or after they had done so. '*And, when he shall die, take him and cut him out in little stars, and he will make the face of heaven so fine that all the world will be in love with night, and pay no worship to the garish sun.*'

'It's just as well you're not playing Juliet,' Jerome told her. 'Or the Lord Chamberlain would close down the theatre.'

Pippa picked up the phone without thinking. She was on her way out to see Jerome perform when it rang, just as Pippa hurried past the hall table. It had been weeks now without any word from her tormentor, so Pippa had put any thought of her out of her mind, and certainly that evening in her hurry to leave the apartment she had forgotten the code, she had forgotten about letting the phone ring to see if it just rang twice for friend, or more for foe.

She picked it up as it barely finished ringing once.

'Oh dear,' said the voice. 'I hope you haven't forgotten me.'

Pippa slammed the receiver back down immediately and stood staring at it, aware that she was shaking all over, and furious that she had forgotten the rule. Then she turned and hurried across the hall. As she reached the front door, the phone rang again, but this time Pippa ignored it, although she could hear it ringing in the empty hallway as she ran down the stairs and into the street, and all the way through the play and well into the night.

The next letter arrived two days later, and again Pippa was caught. Jerome had ordered her to tear up unread any more letters which arrived addressed in that particular childish handwriting, but the name and address on this particular letter were typed, and the notepaper was also different. So Pippa was unaware of the sender as she opened the letter over breakfast.

YOU KNOW THE CAUSE OF MOTHER'S MISERY. YOU'RE MARRIED TO IT.

All in all over the next month there were seven more letters, which arrived at irregular intervals. By the time the third one dropped through the letterbox, different type face, different envelope, but the same postmark – *Haslemere* – Pippa knew the time had long come to tell Jerome.

He was furious. Pippa had never seen Jerome in a temper, a genuine rage, a proper fury. She had seen him cross, irritable, angry, but never like this. He sat across from her at the table, white-faced, gripping her by her wrists.

'Why didn't you *tell* me?' he hissed. Even his lips had paled.

'You know why. I've told you. I thought I could cope with it.'

'By yourself.'

'You were far too involved.'

'For you?' Jerome sounded totally disbelieving.

'With the play.'

'I am *never* – too involved for you, my darling girl. Never.'

It was the way he said the word – *nevah* – just the once, but it was enough to give Pippa the fleeting impression that Jerome was acting. Then she put it from her mind. She was tired, terribly tired, tired out by the mental battle, exhausted from trying to work out not how but *why*. And because she was so devitalized by all the conscious and subconscious worry, for a moment she had even lost her trust in Jerome. Stemming back a tear, biting hard down on her lower lip, she looked up and across the table at Jerome, who when he caught her eyes with his widened his own as wide-as-can-be.

Then he smiled slowly, with just a tinge of regret, and once again Pippa had to remind herself what he was doing was real, and that he was not play-acting.

'I was only angry,' he said, 'because you excluded me. And by doing that, I felt that you didn't trust me.'

'You told me when you're acting to leave you alone.'

'Not about important things, my darling girl. Only the day to day things. Only the day to day. Now, what are you going to do? I'll tell you what you're going to do. You're going to go to the police.'

'I don't want to go to the police, Jerome.'

'You're going to solve this single-handed?'

'It has to be someone in the village. It can't be anybody else. Nobody outside the village could possibly know all – all the details. The village is tiny – what? Hardly a hundred people. And it's a woman, so that probably halves the list of suspects. No – more. Because I haven't counted the children—'

'Sssshhh!'

Jerome tightened his grip on Pippa's wrists, as the expression changed on his face. Pippa watched curiously as he worked the muscles in his jaw, tightening them and slackening them, while he gently drew her closer to him across the table, and wondered why to herself, why did she think this was all so unreal?

'Jerome—' she began.

'No,' he said, firmly, but still with a smile. 'No, you're to listen to me, young lady. You are not going down to Selham to knock on everyone's door and ask all the wives and mothers if they've been sending you poison pen letters. There is no reason why it should be someone *in* the village. It could just as well be somebody *outside* the village, or in the next *door* village, or the next one. It's a close community down there, but it doesn't run into twenty or so suspects, darling girl. It could be a list of *hundreds*. And you won't know by asking, and you certainly won't tell by looking. So you're going to do as I suggest, and hand all this over to the police.'

Pippa was losing touch, but she couldn't say anything, she couldn't tell Jerome, because Jerome was suddenly so far away, and he was so very small, and his voice was echoing only faintly as if they were either end of a long pipe or alleyway underground. She called out to him, but no sound would come, she called again, and again. But still there was silence from her and only the faintest of noises from the other end of the pipe or alleyway where they were, at either end, and where she could just, but only just, about see there was still some light. The light was still there, but growing ever fainter, when at last she managed to call, she called his name and as she did so – *Jerome* – her head suddenly crashed down and forward on to the table as the light disappeared completely.

ELEVEN

'You still call it that over here?' Oscar asked. 'A nervous breakdown?'

This genuinely puzzled Elizabeth and she allowed her brow to wrinkle, but only lightly.

'Obviously you Yanks have a much more up-to-date name for it,' she said. 'Something marvellously technical, something altogether more suitable.'

They were sitting having drinks in Elizabeth's drawing room, discussing Pippa's sudden collapse and subsequent confinement. Elizabeth had thought it a nice idea to ask Oscar round to discuss their affairs, with Sebastian safely out of the way on business abroad, 'off-stage' as she liked to think of it.

'No, no,' Oscar hurriedly corrected her, dropping cigarette ash on Elizabeth's white carpet without noticing. 'We don't have any fancy new word for it, it's just that the term nervous breakdown has been kind of discredited.'

'What a pity,' Elizabeth sighed, eyeing the snail of grey ash at Oscar's feet. 'I always think it has a rather nice dramatic ring to it. *He's suffering from a nervous breakdown.* As if wretched old life has just become far too much. Don't move.'

Oscar frowned as he watched someone who was surely one of the world's most beautiful women get down on her hands and knees to crawl across to him and carefully scoop up his snake of fallen ash with the lip of an unsealed envelope.

'Hell,' he said. 'I'm sorry.'

'Oz, darling,' Elizabeth replied, neatly tapping the ash into his ashtray, 'you know it's said to keep the moths away. Do go on with what you were saying.'

Elizabeth sat back in her chair and ran a moistened finger along the collar of glue on the pale coloured envelope, sticking it down. She put the envelope beside her on a round table, face down, with some other letters.

'Go on,' she urged. 'You were going to tell me the fancy American term for a nervous breakdown.'

'There really is none,' Oscar replied, wishing instead to talk about the play. 'No-one knows where or what the mind is, so the term nervous breakdown can really have no technical meaning. All it can do is loosely, very loosely, be used to describe various mannerisms manifested by those suffering from anxiety, or extreme nervous tension.'

'*Fasc*inating,' Elizabeth said. 'All of which goes for poor Pippa.'

'Have you seen her?'

Elizabeth shook her head. 'Have you?'

'I gather she has to have complete rest. An impossibility I'd say, given the amount of traffic that flows through that apartment.'

'Poor darling. She *must* need a rest. After what she's been through.'

In time Oscar just caught the next half inch of ash in the palm of his hand as it flaked off his Lucky Strike. He tipped it at once into the ashtray, followed by the stub of the cigarette.

'You don't seriously think it's an inside job, Lizzie?' he asked. 'Much more likely it's some batty old dame in that Agatha Christie sounding village.'

Elizabeth picked up the sealed envelope from beside her, and tapped it thoughtfully on the table.

'It was just a thought, darling,' she replied. 'Jerome is *such* a national heart-throb now, you know. I gather he was mobbed nightly at the stage door during his *Romeo*. That they tore the clothes off his back. That young girls *fainted* in the Gods.' Her voice dropped to a whisper. 'That they sent him their knickers through the post.'

As usual, Oscar remained stone-faced, but inside he was astounded. It seemed such a contrary thing to do.

'Do they enclose a covering note?' he wondered. 'You know, something along the lines of Dear Mr Didier, I really enjoyed your Romeo last evening. In all honesty I can say I have never seen a more poetic or spiritually inspired performance. Please find enclosed one pair of black lace panties. Yours sincerely, Jane Doe.'

Elizabeth threw her head back and laughed, and then having smoothed her dark hair back in place, turned her famous green eyes on him.

'Of course,' she said, sighing. 'All jokes aside, I suppose this will mean Jerome won't even *consider* the play.'

'I very much doubt it. Would you? If you were he?'

'I'm going to surprise you by saying yes. Yes, Oz darling, yes I would. You see what poor sweet Pippa needs is a complete rest. From *everything*. And as we're agreed, that apartment of theirs is the next best thing to Piccadilly Circus. When Jerome is home. But if Jerome *wasn't* at home—'

Oscar, who was finishing his Martini, looked up at this, and in doing so missed seeing the olive stick which caught him in the lip.

He ran a finger over the little bruise which was already swelling and frowned at Elizabeth.

'Better still surely,' he asked, 'if they *both* weren't at home. If they took some time off. Went on a vacation.'

'Yes.' Elizabeth invested the adverb with sufficient doubt to make it sound most unaffirmative. 'The trouble being that – or didn't you know?' Now she looked worried, as if she had only just realized something. 'Did Cecil not tell you?' Again the question was loaded differently. It wasn't a *curious* question. Did Cecil not tell you? It was a *you-mean* question. You-mean Cecil didn't tell you? 'We've had to move everything forward, Oz darling. If I'm to do your play, it's going to have to be now.'

'What's with the *if*, Miss Laurence?' Oscar got up and then sat down again. 'Come on – it's never been a question of *if*. This play was written for you. *With* you, dammit! This whole new version is all your idea!'

'I can't believe Cecil didn't say anything.' Elizabeth carefully lit a Sobranie, and blew the smoke out uninhaled. 'Darling, the *on dit* is Hollywood next stop. And *this year*.'

Oscar got up again, asked if he could fix them both another drink, and when Elizabeth declined the offer on her behalf, he went over to the drinks table and mixed himself an extra stiff cocktail.

'Jerome will never agree,' he said finally. 'No chance.'

'I think he might,' Elizabeth said carefully. 'I think I might be able to persuade him.'

'Sorry, Lizzie,' Oscar disagreed. 'Even given your quite unique charms, I don't think anything will persuade Jerome to leave Pippa.'

Elizabeth took a long pull on her cigarette, this time inhaling the smoke, before crushing it to a premature death in an ashtray.

'Come along,' she said, on the rise. 'Let's go and have lunch.'

On their way out, Elizabeth handed her maid, who was also dressed to go out, her batch of letters to post, keeping back just one, the palely coloured envelope which she slipped unseen into her handbag.

'Be a poppet and post these for me, Maggie,' she said. 'Here's the money for the stamps.'

'I won't have time to get the stamps till I get home, Mrs Ferrers,' the maid replied. 'I'm only just going to make the station.'

'I'm *always* doing this to you, aren't I?' Elizabeth laughed.

'It doesn't matter, Mrs Ferrers. As long as you don't mind.'

'Mind, Maggie? I actively prefer it! You know that! You just can't trust the post in London any more. Now off you go, enjoy your afternoon, and I'll see you in the morning.'

Oscar got a cab, and was giving the driver instructions when Elizabeth got in.

'I don't know where I'd be without Maggie,' she said as the cab pulled away from the house. 'She's such a sweet girl, you know. An absolute treasure. Always goes home to mum 'n dad in the country on her half day. It's terribly sweet. They run a little village Post Office just outside Haslemere.'

The mail, which included a brown enveloped letter once again addressed to Pippa in the original childish block writing, and a large pale lavender enveloped letter addressed to Jerome in a loopy backward sloping hand lay waiting to be collected by Miss Toothe in the wire catch basket on the back of the front door. It was twenty-five to nine in the morning, and the secretary was not due in to start her duties until the hour. No-one else was allowed to touch the incoming mail, those were Jerome's strict orders, until Miss Toothe had sorted through it, sifting the personal from the business and the bills, and keeping a strict eye out for any of an immediately suspicious nature. The telephone number of the apartment had been changed the day after Pippa's collapse, as indeed had the number for her Chelsea studio, as a precaution.

Jerome and Pippa were still in bed, Jerome asleep, Pippa wide awake, feeling for the first time in a long time that she couldn't sleep another minute. After her collapse, which Pippa knew to be only a faint, and correctly described it as such, Jerome nevertheless insisted on advice privately taken from both Elizabeth and Cecil that Pippa be examined by a Harley Street neurologist, who pronounced her to be suffering from a nervous breakdown. Pippa had insisted that this was not the case, that she had merely fainted, something she had often done as both a child and a teenager, and that the faint or *syncope* (she remembered the correct term from Dr Weaver who had often treated her for it) had been brought about as might be expected by emotional causes and a lack of proper nutrition. For obvious reasons Pippa hadn't eaten properly or regularly in months.

Mr Sessions, the specialist, a tall, pompous and rapidly balding know-it-all (Oscar called them *swell-heads*) had smiled benignly but briefly at Pippa before continuing to talk to Jerome as if she wasn't there. The patient he advised would need a long bed rest and absolute quiet. Again, Pippa had interrupted him, raising her voice so that the specialist might pay her some attention while she had repeated what in her opinion was wrong with her, and that all she needed was some sleep and a couple of good square meals. And once again the specialist had refused to acknowledge her, informing Jerome instead that such outbursts were a typical symptom of nervous breakdowns, and he must expect other indications, such as sudden tearfulness, loss of temper, marked social withdrawal, and even an overt concern for the patient's own state of health, which as Pippa later remarked to Jerome covered just about everything, particularly for someone who was still in grief, and particularly if that someone was female.

Mr Sessions had left Jerome with a long list of the medications he considered vital for the patient's recovery, which included prescriptions for nerve tonics, brain foods, vitamin complexes, particularly thiamine and riboflavin, tranquillizers, sleeping tablets and a revolting sounding diet based mainly on steamed fish, nuts and undercooked liver, all of which Pippa chose to ignore completely.

She had been out of bed and dressing when Jerome had returned after seeing the doctor out.

'If anyone needs treatment,' she had told Jerome in a rising voice, 'it's not me, it's that over-dressed horse-doctor! I am *not* going potty, Jerome! I am *not* having a nervous breakdown! I am *not* going round the bend!'

Jerome had sat her patiently down on the bed, mistaking the exasperation in her voice for hysteria, and had tried to talk her down gently, reasoning with her that it couldn't do her any harm to spend some time in bed, just resting, and sleeping, and being waited on hand and foot. Nancy would look after her, Nancy the maid and Miss Toothe, they would see to her every need if he was working, and if he wasn't working he wouldn't move from her side. Then the moment she was quite well again, they would take a holiday. They would go off to France, or even better, they would go to Florence – which was the moment when Pippa really despaired.

She had seen the look in Jerome's eyes, a look of such pity and concern that she knew he believed the specialist, that he thought she really was cracking up. It was (again as Oscar would say) a

264

no-win situation. If she fought it, if she raised her voice in protest, it would be taken as a symptom of her diagnosed disorder, while if she didn't, if she just took to her bed and slept and ate and did as she was told, that would equally be read as proof that she was ill. And so she had cried, not because she was really ill, but because she wasn't. Pippa was not in the least neurotic, and she never had been. What she had been for as long as she could remember was a fainter. As she was growing up, she had fainted not frequently, just enough to cause her mother and Dr Weaver concern, although happily it was found there was nothing seriously wrong with her beyond a common overactivity of the *vagus* or *parasympathetic* nerves.

'A faint is just a reflex action,' Dr Weaver had told her. 'All you've got to do if you start feeling faint is just lower your head below the level of your heart, which will soon restore the flow of blood to your brain.'

Unfortunately, the day she had collapsed at the table with Jerome, she had been so upset she hadn't noticed the warning signs in time, so when she had tried to get to her feet it had been too late, with the result that now everyone, including Jerome, thought she was suffering a breakdown.

Which was why when she saw that look in his eyes, she cried, uncontrollable tears, unstoppable tears, sudden tears, which as she did she realized was, of course, a typical symptom of a nervous breakdown.

Pippa remembered all this, she sifted all the facts backwards and forwards through her head that winter morning as she lay in the half-light with Jerome still fast asleep beside her, while the letter which was to change her life lay as yet uncollected in the wire basket. Oddly enough, even though she knew she was not broken down or even breaking down, the enforced rest was doing Pippa good. She would never have believed she could sleep as much as she had. Once she had started to sleep in, having been made to entrust Bobby's walks to either Jerome or Nancy, she found to her astonishment that she could sleep right through the morning with no trouble.

Jerome was delighted, not because he thought it proved him right that Pippa was suffering from some form of crack–up, but because he maintained that people's bodies told them what they needed, and half the modern world's troubles stemmed from people not listening to their bodies. Pippa needed the sleep, her body was telling her that in no uncertain terms, so sleep she must.

'*Innocent sleep,*' he had smiled as he settled her back on her pillows. '*Sleep that knits up the ravell'd sleave of care, the death of each day's life, sore labour's bath, balm of hurt minds, great nature's second course, chief nourisher of life's feast.'*

So Pippa had slept, she had given in to the remorseless fatigue she realized she had felt, and the longer she had slept, the more the wound healed.

She could think sensibly about the play now. When before her collapse Jerome had first mentioned it, worried as always (worried more than ever, Pippa recalled), about the implications and the ramifications and the connotations of what *They* were once again asking him to do, Pippa had found herself for once irritated by the amount of importance Jerome gave the matter when there seemed to be matters more worthy of their concern. Jerome had been oblivious to this, and had worried the issue of Oscar's new play much as Bobby worried his rubber play-bone, endlessly, noisily and at all the wrong times, until surprising herself and surprising Jerome even more Pippa had told him once but in no uncertain terms that there was no point whatsoever in seeking her advice because there was only one person's advice Jerome ever took and that was the person who stared back out at him every morning in his shaving mirror.

'Is this our first fight, Mrs Didier?' Jerome had laughed. 'Is it separate bedrooms tonight? Oh, alas – alack-a-day!'

She hadn't been allowed to read the play in bed, because Jerome knew that would only lead to a long discussion about its merits and its suitability, which he feared would tire the patient unnecessarily. In fact since her faint, the subject of Oscar's new play had never been brought up again, at least not in front of her. Pippa had heard it discussed briefly and in the distance, whenever Cecil called round, and during certain telephone calls if the bedroom door had been left ajar. Jerome was at his most doubtful, and the more Pippa lay in her bed thinking about it, the more she was inclined to agree with him. From what she could gather it seemed Oscar had once again written the play primarily for Elizabeth, with Jerome very much as an afterthought, and from what she overheard from the snatches of conversation, Elizabeth's part was a brilliant creation, almost guaranteed to steal the thunder. So what, she wondered, was in it for Jerome?

Second best, from the way Jerome had described his role, that of a failed painter who becomes obsessed with a strange girl he finds one day when he comes to open up his long locked studio, a beautiful but elusive sprite who becomes his model and his mistress, only finally to vanish as mysteriously as she appeared, from the locked studio just after the painter has completed a portrait of her which is hailed as a masterpiece. The cards were all well and truly stacked in Elizabeth's favour.

'Mind you,' Jerome had said once he had outlined the play, 'it sounds corny, the whole *play* sounds corny, but then what play doesn't when you describe it? Try describing *Hamlet*, and I guarantee you'll be rolling on the floor by the time poor Polonius gets stabbed in the arras. But of course it isn't in the least corny. Oscar is a *wonderful* writer. He can take the most mundane sounding theme and stand it on its head. It is a simply *mar*vellously written play. Witty, full of twists and turns, dramatic, and – I have to say it – finally heartbreaking. But there you are.' Jerome had gestured helplessly. A quick circling move with one raised hand. 'It is a vehicle for Didier and Laurence. Or rather more perhaps one should bill this one Laurence and Didier.

By the time Jerome was bathed and shaved that morning, and padding wrapped in a thick, white, towelling robe barefooted like a cat across the bedroom to draw the big, expensive curtains, Pippa's mind was made up. Jerome must not do the play. Jerome was launched. Jerome had just been acclaimed the finest Romeo in living memory. Jerome Didier was on his own way. So if asked, Pippa would agree with him. Yes, it would be wrong, very wrong to do the play. No, he certainly must *not* do it.

Unfortunately the letter lying in the wire basket was going to make up Jerome's mind long before Pippa got round to him. In fact the contents of the letter lying in the wire were such that Pippa's opinion would not even be sought.

Miss Toothe had all the mail sorted out by the time Jerome was dressed. She brought all the personal letters through to him at the breakfast table, as was the agreed habit. She had placed the brown envelope with the childish writing at the top of the pile, again a part of the agreed procedure. Jerome frowned as he slit the letter open with a long-bladed paper knife, puzzled as to why the anonymous writer should have suddenly reverted to her original form of inscription, and as he noticed when he unfolded the letter, back to her original cheap lined blue notepaper. The message was even more cryptic than ever. It read:

GOD HAS NOT FORGIVEN MOTHER.

'She's losing her touch,' Jerome muttered before screwing the letter up and consigning it to a waste basket which Miss Toothe had as usual placed beside him. 'What else?'

Jerome sifted through the post, seeing if he could recognize any familiar handwriting, or putting to one side any which bore the stamp of any theatrical managements or film studios. This morning there was just one, the expected letter from Locke's, which he cut open, discarding the envelope but leaving the letter unread and still folded beside his plate. He knew more or less what the letter would say, and his eye had been more taken with the pale lavender coloured envelope, the one addressed in the oddly looping and backward sloping hand. He frowned at this one too, though not this time from irritation, but from curiosity. The letter spoke to him, it asked to be seen, it demanded to be read first.

Jerome picked it up, glanced at the London postmark, and then read it, first dismissing Miss Toothe, who departed taking with her the waste basket full of the day's envelopes, and the crumpled anonymous letter, which she would retrieve and read, as part of her own procedure, before consigning it finally to the dustbin.

There was no address on the top of the letter, just a name, written in the same oblique hand:

SYBIL DODONA

At first Jerome considered it might be a letter from an actress, hoping for work. Since *Lady Anne* his mailbag contained many such pleas, and they all were consigned to the waste basket. It wasn't that Jerome was callous, on the contrary. It was simply that he believed if he met and saw one actress and subsequently helped get her work, then he would be obliged to do the same for them all, or rather he would at least have to go as far as interviewing them all. It was an all-or-nothing choice, and Jerome had chosen the nothing option.

This letter, however, was from neither some aspiring nor some failing actress. It was from an astrologer. Jerome immediately put down his half-drunk cup of coffee and leaned forward so that he sat practically on the edge of his chair. Ever since he had been told the story by Elizabeth of the young actress whose dying day had been predicted by a well-known fortune-teller, and who had wished all her friends goodbye on the nominated day before climbing into her bed and dying, even though there was proved to be nothing medically wrong with her, Jerome had become fascinated by the art of astrology.

But this one Jerome didn't know. He had never even heard a mention of someone called *Sybil Dodona*, so his first instinct was that she was a fraud, and that her letter would turn out to be yet another variation of the begging bowl. That is until his skim-reading eye caught a phrase halfway down the first page, which read:

You must take advantage of a disadvantage now or by the end of the year you will be adrift, and your chance of singularity damaged by your determination to plough a single furrow *at any cost*.

That was enough to convince Jerome the letter was genuine. The tone was right, the language confident, and the prediction founded on fact, however speculative. He knew there was an offer on the table from Hollywood for Elizabeth. Not for him or for him and her, at the moment according to their mutual agent the deal was just for her. So perhaps what this stargazer was saying was that what might seem to be a disadvantage now, the point in present contention, could turn out to be one of those much vaunted blessings in disguise.

He therefore laid the letter out flat on the table in front of him, poured himself a fresh cup of coffee, and began to read it from the very top. It ran:

Dear Mr Didier,

You will not know who I am, so I have the advantage of you, because now like millions of others, I know you, and like those millions of others feel, I feel I know you well. There is a fundamental difference, however, because unlike those millions of others, I do know you and know you very well. Please do not be offended. It is my business to know people well, the people I choose to study, and because you are one of the very brightest of stars to rise in our firmament for a very long time I chose to make a study of you the moment I first saw you on stage, in *All That Glitters*.

Knowing that you are a busy man, I will not take up your time as so many astrologians (so-called) would with vague and ambiguous predictions designed to suit a general type of person, rather than a single and singular person (such as yourself). I am only interested in your future, and in helping you to make it secure, and as successful as you deserve it to be. I had the infinite pleasure of seeing your Romeo since when I have been even more assured that you will go on to achieve a fame greater than any English actor before you, and greater than any one who will succeed you for very many years. One hundred and twenty-five years to be precise. That is the predicted length of time which will pass from your death until the appearance of another with your *special* talents.

And they are special, Mr Didier, this I can tell you, along with many other things, and I can tell you with certainty because our future, contrary to what one of your favourite playwrights believes, is indeed in the stars, and not in ourselves. Your fate is already designed and you must go with it, you must flow with the current, and not try to swim against it.

This is the hardest part for those without the vision and the knowledge to understand. You will argue if your future is already predestined, then you have no say in the matter, no choice. You are wrong. We are all given free will, we all have a full say in what we do and how we do it. But since we have choice, we must remember that in choosing, there are good and there are bad choices, which is where people such as I may be asked into your lives *to help you make the right choice*. We can do this, those who are blessed with the ability to read the skies, because we can see what the choices are. I will say nothing more of this, because there is nothing more to be said. It is all in your birth chart, from the moment of your conception, to the moment of your death.

By now I either have your full attention, or I am lying at the bottom of a waste paper basket, or consigned to the fire. But if I have your attention, I am happier than I have been in a very long time, because at this very moment I can help you, and I know from your chart that this is a time when you desperately need help. I took your chart down last night, as I do every week, or when something indicates that I must, and when I saw the five planets of Virgo, I knew your confusion. Alone you will never make this decision a correct decision. Besides the five planets you have a Full Moon in your opposite sign, and the light which it casts is deceptive. It makes you think you can see the problem clearly, but as I said, the light it casts is illusive.

The light is so clear, in fact, it makes you think what you want is right, and what else is wanted of you is wrong, because the truth is hidden in those deep dark moon shadows. It is essential you are not deceived and it is equally essential you understand this turmoil you are in can be very easily explained by the presence of those five planets which are busy whirling around Virgo. So if I may advise you, and I can only offer it as advice, but it is good advice, for I can see where you cannot, please:

You must take advantage of a disadvantage now or by the end of the year you will be adrift, and your chance of singularity damaged by your determination to plough a single furrow, *at any cost*.

You will know what this means in terms of your life. I cannot. I cannot even begin to guess, but I know from your chart that if you miss this turn, then what you seek and what is your due cannot be yours, ever. While if you take this other path, whatever its immediate disadvantages, by doing this you will achieve your goal in life, and it will not be done at the sacrifice of your ambition.

Go then, and turn about face. You think your stars say that two into one will not go, but I have seen the heavens, and I can tell you that this is not so. I have seen the night-cloths, and your name is there for you to see, embroidered in stars, but only if you understand that the way to the stars is not always as signposted.

I shall always be here at hand, when you need me. I do not need to reveal where I am, because I shall know long before you when again you need my direction.

Jerome looked in at Pippa, but she had fallen back fast asleep, her coffee cup still full beside the bed. She looked so lovely when she slept, so innocent and untroubled, one arm up on the pillow crooked round her tousled head, the other dropped in a loose embrace around Bobby, who woke up briefly when Jerome tiptoed in, before settling back to sleep with a contented sigh.

He wondered when he should tell her, and how. He knew he couldn't just announce he was going to do the play just like that, out of the blue and for no reason, not after these weeks of indecision. In the state Pippa was in, the surprise and the shock of his volte-face could well have a detrimental effect on her apparently improving health, particularly if as he already knew to be the case, the play was destined to go out on a tour before coming into town. And Pippa was in no state to tour. Neither was she in a state to be left alone. But equally since the arrival of that morning's mail, neither could Jerome take the risk of ignoring what was already written, not by Oscar Greene, but way up there above him, up in the stars.

On the appointed day, a young and healthy woman had said goodbye to all her friends, climbed into her bed and died.

Carefully Jerome closed the bedroom door shut behind him and tiptoed out to the telephone in the hall. There was only one thing for it, he had decided, and that was to ring Elizabeth. Elizabeth was the friend of both of them. Elizabeth would know the best way to handle it. Elizabeth was the person to ask.

TWELVE

Cecil was chosen as the herald (Elizabeth's term), although he himself preferred the term diplomat. To Cecil's way of thinking there was a tremendous similarity between the life of theatrical agents and those in the diplomatic corps. To him they were both honest men sent abroad to lie for the good of the commonwealth, and this was one of those occasions. Pippa had to be convinced that what he was about to do was for the good of them all, which was something Cecil now believed, thanks to Elizabeth's powers of persuasion. Happily Pippa took little persuading, although there was one very sticky moment, Cecil always recalled, over of all things her dog.

The conversation had run roughly along the lines that for Jerome to accept the offer of Oscar's new play meant going against Jerome's own judgement, which Cecil did not consider a better one than his, or the judgement of certain other parties. His brief had been to convince Pippa that her husband would rather play in the *nth* revival of *The Little Hut On The Mountain* all year in Skegness than appear in the West End once more as part of the Didier-Laurence duo, and this he had done, in Cecil's own opinion, really rather well. If Jerome was going to do Oscar's new play, it was going to have to be for some damned good reason.

Cecil had explained the damned good reason, which he felt sure Pippa could help persuade Jerome to see. Hollywood, in the shape of Metro-Goldwyn-Mayer, wanted Elizabeth and they wanted her badly, but as yet they remained unconvinced about Jerome. This at once made Pippa leap to the defence of her husband and wonder to Cecil what on earth MGM can have been watching if they were convinced by Elizabeth but not Jerome.

'Quite frankly, dear girl,' Cecil had confided, 'one gets the rather distinct impression they haven't so much been *watching* as *listening*, what we like to call – if you'll excuse the vernacular – earholing. When it comes to beautiful and exciting young actresses, the Americans will take things on trust, although I'm inclined to think – and I'm not alone in this – that Americans are simply just inclined to take things. Dog in the manger, you know. *I'd rather have it than have you have it even though I don't know what to do with it now I've got it* sort of thing. And now they've heard of Elizabeth Laurence. In fact all they've heard about from their spies here is Elizabeth Laurence Elizabeth Laurence Elizabeth Laurence. And they've seen her pictures. Not her *movies*, her pictures, the photos in the Press and magazines, and they've gone, *wow*! or whatever the latest American word is. *Gee whiz, guys, just wait till you feast your peepers on this little baby!*'

Naturally Pippa had wanted to know why they hadn't had the same reaction about Jerome, and Cecil had sighed and shaken his head and explained that the people who feasted their peepers were almost exclusively men, the sort of men who preferred, like most men, to feast their peepers on women. Of course, they had sent copies of Jerome's films to MGM, but that was just coals to Newcastle. The last thing film makers wanted to do at the end of their day was to sit down and watch some other film makers' films. No, the only chance they had of getting Jerome considered as seriously as Elizabeth was being considered, was to get him seen in something good, and preferably doing it the day after tomorrow.

Everyone knew there was only one option, and that was to do Oscar's play. This would get him seen, Cecil would see to that. He would invite all the American talent scouts he knew, and he would make personally certain they all saw Jerome, who would be (no guessing) superb in the part. However, Cecil had explained to Jerome (he had explained to Pippa), that should the Americans consequently take as active an interest in him as they had in Elizabeth, this would in no way entail any sort of partnership deal. Cecil would make sure of that. He would make personally sure of it. If Jerome was wanted, it must be, it had to be *only for himself*. For the last time Cecil had explained to Pippa that he had explained this to Jerome, but it seemed Jerome still needed convincing, and the only person who could do that final convincing was Pippa. The vote on that had been unanimous.

They were practically home and dry. Cecil had seen that, he sensed his careful persuasion had won the day, and he could go and collect on his ticket. Which he was just about to do when the subject of Bobby had come up.

'Just suppose,' Pippa asked, propped up against her pillows, looking for all the world like something from a pre-Raphaelite painting, 'suppose Jerome does get an offer from Hollywood, and has to go and make a picture there.'

'Or several,' Cecil had carelessly added, immediately regretting the indiscretion.

'Exactly,' Pippa had pounced. 'Or several. That would mean we'd have to go and live there, wouldn't it?'

'Good heavens, Pip – not for *ever*!' Cecil had laughed, trying to brush such a thought under the mat. But Pippa was nothing if not persistent.

'But even if it was for three months, six, a year say. I mean I wouldn't stay here.'

'Of course not. That would be the last thing Jerome would want.'

'I know,' Pippa had fallen silent then, pulling her knees up under the covers to hug them. 'So what would I do about Bobby, Cecil? I couldn't kennel him, even if it was only for three months say. And I couldn't take him, because of the quarantine laws. So what would I do?'

Cecil had felt a sense of absolute outrage welling inside him, and he had very nearly wondered aloud and really quite passionately (for Cecil) that Pippa wasn't *serious* – that she wasn't really prepared to jeopardize her husband's career for the sake of some flop-eared, tangle-haired, over-active mongrel who had once cocked his leg against Cecil's best Daks casuals? But instead he had held his breath, and kept quiet for a moment, as if giving the matter his most serious attention.

'Bobby could stay here,' he had finally suggested. 'Miss Toothe could look after him.'

'I don't think so, Cecil. Miss Toothe doesn't like dogs. Particularly small, hairy, black mongrels who eat secretarys' walking shoes.'

'Someone will look after him, Pip. We'll find someone.' Although for the life of him Cecil hadn't at once been able to think of anybody. 'That really isn't a problem.'

But from the look on Pippa's face, and her increasingly glum expression Cecil had realized that indeed it was.

'My mother.' An inspired notion, Cecil thought, if ever there was one.

'She'd never keep him in, Cecil. He'd keep running home. Rather where home used to be. He'd keep running back next door.'

'We have a big empty chicken run,' Cecil had remembered wishing to curtail this increasingly dangerous conversation. 'He could live indoors in the boot room at night, and Aggie could let him out every day in the hen run. He'd be perfectly safe, I promise.'

'You're very sweet, Cecil. And I'm sure he'd be fine—'

Cecil had got to his feet quickly before the 'but'. Good, he had said, but all this was something they could discuss, if and when. It was nothing insurmountable. There was an answer to everything. And the most important thing was to get Jerome to do the play, agreed? Pippa had nodded. Of course, she had said. Yes, Cecil was right, it would be terribly unfair if Elizabeth got the chance to go to Hollywood and Jerome didn't, provided it was something Jerome wanted. Oh yes, Cecil assured her, remembering just in time the small box of chocolates he had purchased for Pippa and placing them beside her bed. This was certainly something which Jerome wanted, while thinking to himself that if it wasn't, Jerome could go and find himself another agent, if all Jerome Didier wanted to do was stay in England and fool around in the theatre.

He was quite sure of that? was Pippa's last question. Because if they decided between them that Jerome should do the play, there were to be no strings, and it had to be something Jerome wanted.

You know Jerome, Cecil had said with a smile as he pulled on his brand new calfskin gloves. Jerome only really ever does what Jerome really wants.

It was surprising how readily Jerome had conceded. Pippa had expected more of a fight. Not that she had been the least bit contentious, nor had she advised him one way or the other. All she had done was put the case to him, just as Cecil had put it to her, with nothing added, one way or the other. Jerome had baulked, of course, but only at the *unfairness*, at why Hollywood should be prepared to take Elizabeth on trust, as it were, while he had to go through some sort of public audition. He didn't *have* to, Pippa had reminded him. There was no compulsion for him to do so, unless he really wanted to go to Hollywood. Did he want to go to Hollywood? Well, of course he did! Didn't any actor with *sense*! Even if he didn't know what was on offer? Pippa had reminded him of what he was always reminding her, that any play or film that he did he would do so only after the closest consideration, and for his own reasons. Jerome had his own reasons. England alone could never make him a major international star. He had to go to Hollywood. He knew that now, whereas he hadn't known that before, not in his salad days, when he had thought all you had to do was good work and do it well and fame and success would be the natural concomitant. No, damn it, sooner or later he had to go to Hollywood, and it might as well be now, particularly since to combat the menace of television Hollywood had sacrificed quantity for quality, and was making pictures such as *The Bridge on the River Kwai, Twelve Angry Men, Paths of Glory,* and *The Defiant Ones.* Yes, of course Hollywood was the place to be.

England didn't matter any more?

Of course England mattered! But think! Think what could be done! And think what could be asked! With one, two or even three *internationally* successful films under one's belt! Think! Think! We could take a theatre! Put in our own company! Do a season of plays we wanted to do!

Who's we?

Us, Pickle! *(Pickle was Jerome's new name for her.)* Everything I do and everything I think about doing is not for me! It's for us, my darling girl!

Then you must do the play.

Yes. Yes, I suppose I must. As long as you're quite sure –

It's nothing to do with me, Jeromeo. *(She smiled, took both his hands, and kissed his fingers.)* You mustn't make it anything to do with me. The choice has to be yours.

I think I have to do the play.

I think you have to as well. But that's only a feeling, not an opinion.

Jerome had then turned over one of her slender hands and buried a kiss deep in the palm.

I don't think we'll be sorry, Pickle, he had whispered. I shall bring you the heavens' embroidered cloths. I shall spread them under your feet.

I'd rather have your dreams, she had whispered back.

You have my dreams, Pickle. I'm just going to turn them into the heavens' cloths.

What about Bobby? she asked. What about Bobby?

First things first, he'd whispered back, now taking her to him in the bed, both naked. First let them see me, let them take notice. Don't worry about Bobby. I'd never let anything happen to Bobby. You mustn't worry about a thing. Just fall back, lie back in my arms, let me kiss your white neck, and don't worry. There is nothing to worry about, my Pickle. I am going to spread the cloths beneath your feet.

Later, fully three months later, when she knew, when she was certain, in the middle of that terrible, *terrible* time, once Pippa knew and worked it all out, she realized that was the night that she had conceived.

THIRTEEN

Sebastian arrived back from abroad the day before Elizabeth left on the tour of *Tatty Gray*, and said (not complained) that he never saw her. Elizabeth was heart-broken with regret, and to compensate spent as much of that Sunday afternoon as she could afford in bed with her husband. It wasn't a very successful sexual encounter, as the travel weary Sebastian had drunk too much wine at the lunch they had attended and Elizabeth's mind was quite elsewhere. It was the last time they were to make love as a couple.

After their second attempt at making love, and while Sebastian lay curled up in a deep sleep back in his own bed, Elizabeth lay wide awake thinking how well everything had gone to this point. The Bumpkin had cracked so readily it was almost too good to be true. Of course, the choice of the neurologist that Elizabeth attended herself in Harley Street had been a good stroke. All apparently mild nervous disorders were awarded the blanket diagnosis of a nervous breakdown by Mr Sessions who had long ago come to realize all that most of the highly strung, spoilt and neurotic women who attended his clinic required was a compulsory break from the absurd life they were leading. Bed-rest was a wonderful panacea, and an excellent way of notching up unlimited house calls.

Even so, Elizabeth had anticipated a far greater resistance from her rival, which was why she had given such long and such very hard thought to her plan. First and foremost it had been vital to gain the Bumpkin's confidence, but once again – thanks to Jerome's indulgence, that had been handed to her on a plate the day the Bumpkin had been given the key to her studio. After that, it had more or less been a cakewalk. The Bumpkin had trusted her so readily and opened up so easily that Elizabeth very soon had the material necessary to make both the anonymous telephone calls and letters positively reek (as she liked to think of it) with authenticity. *God Has Not Forgiven Mother.* She was especially pleased with that one, not so much for its content, but for the fact that she had persuaded the Bumpkin not to tell J about her call on the family's perfectly dreadful sounding sanctimonious doctor, which must surely have gone a long way to convincing the Bumpkin that her persecutor was someone if not within her family's immediate circle, then at least it had to be someone in the village.

She was rather pleased with her voice, too, the *caller's voice*, the anonymity of it, the blankness, the impersonality.

You don't know me. You don't need to neither. But I knows you. And I knows who killed mother.

The accent of course had presented no problems. Elizabeth was a born mimic, as indeed was J, with whom she would often and quite deliberately verbally fool around in rustic accents. A hankie placed carefully over the telephone receiver had done the rest.

I knows who killed mother.

Elizabeth whispered it to herself now as she lay in the bath while Sebastian slept on, she whispered it over and over again until she had frightened herself so much her pale white skin goose-fleshed, and then she smiled with deep pleasure as she slid slowly lower into the hot soapy water until the oval of her beautiful face was all that was left above water, framed by the floating strands of her dark wet hair.

'*Sweets to the sweet*,' she smiled to herself. '*Farewell!* Bumpkin.'

The flower-strewn body of Pippa was floating down the stream already, beyond J's reach, beyond the reach of anyone. Elizabeth sighed happily as she sat before the fire, brushing out her drying hair until it gleamed once more like a raven's coat. She had got J to do the play, and how she had done that was her *pièce de résistance*. She had gone for his weakness, one he shared with every actor, she had played on his superstition. *Don't wish actors good luck. Don't come round before a performance. Don't whistle in the dressing rooms. Don't call the Scottish play anything but the Scottish play, never by its true title, never ever* Macbeth. *See a butterfly on-stage and you see the spirit of a dead actor. Find the answers not in your* selves, *but in your* stars. *Follow the yellow brick road.*

He had. She had helped, of course. The letter from Sybil Dodona (*Sybil Dodona!*) had been masterful, although sadly not original. The letter had been composed from speeches gleaned from a perfectly dreadful film Elizabeth had been offered and rejected, in which the young frightened heroine was nearly but not quite

279

lured to her fate by a phoney astrologer. Elizabeth had embellished the letter, of course, with little touches of her own (*unlike those millions of others, I do know you and I know you very well . . . a fame greater than any English actor before you . . . etc.*), but the body of the work had been created by another. Even so, Elizabeth thought, it was her idea to use it, to turn the speeches into a letter of prophesy, and once delivered into J's hands, there was only ever going to be one outcome, because as Elizabeth knew, J would never risk letting his chance of singularity be damaged by his determination to plough a single furrow at *any cost*.

It was all such nonsense, Elizabeth laughed, such a tomfoolery. But J had fallen for it, hook, line and loaded sinker. And bang-bang, she thought, bang-bang *Bumpkin*, you are dead.

She sat back from the fire now her dark hair was dry, and lit another cigarette to take the edge of her increasing appetite. Above her she heard Sebastian moving around the bedroom as he got dressed, and for a moment she felt sorry for him, sorry for what she was about to do to him, sorry that she hadn't been a better wife. He was a nice man, she remembered as she drew deeply on her Sobranie, sitting now in her armchair, Sebastian's silver-framed photograph in her hand. He was nice, honest, decent and certainly more than good enough to be seen with. But frankly he bored her. He always had, because he was a civilian, and she was not. In fact now she came to think of it, she never had been. She had always belonged to the land of *the red and the gold*, always, a land which alas had no room for civilians, none whatsoever. Never mind, she thought, all feelings of pity gone as she replaced his photograph on the table, with looks like his, and with his money, never mind, Bethy darling – he'll soon find someone else.

She tapped some non-existent cigarette ash into the fire and stared at the flames. Why was she so confident? How did she know she was going to succeed? What a silly question, she said out aloud, as she stood and smiled, catching sight of herself in the mirror. Good heavens, as far as J was concerned, right from the word go *it had only been a question of time*. A time that was now coming right, a time that was about to come round at long, long last.

Because Jerome was doing the play and darling Oscar was directing it.

That alone called for a drink, just a small quick gin before Sebastian came down, looking for something to eat. She poured an inch of gin in a tumbler and drank it straight down, before sucking hard on a slice of lemon to remove any trace of alcohol. Then she lit another cigarette, all thoughts of food now firmly banished from her own mind. Instead, while Sebastian ferreted around in the larder, she would concentrate on remembering every small detail of her triumph, right up to the moment she had so regretfully had to veto poor Booble's costume designs for *Tatty*.

'No, darling,' she'd sighed, one pale and slender arm linked lightly through the designer's horrid pink and fleshy one. 'They are beautiful, but *too* beautiful. Like everything you do. Tatty is a sprite, you see, someone who only exists in this man's mind. *We think*.' She smiled here, and squeezed Booble's arm, a moment of mischievous conspiracy which meant nothing whatsoever. 'So I don't think she should wear *normal* clothes, that is to say beautiful clothes like yours which would have needed to be *designed* for her. She's a little wild thing, a phantom. And remember, when she sings, she doesn't sing like a human – *she sings like a bird*. So I think it's that sort of Peter Pan look we want, except updated. I think Tatty Gray is the sort of girl who would wear an old tennis shirt, a pair of boy's shorts, and any old thing on her feet. Like I don't know' – which she did – 'let's say no socks and a pair of plimsolls.'

Oscar had been so delighted when he heard she had rejected Booble's spangly designs that he had clapped, and then hugged his star so hard he had broken the spectacles which he'd just stuck in the top pocket of his jacket.

When Sebastian finally appeared, looking like something out of a Hollywood picture in a white shirt, paisley cravat and dark slacks worn under a handmade silk dressing gown, Elizabeth hardly noticed because she was still laughing so much at the memory of it.

The play was very difficult, much more so than had been imagined. It had been agreed that because of the subject matter *Tatty Gray* represented a new direction for Oscar, but difficult plays are often very much easier to read than to perform (the same goes for the reverse), and initially no-one foresaw any difficulties. As a piece, *Tatty Gray* read seamlessly and enchantingly, and as a play was practically impossible to rehearse.

'It's coming over as whimsy,' a doomy Oscar noted at the end of the second week of rehearsals, 'and whimsy is the very last thing we want. I'd rather it came over as a satire.'

None of the cast laughed at Oscar's literary joke, not so much because they failed to understand it, which they had, but because they didn't really feel like laughing. Jerome felt positively suicidal. He missed Pippa, he couldn't get to grips at all with the part of the diffident and introverted painter, Sam, and because he couldn't he missed Pippa all the more. He needed Pippa badly, not because she offered active criticism and advice, which she didn't, but because her calm and matter-of-fact approach stopped Jerome from going over the edge, which was where at this moment he was most definitely headed.

For as always, when Jerome was uncertain of what he was doing, he was overdoing it, going over the top, relying on a display of vocal and physical pyrotechnics rather than finding the truth from within, with the result that he was fast turning the gentle, ironic, self-teasing Sam into an aggressive, sarcastic and tormented monster. Fortunately for his sanity, Oscar, who after much politicking had been allowed to direct his own work, knew exactly what sound it was he wanted to hear, and so he kept the lid on it all and didn't let it boil over. Most other directors, particularly those whose idea of directing comedy was simply to have everyone play everything faster, louder, bigger and brighter come what may, would have already hit the panic button and the delicate play would have been doomed to an instant failure. But Oscar knew the touch it required, and knew that he must wait until his actors found it, he knew that he mustn't press. One push too hard and too soon and the play would be gone beyond the point of recovery.

Elizabeth too seemed uncertain of where exactly (in Oscar's terms) to pitch it. In the morning she would try one approach and in the afternoon another, *gamin* before lunch, unbridled mischief after it. Then the next day, having settled for one of the two possibles, she would start to build a performance, and the moment that she did the play started to live, and Jerome began to descend from the heights of unreality to the plain of naturalism. And Oscar would sit at his table as a hush came over the rehearsal room and hold his breath, an unlit Lucky in one hand, a pencil stub (for once not taking copious notes) in the other, while magically time was suspended and the world outside the doors of the buildings was put on hold, only for the spell to be shattered by Elizabeth suddenly breaking off, throwing her script down, or picking it up, going to sit in a corner and begging to be left alone, or coming over to hug Oscar and hang her head in silence on his shoulder in contrition.

'It's wrong,' she might whisper. 'It's nearly right. So *nearly*. But I can't go on any further.' Or she would simply apologize to a silent Oscar, over and over again, and Oscar, who by now knew better than to question her repentance since it always led to tears, would call a break instead, gathering the cast of five around for coffee or tea and talk, and let them talk about everything but the play, while all of them, Oscar included, they all delayed the resumption of rehearsals in case inspiration was still lacking and they would once again find themselves stumbling up yet another blind alley.

Privately Elizabeth was enjoying it all enormously. She knew exactly how Tatty should be played. She should do, because she had her role model, a characterization she had perfected *in camera* long before the cast had assembled for the very first rehearsal. But she knew better than to show her hand yet, for if she did and Jerome found the way to play Sam, which Elizabeth knew full well he would – he simply had to the moment she revealed who her Tatty Gray was – then she would have no cards left to play, or rather more importantly, she would not be able to produce her trump card, her ace in the hole.

So she waited. She didn't mind waiting. She had waited this long, so what was a few more weeks? Besides, she loved playing games, she was addicted to her tomfoolery, and this was the very best of games, with the very best of rewards. So while she waited she kept herself amused by pretending she was lost, and unable to find the key for Tatty, while every now and then, for Oscar's peace of mind as well as for her, allowing a sudden flash of the brilliance that was to come, before once more play-acting within the play-acting, and pretending it had vanished, gone as suddenly and as mysteriously as it had arrived.

It infuriated Jerome, as Elizabeth was hoping that it would. He was floundering hopelessly, nowhere near an even halfway acceptable interpretation of a man bent on self-destruction rather than find the courage to face up to the genius he knew lay inside him. He would walk back with her to their hotel, artsick, heartsick and homesick.

'Whose preposterous idea was this to rehearse away from home anyway?' he would moan. 'It's unheard of. Absolutely unknown.'

'It was Oscar's,' Elizabeth would remind him, perfectly truthfully, while hiding the rest of the truth which was that it was she who had sowed the seeds of the idea in Oscar's head by wondering whether a play which would require the actors to strip themselves metaphorically and spiritually bare would not benefit by being assembled well away from the loving security of their homes. This appealed to the amateur psychologist in Oscar just as Elizabeth thought that it would, with the result that the cast, the stage management and their director were despatched to York, three weeks in advance of the play opening there.

'And that's another thing,' Jerome had complained early on. 'This tour. York, Nottingham, Manchester, Leicester, Cambridge – Christ knows where.'

'That's all,' Elizabeth would laugh, as if the whole thing could only be what things should always be – fun.

'Who planned it? Who? This play is a south of England play if ever there was one! We're going far, *far* too North to survive!'

'I understand the idea is – was? Anyway, the whole idea, J, is to give the play on tour the worst possible chance.'

'Meaning if we can survive Nottingham and Manchester with this sort of play, we really have a play?'

'I think that's the general idea, J. And I suppose it has a certain novelty value.'

She had taken to calling Jerome by just his initial the day they remet after he had agreed to do the play. It helped her to reduce him just to his initial, it depersonalized him just enough in her mind for Elizabeth to be able to carry out her plan. Jerome belonged to the Bumpkin, but *J* was going to be hers. She also, much to her delight, found knowing him just as J oddly exciting.

'Bethy,' he said this particular evening as they walked through a light drizzle of rain back to their hotel. In response to the intimacy of her nickname, she slipped an arm lightly through his and smiled. 'Bethy darling—' the *darling* being a groan, rather than an endearment. 'What, my sweet, if you'll excuse the vernacular, *the fuck are we going to do?*'

Not yet, Elizabeth thought to herself, however tempting the feed, not yet, just contain yourself and wait. She laughed instead, in no way outraged by the blasphemy. On the contrary she was encouraged by it, because actors swearing to each other was all part of their code of behaviour. It bonded them, like soldiers in a war.

'I asked you a question, Bethy,' Jerome reminded her. 'It is us, you know, not the play. The play is wonderful, and we aren't. Not very. Not even ever so.' *Ever-so* was done in his stage cockney, a dreadful whinge, with an elongated o that made Elizabeth laugh (this time) quite genuinely.

'You shouldn't laugh, Bethy!' Jerome chided. 'I'm only fooling around because it's so deadly bloody serious! You're just about keeping afloat, darling, you'll probably make the life-boat, but not me. The water is already – in my *lungs.*'

They walked on in silence, the rain heavier now, Elizabeth pulling the collar of her coat up one-handed but not stopping, liking the drama of the rain, thinking how well it fitted the mood of the scene. Their feet started to splash through the quickly forming puddles on the pavement, and Elizabeth could just see the tracking shot of both their legs, hers beautiful, contained in skins of nylon, with the swill of her camel wool skirt swinging below her knees, his feet brogue-shod and his long legs trousered in tapering twill, then the camera travelling up to their faces, to find them as they were, stopped by the kerb, all at once looking at each other.

'I need your help, Bethy,' Jerome said after a moment. 'I'm holding you back, I can see that because you keep showing signs that you're getting there. But I'm not. I'm nowhere near it. *And I need your help.*'

The italics were hers. Elizabeth put them there, she put them there in her head, because these were the words she wanted to hear, the words she'd been waiting for, the words she knew sooner or later he had to utter.

I need your help.

'Well?' he demanded, swinging her round by her arm, almost roughly, and she could hear his breath, shorter, and shorter, as if they were already making love. 'Bethy – I am *serious*. I will not get there otherwise!'

Instead of answering immediately, Elizabeth tightened the grip on his arm and walked him on, across the street and on towards the hotel which was now within sight. She waited until they had passed a milliner's, with, she noted, some rather pretty hats, before she slowed to a halt and turned to Jerome, to *J*.

'I know what our trouble is, darling,' she said. 'In fact I know exactly.'

'What?' Jerome didn't, she could see that from the anxiety in his eyes. Either that or he did! she suddenly thought triumphantly. He did and he was frightening the pants off himself! But the fear wouldn't be a cold fear. Elizabeth knew what this particular fear was like. It wasn't a terror, it didn't take the breath from your body, and make your blood run cold. This was a pleasurable tingle, a sense of excited panic that started somewhere in you, somewhere that it shouldn't and rose until it dried up your mouth and made your limbs weak. And drained the colour from your face, just as it was draining J's.

'What?' he asked again, putting his other hand on her other arm. 'What?'

She went to tell him, made as if to say, then withdrew, a look of private pain crossing her face fleetingly, as she slipped her hand into his.

'I think we both need a drink,' she said, and led him up the steps of the hotel. He could wait to find out until Manchester. That was the date Elizabeth had set provisionally. By which time he would be on his knees and begging.

Oscar did his best to help Jerome, but there is only a certain amount a director or anyone for that matter can do for an actor who has, as they say, gone off the map. Oscar got drunk with him, he stayed up all night with him. He walked on the Moors with him, he played endless games of bar billiards with him. They sang together, with Oscar at the piano, they played Gin Rummy, they got drunk again, they even cried. But when the play opened in York, Jerome was still off the map, and not lost just somewhere in the next county, he'd gone abroad. He was in another country altogether. People walked out. For the first time in Jerome's young life he heard the dreadful sound of the seats going up and the conversation of the deserters. He learned yet another of those terrible theatrical truths, namely that when people walk out on a show they do it so that you notice. They do it not in the interval, but just after, so that you see them and hear them, because they always talk. *I've had quite enough of this*, they say. *Come on, this is terrible. This is rubbish. Get your hat, come on, let's go and have a drink, for God's sake. I've never seen such rubbish*. No-one leaves without being noticed, because they've paid *good money for this rubbish*, and they want you to know it before they bang their seats up, and go out the wrong exit.

It happened in York, and it happened in Nottingham. They played Oscar's beautiful play either to silence or to the crashing of upturned seats and the slamming of brass-barred exit doors. By the middle of the second week in Nottingham, even Oscar was about ready to concede.

'Heck I'm sorry, buddies,' he said in the bar afterwards, to one, two, three, four, five dejected faces. 'Sure, I know you haven't got there yet, but you know, you know maybe there isn't any place to go. Or if there is, who knows? Maybe it's really not that interesting. Maybe I'm saying you haven't got there, *we* haven't got there when it's just not true. Maybe *I* never got there, team. Maybe I'm the one who didn't find the truth and get to tell it, because maybe they're right. This really is just some soft-edged piece of goddam whimsy that I've kidded me and I've kidded you is something else, when it really isn't. Not one person who's seen it so far has liked it, or at least not one person who's seen it so far has *said* they liked it. Everyone has *hated* it, and I mean hated. A guy after the show last night wanted to hit me. Why? I mean if you don't like something – OK, you don't like it. But violence? This is England, everyone,

286

where failure is everyone's prerogative. But this guy went for me. When he found out I was the author, he said first – first he said I had to be a pansy. Because only a pansy could write such soppy rubbish. And even when I denied it, when I said no, I didn't happen to be a *Viola tricolor*, but look I did wear *glasses*, he still tried to punch me on the nose, and I'd have been dead meat, I mean it – seriously. If his wife hadn't pushed him over. So listen, you guys, and you dolls – don't laugh, because I'm serious. If you want out now, you say it. You don't have to stay on board. All hands may leave the deck in the lifeboats, and allow the captain and his colander to go in a dignified silence down right to the very bottom.'

Elizabeth so very nearly gave in at this point. Like everyone in the company she loved Oscar, and she could see behind all his so-called world-weariness how much it was hurting, so much that she wanted to sit on his knee, wrap her arms round his lovely neck with all that thick dark hair showing over the top of his vest and whisper in his ear that he mustn't worry, because the play was beautiful, it was going to be just how he imagined it when he wrote it except even more so, and that all he had to do was *wait until Manchester*. But she didn't. She hardened her heart and looked brave and sad like the rest of the company, and like the rest of the company pledged her allegiance to HMS *Tatty Gray* who was not going to the bottom of the seas, and even if she did, she'd be there as well, on the bridge with the rest of them – saluting.

Then they all got maudlin drunk and sang defiant songs until a weary hotel management told them it was way past the time they should have gone to bed.

Jerome rang Pippa every day, or if he didn't, Pippa rang Jerome. She wanted to come up but he wouldn't let her. Come home then, she suggested, when you finish at Nottingham come home. He couldn't. If he could he would, but he couldn't see it happening, because they only had two more days to play, and if the miracle didn't happen they were to travel to Manchester straight after the show Saturday night so that they could rehearse all Sunday and Monday. You must be tired out, she said. Let me come up. I could come up to Manchester and at least we'd be together. But he said no, no that wasn't fair. This was his disaster, his failure, and he didn't want her to see him like this. He wanted her to see him when he had found it, when he had got there, and just talking to her was helping. She could talk to him in Manchester, she said. She was so much better, in fact she was completely OK, because she'd gone down to Sussex and seen Dr Weaver. And he'd said that she was one hundred per cent. So what had been wrong with her? he asked. There must have been something wrong with her. After all, Mr Sessions was no fool. Mr Sessions looked after half the profession. Pippa laughed and said that was probably the trouble. She wasn't an actress, and she wasn't a socialite. And Mr Sessions had diagnosed what he always diagnosed for people like that, while what someone like Pippa needed was a bit of sleep, granted, which she'd had more than enough of thank you, and some fresh air, which she'd also been taking by the bucket. So why couldn't she come up?

He so nearly said yes, he so very, very nearly did, because he wanted her with him so much. But something inside him said no, and not for the reasons given. Something somewhere inside him remembered that uncontrollable tremor of excitement he had felt when Elizabeth had looked at him in the rain and said she knew what was wrong with them, it was a sensation he couldn't put out of his mind, it was more than a sensation, it was a sense of anticipation, an anticipation of something so intoxicating he got drunk on it every time he thought about it.

So he said no. 'No, don't come up yet, darling girl,' he said, 'I really don't want you part of this, not if it's a failure. I'm too proud, you see. Too proud not of myself but of the way you love me, and I don't want to let you down. Which you will be if you see me being as absurd as I am at the moment. But just talking to you has helped. And I feel refreshed and strengthened by it, Pickle. Strong enough and loved enough now to stop fiddling around and start looking for what it all really means. And when I've found it, Pickle, my darling, darling girl, I promise you, you will be the very first person to know.'

It was as pure and as simple as that. No, a denial, no, I don't want you to see me now, no, I don't know that person, thrice no no no, a rejection which was to rob him of the rest of the life that was rightfully his. As he put the telephone receiver down, Jerome knew, somewhere inside, somewhere where those other dark feelings lay hidden, that what was already only a thought might just as well already be a fact.

The trouble as seen from Oscar's point of view was that both actors were too respectful of each other. He wanted to get up and draw them together, bring them physically closer, because the way they were it was as if they were acting at either end of an empty space, or as if there was an invisible wall between them. Jerome seemed over-awed by Elizabeth, even though he had acted opposite her so often. The thought of her brilliance seemed to knock him off his balance, with the result that he panicked, and over-acted monstrously. For her part, Elizabeth appeared ill at ease, as if she hardly dared do what she knew she was capable of doing, in case by doing so she might blot Jerome out. Oscar had seen her do it before, of course, in *All That Glitters*, but it hadn't mattered so much then because basically the play had been a vehicle for Elizabeth alone and Jerome never had a chance of matching her, from the moment Oscar had first set pen to paper.

But *The Tale of Tatty Gray* was different. Certainly Oscar had written the play around his inspiration, around the girl he had imagined on the train, so logically it should have been another solo vehicle for Elizabeth. But somehow, and he still didn't know quite how, her character in the play had come to resemble the fictional Pippa less and the real one more, and as it did so the nature of the play changed. Tatty Gray became an infinitely more interesting character as a result of the reshaping and the rewriting, the play had developed organically, and there was now more room for the character of Sam, the painter, thus giving the play a proper balance, and Jerome a chance this time of achieving parity. Yet he hadn't seized the opportunity, and nor had Elizabeth helped him do so. This time Jerome needed her brilliance in order to match it, which Oscar knew this time he could, because he had given Jerome the right raw material, but it simply wasn't happening, which was all the more frustrating for Oscar because he knew it was right there, lurking just below the surface, for both of the actors. He had seen it, as the rest of the company had, during one of those rare flashes of Elizabeth's unique brilliance, to which Jerome would at once respond, so that there they were, for all to see and hear, point and counterpoint, her a descant to him the theme, moments of such sublimity that they could only be likened to music, to the liquid beauty of a clarinet dancing above a cello, or the mystic delicacy of a flute hovering over a piano line, a butterfly of notes over the blue of a buddleia.

And then it was gone, and the silence which followed the moment was more cacophonous than the clash of a hundred cymbals. Then Elizabeth would recriminate, weeping or just silently resting on Oscar's shoulder while Jerome paced the room, smoking a cigarette, wreathed in a film of blue smoke as he paced the room in despair, silhouetted against windows lit by the afternoon sun. Dammit! he might cry, Will someone – Oscar! – will you please for God's sake tell me what I'm doing *wrong*!

But Oscar couldn't. No-one could. Because Jerome wasn't doing anything wrong. The person who was doing something wrong was Elizabeth, who knew it, and who loved every minute of it. In fact Elizabeth was beginning to find holding out on them and particularly on Jerome all strangely exciting.

Pippa had been left well attended. Nancy, their maid, had been ordered to move into the spare room so that Pippa would have someone in the apartment at all times, Miss Toothe requested to see to her daily requirements, and Lalla, for whom for once there was no part in the play, had been suggested by Elizabeth as a companion, someone with whom Pippa could go to the theatre or cinema, or simply out shopping and to lunch. Pippa had privately resisted the idea, explaining to Jerome that she was self-sufficient, and would be much happier alone, but Jerome, who was not yet convinced that Pippa had recuperated either well or long enough to be left to her own devices, insisted that Lalla either called her or called in on her once a day. Elizabeth was delighted, because the whole idea was to have a spy in the camp, and she could think of no-one better qualified than Lalla.

At first Pippa was irritated by the conditions Jerome had imposed, since she considered herself now fully recovered from what to her had been simply a bout of exhaustion, physical as well as mental, but she quickly realized that any undue resistance on her part could easily be interpreted by the over-anxious Jerome as neurotic behaviour, with the result that he might confine her totally to the apartment, a restriction which Pippa wouldn't be able to bear. So she played along with Jerome's notions, knowing full well that once he was away and fully immersed in rehearsals, she would find no difficulty in shaking off the attentions of Lalla, and would be able to lead a solo existence, doing the things she wanted to do when she wanted. She would reopen her studio and paint again, she would take Bobby out and go walking again, and tomorrow, she decided having consulted the appointments diary, she would go to Cork Street, and attend the opening of an exhibition of paintings to which she and Jerome had been invited, which next to marrying Jerome, was the most fateful decision Pippa was ever to take in her life.

That was on Sunday afternoon, late, a time while Pippa lay on a sofa listening to a concert on the radio while outside the spring sunshine tried to break through low clouds which hurried across the sky as if in a dream. The programme was Busch playing Mozart, the twenty-second Piano Concerto in E flat, every phrase lovingly shaped, the music wholly sensuous and magical sounding. Pippa lay listening to it, staring at the ceiling and then at the clouds passing by.

While she was listening, Jerome walked with Elizabeth from the stage door of the Theatre Royal, Manchester, where they had just concluded yet another rehearsal designed to attack the play from yet another angle, and which had yet again failed lamentably, leaving the performers at their very lowest ebb.

'God knows it was bad enough yesterday in Nottingham,' Jerome observed, turning the collar of his black overcoat up against the wind and seemingly incessant rain. 'No-one at the matinée, and the bird in the evening.'

'I marginally preferred the matinée,' Elizabeth said, putting up her umbrella. 'I would much rather die in silence than to the sound of upturning seats and catcalls.'

'What are you going to do now?' Jerome asked, as they walked along the street. 'We've got three hours.'

'Go back to the hotel,' she replied very firmly, 'and go to bed.'

'Good idea,' Jerome agreed. 'Not to sleep, of course. I don't think it's good to sleep just before a performance.'

'I wasn't thinking of sleeping,' Elizabeth said, slipping her arm through his.

'What were you thinking of?'

'What were you?'

She didn't even look at him as she said it, she looked instead in a shop window, at some shoes, and then on to the next shop where she looked at a dress.

'I said, what were you?'

Jerome hadn't answered. He knew the question could have been perfectly innocent, should have been perfectly innocent, but it hadn't sounded that way. Had Elizabeth thrown it away, as if to suggest she was going to bed to read, or just to lie there resting, like a soldier on the eve of battle, he would have responded in kind. No, he would have said, I was thinking of perhaps just reading, or simply lying down, like a soldier on the eve of battle. And she might have sighed in return, yes that was what she had been thinking of, too.

But she hadn't thrown it away. She had inflected it quite purposefully. Jerome knew Elizabeth's vocal tones too well now to have mistaken what she had intended. I wasn't thinking of *sleeping*, she had replied, before looking in the window, the intimation being she was thinking of going to bed for the very opposite reason, which was why Jerome had caught his breath, and been *unable* to answer, as he had become immediately gripped by that same delicious terror which had gripped him before, when Elizabeth had said she knew *exactly what was wrong with them*.

'Elizabeth,' he said, turning her away from the second shop window. 'Bethy.'

'No, not here,' she replied, factually, not in warning, but rather as if this was something they had already agreed. 'Wait till we get back to the hotel.'

They went to her room, again as if part of a pre-agreed arrangement. Jerome saw no-one in the foyer, no-one at the desk as Elizabeth and he collected their keys, saw no-one on the stairs as he tried not to hurry, he saw no-one at all anywhere in the hotel because he was hoping that no-one had seen him. If they had, he knew they would have known, they would have known by looking, by his face, by his eyes, by the look he couldn't possibly hide however hard he tried. As he walked up the staircase one step behind Elizabeth he knew he might as well have been naked already.

'No, don't look up and down the corridor, J,' she said, again not in a whisper, in a perfectly normal voice. 'That's what some of your trouble is, you don't *really* think things out. Just look ahead at the door, take my key and open it, as if this was something you and I did every night of our lives. And then no-one will even notice us. That's right. Now those people down the end of the corridor who were coming towards us. I'll bet if they had to go to court they would swear the corridor was absolutely empty.'

Once he had shut the door, he had expected Elizabeth would either fall in his arms, or do as he was doing, lean against the door with her back, waiting to recatch her breath. She did neither. She walked very calmly across the room, undoing her coat and taking off her gloves, shaking some rain from her hat as she peeled it off one-handed from the front, putting her umbrella away in the bathroom, re-emerging without her raincoat, smoothing down her jumper and her skirt, running a hand down her hair, a thumb curled under the braid, checking it was shaped in place, before turning her full gaze on him, as he still leaned against the door, the last drop of rain from his own hair slowly trickling down the back of his neck.

'Oh God,' she said, after she had taken a long look at him. 'I keep forgetting how *beautiful* you are.'

He didn't say anything, Jerome had nothing to say now, he could think of not one word, to impel them further forwards, or to stop them altogether. Instead he just leaned his head back even further, slowly, and closed his eyes.

He heard Elizabeth walking over towards him, quietly. He smelt her scent, felt her breath close by him.

'J darling. We must talk first.'

'First?' He opened one eye first, then the other.

'Very well, if you prefer, the *first* thing we must do is talk.'

'Jaw-jaw rather than war-war.'

'It won't be war, darling, I can promise you that, whatever we decide.' She was taking his hand, leading him across the room, sitting him beside her on the bed, a double bed covered in a thin pale fuschia coloured satin spread, which seemed to hiss as they sat on it. The bed was high off the ground, so that Elizabeth's beautiful legs dangled, unable quite to touch the floor. She still had his hand.

'This is what I've been trying to tell you,' she said. 'And you will probably think I'm mad.'

'No, no, Bethy,' he whispered. 'If anyone is mad, it is I.'

'Wait, J. You must listen. You have to listen to what I have to say, or you'll misunderstand. And there mustn't be any misunderstandings between us, *ever*. Do you see?'

He didn't, but he nodded. All he could see were green eyes, a pale white skin and black hair, against a shiny pale pink satin which was cold under his hand, and which whispered with every move.

'You see, I think you know as well as I do what's wrong with us, why our characters are eluding us, why we can't *get there*. And maybe you haven't said so because either you are a *much* more noble creature that I am, or because you are more cowardly. I don't know which. Maybe you don't want to face up to the truth. Maybe it's as simple as that.'

'I don't know the truth, Bethy, not any more. I'm confused, *God damn it*. I don't *know* what's what any more, what the truth is, what I'm saying to myself, what I'm *doing*. I just know . . . '

'Yes?' She prompted him, out of a silence.

'I just know rather than something happening between us, I know that there is nothing happening between us, Bethy – because—' He moaned, low, and hung his head.

'Because we won't allow it to happen, J.'

'You seem so very certain, Bethy. How can you be so certain?'

'How can you be so dishonest?'

'Bethy – I am *married*, Bethy! What are you talking about dishonesty for!'

'I'm married as well. Don't be such a prig.'

293

'A *prig?*'

'A prig.'

She let go of his hand and stood up, dropping that inch or so to the floor, and then walked away from him, running both hands slowly through her hair. 'Oh, I knew you wouldn't understand, J.' she said, with just the right amount of helpless exasperation.

'Oh Christ!' Again, it was a moan, rather than an expletive, a sound designed to show his suffering, the torment he was feeling as he stared at her back, at her shimmering black hair, at her perfectly proportioned legs, her small rounded backside under the smooth wool of her skirt, her tiny waist, at the entire perfection of her. Ever since they had begun to rehearse this play he had wanted her. Ever since she had begun to work on her character, finding little bits of it here and there, a sudden open look to her face, or a sad bewildered puzzle in her eyes, a glimpse of Tatty's naïvety, he ingenuousness, her frankness, even the way she walked, hopping down from tables, stools, beds, the lightness of her being, and her elusiveness, even though the whole was all still in array and unassembled, those glimpses, those hints of what she could *do*, of who she might be, they had been enough to make him desire her sexually more than he had sexually desired anyone. But he had taken a hold, he had held on and held on firmly, and done his best to shut down on the idea which kept feeding itself every day and night into the back of his mind, the conviction that sooner and not too much later he had to make love to her.

At first he thought he had known why because he thought he had known who she was, and if she was whom he thought she was, then it was only logical he would want to make love to her. All during the early part of rehearsals whenever he got a glimpse of who Tatty Gray might be, or who she might be going to be, he was certain it was Pippa, even if it was only bits of Pippa he was seeing, and if he was right which he convinced himself he was, because that was how actors built their performances, out of bits and pieces of people they knew, then it was only normal to feel the way he did. Elizabeth was basing her character on Pippa, perhaps only subconsciously, and if she was so it was only natural that missing Pippa as he did, he should be attracted to her surrogate, however imperfect and unfinished the impersonation.

But then Pippa disappeared, Elizabeth lost what she was doing, and started to assemble an entirely different character, someone who bore hardly any resemblance to Pippa except in the way she was costumed, which oddly enough meant next to nothing to Jerome since the person wearing them was no longer reminding him of the original. By the time of the first dress rehearsal, all traces of Pippa had been so totally expunged from Elizabeth's performance that Jerome didn't even notice how like Tatty's costume was to the clothes Pippa wore, and by the time the play had opened in York, Jerome was foundering so badly that he had even forgotten why he had wanted Elizabeth so desperately only a few weeks before.

What he hadn't forgotten, however, was that he had wanted her, because he still did. He had just forgotten the reason. Elizabeth hadn't, of course, and every now and then, just in case Jerome's attention might be straying from her, she let him have a glimpse, but only a glimpse, of who Tatty really was, and once she did, Jerome would come back to life as if attached to a live electric cable. His eyes would flash at her, she could almost hear his heart pound, and the clarinet would once more soar above the piano. Then once she knew she still had him, she shut Pippa away, and started playing little-girl-lost-in-the-woods all over again.

'Oh Christ,' Jerome moaned again, behind her on the bed. 'Christ dear God.'

'J, darling?' It was a gentle question, not a rebuke, and so he looked up, a small boy wanting help so badly. 'J there is nothing wrong, not intrinsically, in two people like us wanting each other, wanting to make love.'

'Even if we are married?'

'Who are you married to, darling boy? Who am I? We're married to two wonderful people who understand and love us. But we're also married to our art.' She'd been a little afraid of this, when she'd run it through in her mind, and she tried it all sorts of ways, sad, sad-dramatic, rueful, factual, intense and despairing, finally settling for the shared secret, the you-know-it-as-well-as-I-do approach, which seemed to be working, because instead of staring at her with that mad stare Jerome used on people when they said something calamitous, he was pursing his mouth very slightly instead, looking at her, into her eyes and nodding, she was pleased to see, very slowly.

'Yes,' he said finally. 'I know what you mean. I know what you're going to say, because it's exactly what I've been thinking.'

This was precisely what Elizabeth had prayed he would say, and because of it she felt the triumph rise in her, the surge of adrenalin heating her veins, the tremor of excitement in those hidden parts of her, and that delicious almost unbearable anticipation, but all she did was look sad, as if the conclusion they were slowly reaching was regrettable, but inevitable, as if what they must do was not against their better judgement, but because of it.

She came and sat down beside him again, but kept her hands in her lap.

'It's the only way,' she said, having counted slowly up to fifty without him saying anything, without him even moving. 'We're never going to get there otherwise, J darling. It's like an invisible barrier. And if we don't, what a *waste*. You know and I know, we all *know* what a beautiful, wonderful play this is. And you know and I know, and everyone knows that if there are two people who can make it work, those two people, my darling, are us. But because of our silly old inhibitions, because we're *afraid*, in *every* way, we're going to let everyone down, from Oscar to the last person who buys a ticket before they take the wretched thing off. It doesn't matter that *we* fail, that's something you and I will have to live with, that's entirely to do with us. What matters is why we fail, and who we let down. We just have to break the door down, J. We have to come to each other, we have to know each other, we have to get this out of the way, because, darling boy, *it is completely buggering us up.*'

For a moment his sense of excitement was so intense, Jerome thought he was going to pass out. His mouth was dry, he could only breathe as far as the very top of his chest, and it was as if he was shaking violently inside. He straightened one hand, cautiously, trying not to be noticed as he looked to see if he was in fact trembling, but his hand was still, the shaking was actually inside him.

'Yes?' he asked her. 'You really think that's what it is?'

'I know it is,' she said. 'Don't you?'

'All I know at this moment is that I want to make love to you, Bethy. That's *all* I know.'

'That is all, darling one,' she whispered, 'that you need to know.' Then she quietly and easily moved her hand, so quietly and easily that he hardly noticed, hardly noticed that is until she slid it up between the top of his thighs and held him fast. 'And that,' she smiled, showing the tip of her tongue, 'is all I need to know.'

Like the people in the corridor who might not have seen them, and who might swear the corridor had been empty, Jerome could only really remember that moment and then being in bed. In between was a corridor in which he saw nothing, and in which he heard nothing. Of course, he remembered that they kissed and how they kissed, but in detail it was a long, blank, white-hot corridor. They had taken their clothes off, they had kissed, they had kissed, and kissed and kissed. Elizabeth had almost swallowed him, and he had almost drunk her, and he could recall her undoing him, not how, but the fact that she had, she had opened his shirt, and his trousers, she had slipped them down, when she was already part naked, that he knew. He had started to take her jumper off but she was wriggling, and she was out of her clothes faster than he could get her out of them, although he let him slip her panties down, slowly, she told him so, he recalled that, *slowly*, she said, *very, very slowly*, she had told him this on a breath, *suspirato*, as he slid his hand between the silk of the featherweight garment and the touch of her skin, his hand on her beautiful small and firm buttock – *slowly* she had said, and slowly he had done it, levering the silky garment away from her body with the backs of his hands and slipping them down her thighs, down further, down her legs till they slipped down her legs, like a chrysalis, while she must have undone him by then, although he still couldn't say with certainty, he had just heard her gasp as she took him in her hand, gasp now that there was nothing between her hand and him, no overgarment, no undergarment, just him and her hand, him in her hand, and now they were in bed.

Now they were in bed, and her eyes were looking straight up into his. They looked only a little surprised, but those green eyes were certainly open wider than normal, and fixed on his and into his as she told him to go on, please, she asked, *go on*, my darling, *oh yes, please go on.* She was so beautiful in his arms, with one arm round her for a moment, her black hair falling straight back against the white pillow, her neck arched and exposed while he eased her down on him and himself up into her, she was so, so beautiful as she lay back now, her hips moving with his and her teeth suddenly showing as she bit her lower lip, with more surprise in those wide green eyes now, she was so utterly beautiful and she felt so good he wanted to shout out, and yell, he wanted everyone to know how completely perfect this moment was, but what he did *or whoever this was who was doing this did*, was he opened his mouth suddenly, his face contorting as if in sudden sharp pain. Aaahhh! he said, softly – aaahhh! But she whispered urgently no! No not yet! She told him to wait and he did, smothering her mouth with his, kissing her right inside, deep deep inside, while he heard her groan as he went on, he heard her groan more and more and Christ! she said suddenly as he looked and saw the eyes wide open now, and her hands were off his back and out somewhere in the air – Christ! she almost shouted it but Jerome didn't care because they were one now, wholly one, she was there at the same time, with him exactly and she was saying something over and over and over again and he could feel her hands in his hair, pulling his hair, pulling his head down and he saw blood, just a small dart of dark red blood on her lip where she had bitten herself, and then she was smiling, and licking her lip with a pink tongue before leaning her chin back and kissing him slowly and softly on his mouth, and on his neck, his chest, his neck again, his arms, her arms round him as she sunk down on to him, his sweat falling on her white skin, on her breasts, breasts which gleamed with her own sweat, and which now cushioned their embrace as they just held each other, holding on, holding on in silence, while outside the world picked up again and they could hear the noise of the city, the cars, voices, other people, rain, a clock chiming somewhere, and in the room just their silence, and their breathing, and perhaps the slow easing of the bed springs and the rustle of bed linen, as Jerome turned on his back, pulling the covers up over them to keep them warm, and then raising his arm so Elizabeth could move and lie across his chest, in the crook of his arm, her hair brushed against his cheek, her left arm curled across his stomach.

'Don't ask any questions,' she said.

'I wasn't going to.'

'We can tell each other things, but we mustn't ask any questions.'

'Like how was it for you?'

He couldn't see her smile, but he could feel it.

'Yes,' she said. 'But since you ask—'

'I don't ask. That wasn't a question. It was a for example. I don't have to ask, Bethy. This wouldn't have happened, not like this, not if we had to ask *how it was.*'

'No. No, of course it wouldn't. Of course it wouldn't, darling boy.'

Silence, long and peaceful. Then she moved and propping herself up on her elbows, on him, she smiled into his face.

'But as I said, we can say things. So I'm going to say something. Two things. Firstly, if we haven't broken the door down now, Jerome Didier, then may God help us. And two – I don't know how to say this.'

'Your husband is mad to let you out of his sight.'

'No husbands, no wives. This is for art. And that *was* art.'

'Even so, the man in London who lives in your house with you must be certifiable.'

'If you're thinking what I think you're thinking—' Elizabeth suddenly laughed, and then grew mock serious. 'That's what I was trying to say. It's never happened like that, J. Not once. Not even *remotely* like that.'

Jerome stared back at her. He could hardly believe it. He wanted to tell her she was brilliant, that he had never made love to a woman as dextrous, as agile, as *brilliant* as she, but she was looking at him in truth, there was no misreading the expression on her beautiful face. It had been the same for her as it had been for him, an experience for which there are no known words or phrases.

'I hated making love before,' she said. 'It bored me.'

Jerome began to laugh. Elizabeth pinched him.

'It's true, J! I'd come up with any excuse possible. And if the man who shares my house in London and who lives with me insisted, I would lie there with my eyes closed and think of the next part I was going to get.'

Jerome laughed even more.

'It is *true*,' she insisted, and it was. Elizabeth, the greatest actress of her generation, had not had to fake one thing. Which had surprised, *and* frightened her.

'I believe you,' Jerome said, seeing her expression once again. 'And I have to tell you something. I have never, *ever*, known anything like that, not – in my *whole life*.'

Elizabeth looked back at him, and seeing that he too had been frightened, felt better, felt comforted, and so she sighed and then lay down again across his chest.

'I love the way you say ever,' she smiled. '*Evah*.'

'I love the way you make love,' he replied.

'You shouldn't have said that.'

'It's not a question.'

'No. It's provocation. How long do we have?'

Jerome picked up his wrist watch off the table and looked at it.

'We have a whole hour until we have to be at the theatre.'

'Good,' Elizabeth slid herself slightly further down and kissed him feather lightly on his stomach. Then she looked back up at him. 'Plenty of time to make sure I haven't lost my touch.'

At this very moment, Pippa was standing in front of a painting of an industrial landscape, by coincidence a picture of Manchester, by the eccentric Mancunian artist L.S. Lowry. It was a compulsive work, a composite of reality and the imagination which the artist preferred to call a 'dreamscape', full of small stylized figures, anonymous people without shadows, hurrying through a life dominated by their place of work, a vast green-grey mill. Pippa loved the painter's work, even though the feelings he conveyed were ones of desolation and loneliness, so she stood for an age in front of the canvas, staring into it, lost in the despair of a big smoky city, unaware even that it was Manchester.

At this very moment, the woman who had crossed the Atlantic on the same plane as Oscar when he had returned from America moved into place behind Pippa, back to back, in order to view the small Spencer which hung on the opposite wall. As soon as she did so, the woman felt her eyes close of their own accord, a familiar event which had long ceased to disturb her, as the words began to come into her head. She listened very carefully as always and memorized them, which was no problem since she could hear no other sound. Then when the words stopped, her eyes opened once again and she turned immediately to where Pippa was still standing.

'Excuse me,' she said, laying one hand lightly on Pippa's shoulder.

Pippa turned and found herself face to face with a very handsome, tall, middle-aged American woman, beautifully dressed in an expensive couture suit, and with a fine head of light grey hair pulled up into an elegant and carefully coiffured knot.

'I'm sorry,' Pippa said, noting at once the kindness in the stranger's eyes. 'I've been hogging this canvas rather, I'm afraid.'

'It's perfectly all right,' the woman replied. 'Apparently I'm not here to see the paintings. I'm here to see you.'

'Do I know you?' Pippa stared more closely at the woman, feeling that she did know her, that she was very familiar, and yet totally unable to place her handsome, open face.

'No, you don't know me.' The woman answered calmly, standing quite still, her hands clasped lightly in front of her. She seemed completely relaxed and oddly at ease with herself, Pippa thought, she seemed to radiate happiness. But Pippa knew she didn't know her, because the only American she knew was Oscar. She knew no other American people at all.

'Please, don't look worried,' the woman continued, sensing Pippa's perplexity. 'You don't know me, and I don't know you. But I have a message for you.'

'How?' Pippa wondered. 'How can you have a message for me if you don't know who I am?'

Pippa frowned, sensing something uncommon, something unforeseen, but the woman just smiled kindly at her in return.

'The message is from your mother,' she said.

'You knew my mother?'

'No.'

'Then how—?'

'Please, just listen. You must listen.'

She was still smiling at Pippa, even when her eyes suddenly closed and she fell silent, except for a deep intake of breath, followed by a long sigh. There was so much noise in the gallery, so many people were all talking and laughing, that Pippa knew she shouldn't have been able to hear any of this. She shouldn't be able to hear the woman's soft voice, nor should she have heard the long sigh, which had seemed to have been a sigh of relief. But she had. She had heard the sigh, and she could hear everything the woman said to her, not above the noise in the room, but through it.

And all the time the woman never stopped smiling. For a moment Pippa feared as the woman stood there with her eyes closed that she had been confronted by a mad woman, but nothing about the stranger spoke of madness. Instead the feelings Pippa got were ones of utter goodness, and of peace, while the woman's smile was almost beatific.

The stranger's eyes opened again and she spoke.

'Your mother says she did not tear up the card.'

She felt it then, Pippa felt it in time. She saw and felt the blackness coming, and as her head began to swim she took a deep breath in, she gasped, and folded over, dropping her head below the level of her heart. As she did she knew she was holding on to the woman, holding her by both her elbows, holding on while she fought the darkness, yet the woman never moved or said a thing. She stood still and firm, and Pippa could feel her strength.

'I'm sorry,' Pippa said. 'I thought I was going to faint.'

The woman simply smiled some more and then continued.

'Your mother says she had nothing to do with the card.'

'Which card?' Pippa demanded, suddenly determined to test this woman's plausibility. If she was genuine, she had to know what the card was. 'Which card are you talking about? I have to know which one.'

'The third one. The last card. Your mother wants you to know it was Doris.'

Doris. No-one could have known that. No-one could have known about the card, but even so, Pippa thought, it might have just been some cranky guess, or a practical joke, or *something*, something which had some sort of explanation. But no-one could know about there being three cards. Only someone who knew, who knew about her, who knew about her mother. And only someone who knew all that, who was real, who was genuine, only they could have known about Mrs Huxley, and that Mrs Huxley's christian name was Doris.

'Do you know why Doris destroyed it?'

'She didn't tell me, I'm afraid. Perhaps she didn't think it was necessary. Perhaps she thought you would know why. She just said she wanted you to know that it wasn't her. That was the important thing. That it was Doris. And that she loves you.'

This time she missed it. She missed it because of the glow she felt, the warmth, the light that was flooding through the door. She missed the tell-tale warning signs, as the blood pressure suddenly dropped in the arteries of her brain, as her heart slowed, as the blood vessels in her abdomen relaxed, and because she missed it she had no time to correct the flow, and so her blood rushed down from her head, down from her heart, and into her stomach, as Pippa passed away into darkness.

When she awoke, she was in an office, small, cluttered, smelling of oil paint and leather. A pretty girl was sitting by her, and behind the girl, a tall man in glasses and a pin-striped suit hovered anxiously.

'Oh good,' said the girl who was holding her hand. 'Thank heavens.'

'Absolutely,' the tall man said. 'Oh dear, you have had us worried.'

'The doctor's on his way,' the girl said, pulling the tartan rug which covered Pippa higher up her chest. 'You just lie there now.'

'It's all right,' Pippa said, blinking at the light, and taking slow, level breaths. 'I'm perfectly all right, really.'

'You fainted,' said the girl, smiling.

'Yes, I know. It's not a habit, but it happens. From time to time.'

'Yes,' said the girl.

'The noise probably,' the tall man said, taking off his glasses and holding them against the light. 'I'm afraid it was terribly hot in there. And frightfully noisy.'

'It wasn't the noise.' Pippa folded the rug back and sat up slowly. 'And honestly, I don't need a doctor.'

'Oh, I think you should let the doctor see you,' said the girl. 'You have been out for an awful long time.'

'Surely not?' It was Pippa's turn to be perplexed. 'It's usually only a matter of a minute. Less.'

'No, no.' The man was carefully putting his glasses back on, looping the flexible ends individually over and behind his ears. 'No, you were unconscious for fully ten minutes.'

'More like quarter of an hour,' the girl said.

Pippa sat back in the old leather chair and stared at nothing in particular, because she had never fainted for as long as that before.

'The woman I was talking to.'

She was half expecting, more than half expecting them to tell her there was no woman, to look blank, or to look at each other.

'Yes, the woman I was talking to—'

'She's gone, I'm afraid. Your friend, you mean?'

'My friend?'

'The American lady.' The tall young man leaned forward, and rested his hands on the back of an upright chair. 'She helped bring you in here, but then she had to leave.'

'She told us not to worry though,' the girl added.

'That's right, Mrs Didier.'

'You know who I am?'

'We checked your invitation. I hope you don't mind. We wanted to know if there was anyone we should call, but your maid—'

'We called your home, you see. The number was in your diary.'

'Your maid says your husband is away.'

'The American woman,' Pippa said.

'She told us you would be fine,' the girl said. 'That there was nothing to worry about, you'd just fainted, as you sometimes do. At least according to your mother.'

'My mother?' Pippa sat forward with a start, dropping the rug off her knees, trying to rise. The girl put a hand out to stop her, to ease her back into her chair. 'My *mother*?'

'That's right,' the young man said. 'That's what she said.'

'About you fainting,' the girl added. 'She said your mother had told her.'

Pippa sat with one hand across her eyes, blanking it all out for a moment while she thought. Then she looked at them both, at the sweet-faced girl and the tall, young man.

'Do you know who the woman was?' she asked.

'I'm afraid we don't,' the young man replied, and then frowned. 'Why – don't you?'

At this very moment, Elizabeth leaves her hotel for the theatre and the first performance in Manchester of The Tale of Tatty Gray. *By now Jerome has made love to her not twice but three times within the space of that hour and a half between the end of rehearsal and curtain up. Elizabeth gets dressed first and leaves before Jerome does, because she thinks it best. When she gets to the theatre, she instructs Muzz to lock the dressing-room door, and she refuses all* calls from everyone until she is ready to give her performance. She doesn't see Jerome again or speak to him until they meet face to face across the stage.

Everyone backstage knows that something is up, but no-one knows what. All they know is that since Elizabeth and Jerome have returned to the theatre and sat closeted in their separate dressing rooms, backstage is a different place. Backstage there is this feeling of expectation, although no-one has any explanation for this sudden surge of excitement other than the fact that it's another first night, and that each first night is different, and on a first night anything might happen, and sometimes even does.

Otherwise, there is just this feeling, this tension, this electricity. Oscar sees Jerome and Elizabeth arriving separately, and observing that they are not speaking, fears they've had a quarrel and that as a result the play is going to be an even greater dog than it was in York and Nottingham. But then he too feels whatever it is in the air, and instead of giving his leading players their usual set of notes, or trying to find out what has happened between them, he leaves them alone. He never says one thing to either of them before the curtain rises, he doesn't even wish them the traditional wish of merde because although he doesn't know what it is, or why it is, he knows something has definitely occurred and that a miracle might be just about to happen.

And happen it does. From the moment Jerome, as Sam, opens his derelict studio and finds the girl perched on a high stool by his old easel, disbelief is suspended. He asks the girl what she thinks she is doing in his studio and the girl laughs, she laughs like someone Oscar knows, like Pippa he realizes — that sudden infectious, impetuous and pure laugh, and she tells the artist no, that he mustn't ask questions, that they can tell each other things, but they mustn't ask questions – otherwise the spell will be broken. What spell? the artist wants to know, and the sprite laughs once more, again, just like Pippa, and says as she jumps off the stool, just like Pippa, there you are! That's a question! But that's your very last one!

Now it seems to Oscar that everyone in the theatre is sitting forward, as if the whole audience knows they are about to see magic performed, and that they are all holding their breath, and that no-one breathes out again, not until the curtain finally falls.

Like Oscar, Jerome also senses it from the start, from the moment he sees Elizabeth on the stool. She is even sitting differently, she is sitting, Jerome realizes, just like Pippa does, and when she talks, it's Pippa talking. Jerome now sees she even looks like Pippa, her *clothes, and even her hair which she has done as a wonderful wild cascade. The impersonation is so brilliant, the characterization so fully realized, completely capturing Pippa's open affection, her honesty, her frankness, even her very elusiveness, that Jerome no longer has to worry how to play his part. He knows he has now only to be himself, and show the Jerome whom Pippa knows and loves and who knows and loves Pippa, he knows that's all he has to do for the play to work. And so that is all he does. He plays Sam as himself, because Elizabeth is playing Tatty as Pippa, and all at once they are the clarinet and the piano, they are perfect and sublime music, they are wonderful together, they are in harmony, and the play is an absolute and unqualified triumph.*

They take twelve curtain calls, and they could have taken twelve more. As the curtain finally falls, Elizabeth slips her hand into Jerome's and squeezes it before walking off to her dressing room where she locks herself in. Jerome leaves her alone for the moment, thinking she is overcome, thinking perhaps she is crying, which is what Elizabeth wants him to think, but in fact she's hugging Muzz and opening a bottle of champagne for them both to celebrate her double triumph.

Meanwhile, alone in the stalls Oscar sits, long after the last member of the audience has departed. He has long since worked out what happened at the hotel between the end of the disastrous rehearsal and curtain up, and now he doesn't know whether to laugh or cry. He wants so badly to laugh with delight, to clap his hands and throw his cap in the air, but he knows that what he should really be doing is crying with despair, because whoever is responsible for what has happened, he knows that in fact no-one is more responsible than he. So instead of laughing and instead of crying he determines to get stone drunk, and begins by drinking two large whiskies in quick succession in the pub across the road before going backstage to hug and kiss and thank his leading actors, as well as to congratulate them for giving the two finest performances of their kind he has ever seen.

At this very moment, Pippa came to terms with what had happened to her at the gallery. After the doctor had examined her, superficially, assuming her to be a socialite who had drunk too much champagne, a notion which Pippa had encouraged in order that she could at once return home, she took the taxi provided back to Park Lane. No-one had known who the woman was, and there was no point in trying to find out who she was, because it was perfectly obvious she hadn't known Pippa from a total stranger.

She was some sort of medium, her mother had spoken through her, and that was that.

There was no other explanation, and to look for one would be a waste of time, because in terms of everyday life, of normality-so-called, this was something inexplicable. No-one except her mother could have told the American woman what the American woman had passed on to Pippa, that was indisputable. Her mother had not torn up the postcard, Doris Huxley had, and her mother loved her.

For a long time, so that it all could sink in, Pippa lay on their bed in the dark with Bobby beside her. The traffic passing below swished through the rain, while Bobby snored contentedly and Pippa watched the lights criss-cross the ceiling.

Her mother loved her. She hadn't torn the card up. She hadn't been enraged. Doris Huxley who for some reason had always disliked Pippa had done it, perhaps to make it look as though her mother had suddenly taken leave of her senses, to make it seem she had become enraged about Pippa returning home as a married woman.

But then, Pippa thought, Doris Huxley could only have done that *after* her mother had died. So what had really happened that evening after the Weavers had finally gone home? Pippa reasoned that Doris had wanted to go on drinking, and having managed to get Pippa's mother back on spirits so that like all alcoholics she could have someone to drink with, they had sat up together into the small hours, with her mother just keeping Doris Huxley company, rather than getting drunk. She didn't think her mother could have got drunk because when they had found her she had been in bed, in her nightgown, in an orderly not a disorderly fashion. She must have gone to bed, very late, Pippa decided, obviously having had more than she should to drink, become confused about her pills, exactly as Dr Weaver had indicated, and accidentally overdosed herself.

It wasn't suicide, and it certainly wasn't a revenge suicide, as had been suggested by her anonymous tormentor, that at least Pippa knew now she had received her mother's message. Otherwise why would her mother have said that she loved her? Her mother had died by chance, by accident, just as if she had forgotten to look when she was crossing the road and stepped out under a car. There was no blame. The only blame had been the one Pippa had put on herself, a blame born from contrition and grief, from the guilt people always feel when loved ones die too soon or suddenly. But now the burden had finally been lifted, and Pippa once more could be at one with herself.

She had lain there in the dark, long after she had reached her conclusions, while the tears of relief slid slowly down from the corners of her eyes to dry in her hair. She thought how strange it all was, how very close they were to disaster all the time, all of them, because had she gone to see Jerome in Manchester that evening, she wouldn't have gone to the gallery, so she never would have met the American woman, she never would have got her mother's message, and so she would have gone on thinking an entirely wrong set of thoughts, probably for the rest of her life. She would have remained convinced that her mother had died in anger because of her, because of her marrying Jerome. But she hadn't. Her mother had died accidentally. Her mother loved her. Perhaps she had even loved Jerome.

At twenty-five to eleven she got up and rang the theatre, but the line was engaged. She waited and tried again, but again she couldn't get through. The apartment was still in the dark as she sat in the big chair by one of the windows, waiting to call again, and while she waited Bobby jumped off the chair, and padded through to the kitchen for some water. The line was still busy on her third attempt, and Pippa suddenly sensed that something else had happened that night. She felt it quite suddenly, it was an intuition, but she knew she was right as she stared out across the darkness to the park.

The play had come good. She told Bobby as he wandered back in from the kitchen, his whiskers dripping cold water over her bare feet as Pippa rubbed his head and pulled his ears and told him of his master's triumph. 'The play's a hit, Bobby,' she said. 'I know it. I can feel it.'

She finally got through at quarter-past eleven, catching the last person out of the door, one of the stage management. No, he'd said, they'd all gone, everyone had gone to the pub over the road and then they were going to a party somewhere. Sorry, he'd said, he wasn't sure where, it was at some rich bloke's house, someone who had some money in the play, but sure – of course he'd tell Jerome she'd rung. It had been such chaos back here, he told her, backstage, since they'd come down it was no wonder she couldn't get through. Why? Pippa asked, knowing the reason already, what happened? What happened? the voice laughed delightedly in her ear. What happened? What had happened was fantastic. What had happened was it had taken off. The play was a hit, Mrs Didier, that's what had happened.

Jerome didn't ring, but then Pippa didn't expect him to do so. There would be too much going on, too much excitement after all that *grief*, as Jerome called it, too much celebrating. Pippa laughed happily, out loud, suddenly, infectiously, purely. She laughed because she was so happy. She was so happy because she knew Jerome would be so happy, and she was so happy because she knew her mother loved her. She could hardly wait to see Jerome and tell him.

She had the train timetable in hand now, running a finger down the right page under the light of a table lamp she had just switched on. She saw the first train would get her there shortly after midday, just in time for a late lunch together, provided she could get a message to Jerome. But that proved impossible. There was no-one on the hotel switchboard, at least no-one was answering at such a late hour.

Pippa put the phone down and lifted her dog back up on to her knee.

'Never mind, Bobby,' she said. 'Even better, we'll surprise him.'

They avoided each other studiously at the party, except for when necessary, because since they had become lovers, they had lost their actors' intimacy, something they realized as soon as they congratulated each other afterwards. They could no longer hold each other and hug each other and go *kissy-kissy*, as Elizabeth called it. As soon as they tried to do so, as soon as Jerome threw his arms around her, when Elizabeth emerged looking radiant from her dressing room, it was all he could do not to make love to her there and then. It was the same for Elizabeth, she was thrown totally. She allowed his embrace thinking it was going to be the same as all their other backstage embraces, a bear hug, a *kissy-kissy*, Jerome lifting her up in his arms off the ground, swinging her round in delight and telling her how marvellous she was, before releasing her to turn and hug and kiss and talk to someone else.

This time, as soon as he touched her, she shivered and for some absurd reason found herself wanting to cry. She could also feel him against her, they were both only in gowns after all, Elizabeth in her silk underwear and pale pink robe, Jerome in just a towel round his waist, and his old make-up marked, black dressing gown barely tied. They had hugged like this often before, and although Elizabeth had been secretly thrilled, she had never been aware of him, never felt him up against her like that, never felt his sudden awakening excitement.

It happened so quickly Elizabeth only just disentangled herself in time, as did Jerome, but if anyone had been watching closely they would have seen the look in their eyes, a look which told of some sort of fear, of some sort of loss of control.

'Ozzie!' Elizabeth called, seeing the writer just in time, although unable to resist giving Jerome one more glance over her shoulder, a glance which Oscar saw, and which he followed, finding a shell-shocked Jerome at the end of it, staring wide-eyed and straightfaced back at Elizabeth.

'Ozzie darling!' Elizabeth threw her arms round Oscar's neck and still on the run from that moment of danger kissed him far too hard as a result.

'Wow!' Oscar exclaimed. 'I'm made of the same stuff as all these other guys, you know, Lizzie. I bleed, I tickle, I laugh just the same, right?'

Elizabeth laughed with well-feigned delight and kissed him again, and then Jerome was at his side embracing Oscar, both arms round him, looking over Oscar's shoulder right into Elizabeth's face, her mouth only inches away from his. Elizabeth just closed her eyes, that was all she could do, but it was quite enough for Jerome.

'I have to take a shower, Oz!' he said above the din. 'Sorry – but I'm so *hot*!'

Elizabeth laughed. She had to. She couldn't help it.

And now they were at the party they circled around each other, passing each other by, only talking to each other when others were present, making sure they were never alone for one moment because they knew companies, they knew how everyone in a company read faces for any sign of an affair, they knew how everyone always looked for signs. So they were extra careful not to give the watchers any, they gave them no signs at all, not even the smallest one, which was how everyone in the company knew they were lovers.

Oscar saw it straightaway. He had seen it as he followed Elizabeth's look, and he could see it now every moment they were not together. Jerome and Elizabeth were usually inseparable at these bashes, holding hands, standing with their arms round one another, Elizabeth straightening Jerome's hair, or shirt, Jerome teasing her, pinching her cheek, dancing and flirting. Now they were at opposite ends of the room, their backs to each other, talking to everybody and anybody rather than to each other. No-one said anything about it, because no-one was really that bothered. The more experienced members of the company had seen it all before in other companies, and although they had predicted it happening, previous experience told them it rarely amounted to anything. Infidelity didn't count on tour, it was an unwritten rule. And if, as in this particular instance, it actively helped, if it made life better by making what they were all doing better, then it was to be positively welcomed, not actively discouraged.

Elizabeth left long before Jerome, without, as far as Oscar could see, even saying goodbye to him. She waved to Oscar through a throng of people, her hands to her pretty mouth, blowing him a stream of kisses, mouthing to Oscar that she loved him, and then when he had picked up his glass she was gone. And Oscar still didn't know whether he should laugh or cry.

He took a long draught of his whisky and ginger ale and sank into a chair. What he had seen that evening, what they had all seen, what they had cheered to the rafters were two performances of such total brilliance that they defied description. In all his wildest dreams Oscar had never imagined that anything he wrote could ever be performed with such breathtaking artistry. He had thought Elizabeth brilliant in his first play, he had thought at that moment she could not be surpassed, nor that she could surpass herself. But *All That Glitters* paled into insignificance against what he had witnessed on stage tonight. Elizabeth and Jerome, both of them, they were every word there was in the dictionary which described brilliance, every word, he decided, and then some more.

Jerome came and knelt on the floor beside him.

'You look as though you're about to burst into tears, Oz,' he laughed '*What ails you?*'

'I think I *am* about to burst into tears, Jerome baby,' Oscar replied, totally out of character. 'Just don't ask me why.'

'I know.' Jerome settled down slightly lower, sitting back on his thighs, but still kneeling. 'I feel completely thrashed. *Bouleversed.* Back to front. Upside down. You're a genius.'

'No, pal, I'm a very good writer. *You* – are the goddam genius.'

'We are nothing, Oz, without the words. Without you – we are *dumb.*'

He said dumb *dum-mer*, Oscar noted, delighting as always in Jerome's wonderfully idiosyncratic delivery.

'Hey, tell me, bud,' he said, 'where did you learn to speak that way? I just love it. *Evah. Dummer. Iyah. Lah-ve.* Boy, is it great.'

'Where did you learn to write like that, bud? Beautiful, wonderful, touching, funny. We can all learn to speak, Oz. What we cannot be taught – is how to *write.*'

'Hell, there it is again,' Oscar sighed. 'To *write-ah.* Where did I learn to write? Where does anyone learn to write. I'll tell you where. Wherever I go. Because wherever I go, I watch people, Jerry, *old buddy.* I watch 'em, and I watch 'em damn good.'

He hadn't meant to say that, but Oscar was drunk and no longer in control of his mouth. He was irritated, too, because he saw that Jerome wasn't drunk, and he knew why that was. Because he didn't want to disappoint Elizabeth. Lover-boy wanted to be able to keep it going, on through the night.

'Keep it up, old boy,' Oscar said in a terrible English accent. 'What-ho.'

'Oz – you are pissed,' Jerome laughed. 'You are completely drenched.'

'Oh – you think I don't know what's going on, right?'

'Is that a question or a statement, Oz?' Jerome asked lightly, taking a cigarette from his packet as he did so, so that his eyes wouldn't meet Oscar's.

'I know what is going on, Jerry boy. And I shall tell you. What is going on is serious.' He stared down at Jerome, who was looking up at him completely openly, so openly Oscar knew he was hiding the biggest secret of his life. 'What is going on, Jerome Didier, genius, is that we have a stinking, great, socking big hit, you bastard.'

He leaned over to Jerome, knocking his drink off the arm of his chair but not noticing, and put his arms around his neck, hugging the actor to him. Jerome was pulled off balance, forward from his kneeling position, but he caught hold of the front of Oscar's chair just in time to regain his balance.

Oscar still had hold of him, and was whispering in his ear.

'You bastard,' he was whispering. 'You bastard great son of a bitch.'

When he eased Oscar back into his chair, and took the still smouldering stub of his cigarette from his fingers before Oscar could burn himself, Jerome saw that Oscar was crying.

During the night while Pippa slept, the lovers were reunited. Jerome had wondered what to do when he got back to the hotel, but his instructions awaited him in a note slipped under his door, and he obeyed them, slipping into Elizabeth's room once there was nobody else about.

'You're having doubts, J,' Elizabeth said as he came and sat on the edge of her bed in the dark. 'I feel it. I know you are.'

'Aren't you?' he asked.

'I have no doubts at all,' she replied. 'At least not as far as you are concerned.'

'What about the other people who are concerned?'

'They needn't know. Not ever.'

She put a hand out to him, resting it on his arm when he wouldn't take it. After a moment, he got up and took a packet of cigarettes from his pocket, lighting one.

311

'I'm sorry, Bethy,' he said, after he had walked over to the window and looked out at the silent city. It was time to be brave. 'But I don't think we should go on with this. We've broken down that famous door of yours, we've got through to each other, we have the play now. We have our characters. So I don't think we should go on.'

'I disagree.'

The voice behind him was so icily positive, Jerome spun round, his cigarette still in his mouth.

'I mean it, Bethy,' he said.

'I mean it, J,' she replied. 'It's a condition of doing the play.'

Jerome stared at her, and stared at her, and then laughed, as if she were joking, turning back to look out of the window.

'No, no, Bethy,' he said, drawing on his cigarette and shaking his head. 'There *are* no conditions. Particularly ones which come wrapped in emotional blackmail.'

'You don't understand, J.' He heard her slip from the bed behind him, and pad across the room to stand beside him. 'This isn't emotional blackmail. It's a fact. I can't do this without you.'

She had put her arm through his and now rested her dark head on his shoulder.

'Jesus Christ, Bethy darling!' he whispered as he looked round at her, her beautiful face lit pale by the moon. 'I can't do it without you either! That goes without saying!'

'You don't understand.' She sighed, deeply, keeping her head on his shoulder, but tightening the grip she had on his arm. 'I can't do this play *without* you.'

'Without us making love you mean?'

'Don't sound so astonished, my darling. I can't do this play, I can't do any play – I can't do anything now – not *without you.*'

He wasn't aware she was crying, because her voice was quite level, but when he turned her round to him he saw the glint of tears on her cheek. He put a hand up to her face, but she took it, holding it away from her.

'No,' she whispered. 'Kiss them away. Please. Kiss the tears away.'

'I can't.' It was hopeless, he knew. She just had to touch him, to look at him like that, and it was quite, quite hopeless. So he let go of her, or rather he made her let go of him.

'We know how to do the play now, Bethy,' he said. 'We've found out how to do it. We simply have to be responsible.'

'No,' she said, 'no, no, *no!*' And turning away from him quickly, she threw herself down on the bed, face down, burying her head in the pillows. He had to go over to her, he had to take her up in his arms, gently, carefully, he had to hold her while she cried, and cried, just as she had planned to do earlier in the theatre with Muzz. *If he suddenly gets an attack of conscience,* she said, *I think I shall cry, Muzz, don't you?*

'Bethy, darling,' Jerome said, stroking her thick silky hair. 'Of course you can do Tatty without – without me.'

'No, I can't!' she cried into his chest. 'I can't, J, I simply can't! If you suddenly stopped loving me—'

'Loving you?' He had her by the shoulders, gently but firmly, so that he could hold her away from him, so that he could look at her. Even through her tears she was beautiful, perhaps even more beautiful. '*Loving* you?'

'Yes, J,' she whispered, putting one hand to her mouth, 'loving me. And if you stopped now, I don't know what I'd do.'

'I haven't said I loved you, Bethy. I never said that.'

He felt her body stiffen, and she suddenly threw back her head and those famous green eyes glittered up at him dangerously. 'What do you think you're doing, J? What do you think you did this afternoon? You made love to me, didn't you?'

'Of course we made love, Bethy! But—'

'So what else is making love, J! But loving! At least that's what I understand by making love!' The eyes narrowed, and she tried to pull herself away from him, as if she suddenly sensed real danger. 'Unless—' she faltered, 'unless that's not the way you see it. Perhaps it isn't, J!' She was beginning to struggle harder now, but Jerome had a tight hold on her, he was determined not to let her go, he was afraid of that look in her eyes. 'Oh God – perhaps it isn't! Perhaps you didn't see it as making *love* – perhaps you just saw it as – as *having* me! Oh God!' she moaned. 'Perhaps that's all it is to you, Jerome Didier! Perhaps I'm just another person for you just to *have*!'

'No, Bethy! Don't say that! Don't be such a damn fool for Chrissake!' he said, still holding her as she began to struggle against him now with all her strength. From next door someone shouted at them to keep it down, to shut it up, that some people were trying to sleep, so Jerome frowned darkly at her, and told her to hush, to sshhhh.

'I'll scream,' she said, her eyes fixed on his. 'If you don't say you were making love to me, that you were loving me, that you weren't just doing the traditional thing, *laying the leading lady*, I warn you, J, I shall scream.'

'Of course I wasn't, Bethy!' He didn't want her to scream, he didn't want to be caught in the middle of a scandal, he didn't want his career to be hurt, not now, not ever. So he eased her down on to the edge of the bed, slowly and easily while he changed his pitch to soothing, to soothing reassurance, to calm her, to keep her from screaming. 'Of course we were making love,' he said. 'Of course I was loving you. I couldn't just – oh Bethy – if you thought I was the type of man who could just—'

He got no further because she had suddenly started to giggle, and then to laugh, to laugh with such delighted relief he had to clap a hand to her mouth and hush her once again. He kept his hand there while she rolled her eyes at him, over his hand, which she then softly bit, before sliding her tongue through his fingers, and kissing the palm of his hand slowly and softly while catching his eyes in hers.

'I'm sorry, darling,' she whispered, easing his hand from her mouth. 'I'm so sorry I really thought for a moment you meant—'

'Sssshhhh,' he whispered back, 'it's all right. It's all right.'

She kissed him, and he made no effort to stop her. In fact he welcomed it, kissing her in return, slipping his arms round her tiny waist, drawing her down beside him on the bed.

'I need you so much,' she gasped, 'I can't do without you. I can't do the play! I promise I can't!'

'You won't have to, Bethy my darling.' He was opening her robe, exposing her beautiful body to the moonlight, kissing her white breasts. 'You won't have to, I promise.' Her nipples were so perfect, they were little pink buds. 'You won't have to,' he said, 'because the truth is I can't do it without you.'

'I would die,' she said, her back arching under the delicious thrill of him kissing each pink bud. 'If *Tatty* were to fail now, if we couldn't take it, now that we have it right, if we couldn't take it into town.' Now she gasped, as his hand eased down her stomach. 'But we couldn't, it just won't be possible, not unless oh—' she groaned quietly, 'oh no, not unless we keep loving each other, my darling. So that we don't ever lose it – *Oh!*'

'*Ah*—' Jerome whispered, '*yes, my darling, oh my God yes, Bethy darling, yes!*'

By the time dawn broke, as Jerome was creeping back to his own room and bed, he knew there was no way he could stop now, not until the play was over, not until the play had come off and they had then to part, there was simply no way. Because Jerome was hopelessly addicted.

Pippa's train arrived on time at Manchester Central, from where she took a taxi straight to the hotel. Pippa had intended to ring

Jerome from the station to warn him of her arrival, but when she saw the queue for the phones as well as the growing one for cabs she decided otherwise, knowing that it wouldn't matter because Jerome loved surprises. They were always surprising each other.

She waited at Reception while the clerk rang Jerome's room without success. He then ran his finger along the line of key pegs and seeing that the key for room number seven was still missing, and having checked with the other clerk on duty, he told Pippa that although her husband was not in his room he must still be somewhere in the hotel, and if she would like to wait in the foyer he would have Mr Didier paged.

A waiter took her order for a sherry and showed her to a big comfortable old leather armchair which faced the desk and stairs. Pippa settled into the chair, and watched while the page boy chalked his board with her husband's name. It was still lunch-time, and people were arriving to meet their friends, their business colleagues or their dates, to have an aperitif and then to wander on into the large dining room. The pageboy began to move around the bar area with his board, while above on the first-floor landing, Pippa saw a waiter backing out of the service lift. As he turned she could see he had a trolley set for lunch, white linen, domed silver dishes, a bottle of champagne on ice, even a small vase of flowers, which he carefully wheeled along the landing and then round out of sight down a corridor, leaving Pippa idly to wonder who could be having such a wonderful treat.

As she sat day dreaming, with Bobby sitting as good as gold at her feet, a large man in a check suit arrived on the foyer and stood in front of Pippa, looking around him for the person he was to meet. Bobby growled, and the man smiled affably enough while Pippa came back to earth and put one hand on her dog's head to quieten him. Then the man in the check suit obviously caught sight of his host because he suddenly smiled and went round behind Pippa's chair.

As the waiter put her sherry down in front of her, Pippa heard the two men greet each other and exchange pleasantries. Pippa peered round her chair cautiously, unable to resist taking a look, and saw the second man was also middle aged and sturdy, with a rather lugubrious expression. Both of them were too busy talking to notice Pippa's curiosity, and as she returned to her former position, she heard them call the waiter over and order two large pink gins. Then they sat down in the sofa which directly backed on to the line of chairs where Pippa was sitting.

Bobby growled again, for no particular reason this time, so Pippa gave a small tug on his lead and hushed him to be quiet. Then she picked up a copy of the *Tatler* and began leafing through it.

The men behind were discussing the hotel and the second man, the one with the lugubrious face, was explaining that he always stayed here at the Grand when he came down to Manchester on business because there was simply nowhere else worth staying.

'Mind you,' he added, 'I can't say 'ow I enjoys it, staying in 'otels. I'm an 'omebird, and I likes me own bed. I just don't sleep in 'otels. And I tell you, Stanley, last night were no exception.'

Pippa was staring at a set of pictures of the guests at some Hunt ball, but her attention was on the conversation behind her. It was impossible not to listen, because the men were conversing in such loud voices.

The man in the check suit, the first man, was asking his companion why he hadn't slept, politely, not with a great deal of interest, Pippa thought, as the smoke from their freshly lit cigarettes wafted past her chair.

'It were them theatricals,' the second man replied with a deep sigh. 'Honest to God, they're a right bunch.'

'They're staying here, are they?' the first man asked. 'I thought the likes of them usually stayed in digs.'

'Aye,' the second man agreed. ' 'appen. But this lot's different. This lot's got nobs on 'em.'

Pippa smiled to herself, thinking how Jerome would laugh to hear himself described like that, thinking how much he would laugh when she told him.

The page was coming out of the dining room now, followed by a man Pippa couldn't quite distinguish through the half glassed doors. Thinking it must be Jerome, she put down her sherry and prepared to get up, only to find when the man emerged into the foyer he was a total stranger.

'Pagin' Mr Didier!' the page called in a high voice as he crossed to the bar. 'Pagin' Mr J. Didier!'

'That's 'im,' a voice said behind Pippa, 'that's one of 'em.'

'Oh, aye?' said the first voice, again without much interest.

'Aye,' the second voice said. '*Jerome Didier*. Fancy. Mind you, 'e's some looker. Can act a bit, too.'

'You saw the play then?'

'Aye. I were there last night. George took a party on, after reception. About eight of us all told. It were good, too. I 'ave to say it were really damn good, and I'm not a great one for theatre. Least not unless it's variety.'

'You don't say? Well, who knows? I might take the wife to see it then. She's always naggin' me to take her to theatre. For the life of me, I can't remember last time I were there!'

At this point the waiter arrived with their drinks and the men fell to silence. Pippa couldn't wait for them to get going again, to see if they were going to go on talking about the play, and about Jerome. Because if the play had succeeded in front of an audience composed of people like this, then the miracle surely must have happened.

'No,' the second man began again. 'No I were surprised, I tell you, Stanley, because it's mostly talk, you know. But there's this girl in it, and she's a cracker. We was saying in the bar at 'alf-time what a cracker she was. I tell you, I never seen a lass as pretty, and I've seen a few. Never. Never.'

'You don't say.' The second man laughed. 'In that case, Jack, perhaps I won't take the wife after all!'

'She'll be all right, Stanley, don't you mind. She can feast her eyes on that *Jerome Didier*. Eeee, you should 'ave 'eard all the women. Billin' and cooin', and sighin' and moanin' all over the place they were. Your wife'll enjoy it, don't you worry, if all them other wives is anythin' to go by.'

Pippa smiled in private delight. She found it practically impossible not to turn round to them and tell them who she was, that she was *Jerome Didier's wife*, and that their wives couldn't have him. But she didn't. She just sat and listened.

'Oh yes,' the second man continued, 'they're a right pair, that little lass and Mr 'owsitgoing. And you'd think, when you see 'em, Stanley, they're that good, they're that *sweet*, you'd think that butter wouldn't melt in their mouths.'

'What you saying, Jack? You mean it would?'

'Do I 'eck. Weren't I tellin' you they was stayin' 'ere?'

'Aye. Happen you was.'

'Aye,' said the second man firmly. 'Well then.'

In that second the smile vanished from Pippa's face and she felt suddenly and inexplicably sick. She knew something was about to be said and she knew she shouldn't hear it. And yet she couldn't move. She couldn't get up out of the chair, because she knew she had to know.

'Pagin' Mr Didier!' the boy called again somewhere, on his way to another room. 'Pagin' Mr J. Didier!'

''e should try upstairs,' the second man laughed. 'That's where 'e'll be most likely.' Then he dropped his voice and said something Pippa couldn't hear, but which made the first man laugh out loud, a filthy laugh, a bar-room guffaw.

317

Now Pippa knew she must go, so she looked round for her bag which she'd put behind her on the chair, and which had fallen open, spilling out some of her belongings, her keys, her powder compact.

'No,' the second man said, 'that's what all the 'iatus were last night. Why I couldn't sleep, Stanley. My room's next door to 'em. By 'eck, they were at it like rabbits.'

'Were they by heck? *You don't say.'*

'They were at it all night, Stanley. Like rabbits. *Like rats up a drain.'*

Pippa couldn't gather her things together, her hands were shaking too much and suddenly she couldn't see now, because her eyes were full of tears and she was dropping her things on the floor, her compact, her keys, the little travelling teddy bear Jerome had given her.

'Mind you—' the first man said. 'I have heard, mind. I've heard tell about them theatricals. I remember a friend of the wife saying that as soon as the curtain comes down, they were at it like knives.'

'Like rats up a drain, Stanley. I couldn't sleep a wink.'

The first man laughed, as if the whole thing was a joke, which to him it was, of course, because he'd be dining out on this one, he'd be making his pals laugh in bars everywhere. *You know them two fancy young actors? Didier and Laurence? You know who I mean. Listen lads, them two's like rats up a drain.*

'Course you're sure it was them, Jack?'

'Sure? Course I'm sure, Stanley. I could 'ear the whole thing as if it were on radio! And not only that, I got up to answer nature at some unholy hour 'cos I couldn't bloody sleep, and I saw the bugger sneaking out of 'er room back to 'is.'

Pippa's compact rolled out of her reach, as she tried to pick up everything on her hands and knees, while Bobby licked her face. The compact rolled under the chair and out beside the sofa the men were on. One of them picked it up and held it out to her, round the sofa as she crawled to get it. She took it from him and got up.

'Are you all right, lass?' she heard him saying. 'Here—'

But she was gone, pulling Bobby behind her as she rushed up the carpeted stairs, past a startled couple whom she divided in the middle, while below her she heard one of the clerks calling after her.

But she knew which room he was, because she had seen the clerk checking number seven, not that she wanted his room because she knew *he wasn't there*, she wanted *her* room, she wanted her friend Elizabeth Laurence's room, and she knew that must be on the same floor, in fact she knew it must be one of two rooms, because she had also noticed that the peg for room five and room three still had no key, so she must be in one of them, and if she wasn't she would break down every door until she found her, until she found the *rabbits*.

Number seven was empty, Jerome's room, which she checked anyway, just in case, but it was empty, the bed made, but with Jerome's clothes still on the chair. *So that's who the lunch was for, and the champagne, and the flowers. It was for the rabbits. It was for the rats.* Along the corridor the door of room three swung open, and a maid came out, having obviously just finished making the room up. Pippa could see past her, it was empty, the bed beautifully made. So there was only room five. Which was here, right in front of her now, with a notice on the door, *Do Not Disturb*.

There were voices, too. A girl's laughter, throaty, not Elizabeth's usual light, little laugh, but something altogether different, something altogether more intimate. Then silence. Then his voice, Jerome's voice, which even carried at a whisper. But Jerome wasn't whispering, he was saying something to Elizabeth, something Pippa heard but didn't want to hear, something which she'd never heard him say before, which was why Pippa wrenched the door handle round and found the room was open and saw them look with horror when they saw who she was.

But she had the edge on them, she was on her feet and moving, while they were trapped in bed, him it seemed with nothing on at all, no dressing gown, nothing, while she had just a slip, a petticoat with no bra, the top of one white breast spilling a little out over the edging of lace, her thick black hair for once undone, spilt like ink against the pile of pillows. Pippa heard nothing, not anything that Jerome was beginning to shout at her, she couldn't even hear her own screaming as she threw everything she could find at them, she threw domed silver dishes, empty plates, plates still with food on them, the champagne bottle with its contents corkscrewing into the air, the glasses, the cutlery, she rained them all in a stream at them, she hurled their love feast at their faces, the plates and glasses the knives and the forks the bottle and the shower of wine she saw them all crashing and spilling and splintering and spewing over and around *the rabbits, the rats*, who were trying to protect themselves against the barrage, Elizabeth with her hands first to her precious face, and then hiding under the sheet while Jerome

319

grabbed a pillow for protection and yelled at her, Pippa could now hear him yelling, he was shouting for her to stop but she wouldn't, not until she had killed them, not until they were all of them dead for ever.

Someone now had hold of her arms, someone from behind, and she couldn't move. Bobby was barking furiously, running across at whoever it was, loose with his leash dragging behind. Whoever it was behind yelled suddenly and sharply as the dog bit him hard in the leg, and Pippa, feeling the grip on her arms slacken, escaped and threw herself with all her strength at Jerome, who was stumbling towards her, absurdly dressed in a sheet which he was trying to hold in place, but he only had one hand free so Pippa swung at him, so hard, harder than she had ever swung at anybody and caught him on his nose, pulping it, hearing it squash under her clenched fist and seeing the blood shoot from it and on to the sheet which he quickly pulled up to it. The man behind, the unseen man lunged at Pippa again, but Bobby still had a hold of his trousers and sunk his teeth in the back of his legs again, making the man shout out and fall to the ground, clutching his legs. Elizabeth was screaming in the bed, Jerome was holding a blood-stained sheet to his face, a man in a dark blue suit lay floored, face down moaning and clasping first one leg and then the other, so Pippa suddenly stopped. She stopped and pulled herself up as quickly as she had started, easing her bruised hand, picking up her bag, her keys which had fallen out, her compact, her lipstick, her train ticket, picked up Bobby's lead, and turned and left the room.

Other people were coming up the stairs now, curious people, alerted by the disturbance, but Pippa brushed passed them, hardly even seeing them. She hurried down the stairs, past the reception desk, past the two loudmouths who were both now on their feet, talking animatedly, looking up the stairs, wondering like the others in the foyer *what was going on up there*? out on to the street and into a waiting taxi, which she ordered to take her back to Manchester Central Railway Station, where she was just in time to catch the two twenty-two back to London.

ENTR'ACTE

Those of you who followed the careers of both Elizabeth Laurence and Jerome Didier will know that the official version of the events that day in room five (that the incident had involved no third party, that Miss Laurence had been lunching alone in her room when she had been badly frightened by a mouse, that during this time Mr Didier had been in the theatre resolving some minor technical problems with his director, and that there was no record anywhere, at least not officially, of an unknown young woman and her mongrel dog) was nothing but a tissue of lies hastily assembled by the dog-bitten Cecil Manners and his two panic struck and near hysterical clients, and was ultimately discredited. All of you with an interest in the lives of *The Dazzling Didiers* (as the first biography of them was entitled), know what really happened, whether through reading the slightly sanitized account in the afore-mentioned biog, or from a study later of the highly personalized and dramatically charged ones in the stars' own published versions of their lives and times. What actually happened was that Cecil, who had arrived coincidentally on the same train as Pippa, but who had gone first to the theatre to meet briefly with Oscar, had checked into his hotel room at the precise moment when all hell let loose.

He saw the event through open doors, his room being all but opposite Elizabeth's, but by the time he had dropped everything he was doing to run across the corridor and into room number five, Pippa had already hurled most of the luncheon trolley at the two in the bed. He had grabbed Pippa from behind, but before he could make himself known Pippa's dog had bitten him hard on the ankle, seizing his trouser leg, while Pippa in her manic struggle to get free had elbowed her unknown assailant in the stomach, knocking him off balance and to the ground, where her wretched dog had once again taken the opportunity of savaging his other leg this time. Pippa had then disappeared, and in the confusion, acting on Jerome's shouted orders, Cecil had crawled over to shut and lock the door just in time.

Elizabeth was later to maintain in her autobiography (*To See How Far It Was*, published by Allen & Graham), amongst many other hotly disputed 'facts', that the face-saving enterprise was her idea. Jerome in his autobiography (*Facing Up*, published by Cockerel) not unnaturally contradicts this theory, maintaining that the only one with any degree of sang-froid at that particularly dangerous moment was himself, and that the only person he was thinking of was Pippa. This latter assertion was most probably the only true statement either of them made, as there is little doubt of Jerome's genuine concern for his wife, whom he always claimed

323

he still loved dearly at that moment, a claim which hasn't always endeared him to the more sensitive of his fans, who found his duplicity heartless and hypocritical to say the very least.

But it didn't destroy his then growing popularity, not in the least. Elizabeth in fact claimed it actively helped them, being a firm believer that the worst an actor can suffer is not bad publicity, but no publicity. This, however, was not the thinking at the time, as the three of them sat, lay or crouched, huddled, bleeding or wounded in room number five of the Grand Hotel, Manchester, Elizabeth, one eye blackened from a flying coffee cup, in bed sobbing seethingly that she would *kill the bitch*, Cecil, trouserless on the floor holding cold towels to the bites on his wounded legs and asking for quiet, and Jerome huddled Brutus-like in a blood-stained bedsheet clasped both around his waist and to his still bleeding nose, rocking backwards and forwards and wondering out loud and again and again *what in hell they were all going to do.*

Elizabeth began to moan through her sobs that they were ruined, that their careers were in shreds, and just on the eve of their greatest triumph too, at which point Jerome suddenly decided he should go to his room, get dressed and go after Pippa. Cecil only just managed to catch him by the door, scrambling to his feet and barring his way, warning him that the corridor would be full of people, and that Jerome was all but naked. Jerome got a hold of Cecil by his lapels and tried to hurl him out of the way, determined to go after his wife, but Cecil, although lame, was still strong enough to overcome him, and *sotto voce* informed Jerome that running after his wife now, in full view of most of Manchester, would do the utmost harm and the smallest amount of good. Jerome insisted, wishing the play to hell, and saying that the only thing he was interested in was saving his marriage, but Cecil stood firm, and reminded him that if he tried to get out of the play particularly now that it had come right, the management would sue him till kingdom come, and not only that but he would close the door on Hollywood. Cecil had Hollywood lined up, he had the talent scouts coming to the London opening, but no opening, no Hollywood. For Elizabeth yes, but for Jerome he could kiss the chance goodbye. No, the time to talk to Pippa, he advised, was when he, Cecil, had taken the steam out of the situation as it stood, and if that's what they wanted, Elizabeth and he, for him to take the steam out of it, which it seemed they now did, then they must both *shut up, listen, and do exactly as they were told.* Which they then did, because they knew perfectly well there really was simply no alternative.

Cecil then organized it all. This sort of thing had happened to him on previous tours, although certainly not quite as spectacularly, so he had at least the benefit of experience in the field. He knew there was only one thing which talked at times like this, not reason, but money. Hotel managements, while not exactly eager to encourage scandalous behaviour, were generally reluctant to be seen to condemn them out of hand, lest they deter the rich and the famous from staying in their public houses, since as everyone knew, scandals only ever concerned the rich or the famous. The most the poor or unimportant miscreant was ever capable of making was a disgrace. So Cecil knew of old that as long as sufficient money changed hands, history could as usual be beneficially distorted.

All in all it cost the management approximately three hundred pounds to make sure that the true story didn't break, a not inconsiderable sum of money for those days. But the odd thing was, Cecil really needn't have bothered. He needn't have troubled to buy all the witnesses' silences, nor felt himself obliged to force Oscar to provide an alibi for Jerome with the threat that if he didn't the subsequent scandal would surely mean that *Tatty Gray* would never see London. Oscar hadn't been inclined to believe such a thing at first, but Cecil had been adamant, persuading Oscar that a play of such delicacy would be ruined by any such notoriety, and that if a scandal such as this was to break, they might as well put up the notice backstage that night. It was a terrible dilemma for Oscar, loving Pippa as he did, feeling that he had betrayed her as he had, loving Jerome and Elizabeth for what they had done on-stage, while hating them for what they had done off it, hating himself for being the instrument of this tragedy, loathing Cecil for trying to implicate him further, but loving and loving so much what had happened to his play, which after all might be the only great play he might write in his entire life, and knowing that certainly there would never ever be a finer production of it, at least not as far as the leading performances went. He told Cecil all of this, and Cecil laughed in his face, telling him not to be such a damned fool, that he Oscar couldn't possibly be blamed in any way for what had happened. Of what was he guilty? Writing a play so fine and beautiful that it had turned the heads of two silly, vain and empty-headed young actors? What nonsense. No, no charges could be brought against Oscar, so he must now put aside any personal feelings, any feelings of imagined guilt, and be professional. Like Cecil was. Cecil didn't like this sort of thing at all, he assured Oscar. In fact he hated it. He hated apparently condoning it, but he had to do it for the sake of the play, as had Oscar. *The play was beautiful, at last the play was alive, and wonderful, and they must protect this child of theirs at all costs.* So Oscar, knowing that it was wrong, allowed himself to be persuaded otherwise and took Cecil's pieces of silver, his reason being that even if the play was taken off now, the personal and private damage which Jerome and Elizabeth had done would not and could not by consequence be undone.

Cecil was deeply relieved, although one part of Oscar's confessions had troubled him, namely the information that Oscar too was in love with Pippa. But Cecil soon let this pass, as he couldn't for a moment imagine someone as sweet and beguiling as Pippa falling in love with such a hangdog as Oscar, and now, as a result of the particularly clever predictions made by Elizabeth's friend Lalla, given the necessary amount of healing time Pippa would ultimately be his. So Cecil went on paying the play out of trouble.

But he really need not have bothered. Elizabeth was quite right in her belief that the only bad publicity is no publicity. Certainly some newspapers did run the item, but only as a non-story, a *no-truth-in-the-rumours-that* sort of piece, while the better papers ignored the incident altogether, printing nothing. It didn't matter, however, how they ran it or whether or not they did, because since the world generally believes there is no smoke without something burning somewhere, versions of the story were soon on everyone's lips. Everyone talked of it, it was the talk of every town, and as a result you couldn't buy a seat to see Jerome Didier and Elizabeth Laurence in *The Tale of Tatty Gray* by Oscar Greene for love, money or at least six months.

As for Pippa at this time, what of her? What of the tousle-haired, freckle-faced, open-hearted girl who had fallen so wildly and deeply in love with her passionate, dark-haired, dark-eyed actor? What exactly happened to her at this moment? Where did she get to? Where did she go? What did she do? Pippa never wrote anything about it, she never published her version of their life, although she must have read (we know she read) Jerome's, which can't have been easy, because when it came to recounting their time together, Jerome bled over every page. Yet she never said a thing in public to anyone, never gave an interview, never expressed an opinion intended for publication. So nobody ever knew how she felt, nobody who didn't know her or get to know her intimately that is, and for a long time nobody even knew where she had gone.

What happened in the immediate aftermath was that she

returned to London with Bobby, although to this day she cannot remember a detail of the journey, but still she got herself home, and she got herself packed. It was evening, of course, by the time she got back to Park Lane, but Nancy was there, startled and bewildered to see her mistress back so unexpectedly. Pippa gave no explanation for her return, she just asked Nancy to come and help her pack up all her belongings. Of the events in Manchester she said nothing whatsoever, although Nancy had sensed something was afoot, since Miss Toothe had been fielding a constantly ringing telephone from about mid-afternoon, answering every call with the selfsame answer, that she was very sorry but she could *make no comment.*

And now her mistress was leaving, taking all her own things, her clothes and her books, her records and photographs, her letters, her diaries, everything which was a part of her, however small, she was packing up and taking. Nancy, knowing now she must be leaving for good, carefully enquired if she might ask where her mistress was going, in the hope that she might go with her, and when Pippa told her that she didn't yet know, and that she couldn't possibly take her because it wouldn't be fair, Nancy asked why not? That there was nothing to keep her here, only her job, and she was dashed if she was going to stay on as housemaid in a house with no mistress (Nancy was Irish). She'd far rather go with Mrs Didier and look after her.

Pippa said if Nancy was quite sure that she would take her, realizing somewhere in the back of her mind that she would need her, that she would need someone to take care of her, particularly now because she thought she might be pregnant. She was very grateful to her shy young maid, and told her so, before ordering her to bed because they had a great deal to do in the morning, and because they had, they needed to be up with the dawn.

The phone had been off the hook since Pippa's return, which was how she left it. It had been the very first thing she had done when she walked through the door. She had done it before she had even let Bobby off his leash. She had walked straight in and disarmed the instrument, knowing that if it rang she would finally answer it, and if she did, she would be lost. She had worked all that out on the train. She knew she must neither hear nor see Jerome because if she did, he would persuade her to stay, because he would be able to talk her round, because he would have had every reason for doing what he had done. Pippa knew that if he reached her, by phone or worse, in person, she wouldn't go, because although she wouldn't believe his every reason, she would stay because she loved him. And if she stayed, he would do the same thing to her again, and again, and again, and again and again and again she would be expected to forgive him, since she had done so in the first instance. If she forgave him now when it really mattered, it would be as good as giving him *carte blanche* for the rest of their days.

She had, however, opened and read the two telegrams which had arrived together, because telegrams were inanimate and by necessity cryptic. Not even Jerome could inflect a telegram, not even he with all his vocal magic and physical tricks could make the potency of his presence felt by wire. The telegrams weren't both from Jerome, only one was, the first one she opened which said she was to call him either immediately before the performance at the hotel or immediately afterwards at the theatre *when he would explain everything*, just as she thought he would. The second one was from Cecil which said she was to do or say absolutely nothing until he had spoken to her personally, which he would do by telephone that evening *when he would explain everything*. Pippa tore them both up into small pieces, burned them in an ashtray and left the telephone off the hook.

Now she slept. No-one knows how well or how badly, or if she did at all, because she recorded nothing about that evening in her diary, nothing about the events of the day, nor of her feelings. Later, years later she was to confess how she had surprised herself with the way she had managed, and managed so ably, withdrawing all her money from the bank the following morning, funds which included her half of her late mother's small estate, half of the proceeds from Bay Tree Cottage, half of the proceeds from the furnishings, the few stocks and shares, her mother's jewellery (all which she kept, none of which she sold) and her half of her mother's small savings, before selecting at random, without anyone's advice, the place that Nancy, Bobby and she were to go, getting them all on the boat train, and then on the ferry across to France. In hindsight she was to admit to being amazed not so much at how she had actually done it, but more at the fact that she had, that she had been able to organize her departure from England as if she was simply going away on holiday, rather than walking out of the life of the man whom she knew she still loved with all her heart.

These things you might not know. You would certainly not have been aware of them from reading the books on *The Dazzling*

Didiers, The Daring Didiers, The Darling Didiers, because there were no such details in any of the books about things like these, even in the books written by them, because *The Dazzling, The Daring* and *The Darling Didiers* were not, of course, Pippa and Jerome. By then the Didiers were Jerome and Elizabeth.

ACT THREE

England
Late in the Sixties

Jerome had found Sainthill by chance, while driving round the countryside beyond Bath one afternoon when not required on the shoot of The Heart's A Secret. As soon as he had seen the place he had known he must have it, and so he had instructed Dingo, his private chauffeur-cum-valet, to drive at once into Malmesbury and find the posted estate agency.

He had already had a good look at the outside of the place, which although practically a ruin, was nonetheless the sort of place about which Jerome had endlessly dreamed. To judge from the architecture it had most probably been built as a monastery, or a priory, for it had its own integral chapel, the traditional carp pond, a trout stream and lush pastures for grazing livestock, lands designed to provide a self-sufficient living for whatever order had once occupied the wonderful buildings, and which with recultivation and reshaping Jerome knew would afford the sort of grounds and setting fit for the world famous stars which he and Elizabeth had now become.

So too the house, or priory, or whatever it had been, Jerome had mused as his Rolls-Royce had sped back from Malmesbury, taking back with them to Sainthill a faintly supercilious young estate agent who was doing his level best not to be too impressed by his famous fellow passenger. Jerome in turn had paid him little heed, preferring instead to try and imagine how the splendid property would look when restored. It would be ideal, he had decided as Dingo had headed the Rolls off the road and up the long and potholed drive towards the distant building, it would be absolutely perfect, because without a doubt it was beautiful, and without another doubt far and away the most entirely suitable place he had seen since their recent return from America, which was when they had both started searching in earnest for a house appropriate to their international status.

'It is – sublime,' he had announced, his voice echoing round the vast empty rooms. 'Quite and utterly sublime.'

'The wonderful thing,' the estate agent had told him, 'is that it is utterly unspoilt. In the wrong hands it could so easily have been ruined. Central heating, this new craze for adjoining bathrooms. Knocking out the chapel. You can imagine.'

'I can!' Jerome had laughed, not at anything amusing but rather to try out again the extraordinary acoustics of the place. 'I can! I can!'

His voice had echoed back from where he had thrown it, up the spiralling stone staircase, out of sight round the vast central pillar, and back again down the deeply worn steps.

'Of course,' the estate agent had continued, now warming both to his task and to Jerome, having sensed his client was seriously considering buying this appalling ruin, 'someone like you, sir, like you both, the two of you, this could have been made for you. It's perfect. It's a very dramatic place, it needs people like you. With your artistry, and your theatrical skills, you will make Sainthill famous.'

'Baloney!' Jerome had laughed again, this time into the stone flagged dining room. 'Stuff and nonsense!'

But the following day he had brought Elizabeth down to see it.

She had hated it. She had remained totally unimpressed by the whole place, from the thirteenth-century chapel set to one side of the arched hall, and the great stone vaulted roof, to the intricately mullioned windows, and vast open fireplaces.

'It's a monster,' she had declared. 'This isn't a home, J. This is a film set. This is something straight out of the English version of Citizen Kane.'

'No Bethy, my darling!' Jerome had countered, stretching his arms out wide and turning round where he stood, in the middle of the room he had chosen as the drawing room, and which Elizabeth had denounced as a barn. 'You're not stretching that famous imagination of yours! Think of the parties! Just imagine the parties!'

'I can't,' she had replied, pulling her fur coat around her to protect her from the winds which were howling through the broken window panes. 'All I can think of is going home.'

Elizabeth hated the cold. Sometimes she thought she hated the cold more than anything else. Being cold made her feel physically sick. She also hated huge rooms with high ceilings. Elizabeth was a small house person, a chintz person, a person who liked delicate and decorative things, such as beautifully hand-crafted shelves back lit to show off her collection of antique china figurines. Everything would be lost in a place this size, most of all her.

But Jerome had been determined on it. He had dragged her up the patently dangerous stairs, at the same time proclaiming the merits of the place at the top of his voice, and had paced through the succession of bedrooms pointing out every architectural detail, exhorting her to take notice of them all, while all Elizabeth could think of was the cold, the eternal and the universal cold. She had clutched the neck of her fur coat tightly round her throat, thankful for her cashmere gloves and her elegant, handmade, furlined, high heel boots, as Jerome had explained with mounting enthusiasm where the library would be, which would be his study, and which hers, where would be their bedroom, their bathrooms (individual), their dressing rooms, the guest rooms, the guest bathrooms, the music rooms, the billiards room, before Elizabeth had finally interrupted him to point at the ceiling directly above.

'And what about up there, J darling?' she had asked, mock sweetly. 'More guest rooms? Studies? Music rooms? And what-have-you? According to this –' (here she had shaken the house details at him) '– there are another ten rooms up there!'

'They're for trunks and things, Bethy!' he had shouted back, irritated, as if she should have known better. 'Attics! Junk rooms! You know! Nurseries! Nurseries for the children!'

'What children?'

'When we have children, Bethy! You'd be surprised how quickly you fill a place like this up! And just think of the parties!'

Elizabeth had turned away and gone back downstairs, down those lethal, worn, stone steps, picking her way carefully, holding on to the rusting iron rail. There might well be parties, she had thought, but no, no children. Jerome seemed quite incapable of realizing that she never intended having children. And even if she had been, Elizabeth had thought, nearly falling over on the last two steps, even if she went mad and gave birth to fifty blasted squawling brats, even that wouldn't be enough to fill a God-forsaken mausoleum like this.

She had sat in the car, tucked in under her travel rug, smoking a Sobranie while she waited for Jerome whom she could see inside the ruin walking around room after room with his arms up in the air reciting something to himself. Finally he had emerged just as Elizabeth had been lighting her second cigarette from the dying butt of her first, and with a look of disapproval, had settled in the back of the Rolls beside her.

'Well?' he had said, looking back at the house as Dingo drove away down the drive.

'You're mad,' she had replied. 'Stark, staring mad.'

That was the extent of their conversation all the way back to London. For the rest of the journey Jerome had sat in silence holding on to the strap his side and staring out of his window, while Elizabeth had sat in silence holding on to the strap her side and staring out of her window.

Elizabeth had worked on everyone they knew to talk Jerome out of buying Sainthill, most of all their mutual confidant, 'Booble' Doulton, the resident set designer for the Didier's newly formed and London-based theatrical company, as well as their unofficial interior decorator. A single woman with seemingly eternally young features, she was highly talented, blond, comfortably plump, *although with surprisingly shapely and slender legs and arms, and extremely skilled in the art of theatrical diplomacy.*

'It will cost a fortune to rebuild, Booble darling,' Elizabeth had complained, 'and another fortune to do up. And neither of those fortunes will be small ones. You are going to have to talk him out of it.'

This was after one of their regular lunches, taken at Elizabeth's Chelsea home which she had been allowed to keep after Sebastian had divorced her. As usual Elizabeth had eaten nothing, but had just smoked and drunk champagne throughout the beautifully prepared meal, while Booble had eaten everything that had been put in front of her. Now they were sitting in the newly refurnished drawing room, drinking their coffee from tiny Spode cups that Booble had found for Elizabeth on one of her countless jaunts in the countryside, china which matched exactly the faded colours in the French rug which Booble had also found and which now lay in front of the fireplace. Booble liked harmony, she liked everything to tone in and blend with their surroundings. This was one of the many things she so admired in Elizabeth, her sense of correlation. This day, for example, Elizabeth was most exquisitely dressed, in the most delicate of pale blue silk dresses, pale stockings and shoes, with her jewellery, small sapphires and diamonds, carefully chosen to suit not only her clothes, but the room, and even, it seemed, the mood of the day.

'I had better come and see this place,' Booble had said, finishing her coffee.

'I think you had,' Elizabeth had agreed. 'Jerome will listen to you because he thinks you know what you're talking about.'

'Don't you, Lizabett?' Booble was the only other person in the entourage who was allowed to nickname her.

'You wouldn't be working for us, darling,' Elizabeth had laughed, 'if I didn't.'

The house had seemingly been full of birds the day they visited. As Elizabeth had unlocked the front door with the largest key either of them could ever remember seeing, a whole flock of small black birds rushed with a clatter of wings out past their heads, forcing the two women instinctively to duck.

'Don't faint,' Elizabeth had said as they had walked into the hall. 'And don't say you haven't been warned.'

Booble stared around her, and above her, and then at her surroundings again. The place was simply magnificent, it was everything and more that Jerome had described to her when he had taken her out to lunch and asked her to try and talk his wife into letting him buy it.

'You do see now what I mean, Booble darling, don't you?' Elizabeth had said, leading her friend through room after room. 'I mean what can he be thinking? Parties indeed. We'd have to give one twice a week so as not to die with boredom. I mean can you imagine? Can you imagine sitting in a room this size on your own?'

'It's one of the most amazing places I've ever seen, Lizabett. I don't think I've ever been in a place quite like this.'

'Can you imagine what it would take to do it up, Booble? In time as well as money?'

High above them suddenly, somewhere up in the rafters, a bird had called, a harsh and startling cry, which had echoed bleakly round the vaulted ceilings. Both women had looked up at once, in time to see a huge black bird swooping down towards them, wings flapping in menace, and its beak wide open to shout defiance at them, before gliding with briefly closed wings through a broken window then stretching its wings once more to fly away up in the skies.

'Good heavens,' Booble had said, watching the bird with dismay. 'I think that was a raven.'

'Well?' Jerome had asked. 'Did you talk her round?'

'She'll be fine, Jerry,' Booble had replied, spreading her designs for A Code of Practice on his desk in front of him. 'It's only because you found it first. Leave her to me. I'll get her to help with the interiors, involve her one hundred per cent. Promise, Jerry darling, within a couple of months she'll be swearing to all and sundry the place was all her idea.'

'You're a marvel, Booble. No wonder we all love you.'

Later, after their meeting, when Booble had returned to her own office high under the eaves of the Princes Theatre, the home of the Didiers' New England Players, she had thought with relish as to how much work the restoration of Sainthill would bring her, and had sighed contentedly as she had put away the stage designs. Fabrics would have to be specially woven, furniture bought (masses of it, the place was so vast), the right materials found, paints expressly mixed, window glasses correctly replaced, stone masons hired, and builders of the highest quality engaged, all through and by her. Jerome had given her a free hand. The job would be worth a fortune.

Not only that, Sainthill would secure her reputation. The restoration of such an historic property would immortalize her. She would be known for ever and always as that brilliant woman who designed Sainthill, the place the Dazzling Didiers had lived.

She stared out of her window across the roofs of London and thought, had lived? How odd, she wondered, they hadn't even bought Sainthill, and yet already she had consigned it to the past tense, as if looking forward to a time in the foreseeable future when there would be no such couple as The Dazzling Didiers. And then she had put the thought right out of her head, because such a thought was, when she thought about it, quite unthinkable.

FOURTEEN

This was Oscar's first visit to Sainthill, as it was everyone else's in the car, and in the car behind and, miles behind, in all the other cars making the pilgrimage west. He'd seen photographs of it of course, they all had, all Jerome's and Elizabeth's courtiers, they had all been shown photographs of the great house from the moment Jerome had bought it, they had been shown photographs of every single stage of the conversion, and they had been shown photographs of Sainthill on the completion of works. But this was the first visit paid by the court, this was to be the great and the grand unveiling.

The car in which Oscar was travelling (all the cars had been laid on by their hosts, no-one was required to drive down in their own humble vehicles, or worse – by train) contained besides himself and the driver four members of the New England Players, including Elizabeth's court jester, the actor Robert Dunster, and her still good friend Lalla Henderson. Oscar liked Lalla. Not only had she matured into quite a reasonable actress (she was particularly good in bitchy parts), but she was always excellent company, and a mine of gossip.

But not even Lalla had been allowed a preview of Sainthill.

'Of course I tried, darling!' Lalla laughed, in answer to Oscar's enquiry. 'I even thought of disguising myself as a prospective domestic—'

'Listen—' Oscar interrupted. 'That's not a bad title. *The Prospective Domestic*. I might well use that.'

'It wouldn't do for the New England Company though, darling,' Lalla continued. 'It's a shade too light, I think. Don't you? Not quite worthy of *serious* attention. Anyway – I actually did think of disguising myself as a domestic—'

339

Lalla prattled on while Oscar retreated into himself and thought of the truth behind Lalla's joke. Oscar's work was considered by the management of the New England Players as too lightweight for their repertoire. Oscar was still their number one writer for the Didiers' films, or rather, he thought with a sigh, their number one *re*-writer, but for their seasons at the Princes Theatre, the Didiers wanted real writers, which meant serious writers, writers who had something important to say. Elizabeth had said as much to Oscar's face. She had said no more powder-puff theatre, darling, no more charming little comedies. The public, it seemed, wanted to see great acting, and Jerome and Elizabeth could only oblige their public if they now played only the Great Roles.

At first Oscar had felt bitter. It was difficult not to when he had remembered all their early days, the days when he had sat up through the night to finish *All That Glitters* for the young woman whose beauty had so inspired him, the times when he then had watched them both triumph in his work, the time when they had literally carried all before them in *The Tale of Tatty Gray*, a play which had won every West End award not only for the acting, but also for the writing, and even Oscar's direction. The memory of those golden days, which so far were certainly Oscar's most golden ones, always stirred up that old feeling of resentment in him, because he knew the Didiers' triumph had been built on his back. And now he was their re-write man, the hack they only called when their films needed customizing, dear old Oscar, good old Oscar, the man with the golden pen. So yes, he thought to himself as the car headed deeper into Wiltshire, sure he'd felt pretty bitter about it, but now he just felt ambivalent. He liked the Didiers. He couldn't help liking them, liking them both, although he was one of the very few people who actively did. Most preferred one or the other, and most of the most preferred Jerome. The camp camp-followers loved *her*, of course, they loved Elizabeth's sweet mockery, her delicate bitchery, her charming malice, they thought *she* was a *scream*, and Oscar liked her too, though not for the same reasons. What Oscar liked was not the person, in fact he could barely tolerate Elizabeth as a human being, what Oscar loved was the brilliance of her talent, the singularity of her genius. Elizabeth Laurence was without any doubt the most uniquely gifted actress he had ever seen (and this was not just his opinion, this was the general one). But then Oscar had always been a talent snob.

Oscar had also always been a practical man, the more so as he had matured into an experienced and highly skilled writer, and he realized as he had grown older that the style of his earlier plays was now old-fashioned, and not any more at all *à la mode*. Films, happily, when it came to the writing of them, were less fashion conscious, and Oscar's skills were welcomed in that field. Moreover, films paid well, they paid exceptionally well compared to the theatre, which was something not only Oscar had discovered, but so had the Didiers. Hence his and their continuing relationship.

The Didiers needed the cinema. It was a fact of their professional and private lives. If they did not make their quota of films, they could not possibly afford their life style, and this, Oscar reminded himself, had been the case even *before* the purchase of Sainthill. The Didiers lived like royalty, which they had every right to do, since everywhere they went they were treated like royalty. Wherever they went, whatever they did, wherever they ate, whatever they ate, wherever they shopped, whatever they bought, whoever they met, whatever they saw, whatever they liked, whatever they loathed, whatever they wore, whenever they wore it, every detail of their lives was reported in the minutest detail. Elizabeth gave advice to everyone, even to cat lovers, and not just nationally, internationally. *How Best to Understand Your Cat* appeared on the covers of women's magazines around the world, starting a craze in America and France for Burmese cats, which were now Elizabeth's favoured breed, while all the major journals carried her syndicated advice on diet, skin care, hair care, fashion (*Elizabeth Laurence Reveals Secrets of her Wardrobe*) and even regular counsel on marital problems (*How The Stars Keep Their Men – Elizabeth Laurence Reveals Jerome Didier's Tender Spots* selling a record amount of copies internationally of *Womans Home Journal*). No-one before them in the British theatre and for a very long time afterwards, in fact not even until the present day, no couple had ever afforded such an extravagant and inordinate lifestyle, particularly once they moved court to Sainthill. It was California in England.

The house could now be seen, as the cavalcade turned off a small country road and swung up a flawlessly regravelled drive lined with very old cypress trees. The sight silenced everyone in the car, even Lalla Henderson.

'Good God. My God,' was all she could manage.

It had only taken eighteen months, albeit eighteen months with everyone flat to the boards, and the result was magnificence, not in size, because despite Elizabeth's original fears, the building was extremely manageable (given the staff), but in aspect. Sainthill was

341

truly superb. Set in newly landscaped gardens, against a background of fields planted out with wheat and hay now waving gently in the breeze, the priory could never have looked finer or more perfect. Every pane of glass had been correctly replaced, the plain and the coloured, all the damaged stonework recut and restored, all the joinery rebuilt and returned, and the entire roof stripped, rebuilt and precisely retiled.

'Is it too good to be true?' Lalla wondered as they got out of the limousine. 'Or too true to be good?'

'I can't answer that,' Oscar said. 'All I know is that perfect people and perfect places annoy the hell out of me. There's no way of taking advantage of them.'

'I wonder,' Lalla continued, staring up at the faultless façade. 'Maybe the Bard was right as usual. Maybe striving to better, we do oft *mar what's well.*'

'Now there's a part you could aim at,' Oscar said, wondering what to do with his cigarette.

'Yes, I've always wanted to play Cordelia,' Lalla said.

'I was thinking more along the lines of Goneril,' Oscar replied.

Inside, they all at once fell to whispering, as if they had entered a church, which in a way was appropriate for there were candles everywhere, not ordinary household candles, but grand candles, enormous candles in huge wrought-iron sticks, big, thick, fat candles made of old-fashioned yellowy wax. There were flowers too, just like in Church, not ordinary arrangements, but vast and extravagant compositions, works of art created from blossoms, petals and leaves of exactly toning hues, matchless assemblies of blooms realized into visions and placed to their maximum effect in the great stone hall with its vaulted ceiling, and in the rooms glimpsed beyond, historic stone chambers also lit only by candle and firelight.

'I feel all wrong,' Oscar muttered to Lalla. 'I feel I should be dressed in a habit.'

'Knowing you, Oscar darling,' Lalla whispered back, 'it certainly wouldn't be a clean one.'

'Is it true rather than gonging him they're giving Jerry a bishopric?' Robert (Roberty to his intimates) Dunster sighed as he joined them. 'Or was that just naughty me mishearing things as usual?'

'No, it was just you going *miaow*, Roberty dear,' Lalla whispered. 'You're jealous because Jerry didn't cast you as Titania.'

'Oooh,' Roberty smiled with pained delight. 'And who have we been eating for breakfast?'

Oscar still hadn't found what to do with his cigarette which was now all but just a red hot stub. The fireplace was a little too distant for a flick, so Oscar began to make his way surreptitiously towards it, just at the moment when Elizabeth and Jerome stepped down the last tread of the stone spiral staircase and into a pool of light. Oscar stopped and stared, just like everyone else who had now arrived was doing. The sight arrested everyone.

Jerome and Elizabeth were dressed totally in keeping with their surroundings, which was the brief they had given Booble. Elizabeth wore a full-length red and gold embroidered gown with long medieval sleeves, which was pushed up high at the bosom, where it was cut to reveal the tops of her milk white breasts, and which had at the back a full train with an inset panel of gold. To her own famous hair she had added extra pieces of an absolute match, and someone had brilliantly fashioned it all into a complicated arrangement of plaits, which was finally held in place by an extremely expensive looking burnished gold ornament.

'That thing in her hair?' Lalla whispered behind Oscar. 'Booble designed it. It's specially made. Want to know the cost? *Two thousand quid.* And Cecil still can't get my five pound raise.'

They were all falling into line behind and in front of each other, as if they were at a première, waiting to be introduced to royalty.

'I do like Jerry's choice of frock,' Roberty murmured. 'Absolutely perfect for the young O. Wilde.'

As usual and in his own way, Roberty Dunster was right. Booble had designed Jerome a beautiful dull-red velvet jacket to match Elizabeth's gown, a double-breasted and braided smoker, which fitted and flattered Jerome's marvellous figure absolutely. Even the trousers were especially tailored, cut in what looked like a heavy, dark silk with insets of the dull-red velvet down the sides, and at his neck he wore an extravagant white silk scarf loosely knotted, an outfit which as soon as the pictures of the couple in costume were released, at once became the new man's fashion for evening wear.

The queue was making its way inexorably up and past their hosts, and just in time Oscar managed to chuck the red hot stub of his cigarette towards the fire. But as he feared it fell woefully short and landed on what looked to Oscar like a very expensive piece of matting. He at once made a move to retrieve the smouldering cigarette end, but Elizabeth had already seen it and despatching one of her soberly dressed footmen to repair the damage, pointed a long finger-nailed finger at the culprit.

'Oscar's here, everyone!' she laughed. 'Man the pumps!'

She then kissed him warmly on both cheeks before passing him on to Jerome, who hugged and kissed him Italian style. If Oscar had not been a theatrical, if he'd been a mere *civilian*, he would have been more than a little surprised at the effusiveness of the greeting, since he had seen them both only the day before in London.

'Hey!' he said as Jerome held him away by the hands at arm's length. 'This place! Wow. I guess this is what the Pope would have done with it, if he'd had the money.'

Jerome laughed and releasing Oscar with a naughty-boy pinch to his cheeks, moved on to welcome his next guest. Oscar moved on too, taking a fluted glass of champagne from one of the footmen while looking around for suitable company. Someone took his hand and he looked round to see it was Lalla.

'I'd love to be in a film with a budget this size,' she said, changing her already empty glass for a full one.

'I'd like to write a film with a budget this size,' Oscar replied. 'You seen the labels on the bottles? This stuff was canned before Garbo talked.'

'Odd to think that this is all my fault,' Oscar announced after the banquet which was served as dinner. Lalla had re-attached herself once again to him, having only just discovered that the one man she fancied in the entire company of the New England Players was carrying a torch for someone else, and it wasn't a woman. 'I'm not joking, you know,' Oscar finished.

'I know you're not, Ozzie,' Lalla agreed. 'But you'd *better not*, or I'll take your glass away.'

'It's true though, Lalla,' Oscar continued blithely. 'Without me, none of this would have been possible. And I'm not talking here about what I wrote—'

'I know what you're talking about,' Lalla interrupted, leading Oscar away out of anyone's earshot. 'And you're not to, not here. Didn't anyone tell you what happened to that journalist who asked about her in an interview with Elizabeth? She threw a Waterford glass at him.'

'That's because her majesty knows, Lalla.' Oscar helped himself to yet another glass of the best vintage he had ever drunk. 'That's because her majesty knows everyone loved her. Not just Jerome, not just me, everyone who met her and knew her loved her, Lalla—'

'Yes, yes, I'm sure she was terribly sweet, Ozzie darling, but not *now*.' Lalla looked over her shoulder, and around her, as if Oscar was unveiling state secrets rather than just getting maudlin.

'Come on, Lalla Henderson,' Oscar exhorted her. 'Let's talk turkey. Let's live dangerously.'

'You'll have to talk turkey to yourself, Oscar,' Lalla replied, moving away. 'I want to go on working.'

'You think I don't?'

'If you do, darling, you'll pipe that charming American voice down at least ten decibels.'

Just in time Lalla spotted Elizabeth approaching, and left Oscar in order to head her off. In the mood Oscar had got himself in, Lalla sensed there might well be a confrontation.

So did Oscar, who suddenly realized the last thing he wanted was the drink he had just taken, and the first thing he needed was some fresh air. So he put down his still full glass and wandered solo towards an arched door which opened on to the gardens. As he went, he passed Jerome.

'Are you all right, Oz?' Jerome called. 'Are you enjoying yourself?'

'You bet your ass I am, Jerry!' Oscar replied with a wave. 'There's damn all else here to enjoy!'

On the crest of a welcome laugh from Jerome and some of his courtiers, Oscar shut himself out in the cool of the night. He found himself in a courtyard garden, the fourth side of which was made up by a row of refurbished stables, four of which were occupied. Oscar wandered over to stroke the horses' noses, and enjoy the warmth of their breath on his hands and on his cheeks.

'Jeeze,' he sighed. 'They even have beautiful horses. What is it anyway? Why does the devil always have all the best tunes?'

The horses whickered softly at him, and one of them, the big, dark bay behind him, pushed him unceremoniously in the back with his head.

'Typical actor's horse,' Oscar said, turning round to tug the animal's ears. 'Me, me, me, me. Oh boy, but OK, sure you're beautiful. But you see, Dobbin old pal, you're meant to wait until someone tells you that. You're not meant to say hey! Look at me! Look I'm *gorgeous*! But I'm afraid you are. You are simply gorgeous. And do you know who would have loved you? *She* would. You don't know who she is? OK so I'll tell you. *She* is—' He leaned forward and standing on tip toes, whispered into the horse's ear. '*Pippa*,' he whispered. 'The first Mrs Didier. There now, I've said it. I've said it here at Sainthill, and look-ee. I have not been struck by lightning.'

Oscar turned and leaning his back against the wall between two of the boxes contemplated the courtyard garden, a space carefully and meticulously planted out with a mixture of herbs and oleaginous shrubs whose scent filled the night air, while he thought about her, about Pippa, about the girl who had disappeared totally from view.

For still nobody knew where she was, no-one had ever heard of her or from her again. Oscar had tried. He had tried various routes, through Miss Toothe, Dr Weaver, through friends of hers in that odd little Sussex village, through anybody he could find who had known her, but none of them had known a thing. Nobody knew anything. All Jerome had been able to find out, according to Jerome when he and Oscar had got drunk together on the last date before *Tatty* came into London, was that his then wife had withdrawn all her money from the bank, before quite simply vanishing.

'The lady vanishes, old chum,' Jerome had said, pouring another brandy on top of the one he had hardly begun. 'But not I think to—' He had drunk some brandy then, at that moment, and fallen into a long silence. 'No,' he had finally continued, 'No, I really don't think anyone contemplating anything . . . anything other than just *vanishing* would have taken her belongings, her money, her maid. And Bobby.'

How they had finally fought that night, Oscar remembered, not with their fists, fortunately for Oscar, but with words, unfortunately for Jerome. Jerome had begun it, accusing Oscar of being whimsical, of turning life and people into a shape and substance acceptable to him, and worst – of betraying Pippa by taking her and using her as his model for *Tatty Gray*. He tried to make Oscar responsible for it all, for his own folly and conceit, for his own treachery and adultery, and Oscar finally just wouldn't take it. He had spoken to Jerome very quietly, after Jerome had calmed down, he had spoken quietly and calmly, but he had torn him apart, bit by bit, inch by conceited inch, until he had reduced Jerome to tears, whereupon he upped and left and hadn't spoken to Jerome for another six months, all the way through the triumphant opening of *Tatty Gray* in the West End, throughout the superlative success of the first part of the run, they had never exchanged one let alone two words.

Until the day Jerome had called him, right out of the blue.

'She's alive,' he'd said. No hello, no who it was, no apology, no prologue. Just Jerome's voice in his ear saying that Pippa was alive. 'At least we think that she is.'

'Who's we, Jerry?'

'Toby. You know Toby? Toby Thompson?'

'Of course I know Toby for Chrissake. He was Henry in *Glitters*.'

'Toby was on holiday in France. He's sure he saw her on a train. Or rather get off one. He swore he saw her get off the train at Tours.'

'So what are you going to do, Jerry?'

'What am I going to do?' Jerome had sounded puzzled, not angry, but bemused. 'What can I do, chum? Except get down on my bended knees and thank God – she's alive!'

He could have gone after her, Oscar had thought at the time, but then at the time he hadn't known the hold Elizabeth had over Jerome, he knew nothing of Jerome's enthrallment. No-one knew. No-one knew till much, much later the extent of Jerome's bondage. From the day he first got into his co-star's bed, until the day he agreed to marry her, Jerome was enslaved, and rather than freeing him, on the contrary the news of Pippa's survival had only allowed him to enjoy his captivity the more.

How strange it was, Oscar thought as he continued to stand between the heads of the horses either side of him, listening to the sounds of the party, the wine induced laughter, the power induced gaiety, how odd that Jerome had never seemed to mind being fooled by Elizabeth, by her deceit, by the deception she had played on him by making herself appear through *Tatty* and through the way she had approached *Tatty* as someone quite different from the person she really was. Or is rather, Oscar corrected himself, because the person Jerome had fallen so absurdly in love with was simply a facsimile of Pippa, while the person to whom Jerome was now married bore not even the slightest resemblance to the girl both the men had loved.

Yet the thought had seemingly never occurred to Jerome. It couldn't have done, Oscar reasoned, otherwise he would never have married Elizabeth, or at the very least would not *still* be married to her. Perhaps if he met Pippa again, Oscar wondered, perhaps he would then regain his senses, but then in the next breath Oscar prayed that Jerome never would. He wanted Pippa to be happy, and if she were by some cruel twist of fate to be reunited with Jerome, Oscar knew she would never know another moment's happiness, which was why finally he was so glad Pippa had disappeared.

'In fact it's good all round, horses, believe me,' Oscar suddenly announced out loud, although the reason the horses quickly backed away from him, stomping their hooves and snorting with displeasure was not because he had spoken, but because he had chosen to light a cigarette. 'Seriously, you guys,' Oscar continued, oblivious of the animals' displeasure, 'The best thing that wonderful girl did was get the hell out. Because what's everyone done ever since? You're right. All they've done is talk about her, and wonder about her. And they'll never, ever know. Particularly – her majesty.'

It was true. It was the worst of all possible revenges. Elizabeth had no rival, no-one to fight, no-one who by looking less than Elizabeth in beauty, could – in the eyes of the star's adoring public – explain Jerome's monstrous infidelity. Not even Elizabeth

Laurence, considered by now and by most good judges to be possibly the most beautiful woman in the whole world, not even she could box a shadow, or be more beautiful than a memory.

What was even worse for Elizabeth, was that from the moment Pippa disappeared she remained as she had been in everyone's minds. She remained the age she was when she vanished. She stayed fixed as young, exuberant, hopeful and innocent, while in contrast Elizabeth began to change, imperceptibly at first but still inevitably. Elizabeth aged, she got older, she changed, while Pippa stayed still, treading the waters of time. To everyone who thought about her, and there were so many who did, since so many of Jerome's and Elizabeth's mutual acquaintances had met Pippa and had adored her, Pippa would never change. *She would always be that lovely, beguiling, freckle-faced, sweet girl who was once married to Jerome.*

While Elizabeth would always be the other woman, the one who broke up Jerome's marriage to that *lovely, beguiling, freckle-faced, and sweet girl*. Elizabeth would always be the wrecker, and Pippa would always be the one *you really should have met.*

Maybe that was the day you got your first crow's feet, honey, Oscar thought as he looked over to the house and saw Elizabeth staring back idly out into the darkness, while some man, not Jerome, came up behind and whispered something in her ear. Maybe the day Jerome came across, maybe that day it all began to fade a little. A part of me can't help hoping that's so, he added as he saw Elizabeth laugh, and without turning put an arm up to curl it round the young man's neck. And then he saw the young man lean forward, brought forward probably by Elizabeth's arm, and Elizabeth tilt her head back for the young man to kiss her as near to her mouth as he could. I sure do hope so, he concluded. Otherwise it just ain't fair.

He stayed a little while longer, smoking his cigarette and watching the shadow play within the magnificent house. Then he carefully stubbed out his smoke, and dropped it just as carefully down a drain.

'One last thought, you guys,' he said over his shoulder to the horses, 'before I say good night. If the first Mrs Didier had wanted to choose the best way to torment the second Mrs Didier, she got it. She couldn't have chosen a better way than to disappear. While age gets to withering and custom to destroying that beauty and infinite variety over there, I tell you, fellas, they're not going to be able to do one single thing to the first Mrs Didier. I mean it, guys. To disappear was inspired.'

FIFTEEN

Pippa had disappeared. Nancy couldn't find her anywhere. Neither could Jenny whose real name was Jane. They both thought Bobby knew, they thought he must know from the way he was wagging his old tail, and barking every now and then. But his mistress had told him no, she had told him to stay, and so stay he had, sitting by the open farmhouse door, panting happily in the hot hazy evening sun.

'We give up!' Nancy called. 'We give up!'

'No we do not,' Jenny said very seriously, tugging the maid's hand, although of course Jenny didn't know Nancy as a maid. Nancy was her friend. 'We *don't* give up at all, Mummy!' she shouted at the top of her voice. 'We're going to find you!'

From the top of the tree where she had climbed, Pippa could see them, but they couldn't see her. She had to stuff her knuckles in her mouth to stop herself from laughing, and giving away her hiding place, as down right below her now her little raven-haired daughter was picking her way barefoot across the farmyard, one small hand holding up the front of her faded red frock, the other held to her beautiful little freckled face, thumb firmly stuck in mouth. Some of the chickens followed them curiously, probably wondering whether it was time for their corn, as Nancy, barefoot too and brown as a berry, opened the stable door behind Jenny to peer inside.

'No,' Jenny said. 'She isn't in there. We've *looked* in there, Nancy!'

An apple fell from the tree, a foot or so in front of the child, who at once looked up into the thick branches of the tree.

'I can see you!' she cried in delight. 'I can see you! I can see you!'

349

Nancy lifted the child up and Pippa pulled her up, and for a while they both sat on a lower branch hugging each other and laughing about the game, while Nancy threw the chickens their feed, and Bobby yawned and rolled over on the stoop for another sunny snooze.

'Ah, *oui*,' Pippa whispered to her daughter. '*Mais c'est parfait, n'est ce pas?*'

'*Ah oui, Maman*,' Jenny sighed back, hugging Pippa tightly round her neck. '*C'est absolument parfait*.'

SIXTEEN

Artistically, America was a triumph. Personally it was a disaster and the beginning of the end. This had nothing to do with the country, for both Jerome and Elizabeth had already visited it frequently as actors and privately as a couple when they took a two week vacation in California after Jerome had finished shooting *The Smile* with George Willer. They had enjoyed their transatlantic visits, although Elizabeth later confessed she was only really happy in America when accompanied by her husband. Oddly enough she had been at her most miserable when filming her greatest triumph, which was when she was creating the immortal role of Katie Molloy in *The Forsaken Land*, the role which was to consolidate Elizabeth's reputation internationally and win the actress her first Oscar. She had been miserable because Jerome had been forced to leave her alone in Hollywood in order to fly back to England and prepare for the opening of the new Stratford season in which he was to play a memorable (although not his very best) Mark Antony, and a Hotspur which the critics unanimously hailed as a definitive performance.

Now they were to return to the land which had made them rich, although this time it wasn't in order to bale themselves out financially by making what they described while giving mock yawns to their courtiers as *yet another film*, but to star on Broadway with their own company in the highly acclaimed productions of *Romeo and Juliet* and *Hamlet*. They sailed into New York on board the SS *America* to receive a welcome usually reserved for the country's own and home-grown stars, and were followed by a cavalcade consisting in the main of press photographers and cheering fans all the way to the Plaza. Such was the size of the operation that when the Didiers had announced their plans to bring their two productions States-side, they meant it literally, and so when the great ocean liner docked it contained not only the New England Players company but also the entire London stage sets, props and costumes.

Publicly, all seemed well, deliriously so in fact. Seventy-five per cent of the productions mounted by the Didiers' company in the Princes Theatre, London, had been outstandingly successful, and even the flops were only failures critically. The box office had been beseiged since the company had opened its inaugural season with a glittering and star-studded production of *The Rivals*, with HOUSE FULL signs up almost every night for the runaway successes, and healthy enough attendances even for those plays the critics had adjudged as failures. The only three total failures were the plays in which Elizabeth Laurence had not appeared, even though all three plays had been greeted with highly enthusiastic notices. All three productions lasted barely two weeks.

With *Romeo and Juliet* and *Hamlet*, however, for those who had not booked well in advance it had been a case of either returns or scandalously over-priced black market tickets. Cecil Manners had teased Jerome unmercifully about his decision to play Romeo again, now that the actor was well into his thirties, but Jerome, to Cecil's delight, had defended his decision vigorously without once managing to see the humorous side. He had even gone so far as to inform his agent very solemnly that the part was too difficult to be played by an actor who was the same age as the tragic hero.

'Actors need a long apprenticeship, you see Cecil,' he had said, unconsciously misquoting Pippa. 'Acting is mechanical, dear boy, as well as intellectual. This is why there never have really been nor ever will be any *genuine* great child actors.'

The statement was a nonsense, of course, which Cecil would have known even had he not been familiar with the original Constable quote, but Jerome had, as usual, like most actors been swayed by his own rhetoric and convinced by his meaningless argument. Neither had it mattered, since it might just as well have been true, for Jerome and Elizabeth made an utterly wondrous pair of stage lovers, totally plausible, and finally completely heartbreaking.

The New York critics thought so too, extolling both the Didiers' performances as the finest and most tragic acting ever seen on Broadway. 'I wept,' Mort Lehmann of *The New York Times* wrote. 'The audience around me wept. America, when it sees them, as surely all of America should, as a nation America would weep for these star cross'd lovers, a Romeo and his Juliet so beautifully realized by Jerome Didier and Elizabeth Laurence that you will need to leave the control of your emotions checked in with your hat and your coat. For come the interval even, I will wager you will be already heartbroken at the prospect of what there is to come. This is everything this great play should be. It is true youth, it is true love and it is true tragedy. You will never want to see this play again afterwards, never, not once, in case your cherished memories of these star cross'd actors be dimmed.'

The same went for Jerome's Hamlet and for Elizabeth's Ophelia, Jerome being 'swift, sardonic, passionate ... a Hamlet this time made of steel, keeping his dangerous rage in check until he can stand no more ... a master of repartee as well as swordsmanship, a nettle that must be grasped rather than as others have played it before as a weed to be plucked out ... there is sadness, too, moments of brooding melancholy and introspection, but the final impression gained is of a man with a fiery spirit, all flash and fury when aroused, an angry fire which will not be dimmed ... ' While Elizabeth's interpretation of Ophelia was described as 'the most believable yet, a young girl at first high spirited ... able and ready to laugh with Laertes at her father's foolishness, and then to cry with pain and bewilderment at Hamlet's cruelty ... a performance of such integrity that it breaks the heart ... her descent into madness is all the more moving for being performed with such prosaic deliberation by Miss Laurence ... it is no exaggeration to say that in Miss Laurence's performance we see Ophelia most perfectly realized.'

Both plays did capacity business, and, it was generally agreed, both stars deserved the praises heaped upon them. One or two dissenters hinted that the Didiers' scandalous past and their now world famous marriage was the best explanation for their fabulous success, Roberty Dunster letting it be known privately that he considered that Jerome played Hamlet like a randy sergeant-major and Romeo like a sun-tanned bobbysoxer, while Sally Stanway, who had once played Ophelia to Sir Neville James' Hamlet and was now appearing on Broadway in Virginia Ford's *A Willow By The Sea*, let it be known in a televised interview that she considered Elizabeth Laurence a *one-dimensional actress, far better suited to the screen than the stage, where her famous eyes could feature better and her thin little voice matter less*. Apart from these odd lone cries in the wilderness, however, everyone else was of the same opinion, namely that together Jerome Didier and Elizabeth Laurence were the finest actors in the world.

It was the word *together* that troubled them both the most. It had always troubled Jerome, of course, ever since he had first been artistically coupled with Elizabeth, and now here he was, one half of the creature he had dreaded becoming, the fearful double-headed Hydra. Since the time of *Tatty Gray* (he preferred to think of it thus, rather than *the time when Pippa had left him*), Jerome had been careful to do as much solo work as he could, which had been totally possible, since the prediction Cecil had made about the consequences of Jerome doing Oscar's new play had worked out exactly as Cecil said it would. Jerome made such an impact as Sam in *Tatty Gray* that he had been invited over to Hollywood at the same time as Elizabeth. They had travelled over together, naturally, because by then they did nothing without the company of the other (except act), privately as a duo they were completely inseparable, but when they had arrived in Hollywood they went their own different ways at the Studios, Elizabeth to MGM, Jerome to Warner Brothers, where they both individually secured contracts for major motion pictures, Elizabeth to play Katie Molloy in *The Forsaken Land*, and Jerome to star in the remake of *Captain Blood*. Unfortunately filming was delayed on *The Forsaken Land* due to a change of director, with the result that by the time Jerome had finished *Captain Blood* and was on his way back to Stratford, Elizabeth was still hanging around their rented house waiting to commence shooting.

Elizabeth was not good when left by herself, even as early on in their relationship as this was. She knew no-one out in Hollywood, and the Didiers were not yet rich enough (they weren't even married to each other at this stage) to afford to travel with the retinue which was later to accompany them across the Atlantic and right around the world. The English colony of actors in Los Angeles soon befriended her, but although she was glad of their company, she was in no mood to make close friends, since when she wasn't working, all she could think of was Jerome.

She was surprised how much she thought about Jerome, and more particularly how much she thought of him. When she had started in pursuit of him, although in deadly earnest Elizabeth had never stopped to wonder why or even wherefore. She had just wanted Jerome, and when Elizabeth Laurence wanted something, with hardly an exception she got it. She desired Jerome, she admired him, she wanted him. It was as simple as that. They would be good for each other professionally, and together they would go to the top of the world, of that there was no doubt in her mind. There never had been, from the moment she had first

354

seen him in Cecil's office, and heard him read against her, Elizabeth knew that if only she could catch him, catch him and enthral him, together there would be no mountain high enough.

She hadn't given a thought to what effect they might have on each other personally, not one. She had simply seen them as a couple, a couple who were destined for each other, and as a couple who not *could* but *would* be world famous. What she didn't know because she never once stopped to think about it was that the reason they were both finally so violently attracted to each other was because of a mutual need. Many of their personal critics later said if Jerome hadn't been in love with Pippa when Elizabeth first saw him, and if they both hadn't been married when they finally transgressed, they would probably have not been attracted, or as Roberty Dunster was to put it so delicately, if Jerome hadn't been so remorselessly unavailable *Lizzie L would never have bothered with getting into Jerry's knickers.*

But once she had, once she had taken Jerome into her bed she found to her astonishment that not only did he become totally enthralled but that she did too. What had happened, and what she said to Jerome had happened was all true, that night in Manchester, *the night they had broken down the door.*

Jerome thought of little or nothing else either (except when he was acting). Once he had realized that Pippa had gone and was intending to stay gone, his first thoughts were only ever about Elizabeth, and about making love to her. She excited him like no woman had ever excited him. He could become sexually aroused just by thinking of her, not of specifics, not of what they had done, or of what they might do, but just of *her*, just of Elizabeth simply as a being, as an existence. Often in those first months, which soon turned into their first two years together, they would have to get up in the middle of a meal they were eating and leave the restaurant, to hurry back speechlessly in a cab to either one of their houses where they would make passionate and sometimes violent love in a silence broken only by their gasps, their groans and their cries.

They might be anywhere, in the cinema, at an art gallery, out shopping, or just walking. It happened everywhere and all the time. Once they were both at their dentists, at the same time. Jerome had laughed himself stupid afterwards, howling with mock anguish that if you were going to choose the *most* sexless place in the world, it surely had to be your dentists! But there they were, sitting silently and properly either side of the waiting room in Harley Street, reading back numbers in *Country Life*, and all Elizabeth had done was slip the toe of one high heeled shoe inside one of Jerome's trouser legs, and that was it. Jerome had got up, smiled at the other patients still waiting, taken Elizabeth by the hand and then her arm, apologized to the receptionist without giving a reason for their departure, summoned the lift, hailed a taxi, gone back to Park Lane, dismissed the staff, and taken Elizabeth to his bed, keeping her there for an extremely active twenty-four hours.

Which was why their first enforced separation had been so terrible for Elizabeth, when she was filming *The Forsaken Land*. Any other actress would not have had the time to think about anything except the part she was doing, so difficult was the role Elizabeth had been chosen to play, particularly for an actress as inexperienced as Elizabeth was when it came to the shooting of a film of epic proportions. Yet what occupied her most was not how to sustain such a demanding role, but how she was going to live without making love with Jerome, and born out of that thought what would happen to her should anything ever happen between them and she had *really* to live without making love to Jerome.

In the best book written about her life and career, an unofficial biography by Edward Neil entitled *A Way to The Stars*, his given reason for Elizabeth's superlative and Oscar winning performance as Katie Molloy is that it was the very real private concern which showed in Elizabeth's famous green eyes that made her so believable, and that had she in fact been fully in control of herself and her art she would not have succeeded quite so triumphantly, because she would have made Katie Molloy too knowing, instead of the girl the camera captured, namely a beautiful but insecure young woman, a young woman who had been so cruelly jilted, and as a consequence of that hurt, mistrustful for ever after about love. Neil wrote:

> The camera reveals all. Nothing and no-one hides from the camera, particularly when that camera is being directed by one of Hollywood's old masters, Henry Losch. And what it revealed most of all in *The Forsaken Land*, besides the fact that Elizabeth Laurence was even more beautiful than painted in previous Hollywood pictures, was that like all actresses she could suggest what she was feeling simply by just thinking about it. There is absolutely no doubt at all that this first painful and (it later emerged) potentially damaging separation from Jerome Didier obsessed her, and contributed greatly to her remarkable performance, most of all because it is there for us all to see, behind those wonderful eyes.

*

356

But the most important thing Elizabeth discovered when left behind in Hollywood, without Jerome for the first time since they had become lovers in Manchester, was the devastating realization that she loved him. If it hadn't been for William Devine, Hollywood's favourite resident English actor, it is generally supposed by those closest to Elizabeth at the time she would never have got through the filming of *The Forsaken Land*, and that particularly famous chapter in the history of film-making would never have been written.

William Devine had found Elizabeth in a state of near collapse when he had called at her house the night he and his wife were due to dine with her. Devine wasn't in the picture, he was shooting some incidental comedy for Howard Mann at the time, but he had met Elizabeth at the pre-production party thrown in her honour, and they had at once established a great but totally platonic rapport (Devine was happily married at the time to Kay Silvers). He and Kay were to take Elizabeth to the Brown Derby, but when she didn't show up at their house that evening as arranged, William Devine, unable to raise her on the telephone, drove immediately to the house Jerome and she had rented in case something was wrong.

The front door was open when he got there, and fearing the worst Devine ran in expecting to find the beautiful young actress either raped or murdered. She was neither. She was sitting on the edge of a vast six seater sofa, a tiny figure still in her bathrobe, sobbing uncontrollably. Still imagining she had been the victim of some sort of attack, he went to comfort her, whereupon Elizabeth had gone for him, screaming and shouting incoherently and uncontrollably. When at last the actor had finally managed to calm her down (he had to slap her twice, hard, *and* throw water in her face), Elizabeth threw her arms around his neck and started to laugh.

'Oh my God, Willy!' she had cried. 'You must think me quite crazy! I'm like this because of J! J just called me, Willy, and God! God – I never *realized* how much I loved him!'

From then on both William Devine and his wife Kay had hardly let Elizabeth out of their sight. Every moment she wasn't filming one of them was with her. They both knew what a lonely and frightening town Hollywood was for first-timers, particularly if they were alone, and particularly if they were as sensitive as the Devines supposed Elizabeth to be. So they chaperoned her every move, and because of them and their infinite care, and for absolutely no other reason, Elizabeth pulled herself together, completed the picture without further incident, and – well – the rest is cinema history.

But it was now ten years on and the Didiers were once more back in America, in New York, in triumph, carrying all before them as happened wherever they went. But behind the scenes, in the backstage of their lives, they were by now finding it all but impossible to continue the charade. On this particular day they were in their palatial suite in the Plaza Hotel and it was late afternoon, only two hours, perhaps less, before they had to leave for the theatre and prepare for that evening's performance of Hamlet. Jerome was standing by one of the huge windows, looking out on Central Park, wiping his forehead regularly with the backs of the fingers of one hand, while behind him, seated coincidentally again on an over-large sofa, Elizabeth, with her dark head bowed over, was sobbing into both of her hands.

'What *is* it, Bethy?' Jerome finally asked, yet again. 'You must tell me, Bethy, you know I have to know before we leave for the theatre.'

'It isn't anything, J!' Elizabeth sobbed, still into her hands. 'I told you! I keep telling you! It's just me! It's just me being a damned fool!'

'You should have something to eat. You aren't eating anything, Bethy.'

'It's nothing to do with my diet for Christ's sake! If it was anything to do with my diet, J, I'd be passing out on stage! I'd be fainting, wouldn't I? Or giving a feeble performance! But I'm not, am I!' It wasn't a statement, it was a question of fact, and Jerome didn't deny it. He just kept his back to her, and shrugged. 'It isn't anything to do with eating, J!' Elizabeth shouted. 'Why don't you bloody well listen!'

'Bethy, darling,' Jerome turned and looked at her. 'Bethy we have to go on-stage in less than three hours. We can't have this. We can't have this every day. Not unless you tell me *what is going on.*'

'You wouldn't understand,' Elizabeth said, suddenly stopping her crying and standing up, brushing her blouse and her skirt scrupulously, as if they were covered with dust or animal hair. 'There's no point. You wouldn't understand.'

'Where are you going?' Jerome's heart sank when he saw where his wife was headed.

'I won't be a minute, it's all right,' Elizabeth replied. 'I'm just going to wash my hands.'

You've just washed your hands, Jerome thought. You washed them ten minutes ago. And ten minutes ago before that as well. You're always washing your hands now, Bethy.

But he didn't bother to try and stop her. He'd tried too often and failed. He simply lit a tipped cigarette and went back to staring out over the park as dusk began to fall.

He had tried to put a starting date on it, on the moment she had begun to get so unreasonably upset, when they had begun to argue, not as lovers, but as people opposed to one another, but so far he had failed, beyond what he privately considered to be a spurious notion, namely that it had all begun after that odd meeting she had demanded they convene in the company offices in the Princes Theatre.

Elizabeth had wanted the meeting called because she wished to withdraw from two of the plays in the forthcoming season, one of the Shakespeares and one of the Anouilhs. The latter posed no great problem. If it had been the great French playwright's version of *Antigone*, which Jerome had pencilled in for the following season, that would have been very different, but as it happened it was one of his comedies, *Ring Round the Moon*, in which Elizabeth would not be irreplaceable. The Shakespeare was a different matter altogether. They had planned to open that season with *The Taming of the Shrew*, and without Elizabeth as Katherine, there was no point in even *thinking* about doing it. In the end Jerome had won the argument and Elizabeth had reluctantly agreed to co-operate, but Jerome felt this first major artistic confrontation had left its marks.

'Why?' he had demanded when they had arrived back in their house in Cadogan Square where they now lived. 'Why not ask me in private, damn you, rather than call an extraordinary meeting of the whole wretched committee?'

'Oh, do stop shouting,' she'd replied. 'You're always shouting.'

'I just happen to feel this was a matter between us,' Jerome had continued. 'This was something which could have been settled here, at home, in private. We have that advantage, Bethy! We can discuss things like this between us, without involving committee meetings! Without involving anyone else, dammit!'

Elizabeth had said nothing straight away. She had started to sing softly to herself, rung for the maid and asked her to bring up some champagne, and then stretched herself out full length on the black, silk-covered sofa. When the maid had gone, she had taken Jerome's hand with both of hers as he walked by her.

'I was afraid, my darling man,' she had confessed. 'You can be so very, *very* fierce.'

'Full of sound and fury, Bethy,' he had sighed, sinking on to the sofa beside him. 'Signifying bugger all.'

'Darling,' Elizabeth smiled. 'Signifying *everything*. You know I think you're wonderful.'

'Why didn't you bring the matter up here, Bethy?'

'Because you would have talked me out of it, I know you. You can talk me in and out of anything.' She had lit a Black Russian Sobranie, and lifted one of her sleek brown cats which had padded silently into the room up on to her flattened stomach to scratch the creature just in front of its sticking-up tail. 'You see, I do have my reasons, J,' she had continued, although addressing the cat, not him. 'And the reason was, why I wanted not to do at least one of the plays, was that I think I'm doing *too* much, you see. I'm doing too much, and it's just not fair on you.'

That had been the start of it, Jerome thought as he stared across the heart of New York, definitely, that had been where the derailment had begun. He laughed to himself, though not with any humour. *I'm doing too much, and it's just not fair on you.* She could have put it a little more tactfully, or perhaps she had meant it that way. Perhaps she had meant it as a put-down. It wasn't so much that she was doing too *much*, what she meant was that what she was doing she was doing *much better than he was*. Whatever play they did, as long as she was in it, they filled. Whatever play they did, as long as she wasn't in it, they did not fill. 'QED,' he said out loud, angrily. *Quod erat* bloody *demonstrandum*. Elizabeth Laurence was box office, and Jerome Didier wasn't, at least *not by himself, he wasn't.*

'I think we should talk,' he said in the car as Dingo drove them to the theatre.

'Not now,' she replied, a pair of large dark glasses and a hastily applied make-up as always covering the damage done by her tears. 'We have a performance to do.'

'When then?'

'What is there to talk about?'

'What is there to *talk* about, Bethy?'

'Oh, for God's sake stop being so bloody *theatrical*, J. What *is* there to talk about? I'm just a bit over-tired, that's all. I've just got over-tired.'

She looked out of the car window, her pale face reflected against the dark behind the glass.

'You haven't been eating, Bethy.'

'It has got nothing to do with my diet.'

'You don't eat, you take pills, you drink too much champagne—'

'I shall get out of the car.'

'You don't sleep, you're up half the night partying, dancing, playing games, playing charades, drinking, exhausting yourself—'

'I mean it, Jerry.' She only ever called him that when she was serious. 'If you don't stop—'

'No. No! No if *you* don't stop, Bethy!' He turned to her, his dark eyes flashing, his voice already taking on the ring he had given it for *Hamlet*. 'If *you* don't stop you're going to kill yourself, or something dreadful. You look *ghastly*.'

'Thank you. How sweet you are.'

'I meant ghastly for you, Bethy. You look drawn, tired—'

'I *am* tired, Jerry. I find playing both these parts very, very tiring. Playing them both on top of one another. I find it really rather ennervating.'

'Then you should take more care of yourself,' Jerome said, harshly, already sounding as if he were despatching her to the nunnery as he would do later that evening. *I am myself indifferent honest, but yet better my mother had not borne me.* While she beside him, as she stared out at New York for Elsinore, was preparing herself for her watery grave, *larded with sweet flowers, which bewept to the grave with true love showers.*

'You really should take more care of yourself, Bethy,' Jerome said out of the darkness. 'Some of these things you do to yourself, and to your body.'

'Would you rather I was fat, J? With a greasy skin, and a complexion like *Gertrude*'s?'

'Poor Adrienne can't help it,' Jerome said. 'The wretched actress can't help her complexion.'

'Of course she can,' Elizabeth retorted. 'She doesn't take care of herself. She eats and drinks too much, and as a result, lives over a sewer.'

'I hate that expression of yours,' Jerome sighed, looking out of the car at the crowds gathering outside the theatre which was now in his view.

'Well, I'm sorry,' she said without sounding it. 'But it happens to be true. But, of course, if you'd rather I looked like Adrienne—'

Elizabeth checked her looks in her compact, switching the courtesy light on above her. She applied some more powder before pulling the knot of her headscarf up over her chin, to hide as much of her face as possible. Then she too looked out of the window as the gathered fans started to crowd and jostle around the car as it pulled up at the kerb.

'You might,' Elizabeth said clicking shut her compact.

'I might what?'

'Prefer me to look like poor Adrienne. But I don't think *they* would.'

Elizabeth waved at her adoring fans as she prepared to alight from the car. Dingo was round opening her door, while on the sidewalk the police did their best to control the crowd.

'Oh my!' someone gasped as Elizabeth got out. 'But isn't she just beautiful?'

Every night after the performance it was the same. On to *Sardi's*, and afterwards to a party somewhere. There was always a party somewhere. Sometimes at weekends the party would be out of town, Long Island maybe, or further afield, in New Hampshire or Vermont. Distance was no object. Fleets of limousines would await outside the theatre to transport those in the company lucky enough, and once or twice unlucky enough, to have received invitations to spend what was left of the weekend with the rich or the famous and sometimes both. Jerome tried to sidestep all such occasions, but never once succeeded since Elizabeth was grimly determined to attend whatever was on offer wherever it was. Initially when he had tried to demur, there had been arguments, frightful arguments, screaming matches in their dressing rooms at the theatre, until rather than face a weekend of tearful and hysterical recriminations, Jerome had finally relented and they had taken off for yet another bash in some huge apartment in Manhattan, or some vast estate in New England.

The parties were always the same, Elizabeth saw to that. Whatever the hosts might have had in mind when they invited the stars and some of their entourage was rarely if ever realized. Everyone danced to Elizabeth's tune. She was very skilled at getting her own way, never appearing to upset any applecarts as she went about rearranging people's parties, charming hosts and hostesses everywhere with that irresistible mix of sweetness and mischief, while making sure that nothing was ever done in anyone's house or apartment which was not initially approved of by her. She was, as said, very good at it. Whatever she suggested, the idea always apparently arrived impulsively, on the spur of an inspired moment, completely *impromptu*, never, ever premeditated, and inspired everyone to go along with it by its very spontaneity. It might be an idea for a game or a diversion or a type of dance, but whatever the inspiration was it was always prefaced by the same thoughtful little frown, and then that sudden heart-stopping smile as Elizabeth announced with one clap of her hands that she had suddenly realized she knew *exactly* what they could do. Even if their hosts had hired a band, or a singer, or a singer with a band, the band played what Elizabeth wanted to dance to, and the singer sang what Elizabeth wanted to hear. And the parties would go on all night, if Elizabeth had anything to do with it, which she invariably had, and if it was a Saturday night they would go on into the dawn and sometimes seamlessly and sleeplessly into the next day.

Jerome, who hated parties that were thrown just for the sake of throwing a party, was invariably bored. He couldn't care less if the people who met him socially were disappointed in him, as Elizabeth kept endlessly reminding him they would be if he made such little effort, because Jerome was only interested in exciting or amusing people through his work. When gushy social-ites rushed up to him at parties and seized him, telling him that oh, he was that truly wonderful Jerome Didier, he would politely shake them off and tell them that no he wasn't, not that night, before trying to find somewhere he could have a quiet drink and gossip with a member of the company about the evening's performance, or failing that, a dark corner somewhere where he could simply sleep.

Elizabeth on the other hand appeared to live for these mostly appalling occasions more and more. She seemed almost to be just getting through her work in order to play, although to give Elizabeth her due, no such thing ever showed in her performances. There was never a hint of disinterest or indifference. Elizabeth was both far too ambitious and far too much the professional ever to disappoint her adoring public. It was only apparent off-stage, and only to Jerome. Once she had finalized her performance to her own satisfaction, and locked it away in her memory bank, she rarely if ever again referred to what she was doing on-stage. If Jerome noted after a performance that he thought Elizabeth had mistimed a line, or lost a nuance (the faults were always miniscule, and the note sessions scathingly referred to as Jerome's *nit-picking*), Elizabeth would just shrug and say whatever was lost would soon come back, which at the next performance it invariably did. Other than that, Elizabeth did no further work on her roles, nor did she ever discuss them once she had left the theatre. All she professed herself to be interested in, an in-terest she loved to profess in the native idiom, was *where the action was*.

'I know what it is,' Jerome said mid-sulk one Monday morning, when they were being driven back from a particularly energetic and non-stop party on Long Island. 'You can't bear being with yourself any more, that's what it is.'

'Oh Christ, J,' Elizabeth sighed from behind closed eyes. 'Christ Almighty.'

'It's true, Bethy. We don't have any time together any more, not just you and I. But it's not because you don't want to be alone with me—'

'You flatter yourself, sweetie.' Elizabeth pulled the car rug higher up around her chest and recurled her legs under her. 'You're such a bloody old bore when you're working. You're not you, you is somewhere else altogether, but don't ask me where. And in the meanwhile I'm certainly not going to spend what little time I have to have fun sitting around with moody old Hamlet, or dreary little Romeo boring my beautiful tits off.'

'It's nothing to do with that, Bethy, and you know it!' Jerome retorted. 'I don't know what's happened. I don't know what it is, but whatever it is, you've become a completely different person these last months – this last year.'

Elizabeth opened one eye and stared at him, glintingly.

'Shut up, darling,' she said. 'All right?'

'I can't even remember the last time we made love.'

'Ask Dingo.' Elizabeth nodded in the direction of their chauffeur. 'Dingo probably knows.'

Jerome leaned forward quickly and pushed shut the glass division between the compartments which wasn't fully closed.

'Well?' he said, leaning back.

'Well what, darling?'

'Can you remember when we last made love? Darling?'

'J sweetie,' Elizabeth sighed, taking her dark glasses off to look at him with eyes dark-rimmed with fatigue. 'This is my last word on the matter, all right? Because I was asleep. And I really couldn't care less how you answer this, just as long as it stops you *banging on*. I can either be Elizabeth Laurence, and all that it entails, or I can be little Mrs Didier, the dutiful and loving wife. Now which do you want to be married to, darling? Elizabeth Laurence? Or little Mrs Mouse? Because I cannot be both things at once, do you understand? I cannot possibly play Ophelia, Cordelia, Juliet, Cleopatra, Lady Macbeth, Lavinia, Desdemona and all these other poor tragic, lamentable bitches you want me to play all the time *and* be your dutiful little wife. Do you understand, sweety-pie?'

Jerome stared back at her, stroking one side of his unshaven chin with two fingers.

'Go to sleep,' he said after a very long time. 'You look awful.'

*

The trouble with all the women Elizabeth had mentioned was that they all died. They all either died young, were murdered or killed themselves, and she really was finding the whole thing frightfully depressing. Some of the roles she had yet to play, admittedly, but she knew they were all there lying in wait, they were all on the agenda, and frankly, at this particular moment in her life she wasn't sure she wanted to play them. She wanted something that was a bit more fun, something that was a bit more glamorous, something that was a bit more suited to her mischief, her sense of devilment, something in which she could radiate.

Some Shaw, perhaps. *Pygmalion*, perhaps. Perhaps *Caesar and Cleopatra*. Or even some more Sheridan, *The School for Scandal* this time, or something American, and sexy, like Tennessee Williams, like *Cat On A Hot Tin Roof*, something in which she could be sultry and seductive, or just downright provocative. (She made a little *moue* at herself in her dressing mirror – *mmmmm*!) Something, anything as long as it wasn't another of the Bard's infernal tragedies. She was sick of the Bard. She was sick of weeping and wailing. She was sick of playing mad. She was sick of dying. She was sick to the teeth with it all. It was all of it *getting her down*.

And she didn't look awful. Jerome was talking through his hat. She didn't look at all awful. She hadn't even looked awful on her arrival that night, before she'd put on Ophelia's face, not even a tiny bit awful. Tired perhaps, but then it had been a terrific party, simply terrific. Frank Sinatra in person, among all those other famous faces. But no-one like Frank Sinatra. And he had sung, to her. Sinatra had sung to her. He'd sat by her on the sofa and sung her 'The Nearness of You' while holding her hand. Elizabeth sighed and wondered to herself what she would have done if Jerome hadn't been there.

But she didn't look at all awful, then or now. Then, at the party, everyone, *everyone* had said how beautiful she was looking, how young, how she hadn't changed at all. They wanted to know how she did it, working as hard as she did, playing as hard as she did, how *did* she do it? How did she do it? she wondered, looking at her made-up reflection. How did a woman in her thirties (her early thirties) manage to look like this? Like a child of sixteen? It was wonderful. She was wonderful, and it was worth all the unpleasantness, and all the discomfort. Jerome was just being horrid, and she hated him for it. He was jealous of her, that was the trouble, jealous of her seemingly indestructible beauty, and of her ineffable talent. She could fill, and he couldn't. He could do what he liked, play what he liked, but without her, there were always some empty seats.

The boy called the five. He knocked on her door and she called back yes, my darling one? And he popped his gorgeous young head round the door and said five minutes please, Miss Laurence, and she smiled at him sweetly in the mirror. Thank you, darling boy, she said, but I'm ready. Then when he was gone she called Muzz over, with a conspiratorial look and a wave of one finger.

'Perhaps really I should feel sorry for him,' she said in a stage whisper. 'What do you think? Should Elizabeth feel sorry for him?'

'I don't know who you're talking about, dear,' Muzz replied, smoothing out the shoulders on Elizabeth's costume. 'I never know what you're talking about half the time nowadays.'

'I'm talking about Jerome, darling. He was beastly to me today, and made me cross. But really I think what I should be doing is I should be feeling sorry for him.'

'He's doing all right, never you mind. Jerome can look after himself.'

'Oh, I know he can. J can look after himself very well.' She smiled at herself in the mirror, putting her head a little to one side. 'But even so, sometimes he's such a poor old thing. And the last thing Bethy wants is for it all to go wrong, not after all this. Not after all we've done. Don't you agree, Muzz dear?'

Muzz finished straightening Elizabeth's costume and then stood back to look at Elizabeth in the mirror.

'I don't know,' she said, 'I really don't. Sometimes I really wonder where you get it from, you know, Elizabeth. I suppose it must have been from your father. Because it most certainly wasn't from me.'

Elizabeth's eyes glinted back at her in the mirror.

'Be careful, Muzzie darling,' she said with one of those smiles which never reached her eyes. 'After all, we don't want to lose our precious job now, do we?'

'I'm sure I could get another one,' her mother replied evenly.

'I'm sure you could,' Elizabeth countered, never taking her eyes off her mother in the mirror. 'But that's not what you thought when you arrived back in England, penniless, and without a husband, and I took you in, gave you a job, gave you your respect back, was it? When you suddenly and so conveniently remembered you had not just a dead son, but a living daughter? It was all very well when you were living it up in Ceylon, but when hubby runs off with a native girl and leaves us high and dry and middle aged, we suddenly remember, oh, so conveniently our little daughter who was *such* a bore before.'

'We have been over this before, Elizabeth, time and again. And time and again, dear—'

'Stop calling me dear, I'm not your dear. Now let's hear again why it was that you left Peter and me in England.'

'You know why we did, Elizabeth,' her mother replied suddenly sounding weary.

'No, I don't know the reason, Muzzie,' Elizabeth sighed. 'I only know the *excuse*.'

'Beginners please!' the boy called in the corridor, before knocking and putting his head round her door. 'Beginners please, Miss Laurence!'

'Thank you, darling!' Elizabeth waited until the boy had gone before staring once more at her mother in the mirror. '*Oftentimes excusing of a fault, doth make the fault worse by the excuse.* Did you know that? No? Well you know it now. So go and pour me a drink and shut up. I have a performance to give.'

SEVENTEEN

In response to the call Cecil caught the first plane he could and
Jerome met him at the airport.

'She's not going to be able to do the film,' he said to his agent
on the way back into town.

'Why not?' Cecil asked, alarmed by the note of controlled fury
in Jerome's voice.

'You'll see.'

Jerome said very little else as the limousine sped across the
bridge and back into Manhattan. He just smoked tipped cigarette
after tipped cigarette, and drank whisky poured from a cut glass
decanter. Cecil knew this mood, he knew how dangerous it was,
so he stayed quiet, and sipped the drink Jerome had silently offered
him while enjoying the Manhattan landscape.

Elizabeth was in bed when they arrived up at their apartment.
A maid was busy clearing up what looked like debris from a party
the night before, while Miss Toothe was already busy at her desk.
Miss Toothe nowadays travelled everywhere with them, as indeed
did Dingo and the monosyllabic Miss Page, whom Elizabeth had
put on her personal payroll.

'Go in and see her,' Jerome instructed Cecil, before Cecil had
even had time to remove his top coat. 'It's perfectly all right. She's
heavily sedated.'

The maid held open the bedroom door and Cecil went in. There
was a nurse sitting by the bed, who looked up briefly when Cecil
came in before returning to read her book.

Elizabeth was propped up in bed, but fast asleep, just as Jerome
had indicated she would be. She was wearing a black silk négligée
trimmed with jet black fur which matched the hair which was

spread out on the pillows. She looked for all the world just like something out of a film she might make, except for the four deep, red and wickedly angry weals which ran in identical formation down each of her cheeks.

Cecil then noticed her hands which lay either side of her outside and on top of the bed linen. Both her hands were heavily bandaged into mitts, and taped tightly round the slender wrists, so that no more damage could be done. The sight of Elizabeth like this deeply troubled Cecil, so he backed quickly out of the room and was only too happy to accept the ready offer of a stiff drink from the waiting Jerome.

'Dear God, dear boy,' was the best Cecil could initially muster. 'What the devil's been going on?'

'She got in a bit of a temper, *dear boy*,' Jerome replied. 'Most probably because for once she couldn't get her own way.'

'But I don't understand.' Cecil was totally bewildered. 'To do that to herself. She must have lost her reason. What's she been doing?'

'What's she been doing?' Jerome examined the question over deliberately and calmly.

'You know what I mean, dear boy. Has she been drinking? Has she been drugging? I mean what has she been *doing*?'

'What has she been doing?' Jerome nodded as he repeated the question. 'I'll tell you what she's been doing, dear boy. She's been drinking, certainly. Only champagne, I'll grant you, and only one bottle at a time. She hasn't been eating. She's been staying up all night, and I imagine to do that she's been popping a few bennies, but then that's how it goes, isn't it? That's show business. But besides that, all she's been *doing* is injecting herself with cows' piss – there's no need to look like that, dear boy. They *all* do it! All the actresses! How do you think they keep those fabulous figures? *With regular injections of cows' piss.* And besides the cow piss injections, and the diuretics, and the twice a week colonic washouts kindly arranged and performed by Miss Page, she has been sticking her pretty little fingers down her pretty little throat on the rare occasions when she does eat something, so that she can sicky-it-all-up-again, and not get fat, and just to make doubly sure she doesn't get fat or worse – feel like eating something, she has been smoking about sixty cigarettes a day. That's about the size of it, Cecil, dear boy. Get the picture? That is what little Miss Laurence has been *doing*.'

Cecil stared into his drink and then up at Jerome, who was chain-smoking and pacing the room, up and down, up and down, immaculate as ever in a beautifully tailored double-breasted grey suit, his hair brushed and brilliantined back in the style he now liked to wear it.

'Yes?' Jerome said in answer to Cecil's stare. 'Well?'

'You're going to have to take her home, dear boy,' Cecil said.

'Correction,' Jerome replied. '*You're* going to have to take her home. One of us has to do this blasted movie.'

'But you said she won't fly.'

'She won't. You're going to have to go back by boat.'

Over lunch, Jerome told Cecil what had happened. It had all come to a head on the Sunday, the day after the end of their triumphant Broadway season, in the hangover of a huge last night party thrown by Gloria Van Der Post.

'For once it had been a rather good bash,' Jerome said. 'Rather civilized as it turned out, rather *fin de saison* rather than *fin de siècle*. Bethy was in her element, and, I have to say, looking a million dollars once again. Probably because the season had finished. She'd kept complaining towards the end of it of depression. Said it was all the fault of those dreary cows Juliet and Ophelia, as she liked to call them. She found Ophelia's mad scene particularly taxing.'

'I can believe that,' Cecil said. 'I've never seen it played so well. She was tremendously convincing.'

'Yes, but Bethy's not usually one for all this agonizing about internals,' Jerome said. 'All this Strasberg bollocks. All this methodizing they go in for over here, this agonizing in corners. She doesn't give it that.' He snapped his fingers on *that*, right on the beat, sharply like a castanet. Jerome never missed an effect. 'So all the more surprising,' he continued, 'that she let her *dreary cows* get to her. I mean last week, dear heart, I came back late one afternoon from the Guggenheim, and walked straight into *Hamlet*, Act Four, scene five. At least it might as well for all the world have been. There she was, wandering round the apartment half naked, her hair all over the place, muttering to herself with the tears streaming down her cheeks.' Jerome put down his knife and fork and stared at Cecil. 'I was seriously worried, Cecil. *Was?* What am I saying? I *am* seriously worried! *There are times when I think she may be losing her mind*,' he said, dropping his voice to a suitably *sotto* pitch. 'She won't stop washing her hands. She washes her hands all the time, just like Mrs Macbeth. And yet at other times, like on Saturday night at the party, like most nights when she's partying, she's her old self. Funny, mischievous, witty, flirtatious, a little dangerous, very much the original coinage, very much the Elizabeth Laurence we all know and love.'

Cecil drank some wine and wondered about everyone loving Elizabeth. Not many people loved her, not those who really knew her. They treated her with a healthy respect, because they knew how formidable she could be, how wilful, and how utterly singleminded, but few of her acquaintances actually loved her. Her coterie did, her famous *camp-followers*, they *adored* her, and the worse she was, the more they worshipped at her shrine. But probably even they didn't actually love her, Cecil thought, before briefly glancing across the table and wondering if Jerome still really loved her, or if in fact he ever really had done.

But Jerome was talking, carrying on with his story, so Cecil put down his wine glass and paid him full attention.

'She got very drunk at the party, of course,' he said. 'But then she always does on these occasions, because she never eats a thing. Mind you, you would have to know her pretty well to know that she was drunk. She doesn't make a nonsense, slur her words, or fall about the place, she's not at all the stage drunk. She just gets very beady, very glittery, and – and this is the frightening part – even more coherent than ever. She was very coherent around about dawn on Sunday, dear boy, I can tell you. *Very* coherent. *Ever so.*' Jeremy threw in a little of his stage cockney, not to lighten the telling, but to flavour his sarcasm. 'It was the film apparently. One of her fairy crew had put it about at the party, particularly in Bethy's hearing, that Goldberg had only agreed my being in the film in order to secure her.'

'They always say that,' Cecil said heedlessly, and then realized his gaffe as he saw the dark look in Jerome's eyes. 'Sorry, dear boy. What I meant was that surely you must be used to that by now.'

'Go on,' Jerome said icily. 'It's getting better by the moment.'

'You know what I mean,' Cecil floundered on helplessly. 'I mean that you two cause such an enormous amount of professional resentment you can't any longer be surprised by what people say.'

'Of course I'm not!' Jerome snapped, pushing his plate away and then beckoning for a waiter to come and remove it at once. 'What *surprised* me was that it bothered Bethy. Apparently all hell let loose at the party and she took herself home in a high old dudge, long before yours truly, for once. And when I crawled in with the dawn, there she was, like Medusa, in a blind, white-hot rage. She said nobody said things like that about me, nobody, it didn't matter who they were. And to show them how utterly untrue such a stupid bloody rumour was, she was going to withdraw from the film. She was not going to do the film, because she knew better than anyone that the person MGM really wanted was not her, but

371

me. And she would stake her reputation on it. She was going to scotch this nonsense once and for all—'

'What nonsense?'

'What nonsense, dear boy?' Jerome looked at Cecil with amazement, as if he couldn't understand the naïvety of the question. He then pushed his chair back and leaned away from the table before continuing, seemingly unaware (although Cecil very much doubted that he was) that he now had most of the restaurant as his audience. 'The nonsense she was going to scotch, once and for all, was this blatant misconception that I play second *fiddle*. That without her I am just another starry actor, and not the genius she knows I am, and that everyone knows I am. So to show them, she was going to walk off the blasted movie, she wasn't going to do *Encounter in the Park*.'

'She's mad,' Cecil said, thinking of his lost commission and earning himself another very hard stare from his client. 'I'm sorry, I didn't mean that either. I didn't mean Elizabeth is mad. I meant that was a mad thing to say. To think of doing.'

'Of course you did.' Jerome rocked on his chair for a moment, staring up at the ceiling, then he set it back down on all four legs, sat forward and folding both arms on the table in front of him, buried his head in them. 'Anyway,' he muttered, but quite loudly enough for Cecil to hear everything. 'The long and the short of it was this. I said no, she was not walking off the film for my sake, I said it was a wonderful part, they were both good parts, but for her and for once, recently, it was an extremely well-written and realized role and she must play it, I didn't *mention* the money, the bills here, the bills at home, the vast and ever increasing budget it costs to run this goddam roadshow, I never once said she had to do it for that reason, although she knows full well we have to make movies to pay our way. For Christ's sake, Cecil, *we haven't made a penny out of this blasted tour!* Not a dime! Not a nickel, not a goddam cent! Not on top of our salaries! This tour has eaten up all the money we made from the last *three* movies! From *Dinner Date*, *The Silver Fox* and *Meet Me at Nine*. That's what this tour has cost us. It's the blasted management who's coined it. It was a crazy idea having us bankroll ourselves, and bring everything over including the kitchen sink! Whoever dreamed up such a lunatic deal?' He looked up briefly at his agent, to stare at him beadily, before burying his head back in the fold of his arms. 'Anyway – where was I?'

'You were saying you hadn't mentioned the financial necessity for you both making *Encounter in the Park*,' Cecil reminded him, resisting the temptation to remind him also that the lunatic who had thought up the deal for the Broadway season was none other than Jerome himself, although Cecil suspected that Jerome remembered this was the case from the speed with which he resumed his story.

'Good. Yes, well I didn't. I didn't say a word about money, because I happen to think it's a damn good movie anyway, and it *is* a film she should make. But in hindsight, it probably would have been better if I had made money the reason, because she might have seen sense.' Now he sat up, bolt upright, and placed both his hands palm down on the table-cloth. 'Instead of screaming and yelling at me that if I wouldn't allow her to walk off the movie,' he concluded, 'then she would make it impossible for her to do the film her own way. Whereupon she shut herself in the bathroom and tore her face to ribbons. With her wretched fingernails.'

Cecil accepted some more wine from the waiter, knowing that he needed it, and that he was going to need even more.

'I know what you're thinking, Cecil,' Jerome sighed, 'but it won't wash. They won't delay shooting, I've already talked *unofficially* to Mort Goldberg and he says much as he'd love to—' Jerome shrugged his shoulders high, and left the rest of the sentence hanging in the air. 'And even if they did, Cecil, Madam promised me before I got the doctor to her that if I insisted that she do the movie, she would continue to carve her lovely face up at every given opportunity. So negotiate, Cecil. I have to do this movie. I need to do a movie right now, and I need to do this movie, because it's a good one, and you got us very good money. I don't want to lose this one, Cecil. So convince them I can carry it. They can find another actress. I do not want to lose this job, Cecil. Because I do not want to have to sell Sainthill.'

It was the house, Cecil thought morbidly as the liner pitched and heaved in the heaviest seas Cecil had ever encountered. All Jerome cared about was the house, and all that absurd posing as the country squire. He didn't care about anything else. All he seemed really concerned about was Sainthill.

There were storms and high winds all through their first night and day at sea, making it practically impossible to eat, sleep, or do anything other than drink. By mid-morning, tired of trying to stay upright on his feet, like most sensible passengers Cecil had taken to his cabin and was lying on his bed, thinking over the events of the last twenty-four hours. There had been the most frightful scene on embarkation, when having successfully smuggled the semi-sedated and heavily veiled and caped Elizabeth on board the liner, she had managed to escape from her cabin while the doctor was trying to give her the other half of the sedative. She had then run riot through the First Class lounges and bars, shouting and screaming that everyone was trying to kill her, with Jerome, Cecil, Miss Toothe, and the doctor in pursuit. They had managed finally to run her to ground in the library, where under the noses of four elderly passengers already settled at the bridge table, Elizabeth put up a spirited defence, kicking and lashing out at her pursuers while filling the air with expletives, until quite unexpectedly and all of a sudden she burst into fits of uncontrollable laughter and allowed herself to be led quietly away back to her suite of cabins.

She would not allow herself to be sedated, however. She made that perfectly clear, giving warning to the entourage that if any attempt was made to drug her without her direct permission, whenever she awoke from the enforced sedation the very least she would do would be to attempt further self-mutilation.

At this point Jerome had requested to be left alone with her and afterwards told Cecil what had occurred between them, since Cecil was to be in charge of her on the journey home. Jerome said he had asked his wife why she was doing this to herself, to him, to both of them in fact, to which Elizabeth had replied very calmly that there was nothing to worry about, not any more, because she was herself again. The problem was simply one of total exhaustion, she'd explained, something which no-one had seemed fully to have taken into account. She needed rest and the journey back could be the beginning of that rest, but, and this is why Jerome had to spell it out to Cecil, she had made it quite clear she was not going to travel under sedation because the thought of it terrified her. Suppose something happened when they were at sea? She had wanted to know what would happen to her if there was a fire on board, or a collision with another ship, and she was just lying there unconscious. Is that what Jerome wanted? she had asked. And even if there wasn't to be an accident, if she was sedated she would worry, whenever she was awake, that there might be, that something might happen when she was drugged and helpless, and so she had told Jerome she simply couldn't take that worry. It would kill her, she said. Or worse, she might even kill herself.

That, of course, had been enough to convince Jerome to persuade the doctor to give her nothing more than a mild tranquillizer then, and to promise in front of Elizabeth to recommend to the ship's doctor not to prescribe anything stronger than the dosage he had administered thereafter unless the circumstances truly demanded it.

'Which they won't, darling,' Elizabeth had promised Jerome after he had helped settle her down. 'I have Toothy here to help me. And Maggie, my maid. *And* dear Muzz to look after me. As well as Cecil Fussbudget to make sure I behave. Besides—' She had put an arm up around Jerome's neck and eased him down so that she could confide in him. 'Besides,' she had whispered, 'Bethy's all better now. Bethy's quite herself, darling. You really don't have a thing to worry about as long as Bethy's in charge.'

Shortly before midday Cecil arose and went to the bar for a medicinal brandy. Having downed a double Courvoisier, he then went as he had been instructed by Jerome to visit his charge and monitor her behaviour, and was both relieved and pleasantly surprised to find Elizabeth sitting up in bed, smoking one of her favourite Sobranies and playing gin rummy with her ever-faithful dresser. Muzz left them alone to talk, and Elizabeth was her old bright and cheerful self, gossiping and chattering away about the season in New York, and even discussing plans for the forthcoming season in London. Finally, when she had sent Muzz off on some errand or other and they were alone in the cabin, Elizabeth told Cecil that she wished to confide in him.

'That's what I'm here for, dear girl,' Cecil said, lighting a cigarette. 'Shoot.'

'It's not me that's causing all this trouble, Cessy,' she said, dropping her voice. 'I want you to understand that.'

'I see,' Cecil said, not seeing at all, but needing to say something in the long silence which had ensued. 'I see.'

'Cecil.' Elizabeth's voice now had a hard edge to it, as if she was irritated and doing her best not to show it. 'The point is, Cecil,' she continued, 'no-one seems to understand. They all think it's me, but it isn't. It isn't at all.'

'I see,' Cecil said again, trying to buy time so that he could work out what Elizabeth could possibly mean. 'Ah. You mean it's Jerry?'

'What is?'

'Jerry's the problem, is he?'

'Oh.' Elizabeth dropped her cigarette which was still alight into the ashtray and immediately lit another, talking as she did so. 'So you don't want to talk about my problem.'

'I want to talk about whatever you want to talk about, Lizzie,' Cecil replied, stubbing out Elizabeth's still smouldering cigarette.

'Oh, for Christ's sake!' Elizabeth suddenly snapped. *'Who's Lizzie?'*

'I'm sorry, dear girl, I was forgetting.' Cecil had indeed momentarily forgotten how Elizabeth could suddenly take against any unwarranted or unauthorized abbreviation of her name, and Cecil had never really been given formal permission to call her by anything other than her proper name. 'You were saying?' he asked.

'No, *you* were saying. Actually, I don't know what you were saying. I didn't understand one word of what you were saying.'

'I'm sorry. Perhaps I wasn't making myself very clear.' Cecil was confused, and not really feeling at all well. 'Let's start again, shall we? What I was going to say was – I wonder what the best way is of putting this?'

Elizabeth looked up at him, quickly, her eyes glinting through half closed lids, and she began to smile slowly, and beguilingly.

'Yes, let's,' she agreed. 'Let's find the best way of putting it we can. I like that. I like putting it the best way.'

Cecil was temporarily mesmerized, a snake caught by its charmer, a moth fluttering round the light. Then the music stopped, and the light went out, as Elizabeth closed her bright green eyes and began to laugh, rather raucously. Even so, Cecil laughed too, seeing that what Elizabeth had said had after all been a joke, that she had as usual been lightly making fun of him.

'To get back to Jerry,' he said. 'I think Jerry's problem—'

'Who's *Jerry?*'

'Sorry. Jerome.'

'Who's – *Jerome?*'

'Your husband, dear girl.' Cecil laughed. 'Who's Jerome indeed?'

'My husband,' Elizabeth said slowly. 'Ah. The black man. The naughty black man.'

'Yes,' Cecil agreed, 'probably.' He was quite used to Elizabeth's games. She was always inventing names and identities for people, particularly Jerome. Last time they had all talked and Elizabeth had been patently cross with Jerome, she had spent the entire time referring to him as *the Boeotian.* So now he was a black man, Cecil thought, and who cares? Just as long as Elizabeth doesn't start scratching her face to pieces again or trying to cut her wrists, as far as Cecil was concerned Jerome could be the man in the moon.

'Anyway,' he continued, 'your husband's problem really is only a question of confidence. Self-confidence. He seems to be brimming with it, but in fact like all great actors—'

'No!' Elizabeth suddenly sat bolt upright in her bed, her cigarette still stuck absurdly and quite out of character in the middle of her mouth. 'No.' She repeated slowly and firmly. 'The black man is not an actor, you dope. The black man is a drummer. In a jazz band.'

These were the moments Cecil always dreaded, the moments Elizabeth started playing her games and he was expected to join in, either in some terrible telephone jape, some not always kind practical joke, or some fantasy conversation she would force him into making in public, all of which Elizabeth would find screamingly funny afterwards, while Cecil, who was hopeless at doing anything impromptu, always and resolutely failed to see the joke.

'I'm sorry, dear girl,' he began, 'but I don't really think this is quite the time or place, you know, do you?'

'Oh, Cessy!' Elizabeth interrupted him with a laugh of delight. 'Cessy don't be such an ass! You don't want to listen to a word she says! You're such an ass!'

'Who? A word who says?'

'There *is* no black man. There is no black man who's a drummer in a band! Don't be such a complete ass! What else do you believe?' She leaned forward suddenly, so that her face was only inches from Cecil's. She smelt faintly of nicotine, but more of violets, mixed with some very pungent and exotic scent. 'What else do you believe?' she repeated. 'Do you believe in fairies?'

Cecil smiled and extinguished his own cigarette. The sea had become even rougher, and the brandy hadn't done quite the trick Cecil had hoped. He got up, holding on to the edge of the bed.

'Look,' he said, 'perhaps this isn't the best time to talk, dear girl.'

'No perhaps it isn't, *old boy*,' Elizabeth giggled. 'You are looking a little green round the edges.'

'I'll pop in again at tea-time,' Cecil said, clutching on to whatever he could as he swayed towards the door. 'I'll look in then to see how you are.'

'Why not?' Elizabeth said gaily. 'One of us is bound to be here.'

If Muzz hadn't returned at that very moment, and been opening the door as Elizabeth spoke, perhaps Cecil would have questioned exactly what Elizabeth had meant. But because there were now two women in the room and because Cecil feared he might be sick at any moment, he simply smiled in response to Elizabeth's cheery wave and hurried out. Muzz clutched the large handbag she was holding as Cecil went, and then closed and locked the outside door.

'You took your time,' Elizabeth said, smoothing her top bedsheet back with both hands to get rid of the creases, her cigarette still stuck in the corner of her mouth. 'You certainly took your time.'

'I'm sorry, dear, but it's difficult to hurry when it's as rough as this,' Muzz said, fetching a glass from the storm holder on the wall before sitting on the edge of Elizabeth's bed and opening her copious handbag. 'And they only had Moët. No vintage Bollinger, I'm afraid.'

'That's all right,' Elizabeth said reaching under her covers for the empty bottle she had hidden there from Cecil. 'We'll forgive you.'

With that and a little smile she handed her mother the empty champagne bottle in exchange for a full glass.

After successfully staving off what he'd considered to be a surefire bout of sea-sickness by the quick intake of another two brandies, Cecil made his way topside to the wireless room and cabled a message to Jerome in the style in which he had been instructed. The message read:

NANNY'S CHARGE A.1. IN FACT QUITE HER OLD NAUGHTY SELF.

Then he retired to his cabin to try and sleep until it was time for him to look in on his charge once more.

Apart from the terrible weather, the rest of the journey passed uneventfully enough, with Elizabeth behaving herself impeccably. Whenever Cecil made his rounds early morning, midday, mid-afternoon, and twice in the evening, his charge was either sitting up in bed playing cards with her dresser, or lying propped up on a pile of pillows reading or sleeping. Apart from the scars on her face, she was beginning to look her old self, and far less fatigued, Cecil also noted happily, putting down the improvement in her appearance and attitude to the enforced rest and his careful management.

By the end of their third day at sea, Cecil had every reason to be pleased with himself. Elizabeth was now up and about in her suite, and he had even managed to get her to eat a light lunch with him, which he ordered to be served to them in her state room. She was in high spirits throughout the meal, and now that the seas had calmed down dramatically, Cecil was fully able to enjoy himself and the excellent fare, even though he was forced to accompany the superb Dover Sole with a glass of barley water. After lunch Cecil sent another cheering cable back to Jerome to report the continued good progress, before returning to his cabin for a well-earned cognac and a post-prandial slumber.

He was awoken an hour later by Elizabeth's maid knocking on his cabin door.

'Is something the matter?' he asked through the half open bedroom door as he hurried to get himself dressed. 'Do we need the doctor?'

'I don't think so, sir,' the maid replied, admiring herself privately in a mirror. 'Muzz just asked me to fetch you. Quick as is possible.'

Elizabeth was in her state room when Cecil arrived, sitting in an armchair with an open book on her knees. Tears were flooding down her face, but there was no sound of her sobbing. She just sat as still as a waxwork, a silently weeping doll-like figure.

Muzz was sitting in the armchair opposite, which she vacated as soon as Cecil entered.

'How long has she been like this?' Cecil asked *sotto*.

'Like what?' Muzz answered, as if there was more than one answer.

'Like this,' Cecil repeated. 'Crying like this?'

'Oh.' Muzz thought for a moment, while turning to stare back at Elizabeth. 'Since you left I'd say,' she said. 'Since after lunch.'

'Do we need to call the doctor?' Cecil asked, taking Muzz by the arm to stop her leaving.

'You tell me, Mr Manners,' she replied. 'You're the one in charge.'

Cecil postponed calling the ship's doctor until he had taken the chance to talk to Elizabeth and see if there was anything he could do. Left alone in the state room with her now, he sat down in the vacated armchair and smiled across at his charge, who so far had given him no indication at all that she even knew he was there.

'Now then,' Cecil began in his best avuncular fashion. 'What exactly seems to be the matter, my dear?'

Elizabeth made no reply. Instead she began slowly to wash her hands in her lap, staring at them as she did so, as if to make sure she had removed every mark.

'Elizabeth?' Cecil said, suddenly worried, suddenly sensing a dread, a dread that Elizabeth might indeed be going insane. 'Elizabeth, it's Cecil. Elizabeth – do say something.' She still said nothing, just continued with her dry handwashing. 'Elizabeth dear,' Cecil said hopelessly. 'It's me. It's *Cessy*.'

It was to no avail. Elizabeth said nothing, she didn't even look at Cecil. She just concentrated all her attentions on trying to remove whatever it was on her lily-white hands. Cecil eased himself out of the chair, intending to reach for the telephone and call the doctor, but as he did, Elizabeth suddenly spoke.

'Look,' she said, holding out her hands. 'I can't get rid of them, you know. Whatever I try, I cannot get rid of them.'

'What, old girl?' Cecil asked, sliding back into his seat. 'What are you trying to get rid of?'

'You can't see them, can you?' Elizabeth sighed, turning each hand up to stare down at the palms. 'Of course you can't. It's only the people who've done something who can see the marks.'

'What marks?'

'The marks, you oaf. The marks of what you've done. And they're all over my hands.'

'But what have you done, old girl?' Cecil tried a laugh, as if to make light of the whole thing, but Elizabeth paid it no heed. 'You haven't done anything, Elizabeth,' he said.

'Oh I have, I have. I've done something dreadful. I have killed somebody.'

'No, you haven't, Elizabeth,' Cecil said finally. It was all he could think of saying. It was all he could do to stop himself shaking he was so frightened. 'You haven't killed anybody,' he assured her. 'Don't be so silly. Who could you have possibly killed?'

'Oh, stop being such a complete and utter oaf, you clodhopper!' Elizabeth suddenly rounded on him, staring across at him for the first time. 'You know bloody well what I'm talking about! Because you conspired too! But I was the one who killed her! *Juliet*! I was the one who killed *Juliet Bumpkin*! And I have her blood on my hands to prove it! Look, damn you! Look!'

She thrust her hands out for Cecil to see, and the next thing he knew as he bent forward was that she was at his throat, and his face, and even his eyes. She was like a demon, possessed with great strength, while she fought to tear at his skin, hissing her hate at him while moving with the speed and agility of a wild cat.

'You should have her blood on your hands as well, you bastard!' she seethed. 'You were all too willing to listen to Lalla and to go along with what I'd planned! Because and damn you to hell, Cecil Manners, because you were in on it too! You were a part of it, damn you! Yet there's not a mark on you! There's not a mark anywhere! But there will be, you bastard! There will be! Because I'm going to tear your eyes out!'

She might have succeeded too, such was the ferocity of her unexpected attack. But fortunately for Cecil the extra two stones he had put on over the years gave him an enormous advantage in weight, and after being totally overwhelmed in the initial wave of

Elizabeth's attack, losing his glasses and a handful of hair, having two deep cuts gouged out of one cheek and suffering near asphyxiation when Elizabeth with superhuman strength managed to get both hands on his neck in an attempt to strangle him, he managed to wrestle her around under him and simply fell on top of her on the cabin floor, immobilizing her with his sheer weight.

They lay there for how long Cecil couldn't say. He just held Elizabeth down, kneeling on her upper arms as if back in the school playground, holding her down by the wrists with his hands, while they both fought to regain their breath, and while the blood from the wounds on Cecil's face dripped down on to the white swansdown of the négligée and nightdress worn by the most beautiful woman in the world.

Then suddenly Elizabeth went totally limp under Cecil and in his grip. He could feel it, as if all the life had abruptly left her body. Her eyes glazed, and her beautiful head rolled to one side, with the tip of her tongue lolling out of the corner of her mouth. For a moment Cecil was sure she had died, and scrambling awkwardly to his feet, he stood above her, still panting, still short of breath while the most beautiful woman in the world lay on a patterned beige carpet, motionless and white as driven snow.

He bent down to pick her up, to see if she was alive, and as he did, she took a massive intake of breath, the whole of her frail body heaving with the effort. Cecil got an arm round her waist, holding on to the side of a chair to steady himself against the pitch of the great liner as she still gently rolled, and as he eased Elizabeth up off the floor she fell backwards, faint in his arms. She was so light, there was simply nothing of her, Cecil thought, as he carried her through into her bedroom and laid her down on the bed. He simply couldn't imagine where all that brute strength had come from, because he could carry her practically in one arm.

As he quickly washed the blood off his face and took a clean towel to dress the wounds, he could safely see her in the bathroom mirror, but she was still lying absolutely motionless, a beautiful doll someone just dropped on the bed, one arm across her stomach, the other palm up sticking out to one side, her head turned the other way, her legs splayed apart. Cecil held the towel tightly to his throbbing face, trying not to look at the pathetic sight, a sight which he found deeply distressing.

Still holding the towel to his face, and uncertain of quite what he should do next, he went and sat beside her on the bed. Again, he didn't know how long he sat there as the ship gently pitched and rolled in the seas off the south of Ireland, but it must have been a long time, certainly long enough for Cecil to have reviewed in his mind everything she had said, everything of which he stood accused, and certainly time enough for him to find himself guilty, an accessory before and after the fact of what Elizabeth chose to call Pippa's murder.

After a very long time, Elizabeth stirred, awakening as if from a dream. She stirred back to life and seeing the sad hump of a man sitting with his head bowed beside her, she put a hand out, first on his back, which made the man flinch, and then as he half turned his head, she put her hand on one of his and took it. The man turned to her and she saw he had cut his face, there were two or three very deep cuts on one of his cheeks and several scratches elsewhere. She knew who the man was, of course, even without his glasses, she knew it was poor dear Cecil, and she knew at once who had done this awful thing to him, and she sighed, she sighed hopelessly and helplessly. Even worse, there was blood all over her best night things, her favourite night things, things J had bought her on their first trip to New York, the négligée and nightdress in which Vogue *had photographed her for their piece on* The Most Beautiful Women In The World.

'Poor Cecil,' she whispered as he turned further round to her. 'Poor dear Cessy. Are you all right, darling man? Do you want a doctor?'

'Are you all right, Elizabeth?' Cecil asked by way of a reply. 'I think if we're thinking of getting the doctor—'

'I don't want a doctor, Cess,' Elizabeth sighed. 'It's not me who needs the doctor.'

'Even so,' Cecil said unsurely. 'I think perhaps he'd better come down. And take a look at us both as it were.'

'You're shaking,' Elizabeth remarked, as she watched Cecil reach for the telephone. 'You're shaking like a leaf.'

'It was quite an attack, dear girl,' Cecil replied, doing his best to laugh it off. 'It was rather like being hit by a windmill.'

'Oh dear,' Elizabeth sighed, biting her lip and sinking back on her pillows. 'Oh dear, what is going to happen, Cessy?' she asked. 'What *are* they going to do with her when we get home?'

They had to wait, of course, to do with her what the doctors all said they must do with her. They had to wait until Jerome could sign the papers, but Jerome was away in Hollywood, deeply engrossed in the filming of *Encounter in the Park*, thanks to Cecil's astute and diplomatic negotiations, filming opposite the last minute but inspired replacement casting of Dorothy Brookes. From all reports

Cecil gathered the stars had finally hit it off after a very awkward start, the chemistry was magical, and the prediction was for the film to be everything and more the studio had hoped it would be when they had finally given the go-ahead.

So Cecil had a difficult hand to play, some would say impossible. The longer he waited approaching Jerome, the worse Elizabeth's condition was becoming, but if on the other hand he broke the news too early, he could wreck Jerome's chance of scoring a solo hit with the movie. Finally, after long and private transatlantic calls to the producers and the director, Cecil chose the moment to fly in, namely the last week of the shoot when all the difficult scenes had been safely and successfully filmed. He arrived on the Monday in Los Angeles and drove straight to talk to Jerome privately. After a three hour meeting with him in his luxury caravan on the studio lot, Cecil finally made Jerome see sense and secured his signed permission for Elizabeth to be admitted to The Hermitage at Beckhampton, a nursing home which specialized in the treatment of mental disorders.

EIGHTEEN

Pippa read about Elizabeth. She read about her quite by chance because she never took English newspapers and listened only to the French radio. She also read and listened selectively, persuading herself that because she no longer had any interest in films or theatre there was no point in reading about them. But the real reason was that she was afraid. Pippa was still afraid of what her reaction might be if and when she saw a news item on or more importantly a photograph of Jerome, which if she did not censor her reading carefully sooner or later she knew she was almost bound to do.

They say snakes hide where you least expect to find them. This time the snake was hidden in a box of books for which Pippa had sent away to Foyles in Charing Cross Road, hidden in the rolled up newspaper sheets used to pack the ordered volumes tightly in the bound and sealed cardboard container which had just arrived at the small farmhouse in the Loire that sunny spring morning. Jenny was helping her mother unpack the books, sitting at the scrubbed wood table with old Bobby asleep at her feet, and smoothing out the crumpled newspaper as Pippa stood examining and leafing through each precious book. Occasionally Jenny would read something out in English from one of the sheets of newspaper, or intrigued by some strip cartoon she had never seen before, like *Flook*, or *Fred Basset*, she would sit with both her elbows on the table and her chin resting on her clenched fists while she earnestly studied the comic activities of the strange comic strip characters.

'What is this, *Maman*?' she would ask occasionally. Or, 'why are they doing this? Who's this meant to be, *Maman*? And why is he saying that?'

It was during one of these enquiries that Pippa saw her, on the other side of the double page Jenny had just straightened out in order to read. It was the lead story, with a large picture of Elizabeth and a smaller picture of Jerome inset into the paragraphs below. STAR FORCED TO QUIT PICTURE the headline read, and then underneath: ELIZABETH LAURENCE HOME IN ILL HEALTH.

Pippa took the page, having torn the strip cartoons off for Jenny, and sat down on a sun dappled seat under one of the kitchen windows. For a while she just stared at the news pictures, testing herself, curious to see how she felt now that she was seeing Jerome for the very first time in twelve years, since the day she had found him lying in bed with this *little old woman in dark glasses and silk headscarf who was coming down the gangway on the arm of Cecil Manners.*

The photograph was good enough and big enough to show quite clearly the state of Elizabeth's physical health. She was bird-like, her once slender and elegant hands claws hooked round Cecil's elbow, her previously flawless skin stretched tightly over hollowed cheeks and too prominent bones, her once enviable mouth no longer a rosebud, but now a thin tense line pursed shut, and the world famous eyes hidden behind the black orbs of her sunglasses. And even though her body was invisible under her mink coat, Pippa could sense its sickness and its infirmity from the way Elizabeth was stooped round-shouldered, appearing to lean all of what little weight she now was on the arm of her agent. Even her beautiful legs looked emaciated and shapeless.

Pippa was horrified. The sight of Elizabeth in such obvious distress gave her not one frisson of pleasure, not one moment of *schadenfreude*. The woman looked as if she was dying. This fabulous creature whose beauty had defied description seemed to have aged beyond belief, and to have withered into nothing.

On the other hand, Jerome looked marvellous, Pippa noted, more handsome and compelling than ever. The photograph of him was obviously a publicity still, taken and processed to accentuate his stunning good looks, but even so there was no doubt in Pippa's mind that those looks had improved with maturity, because the slight weakness around his mouth had gone, and while the vulnerability was still there in those famous eyes, those eyes were now more determined, and the jawline more square.

And yet all Pippa could think about was Elizabeth. She studied the picture of her ex-husband, of the only man she had ever loved with an almost clinical detachment, almost as if all she had been was one of his fans, perhaps his most adoring fan, but one who nonetheless had stopped admiring her hero after he had made a picture or been in a play she had hated. Her feelings didn't frighten her at all. They might have surprised her, she may well have been confounded that her heart no longer beat the faster and that her breath caught no more in her throat at the very sight or thought of him, but she wasn't appalled, she wasn't devastated. What she was, as she later discovered when analysing how she really felt about seeing his image once again, was purely grateful, *deeply* grateful because emotionally she found she felt nothing whatsoever, not even rage.

He could have been anybody, Pippa eventually realized as she walked the banks of the Loire later with her daughter running ahead of her, and her old and faithful dog following slowly on behind. She had been so untroubled by it, the photograph could have been of any famous actor, or more accurately of anyone, famous or not. Jerome was no longer someone, he was just anyone. Jerome was now not just in the past, Jerome was the past.

Elizabeth was the past as well, Pippa realized, which was why she was able to feel concern and compassion. If Elizabeth Laurence had still been what Pippa thought she was, someone to hate, someone to curse, someone she had once wanted to harm, she could never have returned to look at that terrible photograph, and reread the accompanying story, nor could she ever have picked up the telephone and called Cecil to find out how Elizabeth now was.

'Oh, she's *fine*,' Cecil told her, after he had got over his initial surprise and delight at this out-of-the-blue call from Pippa, particularly since no-one had heard another thing from her since the formality of the divorce. He, Cecil, had it seemed been the first person to hear from her again, a designation which added relish and pleasure to his joy. 'No, no, it was just a case of nervous exhaustion, nothing more and nothing less, Pippa, than a case of burning the famous old candle at both ends,' he continued. 'Elizabeth has never been, as I'm sure you appreciate, one for half measures.'

'But how is she now, Cecil?' Pippa asked. 'I mean there's nervous exhaustion and there's nervous exhaustion. That photograph. I simply wouldn't have known that was Elizabeth.'

'Oh, it was a terrible picture,' Cecil said dismissively. 'You know the Press. They print what they want to show. *World Famous Star Collapses*. You know? You can't exactly head some trumped-up story with a photograph of the so-called collapsed *World Famous Star* smiling and waving now, can you? No, no, it had been a *particularly* horrendous crossing, we were all as sick as dogs, and that's what did poor Elizabeth in, that on top of the sheer exhaustion.'

It all came trippingly off Cecil's tongue, as indeed it should have done, so often had Cecil recounted the official reason for Elizabeth Laurence's dramatic and pitiful return to her native shores. Except for the one unguarded moment on the ship's gangway, when a press photographer disguised as a sailor got close enough to take that one all-too-revealing photograph, Cecil had done his job admirably, keeping the reporters at bay with his well-phrased bulletins, while managing to complete the advance arrangements for Elizabeth's admission to The Hermitage in absolute secrecy. By the time the story broke about the nursing home, Cecil and the doctors had already drafted their explanatory and carefully sanitized statements, and no-one had seemed any the wiser. Certainly no-one knew what had gone on behind the scenes.

It seemed, however, that Pippa's concern was not to be so easily assuaged.

'But why The Hermitage, Cecil?' she was asking, in precisely the same tone she had used to use, Cecil noted irritably, when questioning his selection of shot on the croquet lawn. 'The Hermitage, as far as I remember, that's a place for the seriously disturbed. They don't take you in there just for fun. Just to get over a few late nights.'

Fortunately Cecil had fielded this one countless times before as well, so this answer, too, came well rehearsed.

'That was a slight backfire,' he said. 'The point was we needed somewhere where Elizabeth could have a complete and undisturbed rest, somewhere where the phone doesn't ring, and the traffic doesn't stream past, where people don't bang the doors, and turn the television on, so what better than a nursing home, and what double better than probably one of the most secure nursing homes in the country? No-one could bother the patient there, and after all, money was no object.'

'So what happened?'

'There must have been a spy, a paid informer on the staff. The wretched newspapers have them everywhere. The next thing we knew they were running this ridiculous story – this ridiculous and *damaging* story – about a total crack-up and all sorts of things.'

Cecil did the best he could to control the anger in his voice because he was still furious about the betrayal. It hadn't been anyone in The Hermitage. It had been one of Elizabeth's wretched *campfollowers*, anxious both for a little extra pocket money no doubt, and the chance to make Jerome look unlovable and uncaring. Cecil had more than just a faint idea who that particular person was.

But Pippa, it seemed, had read or heard of no such thing. Or else, he suddenly realized, she might be trying to test his mettle, to fault his story.

'What do you mean *crack-up?*' she asked. 'And *all sorts of things?* They obviously weren't referring to another of her so-called nervous breakdowns, were they? You mean they were trying to make it look like something different altogether. The real McCoy, in other words.'

'You know papers,' was all Cecil was prepared to add, anxious to close the subject, convinced that Pippa knew more than she was letting on. If she did, he had absolutely no desire whatsoever to find himself once more arguing the pros and cons of electroconvulsive therapy. 'Papers will have you believe what they want you to believe and most particularly when it isn't true,' he said. 'The point is Elizabeth is fine now, Pip, she is one hundred and one per cent her old self. She's been home for four months now, and Jero – um – and she's back home in the bosom of her family—'

'It's all right,' Pippa cut in. 'You can say his name. You can say *Jerome*. If I can, then you most certainly can, Cecil.'

'The point is, Pip, and I can't tell you how sweet it was of you to call, and how lovely it is to hear your voice again, the point is, my dear, all is well. There are no problems, Elizabeth is quite recovered, and the world's most famous couple—'

'Show business couple,' Pippa corrected him.

'The world's most famous *show business couple* are about to launch their new season at the Princes,' Cecil finished. 'They open with *Antony and Cleopatra*, followed with *The School for Scandal.*'

'They should make the perfect Antony and Cleopatra,' Pippa said, without a trace of rancour, 'and a simply marvellous Sir Peter and Lady Teazle.'

'You should come and see for yourself,' Cecil said magnanimously and foolishly. 'Everyone would love to see you.'

'You are a chump, Cecil,' Pippa laughed. 'Anyway, I don't go to the theatre any more. Goodbye.'

She hung up before Cecil had time to ask where she was, which was what she intended, since she had never let it be publicly known where she now lived, even during the divorce proceedings. And Cecil was dismayed, because he knew he would look foolish if he said he'd spoken to her but he hadn't an idea where she was actually speaking *from*. But that was the only reason for his dismay. The hopes he'd secretly nursed that Pippa would one day be his had long since gone, gone since that horrendous transatlantic crossing, since the time Elizabeth had reminded him of his part in their famous conspiracy, since the moment he realized as he had nursed Elizabeth on that last and fateful day of their journey that it wasn't Pippa whom he loved, but the mad woman entrusted to his care.

As for Pippa, she had known Cecil was lying from the start. She had known Cecil too long both as boy and man not to know when he wasn't telling the truth, and Cecil, like most other bad liars, was always lying when he sounded most as if he was telling the truth. Not that there was anything she could do about Elizabeth and not that she was any of her business, far from it. Pippa was simply concerned because she couldn't help feeling sorry for the wretched creature, and for the unhappiness she must have been suffering from to induce a nervous breakdown, a proper nervous breakdown. Pippa sympathized deeply, because although her own malaise had been nowhere near as severe as she imagined Elizabeth's to have been (from the look of her and from the sound of Cecil's glib prevarications), Pippa had been near enough the edge to see how high the clifftop was.

She found the newspaper cutting again, where she had screwed it up in the fireplace and took another look, not at the photographs but at the date, and sure enough it was an old newspaper, a six-month-old edition of the London *Daily Mail*. Then curious to see what else the box from London had contained in the way of old news, Pippa sorted through the packing and found several pages from papers only weeks, and in some cases, only a few days old. On one quite recent page she located the columns with the theatre advertisements, and scanning them for any announcement of forthcoming productions, she found a box containing details of the New England Players' forthcoming season at the Princes. It was headed simply:

The Didiers
in

and followed by the titles of the plays in which they were to appear.

For one brief moment Pippa suffered, as always just at the moment which is least expected. For an instant there was a stab of pain in her heart, and very nearly tears, and all because of the name, *The Didiers*, who were the people she and Jerome had once been, the two halves of what they had sworn would be an inseparable couple, two people to be parted only by death.

But then she recovered, screwing the paper again into a ball and tossing it into the unlit fire. She knew she mustn't weaken, particularly over something so trivial, particularly as she had long since ceased being a Didier, having renounced the name the day she left England, the day she had reverted to her maiden name, the day she had landed in France and become *Madame Nicholls*, which very soon had become *Madame Nichole*.

'Madame Nichole! Madame Nichole!'

At first, so immersed was she in her thoughts, Pippa only vaguely heard the agitated cry of her neighbour, Madame Theroux. And then she heard it clearly, and noting the sound of urgency in her voice, hurried outside into the sun filled farmyard to see what the matter was.

Her neighbour, a large, red-faced woman, with a shock of bright white hair, was hurrying towards her as fast as she could, scattering the chicks and chickens, her one arm raised in alarm, the other hand clasping her voluminous skirts.

'Oh, Madame, Madame!' she cried as soon as she saw Pippa. '*C'est votre petit vieux chien! Oh Madame! Madame Nichole! Mais il est mort! Je pense qu'il est* mort!'

Pippa began to run, stumbling on the cobbles, nearly tripping over the squawking chickens as she followed Madame Theroux out of the farmyard and along the grassy path, away from the old house and down across the meadows. There was no sound but the two women's breath as they hurried across the lush grass, putting up wild birds which cried in sudden fright and scattering a line of ducks which were crossing their path. She had wondered where Bobby had gone, for one minute he had been asleep as usual by her feet, but then when she had telephoned London she remembered him wandering a little groggily as he did nowadays out of the shade in the kitchen and into the warmth of the sun. She had assumed he had just gone outside for his usual sun-drenched nap, his regular late afternoon habit, but he must have strayed, which was so very unlike him.

They were on Madame Theroux's land now, running in the woods, the sun flashing and glinting through the gaps of the trees, and Jenny was with her, by her side. Pippa suddenly became aware that her daughter was beside her, grabbing her hand and wanting to know what was wrong.

'I don't know,' Pippa replied breathlessly. 'There's something wrong with Bobby.'

Suddenly Madame Theroux stopped, grabbing hold of a tree to do so, to stop her running past the appointed place. With a hand clapped to her mouth, and her eyes filled with tears she pointed to a place on the ground, at the foot of the tree.

Bobby lay there, curled up, as if fast asleep, his head tucked down into his chest as always, and one paw over the end of his grizzled grey muzzle. He looked so sweet and so comfortable as he always did when he slept. But this time there was no light in his eye, this time his eye was fixed open.

No-one said anything, there was nothing to say. They knew he was old, very old, and they knew his time was near, but their hearts ached with sadness all the same. Pippa picked him up, his body still warm from the last of his life, still warm from the sun, and she carried him back to the farmhouse where Jenny and she buried him by the stream that ran down from the hill behind the house and from which he had loved to drink.

Her ever faithful and beloved dog had gone. He had got up and left as if someone had called for him, and had wandered off in the late spring sunshine to find himself the very best spot to go to his final sleep. Pippa cried now, as did her daughter, hand in hand they both cried as they stood where Bobby lay, Jenny for her dearly loved old friend, and Pippa also. But Pippa was also crying because she knew that now with Bobby gone, that was the last full stop in the chapter which had been Jerome.

ACT FOUR

Later
Some time in the Seventies

NINETEEN

'It will restore your reputation, Dmitri,' Jerome said.

'And consolidate yours,' Boska replied.

'A filmed classic would help,' Jerome admitted, pushing the box of Havana cigars across the table to his guest. 'It would certainly be a feather in the cap.'

'Or the jewel in a crown.' Boska clipped the end of his cigar and lit it, deliberately leaving the band still in place. Boska was known to delight in the making of such social solecisms. 'Any rate, what's wrong with my reputation?' he asked. 'My reputation's not so rusty.'

'I think you mean *dusty*, my dear chap,' Jerome smiled across at Boska as he lit his own cigar. 'And no, it most certainly isn't. You're responsible for making some of the most notable British films since the war. The only trouble is, Bossy, the war's been over some while now, and man can neither live by bread alone, nor by reputation. You *need* to make another film, my dear friend, and it needs to be something remarkable.' Jerome rose, and began to pace the flag-stoned dining room. 'It needs to be the sort of film no-one else is making in this country now, or anywhere for that matter. A film which shows the depth of our native talent, on both sides of the camera, a technical and artistic *tour de force*. So naturally it must be a classic, and equally naturally it must be Shakespeare. No other country – *not in the final analysis* – they can't do Shakespeare. The Americans had a go, and not a bad go at that with *Caesar—*'

'Not bad?' Boska wondered, eyes widening. 'Not *bad*? You're talking about *Johnny Gielgud Meets The Wild One*? Pah! It had shoes of lead on, Jerry. Shoes of lead.'

395

'Mason was very good I thought,' Jerome said. 'I remember being most impressed by James Mason at the time.'

'Pah!' Boska wasn't interested in what Jerome thought critically, he was too busy remembering and savouring the film's pre-publicity. 'You remember how they bill it? It's magic. *Greater than Ivanhoe!* you remember? *Thrill to ruthless men and their goddesslike women in a sin-swept age! Thrill to traitors and heroes, killings and conspiracies, passion and violence in Rome's most exciting time!* You tell me – whoever thought up such things!'

Jerome roared with laughter, having quite forgotten the utter absurdity of Hollywood's publicity machine.

'It was like *Lust for Life*, Bossy, yes?' Jerome recalled. 'The story of Vincent Van Gogh, or *Van Goe* as they call him over there. Do you remember? *This man doesn't kiss – he crushes!*'

Both men had overlooked the main topic of their conversation and were helpless with laughter as they recalled more and more absurdities from various publicity departments when Elizabeth opened the heavily studded oak door and stared into the dining room.

'Are you two children going to stay in here all night?' she asked. 'Because if you are, I shall lock the door.'

'We're just coming, Bethy,' Jerome told her, swinging round and turning his back on Boska so that their guest couldn't see the go-away-and-leave-us-alone frown Jerome was giving Elizabeth. 'We won't be a minute.'

'You'd better not be, Jerry,' Elizabeth warned. 'I've persuaded darling Rozzie to sing, and Walter's going to do his impersonation of Charles Laughton impersonating Alfred Hitchcock.'

'We shall be with you, Bethy—' Jerome said, leaning further towards her and narrowing his eyes, 'in *five minutes*.'

'You had better be,' Elizabeth replied, brandishing the huge iron doorkey. 'Because look what Bethy's got.'

She went, banging the door deliberately hard so that it echoed across the huge room.

'Lizzie looks fine,' Boska said, drawing on his cigar. 'She looks as good as she's ever done.'

'She is fine, Bossy,' Jerome assured him. 'What is it now? It's over six years – nearly seven.'

'And no repercussion,' Boska said, as a statement of fact rather than as a question.

'Christ, man!' Jerome laughed, but his eyes didn't. 'You've seen what she's done in that time? You've seen all the work she's done!'

'Oh yes,' Boska smiled casually, 'but me – I'm not the one what live with her. That's you. You know how she really is. So you want to tell me?'

That was the last thing Jerome wanted to do. If he told Boska the truth, not only would they never get to make the film, he doubted if Elizabeth would ever work again. There were rumours, of course, there were always rumours, but rumours need to be substantiated when they concern stars of Elizabeth's magnitude, and so far, Jerome thanked God, his wife and partner had always behaved impeccably in rehearsal, on the set, and in performance. In fact never once in public had she shown any signs that all was still not entirely well with her, thanks to Jerome's careful monitoring of her condition, and the skill of her extremely private doctors.

It helped considerably, of course, that all of Elizabeth's treatment was now carried out at Sainthill, in the greatest secrecy and under the tightest possible security. The whole operation was so well organized that Jerome doubted if anyone except those immediately involved with the medication had any idea at all of what was going on, not even Miss Toothe, or the omnipresent Miss Page. Elizabeth would certainly not have confided in anyone. She was far too concerned with the keeping up of appearances, and had been well and truly warned that one indiscretion could mean the end of her illustrious career.

Oddly enough it was Elizabeth's much detested third floor at Sainthill which provided her salvation. During the summer after her release from the Hermitage, and upon the advice of her doctors, while the staff were on holiday Jerome had arranged for four of the rooms on the third floor to be converted into a private nursing suite, complete with treatment and recovery rooms. He had been persuaded of the wisdom of such a move by Sir David Appleby, Elizabeth's specialist, who was of the opinion that Elizabeth's condition could be kept in check only with regular therapy, and if this was the case then it must be carried out in private obviously, because if his patient was constantly readmitted to clinics well known for the treatment of mental disease, there would naturally be no possible chance of concealment.

So instead a private nursing home was built under the eaves of Sainthill, where if needs be Sir David Appleby and his staff could carry out any further courses of electroconvulsive therapy. Since it was now the practice lightly to anaesthetize patients before applying the electric shocks to their brains, proper facilities had to be inbuilt into the suite of rooms, so that Elizabeth could be both safely treated and her recovery properly monitored. The electric shock treatment had been deemed necessary because of the profound nature of Elizabeth's depression, and although Jerome had been aghast initially when he discovered what was proposed, he had to admit that the three courses Elizabeth had been obliged to undergo over the period of six years had removed practically all traces of her seriously depressive tendencies.

Elizabeth's diagnosed schizophrenia had, however, been a different matter, and occasioned far greater use of the private suite in the attics. Because the schizophrenia was allied with very positive manic-depressive symptoms, Sir David Appleby was confident that not only was the patient treatable but that there was a very real chance of her total recovery, provided she endured the prescribed treatment. Early on in her medication, Elizabeth, or rather the *other Elizabeth*, had fought like a wildcat both with her doctors and with her nominated psychotherapist, but once they had managed to get her on a regular course of antipsychotic drugs, in this case *chlorpromazine* administered through a series of long-acting depot injections, Elizabeth had started a remarkable recovery, one which was deemed by her doctors to be proceeding so successfully that she was allowed to return to work exactly one year after her calamitous collapse in America.

There had been setbacks, of course, occasional reappearances of the *other Elizabeth*, one or two bungled attempts early on in the treatment at self-mutilation, and one horrific but hamfisted attempt at suicide (Jerome had woken up one night to find Elizabeth trying to hang herself from their four poster bed with his dressing-gown cord), but once the anti-psychotic drugs had begun to work fully, despite some unpleasant side-effects caused by the uneven release of the *chlorpromazine* into her blood stream, the *other Elizabeth* disappeared, and the *old Elizabeth* re-emerged, bright, energetic, impulsive and mischievous, *Bethy* reborn in fact, seemingly mended and whole.

Sir David had warned Jerome that the case would never altogether be closed, because Elizabeth's behaviour needed to be monitored regularly. However, if all went well, a time would come when Elizabeth could be taken off the drugs altogether and allowed to try and lead a normal life without medication. And this was the time they had arrived at now, the time Jerome was approaching Dmitri Boska with his suggestion, a time when except for her psychotherapy, Elizabeth had been off all medication and treatment for six months without the occasion of one undue incident.

'You want to know if she can cope?' Jerome asked Boska. 'If she can hold out to the end?'

'The role's a real ballsbreaker, you know that,' Boska said. 'It's driven totally sane people monkey nuts.'

'Bethy's not insane,' Jerome retorted, annoyed. 'She never has been. She suffered a breakdown, that's all. She's a very highly strung person, she always has been. Ever since I met her, she pushed herself to her limits, as if it's a sort of challenge. To see just how hard and just how far she can stretch that prodigious talent. But insane – no. No, no, no madder than the rest of us. Because we are all mad, Bossy. That's what a lot of people have maintained, from Samuel Beckett to Mark Twain. Mark Twain said it's only when we remember we're all mad that the mysteries disappear and life stands explained.'

'That don't answer my question, clever-dick,' Boska replied, tapping an inch of smoked Havana into the saucer of his coffee cup. 'Suppose we do the film, suppose I get the money—'

'You'll get the money, Bossy, on our names alone.'

'So, supposing I do. Will she hold out?'

'Yes.' Jerome came back and sat down again opposite Boska. 'Yes she'll *hold out*, I'll stake my life on it, Bossy. And not only that, she will be the greatest *Lady Macbeth* ever.'

Boska looked at Jerome, and looked at him hard. Then he nodded and rose.

'So, OK,' he said. 'So now we go and join the party.'

TWENTY

When *Le Parc* was to be shown in Tours, Pippa considered it time to tell her daughter more about her father. When Jenny had been four Pippa had explained in the simplest terms the reasons why unlike her friends, her daughter had no father. You have a *papa*, she said, of course you do. But your *papa* doesn't live here in the farm with us because he lives in another country with another lady. Of course you'll meet him one day, darling, she'd said as the child sat on her knee by the fire, when you're bigger, when you've grown up I'm sure he'd love to see you, and see what a beautiful girl you are. But not now, *ma petite*, because he's very far away, in a far, far away land, and he's *very* busy.'

There was no point then in telling her daughter anything more, because there was nothing more a child that age could understand. As Jenny got a little older, so some of the gaps were filled in, such as how Jenny's *père et mère* had met when they were young and fallen headlong in love, but how perhaps because they were too young they were impetuous and had made a mistake. This often happened, Pippa explained, lots of people's parents married too young or too quickly and when they realized it was a mistake, they stopped being married so that they wouldn't go on hurting each other. That was all. Marriage was like all things, mistakes could be made, and it was better to realize when you'd made a mistake and call it a day, particularly when there were no children involved.

When Jenny was old enough she asked why that should be so. She said some of her friends at the *lycée* had parents who were not happy together but they stayed married because of their children. Pippa agreed this was possible, that some people would endure an unhappy marriage for the sake of their family, particularly in

Catholic countries such as France where every effort was made
to save a marriage rather than to abandon it. But when Pippa had
left Jenny's father, she was living in England, she wasn't Catholic,
and Jenny hadn't been born. Did that mean her father had never
seen her? Jenny had wanted to know. No, her father had never seen
her, Pippa had replied, without telling her that her father didn't
even know she existed, that he had no idea whatsoever that when
Pippa had left him she was in fact pregnant.

Time passed, and there was little further curiosity on Jenny's
behalf. She seemed to know all she needed to know, that her
father and mother had once loved each other, that they'd made
a mistake and parted and that it was better, much better, that
they had, because her mother was happy now, and fulfilled, and
her father was married again and he, too, was happy. Jenny was
happy, too. She loved her mother, she loved where they lived,
she was happy at school, she had many good friends, and really
she wanted for nothing. Growing up she had never really missed
having a father, because just as they say, what you never have you
never miss. Her friends used to ask her how she felt having only
a mother, having never known her father, and Jenny would tell
them the conclusion she had long ago reached, that it would have
been much, much harder if she had known her father, and if he'd
left her mother and her when Jenny could have remembered him.
As it was, he simply didn't exist, and because he didn't exist, there
was no sense of loss.

'*Non, non! Pas du tout!*' she would exclaim when it was inferred
by some of her friends that Jenny was deceiving herself. '*Ma mère
est sensas! Ma mère et moi, on est copines!*' Which was true.
As Jenny had grown up, so the bond between Pippa and she
had strengthened, until by the time Jenny was sixteen, they
were more like sisters than mother and daughter. They went
everywhere together, did everything together, argued together,
cooked together, tended their little farm together, swam in the
river together, fished together, bicycled together, and even learned
together. Both were totally bilingual, able to think and speak in
both French and in English, both were slender, both were wiry
and strong, strong from all the hard work they did together on
the farm, fit and strong from their brisk swims all the year round
in their fast flowing stretch of the Loire and from their long, hard
bicycle rides into the local towns and countryside, both had heads
of brown tousled hair and beguiling freckled faces, and both were
determined that life should never best them, Pippa because once it
had so nearly done so, and Jenny because instinctively she knew

that since her mother had left her father she had needed to fight every inch of the way, and so in return she was going to make her mother proud of her, somehow she would one day repay the debt she owed her mother, for giving her against all odds such a wonderfully happy and secure upbringing.

'I could never have done it if it hadn't been for you,' Pippa would tell her, and Jenny would laugh it off dismissively. But her mother would insist, as always getting very serious at such times. '*Mais non, Jenny,*' she would repeat, '*tu ne comprends pas, chérie. Sans toi?*' And then she would shrug. '*Rien. Sérieusement. Très sérieusement. Sans toi ma vie aurait été vide. Mais complètement vide.*'

It was true. It wasn't that Pippa couldn't have existed without Jenny, that her life would have been empty, the point she was making was that she would not have done. Often in those early years, when the money was running low, Pippa would lie awake at night, frightened and lonely in a country that was still so strange, and so real were her worries she thought seriously and regularly that she would have to concede defeat, sell up and return to England and some menial job in order to bring up her daughter. But then the next morning when she saw the sun rise over the Loire Valley, and rose to find her daughter and Nancy up as usual before her, Nancy letting the chickens out and feeding them, while Jenny collected the warm eggs up in her little apron, with Bobby at her side, barking and chasing his tail with delight as the farmyard came to life, all thoughts of failure went from her head and she would pull on her old dressing gown and hurry downstairs to breakfast in the sun-filled kitchen on home-baked baguettes and thick, sweet chocolate.

'*Au contraire, Maman,*' Jenny used to love to contradict her mother, '*rien n'était possible sans toi. Rien ici! Tu as été mon inspiration.*'

In fact the reverse was the truth. It had all been possible because of Jenny. Jenny had been Pippa's inspiration. She had been such a beautiful baby, Pippa had been inspired to draw and to paint her, and it was these early pencil sketches, pen and washes and then the subsequent oils of her daughter growing up in the charming little farmhouse in which Pippa had finally settled deep in the heart of the Loire Valley that proved their salvation. She had been persuaded to exhibit them in a local café by their postman, who was a friend of their neighbour Madame Theroux, and who fancied himself as a bit of an art connoisseur. Pippa was flattered to be asked, but also reluctant to show, since as she explained none of the pictures of Jenny were for sale.

This not unnaturally exasperated *le facteur*, who over his morning coffee and croissant in the farmhouse kitchen went into a long tirade about the absurd attitudes of amateur painters, the best of whom were always the same – they would paint first class pictures and then refuse to sell them.

'Because they don't have to,' Pippa had argued. 'Because they are amateurs.'

'But not you!' the postman had growled. 'You may be amateur, but you – you *have* to sell!'

In the end they evolved a mutually satisfactory plan of action. Pippa would show the best of her work, but it would all be marked *sold*. This way she would create an advance reputation for herself, and if anyone wanted her work, she would take commissions. By the end of the second week of her first café show, Pippa had a book full of orders, her subject matters ranging from children to their parents' prize bulls.

And now her very first model and the start of her success as a professional painter was eighteen years old this week, and the very next week her father was coming to town. Pippa had seen the advertisements for the film in the local newspaper, where it had been given a lot of coverage because the French, deciding that for once the Americans had made an unusually sensitive and intelligent movie, had given it their seal of critical approval, despite the fact that it had been garlanded with Oscars for best script, direction and acting, Jerome winning his first Oscar, and Dorothy Brooks her second. As a result of the universal good notices in Paris, *Encounter in the Park*, retitled for French consumption simply *Le Parc*, enjoyed a record breaking run and was about to go on general release throughout the country.

Of course, there was no need for Pippa to tell her daughter. There was no way Jenny could ever find out her father's real identity, because no-one from Pippa's past knew where or who she now was. She had been careful not to tell Cecil when she rang him even from which country she was calling, and where she and Jenny lived no-one called unexpectedly. Besides, now that she was accepted as a local, no-one referred to her any more as English. To the inhabitants of the village, the town and the countryside around, Pippa was simply Madame Nichole, a local smallholder and professional painter.

Even so, as she saw the advertisements for the forthcoming film posted all around the village and the town, she felt the presence of Jerome looming ever stronger in her mind, and the compulsion grew within her to tell Jenny her father's true identity. There were posters on walls everywhere in the village, of Jerome locked in an embrace with a beautiful, haunted looking blonde, and he looked so handsome, so debonair, and so unique the more Pippa stared at his image the more she felt it only right that Jenny should know exactly who her father was. It wouldn't be fair otherwise. If Pippa kept the secret, then her daughter would never have the chance to make sense of herself, to understand herself, to get herself into a proper perspective. Her father was one of the most famous actors England had ever produced, and his daughter had the right to know this, and to find out whether or not she wanted to be part of it, part of what was after all her inheritance.

It wasn't the thought that Jenny might find out later by accident, from someone other than her that decided Pippa. Pippa wasn't that sort of person. What concerned her were simply the rights and wrongs of the matter. When Jenny had been conceived, Pippa and Jerome had loved each other, so their daughter was part of that love and therefore she really had every right to know both her parents. It simply wouldn't be fair for Pippa to deny her this right, even if in the final analysis Jenny chose to go and find her father and make herself known to him, rather than stay in France with her mother and remain ignorant of who he was and what he did.

She had told Jenny that he had been an actor, naturally. Pippa knew she had to tell the truth about what Jenny's father was when Pippa was married to him, but she chose quite intentionally not to tell her daughter any more details. Too often she had heard tales of the children of the famous being victimized for their parents' notoriety, so she had kept the profile deliberately low. Whenever Jenny had asked if her father had been good, and if he had been successful, and if he was still acting, and if so in what, rather than tell her child a wilful lie, Pippa had answered the question by saying the child's father had been an actor when they were married, he had been a very good actor, a successful one, but once they had parted Pippa had no longer followed his career. So what was he called? Jenny had asked. What was his name in case he's someone we've all heard of? To which Pippa had replied with complete truth that his name was Jeremy Norman, which is what Jerome's baptized name was, and which is what his name had been up until the moment he had changed it for the now world famous name of *Jerome Didier.*

And now finally the circus was coming to town. Pippa put off the moment of revelation for as long as she could, afraid that once she had told her daughter the spell between them would be broken.

She delayed as long as possible, and afterwards she often wondered whether or not she would in fact have finally revealed her father's true identity at all had fate not forced her hand.

'*Maman? Maman!*' Pippa heard Jenny calling for her from outside after her best friend Odette's old Citroën *deux chevaux* had squeaked and clattered to a halt in the farmyard.

'I'm upstairs, darling!' Pippa called down from the top of the stairway as she heard the girls come into the kitchen. 'I was in my bath!'

'Oh—' Jenny groaned in impatience. 'Hurry up, *Maman*! I want to ask you something!'

Pippa dried herself off roughly and then pulling on her white cotton underwear and a sunfaded cornflower blouse and denim skirt, hurried barefoot down the stairs to see what the problem was.

The two girls were sitting by the fire which Nancy had laid and lit earlier against the coming chill of the evening. The October days were still warm and benign, but once the sun had slipped down behind the forests, there was already a hint of winter in the air. Jenny had Bobby's replacement on her knee, a tangle-haired bundle of mischief and unknown parentage they had rescued when it had been abandoned as a puppy in the village by some itinerants.

'Well?' Pippa asked, pouring herself a glass of wine. 'You rang?'

'Are you doing anything tonight, *Maman*?' Jenny asked, her dark eyes shining with excitement. 'Because if you're not, we'd love you to come into Tours with us. And come and see *Le Parc.*'

Pippa's heart missed a beat, and to cover her confusion she smiled vaguely and got up from her chair to check a pot on the stove which wasn't even lit. She had been meaning to tell her daughter that evening over dinner, but now events had overtaken her.

'I can't,' she said, still with her back to her daughter. 'I have to cook for tomorrow. For your birthday dinner.'

'You said you weren't going to start cooking till the morning,' Jenny countered.

'No,' Pippa said. 'I decided there's too much to do to leave it all until tomorrow. I really have to make a start this evening.'

'Oh—' Jenny moaned with genuine disappointment, the way only the young can, making the one plain syllable into at least two, if not three. Pippa smiled but remained resolute. '*Please,*' her daughter pleaded. '*Please?*'

'Please,' her friend Odette added for good measure.

'It won't be the same without you,' Jenny said.

'Nonsense,' Pippa laughed. 'You can tell me all about it when you come home. And if it's good, perhaps we can all go at the end of the week.'

'*Bien sûr*,' Jenny said. 'Lots of people at school have already seen it in Paris, and they say it's *sensas*. At least they say he is *sensas*.'

'Yes?' Pippa heard herself saying from somewhere far away. 'And who's *he*?'

Jenny groaned again, this time in mock despair as she and Odette rose to leave.

'The man in it,' she said. 'This very famous actor, Jerome Didier.'

Pippa made supper in advance of the girls' return, but she ate nothing herself as she waited. Instead she took the bottle of wine and sat in her favourite window seat in the sitting room watching the sun set and then the night fall, while she wondered what her daughter was thinking, and how and exactly when she was going to be able to tell Jenny the real identity of the man she would be watching at this very moment, a man who would undoubtedly as always be lighting up the big silver screen.

She couldn't tell her over supper, because Odette stayed. Not that Pippa could have got a word in edgeways, so intense and non-stop was the girls' conversation. The film was fantastic. It was the best film they'd ever seen. It was brilliant. It was amazing. It was incredibly exciting, and so moving. The girl was wonderful. The girl was brilliant. She was fantastic, you really believed her, you really believed in her, she was so convincing. And she was so *beautiful*. Pippa *had* to see it. She just had to, she had to see it straightaway. They'd go and see it on Wednesday. The girls couldn't wait to see it again, it was utterly and completely brilliant. And as for *him*. They sighed. They closed their eyes. They opened them and looked at each other, and laughed, then they closed their eyes again and sighed. While Pippa asked carefully, yes? Well? What about him? Oh, he was *something else*. Something else? Pippa shook her head and wanted to know what this something else was. And Jenny laughed and said her mother knew, she knew something else was something other, that it was American *argot* for something, or someone, Odette prompted, for something or someone who defied description. Which was what *he* was. He defied description, he was *so* handsome, so brilliant, such an incredible actor, and *so sexy*.

Pippa started to clear the plates away and apologized for breaking up the party.

'I don't want to spoil the fun, Odette,' she said, 'but it's very late, and it's a big day tomorrow.'

'Of course,' Odette agreed, and then with a mock horrified look at her watch admitted she had no idea of the time. Jenny saw her friend out to her car, and while they were gone, Pippa drained half a glass of wine in one and sat herself down by the remains of the fire.

Jenny came back in, singing some new song as she started to clear away the table.

'Come on,' she said to her mother. 'I'll help you do these or we'll never get to bed.'

'No, darling,' Pippa said. 'Pour yourself a drink and come and sit down.'

'I don't really want any more to drink,' Jenny said. 'I'll just finish up the coffee.' She poured herself a half-cup and then came and sat opposite her mother. 'I thought you wanted to go to bed?' she asked.

'I had to get rid of Odette,' Pippa explained, 'because I have to talk to you.'

'*Zut*,' Jenny grinned. 'I hope it's nothing *sérieuse.*'

Pippa drank some more wine, and then eased herself over in her chair to make room for her dog who had just jumped up, deciding he wished to sleep alongside her leg.

'Are you all right?' Jenny asked. 'You never normally drink so much wine.'

'No, I don't,' Pippa agreed. 'I'm trying to summon up the courage of my convictions.'

'Something is wrong, isn't it, *Maman*?'

'No, cuckoo. Nothing's wrong. Nothing's wrong except for my timing.'

'Come on, *Maman*,' Jenny said sweetly. 'You know you can tell me. You know we can talk about anything.'

'I know, darling. I know.' Pippa took a deep breath, and then dived straight in. 'Very well. It's about your father.'

'Yes? What about my father? Has something happened to him?'

'Only indirectly. You've just seen him. Although he didn't see you.' Pippa looked at her daughter and smiled, hoping her attempt at being enigmatic might remove or at least lessen any possible shock wave.

'I don't understand,' Jenny said, leaning forward. 'How could I possibly have just seen my father?'

'Think about it, cuckoo. Think about what you have just seen. Think about everything I have ever told you. About you, about me, about your father. About the father you have just seen.'

'What I have *just* seen,' Jenny said, slowly, cautiously, 'is a film. What I've just seen is *Le Parc*. And my father was an actor. No. You mean? You mean my father was in *Le Parc*?' Pippa nodded. 'My father was in *Le Parc*? Which one was he? *Maman* – there are masses of people in the movie! Which one was he?'

'I haven't seen the film, Jenny,' Pippa said. 'So if I know, how do I know?'

'Stop playing games!'

'I don't mean to.'

'Well, you are! You're playing games! You're teasing! And I don't like it!' Jenny was on her feet now, standing in front of her mother. 'Which one was my father?'

'*Ma petite—*' Pippa said, extending both her hands to her daughter. 'I'm sorry. I don't mean to tease. Not at all. I'm just trying to find in my clumsy way the best way of telling you.'

And then Jenny knew. She knew at once, and at first she smiled and raised her eyebrows, and her shoulders, and then she suddenly looked like crying, as her forehead creased into a sudden troubled frown, and as she bit hard on her lip.

'You mean that man in the film?' she whispered, 'that man? The man in the film – Jerome Didier? Jerome Didier is my father?'

'*Oui,*' Pippa nodded almost mechanically. '*Oui, ma petite, c'est vrai.*'

'*Sacre bleu,*' Jenny murmured as she sank back down into her chair. 'Jerome Didier? 'Oh *Maman. Oh merde.*'

Upstairs, later, talking it over together in Jenny's room, Jenny would keep getting up off her bed to take a long look at herself in her dressing mirror as if to make sure of who or what she looked like now she had ascertained who she really was. Whenever she did, she'd ask her mother who she thought she most looked like, her or her father, to which Pippa always replied the same.

'You don't look like either of us. You look like you.'

Pippa knew it would take time to sink in. More importantly she knew she must give it time. Jenny would have all sorts of adjustments and decisions to make, and the making of them would all require time as always. During the night she had learned the truth of her parentage, Pippa had witnessed her daughter's incomprehension, her stupefaction, her incredulity, her confusion, her wonder and finally her quiet pride, but she knew that all this

408

mixture of emotions needed to be put into the melting pot, brought to the boil, allowed to simmer and then put aside until set into their final shape.

In a way Pippa deeply regretted telling her daughter, because she knew that her hard won peace was over, and that now there would be new mountains to climb and new valleys to be negotiated. And she also knew she had made a great problem for her child, since it would be hard enough for any young person finally to discover the identity of a previously unknown parent, let alone to realize that person was one of the most idolized people of the time. But great though her present regret was, Pippa knew in her heart that it had been the right thing to do, and that had she not done it, any regret she would have felt at a later date would by then have turned to remorse, and quite possibly finally to sorrow.

For the rest of that week, and most of the week after that, Jenny was never home until late evening. Pippa knew where she was, but made no reference to these continued absences. Instead she just cooked dishes that could wait, and Pippa would wait too, until Jenny bicycled up the lane and into the farmyard at around a quarter past nine every night, at the precise time it would have taken her to catch the bus back from Tours after the first showing of *Le Parc*, pick up her cycle from behind the café in the village and complete the second leg of her long journey. Finally, mid-way through the second week, Jenny put down her knife and fork and stared across the lamp-lit kitchen at her mother.

'*Alors, Maman,*' she said. '*J'ai pensé que ça serait sympa si nous allions voir le film de Papa tous ensemble, n'est ce pas?*'

'*Je ne sais pas, chérie,*' Pippa replied. '*Je ne sais pas ce que je pense en ce moment.*'

And for once Pippa really didn't know what to think, or what to make of such a suggestion, Jenny's idea that they should go into Tours together and sit together in the darkened cinema watching a long lost lover and a newly found father up there on the screen. She was frightened, afraid for the first time for a long time that all those old and now well-buried feelings might be awoken somewhere in her, and that the sight of Jerome would resurrect her love for him, a love which for all she knew might never have really died.

'You're going to have to, sooner or later you know, *Maman,*' she heard her daughter saying.

'I'm going to have to what, Jenny?'

'You're going to have to face it sooner or later. Or rather – *him.*'

'You said that just like your father.' Pippa smiled and cut herself some cheese as a distraction. 'Or rather – *him.* A great one for the

409

telling pause, your *Papa*. Something he was taught as a young actor. How to surprise. How to take the breath in the wrong place, how to fool the audience, how to stop, to stall almost, like a car – and then – finish – *comme ça*.'

'He does that quite a lot in the film.'

'He always does it. Did it.' Pippa ate some of the local brie off her knife.

'Come on *Maman*. We really should go together.'

'Why, Jenny? Why should we?'

Her daughter smiled at her and stretched out a hand.

'Because I don't want you going by yourself.'

It was a simply wonderful film, everything Jenny had said that it was, enthralling, exciting, passionate, and finally very moving. Dorothy Brooks moved Pippa to tears, and Jerome broke her heart.

'But only on screen,' she laughed on the journey home. 'Only in the film. Otherwise, and it really is most odd, otherwise he really could have been anybody.'

'But then surely that's because it was a film?' Jenny asked, carefully breaking a bit of chocolate off and handing it to her mother. 'I mean I feel a bit the same. I look at the screen and I say that man is my father. And then another part of me says don't be so silly, that man is a murderer, or at least we think he's a murderer – oh God – isn't it awful when you think he's going to push her off the building?'

'It's terribly good,' Pippa agreed, looking for the turn they needed, 'in fact it's a marvellous film altogether.'

'Did you *think* he was a murderer? That he really was going to kill her?'

'I have to admit I have read the book. Some time ago, but I remembered the end.'

'They could have changed the end. And anyway, if you knew, *Maman*, why did you keep blocking your ears?'

'I always block my ears in the exciting bits,' Pippa laughed. 'You should know that by now.'

They drove on for a while in silence, along a straight and deserted road lined with trees.

'Are you glad you came?' Jenny finally asked. 'Are you glad you saw it?'

'Yes, darling, I am,' Pippa replied. 'And I have you to thank for it. I don't suppose I'd ever have been quite sure otherwise. Not absolutely.'

'And you are now?'

'I think so.'

'Supposing you saw him again not on the screen, but really, *Maman*. In the flesh. Would you still be sure?'

'Oh, I think so, yes. Yes. I'm sure I would.'

'Yes? How can you be so sure?'

Pippa looked sideways at her daughter, and seeing how genuinely perplexed she was, she smiled.

'I'll tell you why, *ma petite*,' she said. 'Because I didn't feel a thing when he kissed the girl. I thought I might feel a twinge of jealousy, something, but I didn't. I didn't feel a thing. I couldn't have given two hoots.'

Pippa sounded her car horn twice as she drove on with a laugh and a feeling of very real relief into the still, dark autumn night.

What Jenny did next took Pippa unawares. When she thought about it afterwards, of course, she realized such a move was entirely predictable, and if she'd had her senses about her it wouldn't have taken her so much by surprise. As it was, she was so busy preparing for her latest and biggest exhibition, to be held in the *Galerie Lefebre* in Tours, she was caught on the emotional hop. What happened was Jenny decided wanted to try acting.

She was going to play St Joan in the annual school production. She hadn't won the part by declaring her real name, because she had decided to keep her real name a secret. She had won the part by taking her chance like everyone else at the auditions, which made Pippa's concern all the greater. If somehow Jenny had been given the role as some sort of favour, since it was her last year, or if they had found out she was Jerome's daughter and cast her for that reason, Pippa would have paid little heed to the event, and while she would have enjoyed seeing Jenny attempt the role, she wouldn't have had the worry she now had, which was that Jenny might be seriously contemplating becoming a professional actress, the very last thing Pippa wanted for her. She had seen enough of the theatre and met enough of its incumbents to know that this was not the world in which she wanted her daughter to live and work. She had got to know Jenny so well, she had got to know how bright and clever Jenny was, and she knew such an intelligence could and would only be blunted in the world of the theatre.

Previously, all Jenny had been interested in doing was painting, a subject at which she excelled, her interest in art growing profoundly since her teens. Pippa had converted one of the old barns into a huge studio for them both, where they spent much time together when the work was done on the farm, or when

411

Jenny was on holiday, or at weekends when sometimes there was nothing else to do but paint. Pippa considered her daughter to be so much more talented than she herself was, but left that for her teachers to say, knowing full well that such remarks from a parent only sounded like flattery, and carried no real weight. Happily Jenny's teachers were even more enthusiastic than Pippa privately was, with the result that Jenny's work was always the centrepiece of the yearly exhibitions at the *lycée* and there was already talk of a scholarship to Paris or to London, whichever Jenny would prefer.

In fact Pippa and she were just preparing a portfolio of Jenny's work for both the nominated art colleges when Jenny broke the news she was going to play St Joan.

'What about your painting?' Pippa asked. 'What about the chance of these scholarships?'

'I didn't say I wasn't going to apply for the scholarships, *Maman*,' Jenny replied. 'All I said was I was going to play St Joan. It's only at the *lycée*. It's not at the *Sarah Bernhardt*.'

'You'll neglect your studies, Jenny,' Pippa said. 'Painting's a discipline—'

'So you always say, *Maman*,' Jenny interrupted her. 'But don't worry. I won't stop painting.'

But she did. The deeper she became involved in rehearsals, the more she neglected her work, until she finally stopped painting altogether. All this was only over the space of a few weeks, but it was long enough and the change in Jenny was profound enough to cause Pippa concern.

What caused her even more concern was her daughter's performance. Naturally Pippa was allowed nowhere near rehearsals, and while she heard Jenny practise her lines, these were just repetitions to consign the part to memory, and from listening it would have been impossible to guess either how good or how bad Jenny was going to be in the part.

She was neither. She was in truth astounding. She was defiance and she was humility, she was strength and she was frailty, she was the peasant girl and she was the martyred saint. Jenny captured everything there was to capture of the Maid, her confidence, her faith, her appeal and her rebellion. At the curtain calls, the packed audience threw their hats in the air, stood on the benches and cheered her to the rafters. That night she was without a shadow of any doubt her father's daughter.

Pippa sat while around her everyone stood. She sat not knowing whether to laugh or to cry, and then finally as the cries of *Bravo!*

echoed all around her, she too rose to her feet, climbed on her bench, and cheered her brilliant, talented daughter until she was hoarse and her tears had finally run dry.

There were only five performances, but even that number was one more than intended, the fifth performance being hastily programmed for the Saturday afternoon in response to the demand for tickets. From Wednesday to Saturday night, there wasn't a seat to be had, nor a standing space to be found which wasn't taken an hour before curtain up. Jenny's performance was the talk of Tours and its environs. Had the play been mounted in a professional theatre, everyone said it would have run for months. As it was, those who saw it counted themselves lucky, and swore they would never forget the experience.

'So,' Pippa said, after all their Sunday lunch guests had gone, after all the parties and all the celebrations were over. 'You know, I don't know what to say.'

Jenny laughed as she helped clear away.

'You don't have to say a thing, *Maman*,' she said. 'I'm the one who has something to say.' She put the pile of dishes down by the sink and then having carefully wiped her hands on her apron, came back to her mother to hug her very hard and to kiss her. 'Thank you,' she said.

'Thank me, *ma petite*? What on earth for?'

'Oh – nothing.' Jenny smiled again, and then hugged her mother once more, laughing as she did so. 'Just for being such a wonderful mother, that's all. For being you. For not asking me why? Or are you sure? Or saying I shouldn't, that you didn't want me to.' She held both her mother's hands and stood away slightly, her expression now grown serious. 'I know what you've been thinking. I know you've been worrying. But don't. There's no need to. It's just something I had to do. It's something I had to find out. And what better way? I might never have got the chance otherwise, and I'd have wondered, I'd have wondered for evermore. Which is why I love you more than ever, and which is why I say *merci, merci, merci beaucoup, Maman*.'

The very next morning when Pippa arose, she saw a light already on in the studio, and when she looked in, she found Jenny already hard at work preparing her portfolio. It was not yet seven forty-five.

At exactly seven forty-five, having filled his hired Mercedes up with gasoline, and thrown his suitcase in the trunk, Oscar Greene got in, fired the ignition, and drove off from Cannes.

413

On the fourth day of his leisurely progress through France, Oscar left Bordeaux, drove up along the Gironde estuary as far as Royan where he lunched, then rather than going on to Nantes straight- away which had been his plan, he decided instead to go east cross country through Saintes and Cognac and then further east to Limoges. He stayed overnight in Limoges, in a city famous in the sixteenth and seventeenth centuries for its porcelain and enamel, exploring it, sightseeing and buying some presents for his family before leaving on the next leg of his journey which was to take him north across country through Lussac and on to Poitiers and thence to Tours, his next designated overnight stop. Such are the vagaries of fate.

Such indeed are the vagaries of fate that if he had stuck to his original itinerary he would have missed Tours out completely and instead gone as planned to Nantes, on up to Brittany through Châteaubriant, Rennes and finally to Cherbourg for the ferry. Of course, had he done so, had he missed out on Tours, had he not seen the painting, this story would have ended with Jenny taking up one of the two scholarships which predictably enough she won, and with Pippa living peacefully and working alone (except for Nancy and Frizzle, her new dog) at the farm in the Loire Valley, her life well ordered and herself content.

Oscar's meanderings would mean a quite different conclusion. Oscar's vacational wanderings, and his last minute change of direc- tions would totally alter everyone's plans, and not just their plans, their very lives. The road north from Bordeaux is marked in two quite different directions, one road to Nantes and one to Tours. But it is pointless wondering what might have happened if Oscar had taken the left fork rather than the right and had gone to Nantes instead of Tours, because he didn't. Because he obviously wasn't meant to do so. Oscar was fated to turn right, change direction, and go to Tours instead. That was also something that was written in the stars, and not in anyone's self, not anybody's.

TWENTY-ONE

The picture, the only painting which hung in the window of the gallery, was of a small, simple, sunlit farmyard. In the right foreground a beautiful dark-haired child barefoot and dressed in a plain, faded, blue smock was sitting on her haunches feeding the chickens which had gathered round her, while behind her a slim and deeply sun-tanned woman in a plain black dress, her feet in open sandals, her bright red hair swept away from her face and tied at the back of her head by a large green ribbon, was sweeping out an empty stable. The occupant of the stable, a bay cob with a bull neck on him and a big white blaze stood in a rope bridle loosely tethered to a hitching post feeding from a haynet, the dapples on his summer coat shining in the bright, clear sunlight, while outside the yard door of the stone-built and red-tiled farmhouse with its blue painted woodwork a nearly black dog lay fast asleep, his head in his chest, and one paw curled over his muzzle. Beyond the yard and the house lay the hills and forests of the valley, a background of greens which in the distance became blues, under the light of an azure summer sky. It was oil on canvas, about 24" x 18", signed indecipherably in the bottom right hand corner, absolutely exquisite, and Oscar knew he had to have it.

'But it is sold, monsieur,' the patron informed him most regretfully. 'You do not see the small red dot, no? Ah yes, it is sold, and we could have sold him more than twenty time.'

'You don't sound exactly overjoyed it's sold,' Oscar said. 'And I have to tell you, I feel exactly the same.'

'No, no, monsieur. I like him to be sold. My regret it is these artists are so slow. So slow. This artist – I could sell six a day! I

415

could! Oh yes!' The owner of the gallery laughed, and with a shrug pointed to all the paintings on the walls. 'You see?' Oscar hadn't. He'd been too busy examining the painting in the window. Now he turned and saw all the other paintings on exhibition. 'Every one sold, monsieur. Every single one.'

Oscar stared at what must have been a collection of at least two dozen oils, and a dozen or so pencil or pen and ink drawings. 'You mean it?' he said. 'Every single one?'

'The day of the private view—' the owner shrugged his shoulders, pursed his lips and then exhaled emphatically. 'I sell them all.'

'Excuse me.'

Oscar went and walked round the gallery, quickly at first to make sure they were indeed all sold, which they were, and then slowly, to examine each and every exhibit. Oscar had started collecting paintings in earnest after the success of *Tatty Gray*, mostly the works of little-known English and French painters from about 1920 to around 1950. He only ever bought what he loved. He never bought anything he was advised to buy, nor anything that was fashionable. He simply looked for paintings which had he been able to paint, he would have painted, and when he found such paintings, he bought them.

Every one of these exhibited works fell into that category. Most of the drawings were of one particular child, the child in the farmyard, and Oscar could understand why because the girl was so enchanting, with her mop of dark hair, her wide, honest eyes, and the smudge of freckles which ran over her pretty nose. There were studies of the girl when she was a baby, some lying on her mother's bed while the red-haired woman in the farmyard painting was dressing her for bed, or drying her after her bath, or simply just playing a game with the baby, and there were studies of the child from what looked like its first uncertain steps, holding on to a hand belonging to an unseen and unportrayed person, to sketches of her bending down to stare at a baby chick, of her curled up asleep on an old sofa in the corner of a sunny room, of her sitting at a kitchen table with a glass of lemonade, and an absolutely exquisite study in pen and brown ink of the child aged about five, Oscar guessed, standing between the mighty front legs of the big bay cob, while the horse looked down curiously and tenderly, his white-blazed nose just nuzzling the top of the child's mop of curly brown hair.

The paintings were mostly landscapes, of either the countryside where the artist lived, or of the surrounding villages. There were some interiors but these were in the minority, although Oscar considered they were probably the best of all the paintings, particularly one of a simple, sparely furnished café, inhabited by just three men and the patron, the men standing at the bar in the uniforms of their work, a postman, a workman in his dusty blue overalls, and a railway employee, while behind them *le patron* stood sideways, reading his daily paper. It was an immensely atmospheric painting, and the artist had precisely captured a moment in a day, and the light of that day, a sunlight which had been filtered down to a bluish haze through the smoke of the men's cigarettes. Oscar stood staring at this painting longer than at any of the others, with the exception of the little masterpiece in the window, totally absorbed by it, drawn into its depicted world, and into the actual moment the painter had so brilliantly captured for all time.

'You have good judgement, monsieur, if I may say it,' the gallery owner murmured behind him, 'if, as I think, you think this the best.'

'I'd say it was outstanding,' Oscar replied. 'But then the entire collection is remarkable. Do you really have nothing else by this artist? I simply have to buy some of his work.'

'No, monsieur.'

'You have nothing else?'

'No, I have nothing else, and no, the artist is not a *he*. The artist is a woman, monsieur.'

Oscar gave him a look of surprise and then leaned forward in another attempt to decipher the signature.

'No,' he sighed. 'I give up, I'm afraid. I can't make it out at all.'

The owner nodded, and then produced a catalogue from his pocket which he handed to Oscar.

'Philippa Nichole,' he said. 'She is a local artist.'

Oscar flipped through the catalogue in the hope of finding out some further information about the painter, but there was only the briefest of biographical sketches, and no photograph, nor any indication of where she lived and painted beyond saying it was in a small farm somewhere in the Loire Valley.

'Look,' Oscar said, handing the gallery owner back the catalogue which the owner insisted Oscar keep. 'Thank you,' he said, 'but I really have to buy something of this artist's. Does any other gallery carry her work? Could you tell me where she lives? Do you have a phone number?'

The owner smiled, and Oscar knew the smile, because he had seen it so often. It was the *you-Americans* smile, but Oscar had long since grown used to it, and it no longer infuriated him.

417

'I'm a serious collector,' Oscar added, instantly regretting doing so, because the remark simply earned an even more patronizing smile.

'I'm afraid I cannot tell you Madame Nichole's address,' the owner said. 'It is against the gallery's policy. I could, perhaps, telephone her on your behalf? Yes? Although you must understand that any transaction would have to come through here. Through the gallery.'

'Sure,' Oscar said, deliberately allowing his impatience to show. 'You bet. Now I have very little time here, so if you'd be so kind.'

Again, the *you-Americans* smile. We know you, *here today, gone today.*

'Of course, monsieur. If I could perhaps have your name?'

'Sure,' Oscar said, turning back to his favourite picture of the bar. 'It's Mr Greene.'

The line was very bad, and Jenny could hardly hear what Monsieur Pinguet was saying as she wrote down the message, having told him her mother had gone to the village to collect her car from the garage.

'No, no!' she shouted back down the line. 'Don't make the poor man wait! My mother won't mind – not at all! Please, Monsieur Pinguet – can you still hear me? Good! No – listen to me – send him out here now! Yes – today is fine! My mother will be back by the time he gets here – and I know she won't mind! If you remember she has the St Cholet canvases! And all the sketches she did at Chaumont! At the fair! I know, monsieur! I know the arrangement! Don't worry! I will remind her!'

Nancy came in from outside, attracted by Jenny's shouting.

'Oh heck,' she laughed. 'It's you on the phone! I thought you were being strangulated.'

'Fetch up some wine, Nancy,' Jenny said on the move, 'while I go and open up the studio. Some rich Yank's on his way out here, who apparently will buy anything with *Maman*'s name on it!'

'You don't say, Jenny,' Nancy replied, looking for the key to the cellar. 'Who is he? Nelson Rockefeller, I hope.'

But Jenny had gonesed all the way across to the studio by Frizzle. So Nancy glanced at the paper with the details of the telephone message and saw their caller was alas not to be Nelson Rockefeller, but someone called plain Mr Gray.

*

Oscar had never seen anywhere as idyllic. He had no idea of the climate of the Loire Valley, so he couldn't imagine what winter in such a remote spot might be like, but even if it snowed solidly for six months Oscar knew he could take it. He could take anything to live in such a profoundly beautiful place. It was nothing but superb woods, forests, lakes and chateaux, and towns and villages of such inordinate charm that Oscar felt he could move into this part of France tomorrow, except when he saw the farmhouse, he realized that even tomorrow wouldn't be soon enough.

He had left his car at the foot of the track under the shade of an enormous chestnut tree and by a field full of wild flowers and songbirds, to walk the last hundred yards or so up to the house which he could see before him. As he stood to drink in the setting and the view, the red-haired woman in the painting appeared at a gate ahead, leading in two cows which were ready for milking. She didn't see Oscar, as she walked into the farmyard in front of the cows which were ambling happily behind her, nor did she pay any attention to a white goat on top of a nearby wall, who seemed to be busy consuming what looked to Oscar suspiciously like an article of clothing.

The dog saw him first as he shot out of the field after the cows and the red-head, stopping at the entrance to the yard the moment he sensed there was a stranger about. Then he turned and staring back down the track with his tail sticking up like a flag, flattened his ears and began to bark a loud warning.

'OK!' Oscar called. 'Good dog! It's OK!' while continuing to walk up towards the house. He wasn't altogether sure about the dog. It was big, lean and tough looking, with a long pointed muzzle and short, grey, wiry coat, some sort of cross, Oscar reckoned, between a sheepdog and a hound, some sort of very cross cross, because the dog had full control of the right of way and didn't seem inclined to relinquish it.

The red-head rescued him, appearing momentarily from behind a farm building in the process of steering one of the cows back into the yard by means of a stick laid on its quarters.

'It's all right! He won't harm you!' she shouted, and then called the big dog off. 'Frizzle!'

The dog stopped barking for a moment until the red-head disappeared again, then he picked up a large stick and ran down the track towards Oscar, who was wondering what on earth an Irish girl was doing in the middle of the Loire. The dog dropped the stick at Oscar's feet and resumed barking, a different bark this time, a come-on-and-throw-my-stick sort of bark. Oscar hurled the stick into the adjacent field and the dog hurled himself after it.

There was no-one visible in the yard as Oscar strolled in, the dog back by his side now, jumping up behind him and nearly knocking Oscar over in his determination to get his stick thrown again. Oscar wrested it from the dog and chucked it obligingly out of the yard before taking stock of his surroundings. It was exactly like the painting. Except the red-head wasn't sweeping out any stable, he could see her now in the far barn, setting about milking one of the cows. There was no child either, and no sleeping black dog. But there were the chickens, and he could see the horse in the field behind the house, two horses in fact, and he was right, the goat had been eating an article of clothing, and it still was. It was up on the wall above him happily munching its way through what looked like a pair of girl's cotton briefs. And there was someone at the window of the farmhouse, someone he could only vaguely make out since the sun was shining directly on the windows. Oscar put his hand up to his eyes to look at the person who was looking back down at him, and as he did so something hit him with terrific force in the back, giving as it did so a huge whoop of canine pleasure.

He'd have kept his footing had it not been for the cows. As it was the dog knocked him forward into something one of the cows had conveniently dropped and Oscar lost his legs, went up in the air, and performed a classic pratfall straight back down into the freshly deposited pat.

In the midst of his confusion and embarrassment he heard laughter from within the house and then, as he tried to get back up to his feet, someone running down stairs and out across the cobbled yard.

He'd already recognized the laugh, he'd sworn he knew the laugh the moment he'd heard it, and when he looked up he found he was right, when he looked up and found himself looking into a face he had thought he would never, ever see again.

'I don't believe it!' Pippa said, still laughing all the while the tears filled her eyes. 'I just don't believe it. Oscar.'

'You've lost some weight.'

'I found a great diet. You get influenza and then you go on holiday to Spain.'

'I wonder. If I'd seen you in the street, I wonder if I'd have recognized you.'

'You mean it was only me falling for your cow's practical joke that gave me away?'

'You do look different.'

'That's just cosmetic. I was getting tired of people asking me whenever they saw me dressed up what happened – had I fallen over?'

Pippa laughed and poured Oscar some more wine.

'I'm not sure I should,' Oscar said. 'I have to drive home.'

'Where's home?'

'Oh, still America. The land of the Free and the Easy. The land with thirty-two television channels and only one sauce.'

'And you never married.'

'No, Madame Nichole, no, I never married. I guess I've never been that cold.'

'Sorry. I don't understand.'

'Shelley Winters said she was so cold once she almost got married.'

'Stop it,' Pippa laughed. 'Jenny's going to be sick.'

'It's not that I haven't thought about getting a playmate,' Oscar continued, the wind now well and truly under his tail. 'It's just that if I ever do, I'm not sure I'll purchase. I think maybe I'll just lease.'

'No, please stop it,' Jenny begged. 'Please.'

'At least I still have my hair,' Oscar sighed. 'Not like poor old "Bossy" Boska. You remember Dmitri Boska, Madame Nichole?'

'You know who Mr Greene means?' Pippa said to her daughter. 'He produced most of your father's first films.'

'Didn't he also just produce his *Macbeth* as well?' Jenny asked.

'You got it, Mademoiselle Nichole,' Oscar said. 'Well, the poor guy's completely bald now. But that's about all he's lost, his hair. He's still the same old Boska. He's still got his teeth. He was sitting in his club recently, so they tell me. And this other producer, one of his rivals, he comes up behind him and runs his hand over Bossy's bald head. "My, Bossy," he says, "that feels just like my wife's behind." So what does Bossy do? He strokes his own head thoughtfully and he says "Yah, Michael," he says, "yah, so it does." '

'That's quite enough, Oscar,' Pippa said, as helpless as her daughter was with laughter. 'This daughter of mine hasn't left school yet.'

'Not yet, but nearly,' Jenny said. 'One month exactly.'

'What are you going to do then, Mademoiselle Nichole?' Oscar asked.

'I'm going to London,' Jenny said. 'I've got a scholarship to the Slade.'

*

421

'She's a better painter than I am,' Pippa said later in the evening as she was showing Oscar round their studio. 'Or if she isn't now, she's certainly going to be.'

'I don't think that's so,' Oscar said. 'Jenny's a very different painter to you. And when she's older, she's going to be even more different.'

'Have you got different, Oscar?' Pippa asked. 'Now you're older?'

'You bet,' Oscar said. 'I'm even more different than I was before.'

'Seriously, Oscar.'

'Seriously. I guess I was odd before, but you should see me now.'

'*Seriously*, Oscar.'

'I've always found it hard to be serious, Pippa, in public. You know that. But if you really want to know—'

'I wouldn't have asked otherwise.'

'OK. So yes, yes I am different. I no longer jump Jim Crow – you know, *rewrite this, Oscar will you? Here, Oscar, this needs breathing on. Oscar? You got time to cast your eye over this? For old times, Ozzie, know what I mean?* I stopped all that some time ago, stopped being the rewrite man. I thought it was time I did my own thing again, rather than being a paid lackey the rest of my so-called life.'

Oscar picked up one of the St Cholet canvases, a woodland painting of foresters at work, an oil full of movement and vigour.

'Were you anyone's lackey in particular?' Pippa asked, sorting through some more canvases in the corner.

'Sure,' Oscar said. 'I'd become the resident Yank at the court of King Jerome.' Pippa glanced up at him, and Oscar handed her back the painting. 'It's no good,' he said. 'I'm going to have to buy all your stuff.'

'Go on about Jerome,' Pippa said, handing him another painting, a river view this time, a quiet stretch of the Loire late on an autumn evening.

'I can just feel it,' Oscar said, standing back from the easel he had set the painting upon. 'I can feel the end of the day's sun, that damp you get in the air, right? Late September, early October, the moment the light fades and the dew comes out of the ground. The gentle but persistent surge of the water. It's all there.'

'Go on about Jerome.'

'I was Master of the King's Remington. Lord Fixit of the Cock-up. Whatever needed rewriting, I rewrote it. Not plays, mind you, I wasn't allowed near the plays. The plays were reserved for serious writers. You know, guys with the beginnings of beards in black leather jackets who think while they write, right? Which just isn't possible. You know anybody who can do two things at the same time and do both of them equally well? I don't. Anyway, my job was to rewrite all these films Jerome and Lady Jerome had to make to keep the Court of the Didiers going. You sure you want to hear all this, Pip?'

'I just want to hear what happened to you,' Pippa said. 'What happened to make you different.'

'You mean that?'

'Yes. Why shouldn't I?'

'You don't want to hear it because you're curious about Jerome.'

'I want to hear it because I'm curious about you.' Pippa handed him the last painting, the only one he hadn't seen. Oscar didn't even look at it.

'Why?' he said. 'Why are you curious about me?'

'Because I've thought of you often,' Pippa said. 'That's why.'

'You know something, Madame Nichole?' Oscar grinned. 'If I was a bell, I'd go *ding-dong ding-dong ding*.'

Back by the fireside, with all the rest of the household asleep, Pippa and Oscar sat on the floor drinking Armagnac and talking it all over. Pippa told him all that had happened to her, right up to Jenny's discovery of the full identity of her father, and the subsequent discovery of her prodigious acting talent, and her decision to go to art rather than drama school, then Oscar brought Pippa up to date on how he had excused himself from the court of Sainthill, returned to America to do, as described, his own thing, and languished for two years in the Hollywood wilderness, until a director named Jim Asher who'd just made a big hit with a movie called *Dumb Talk*, read an original script of Oscar's over one weekend he was hiding out from his about-to-be ex-wife at Oscar's apartment, and called him the following weekend to say he had the go-ahead from Columbia to put Oscar's script in production.

'That script had been through every goddam production office in that crazy town,' Oscar said. 'But then that's Hollywood. And that's something you learn out there. You learn that there are more of them than there are of us. I've written four movies since, and they've all been made. They just showed my latest in Cannes, *The Streetfighter*, with Robert Nissen. It didn't win any prizes, but then it wouldn't. It's got a story line. But it's doing great at the box office. In fact it's doing so well, next month they're going to show it in the cinema. So there you are. The story so far. Here I am. I got about as far as I can go. I know that's the case because I now have detractors. When you're nobody, all you have is friends. But when you're somebody, you have detractors. No really, people write things about me, really rude things, which is a compliment, it shows I've arrived. You know, they do things like wonder out loud in print why such lousy writers as me should be successful. They don't see the reason. They don't see the reason why so many lousy writers are successful is because so many people have such lousy taste.'

Pippa laughed and shook her head.

'You don't believe that for one minute, you don't believe any of it, and neither do I, Oz,' she said. 'And you certainly don't believe for a moment you're a lousy writer.'

'You're kidding, Pip,' Oscar replied. 'If I didn't I'd never write another goddam word. Now will you marry me?'

Pippa stared at him speechlessly, her glass of Armagnac halfway to her mouth, frozen *en route*.

'What are you looking like that for?' Oscar asked, lighting a cigarette.

'What do you mean, *now* will I marry you? I don't remember you asking me before.'

'I didn't,' Oscar agreed. 'What I meant by now will you marry me, was I reckon that now is a good time.'

'For what, Oscar?'

'For us to get married, Pippa.'

He leaned over and gently took the glass of brandy which Pippa was about to spill down her front.

'So?' he said. 'Oscar's waiting.'

'I don't know what to say, Oz,' Pippa replied. 'I'm sorry. I really don't.'

'OK,' Oscar agreed, 'so I'll do the talking. I'll tell you why this is a good time. I'm doing very well. Better than I've ever done, maybe better than I'll ever do. But whatever happens, from now there's no chance of me starving. Sure I was kidding about being a lousy writer, but I wasn't kidding about not thinking that I'm any good. Because I don't. I just know I can write. If I knew *what* I could write, I wouldn't write. More importantly, you're terrific.'

Pippa looked at him, but Oscar was poker faced. 'A terrific painter I mean. You really are.'

'No, I'm not.' Pippa interrupted.

'There you are! You must be!' Oscar exclaimed. 'Because you think you're not. Anyway, the point is—' Oscar frowned, and drew deeply on his cigarette. 'The point is I love what you do. What you have in you. As they say nowadays where I come from

424

– I love where you're at. When I saw that painting, the painting of Jenny in the farmyard, when I saw all your other paintings, I had to have them. All of them. I never felt like that before in my whole life about anything. Because it wasn't just wanting the paintings, although I didn't understand that. I wanted the person who painted them, the person who had all that inside them, not necessarily the talent, but that spirit, the feeling that was in the paintings and the drawings, whoever had all that inside of them I wanted.'

'Supposing it had been a man?' Pippa asked.

'Very funny,' Oscar replied. 'OK, so if it had been a man, I'd have had a sex change. Now may I continue?'

'If it means you're going to buy some more of my paintings, fire ahead.'

'I can't remember where I was now, smarty-pants.'

'You wanted this painter, whoever he or she may be.'

'You're damned right I did.'

'And now that you've met her?'

'Now I know why I wanted those paintings. Look, I've bought paintings in all sorts of places, but I can tell you, having met some, the last people I ever want to meet are the artists. Most of them are – what did Shaw call them? *Dubedats*. Why your paintings spoke to me, is because it was *you* speaking, Pip. And you see, you see – I'm afraid I'm not going to be able to finish this,' he said.

'It's all right,' Pippa put in. 'You don't have to.'

'I do, Pippa, you're wrong,' Oscar said. 'I have to finish it. I have to find some way to tell you I love you. I have to find some way to tell you that I've always loved you. And have you got any suggestions?'

Pippa sighed deeply, and took one of Oscar's strong square hands in her slim brown ones.

'I don't know, Oz,' she confessed. 'You could try saying it.'

'I don't think so, Pip. You know me. I'd probably bite my tongue.'

They stared at each other in silence for a while, and then Oscar put his other hand over Pippa's.

'I'll tell you what,' he said. 'Maybe if you said how you felt. Maybe that would help.'

'We could try,' Pippa agreed, and then thought for a while. 'Can I have a cigarette?' she asked.

'You don't smoke.'

'I know. I just thought I'd like to try one.'

Oscar lit her a Lucky Strike, and passed it over to her. Pippa took it and took a puff, taking care not to inhale.

425

'OK,' Oscar said. 'So now you're having your first cigarette. So now you're a grown up. So put away all childish things, and now tell it like a woman.'

Pippa handed him back the cigarette, and pulled her knees up under her chin.

'There was only one person I missed,' she said finally. 'After I left Jerome, I didn't miss anybody, besides Jerome obviously. But then when I stopped missing him, when I really did a spring clean and knew I had to start all over again, there wasn't anyone, or anything, or anywhere I missed, except you.'

'Hey,' Oscar said. 'I like that. Or are you just saying what I would have you say?'

'I've just said it, Oscar, and I meant it,' Pippa warned him, 'and if you're going to barrack. If you're going to be facetious—'

'I'm sorry, Pip,' Oscar said, meaning it. 'I hate the fool in me. Really. It's just that this is a place I never expected to be.'

'What is? This house? The Loire?'

'No. I never expected to be *here*. At a moment like this, I mean. With you. Now please go on.'

'I don't know why I missed you,' Pippa continued, almost defensively. 'At least I didn't. I didn't then. I thought it was just because you were a friend, because we'd been such friends, in fact I suppose you were my only real friend.'

'Besides Jerome.'

'Besides Jerome.'

'And?'

'And then. Then I often used to sit and think why were we such friends. And I came to the conclusion we were such friends because we liked so many of the same things, and because we could talk, and because you made me laugh. No-one, at least this is what I thought, no-one ever made me laugh like you did. Not even – not even Jerome. I used to sit here late at night, or up in my bed, and remember how you would talk, and tell me stories, and tease me, and crack jokes, and all I could think about was all the laughter we had shared, and now, then, then suddenly there wasn't any. Not for a long time here, at least it seemed like a long time. There was no laughter, no-one to laugh with, no-one who could make me laugh. Because there was nothing to laugh at. Which is why I thank God for Jenny. When Jenny was born, and as she started to grow up into herself, and become a person – however small at first – it sort of came back. The ability to laugh. And when it did, when Jenny and I used to play together, simple games at first, when she was tiny, and then hide and seek, and that sort of thing as she grew

426

older, and we all used to giggle and laugh, Jenny, and Nancy and me, then I remembered you again. Every time I laughed, I used to remember the other times, and somehow you were always there. Which was why I never thought about you. I couldn't bear it any more, to think that I'd never see you again, I suppose, at least I suppose that's the reason why I put you out of my mind. Why I refused ever to think about you again. I haven't thought about you for years.'

'And now?' Oscar asked, looking at the face he had always loved, warmed by the glow of the firelight. 'Now that we're laughing again, together. Because you have laughed today. And so have I, and for real. Probably for the first time since I last laughed with you. I mean if I manage to say it, if I find a way somehow to tell you I love you, what would you do?'

'I don't know, Oz. I don't know.'

'OK. I'm going to give it a go. I love you, Pip. You hear me? I love you. So what are you going to do?'

'I don't *know*, Oscar!' Pippa repeated. 'I don't honestly know!'

'You don't know what to do? Or you don't know if you love me?'

'I don't know anything, Oscar! I'm the most useless, stupid bloody woman in the world!'

He was on his feet in a second, and he had her up on her feet too, long before she could start crying the tears she wanted to cry.

'Oh no you don't,' he said. 'That's not an answer to anything.'

'What isn't?'

'Tears. You can't see your way through tears.'

'Have you got a better idea?'

'Yes. If you don't know whether you love me, but I do,' Oscar replied, 'then I think the only thing for it is to go to bed.'

'Us, you mean? You mean for us to go to bed?'

'You got it. I think we should go to bed and make love.'

'I haven't made love to anybody since I left Jerome.'

'You won't have forgotten how.'

'What about you?'

'I haven't forgotten how either.'

'I meant— I meant—'

'I know what you meant, and I don't think it's any of your dam' business.'

Pippa looked at him and saw the spark in his eye.

'All right. Then why do you think we should go to bed?'

'Why do I think we should go to bed.' Oscar rubbed his chin. 'OK – one: I think it would be fun. In fact I'm sure it would be. Sex is

427

certainly the most fun you can have, you know, without smiling.'

Pippa smiled.

'Good,' said Oscar. 'And two: I think you might find out that way, whether or not you love me. And if you don't, OK. If you don't, at least I'll have a reason for going away unhappy.'

Oscar didn't have to wait that long, and he didn't have to go away unhappy. Pippa knew she loved him the moment he took her in his arms there and then and kissed her. But she didn't tell him. She made him wait. She made him wait until he'd made love to her, and then she told him.

'All right, Oscar,' she whispered to him. 'I love you.'

'Of course you do,' Oscar sighed. 'You'd never have come to bed with me otherwise.'

They were married two months later on a blazing hot day in July. It was a civil ceremony, and afterwards there was a party for all Pippa's friends and neighbours in George's Bar in the village. The celebrations lasted long into the night, but by then Oscar and his bride were on their way to Provence, for a weeklong honeymoon which they spent at a small hotel high in the hills above Grasse. On their return they continued their honeymoon, lazing the long hot August days away at the farm, walking, bicycling, swimming in the river, fishing, Pippa painting, Oscar writing, and both of them making love. Come September they began making preparations for Jenny's departure to London and art school, with Oscar making discreet arrangements for his stepdaughter's accommodation, since it had long been agreed between mother and daughter that she would travel and study under her mother's 'adopted' French name of *Nichole*.

'As a matter of fact, *Maman*,' Jenny concluded during the preparations for her departure, 'it's even easier now, now that you've remarried. I can be Jane Greene, which is even more anonymous. There's no way they could ever connect me with my father now.'

It was a sensible precaution, since Pippa had always worried just in case someone had made the connection between her as Philippa Nichole and her as Pippa Nicholls. It would be most unlikely, but there was always the slim chance of a coincidence, or a clever piece of detective work, or of some connection or other being made, and the last thing she wanted was her daughter being hounded by the Press. At least that is what she told herself, that is what she allowed to be known. Privately and in truth what Pippa really dreaded was Jerome finding out and claiming her, not legally because he had no grounds, but emotionally.

She had been very honest with Jenny about this, as was always Pippa's way.

'Your father is not just a very attractive man,' she had said. 'He is one of the most attractive men you could imagine, just as attractive off-screen or stage as he is on. This isn't usually the case, Jenny. Actors in their private lives can sometimes be much less than the sum of their parts, and are either shy, shallow or just plain dull. Your father is irresistible. So if you do ever meet him, be careful, that's all.'

Jenny had laughed dismissively, and said firstly she had no plans to meet her father, and even if she did, she'd be so overcome in advance that she would run a mile at just the thought of it. And then when she had seen the doubt cloud her mother's face, she had hugged her reassuringly, and told her she had no desire whatsoever to meet her father, because since he was such a famous actor she had the privilege of always making the best of him, without ever having to know the worst.

'So now here you go,' Pippa said as she helped close up Jenny's suitcases. 'It seems such a very little time, and now you're leaving home.'

She said it very factually, not despondently or remorsefully, although she naturally felt regret. But she had to say it because she felt it, she felt how short the time had been since Jenny was a child, a child playing outside in the yard, the child in the painting.

'You know,' Jenny said, squeezing her largest case finally shut. 'I was thinking last night as I lay awake. That if you hadn't remet Oscar, I think I'd have cancelled. I don't think I could have left.'

'I'd have been all right. I've managed before.'

'Not really, *Maman*,' Jenny smiled. 'You've always had me. You were carrying me when you arrived here. We've always been together.'

'I shall miss you, darling,' Pippa said. 'It's no good pretending. Then it never is. But you're right, if I hadn't married Oscar, you wouldn't have gone. Because I don't think I could have let you go.'

'I'm not leaving home, *Maman*,' Jenny said as they embraced. 'When you've been as close as we have—'

'Past tense,' Pippa said. 'There you are, putting us in the past tense.'

'OK,' Jenny laughed. 'When two people are as close we *are*, you don't leave home. You never leave home. You can't leave where your heart is.'

'Until you fall in love.'

'But you're in love! So what are you talking about! You'll be thrilled to pieces once I'm on that plane! You and Oscar will have this wonderful place all to yourselves!'

'Damn. You've seen through me. I thought I was putting up a pretty good show.'

'You were, *Maman*,' Jenny said, and kissed her. 'But then you always do.'

Oscar accompanied Jenny to London. The plan was that he should help settle her in, since he had to be in London for business before flying back to New York to wind up his domestic affairs there, although it was agreed between Oscar and Pippa that Oscar should keep on his apartment in Manhattan as there was no doubt he would be having to commute to the States regularly.

'Don't you count on it,' he'd said. 'The game plan is with decreasing regularity. If you want to be a popular writer, be dead. And if you can't be dead, be the next best thing, absent.'

As far as settling Jenny in, everything went according to plan. Oscar had chosen lodgings for her with the greatest circumspection, in the house of a second cousin of his who had married a banker, a household which had no connection with the theatre or the cinema whatsoever. Jenny took to the family at once, and they to her, the house was extremely convenient to the college, and Oscar's second cousin had a pretty daughter called Susie who was the same age as Jenny and in her second year studying English at London University. When Oscar stopped by on his way home from New York, again having been diverted to London for some further talks on his latest movie, he found Jenny more than happy with her situation. She loved the Slade, she loved her lodgings, she was great friends with Susie, and had made plenty of new friends at college.

'Tell *Maman* not to worry,' Jenny instructed Oscar. 'Tell her it's like a second home.'

All this Oscar duly reported back to Pippa, who was delighted to hear it. She had been worried that she might have made the wrong decision, allowing Jenny to go to London rather than insisting she went to Paris, but Oscar praised the decision, because it was something Jenny wanted, and when people got what they wanted, the responsibility for the decision and the consequences of making it were theirs and theirs alone.

'So now let's have a drink, sweetheart,' Oscar said, mixing them a Martini apiece, 'and then some of that food you've been cooking that smells just out of this world.'

'Oz,' Pippa began at one point over dinner.

'No,' Oscar said at once. 'No dice, Mrs Greene. Jenny is fine. She couldn't be happier. So raise your glass, and drink to us. Believe me. You really have nothing to worry about.'

As a writer, Oscar should have known better than to be quite so confident. Oscar knew his Somerset Maugham. As a student of English he'd read *The Summing Up* time and time again until he practically knew it by heart. So if he'd really given it some thought he'd have recalled Maugham's dictum that really the only thing you can be utterly certain about is that there is very little about which you can be certain.

Which indeed was the case in this instance. For the time Oscar had chosen to give Pippa such a confident assurance that all was well was the time Elizabeth Laurence decided she was going to leave Jerome, and it was that decision and none other which drew Pippa's daughter inexorably into her father's life.

TWENTY-TWO

Elizabeth blamed it all on *Macbeth*. Not that she ever called the play by its rightful name. In the superstitious tradition of the theatre she elected to refer to it at all times as *The Scottish Play*, maintaining like all actors that the play was bad luck, and with good reason since practically every previous production of the tragedy had either suffered terrible luck, freak accidents, or sometimes had even been tainted with tragedy of their own, such as the death of one of the leading players. No-one ever enjoyed doing *The Scottish Play*, it was said, and Elizabeth Laurence was determined not to join their number.

She had argued and pleaded with Jerome about the wisdom of them performing it, but in the end he had prevailed, mostly by dint of persuading her that she would make the greatest Lady Macbeth of them all. And he had been proved right. When the film, which Jerome himself directed, was finally shown it was an unparalleled artistic, critical and popular success, winning five Oscars, for best actor, best actress, best director, best cinematography and best costume, and it established the Didiers beyond any reasonable doubt as the undisputed monarchs of both the British theatre and its cinema. It also ended their marriage.

Afterwards Jerome argued to his friends that the marriage had been foundering for some time, and his friends had all done their best to express the necessary surprise, since most of them had seen the writing on the wall well in advance of Jerome. They all knew of Elizabeth's affairs, which equally they all knew Jerome liked to think of as just flirtations, and likewise those with their ears closest to the ground knew that once or twice these *flirtations* had very nearly ended with Elizabeth doing a bolt over Sainthill's old

432

monastic wall, particularly when she became hopelessly infatuated with Russ Jason, the American actor who had co-starred with her in the psychological thriller *Someone At My Door*. Jerome had become very agitated at this time, and had stepped very quickly in once filming was over to rush Elizabeth away to the other side of the world for an unscheduled holiday, his given reason being that the content of the film had greatly upset Elizabeth and as a consequence she had been ordered to take a complete rest.

What happened when they got to their island was the very opposite of the publicly imagined peace and quiet. From the moment they landed on Paradise Island to the moment they upped and left prematurely, Jerome and Elizabeth fought incessantly and violently. In her memoirs Elizabeth was to claim that Jerome mocked her and beat her constantly, in an effort to break her will and get her to agree to the filming of *Macbeth*, a project she claimed he knew would set the seal on his reputation, after which she said he had planned to discard her for an actress called Catherine 'Kikki' Bentall. In his own autobiography, while admitting that he had enjoyed a brief affair with Catherine Kendall, Jerome claimed there were no serious intentions on either side, while discounting totally Elizabeth's allegations of violence. In fact Jerome was to argue that the very reverse was true, that he himself had been the subject of constant verbal and physical assaults by Elizabeth, and fearing once again for her sanity he had relented to her persistent demands that they return home immediately.

That was the only concession Jerome made. Again, they both would have differing accounts of what happened on their arrival back in England, Elizabeth maintaining that Jerome kept her a virtual prisoner at Sainthill with the connivance of her doctors, while he visited her American lover who had stayed over in London, and successfully deterred him with such wildly exaggerated accounts of Elizabeth's mental instability that the actor took fright and the very next plane out, back to his long-suffering wife in California. For his part, Jerome would later dismiss these assertions as nonsense, arguing that Russ Jason had already got wind of the rumours concerning Elizabeth's mental health and had long since flown by the time the Didiers returned from their truncated holiday. His argument was the most convincing since it proved conclusively that from the moment filming stopped on *Someone At My Door* and Jerome whisked Elizabeth out of the country to the time they returned from abroad, Elizabeth never saw or heard from her American co-star again, which would mean there was no way of her knowing whether or not Jerome had visited Jason or indeed what he might have told him.

In the Hebrew culture, there is a maxim which runs that there is *your story, there is my story, and then there is the true story*, which was doubtless the case in this instance, because when Jerome and Elizabeth arrived back in England, what happened was something different altogether. What happened was that Elizabeth went to bed with Cecil.

Like Jerome, over the years Elizabeth had become inordinately interested in horoscopy, and by this time there was even an astrologer as a paid up member of her staff, one Rupert Hunter, a large, sycophantic ex-actor who just happened also to be the boyfriend of Roberty Dunster. In his latest prediction, Hunter foresaw nothing but doom and gloom for Elizabeth should she obey the wishes of another, and bend to the will of someone who was really opposed to her. The stars and their moons could not be in a worse possible position, Hunter told her, for the making of any major decision. A conclusion reached now while Neptune was in such a revolutionary location could be disastrous and might reverse all her previous good fortune. Proper health care was imperative. This was not a time but *the* time to rest up, to do nothing untoward, to take the greatest care, and above all not to be influenced by any one particular person or contact, because that person's influence could make her overstep her mark. Most disturbing of all, however, was that Hunter could see something in the skies, something falling to earth, a very bright light, and he was afraid of it, whatever it was, and he was most afraid of it for Elizabeth.

Elizabeth listened intently, her hand in Rupert Hunter's as he looked at and checked her palm, taking all this to mean that she must not agree to play in *Macbeth*, which suited her purposes admirably, because she had privately determined not only now but never to play a part she truly believed to be genuinely cursed. Then she thanked her friend and astrologer with an intensity which surprised him, before kissing him goodbye. Roberty thanked him and kissed him as well when Rupert returned to London, although Roberty's other reaction was nothing but pure, undiluted mirth.

'You're a great, fat wobbly wonder, Roopie dear,' he exclaimed. 'I sometimes don't know where we'd be, dear, without your *magic*. My – but you could have been straight off the *deserted heath* yourself! *Double, double toil and trouble, fire burn and cauldron bubble*, you naughty old witch, you.'

It had been Roberty who had prompted his friend to make Elizabeth's latest horoscope as doomy and gloomy as possible (without being too obvious) because Roberty had career reasons of his own for not wanting Jerome to do *The Scottish Play*. For should Jerome fail to get the finance for the film of *Macbeth* the contingency plan was for Jerome and Elizabeth to star in the première of David Pursar's new play *The Magnate*, in which Elizabeth as part of the deal had made Jerome secure the main supporting role for Dunster.

'*By the pricking of my thumbs*,' Roberty sighed in blissful anticipation, '*something wicked this way comes.*'

He was right, although no-one, not even Roberty Dunster in his wildest moments, could ever have foreseen Nemesis in the shape of the tall, balding and by now semi-corpulent Cecil Manners.

'It's no good, Cecil darling,' Elizabeth told him, trying her hardest not to watch Cecil eat. 'Jerome's being a complete and utter bastard and he won't even listen.'

'He's all but got the money, Elizabeth dear,' Cecil said, carefully boning out what was left of his Dover Sole. 'You do know that, don't you?'

'I don't care whether he's got the sodding keys to Fort Knox, Cecil,' Elizabeth replied, 'I am not playing Lady Fruitcake.'

She lit up another cigarette before she had quite extinguished her last and stared up at the ceiling, unable to watch any more of Cecil stuffing food into his mouth. It wasn't that Cecil was an untidy eater, on the contrary, he was fastidious to a degree. It was simply that Elizabeth could not bear to watch other people eat. So for the next five minutes all her conversation was directed upwards, at the chandelier overhead.

'Couldn't you be ill perhaps?' Cecil suggested rather feebly. 'Suffer a slight relapse?'

'Ha!' Elizabeth dismissed the idea contemptuously. 'I'm monitored practically every minute of every day and every night! They know when and if there's anything wrong with me, darling. And even if there was, even if I was *dying* – Jerome is so obsessed with making this blasted film, he wouldn't let me die! Heavens, he'd drag me on! He'd drag me from my death bed on to the studio floor and film me dying! *The Queen, my lord, is dead*, Seyton would say. But all lovely J would be interested in was whether or not he'd got me shuffling off the mortal coil safely in the can.'

'It is something he feels very strongly about,' Cecil agreed, carefully wiping his mouth and draining the last of his white Burgundy. 'But for once, I don't really see what I can do, dear. Do you?'

435

'Yes I do, *dear*,' Elizabeth said. 'You can stop him, *dear*.'

She ceased gazing at the cut glass chandelier above her head, and slowly let her eyes find Cecil's eyes. And when they did, she turned the headlamps on full beam.

Cecil really didn't know whether he was coming or going, starting or stopping, or alive or dead for the next few weeks. Only in the most private of his private thoughts had he ever contemplated actually making love to Elizabeth, yet now here she was regularly in his bed. He knew she had ulterior motives, of course he did, he knew exactly what she wanted, which wasn't very difficult because it was Elizabeth's habit to be extremely explicit, but he wasn't going to let that ruin his pleasure. Ever since their traumatic transatlantic crossing, Cecil had seen himself cast as nothing more than Elizabeth's guardian and trusted friend, which was really more even than he felt he deserved, but never for a moment had he dared to think beyond that point. Yet here they were now lovers. The woman who had once been the most beautiful woman in the world, and who was without doubt still one of the planet's most desirable and exquisite females, had given herself to him, humble, ordinary Cecil Manners, and allowed him to make love to her twice a week on the days she came up to London to have her hair done. Cecil was so enthralled by her and so besotted with her he would have killed for her, had he been capable of inflicting harm on anyone, which he wasn't. Even so, he most certainly would have done anything for her, anything she asked, simply anything, the only trouble being that he was about as incapable of successful politicking as he was of committing murder.

Nonetheless, he tried. In response to Elizabeth's request that he get her off the film, he tried his best (which in Cecil's case wasn't very much) firstly to persuade Jerome that the filming of *Macbeth* was a worthy but a financially and artistically misguided venture, and then, having failed in that, to convince him that Elizabeth would be miscast.

'Elizabeth is too divine, too lovely, she's altogether too *nice* for Lady Macbeth,' Cecil reasoned. 'Alison Agate would be a much better choice. For a start she's just done it at Stratford and she was sensational. Or there's Cora Thackeray. You saw her *Lavinia* last season. She's already a great tragedian. I just feel that Elizabeth isn't. Elizabeth is much more the doomed heroine, which is why she made such a wonderful Juliet. And Ophelia. Or perhaps best of all, what about Peggy Franklyn?'

'What about suggesting somebody who isn't on your books, you clot!' Jerome laughed, slapping Cecil on the back. 'Anyway – the answer's no. Elizabeth has to play the part because of the very virtues you extol. Because of that wicked innocence. And most of all because of her *plausibility*. She was born to play Lady Macbeth.'

'Perhaps,' Cecil said, 'but she happens to believe she could die playing it. She's convinced the part is bad luck.'

'Oh balls,' Jerome said. '*Macbeth* is a play like any other play, Ces. It hasn't any hidden powers, any special black magic. It might be a difficult play, it might be an exhausting play, but that's all it is, dear chap. It's a *play*. And the men and the women who are going to perform it are merely *players*. Pass it on.'

Cecil wasn't quite sure about Jerome's last remark. For a moment from the look in Jerome's eye and the inflexion he gave the phrase, making it sound childishly conspiratorial, Cecil imagined that Jerome knew about Elizabeth and he. But then he knew he was just imagining, because Jerome gave him a dazzling smile, another slap on the back, and then wandered off whistling happily to go and talk money with Boska.

Cecil had already approached Boska on the subject. He had hinted to Boska that Elizabeth might not be physically up to the role, that she might not be able to stand the strain, without realizing these had been Boska's own initial concerns, and for a while he thought he might have won, as Boska appeared to take this second opinion on Elizabeth's condition very seriously.

'There's too much money at stake here, Cecil,' he'd said, rubbing the stubble on his chin, a five o'clock shadow which appeared daily around noon. 'The dibs is too big for any might or might-not-haves. I have to check this out, so just leave it with me on my desk, OK? You just leave it with me for a day or so.'

Cecil was only too glad to do so, and when the call finally came back from Boska nearly a week later, Cecil was convinced he had pulled it off. He had indicated this to Elizabeth the day before, just before she left to go to her hairdressers in Hill Street, and in return for his high hopes and in anticipation of a hard earned victory, she had rewarded him with what she referred to as a *Mistress-Quickly* before pulling her clothes back on, kissing him haphazardly in one eye and dashing out to catch a taxi.

'Well done, Cecil,' Boska said down the phone, raising Cecil's hopes even higher. 'Your remark about your worries, good for you, dear boy. It reminded me to check through the insurance cover, in case they were thinking of penalizing us for Lizzie's previous collapse. But happy day, Cecil – they see that as a *one-off*, there's no exclusions, and they haven't even loaded the premium. Even so, I owe you for making me check it out. You never know with these insurance shock-a-lollies.'

Cecil called Elizabeth at her hairdresser's.

'Can you come and see me before you go home, Elizabeth dear?' he asked.

'Cecil, *dear*,' Elizabeth replied, as heavily as she could even though she knew her sarcasm was wasted, and that Cecil would persist in calling her the dreaded *dear* come what may. 'Cecil, dear,' she repeated, 'no. You are *insatiable*, and anyway I've just had my hair done.'

'And I've just had Bossy on the phone, Elizabeth dear,' Cecil replied, 'and it's not good news. In fact it's very bad news, I'm afraid.'

'What's very bad news, Cecil dear?'

'I've done my very best, Elizabeth, but I'm afraid it's a lost cause. You start filming three weeks on Monday.'

Elizabeth said nothing. She just dropped the telephone so that it dandled on its cord, and returned to her seat, leaving Cecil to call after her in vain.

She had dropped the phone because she was dropping Cecil, because there was no point in persisting with him any longer. Elizabeth thought it all out as she sat having her hair dried. Cecil was out, and even the thought of him irritated her. It wasn't the sex, it was the boredom of it all, the time wasted in his boring company. She really hadn't objected to having sex with him, even though the experience had been totally unremarkable, she hadn't minded the sex at all because it hadn't meant anything. It never did, not any more, not to Elizabeth. Sex meant absolutely nothing to Elizabeth. Bethy wouldn't have done what she'd just done, because it mattered to Bethy. Bethy only did it with J, and when they did it, it was fantastic. Even just thinking about it, Bethy got a thrill, even though she couldn't quite remember the last time Elizabeth had allowed Bethy to do it with J. But Bethy wouldn't have done it with anyone else, she never had.

Elizabeth had, and Elizabeth did, and she didn't care, because nothing happened when she did it, it had no resonance, the reason for this being simple, the simple reason why it had no resonance being that Elizabeth had no feelings. They had taken away Elizabeth's feelings when they had taken him away out of the house. Go and say goodbye to him, she'd been told, say goodbye to him and don't mind the pennies, everyone has pennies on their eyes, dear. You wouldn't want him staring at you and

438

frightening you now, would you? When they'd taken him away at last, after what might have only been days but had seemed to the seven-year-old Elizabeth like weeks of him in constant pain, forever groaning, and then moaning, and then finally screaming in what was no longer pain but had become agony, after him lying there screaming with the pain, when he had died so suddenly and they'd come and taken all that was left of him away, they'd taken Lizzie's feelings away as well. Her feelings had gone with him in the box, and been buried deep down into the dark earth. Elizabeth had watched as they lowered her feelings into the ground with his cheap coffin and thrown earth that was already sodden with the winter rain on top of him and on to her feelings, and so it really didn't matter what they did to Elizabeth now. It didn't matter what they put in her body with their needles, or what they put on her head when she was asleep, because there was no feeling left anywhere, they wouldn't be able to find one anywhere, not in her fingers or her hands, not in her heart or in her soul. When her foster parents had put her dead twin brother in the ground, Elizabeth's heart had been buried in the coffin with him.

'What is it?' someone was saying. 'Is everything all right, Miss Laurence? Are you all right?'

'Of course I'm all right!' she laughed, looking up at herself in the mirror, seeing Elizabeth with her wonderful green eyes. 'Of course I'm all right, darling! Why shouldn't I be all right?'

'Is there something the matter with your hands?' her hairdresser was asking, and Elizabeth saw he did look rather worried. She frowned at him in the mirror. 'I wondered if there was something wrong,' he continued, dropping his voice, 'because you keep – you keep washing them.'

'I'm washing my hands, darling boy,' she said, 'because they're *very* dirty.'

'But there's no water in the basin, Miss Laurence,' the young man said. 'The handbasin's empty.'

She looked at him, again through the mirror, but this time she saw Elizabeth's eyes were now glinty little slits.

'Really?' she heard Elizabeth saying. 'Isn't there? Then run some water in, you stupid little bastard!'

Fortunately both Jerome and Sir David Appleby were in London and at hand when Cecil called them. By good judgement rather than luck, Cecil had hurried straight round to Hill Street once he realized Elizabeth had left him hanging on the phone, suddenly fearing that if Elizabeth interpreted the news he had just given

439

her as calamitous, it could precipitate an attack. He could never explain to himself or others why he felt it necessary to leave his office and rush to Elizabeth's side. It was a perception, a sudden intuition. At that moment all Cecil suddenly knew was that he had to go to Elizabeth.

His offices were in Old Bond Street, just a block or so away, and Cecil got to Hill Street just in time, just as *Elizabeth* was about to establish her total superiority over *Bethy*, just as *Elizabeth* was beginning to turn on the other women in the salon, just as *Elizabeth* was beginning to berate them for being what they were, just before *Elizabeth* managed to get hold of her hairdresser's scissors.

'It's all right,' he told the proprietor who was about to call for help. 'There's no need to call anybody. It's perfectly all right.' He had hold of Elizabeth now, firmly by her arms above the elbows, holding her close with her face towards him, so the other women in the salon couldn't see the contortions which were transfiguring what had once been the most beautiful face in the world. 'It's perfectly all right, just get Miss Laurence's things, and call me a cab. I'm her doctor, and I'm afraid Miss Laurence is taking some particularly strong medication, which can have delirious side effects.' Cecil didn't know where all this was coming from, and he didn't stop to wonder. He just hoped it would keep coming. He glanced back down the salon and noticed to his relief that most of the women were under hairdriers and couldn't hear the stream of verbal abuse Elizabeth was now directing at him as he manhandled her into the lobby away from their quiz-zical stares.

'Now please don't say anything about this,' Cecil said to Eliza-beth's hairdresser as a cab drew up. 'This is a purely chemical reaction, and we don't want something which is purely medical being misinterpreted, do we? It wouldn't be good for you either, I feel. Because I'm quite sure you don't wish to lose Miss Laurence's valued custom.'

With that, Cecil bundled the still screaming Elizabeth into the cab and took her straight back to his flat.

They had her sedated and down to Sainthill by the end of the afternoon, and no-one was any the wiser. Sir David Appleby accompanied them, and stayed overnight in order that he could supervise and set in motion another course of ECT. By the end of the week, after her enforced sojourn in the suite on the third floor, Elizabeth's condition had completely stabilized, and one week later shooting commenced on *Macbeth*. In deference to her condition, however, Jerome altered the schedule so that Elizabeth didn't

440

have to begin work on what was to prove a highly arduous and gruelling shoot until her doctors expressed complete confidence in her recovery.

They did so unanimously one week later.

It was an extremely difficult shoot, not because it was beset by difficulties because it wasn't. Jerome had done his homework and done it thoroughly, so technically any difficulties encountered were only small ones. What made the work so intense was the level Jerome had decided to pitch the film. He had eschewed any thought of it being a spectacular, or a blood and thunder epic (all the murders were filmed in long-shot and as a consequence were that much more disturbing), and had chosen to concentrate instead on the ambitions and the anguishes of the main protagonists, of Lord and Lady Macbeth. The end result, shot entirely on location in and around a castle in Northumbria, was a very dark, and deeply disturbing version of the play, a sort of tragic *film noire*, with daylight only ever being glimpsed through the arrow slits of the castle, or distantly high on battlements seen from the foot of stone stairwells. Otherwise all seems to be perpetual night, a gloom which was finally relieved only when Macduff severed Macbeth's head from his body.

Elizabeth found her time filming almost intolerable. For once she was unable to lock a performance up and just turn it on, as Jerome so often accused her of doing, and instead she had to search deep inside herself each and every day she was on the set. What she found there deep down the camera read and loved, but Elizabeth hated. It was much too real, much, much too real.

Several times she tried to make Jerome temper the demands he was making on her as an actress, but he refused, pushing her harder and harder, and causing her to search herself more and more. For once he even made her watch her rushes in an attempt to get her to realize the brilliance and scope of her performance.

'No-one will ever better you, Bethy,' he used to whisper to her in the dark of the viewing theatre. 'In fact no-one will ever even get near you. Believe me, this is going to be the definitive Lady Fruitcake.'

The *Fruitcake* joke was the only one they shared on the whole film. Jerome was sensible to the feelings Elizabeth had about the roles they were playing, and while he refused to give in to superstition, he did at least go along with his wife's insistence that the Macbeths at all times be referred to as Lord and Lady Fruitcake.

441

It was a good move, it seemed, because somehow the joke never staled and kept the atmosphere on the set as light as was possible under what were proving daily to be the most taxing of emotional conditions.

It was in fact a dark and searching time for the leading actors, a time finally when they had to dig a little too deep, and when they did, what they found put their private relationship beyond redemption.

Jerome had left shooting the sleepwalking scene until last. He knew Elizabeth would find it difficult, in fact she had already inferred that she couldn't find a line on it, and that as a consequence she was frightened of over-playing it. She had even pleaded with Jerome to shoot the scene in such a way that she could dub the voice on afterwards and simply go through the physical actions for the camera.

'It's a *pig*, Jerry,' she had said, 'you know it's a pig. *Out, damned spot, out I say* – it's become a melodramatic cliché, and until I find a way of doing it, I won't. I can't.'

'You'll have to do it some time, Bethy,' Jerome had warned. 'This isn't like a difficult *Dumb Crambo* at a party. You can't pull a face at this one and say oh no, Jerry! Do I *really* have to do this one? But don't worry. Just put it out of your head and don't think about it. Allow it to happen, let it just emerge. We'll leave it until you're ready. We'll leave it right until the very end if you prefer.'

'What I would prefer, Jerry darling,' Elizabeth had sighed, 'is to leave it out altogether.'

Jerome thought it might be the *hand-washing* that was causing her this advance distress, that Elizabeth was frightened in case she would not be able to reproduce in the playing a symptom of guilt and madness which she herself had manifested. He had always known at the back of his mind that this might prove Elizabeth's undoing, but had gambled on her professionalism. He had never known anyone as professional as Elizabeth, and when he had finally decided that she was fully capable of playing the part, it had been this that had counted for most, for Jerome thought that once Elizabeth could be persuaded to undertake the role, her innate professionalism would see her through.

Even so, he himself dreaded filming the sleepwalking scene in case of uncontrollable repercussions, so the reason he was leaving it until the very last was not altogether altruistic.

He closed the set on the last day to all but those immediately involved in its making, the two actors playing the Doctor and the

442

Gentlewoman in waiting to Lady Macbeth, Elizabeth herself and a skeleton technical crew. Elizabeth refused to rehearse the scene except for her designated moves, which she walked through saying nonsense in place of the text.

'I want to shoot all your stuff, from the moment you appear with the taper,' Jerome said to her privately, 'I want to do it all in one take, right up until *what's done cannot be undone – to bed, to bed, to bed.* I'm just going to be on you for the master, and then once we see what we've got, I can decide afterwards on the close-ups or two shots of the Doctor and the woman, and on where to go closer on you. So just pretend you're onstage, Bethy. Play the whole scene like you'd play it onstage and think of nothing else but what has gone before.'

'What has gone before,' Elizabeth said.

'Yes, Bethy,' Jerome replied. 'What is locked in Lady Fruitcake's mind.'

'What has gone before,' Elizabeth repeated, as her make-up girl moved in for the final repair, and wardrobe adjusted the drape of her nightgown. 'What has gone before.'

Jerome then banished all those who weren't required, disappeared into the darkness behind the camera and called for quiet.

'Sound running,' someone said and the clapperboy snapped his board shut to mark the scene and the point on the soundtrack, but Elizabeth heard nothing. Elizabeth was deep in character, thinking of *what had gone before.*

There was no problem with the *hand-washing.* Jerome stood to the side of the huge film camera, in the dark, hardly daring to look, but when he did he saw Elizabeth was being brilliant, making magic, making the moment real, so real and disturbing that Jerome felt the hairs on the back of his neck prickle.

'*Yet here's a spot,*' she said, almost too lightly, taking an enormous risk, as if she was about to laugh at the blood she imagined on her hands. But then when she wished it away, when she saw the murkiness of hell, when she remembered *how much blood the old man had in him*, the lightness vanished, and the ensuing anguish was almost too much to bear.

Yet Jerome still held his breath because he had seen the look in Elizabeth's eyes, and he knew all was not well. Because the look in her eyes had suddenly changed, from a skilfully feigned dread to what Jerome knew was the real thing, to sheer terror, and predictably on her next line, there was silence. Jerome waited, but the silence seemed interminable. He waited in case Elizabeth recovered and could continue, but she just stood there in her key light, washing her hands over and over and over again in an agony of silence.

Jerome was about to call for the camera to cut, when suddenly Elizabeth came back to life, tears coursing silently down her beautiful white face.

'*The Thane of Fife had a wife,*' she whispered, her voice breaking, '*where is she now? Where is she now? Where is she now!*'

The last question arrived as a scream, out of a whisper of fear seamlessly to a scream of terror, and as Jerome shouted *Cut!* Elizabeth turned from the camera and ran out into the darkness off the set.

Jerome ran in pursuit, unsure at first where she had gone. They were on the first floor of the castle and she could have gone any way, either up or down the spiral stone staircase, or away down one of the endless corridors. Where she had disappeared there were no bystanders, the castle was deserted, so there were no witnesses to her flight.

Then he heard her shoes somewhere above him, on the stairs, and he sprinted up after her, taking the stairs two at a time, hurling himself round the corners as he hung on to the rail. He caught her on the battlement, as she was running for the edge.

'Elizabeth, for Christ's sake!' he shouted, catching her by the arm as she seemed about to try and leap over the parapet. 'What in hell do you think you're doing!'

'The Thane of Fife had a wife!' she hissed up at him as he took firm hold of her, 'where is she now! Nobody knows!'

There was a small windowless room at the top of the stairs which was unlocked, and into which Jerome gently guided his still weeping wife.

'Nobody knows, you see, Jerry,' she was saying. 'Not even you.'

Someone was running up the stairs after him, his first assistant who was calling out if everything was all right. Jerome assured him it was, to go back down and call a break, and they would both be down in a few minutes. Then he shut the door of the turret room and locked it behind him.

'What's the matter, Bethy?' he asked. 'Would it help if you told me?'

'What did you say?' she asked rather harshly.

'I said would it help if you told me what the matter was, Bethy?'

Jerome used his abbreviation of her name deliberately, as Appleby had taught him to do at such times, at times when he thought it was *Elizabeth* who had the upper hand, and sure enough after a long moment, after a long silent time when she just sat staring at him, her tears staining her make-up as they dried, *Elizabeth* slowly disappeared, and someone else stared out of that beautiful face, someone altogether softer and more sweet, someone who suddenly laughed, but who laughed very lightly, as if what she was about to say wasn't very important. Which of course it was, because once she had tucked her small lace handkerchief away, and smoothed her hair back from her forehead, Bethy now proceeded to tell Jerome in great detail everything that horrid *Elizabeth* had done to poor Pippa and why.

By the time she had finished, she had talked well through the lunch hour, so Jerome took her back downstairs and into make-up where they set about repairing the damage done by Elizabeth's hysteria. Then together Jerome and she returned to the set where throughout the afternoon they filmed the entire sleep-walking scene without another hitch. Nobody said a word as they set about their work, nothing which wasn't necessary, because the handful of people present knew that what they were witnessing was work of pure genius. It was inspired acting, it was faultless, it was sublime, and to the minds of all those who watched and to those who later saw the film there was no doubt at all that this notoriously difficult scene would never be equalled let alone bettered.

At a little after seven o'clock when the last shot was in the can, and Jerome had called the wrap, for the second time in the actress's illustrious career, the entire crew and cast broke into a spontaneous ovation. In response, Bethy stood there smiling her sweetest smile before blowing everyone a marvellously theatrical but deeply felt and grateful kiss. Then she turned and walked away. They still clapped her, all the way into the darkness far out beyond the set, a set where Bethy left the best work she had ever done, Jerome and her marriage all behind her.

They remained together for just six more months, and then in name only. Once the film was premièred and the plaudits gathered, the nation's most illustrious acting partnership announced their separation, due to *irreconcilable differences.*

445

TWENTY-THREE

'Look at this,' Oscar said, waving a letter from London.

'I can't look,' Pippa said, who was busy varnishing a canvas. 'Read it.'

'But only if it's good news,' Jenny said who was helping her mother. 'Not if it's one of those you'll-never-guess-who-they've-offered-my-new-film-to litanies of woe.'

'It isn't, Picasso,' Oscar replied, 'so just zip up and listen. They're going to revive *Tatty Gray*.'

'Oh wow,' Pippa said, setting the varnished landscape to one side. 'Why should we listen to that? *Tatty Gray*'s become one of those statistics, hasn't it? Once a day at some time on this globe someone somewhere is performing *Tatty Gray*.'

'You think you're kinda sassy, right?' Oscar said, waving the letter under Pippa's nose. 'Just because you married the greatest writer ever to come out of Little Woodsville, Vermont. But you just listen here, Mrs Greene. I didn't say they're going to *do Tatty Gray*, did I? I said they're going to revive it. In London. They're going to revive the old girl, they want me to rewrite it, and for guess who? They want me to rewrite it for the first Mr Greene.'

'I take it by that you mean the first Mr Nicholls,' Pippa said.

'I take it by that you mean my first father,' said Jenny.

They discussed it over Sunday lunch, which they ate outside in the old orchard. Jenny, who was home on holiday before her last term at art college, wanted to hear all about a play which she knew only by repute, having never seen or read it, while Pippa wanted to know what on earth the thinking was behind wanting it revived and rewritten for Jerome.

Having answered Jenny's question first and briefly, and with typical modesty, Oscar turned to Pippa's.

'I think the career's gone into hold,' Oscar said. 'You know, ever since the split, Jerome hasn't really kept up the good work. All this deliberately turning his back on the classics. I mean he's a classical actor. Sure, he's a fine comedy actor, but then to be a really great actor you have to be able to play comedy. And it's not as if he's ever done that. He's chosen to do all this modern work, which would be fine if it was good modern work, but that it ain't. Not judging from what I've seen on my trips to London. I mean this last play – *The Garden Wall*. The one thing Jerome can't play, at least this is in my reckoning, the one thing he's actually *bad* at being is ordinary. Yet here he was again. And not only trying to be ordinary yet again, but extraordinarily ordinary. You know what people are saying.'

'No, I don't,' Pippa said, peeling an apple.

'Yes you do, because I told you. They say maybe she got custody of the talent.'

'I saw her in *Separate Beds*,' Jenny said, 'and she was awful. The people in the row behind us said she was drunk.'

'OK,' Oscar agreed. 'She does the odd dog, agreed. But then what about her Madame Ranevsky in *The Cherry Orchard*? Probably never been bettered since Olga Knipper created the part in Moscow in 1904.'

'You wouldn't remember that,' Pippa said straight-faced to her daughter. 'But to your stepfather it's as fresh as yesterday's paint.' Jenny laughed, taking the piece of apple on offer at the end of her mother's knife. 'So come on, Oz,' Pippa continued, 'are you or aren't you?'

'I think that's rather up to you, sweetheart,' Oscar said. 'If you'd rather I didn't—'

Pippa stopped her teasing, and looked very seriously at Oscar.

'Darling,' she said, 'it's a play, and he's an actor. That's all.'

'It's not as if I have to get involved,' Oscar continued to defend himself. 'I can do the rewrites and just send them over.'

'You weren't listening, Oz,' Pippa said. 'I said it's a play—'

'I heard what you said, Pip. And thanks. As a matter of fact, I wouldn't mind having a shot at it. I think it might work even better with the artist older, with him around about the age Jerome is now. And I think the play still has something to say.'

'It must do you chump,' Pippa smiled. 'Or else they wouldn't keep doing it everywhere. What about the girl? Will you make her older?'

'Oh no, no I don't think so,' Oscar replied. 'In fact most definitely not. Tatty's whole thing is being a sprite. You can't very well have middle-aged sprites.'

Pippa smiled and poured them all some more coffee. He had long since explained who Tatty was and why, and Pippa had long since forgiven him. (It had taken all of two minutes on her part, after a whole evening of explanation from Oscar.) And she was glad that he wasn't going to change Tatty. She'd never seen the play, only read it, but she loved it and she wouldn't want one word changed.

Jenny drove into Tours with Oscar the following morning, leaving Pippa behind to continue packing up her canvases for her first ever show in Paris.

'Can we meet for lunch?' she asked *en route*. 'Or are you tied up?'

'I can't think of anything nicer,' Oscar said. 'I'll be through at the bank at twelve, so let's say half-past, at *La Petite Maison Blanche*.'

Jenny was early, deliberately so. She'd finished what she had to do in plenty of time, so she settled in at the table in the window, ordered an *anis*, and then reread as much as she could of the copy of the play she had found in Oscar's room just to make sure.

'I take it *Maman* knows?' Jenny asked her stepfather, when he had agreed halfway through the meal the character of Tatty was based entirely on her mother.

'Yes, Sherlock,' Oscar replied. 'She knows now. In that I didn't tell her at the time. I don't know whether she'd have guessed or whether she wouldn't if she'd seen the original production, but your father wouldn't let her till he considered he'd got it right.'

'She didn't see the original production?' Jenny jumped in, picking up Oscar's inadvertent error.

'No,' Oscar said, cursing his strict upbringing and wishing he wasn't quite so much like George Washington. 'I guess I thought you knew that.'

'How could I? We've never discussed this in detail before, any of us.'

'Let's talk about you instead,' Oscar suggested, trying to change tack. 'This is your last term, right? Hey – how time flies.'

'I want to talk about the play, Oz,' Jenny replied. 'If it's all the same to you. Because there's something I don't understand. *Maman* knows that Tatty Gray is her? That your most successful play—'

'It's not my best.'

'I said your most successful play in a way owes it all to her—'

'That's kinda true, but—'

'Yet she never saw it?'

448

'I only said she never saw the original production.'

'Did she ever see it?'

'Nope. Come on – let's dish some dirt. Tell me the rude things you all draw when teacher's not looking.'

'She couldn't have ever seen it, could she?' Jenny persisted. 'Because she left my father before the play had premièred in London. And he wouldn't allow her to see it on tour. So how did it happen?'

'You got me, Jen. How did what happen? I can't tell you how something happened if I don't know what that something is. You know what we used to do at High School when the teacher wasn't looking?'

'Oz, please. This is important. Because I sense something here.'

'You artists. All you're after is the truth. It's much easier being a writer. Writers can make up the truth.'

'I want to know how it happened. How my mother and father broke up.'

'Don't you think you maybe ought to ask your mother? After all, I'm not part of the original cast.'

'I've asked my mother. And she said I'd find out one day, in my own way.'

'So there you go.' Oscar raised his glass. 'Here's to that day.'

'This is it, Oz,' Jenny said. 'This is my way of finding out.'

Oscar didn't actually get round to telling her the whole story until they were driving home. Over the rest of lunch he talked mainly about the play and how he had drawn the character of Tatty Gray and why. He felt it was important that Jenny should know just how madly in love with her mother Oscar was when she was married to her father, as if by doing so in some way he could take some of the blame. But while Jenny was interested in what he had to say about Tatty, she saw no harm in what Oscar had felt during that time because he had done nothing. He hadn't even professed his love for her mother.

'Thou shalt not covet thy neighbour's wife, you dig?' Oscar said.

'Thou shalt not commit adultery,' Jenny replied. 'You dig?'

Jenny was bright, like her mother, and Jenny was persistent too, just like Pippa. She managed to wheedle it all out of Oscar by the time they were halfway home. When he told her, he told her the truth, the whole truth and nothing but the truth, just as Pippa had told him, and Jenny listened to him in total silence, never interrupting him once.

'The bastard,' she said, but not until he'd finished. 'The bastard.'

'The bastardess,' Oscar said. 'I mean surely.'

'Look – Elizabeth is just wicked, obviously,' Jenny replied. 'And she's probably nuts as well. But my father. To do that to someone like *Maman*. He must have been mad. I mean seriously. The bastard.'

'It is a form of madness certainly,' Oscar agreed. 'That good old ass's head.'

'The ass's head symbolizes love. That wasn't love. That was just sex.'

'There's no such thing as just sex, Jen. No-one ever got off by pleading they didn't mean any harm, all they were having was just sex.'

'The bastard,' Jenny repeated, looking out of the car window. 'Of all the people to do it to. I mean can you imagine? Of all the people in the world to hurt like that. To do something like that to.'

'I know,' Oscar said. 'I agree.'

Jenny turned to him, her eyes flashing.

'What do you mean?' she asked. 'You're just going to rewrite the bloody play for him!'

'*Touché*.' Oscar nodded. 'Your round.'

'Well why, Oz? Why are you doing it?'

'Literary vanity. A playwright's conceit. Allied to incipient greed. I did, however, ask permission of your mother.'

'My mother's a saint,' Jenny said, and then looked back out of the window. They drove the rest of the way in silence, before Jenny asked Oscar to stop the car and let her out.

'I'm fine, Oz, really,' she said in answer to his expressed concern. 'I'll walk from here. I'd like to walk. I need to walk.'

They were only a mile or two from the farm, where the country road forks into the beginning of another road which later turns into their lane.

'You'll be OK, kid,' Oscar said. 'Your mother is.'

Pippa knew it the moment Oscar ambled into her studio, she knew something had happened.

'What was it?' she said, pouring him some wine. 'You have words?'

'Words,' Oscar wondered. 'Sure we had words, Pip. All we did was talk.'

'What about?'

'You know. I can see it on your face, and you can see it on mine.' Oscar sat down, looking rather crumpled. 'I wish it had been you

450

who'd have told her,' he said. 'I guess it would have sounded better coming from you.'

'I don't think so, Oz,' Pippa said, sitting beside him on the old studio sofa. 'I'd have sounded too sorry for myself.'

'Oh sure,' Oscar said. 'That'll be the day. I've never once heard you indulge in the smallest amount of self-pity. You don't know the meaning of the word.'

'How did she take it?'

'Let's say I don't think she'll be taking in too many Jerome Didier movies for a while.'

'Do you think she had to know, Oz?'

'You tell me, Pip. I'm just a writer. I just make things up.'

'I think perhaps she did. She'd always have wondered otherwise. And you can do more harm that way, to yourself, I mean. I think really she had to know sooner or later.'

Oscar sighed and curled up beside her on the sofa, putting his head in her lap, a big weary bear.

'Sooner or later,' he repeated. 'Yeah. Well, as my old grannie used to say at times like this, later's plenty soon enough for me.'

Jenny cooked them all dinner, serving them one of her favourite dishes, *Poulet au Fromage*, a chicken cooked in wine, mustard and cheese sauce, served with *Gâteau de Pommes de Terre*, *Purée de Fenouil* and accompanied by a well-chilled white burgundy. She was in high spirits throughout the meal, which, as was usual from spring-time onwards, they ate outside.

When Oscar disappeared inside to brew the coffee and fetch the Armagnac, Pippa asked her daughter if she was all right, or if there was anything more she wanted to talk about.

'Not a thing, *Maman*,' she assured her with a squeeze of her hand. 'We talked it all away, Oz and I, really. So stop looking so worried. I understand everything now.'

'Are you sure?'

'Totally positive.' Jenny cut herself an extra slice of cheese and then turned to stare out into the dusk. 'Have you any idea when they're planning to revive *Tatty Gray*?' she asked.

'Why?'

'If you really want to know, *Maman*, because I'd like to see it. I'd love to see you, or rather the young you on-stage. Not many children could claim that privilege.'

Pippa laughed. 'That's true, I suppose,' she said. 'I think they're hoping to get it in production for the autumn. Oscar doesn't see why the rewrites should take more than a month.'

'The autumn,' Jenny reflected. 'What, sort of September?'

'Sort of September,' Pippa agreed. 'But where are you going to be? You'll have finished at college. Have you thought what you're going to do?'

'I was going to go to America,' Jenny said. 'Oz said he'd get me some introductions over there. But in fact I don't think I'll actually go until the spring now.'

'Any particular reason?' Pippa couldn't put her finger on it, but there was something that was worrying her, a difference in the tone of her daughter's voice, or a difference in her determination.

'No. No particular reason.'

'Have you decided how you're going to use this talent of yours more importantly. Whether you're going to be a painter plain and simple, or whether—'

'You know what we were discussing the other day, *Maman*, and I'm sorry for interrupting. But you know when we were discussing various possibilities.'

'Yes.'

'And now that Oscar's come up with some really useful contacts over the pond—'

'Yes.'

'Well, I thought why not? I mean it's in the blood. I thought why not stage design? Why not be a designer? What do you think?'

'Yes,' Pippa replied, with a smile, thinking she now had found the reason for the change in her daughter's determination. 'Why not? How funny.'

'How funny, *Maman*? I don't understand. Why?'

'Because when I met your father, that's exactly what I was hoping to be. A set designer.'

Jenny read the play again that night, twice. She read it every night (and always at night, never during the day) until she left the Loire to return to London, by which time she knew and understood the part of Tatty Gray perfectly.

TWENTY-FOUR

Jenny had laid her plan well and was equally meticulous in its execution. The beauty of it was that if she failed, even at the final hurdle, no-one except herself would be any the wiser, while if she succeeded the account would be squared, and she would have given measure for measure.

Initially, there were only two problems and both of them logistical. The first one, *where and when*, Jenny overcame by the judicious manipulation of her stepfather. Whenever she wrote or called home, she made sure to enclose a separate note to Oscar or to talk to him directly on the phone. That way she kept herself fully abreast of all the developments. Once the time and the place were fixed, and she had learned them, the rest was up to her.

The second problem, that of union membership, was a bigger worry since it seemed to be a *Catch 22* situation – she couldn't enter the shop without a ticket, and she couldn't get a ticket without being in the shop. There was no-one she could ask for advice either, not without revealing her intention, or at least not without arousing suspicions. She had to work that wrinkle out herself, and after a long private debate she decided the only thing to do was to brazen it out, a decision she reached when she remembered something Oscar had once said.

'The great thing about movies, and about show business in general,' he'd told her, 'is that nobody ever checks. Most of the time the game you're playing is a game of bluff. So you play along. You bluff 'em. And if you succeed, and they want you, by the time they check you out, it's either too late, or it's irrelevant. The great thing about this business is that anything is possible. And if it isn't, you find a way round it.'

453

The first diversion she created was round the woman in charge of the appointments.

'Hello, darling,' she said when a secretary put her through to a Miss Stanway. 'This is Abigail, darling, from Leslie Stone's office.' Jenny had got the agency name from a doorway in Soho. 'I'm sorry to trouble you, darling,' she continued, 'but I'm just checking on the calls for tomorrow.'

'Who in particular, darling?' a rather tired voice answered. 'I've a list as long as your bloody arm. If you ask me they're seeing every girl under twenty-five in the whole of bloody England.'

'It's a new client, darling,' Jenny continued, in her best blasé voice. 'Greene. Jane Greene.'

'Got a Sara,' the woman replied. 'Got a Helen. Got a Susan. No Jane, darling, sorry.'

'Oh Christ,' Jenny sighed. 'I thought this might have happened. It's this wretched temp we've got. You can't entrust anything to her. Leslie wants you to see this girl, because he's just taken her on, and he thinks she's very right.'

Jenny had gleaned the terminology from listening to Oscar over countless wonderfully funny lunches and dinners shared with her mother in the sun filled gardens at the farm. She hadn't made a conscious effort to memorize the patter. It had just apparently seeped into her memory by some form of osmosis, and was now there to be called upon, when and if required.

'It'll have to be the day after tomorrow, darling,' the woman said. 'Wednesday at a quarter-past four.'

'At the Apollo.'

'At the Comedy, darling.'

'I'll get something right in a minute,' Jenny laughed.

'Jane Green, wasn't it?'

'That's right, darling. With an E. Bless you darling,' she said. 'Bye!' And hung up quickly before the woman was reminded to ask again exactly from which agency it was she was calling.

She dressed very carefully and simply, in an old but clean short sleeved white tennis shirt, a well-faded denim skirt, and a pair of black canvas beach shoes, leaving her still sunburned long legs bare. She did nothing to her face, nor to her hair, just running her fingers through it to tousle it the moment she was called.

Which was the only moment she'd been truthfully dreading. Oscar, again inadvertently, had taken her through this moment countless times in the course of his stories and his anecdotes, but Jenny was wise enough to know that nothing could prepare her for the actuality. She could learn the ritual from listening to Oscar, and by such study she could prepare herself for the ordeal by knowing what the people out there were thinking, and what they were looking for, and how they set about finding it. But nothing could prepare her for this stomach churning moment as she stepped out from the shadows and into the glare of the overhead lights which prevented her from seeing little beyond the first row of seats.

They weren't sitting in the first row of seats, of course. She knew they wouldn't be, because Oscar had often reported the ploys which were wilfully used at these times, little tricks and ruses designed to disconcert but not to deter. It was the light which unsettled her most, not being yet able to see the faces behind the voices, not being able to see *him*. But she resisted the temptation to put a hand up to shield her eyes against the light, because she remembered in time Oscar's story about the *ingénue* who had done so, and immediately inspired the shout of *Ship Ahoy!* from someone in the stalls. Jenny didn't want any such barracking. At this particular moment a chance remark or joke could destroy even the most assured of confidences.

'Name please!' someone called from the dark beyond. 'We seem to have lost count!'

'Jane Greene!' she called back. 'That's Greene with an e!'

'Now there's a thing.' He appeared now, from the darkness to lean on the back of a seat in the front row, but she still couldn't see him clearly because of the lights. She just heard this wonderful voice, and felt his presence. 'Greene,' he said slowly, relishing the word. 'With an "e". Like our revered playwright. Like the writer of this piece. Are you by any – chance a relative?'

There was the famous *gap*, the pause taken in the place you least expect it. For a moment, bewitched by the voice and its sorcery, Jenny almost allowed herself to be thrown by the question, she very nearly took it at face value and only just recovered herself in time.

'Wasn't Oscar Greene an American?' she asked guilelessly.

'*Wasn't?*' He laughed. 'Isn't, dear girl, *isn't* he an American! The dear pensmith is still very much alive – I trust! And kicking!'

There was then a silence, during which Jenny calmly looked down to where he was standing, half in and half out of the shadows. But all she could see was the glint of his glasses.

'Have I seen you before?' he suddenly asked. 'Have I seen you before in something?'

'I don't think so, Sir Jerome,' she said, from nerves nearly forgetting to call him by his recently bestowed title. 'I've only just come to London.'

'From where, dear girl?'

'From the country.'

There was another silence, and then he turned his back on her and announced perhaps to the other people hidden out there, or perhaps just out loud to himself, 'I feel certain that I have seen her – in *something*.'

Now someone else appeared at the orchestra rail, a youngish man, with thin brown hair that fell into his eyes, and a cadaverous face. He handed her up a script.

'Act Two, scene two, page two, two, twenty-one.'

'That's page two for Act Two,' the stage manager said leading her back to a chair centre stage. 'Small two for scene two, page twenty-one for twenty-one of the scene. You have five minutes to read it through.'

'Only five now mind you, Wilkie!' Jerome called from the stalls, barely having to raise the famous voice. 'We are running most dreadfully – behind!'

'If you are running behind,' Jenny called back, 'I really don't mind sight-reading.'

Another silence, furnished with just a few distant whispers.

'Very well, dear girl!' he called again. 'Then let you sight-read!'

Jenny turned the script on to the totally wrong page. She didn't need the words, because she knew them, and she didn't want to see the right words in case they threw her. So she found a blank page at the end of the play, bent the manuscript around so no-one would notice, cleared her throat and began.

'You don't see my point,' she said. *'You really don't see the point at all. You have to look in your own heart, Sam. That's the place you have to search. It's really no good, no good at all always trying to lay the blame elsewhere, to make the excuse that other people aren't up to you, or as you like to put it, not in your emotional league. Look inside yourself, Sam. See what you can find there. I'll bet what you find lacking in others is the very thing you'll find lacking in yourself.'*

'I'm most intrigued,' the stage manager read. *'And what do you think that particular thing might be, Tatty?'*

'Honesty in its hardest shape, Sam. The honesty we all pride ourselves in having, practically every day of our lives. Honesty about our self. We boast about it all the time. Now the one person who should know about that is me! we say. Come on! You're teaching your grandmother to suck eggs! Who do you think you're kidding! Who are you to tell me that! I'll be the best judge of that! And so on and so forth! And it's just not true. Because we're

456

all afraid of looking inside ourselves, afraid of what we really might find out! Look at you! Everything you have done, and most of all everything you haven't done – it's all the fault of others! Never once in all this time I've known you—'

'All what time, Tatty?' the stage manager finally interrupted, after far too long a pause. Jenny didn't mind. She knew this speech backwards, sideways, and most importantly forwards, and nothing was going to throw her off her stride now she was into it. So she paused back, after the stage manager had fluffed his interruption. She made a moment of it, sly-eyeing the stage hand, and then sighing wistfully.

'For a moment I thought you'd dropped off to sleep, Sam,' she improvised, and was delighted to hear a roar of approving laughter rise from the stalls, as well as one loud handclap. *'The time I've known you, Sam Buxton, is for all time. I was there the moment you were born, and I shall be there when you go. No – no there's no good in looking like that. I've told you it's no good pretending I'm something that I'm not, something which you can categorize and then pigeon hole the way you do with everyone who comes before you, with those who stand up to you. Oh she's just a nuisance, that one. That one's a scold, that one just is after me for her own purposes, that one thinks she can reform me, this one is some figment of my imagination – well, I'm not. I'm as real as the moment, as all the moments we have shared, and even though I may be gone with the day, gone with the light, nothing more than a memory, an angry buzz fading to a faint echo in that furious head of yours, I shall still be here. I am always here. Because I shall always be a part of you, like I am a part of all people. But before that time, before I slip out under the door, or away through a crack in that window, or perhaps this time even blown away with the cobwebs—'*

'No. No!' This time the interruption came well on time, and was said with great meaning.

'Then listen to me, Sam. Before I go, you're going to do what you should have done when she left you. When Lucy walked out. You're going to do what you've refused to do since then, what you've refused to do all of your life. You're going to look into your heart, a long hard look and you're going to find out who you really are and where you went wrong. And then at last and at long, long last! Then maybe you will start asking those questions which you should have asked before of yourself! Questions which will begin to illuminate the world around you! Questions which will become the key to your experience of others – of all the

457

people around you and when they do – you will have begun the process of understanding! Put away your "shoulds" and your "should-haves". It's no good saying you know what you should do unless you do it! Like it's no good doing it, unless you know what it is you should be doing! And the only way you will find out what those things are is by searching way down deep inside yourself. It won't matter if you fail, if you fall short of achieving the final bliss. As long as you fight, and fight bravely – with the marks of your battles before! Not on your back – but borne proudly on your front! But you won't fail, you won't, believe me, Sam. Not if you judge your chances properly, and really come to terms with your capabilities. You won't fail, I promise you that you won't. You will not fail.'

Jenny closed the script and looked out into the pitch darkness beyond the bright light. There was silence. There was no movement, and there wasn't a word exchanged. Jenny could feel her heart beating faster now, now that she'd stopped being Tatty, but she took a slow, and well-concealed deep breath, straightening the playscript out carefully before handing it back to the stage manager who she found was staring at her intently.

'Thank you!' she called out to the still silent auditorium, and then turned to go. So far it had all worked out perfectly, but she knew the next few moments were the really crucial ones.

'No wait!' It was him who called, she was pleased to hear, Sir Jerome, her father. She turned back and waited, not even bothering to try and peer into the gloom. 'Wait – don't go!' He appeared at the orchestra rail and stared up at her, his eyes, behind a nondescript pair of horn-rimmed spectacles, fixed on hers, and on her face.

'Yes,' he said at last. 'We want to know what else you have done, please. That was very good. Very, *very* good.'

'Why do you want to know what else I have done?' she asked. 'Is it particularly relevant?'

'What previous experience have you had, dear girl?' He sounded more than a little impatient. 'I need to know what you have done.'

'Can I ask you a question?' Jenny said.

'Why not?' Her father smiled up at her, removing his glasses. 'Why not?'

'How did you think I read?'

'Very well. Extremely well, if you must know.'

'Yes, I must. Did I read well enough for you to consider me for the part?'

'Yes.'

458

'Do you think I could play the part?'

'Yes. Do you?'

'Yes. So why do you need to know what else I have done?' Jenny said. 'You can't have done anything before your very first part.'

'I went to drama school.'

'Not every successful actor went to drama school.'

Her father pursed his lips, and tapped them with his folded glasses.

'Did you go to drama school, young lady?'

'No.'

'And you don't want to tell me what you've done before?'

'I don't see that it's relevant. I might have played something so unlike this part and been so good in it, that you might think less of my chances.'

'Very good!' Jerome laughed, leaning forward on the brass rail. 'The best answer I have ever heard to that question.' He turned and marched off back into the darkness. 'We have your agent's name I take it?' he called, not even over his shoulder.

'Yes!' Jenny replied. 'At least—'

'She's with Leslie Stone, Sir Jerome!' Jerome's assistant called.

'Thank you!' the voice called back. 'Next please Wilkie!'

Before she left the theatre, Jenny rang Leslie Stone's office in Soho and asked for an appointment.

'Any particular reason why I should see you?' a rather gruff voice asked.

'Yes,' Jenny said. 'I think I might be playing the lead in the revival of *Tatty Gray*.'

'You realize that was *her*?' Jerome asked his junta, now gathered around him in the stalls with all auditioning done. 'The girl in the tennis shirt. The denim skirt. That mop of brown hair. *That was her*.'

'No-one seems to know who on earth she is, Sir Jerome,' Wilkie said, running his finger down the list of names on his clipboard. 'No-one's ever heard of her.'

'Does that *matter*, d'you think, Wilkie?' Jerome asked, pacing up and down one aisle of the auditorium. 'This part requires total innocence! And that girl had it! That girl in her tennis shirt, her old blue skirt, and those long brown legs.'

'I agree that she read the best,' a man in an ill fitting suit and clear spectacles said from where he was sitting, long legs draped over the back of the seat in front. 'Far and away the best.'

459

'The rest were no competition,' Jerome said, almost with a groan as he sunk into a seat on the other side of the aisle, ahead of the man in the clear glasses, Andrew Black, his new producer. 'I have never seen a contest so one sided.'

'Do you want me to call her back?' Black enquired.

'No,' Jerome replied. 'I want you to call her agent. And offer.'

'Don't you think we should find out just a little bit more, Jerry?' His producer had got up and was walking down to where Jerome was slouched on the edge of his seat, his chin resting on hands which were folded flat on the back of the stall in front. 'I'll ask Leslie for her details,' Black said. 'Get him to send round her c.v.'

'Do what you like,' Jerome replied. 'It won't make any difference. That is the girl. That girl is *Tatty Gray*. I should know, for God's sake.'

'OK, Jerry,' his producer said. 'It's your show.'

'Yes,' Jerome agreed, before continuing, more to himself, 'I just wish I knew what I'd seen her in.'

'Saint Joan,' said the red-faced man behind the untidiest desk Jenny had ever seen.

'Yes.'

'Where?'

'In the *Lycée* Theatre,' Jenny replied.

'Do you mean the Lyceum?' Leslie Stone asked, growing more bewildered by the moment.

'No, the *Lycée*,' Jenny said. 'In Tours. I studied in France.'

She placed a batch of cuttings in front of the bemused agent. He put on a pair of glasses with heavily finger-printed lenses and stared at them.

'These are in French,' he said. 'I don't speak French.' He handed them back to her. 'Read me out the relevant bits.'

Jenny smiled. 'Do you trust me?' she asked. 'If you don't speak French, I could tell you what I liked.'

Stone stared at her through his smudged spectacles, and then pressed the intercom on his desk.

'My secretary understands French,' he said. 'Maureen can translate.'

The secretary spoke tolerable schoolgirl French, enough to decipher the passages in the cuttings Jenny had outlined in pencil. Leslie Stone sat and listened impassively while rave notice after rave notice for a young actress called Jenny Nichole were slowly decoded, notices which Jenny had carefully edited with her black marker pen so that all references to the performance being not only an amateur one but a school one were excised, and which pronounced her interpretation of St Joan to have been *la meilleure* (the very best, prompted Jenny) in living memory, a performance of such fire, integrity, poetry, passion and *éclat* (brilliance, Jenny prompted again) that the critics jointly couldn't wait to see what she would turn her hand to next.

'I thought your name was Jane Greene,' was about all Stone said after the eulogy was over. 'So what's with Jenny Nichole?'

Jenny explained that her mother had remarried since that time, and she had decided to take the new family surname for her career in England, and that Jane was her baptized name.

'I don't see what that's got to do with it?' Stone grumbled. 'Equity, was it? Some other actress called Jenny Greene, I suppose.'

'Yes,' Jenny agreed blithely, showing him her passport lest he should think she had stolen some other girl's press cuttings.

'It doesn't really matter, love,' Stone sighed. 'If *Sir* wants you, and I tell you he wants you all right. His bloody office was on to me twice before you got here. Maureen had to cover. Say I was at the dentist. Anyway, as I was saying, if *Sir* wants you to play Tatty, if *Sir*'s made his mind up, it won't matter what you have done or what you haven't done. And it doesn't matter a toss to me either.'

He flipped Jenny back the batch of press cuttings and leaned back in his chair to light a fresh cigarette.

'Does that mean you'll represent me, Mr Stone?' Jenny asked.

Leslie Stone started to laugh and cough excessively, both at the same time.

'If Jerry Didier wants to star you in a play with him, my darling girl,' he sputtered, 'it shouldn't be you asking me. I should be the one doing the bloody asking.'

News of the revival of *Tatty Gray* had already created great interest. It had after all been the play which had indisputably established the young Jerome Didier as a star and an actor of exceptional merit, and now that he had chosen to revive it, albeit a revised version, theatrical tongues had really started to wag, the *on dit* being that he was *playing safe*, that because he had just endured a string of flops both onstage and on screen since his all conquering version of *Macbeth*, he was playing for percentages, he was making assurance double sure rather than persisting in his attempt to find a new image. Some even had it, particularly Elizabeth's still loyal *camp-followers*, that the nerve had gone since *Macbeth*, the theory being that with that particular performance he had peaked, and now found himself hoist with his own petard.

'Well, think of it,' Roberty Dunster would ask whenever and wherever possible. 'It's rather like the greatest sex ever, isn't it? You think well, my dear, what *ever* can we do next? Talk about *follow that*.'

In a way all of these rumours were true, and in another way none of them were. Yes it was true Jerome had lost his way since *Macbeth*, and had taken the wrong turning in trying to establish himself as a modernist. Jerome's acting had always been just slightly larger than life, and therein lay its appeal. He could be truly heroic, truly tragic, or truly comic, but to be any of these things successfully, let alone to be able to be all three of these things successfully, required acting of a certain dimension, a size which was not necessarily always suited by the minimalist style of the new and fashionable playwrights. So he was right to choose something tried and true from his repertoire. *Tatty Gray* might have been written by a living playwright, but it had an old fashioned feel to it, a sense of romance, mysticism and poetry which the modern writers were deliberately eschewing. Furthermore, the role of the tormented painter had been expressly written for him, and now rewritten for him, so he knew the suit fitted him. There was nothing untried or off-the-peg about *The Tale of Tatty Gray*.

But it wasn't true to say that Jerome had lost his nerve. It actually took a lot of nerve to revive a role which had already passed into theatrical legend, particularly over two decades later. It also took courage to request that the role be rewritten, for there was no guarantee that *Sam* at forty-five years old would have the same magical appeal as *Sam* at twenty-five. It would be a different ball game altogether, and given someone brilliant opposite him as the wilful and savant sprite Tatty Gray herself, there was every chance of Jerome coming home an also-ran. So no, Jerome couldn't rightly be accused of losing his nerve. Jerome had not lost his nerve in any way. All that was to come.

Jenny's main concern was with the publicity. The fact had at least occurred to her that at some time there would be a blaze of publicity, but what she hadn't counted on was the blaze being so early. Like the day after she was offered and had accepted the role.

Of course, it was only the national Press, because the story was of little interest outside of England, but even so, there would, Jenny imagined, be pictures and news in the trade papers, and as Jenny was well aware, the only foreign papers Oscar took were the trades, most notably *Variety* which he read religiously from cover to cover. Besides that, there was just the off-chance that Oscar would go back on his word and take some interest in what was happening to his old warhorse, as he described the play, and in whom was in fact going to take the role of Tatty. Again, taking indirect advice from her stepfather, Jenny had decided to *busk* this one. Oscar was a great believer in *busking*. So taking a leaf out of his book Jenny decided to do nothing until asked. If she didn't get the part, which was just as likely if not more so than her actually being cast, then there were no worries. Nothing had been gained so there was nothing to lose. But if she did win the role, then she would have to think of the best way of handling the problem. Like maybe taking Oscar into her confidence.

Fortunately and unfortunately he wasn't there when she rang, he wasn't at the farm. Neither was her mother, but then Jenny knew that. She knew her mother was in Florence for an exhibition of her paintings, but she didn't know Oscar was in America. Nancy told her. She said her stepfather had left a week ago, that he had been called to Hollywood to work on the final shooting script of his latest movie, and that he would be gone a month at the very least.

This would not stop the news from reaching him, however, Jenny thought after she had put down the phone. He would either read it in *Variety*, or if he was really interested, he'd find out from his agent. Somehow Jenny saw she had to stop up both loopholes.

The photo call was for twelve o'clock the following morning at the Savoy. It was now half-past eight on the evening before, the evening of the day Jenny had formally been offered the role, and by quarter to eleven that night her father at long last got home.

Jenny was waiting for him, on the doorstep of his new home in Montpelier Square. Under her old raincoat which was open she was wearing exactly the same clothes as she had worn for her audition, as if they were the sort of clothes she always wore. She was sitting on the doorstep, legs together, with her arms linked tightly round the front, just as Sam sees Tatty sitting on the stool when he reopens up his studio.

But unlike Tatty in the play, Jenny had been sitting on her father's doorstep waiting for over two hours.

'Hello,' she said as he walked alone from the cab towards his front door.

'Good God,' he said after a moment. 'What the hell are you doing here?'

'*I've always been here,*' Jenny said, her first line in the play. '*You just haven't seen me.*'

Making a poor show of reluctance, her father took her in, telling his ever-faithful Dingo to bring them up a hot drink and some biscuits. Then he poured himself a drink while Jenny watched him.

She hadn't been able to judge him at all in the half-light of the theatre, but now she could size him up properly. He was shorter than she had imagined. In his films he gave the impression of height, of being nearer six foot than the five foot eight or nine he most probably was, but he was in excellent physical shape. Hand-made suits were made to flatter the figure, Jenny knew that, but nonetheless she could see her father was perfectly proportioned and built like an athlete. As if to demonstrate the fact, once he had poured himself a whisky, Jerome unbuttoned and peeled off the jacket of his suit as only a skilled actor can, tossing the expensive garment casually aside and loosening the top button of his hand-made shirt with one square tipped finger, while staring at the girl in his armchair through his extraordinarily ordinary eye-glasses.

'Why do you look at me that way?' he said, standing in front of her.

'I was wondering about your spectacles,' Jenny replied. 'They're rather mundane.'

'They're spectacles,' he said, whipping them off and dropping them on to his desk. 'What do you expect them to look like? A rose is a rose is a rose.'

'You can get much better spectacles than those nowadays,' Jenny said. 'Much more flattering ones.'

'I am quite sure,' Jerome said, spinning out the first few words of the sentence, 'you did not come here to discuss my – *spectacles*.'

Jenny laughed. She couldn't help it. His annunciation was almost like a parody of himself, but even so there was much good humour behind the intended sarcasm, even an element of self-mockery, and Jenny found herself laughing. Which she considered to be all to the good, since she knew her first consideration was to flatter him.

'No, I'm sorry,' she confessed. 'That was very rude, and I only remarked on your glasses because I suppose I don't think of you wearing them. I don't suppose anyone does. I don't suppose anybody in the world does. I suppose we all see you as we think you are.'

'And how would that be?'

'As we've seen you. As we imagine you. As millions of people I suppose must dream of you.'

Jerome frowned at her, suddenly, and bent himself forward, a well-rehearsed and much-employed move, Jenny concluded.

'And what about you, Jane Greene?' he said. 'Do you dream of me?'

'No,' she replied. 'But then I have very weird dreams.' It was her turn to pause. 'I'd rather dream of you,' she said, as factually as she could, 'than of *fragments dropped from day's caravan.*'

'I like dreaming,' Jerome said, still looking at her before topping her quotation. '*In bed my real love has always been the sleep that rescued me by allowing me to dream.* Now tell me why you're here.'

'Very well.'

'Wait.'

Her father's manservant had arrived with a tray of hot chocolate and what looked like home-made biscuits, which he was directed to place on the table in front of Jenny.

'This is Miss Greene, Dingo,' her father said. 'This is my new Tatty Gray.'

Dingo smiled at her and handed her a white napkin, but said nothing, not to either of them. He just turned and walked soundlessly out of the room, his feet cushioned by immaculately white tennis shoes.

'Well?' Jerome reminded Jenny. 'You were going to tell me why you are here. And I should tell you I can't spare you more than half an hour.'

'Oh, it won't take nearly that long,' Jenny said. 'The reason I'm here is to tell you I won't be at the photo call tomorrow.'

She knew he'd have the right reaction to that piece of news, but even the well tried look of wide eyed and stunned surprise, followed by a light and disbelieving laugh couldn't quite conceal the real shock he was feeling at her insouciance. Jenny said nothing more, quite deliberately, determined not to throw him any sort of life line.

'All right,' he said, finally breaking the silence. 'Any particular reason? Or do you perhaps simply have another and more pressing appointment?'

'I just have a better idea than simply announcing me to the Press, that's all. That's what everyone does. *Ladies and gentlemen, I'd like you to meet the latest discovery.* Then they all take their photographs, they all publish them and their stories at the same time, and after that, your story is just something to put down on the floor to train the new puppy.' *(Pure Oscar.)*

'While?' her father enquired, slowly raising both eyebrows. 'Your suggestion please?'

'You call the photo call and I don't turn up,' Jenny said, again having found her inspiration in her stepfather and his tale from Hollywood, this particular anecdote being *How They Launched A No-Talent Actress Called Madison Williams*. 'Everyone asks not who am I, but where am I?' Jenny continued, ice-cool. 'And you don't know. Not any of you. All right, the Press ask, then at least tell us who she is. Which you refuse to do until you have located me and made sure that I'm all right. The hunt goes on, right up to when rehearsals start, and maybe even a day or so into them, who knows? By which time, of course, you have *found* me, but for reasons you won't disclose (you're afraid I might bolt again. I'm an unknown, remember. Over-awed by what's happened to me), you keep my identity secret until the very last moment. I'm never seen outside rehearsal in anything other than dark glasses and with a protective entourage. You have to play it day by day, you tell them, because although I'm a discovery, maybe the most exciting discovery you've made since I don't know—'

'Since Elizabeth Laurence perhaps,' her father interjected calmly.

'Why not? If you say so. I'm your most exciting discovery since Elizabeth Laurence, and you have every confidence in my ability, but what you're not *really* sure about is my temperament. Will you or won't you get me to post?' *(Thanks again, Oscar.)* 'Just think of the mileage. You can keep the story going until we open.'

'And if we close?' Jerome asked. 'Say the day after we open?'

'You can put me back down on the floor to help train the new puppy,' Jenny said.

She looked at him, and she smiled at him, and her father was enchanted, not realizing it was the smile on the face of a tiger.

'Good,' he agreed. 'Very good. Not only are you an exceptionally talented young actress, my dear child, you are also a formidable entrepreneur.'

'Thank you.'

'I just wish I could remember where I've seen you before.'

'You haven't,' Jenny said, getting up to go. 'Don't worry.'

The *scam* worked. Jenny *disappeared*, every paper ran the story, and the popular ones kept running it right the way into the rehearsal period, during which time they tried to break it. But Jerome had organized his forces well, and the identity of his new and rumoured to be brilliant discovery was successfully kept secret.

In the end, it was in fact a surprisingly easy enterprise, once a few false trails had been laid as to where rehearsals were being held. It was almost as if the Press didn't really want to know, at least not until around the time of the first night, when it would either make a sensational story, or just peter out into a squib. They kept running teasers every now and then, to keep up the public's interest, and somebody even leaked a list of the auditionees to one of the popular papers. But even that backfired, as rather like Cinderella's Ugly Sisters trying to fit their feet into the glass slipper, many of those actresses who had tried and failed either became incredibly coy about what they were engaged in working on, or simply went to ground, hoping that if someone somewhere really believed they were the missing discovery, fiction might become fact and they would wake up one morning to find themselves starring opposite Sir Jerome Didier.

Meanwhile, in an inner room in a secret location somewhere off Tottenham Court Road, rehearsals for *The Tale of Tatty Gray* were well under way. Or to put it more accurately, rehearsals were under way but all was not well. Because if there was a case of someone disappearing, that someone wasn't Jane Greene. The person who was lost was Jerome Didier.

At first it was thought that all that was wrong was the fact that Jerome had chosen not only to star in the play but also to direct it. At the end of the first week of rehearsals the management in the shape of one Andrew Black, the latest in the line of whizz-kid entrepreneurs who seemed to have taken over the West End, suggested bringing in an outside director, one who while sticking religiously to Jerome's ground-plan for the play would nonetheless be able to cast an objective eye on matters and see where he was going wrong. Jerome resented the suggestion, but finally had to concede when he realized quite how far out to sea he was.

They brought in a very skilled theatreman, one Douglas Davis, a no-frills and no-flannel expert who had directed name cast plays all around the world. When asked for his candid but private opinion by Andrew Black at the end of his third day at work, Davis replied that if it was anybody else other than *Sir* he would fire him.

'But what do you think it is?' Black asked, doing his best to conceal his ulcerating worry. 'I mean what's the trouble? It's not as if we're not quite sure whether the guy can act or not, is it.'

'It's the girl,' Davis said. 'She's brilliant, and *Sir*'s pressing too hard. He's scared sick he won't be able to match her.'

'Well, tell him then. Tell him, Duggie, if that's the case.'

'I've told him, Andrew. I tell him every day, six times a day.'

'And what does he say?'

'An obscenity which varies according to his mood.'

467

Davis' next move was to work on Jenny and try and get her to rein back, to come back to a level of performance which Jerome would have no trouble matching, which once he did would then allow him to re-establish his confidence. Jenny at once agreed, apparently appalled to think that she could be the cause of the great man's trouble, and immediately started rehearsing like someone who had never even read out loud before let alone stood up and tried to act. The effect on Jerome was devastating.

'I see what you're doing, you bastard, Douglas!' he roared. 'And I won't have it! I will not be bloody well patronized! I will not bloody well be patronized by some rookie bloody actress and some hired-gun old director! If everyone was doing their jobs properly round here! Instead of standing around with their mouths agape! Like a lot of spare dicks at a wedding! I could get on with *my job*, you jackanapes! And I do *not* need – thank you – a lead down to the starting post like some nervous two year old! And if I did need a lead, which I do not, I would most certainly not choose to take it from someone who is still so green and so wet behind the ears that she has chosen to play this wonderful part of Tatty as a *sort of lobotomized Peter Pan!*' He turned and glared his very hardest glare at Jenny, who decided the time had now come for some tears, and some really good ones at that. So she crumpled up her pretty little face in horrified anguish, clapped both hands to it over her mouth and over her nose, and ran from the rehearsal room not quite muffling her little but (she hoped) quite heartbreaking choking and gasping cries.

'Well done, Jerry,' Andrew Black sighed. 'Now with a bit of luck we'll have lost the one decent performance we did have.'

Jerome left that instant. He picked up his things, coat, script and case in one broad sweep and stormed black-eyed out of the room.

'Go after him,' Black asked Davis.

'He can go to hell,' the director replied. 'I'm going back to Brighton. At my age this is the last thing I need.'

Jenny remained locked in the Ladies for the best part of half an hour, passing the time reading her new paperback, while making dreadful racking sobbing noises every time Edie the assistant stage manager called at the door to see if she was all right. When she finally emerged, her face powdered white and her unswollen eyes hidden behind her heavy dark glasses, Andrew Black apologized to her profusely and drove her home personally in his six-week-old Rolls-Royce.

Jerome on the other hand walked as much of his way home as possible, trying hard to exorcise whatever it was that now had taken refuge inside him. He knew he was trying too hard, he knew poor old Duggie Davis was right, and he would telephone him and apologize to him unconditionally as soon as he got home. He would even offer the wretched director the unencumbered chance to direct the very next play Jerome did, but in the meantime he had to discover how to pull back. It had happened before to him with Elizabeth, he could remember those times all too well. So what had he done then? What had they done then? They had worked privately together, they had talked their problems through, on *All That Glitters* he had sorted her out, and on *Tatty Gray*, she had sorted out them both.

Jerome stopped on the corner of where Newman Street joins Oxford Street as he remembered exactly what Elizabeth had recommended they do when they had found themselves cast-away and drifting so helplessly in the self-same play. But no, he thought, no, no, no, this couldn't be the same sort of instance, a similar sort of case, surely not? With this child, this girl? He almost laughed. Why, he was old enough to be her father. The reason why he was not finding his performance, why he was nowhere near the truth was nothing to do with any chemistry which there might or there might not be between the two of them. All this girl did, between *cleaning* him in rehearsals, was to mock him, and tease him or simply to ignore him. She was just a typical actress. She might not be a very experienced one, but oh yes – yes she certainly had all the markings of being nothing other than a *typical bloody actress*, regardless of her quite stunning and original talent.

He walked on, crossing Oxford Street on to the south side, as far as Oxford Circus and then across Regent Street into Princes Street and on round Hanover Square, and the further he walked the further he knew he was from the truth. He didn't believe a word of what he was telling himself, not one word of it. The reason why he could not recreate Sam was because of the girl, not because of her brilliance, but because of her. Because he was enthralled by her, and had been since the moment she had walked on stage in that white tennis shirt, that faded blue skirt, her black canvas shoes, with her long, brown, beautiful legs and her tousle head of thick brown hair. She even had a smudge of freckles across her nose. Christ! he thought and almost laughed. Christ, she could almost have been her! She could have been the girl on the lawn, the girl on the Downs, the girl on the swing, oh Christ, yes, *it could almost have been her*!

It wasn't though. It was just some girl in her early twenties who read like someone inspired and who was now proving she could act like someone inspired too. It was an actress pretending to be her, just as Oscar had intended the part should be played, and he mustn't be fooled by it, he mustn't allow himself to be seduced again by falling for the paste instead of the pearl, by ordering the mock rather than the real, or by mistaking Granada for Astbury Park.

And yet, and yet, and yet. He knew that wasn't the reason this time, he knew that wasn't what was dragging him down, what was giving him this dull, dull heartache. It was that something about this particular girl's eyes, about her pretty little mouth, something about her very presence that made him feel she belonged to him, that gave him the feeling he must claim her as his. She only had to look at him and he was lost. That was the truth of the matter. He couldn't ever get any further than the very first lines of the play before he was gone, hopelessly lost, swept overboard, and not waving, but drowning, drowning, drowning. *What the hell are you doing here? I've always been here. You just haven't seen me.*

That was as far as he got daily, to ask her that, what she was doing there, and then he was in the water and he had forgotten how to swim. All she needed to do was look across at him from where she sat on the stool and catch his eyes holding them fast with hers, those strange lovely speckled grey eyes that looked at him in a way only one other person had ever looked at him, and then she would smile at him, a smile which would stretch that pretty mouth and turn it up at the corners, a smile which stopped his heart, a smile which turned him instantly into a nonsense. It would turn him from being a man of sublime skill into a ranting, noisome, foolish nonsense, while she just looked and talked, and laughed and smiled, and cried and listened, just as someone else once had, just as the girl who Tatty really was had once upon a long time ago.

Unable to bear the ache and the anguish any longer, Sir Jerome Didier hailed a cab and told the driver to head as fast as he could back to Montpelier Square.

She knew who it was the moment the telephone rang, but she didn't answer it. After all, that had been the plan. To bait the line, to leave it out, to wait till the float bobbed and flipped over on its side, just like it did when she and her mother fished the Loire, and then to strike. She had struck that day. She knew the exact moment. She had seen the look in his eyes as she had pulled and the hook had gone home, deeply into his heart, embedding itself there. It had happened after he had turned on her, and berated her so feebly, yelling at her not to give him a lead, and insulting her ability. The insults would have been sufficient evidence, but she had wanted more so she had looked at him, first with a stare of blank bewilderment, and then with a look of such anguish (so brilliantly pretended) she had frightened him, and he had dropped his defences. She knew then by the look of him and the look he had given her that he was hers. He had taken the bait and swallowed it, along with the hook, the line and even the very sinker.

So now she could play him, she could let out some line and let him thrash around while she sat in the sunshine on the riverbank and hoped that in his agony he would remember the dreadful pain he had inflicted on the one and only person who had ever truly loved him, on the person who had never wronged him for one moment, or even for a half a second of one moment. She sat on the riverbank and listened while the telephone rang, knowing that it was him, knowing that he thought he had found out what was wrong, knowing that it was him out there, deep in the dark waters, thrashing helplessly and hopelessly and agonizingly around.

Yet somehow Jenny kept getting this feeling that it had been all too easy. It seemed not for one moment had her adversary stopped to think or to look where he was going. From the moment she walked on stage in her carefully chosen outfit and from the moment he had walked out of the shadows to look at her the way he had looked at her, she had known then not that it was only a matter of time, but that it might merely be a matter of a moment.

The telephone rang again so rather than sit and be irritated by its persistent ringing, Jenny got up and went out to the shops. She had some shopping to do anyway, so she went up the King's Road and bought a very pretty but simple sort of dress, the sort of dress she thought her mother might have bought at her age and if she had been about to go out on an all important date. The dress was dark red, a damask red, made of a sort of crushed velvet, open in a square at the bodice, and with a beautifully cut skirt. She also bought some very sheer stockings, a pair of shoes to match the dress, and a ribbon for her hair. Then she caught a bus back down to World's End where she now lived, where she had lived since her last term at art college.

No sooner was she in the door than the telephone rang again. For all Jenny knew, it might have been ringing constantly all the time she was out, but now the time had come for her to answer it.

'Hello?' she said very carefully in a French accent, as the management had advised her to do in case it was the Press. 'Who is this please?'

471

'Dear girl,' said a voice, but not at all theatrically, sounding instead as if it belonged to someone who had just suffered a tragedy. 'Where have you been?'

'Is that you, Sir Jerome?' Jenny asked, sitting down in an armchair and trying to keep a Cheshire-cat like smile from her face.

'If you don't know my voice by now, Jane Greene, I may as well give up,' her father said. 'Look. I owe you an apology, but I'm not going to make it over the phone. The telephone is a damnable instrument at the best of times, and it certainly wasn't invented for the regretful acknowledgement of faults and failures.'

'What are your faults and failures, Sir Jerome?' Jenny enquired. 'Besides your rudeness and bad temper.'

'I shall tell you when I see you,' Jerome replied. 'If you will allow me to see you. And for God's sake, I've told you to drop the blasted *sir*. You're to call me Jerome.'

'Very well, Jerome. Look, if you want to make a *formal* apology—' Jenny made it sound as if she hadn't got much time, as if she possibly was in a hurry to get changed and go out, at least that was the subtext she was enacting. 'I take it you'll be in to rehearsal tomorrow?'

'I have to see you before tomorrow, Jane Greene,' her father replied after a pause. 'I want you to have supper with me.'

'Oh,' Jenny paused. 'I was going out.'

'This is more important than your damned social life,' her father insisted. 'Can't you cancel? I really do have to see you.'

'You sound upset.'

'That is because I am upset.'

'Still?'

'Still! Dear God – what's so blasted remarkable about that?'

'Nothing. All right, look – I'll cancel what I was doing, it wasn't that important. Where shall I meet you?'

'I want to go somewhere we can talk,' her father said. 'Not some damned noisy Tratt or beastly Bistro. Meet me at the Connaught, in an hour.'

After she had put the phone down, Jenny hung up her new dress, unpacked her shoes and stockings, and selected her most expensive underwear, the set her mother had brought her back from Paris in celebration of the success of her first show there. Next she had a bath, washed her hair, powdered herself lightly, and put on just a little scent, about the same amount her mother always wore, and then she dressed very carefully and very precisely, because she knew she must look just right, and she must feel just right, just as if she was going to appear on stage.

The dress was perfect. She was very glad she had bought it, even though it had cost a little more than she had planned to spend. However, she knew she would have to buy something good, because she knew her father wouldn't want to take her to some noisy Tratt or beastly Bistro. She had guessed he would most likely choose a hotel, she guessed he would choose somewhere exactly like the Connaught.

He was waiting for her in the lounge with well-concealed impatience, impatient because she was twenty minutes late. He rose when he saw her through the open door, and the moment he saw her he wanted to die. He felt he would die when he looked on her, she was so beautiful, the colour of her hair and her fair skin set off so wondrously against the dull laky red of her crushed velvet dress.

'Hello,' she was saying, 'I'm sorry if I'm late, but then you didn't exactly give me much notice.'

Jerome couldn't speak. He was neither able to speak, nor could he find anything to say, so he fell back on the use of mannerisms, a slow closing of the eyes, a raising of the eyebrows, a thoughtful purse of the mouth, and then a slight shrug of the shoulders as he pulled a chair round for her to sit down.

'I'm drinking champagne,' he said. 'Will you?'

'No, I'll just have an orange juice, thanks,' she replied. 'Strict training. In this play you need to have all your wits about you.'

She would have loved a glass of champagne, but tonight she wanted to keep a very clear head.

'Very well,' he said, and summoned a waiter over to take his order, without looking for one, without snapping his fingers, simply it seemed by thinking about one. Then moments later he summoned the head waiter over to whisper something in his ear, again it seemed to Jenny, simply by willing the attendant over.

'Excuse me, won't you?' he asked when the head waiter had gone. 'I had to make sure they've given me my usual table. It's a corner table, so I can sit with my back to the room, and they can't stare at me. And where we can safely sit and talk.'

'So what do you really want to talk about?' Jenny asked, after they had finished their drinks and been shown to a beautifully laid table in the far corner of the dining room. They had only exchanged the smallest of talk before they had sat down at table, idle chatter about absolutely nothing in particular.

'I could have told you that earlier,' her father said, spreading out his linen napkin on his knee, having refused the waiter permission to do it for him. 'If you'd asked me as I was walking round Hanover

Square this afternoon what I wanted to say to you, or if you'd asked me during the taxi ride I had back to my house, I could have given you a full and very detailed answer. But now you are here, sitting opposite me and you ask me, I cannot think of one thing.'

'Would you like me to do the talking?' Jenny said. 'I could tell you all sorts of things. I could tell you all about my childhood, where I grew up, about my family—'

'I don't want to hear about your family,' her father interrupted, wrong-footing her. 'I don't need to. I know all about your family, Jane Greene. I know about your father, and I know about your mother. I know all about them.'

Jenny did her best not to stare open mouthed at him. Instead she slowly lowered her head and pretended to adjust her own table napkin. She felt her cheeks colour deeply, and she knew if he saw a blush, if he saw any sign of weakness, she was lost.

'What do you know about my family?' she asked, still looking down at her lap.

'Your mother was, I should think *still is* – a most beguiling woman. A beautiful, kind and sensitive creature,' he said, 'full of forgiveness and love. I should imagine you have her looks, although that's a presumption. For all I know you could look like your father. But I would say you probably have your mother's looks and your father's character.'

That was the moment Jenny was sure he knew, and she was about to say what she had to say there and then, blush or no blush, she was about to tell him what an unforgiveable bastard he was and how much she hated him and to hell with the sepulchral quiet of the famous dining room, when her father continued.

'I would think your mother gardens very well,' he said. 'I should imagine she has a way with plants like she does with people, that she can make parsley grow – did you know that was the sign of a real gardener? If you can make parsley grow? Oh, I should imagine parsley grows for your mother, and roses too. While your father, who I imagine to be a countryman – something to do with horses perhaps. Yes, a distinguished trainer, a breeder of fine hunters, but he's a quiet man. Strong, very obviously good looking, but taciturn. And not a man with whom one should ever *truck*. Tell me, Jane Greene, am I right?'

Jenny looked up at him now, her composure returned, the blush gone. He had simply been playing games, he had been amusing himself, he had perhaps even been poking fun.

'Am I right?' he repeated.

'No,' she said. 'You're absolutely and completely wrong.'

474

'Of course I am.' Her father smiled at her, gently and rather sadly. 'But don't be so angry. I was only trying to be light hearted, Jane Greene. Which I promise you is far, far removed from the way I really feel.'

'Why? What is it? Are you worried about the play?'

'I shall answer the second part of your question first, and the first part of your question second. No, I'm not worried about the play. The play is wonderful. Oscar Greene, your namesake—' He smiled. 'Oscar has done a wonderful job, but then he is a wonderful writer. And I'm not worried about you. You are going to be quite and utterly – brilliant. I am, and I'm sure you're not in the least surprised to hear it, I am, however, more than a little worried about me, aye – and there is the rub.'

The waiter arrived with their first course, and Jerome fell to silence while the dishes were placed before them, staring implacably down at his plate.

'Why are you worried about you?' Jenny asked when the waiter had gone. 'Isn't your problem just a question of familiarity? The fact that even though the part has been rewritten, you're going over old ground? And that the character of Sam hasn't changed at all, not really, not from the original draft. The changes are just changes of reference more than anything. They don't mark any real changes of character.'

She stopped, knowing she'd gone too far. She could tell that by the look in his eyes. He was staring at her very intently. All that about *changes of reference, real changes of character*, that was Oscar verbatim, and she knew *Sir* had spotted it, he'd certainly spotted something.

'The original,' he mused. 'You certainly can't have seen the original, so am I to believe you read it?'

'Yes.'

'What edition? I'd be most interested to hear, Tatty Gray, in which edition you learned the original you.'

'Why are you calling me Tatty Gray?'

'Because that's who you are, aren't you? *You've always been here. I just haven't seen you.*'

There was silence. Neither of them had touched their first course. Jenny picked up her fork and made a start on hers, but more by way of a diversion than from any real interest.

'I read it at school,' she said, in a blind wild guess.

'Ah,' he said. 'French's.'

She looked up at him, and the look must have been a giveaway. She saw that, too.

'French's Acting Editions,' her father said, as if addressing an idiot. 'The editions published for Amateurs, for Drama Societies. Repertory companies.'

'Probably,' she said. 'Yes. I think it was French's.'

Her father looked at her longer, and then started to eat his first course. Jenny breathed quietly out, the moment of danger seemingly past.

'Part two of your question,' he said. 'Concerning how I feel. What is it? you asked, by which I take it to mean you want to know why I am *thus distemper'd*. Why I'm so heavy of heart.'

'Are you?'

'Oh, Jane Greene,' he sighed. 'I am, I am. I who am old enough to be your father.'

Jenny just caught her wine glass as she all but knocked it over.

'Sorry,' she said, and then put her shaking hands in her lap. 'I don't understand.'

'I don't blame you,' Jerome laughed. 'Good God – why should *you* understand, child? *I* don't understand, God damn it. I only once ever felt like this before. And I have a memory it was just exactly like this.'

'Yes?' In a way, Jenny didn't want to hear any more, because this was not what she had planned, not at all, not one bit. She had known he would be a skilled player. He was one of the greatest *players* the world had ever seen. She thought she had catered for his skills, and she had known or thought she had known how and where he would use them. If so, if that had been the case, then the rest of it would have been easy as the beginning, as easy as the baiting of the hook had been. She would have heard him out, listened to his self-pity, apparently sympathized with his dilemma, while wondering how they could possibly work it out, the two of them in concert, how together they could get his performance back on the rails. She would have appeared to have been as worried as he was about it, and she would have tried certain things in rehearsal, which wouldn't have worked because she wouldn't have let them work, because she knew she had the upper hand, a hand that had him held tightly by the throat.

She had listened as well, she had listened carefully and unostentatiously to what everyone else was saying, and she had heard the whispers. *It's history repeating itself,* they'd said. *She's going to walk away with it, just like Elizabeth Laurence did in* All That Glitters. *It's going to be just like Elizabeth Laurence all over again, you wait, you'll see. He's going to flop, then he's going to throw himself on her mercy, and that's how it'll be. She won't be able*

476

to resist it, it'll be Elizabeth Laurence all over again, because Sir *now believes he can't go it alone. He can't do it without someone. His nerve has gone. He's convinced himself he needs another Elizabeth. You just wait and see. And he thinks he can get back up there with this one, because she's brilliant. He's got to get up there with her, or else she'll walk away with it.*

But it wasn't going to be just like another Elizabeth Laurence, not this time round. The plan was so simple, and yet so effective if it worked, and it was working so far, it was up and running beautifully. Jenny walks away with it, that part was right, because given her proven ability to act, she was bound to do, because *Sir* wouldn't be able to see the wood for the trees. He didn't stand a chance. He would confuse her with Elizabeth, and with her mother. He wouldn't be able to see straight by the time Jenny had reproduced her mother, because this time it would be an even more accurate and telling portrait of the woman he had loved, because it would be painted by someone who still loved her, and who knew her even better perhaps than he had. Jenny would see to that. She had planned it all. She would stun him from the moment she walked into his life to the moment she walked out, a moment she had fixed to be after all the hands had been declared, after he had fallen in love with her, after she had triumphed on the first night, after she had captured all the notices, after he had discovered he was back sitting in second fiddle's chair, after all the celebrations and the hidden disappointments, after he had woken up on the day after the first night and decided that he was best in partnership, and that thank God he had found the perfect new partner, after that she would disappear, like her mother had done, like Tatty Gray was said to do. Before the second night she would vanish, slipping out under the door, or through that crack in the window. Or maybe this time even blown away with the cobwebs. Because Jane Greene *was* Tatty Gray.

And that was her undoing.

Jenny discovered it now, too late for her own good, as she sat opposite her father, and saw through all the play acting, and the vocal effects, the mannerisms and the inflexions, she found out who Tatty Gray was and what Oscar had meant by her as the man across the table stopped make-believing and told to her the truth. For now she saw what really was in his eyes, what that look really was, a look of real pain and of love. It had been all very well in the abstract, it had been all so very, very easy. In the abstract she could have killed him. She could have shot him dead. She could have stabbed him through his heart and left him to bleed to his death.

But here in the light of reality he was her father, and nothing was even remotely as she had so blithely imagined it. They were father and daughter, she was his flesh, she was his blood, and the look that was now in his dark brown eyes made her want to reach out to him, to take his hands and put him out of his agony.

Instead, they again sat in silence while the waiter took their half-eaten food away, and then served them with their second course. While he did so, carefully placing the food on their plates, arranging the perfectly cooked vegetables, and while another waiter poured a different wine out into the larger glasses, a fine claret with a brownish tinge, Jenny knew what she had to do, although she was dreadfully uncertain as to whether she could in fact do it. She knew what she had to do because she understood Tatty Gray. Before, she had just seen the part as a means to an end, but now she understood the part she really had to play. Tatty Gray wasn't a Fury, she wasn't *Megaera*, the avenging spirit. Tatty Gray was the undivined truth, Tatty Gray was the bringer of light.

'Yes?' she found herself asking, picking up the conversation. 'It was just like this you were saying. But just like what? What did you mean exactly?'

Or perhaps *what do any of us mean?* as Tatty asks him in the play.

'I mean what I think I feel for you seems to go back into the past,' her father said, 'and please don't laugh. I'm not being fey. I've thought this out very carefully. There were all sorts of things I had planned to say to you, all sorts of things I was going to suggest that we do, things we could do to find an understanding in the play, things we could do to make me work, things we could do to get my character right. Ways to establish intimacy. Tricks. And worse. Oh, I was going to go through with them, too, and I probably would have been able to convince you. I seem to be able to convince most people. But that was all very fine and large, because that was all just theory.'

Just like hers, just like Jenny's.

'And theory went out of the window, the way it always does when reality intrudes. The way it intruded this evening, the moment you walked through that door, out there, in the lounge this evening, looking like that, like the way you do. I knew then there wasn't one thing I could do but to tell you the truth. The truth, mind, not a version of it. And the truth is that once before in my life, there was this one moment which I can recapture right now, I can feel it exactly as I felt it, and as if it were yesterday. The moment I walked out into the sunshine of an English garden and there

478

was this girl. She was just like you. She was dressed in an aertex shirt – you probably don't know what aertex shirts even are, your generation—'

'Yes I do,' Jenny said. 'My mother has some.'

'Well then.' Her father smiled at her. 'This girl was wearing an aertex shirt, a pair of what looked like her brother's old shorts, tennis shoes, she even had hair like you. Freckles on her face, over her pretty nose. And I had a *coup de foudre*. Do you understand what I mean by a *coup de foudre*?'

'*Ah mais oui, certainement,*' Jenny shrugged, by force of Gallic habit. '*Je comprends exactement ce que vous voulez dire par un coup de foudre. Vous voulez dire* love-at-first-sight, *quelque chose qu'en France nous appelons parfois le regard rouge.*'

'What beautiful French you speak,' her father said, with a very deep frown.

'I'm so sorry,' Jenny replied. 'It's second nature. I'm bilingual. What I was saying was—'

'I know what you were saying,' her father nodded. 'And I was saying that I had a *coup de foudre*, or suffered *le regard rouge*, because that is exactly what happened. I fell in one moment wildly, madly, insanely and passionately in love. This was my first wife, and I don't know whether or not you know—'

He stopped and sighed, not for effect but because he needed to do so. While he stopped, Jenny looked at him and nodded.

'I know,' she said. 'Go on.'

'It should never have happened but it did. I loved her so much, you see. She was called Pippa, and I loved Pippa more than life itself, and she loved me in precisely the same way. We were so happy, and truth to tell, I don't think I've known a moment's happiness since. Since she left me and disappeared. Not one moment of true happiness, not that is until I saw you, Jane Greene. I don't even know what happened to her, you know. To Pippa. Cecil, my agent, he heard from her – I didn't, not ever. But then why should I? Christ – why should I? But old Cecil heard from her and so we knew she was alive, thank God. But where, oh Christ only knows!'

Her father stopped and looked down, dabbing with his napkin at the tablecloth at a non-existent spot or crumb. Then he drank a deep draught of the almost brown wine before looking up at Jenny over his glass, and smiling.

'Please don't think I'm asking for sympathy, or trying to win your heart by melodramatic heroics. I'm not. I just want you to know the truth. I don't know why. Yes I do. I do. And the truth is I didn't deserve her, I didn't deserve Pippa. Anyone will tell you that. She was far too good for me, and her mother was right. Everyone said the same thing about her, and you would, too, if you had known her. You would say she was the most wonderful and the sweetest natured person in the world, and what did I manage to do with such a girl? I managed to break her heart. So there you are.' He stopped and again brushed at the imagined crumb. 'You know, I have to say,' he said, with another look up at her, 'that I've never really talked like this to anyone before.'

'I think you have. In fact I feel sure you have.'

'No, no. I've never ever talked about this with anyone. That's what I mean.'

'I know. And I mean I'm sure that you've talked in this way to someone before. With total honesty. Telling the absolute truth. I'm sure you must have talked to – talked to your first wife like this.'

'Yes,' her father said. 'You're right. Of course. But she was exceptional. She was the one person I could ever really talk to, with whom I could be my actual self. I never talked to *anyone else* in such a way. That is, until now.'

'And you think you can talk to me.'

'I know I can talk to you. I'm talking to you now, can't you hear me?'

'But why do you think that is? I mean have you any idea?'

'Not really,' her father replied. 'I just feel I can. Because in some strange way I feel that I know you.'

'Yes,' Jenny nodded. 'And so you should. Because you see, I'm your daughter.'

TWENTY-FIVE

There was nothing in the play which could prevent Jenny performing it. Jenny had noticed that when she had first started out on her plan of revenge, that *Tatty Gray* was not a love story. There was no physical contact of any kind in it between the painter and his *genius*, so it was a piece that could quite safely be played by a father and a daughter, albeit a father who did not know that the girl playing opposite him was in fact his child.

Nonetheless, nothing that Jerome could say could persuade Jenny not to resign. He said that she was far too brilliant not to be seen, and that it would make her name overnight, but Jenny had to tell him that wasn't what she wanted. She had to explain that she didn't want to act, but without giving the exact reason why, namely that she sensed being just an actress would finally bore her. That would have been too cruel, and an unnecessary slight on her father's profession. She told him the truth, that she wanted to paint, to be a set designer, and having apologized for it, said they would have to leave it at that.

Her father couldn't believe it. Jerome refused to accept it. He had paced his drawing room in the small hours of that long night which had now become morning giving Jenny every reason why she couldn't stop acting, why she mustn't, not someone with her tremendous gift, not someone with her prodigious talent, and although Jenny knew she was hurting him by not accepting her inheritance, this wasn't a game, this was all part of telling the truth. Still Jerome wouldn't let go. He had begged and beseeched her to do just this one play, trying to persuade her that if anyone had been born to play *Tatty Gray* it was her. And such were the powers of her father's persuasion that Jenny had very nearly weakened and given in, when she saw how much it meant to him, to have discovered that not only had he a daughter, but that the daughter he had had inherited his talent.

Nevertheless, Jenny had held out, and the reason she had been able to do so was because she wasn't doing it for herself, but for her father.

'Who shall I get instead?' he'd asked hopelessly as dawn began to break. 'Who can I possibly get to play it now? Nobody, *nobody* could possibly measure up to you.'

'OK, *Papa*. So far you've done most of the talking. Now let me tell you a thing or two,' Jenny commanded.

Whereupon she'd sat him down in his favourite chair and explained exactly where and how he had gone wrong.

'You've always seen this play as Tatty's play,' she'd said, holding up her hand to stop him interrupting. 'No interruptions,' she'd made him promise, 'or I won't go on. OK? OK. Now I know you've always thought of it as the girl's play because Oscar told me, and if anyone knows about this play, it should be the man who wrote it. He said you were always overcome by Tatty, firstly because you convinced yourself the play was initially written around her, and then when Elizabeth was so brilliant in it, it seemed to underline your argument. But according to Oscar what you've always conveniently forgotten is how brilliant you were in the play as *well*. And exactly how many people thought that not only were you brilliant, but that you were even more brilliant than Elizabeth – no interruptions! Oscar told me, *Papa*! He said you always let Elizabeth talk about the play as if it was *hers*, which Oscar says is nonsense. Oscar says – and I agree with him now that I've had a chance to see it from the inside – Oscar says your part is the much, much harder one, which is why – although he pretended only to be half interested in what happened to it this time round – that's why sooner or later Oz would have wanted to know who was playing the girl. Because his bet was that you'd do it all over again, that you'd let yourself be overpowered, because you were convinced *Sam* comes after and below *Tatty* in importance.'

'Oscar was right,' her father had suddenly agreed, getting up and walking the room again. 'Oscar is always right, damn him! I've made this blasted play into a hair shirt!' And here he had started to laugh, taking his daughter by the hand and leading her gracefully around the room. 'And how funny, my darling!' he'd laughed. 'How very, very funny! Because I very nearly made the same stupid damned mistake again with *you*!'

After that it had been easier. Once her father had accepted that not only had he equal footing in the play, but there was actually a very real chance the play belonged in fact to *Sam*, Jenny had sworn later to her mother she could actually see his confidence returning. It was as if *Tatty Gray* had been his Pilgrim's Hump, and that he'd finally cast it off. Furthermore, Jenny was convinced and she convinced her father too, that as long as he could find the right girl for Tatty, and by that she meant an actress who wasn't quite up to the part, not anyone like Elizabeth—

'Or anyone like you,' her father had interposed.

'Forget about me, *Papa*. The point is – and this isn't me talking, this is still Oscar. He says you don't have to try and discover somebody new and brilliant, but instead you should cast a good, experienced actress, one whose limitations you know, so that you can be free to play it against someone who doesn't threaten you, against someone who'll be so grateful for the part they will be wonderful – which they're bound to be because the part is almost foolproof – without being sensational, then you'll be playing the play he wrote. And this, remember *Papa*, this is from the horse's mouth.'

Her father had listened to this advice intently and he had acted on it, after duly deliberating with his management, going ahead and casting an established young actress called Marty James in Jenny's place, a girl who had all the necessary expertise and none of the troublesome inspiration.

'Because you are my daughter,' he concluded at dawn that famous morning, 'I shall embrace you, and because you are my daughter I love you, and as soon as Harrods is open I shall take you over the road and buy you anything you want.'

'I don't want anything, *Papa*,' Jenny told him. 'And I don't want for anything now either.'

'I'm not that unselfish, I'm afraid,' Jerome replied, straight faced. 'Even though I reciprocate the feelings, I shall want one more thing from you.'

'Yes, *Papa*? And what –' Jenny wondered, 'is that?'

'I shall want you to be there on the opening night.'

The chance to attend the opening night of the revival of *The Tale of Tatty Gray* was an event few Jerome Didier fans would have forsworn, and Jenny who now counted herself firmly among their number was no exception. She promised her father that nothing could shake her determination to be there when he rang each day to make sure she was still coming.

'I won't be able to do it unless you're there,' he warned her on his final call, the night before the opening.

'Oh nonsense, *Papa*! It'll be like falling off a log.'

'You sound just like your mother when you laugh like that,' her father said suddenly and hung up.

Jenny had left plenty of time to get to the theatre so it certainly was through no fault of hers that her seat was still untaken when Jerome checked through the spyhole five minutes before curtain up.

'She's probably in the bar,' Wilkie said, when Jerome arrived back in his dressing room, his handsome face clouded with anxiety. 'Stop worrying, Sir. Believe me, she's out there somewhere.'

'Out where, Wilkie?' Jerome asked, leaning over the back of his chair, like a man at a basin about to be sick. 'Out where – out there in the crowd? Or out somewhere there?' He pointed to the window, without looking up. 'I won't be able to do it, you know,' he stage whispered. 'Not if she isn't here.'

By then, Jenny was running down Piccadilly, having abandoned her taxi in the Hyde Park underpass where it had been stuck in an unmoving traffic jam for the last twenty minutes. Piccadilly was jammed solid as well, so she decided there was no point in trying to get another cab. She might as well run for it and run all the way. She looked at the clock above Fortnum & Mason as she sprinted past. Four minutes past. Four minutes late already.

At Jerome's request they held the curtain for as long as possible, until the audience showed signs of becoming restless.

'We can't wait any longer, Jerry,' Andrew Black told him. 'We've waited over eight minutes. And if you want any notices in the morning—'

'Very well,' said Jerome, after one last look through the spyhole and seeing the seat in the second row still empty. 'Take it up.'

He made his way to the wings, to the outside of the door he was to open in ten seconds time. Through the sugar glass window he could see the outline of the girl on the stool in the shadows of the darkened set as she made a last adjustment to her costume and to her hair, and as a voice behind him prepared them all to stand by.

'*Merde*,' someone whispered from the dark.

'Thank you,' Jerome whispered back, and then closed his eyes tightly to pray.

She was in the theatre now, hurrying across the foyer with some other latecomers and then down the stairs which led to the stalls. Someone barred her way at the door, a large usherette who hissed at her to be quiet because the curtain had risen.

'I have to get through!' Jenny whispered back. 'I have to get to my seat!'

'Management orders,' the girl hissed back. 'All late-comers to stand until the end of the first scene.'

'You don't understand!' Jenny replied sotto. 'I have to be in my seat!'

'You should have thought of that when you were going to be late,' the usherette retorted, standing firmly across the doorway.

'I'm Jerome Didier's daughter,' Jenny said finally. 'Now please let me through.'

The usherette stared at her, and then sniffed.

'Very well,' she muttered almost under her breath. 'If you're who you say you are, you can stand at the back.'

She was just in time to hear the opening lines of dialogue, just in time to hear Jerome as Sam ask the girl what the hell she was doing there, and just in time to hear Tatty's now famous reply.

'I've always been here. You just haven't seen me.'

But judging from the sudden silence that followed the line, Jenny knew she was too late.

Jerome had tried not to look down in case the seat was still unoccupied, just as it had been once before, just as it had been his first night in London, when her mother had failed to make it, when Pippa hadn't shown.

'What in hell – what the hell are you doing here?' he had asked, looking at the girl playing Tatty, but not seeing her, not taking her in, his mind elsewhere, his inner thoughts on whether or not she'd arrived. And he'd heard the girl answer back. He'd heard Tatty's reply all right, he heard her say *she'd always been there, that he just hadn't seen her*, and he knew exactly what he was to say next. But then someone moved, someone down there in the hush of darkness had moved, someone was taking their seat, and so he looked. No-one in the audience would have noticed his eyes, so skilfully did he disguise his sideways glance, but he managed to look as he pretended to sweep a lock of hair from his eyes, he looked and he could see the seat, and the seat was still empty.

'I've always been here. You just haven't seen me.'

Jerome heard the girl repeat the line and wondered vaguely what the point was because he'd heard her well enough the first time, so why she should want to repeat it, he couldn't for the life of him imagine.

So he turned his eyes back round to her and told her.

'It's perfectly all right,' he said. 'I heard you.'

485

'*Perhaps you want to know how I got here,*' Tatty replied, feeding him with his own line.

'No,' Jerome said, shaking his head slowly. 'No, no.' No that wasn't his concern. It was what someone was not doing there that concerned him.

You see, Cecil really should have told him that she wasn't coming. At the very least he should never have shifted his top coat and put it on her seat, to show that he knew she wasn't coming. If he hadn't done one or both or either of those things all that time ago, Elizabeth might not have won, she might not have overpowered him as she had that famous first First Night, and had she not done so, who knows? He might very well still be married to Pippa.

'*This place has been locked up for five years,*' someone prompted him from behind. '*No-one's been near it in all that time.*'

'In a minute,' Jerome said. 'I'm just trying to remember something.'

'He's trying to remember his lines,' a woman muttered rather loudly in the last row of the stalls, just in front of Jenny. 'Someone said he'd lost his touch.'

Sensing an impending disaster, the audience had at first grown restless before falling into an ominous silence, and as they did, in the moment they fell silent, Jenny knew what she must do. She pushed the large usherette out of her way and drawing as much attention to herself as she could, she hurried down the aisle and made her way to her seat, drawing them off, laying a false trail as she saw the audience looking round at her, away from her father who was now looking down on her from the stage.

'Sorry,' Jenny said in a loud whisper as she eased herself past people half-standing to make way for her in the row her seat was in. 'So sorry. Sorry.' Then she looked up at the stage and deliberately caught her father's eye. 'Sorry,' she said almost out loud, for his benefit, although everyone took it to mean them.

Jerome looked back down and smiled. The seat was taken after all. She had arrived, she was there and he could see who she was. The audience was still utterly silent, however, still holding its communal breath as they waited and waited as one to see whether or not it was really true, whether or not Jerome Didier had actually lost his touch.

But Jerome was now back in place, back in the studio, back where he should be. He looked over to Tatty, and this time he saw her, this time he could see her quite clearly, he could see she was dressed in an old white aertex shirt, a pair of boy's shorts, her legs were bare, she wore old white tennis shoes on her feet, and her head was a wonderful cascade of tousled brown hair. He looked at the sprite sitting smiling at him on the stool and he smiled back, because the person who was sitting there in his studio, the sprite of light, that person was Pippa.

'*I don't know how you can have got in here,*' he said. '*This place has been locked up for years. And years. No-one's been near it in all that time.*'

And when he spoke, as he said it, he had his hand upon his heart.

REPRISE

There is very little else to relate. Jerome enjoyed what was in retrospect his first single triumph, and a triumph it certainly was. The critics and the public alike enjoyed the revised version of Tatty Gray even more than the original one, and it played to capacity for over three years, Jerome playing the first nine months, before bowing out for Paul Britten to take over.

After the celebrations, Jenny returned first to France where she confessed all to her mother and stepfather. Oscar was delighted, hugely amused and finally very touched by the story, which he called the play within the play, while her mother sat and listened impassively. Jenny was worried in case what she had done had upset her mother, and she asked her if this was the case, to which Pippa replied the very opposite was true, and that in fact she was very proud of her daughter. Her only regret was that she and Oscar hadn't known, which she realized, of course, would have been an impossibility, because she knew they both would have loved to have been there for the opening night.

Jenny later left France to travel to America and pick up on her stepfather's many contacts. Six months later she got her first major commission to design a production of The Seagull on Broadway. She revealed an even more prodigious ability at design than she had as an actress, and at present she is working in London for the National Theatre. She goes back to the Loire whenever possible, with her fiancé Wilkie Maxwell, who is now Sir Jerome Didier's personal assistant.

Oscar and Pippa hardly ever move from their farmhouse, both of them more than content to work as well as live there. Pippa always has been, of course, and Oscar always had in the back of his mind finally to refuse to travel in order to do the final rewrites or polishes on his films and plays. Shortly after the rebirth of Tatty Gray, which was later filmed (and very successfully so with Jerome and a young American actress called Jodie Street playing the leading roles), Oscar at last said boo to the goose and found to his great delight that doing just that thing didn't stop it laying golden eggs. His most recent film was as you may remember the highly acclaimed The Moon in Vermont, a wry and self-deprecating look at his boyhood, while almost every important collection of contemporary paintings nowadays has at least one oil or drawing by Philippa Nichole RA. Her last exhibition, which was her first in New York, was like all her other recent exhibitions, a sell-out. Pippa's happiness was finally made complete by a letter she received quite unexpectedly from a sick and remorseful Doris Huxley in which she confirmed everything the stranger had told Pippa that day in the art gallery.

Jerome remarried a year later, not to an actress, but a concert pianist who promptly and willingly retired and bore him a son. Her professional name was Helena Donlan, and she is a fine amateur tennis player, a tall, slender, brown-haired woman, with extremely long and shapely legs. Jerome and she and Pippa and Oscar have become great friends, being brought back together by Jenny and Wilkie one summer when the Didiers came for a long weekend at the farm and stayed for three weeks. Oscar and Jerome like nothing better than to spend their days angling and wrangling, while Pippa and Helena play very serious tennis on the lawn. Pippa and Oscar have now added to their family, but not by the addition of children. Instead they rescue stray or abandoned dogs, and the last head count showed the number to be a round dozen. Oscar has suggested that they leave it at that, while Pippa gives the dogs as the reason why they never take holidays, although everyone knows that if you live somewhere as beautiful as the Greenes' farm in the Loire, you would never want to leave it even for a moment.

So finally, what of Elizabeth? When last heard of she was announcing her separation from Jerome. Her fans will know, of course, that she is alive and well and making films, but perhaps even they don't know the full story. Briefly, immediately after her separation from Jerome, she left Sainthill (which was immediately put on the market), and went to America. There she heard about and later admitted herself into a private clinic in Northern California which was specializing in a revolutionary new treatment for schizophrenia, a treatment (now widely recognized) which had no use for ECT or anti-psychotic drugs. Instead it relied entirely upon analysis and therapy. Elizabeth was an in-patient for six months, and an out-patient for a year. During the last six months of her treatment she was pronounced well enough to begin working again which she did, sharing the lead in a small budget film called The Moment *which proved in fact to be a box office sleeper, costing less than eight million dollars to make, and grossing well over twenty-five million dollars once it had come awake in the public's mind. Then, pronounced totally cured of her illness, she returned to live once more in London, turning her back on the theatre and preferring to work instead almost entirely in films, which she found far less demanding than the repetitious work of the theatre. Both her physical and her mental health stayed good, and as far as it can be ascertained, since her treatment in America Elizabeth has never reappeared. But just in case, nowadays everyone is instructed to call her either Lizzie, or Lizabett. In private no-one in the know calls her by her proper*

Christian name, and no-one ever calls her Bethy, most particularly her husband Cecil Manners.

Cecil had stood by her for so long Elizabeth thought the only way to stop him being so remorselessly interested in her was to marry him. The move was very successful for them both. Cecil, still her agent and sole representative, is the most diligent of managers, and works so hard at his wife's career he is rarely home except for weekends, which are usually spent in Cecil's country house in Sussex which he inherited from his mother, and which Elizabeth's mother (Muzz) housekeeps, and to which Elizabeth frequently invites friends who are mainly hers. But there is no need to feel the least bit sorry for Cecil. Cecil Manners is an extremely happy man because he is very rich, and most of all, which is a proud boast for one so apparently unexciting, he is married to the woman who in her prime had been considered beyond all doubt to have been one of the most beautiful women in the entire world.

CURTAIN